Grace Livingston Hill

America's Best-Loved Storyteller

LOVE ENDURES

COLLECTION #2

BARBOUR
PUBLISHING

Re-Creations © 2012 by Grace Livingston Hill
Tomorrow About This Time © 2012 by Grace Livingston Hill
Crimson Roses © 2012 by Grace Livingston Hill

Print ISBN 978-1-62416-758-4

eBook Editions:
Adobe Digital Edition (.epub) 978-1-62836-277-0
Kindle and MobiPocket Edition (.prc) 978-1-62836-278-7

All scripture quotations are taken from the King James Version of the Bible.

This book is a work of fiction. Names, characters, places, and incidents are either products of the author's imagination or used fictitiously. Any similarity to actual people, organizations, and/or events is purely coincidental.

Cover design: Faceout Studio, www.faceoutstudio.com

Published by Barbour Publishing, Inc., P.O. Box 719, Uhrichsville, Ohio 44683, www.barbourbooks.com

Our mission is to publish and distribute inspirational products offering exceptional value and biblical encouragement to the masses.

Member of the
Evangelical Christian
Publishers Association

Printed in the United States of America.

RE-CREATIONS

Chapter 1

1920s Eastern United States,
near Philadelphia

Cornelia Copley pressed her face against the windowpane of the car and smiled with a brave showing of courage as the train moved away from the platform where her college friends huddled eagerly for the last glimpse of her.

"Don't forget to write, Cornie!" shouted a girl with black eyes and a frantic green sweater over a green-and-yellow striped sport-skirt.

"Remember you're to decorate my house when I'm married!" screamed a pink-cheeked girl with blue eyes and bewitching dimples.

"Be sure to come back for commencement!" chorused three others as the train got fairly underway.

Cornelia watched the staid old gray buildings penciled over with the fine lines of vines that would burst into green tenderness as soon as the spring should appear, and thought how many good times she had had within those walls, and how terrible, how simply unthinkable it was that they were over forever, and she would never be able to graduate! With tears gathering in her eyes and blurring her vision, she watched till the last flutter of the flag on the top of Dwight Hall vanished, the big old cherry tree, gnarled and black against the November sky, faded into the end of the library, and even the college hedge was too far back to discern; then she settled slowly back into her seat, much as a bit of wax candle might melt and droop before the outpouring of sudden heat. She dropped into her seat so sadly and so crushingly that the sweet-faced lady in the long sealskin coat across the aisle turned and looked commiseratingly at her. Poor child! *Now what was she having to endure?* she wondered, as she watched the sweet lips drop at the corners, the dimples around the eyes disappear, and the long lashes sweep down too late to catch the great tear that suddenly rolled out and down the round, fair cheek.

Cornelia sat with her face turned toward the window and watched the familiar way for a long time through unseeing eyes. She was really looking into a hard and cruel future that had suddenly swooped down upon her and torn her from her friends, her career in life—all that she thought she held dear—and was sending her to an undesirable home among a family who did not understand her and her aspirations nor appreciate her ability. Her mouth took on hard little strange lines, and her deep, dreamy eyes looked almost steely in their distress. It all seemed so unnecessary. Why couldn't Father understand that her career meant so much, and another year or two in college would put her where she could be her own mistress and not be dependent upon him? Of course she couldn't argue with him about it just now after that rather touching letter he had written; but if he had only understood how important it was that she should go on and finish her course, if only *any* of them had ever understood, she was sure he would have managed someway to get along without recalling her. She took out the letter and read it over again. After all, she had scarcely had time to read it carefully in all its details, for a telegram had followed close upon it bidding her come at once, as she was badly needed, and of course she had packed up and started. This was the letter, written in a cramped, clerkly hand:

Dear Daughter,

I am very sorry to have to tell you that your mother, who has been keeping up for the last six months by sheer force of will, has given out and seems to be in quite a serious condition. The doctor has told us that nothing but absolute rest and an entire change will save her to us, and of course you will understand that we are so rejoiced over the hope he holds out that we are trying to forget the sorrow and anxiety of the present and to get along as best we can without her. I have just returned from taking her, with the assistance of a trained nurse, to the Rest Cure Hospital at Quiet Valley over at the other end of the state, where the doctor tells me she will have just the conditions and treatment that her case requires. You will be glad to know that she was quite satisfied to go, feeling that it was the only possible thing left to do, and her main distress was that you would have to leave college and come home to take her place. My dear Nellie, it grieves me to the heart to have to write this and ask you to leave your beloved work and come home to help us live, but I see no other way out. Your Aunt Pennell has broken her leg and will not be able to be about all winter; and even if she were well enough, she never seems to understand how to get along with Harry and Louise.

And then, even if there were anyone else, I must tell you that there is another reason why coming home is necessary. It is that I cannot afford to let you stay at college. I cannot tell you how hard it looks to me written out on paper and how my spirit sinks beneath the thought that I have come to this, that I cannot afford to let my daughter finish her education as she had planned because I have not been able to make money enough to do all the other things that have to be done also. I have tried to keep the knowledge of my heavy losses from you until you should be through with your work at college. Mother and I thought we could get along and not let you know about it, because we knew you would insist on coming right home and helping; but now since Mother has broken down you will have to be told the truth. Indeed, I strongly suspect that your mother in her great love for you and the others has brought on this weak state of health by overdoing, although we tried all we could to keep her from working too hard. You will, I know, want to help in every way you can, so that we shall be able to surround your dear mother with every necessity and even luxury that she should have and so make her recovery more sure and speedy. It costs a good deal at Quiet Valley. It is an expensive place, but nothing is too good for your dear, patient mother, who has quietly been giving her very life for us all without letting us know how ill she was.

There is another painful thing I must tell you, and that is that we have had to move from our old home, also on account of the expense, and you will not find it nearly so pleasant or convenient here as at the old house, but I know my brave daughter will bear it like a soldier and be as helpful and resourceful as her mother has always been. It gives me great comfort to think of your immediate coming, for Louise is working too hard for so young a girl. Harry helps her as much as he can. Moreover, I feel troubled about Carey. He is getting into the habit of staying out late with the boys, and—but you will know how to help him when you get here. You and he were always good friends. I cannot tell you what a tower of strength you seem to me to be just now in this culmination of trials. Be sure to telegraph me on what train you will arrive, and we will meet you.

With deep regret at the necessity of this recall, which I know will be a great trial to you,

Your loving father

Cornelia looked like anything but a tower of strength as she folded the letter and slipped it back into her handbag with a deep-drawn sigh. It had given her the same feeling of finality that had come when she first read it. She had hoped there might be a glimmer, a ray, somewhere in this second reading that would help her to hope she might go back to college pretty soon when she had put the family on its feet again and found the right person to look after them. But this money affair that Father laid so much emphasis upon was something that she could not quite understand. If Father only understood how much money she could make once she was an interior decorator in some large, established firm, he would see that a little money spent now would bring large returns. Why, even if he had to borrow some to keep her in college till her course was finished, he would lose nothing in the end.

Cornelia put her head back against the cushion and closed her eyes wearily. She hadn't slept much the night before, and her nerves were taut and strained. This was the first minute in which she had done anything like relax since the letter came—right into the midst of a junior show in which she had had charge of all the stage settings! It really had been dreadful to leave when she was the only one who knew where everything should be. She had spent half the night before making drawings and coloring them and explaining to two half-comprehending classmates. But she was sure they would make some terrible mistake somewhere, and she would be blamed with the inharmony of the thing. It was too bad when she had acquired the reputation of being the only girl in college who could make such effects on the stage. Well, it couldn't be helped!

Of course, she was sorry her mother was sick, but Father spoke hopefully, confidently about her, and the rest would probably do her good. It wasn't as if Mother were hopelessly ill. She was thankful as any of them that that had not come. But Mother had always understood her aspirations, and if she were only at home she would show Father how unreasonable it was for her to have to give up now when only a year and a half more and the goal would be reached and she could become a contributing member of the family, rather than just a housekeeper!

Over and over the sorrowful round Cornelia's thoughts went as mile after mile rushed away under the wheels and home drew nearer. Now and then she thought a little of how it would be when she got home, but when one had to visualize an entirely new home about which one had not heard a thing, not even in what part of the city it was located, how could one anticipate a homecoming? They must have just moved, she supposed, and probably Mother had worked too hard settling. Mother always did that. Indeed, Cornelia had been so entirely away from home during her college life that she was almost out of harmony with it, and her sole connection had been cheerful little letters mostly filled with what she was going to do when she finished her course and became an interior decorator.

It was almost two years since she had been at home, for last summer and the summer before she had spent in taking special courses in a summer school not far from her college, and the intervening Christmas she had been invited to a wonderful house party in New York at the home of one of her classmates who had unlimited money and knew just how to give her friends a good time. Mother had thought these opportunities too good to be wasted, and to her surprise Father also had been quite willing for her to spend the extra time and money, and so she had grown quite away from the home and its habits. She began to feel, as she drew nearer and nearer to the home city, almost as if she were going among strangers.

It was growing quite dusky, and lights were glinting out in stray farmhouses along the way. The train was due in the city at seven o'clock. It was almost six, and the box of fudge that the girls had supplied her with had palled upon her. Somehow she did not feel hungry, only sick at heart and woefully homesick for the college and the ripple of laughter and chatter down the corridors; the jokes about college fish and rice pudding; the dear, funny exchange of secrets; even the papers that had to be written! How gladly would she go back now and never grumble about anything if she only knew she could finish without an interruption and then move to the city to live with Mable and Alice as they had planned, and get into big work! Oh the dreams, the bubbles that were being broken with all their pretty glitter of rainbow hues gone into nothingness! Oh the drab monotony of simple home life!

So her thoughts beat restlessly through her brain and drove the tears into her smarting eyes.

Presently the train halted at a station, and a small multitude rushed in, breezy, rough, and dirty, with loud voices and garments covered with grease and soil; toilers of the road, they were going back to the city, tossing their clamor across the car, settling their implements out of the way under their big, muddy shoes. One paused before Cornelia's empty half seat, and suddenly before he could sit down a lady slipped into it, with a smile and a motion toward a whole empty seat across the aisle. The man accepted the offer good-naturedly, summoning a fellow laborer to share it with him, and Cornelia looked up relieved to meet the smile of her seal-clad former neighbor across the aisle.

"I thought it would be more pleasant for us both, dear, if I came over here," she murmured with a smile. "They were pretty strong of garlic."

"Oh, thank you!" said Cornelia and then grew shy as she noticed the jewels on the delicate hand that rested on the soft fur. What part had she in life with a woman like this, she who had to leave college because there wasn't money enough to let her stay till she had finished? Perhaps she was the least bit ungracious to the kindly woman who had made the move obviously for her protection, but the kindly stranger would not be rebuffed.

"I've been watching you all the afternoon," she said. "And I'm glad of this opportunity of getting acquainted with you if you don't mind. I love young people."

Cornelia wished her seatmate would keep quiet or go away, but she tried to smile gratefully.

"I was so interested in all those young people who came down to see you off. It reminded me of younger days. Was that a college up on the hill above the station?"

Now indeed was Cornelia's tongue loosened. Her beloved college! Ah, she could talk about that even to ladies clad in furs and jewels, and she was presently launched in a detailed description of the junior play, her face glowing vividly under the opened admiration of the white-haired, beautiful woman, who knew just how to ask the right questions to bring out the girl's eager tale and who responded so readily to every point she brought out.

"And how is it that you are going away?" she asked at last. "I should think you could not be spared. You seem to have been the moving spirit in it all. But I suppose you are returning in time to do your part."

Cornelia's face clouded over suddenly, and she drew a deep sigh. For the moment she had forgotten. It was almost as if the pretty lady had struck her in the face with her soft, jeweled hand. She seemed to shrink into herself.

"No," she said at last sadly, "I'm not going—back *ever*, I'm afraid." The words came out with a sound almost like a sob and were wholly unintentional with Cornelia. She was not one to air her sorrows before strangers, or even friends, but somehow the whole tragedy had come over her like a great wave that threatened to engulf her. She was immediately sorry that she had spoken, however, and tried to explain in a tone less tragic. "You see, my mother is not well and had to go away, and—they needed me at home."

She lifted her clouded eyes to meet a wealth of admiration in the older woman's gaze.

"How beautiful! To be needed, I mean," the lady said with a smile. "I can think just what a tower of strength you will be to your father. Your father is living?"

"Yes," gasped Cornelia with a sudden thought of how terrible it would be if he were gone. "Oh yes; and it's strange—he used those very words when he wrote me to come home." Then she grew rosy with the realization of how she was thinking out loud to this elegant stranger.

"Of course he would," asserted the lady. "I can see that you are!

I was thinking that as I watched you all the afternoon. You seem so capable and so—*sweet!*"

"Oh, but I'm *not!*" burst out the girl honestly. "I've been real cross about it ever since the letter came. You see"—and she drew her brows, earnestly trying to justify herself—"you see, I can't help thinking it's all a mistake. I'm glad to go home and help, but someone else could have done that, and I think I could have helped to better purpose if I had been allowed to stay and finish my course and then been able to help out financially. Father has lost some money lately, which has made things hard, and I was planning to be an interior decorator. I should soon have been able to do a good deal for them."

"Oh, but my dear! No one can take a daughter's place in a home when there is trouble, not such a daughter's place as you occupy, I'm sure. And as for the other thing, if you have it in you it will come out, you may be sure. You'll begin by decorating the home interior, and you won't lose anything in the end. Such things are never lost nor time wasted. God sees to that, if you are doing your best right where He put you. I can just see what an exquisite spot you'll make of that home, and how it will rest your mother to know you are taking her place."

Cornelia sadly shook her head.

"There won't be any chance for decorating," she said slowly. "They've had to move away from the home we owned, and father said it wasn't very pleasant there."

"All the more chance for your talents!" said the lady with determined cheerfulness. "I know you have a sense of the beautiful, for I've been studying that lovely little hat you wear and how well it suits your face and tones with your coat and dress and gloves. However unpleasant and gloomy that new house may be, it will begin to glow and blossom and give out welcome within a short time after you get there. I should like to look in and prove the truth of my words. Perhaps I shall sometime, who knows? You just can't help making things fit and beautiful. There's a look in your face that makes me sure. Count the little house your opportunity, as every trial and test in this world really is, you know, and you'll see what will come. I know, for I've seen it tried again and again."

"But one can't do much without money," sighed Cornelia, "and money is what I had hoped to earn."

"You'll earn it yet, very likely, but even if you don't, you'll do the things. Why, the prettiest studio I ever saw was furnished with old boxes covered with bark and lichens, and cushioned with burlap. The woodwork was cheap pine stained dark, the walls were rough, and there was a fireplace built from common cobblestones. When the teakettle began to sing on the hearth and my friend got out her little cheap teacups from the ten-cent store, I thought it was the prettiest place I ever saw, and all because she had put herself into it, and not money, and made everything harmonize. You'll do it yet. I can see it in your eyes. But here we are at last in the city, and aren't you going to give me your address? Here's mine on this card, and I don't want to lose you now that I've found you. I want you to come and see me sometime if possible. And if I get back to this city again sometime—I'm only passing through now and meeting my son to go on to Washington with him in the morning—but if I get back this way sometime soon I want to look you up, if I may, and see if I didn't prophesy truly, my dear little Interior Decorator."

This was the kind of admiration Cornelia was used to, and she glowed with pleasure under it, her cheeks looking very pretty against the edge of brown fur on her coat collar. She hastily scribbled the new address on one of her cards and handed it out with a dubious look, almost as if she would like to recall it.

"I haven't an idea what kind of a place it will be," she said apologetically. "Father seemed to think I wouldn't like it at all. Perhaps it won't be a place I would be proud to have you see me in."

"I'm sure you'll grace the place, however humble it is," said the lady with a soft touch of her jeweled hand on Cornelia's. And just then the train slid into the station and came to a halt. Almost immediately a tall young man strode down the aisle and stood beside the seat. It seemed a miracle how he would have arrived so soon, before the passengers had gathered their bundles ready to get out.

"Mother!" he said eagerly, lifting his hat with the grace and ease of a young man well versed in the usages of the best society. And then he stooped and kissed her. Cornelia forgot herself in her admiration of the little scene. It was so beautiful to see a mother and son like this. She sighed wistfully. If only Carey could be like that with Mother! What an unusual young man this one seemed to be! He treated his mother like a beloved friend. Cornelia sat still, watching, and then the mother turned and introduced her.

"Arthur, I want you to meet Miss Copely. She has made part of the way quite pleasant and interesting for me."

Then Cornelia was favored with a quick, searching glance accompanied by a smile, which was first cordial for his mother's sake and then grew more so with his own approval as he studied her. The girls his mother picked were apt to be satisfactory. She could see he was accepting her at the place where his mother left off. A moment more, and he was carrying her suitcase in one hand and his mother's in the other, while she, walking with the lady, wondered at herself and wished that fate were not just about to whirl her away from these most interesting people.

Then she caught a glimpse of her father at the train gate, with his old derby pulled down far over his forehead as if it were getting too big and his shabby coat collar turned up about his sunken cheeks. How worn and tired he looked! Yes, and old and thin. She hadn't remembered that his shoulders stooped so, or that his hair was so gray. Had all that happened in two years? And that must be Louise waving her handkerchief so violently just in front of him. Was that Harry in that old red baseball sweater with a smudged white letter on its chest, and ragged wrists? He was chewing gum, too! Oh, if these new acquaintances would only get out of the way! It would be so dreadful to have to meet and explain and introduce! She forgot that she had a most expressive face and that her feelings were quite open to the eyes of her new friends, until she suddenly looked up and found the young man's eyes upon her interestedly, and then the pink color flew over her whole face in confusion.

"Please excuse me," she said, reaching out for her suitcase. "I see my father," and without further formalities she fairly flew down the remainder of the platform and smothered herself in the bosom of her family, anxious only to get them off to one side and away from observation.

"She's a lovely girl," said the lady wistfully. "She wants to be an interior decorator and make a name and fame for herself, but instead she's got to go home from college and keep the house for that rabble. Still, I think she'll make good. She has a good face and sweet, true eyes. Sometime we'll go and see her and find out."

"M'm!" said the son, watching Cornelia escape from a choking embrace from her younger brother and sister. "I should think that might be interesting," and he walked quite around a group of chattering people greeting some friends in order that he might watch her the longer. But when Cornelia at last straightened her hat and looked furtively about her, the mother and son had passed out of sight, and she drew a deep sigh of thanksgiving and followed her father and the children downstairs to the trolley. They seemed delightful people, and under other circumstances she might have heartily enjoyed their company, but if she had hard things to face she didn't want an audience while she faced them. Her father might be shabby and old, but he was her father, and she wasn't going to have him laughed at by anybody, even if he didn't always see things as she thought he ought to see them.

Chapter 2

$\mathcal{I}$t was a long ride, and the trolley was chilly. Cornelia tried to keep from shivering and smiled at everything Louise and Harry told her, but somehow things had gotten on her nerves. She had broken out into a perspiration with all the excitement at the station and now felt cold and miserable. Her eyeballs ached with the frequent tears that had slipped their salty way that afternoon, and her head was heavy, and heavier her heart.

Across the way sat her father, looking grayer and more worn in the garish light of the trolley. His hair straggled and needed cutting, and his cheeks were quite hollow. He gave a hollow cough now and then, and his eyes looked like haunted spirits, but he smiled contentedly across to her whenever he caught her glance. She knew he meant that she should feel how glad he was to get her back. She began to feel very mean in her heart that she could not echo his gladness. She knew she ought to, but somehow visions of what she had left behind, probably forever, got between her and her duty, and pulled down the corners of her mouth in a disheartening droop that made her smiles a formal thing, though she tried, she really did try, to be what this worn old father evidently expected her to be—a model daughter, glad to get home and sacrifice everything in life for them all.

These thoughts made her responses to the children only halfhearted. Harry was trying to tell her how the old dog had died and they had only the little pup left, but it was so game it could beat any cat on the street in a fight already, and almost any dog.

Louise chimed in with a tale about a play in school that she had to be in if Nellie would only help her get up a costume out of old things. But gradually the talk died down, and Louise sat looking thoughtfully across at her father's tired face, while Harry frowned and puckered his lips in a contemplative attitude, shifting his gum only now and then, enough to keep it going, and fixing his eyes very wide and blue in deep melancholy upon the toe of his father's worn shoe. Something was fast going wrong with the spirits of the children, and Cornelia was so engrossed in herself and her own bitter disappointment that she hadn't even noticed it.

In the midst of the blueness the car stopped, and Mr. Copley rose stiffly with an apologetic smile toward his elder daughter.

"Well, this is about where we get off, Nellie," he said half wistfully, as if he had done his brave best, and it was now up to her.

Something in his tone brought Cornelia sharply to her senses. She stumbled off the car and looked around her breathlessly, while the car rumbled on up a strange street with scattered houses, wide-open spaces reminding one of community baseball diamonds, and furtive heaps of tin cans and ashes. The sky was wide and open, with brilliant stars gleaming gaudily against the night and a brazen moon that didn't seem to understand how glaringly every defect in the location stood out, but that only made the place seem more strange and barren to the girl. She had not known what she expected, but certainly not this. The houses about her were low and small, some of them of red brick made all alike, with faded greenish-blue shutters and a front door at one side opening on a front yard of a few feet in dimensions, with a picket fence about it, or sometimes none at all. The house her father was leading her to was a bit taller than the rest, covered with clapboards, weather-beaten and stained; guiltless of paint, as could be seen even at night; high and narrow, with gingerbread-work in the gable and not a porch to grace its poor bare face, only two steps and a plain wooden door.

Cornelia gasped and hurried in to shut herself and her misery away from the world. Was this what they had come to? No wonder her mother had given out! No wonder her father— But then her father—how could he have let them come to a place like this? It was terrible!

Inside, at the end of the long, narrow hall, the light from the dining room shone cheerfully from a clean kerosene lamp guiltless of shade, flaring across a red and white tablecloth.

"We haven't done a thing to the parlor yet," said the father sadly, throwing open a door at his right as Cornelia followed him. "Your mother hadn't the strength!" He sighed deeply. "But then," he added more cheerfully, "what are parlors when we all are alive and getting well?"

Cornelia cast a wondering look at him. She had not known her father thought so much of her mother. There was a half-glorified look on his face that made her think of a boy in love. It was strange to think it, but of course her mother and father had been young lovers once. Cornelia, her thoughts temporarily turned from her own brooding, followed into the desolate dining room, and her heart sank. This was home! This was what she had come back to after all her dreams of a career and all her pride over an artistic nature!

There was a place set for her at one end of the red-clothed table and a plaintive little supper drying up on the stove in the kitchen, but Cornelia was not hungry. She made pretence of nibbling at the single little burned lamb chop and a heavy soda biscuit. If she had known how the children had gone without meat to buy that lamb chop, and how hard Louise had worked to make these biscuits and the applesauce that accompanied them, she might have been more appreciative; but as it was she was feeling very miserable indeed and had no time from her own self-pitying thoughts to notice them at all.

The dining room was a dreary place. An old sofa that had done noble duty in the family when Cornelia was a baby lounged comfortably at one side, a catchall for overcoats, caps, newspapers, bundles, mending, anything that happened along. Three of the dining room chairs were more or less gone or emaciated in their seats. The cat was curled up comfortably in the old wooden rocker that had always gone by the name of "Father's rocker" and wore an ancient patchwork cushion. The floor was partly covered by a soiled and worn Axminster rug whose roses blushed redly still behind wood-colored scrolls on an indiscriminate background that no one would ever suspect of having been pearl-gray once upon a time. The wallpaper was an ugly, dirty dark red, with tarnished gold designs, torn in places and hanging down, greasy and marred where chairs had rubbed against it and heads had apparently leaned. It certainly was not a charming interior. She curled her lip slightly as she took it all in. This was her home! And she a born artist and interior decorator!

Her silence and lack of enthusiasm dampened the spirits of the children, who had looked to her coming to brighten the dreary aspect of things. They began to sit around silently and watch her, their sharp young eyes presently searching out her thoughts, following her gaze from wallpaper to curtainless window, from broken chair to sagging couch.

"We haven't been able to get very much in order," sighed Louise in a suddenly grown-up, responsible tone, wrinkling her pink young brow into lines of care. "I wanted to put up some curtains before you got here, but I couldn't find them. Father wouldn't let me open the boxes till Carey came home to help. He said there was enough around for me to tend to, all alone, now."

"Of course," assented the elder sister briefly and not at all sympathetically. In her heart she was thinking that curtains wouldn't make any difference. What was the use of trying to do anything, anyway? Suppose the beautiful stranger who had been so sure she would make her home lovely could see her now. What would she think? She drew a deep sigh.

"I guess maybe I better go to bed," said Louise suddenly, blinking to hide a tendency to tears. It was somehow all so different from what she had expected. She had thought it would be almost like having mother back, and it wasn't at all. Cornelia seemed strange and difficult.

"Yes," said the father, coming up from the cellar, where he had been putting the erratic furnace to bed for the night. "You and Harry better get right up to bed. You have to get up so early in the morning."

"Perhaps you'd like to come, too," said Louise, turning to Cornelia with one more attempt at hospitality. "You know you have to sleep with me; that is, I sleep with you." She smiled apologetically. "There isn't any other room, you know," she explained as she saw the look of dismay on Cornelia's face. "I wanted to fix up the linen closet for me, but father couldn't find another cot yet. Harry sleeps on one cot up in a little skylight place in the third story that was only meant for a ladder to go up to the roof. Carey has the only real room on the third floor, and there aren't but two on the second besides the little speck of a bathroom and the linen closet."

A sudden realization of the trouble in the little sister's eyes and voice brought Cornelia somewhat to her senses.

"That's all right, chicken," she said, pinching the little girl's cheek playfully. "We won't fight, I guess. I'm quite used to a roommate, you know."

Louise's face bloomed into smiles of hopefulness.

"Oh, that will be nice," she sighed. "Are you coming to bed now?"

"You run along, Louise," put in her father. "I guess Nellie and I will have a bit of a talk before she comes up. She'll want to know all about Mother, you know."

The two children withdrew, and Cornelia tried to forget herself once more and bring her reluctant thoughts to her immediate future and the task that was before her.

"What is the matter with Mother?" she asked suddenly, her thoughts still half impatient over the interruption to her career. It was time she understood more definitely just what had come in to stop her at this important time of her life. She wished that Mother herself had written; Mother never made so much of things, although of course she didn't want to hurt her father by saying so.

"Why, she was all run down," said Mr. Copley, a shade of deep sadness coming over his gray face. "You see she had been scrimping herself for a long time, saving, that the rest of us might have more. We didn't know it, of course, or we would have stopped it." His voice was shamed and sorrowful. "We found she hadn't been eating any meat"—his voice shook like an old man's—"just to—save—more for the rest of us."

Cornelia looked up with a curl on her lip and a flash in her eyes, but there was something in her father's broken look that held back the words of blame that had almost sprung to her lips, and he went on with his tale in a tone like a confession, as if the burden of it were all on him and were a cloak of shame that he must wear. It was as if he wanted to tell it all at its worst.

"She didn't tell us, either, when she began to feel bad. She must have been running down for the last three years—in fact, ever since you went away. Though she never let on. When Molly had to go home to her folks, your mother decided not to try to keep a servant. She said she could get along better with sending out the washing, and servants were a scarce article and cost a lot. I didn't want her to, but you know how your mother always is, and I had kind of got used to letting her have her own way, especially as about that time I had all I could do night and day at the office to try to prevent what I saw was coming for the business. She worked too hard. I shall never forgive myself!" He suddenly buried his face in his hands and groaned.

It was awful to Cornelia. She wanted to run and fling her arms about his neck and comfort him; yet she couldn't help blaming him. Was he so weak? Why hadn't he been more careful of the business and not let things get into such a mess? A man oughtn't to be weak. But the sight of his trouble touched her strangely. How thin and gray his hair looked! It struck her again that he looked aged since she had seen him last. It gave her the effect of a cold splash of water in her face.

"Don't, Father!" she said, her voice full of suppressed pain and a glint of tenderness.

"Well, I know I oughtn't to trouble you this way, daughter," he said, looking up with a deprecatory smile, "but somehow it comes over me how much she suffered in silence before we found it out, and then I can't stand it, especially when I think what she was when I married her, so fresh-faced and pretty with brown hair and eyes just like yours. You make me think a lot of her, daughter. Well, it's all over, thank the Lord," he went on with a sigh, "and she's on the mend again. You don't know what it was to me the day of the operation."

"Operation!" The word caught in Cornelia's throat, and a chill of horror crept over her. "Why, you never told me there was an operation!"

"I know," her father said apologetically. "That was Mother, too! She wouldn't have you troubled. She said it was just your examination time, and it would mean a great deal to you to get your marks; and it would only be a time of anxiety to you, and she was so sure she would come out all right. She is wonderfully brave, your mother. And she hoped so much she'd be able to get up and around and not have to bring you home till your course was over. We meant to manage it somehow, but you see we didn't know how serious it was and how she would have to go away and stay a long time till she was strong."

Cornelia's eyes were filled with tears now. She had forgotten her own disappointments and the way she had been blaming her father and was filled with remorse for the little mother who had suffered and thought of her to the last. She got up quickly and went over to gather the bowed head of her father into her unaccustomed arms and try somehow to be daughterly. It was strange because she had been away so long and had gotten out of the way of little endearments, but she managed it so that the big man was comforted and smiled at her and told her again and again how good it was to have her back, almost as good as having her mother. Then he stroked her hair, looked into her wise young eyes, and called her his little Nellie-girl, the way she could remember his doing before she went away to school.

When Cornelia went upstairs at last with the kerosene lamp

held high above her head so that she would not stumble up the steep, winding staircase, she had almost forgotten herself and her ambitions and was filled with a desire to comfort her father.

She dropped into her place beside the sleeping sister with a martyr-like quiet and failed to notice the discouraged droop of the little huddled figure and the tear-stained cheek that was turned toward the dingy wall. The dreariness of the room and the close quarters had brought depression upon her spirits once more, and she lay a long time filled with self-pity and wondering how in the world she was ever to endure it all.

Chapter 3

In the dimness of the early morning Louise Copley awoke with a sigh to consciousness and softly slid her hand down to the floor under the bed, where she had hidden the old alarm clock. With a sense that her elder sister was still company she had not turned on the alarm as usual, and now with the clocklike regularity and a sense of responsibility far beyond her years she had wakened at a quarter to six as promptly as if the whir of the alarm had sounded underneath her pillow.

She rubbed her eyes open and through the half-lifted fringes took a glance. Yes it was time to get up. With one more lingering rub at her sleepy young eyes she put the clock back under the bed out of the way and stole quietly over the footboard, watching furtively her sleeping sister. How pretty Nellie was even in the early gray light of morning, with all that wavy mane of hair sweeping over the pillow, and her long lashes lying on the pink curve of her cheek! Louise wondered incredulously whether she would be half as pretty as that when she was as old as her sister.

It was nice to have a big sister at home, but now that she was here, Louise wondered in a mature little housewifely way what in the world they were going to do with her. She didn't look at all fit for cooking and things like that, and Louise sighed wearily as she struggled with the buttons and thought of the day before her and the endless weeks that must go by before they could hope for the return of the dear mother who had made even poverty sweet and cheerful. And there was that matter of a spring hat and a costume to wear at the school play. She stole another glance at the lovely sleeping sister and decided it would not do to bother her with little trifles like that. She would have to manage them somehow herself. Then, with the last button conquered and a hasty tying-back of her yellow curls with a much-worn ribbon, she tiptoed responsibly from the room, taking care to shut the latch securely and silently behind her.

She sped downstairs and went capably at the kitchen stove, coaxing it into brightness and glancing fearfully at the kitchen clock. It was six o'clock, and she could hear her father stirring about in his room. He would be down soon to look after the furnace, and then she must have breakfast on the table at once, for he must catch the six fifty-five car. The usual morning frenzy of rush seized her, and she flew from dining room to pantry cutting bread, and back to the stove to turn the bacon and be sure it did not burn. It was a mad race, and sometimes she felt like crying by the time she sat down to the table to pour her father's coffee, which somehow, try as she would, just would not look or taste like Mother's. She was almost relieved that her sister had given no sign of wakening yet, for she had not had time to make the breakfast table look nice, and it was kind of exciting to try to eat in a hurry and have "sort of company" to think about at the same time.

The father came downstairs peering into the dining room anxiously, with an apology on his lips for his eldest child.

"That's right, Louise, I'm glad you let her sleep. She looked all wearied out last night with her long journey, and then I guess it's been a kind of a shock to her, too."

"I guess it has," said the little girl comfortably and passed him his cup of coffee and the bread plate. They both had a sense of relief that Cornelia was not there and that there was a legitimate reason for not blaming her for her absence. Neither had yet been willing to admit to their loyal selves that Cornelia's attitude of apathy to the family hardship had been disappointing. They kept hoping against hope.

Mr. Copley finished his coffee hurriedly and looked at his watch.

"Better let her sleep as long as she will," he said. "She'll likely be awake before you need to go to school, and if she isn't, you can leave a note telling her where to find things. Where's Harry? Isn't he up?"

"Oh yes, he went to the grocery for the soup bone he forgot to get last night. I was going to put it on cooking before I left. I thought maybe she wouldn't know to—"

"That's right! That's right! You're a good little girl, Louise. Your sister'll appreciate that. Make Harry eat a good breakfast when he gets back. It isn't good to go out on an empty stomach, and we must all keep well and not worry Mother, you know."

"Yes, I know," sighed the little girl with a responsible look. "I made him take a piece with him, and I'm saving something hot for him when he comes back. He'll help me with the dishes, he said. We'll make out all right. Don't you worry, Father, dear."

The father, with a tender father-and-mother-both smile, came around and kissed her white forehead where the soft baby-gold hair parted and then hurried away to his car, thankful for the mother's look in his youngest girl's face, wondering whether they had chased it forever away from the eldest girl's face by sending her too young to college.

It was to the soft clatter of pots and pans somewhere in the near distance that Cornelia finally awakened with a sense of terrible depression and a belated idea that she ought to be doing something for the family comfort. She arose hastily and dressed with a growing distaste for the new day and what was before her. Even the view from the grimy little bedroom window was discouraging. It was a gray day, and one could see there were intentions of rain in the messy clouds that hurled themselves across the distant rooftops. The window looked out into the backyard, a small enclosure with a fence needing paint and dishearteningly full of rusty tin cans and old weather-stained newspapers and trash. Beyond the narrow, dirty alley were rows of other similar backyards, with now and then a fluttering dishcloth hanging on a string on a back porch and plenty of heaped-up ash cans everywhere you looked. They were the back doors of houses of the poorer class, most of them two-story and old. Farther on there was an excellent view of a large dump in a wide, cavernous lot that looked as if it had suffered from an earthquake sometime in the dim past and lost its bottom, so enormous it seemed as its steep sides sloped down, liberally coated with "dump." Cornelia gave a slight shiver of horror and turned from the window. To think of having to look at a view like that all summer. A vision of the cool, leafy camp where she had spent two weeks the summer before floated tantalizingly before her sad eyes as she slowly went downstairs.

It was a plaintive little voice that arrested her attention and her progress halfway down, a sweet, tired young voice that went to her heart, coming from the open kitchen door and carrying straight through the open dining room and through the hall up to her.

"I guess she doesn't realize how much we needed her," it said sadly. "And I guess she's pretty disappointed at the house and everything. It's pretty much of a change from college, of course."

Then a young, indignant high-tenor growl:

"Hm! What does she think she is, anyway? Some queen? I guess the house has been good enough for us. How does she think we've stood being poor all these years just to keep her in college? I'd like to know. This house isn't so much worse'n the last one we were in. It's a peach beside some we might have had to take if these folks hadn't been just moving out now. What does she want to do anyhow? Isn't her family good enough for her, or what? If I ever have any children, I shan't send 'em to college, I know that. It spoils 'em. And I don't guess I'll ever go myself. What's her little old idea, anyway? Who crowned her?"

"Why, she wants to be an interior decorator," said the little sister, slowly hanging up the dishcloth. "I guess it's all right, and she'd make money and all, only we just couldn't help her out till she got through her course."

"Interior decorator!" scornfully said the boy. "I'd be satisfied if she'd decorate my interior a little. I'd like some of Mother's waffles, wouldn't you? And some hash and Johnnycake. Gee! Well, I guess we better get a hustle on, or we'll be called down for tardiness. You gotta wake her up before you go?"

"Father said not to; I'm just going to leave a note. It's all written there on the dining room table. You put some coal on the range, and I'll get my hat and coat," and the little sister moved quickly toward the hall.

Cornelia in sudden panic turned silently and sped back to her room, closing the door and listening with wildly beating heart till her young brother and sister went out the door and closed it behind them. Then, obeying an impulse that she did not understand, she suddenly flung her door open and flew to her father's front bedroom window for a sight of them as they trudged off with piles of books under their arms, two valiant young comrades, just as she and Carey used to be in years so long ago and far away that she had almost forgotten them. And how they had stabbed her, her own brother and sister, talking about her as if she were a selfish stranger who had been living on their sacrifices for a long time! What could it possibly mean? Surely they were mistaken. Children always exaggerated things, and of course the few days or perhaps weeks since their father had lost his money had seemed a long time to them, poor little souls. Of course it had been hard for them to get along even a few days without Mother, and in this awful house. But—how could they have talked that way? How terrible of them! There were tears in her eyes and a pain in her heart from the words, for after all, in spite of her self-centered abstraction she did love them all; they were hers, and of course dearer than anything else on earth. Yes, even than interior decorating, and of course it was right that she should come home and make them comfortable, only—if only!

But presently the tears had spent themselves, and she began to wipe her eyes and look around. Her father's room was as desolate as any other. There was no evidence of an attempt to put comfort into it. The upper part of the heavy walnut bureau, with its massive mirror that Cornelia remembered as a part of the furniture of her mother's room since she was a baby, had not been screwed to the bureau but was standing on the floor as if it had just moved in. The bureau top was covered with dust; worn, jumbled neckties; soiled collars; and a few old letters. Her father's few garments were strewn around the room, and the open closet door revealed some of her mother's garments, old ones that Cornelia remembered she had had before she herself went to college.

On the unmade bed, close beside the pillow as if it had been cherished for comfort, was one of Mother's old calico shawls. It was lying where a cheek might conveniently rest against it. Somehow Cornelia didn't think of that explanation of its presence there at first, but later it grew into her consciousness, and the pathetic side of it filled her with dismay. Was life like this always, or was this a special preparation for her benefit?

Somehow, as she sat there, her position as a selfish, unloving daughter became intolerable. Could it be possible that the children had spoken truly and that the family had been in troubled circumstances for a longer time than just a few weeks, on account of keeping her in college? The color burned in her cheeks, and her eyes grew heavy with shame. How shabby everything looked! She didn't remember it that way. Her home had always seemed a comfortable one as she looked back upon it. Somehow she could not understand. But the one thought that burned into her soul was that they had somehow felt her lacking, ungrateful.

Suddenly she was stung into action. They should see that she was no selfish, idle member of the family group. At least, she could be as brave as they were. She would go to work and make a difference in things before they came home. She would show them!

She flew to the unmade bed and began to straighten the rumpled sheets and plump up the pillows. In an instant she had it smoothly made. But there was no white spread to put over it, and there were rolls of dust under the bed and in the corners. The floor had not even a rug to cover its bareness. Worn shoes and soiled socks trailed about here and there, and several old garments hung on bedposts, drifted from chairs, and even lay on the floor. Cornelia went hastily about, gathering them up, sorting out the laundry, setting the shoes in an even row in the closet, straightening the bureau, and stuffing things into the already overflowing drawers, promising them an early clearing out as soon as she had the rest of the work in hand. Poor Father! Of course he was not used to keeping things in order. How a woman was missed in a house! She hadn't realized it before. The whole house looked as if the furniture had just been dumped in with no attempt to set things right, as her father had said. She must get the broom and begin.

She hurried out into the hall, and a glimpse of the narrow stairway winding above her drew her to investigate. And then a sudden thought: *Carey.* Where was Carey? Hadn't he come home at all last night? She had no recollection of hearing him, and yet she might have fallen asleep earlier than she thought. She mounted the stairs and stood aghast before the desolation there.

The little closet Louise had spoken of with its skylight and its meager cot of twisted blankets, its chair with a medley of Harry's clothes, and its floor strewn with a varied collection, was dreary enough, but there was yet some semblance of attempt at order. The muddy shoes stood in a row; some garments were in piles, and some hung on nails as if there had been an attempt at good housekeeping by the young owner. There was even a colored picture of a baseball favorite and a drawing of a famous game. One could feel that the young occupant had taken possession with some sense of ownership in the place. But the front room was like a desert of destruction where lay bleaching the bones of a former life as if swept there by a whirlwind.

The headboard and footboard of the iron bedstead stood against the wall together like a corpse cast aside and unburied. On the floor in the very middle of the room lay the springs, and upon them the worn and soiled mattress, hardly recognizable by that name now because of the marks of heavy, muddy shoes, as if it had been not only slept upon but walked over with shoes straight from the contact of the street in bad weather. Sheets, there were none, and the pillow, soiled and with a hole burnt in one corner of its ticking, lay guiltless of a pillowcase, with a beaten, sodden impression of a head in its center. There was a snarl of soiled blanket and torn patchwork quilt across the foot, tossed to one side, and all about this excuse for a bed was strewn the most heterogeneous mass of objects that Cornelia had ever seen collected. Clothes, soiled and just from the laundry, all in one mass; neckties tangled among books and letters; cheap magazines and parts of automobiles; a silk hat and a white evening vest keeping company with a pair of greasy overalls and two big iron wrenches; and over everything cigarette buds.

The desolation was complete. The bureau had turned its back to the scene in despair and was face to the wall, as it had been placed by the movers. It was then and not till then that Cornelia understood how recent had been the moving and how utter the rout of the poor, patient mother, whose wonderful housekeeping had always been the boast of the neighborhood where they had lived, and whose fastidiousness had been almost an obsession.

Cornelia stood in the door and gasped in horror as her eyes traveled from one corner of the room to another and back again, and her quick mind read the story of her brother's life and one deep cause of her dear mother's breakdown. She remembered her father's words about Carey and how he hoped she would be able to help him, and then her memory went back to the days when she and Carey were inseparable. She saw the bright, eager face of her brother only two years younger than herself, always merry, with a jest on his lips and a twinkle in his eyes, but a kind heart and a willingness always to serve. Had Carey in three short years fallen to this? Because there was no excuse for an able-bodied young man to live in a mess like this. No young man with a mite of self-respect would do it. And Carey knew better. Carey had been brought up to take care of himself and his things. Nobody could mend a bit of furniture or fix the plumbing or sweep a room or even wash out a blanket for Mother better than Carey when he was only fifteen. And for Carey, as she knew him, to be willing to lie down for at least more than one night in a room like this and go off in the morning leaving it this way was simply unthinkable. How Carey must have changed to have come to this! As her eyes roved around the room, she began to have an insight into what must be the trouble. Self-indulgence of a violent type must have got hold of him. Look at the hundreds of cigarette buds, ashes everywhere. The only saving thing was the touch of machinery in the otherwise hopeless mass, and that, too, meant only that he was crazy about automobiles and likely fussed with them now and then to repair them so that he would have opportunity to ride as much as he liked. And Carey—where was Carey now?

She turned sadly away from the room and shut the door. It was a work of time to think of getting that mess straightened out into any sort of order, and it made her heartsick and hopeless. She must look further and learn the whole story before she began to do anything.

She stumbled blindly downstairs, only half glancing into the messy bathroom where soap and toothbrushes got standing room indiscriminately where they could; took a quick look into the small enclosure that Louise had described as a "linen closet," probably on account of a row of dirty-looking shelves at one end of the room; and looked hesitatingly toward the door of her own room, wondering whether to stop there long enough to make the bed and tidy up but shook her head and went on downstairs. She must know the whole thing before she attempted to do anything.

The stairs ascended at the back of the hall, with a cloak closet under them now stuffed with old coats and hats belonging to the whole family. Opposite this closet the dining room door opened. All the space in front was devoted to the large front room known as the "parlor." Cornelia flung the door open wide and stepped in. The blinds were closed, letting in only a slant ray of light from a broken slat over the desolation of half-unpacked boxes and barrels that prevailed. Evidently the children had mauled everything over in search of certain articles they needed and had not put back or put away anything. Pictures and dishes and clothing lay about miscellaneously in a confused heap, and a single step into the room was liable to do damage, for one might step into a china meat platter under a down quilt or knock over a cut-glass pitcher in the dark. Cornelia stopped and rescued several of her mother's best dishes from a row near the first barrel by the door, transferring them to the hall rack before she dared go in to look around.

The piano was still encased in burlap, standing with its keyboard to the wall, an emblem of the family's desolation. As her eyes grew accustomed to the dim light, Cornelia gradually began to identify various familiar objects. There were the old sofa and upholstered chairs that used to be in the nursery when Louise and Harry were mere babies. The springs were sagging and the tapestry faded.

She searched in vain for the better suite of furniture that had been bought for the living room before she went to college. Where was it? It hadn't been in the dining room the night before, she was sure; and of course it couldn't be in the kitchen. Could there be a shed at the back somewhere, with more things that were not as yet unpacked? With a growing fear she slipped behind some barrels and tried to find the big bookcase with the glass doors, and the mahogany tables that Mother had been so proud of because they had belonged to her great-grandmother, and the claw-legged desk with the cabinet on the top. Not one of them was to be found.

A horrible suspicion was dawning in her mind. She waited only to turn back the corners of several rolls of carpet and rugs and make sure the Oriental rugs were missing, before she fled in a panic to the back of the house.

Through the bare little kitchen she passed without even noticing how hard the children had worked to clear it up. Perhaps she would not have called it cleared up, her standard being on an entirely different scale from theirs. Yes, there was a door at the farther side. She flung it open and found the hoped-for shed, but no furniture. Its meager space was choked with tubs and an old washing machine, broken boxes and barrel staves, a marble tabletop broken in two, and a rusty washtub. With a shiver of conviction she stood and stared at them and then slammed the door shut, and flinging herself into a kitchen chair, burst into tears.

She had not wept like that since she was a little girl, but the tears somehow cleared the cobwebs from her eyes and heart. She knew now that those beautiful things of her mother's were gone, and her strong suspicions were that she was the cause of it all. Someone else was enjoying them so that the money they brought could be used to keep her in college! And she had been blaming her father for not having managed somehow to let her stay longer! All these months, or perhaps years for all she knew, he had been straining and striving to keep her from knowing how hard he and her dear mother were saving and scrimping to make her happy and give her the education she wanted; and she, selfish, unloving girl that she was, had been painting, drawing, studying, directing class plays, making fudge, playing hockey, reading delightful books, attending wonderful lectures and concerts, studying beautiful pictures, and all the time growing further and further away from the dear people who were giving their lives—yes, literally giving their lives, for they couldn't have had much enjoyment in living at this rate—to make it all possible for her!

Oh! She saw it all clearly enough now, and she hated herself for it. She began to go back over last night and how she had met them. She visualized their faces as they stood at the gate eagerly awaiting her, and she, little college snob that she was, was ashamed to greet them eagerly because she was with a fine lady and her probably snobbish son. Her suddenly awakened instinct recalled the disappointed look on the tired father's face and the sudden dulling of the merry twinkles of gladness in the children's eyes. Oh! She could see it all now, and each new memory and conviction brought a stab of pain to her heart. Then, as if the old walls of the house took up the accusation against her, she began to hear over again the plaintive voices of Louise and Harry as they wiped the dishes and talked her over. It was all too plain that she had been weighed in the balances and found wanting. Something in the pitiful wistfulness of Harry's voice as he had made that quick turn about interior decoration roused her at last to the present and her immediate duty. It was no use whatever to sit here and cry about it when such a mountain of work awaited her. The lady on the train had been right when she told her there would be plenty of chance for her talents. She had not dreamed of any such desolation as this, of course, but it was true that the opportunity, if one could look on it as an opportunity, was great, and she would see what she could do. At least things could be clean and tidy. And there should be waffles! That was a settled thing, waffles for the first meal. And she rose and looked about her with the spirit of victory in her eyes and in the firm, sweet line of her quivering lips.

What time was it, and what ought she to do first? She stepped to the dining room door to consult the clock, which she could hear ticking noisily from the mantel, and her eye caught her sister's note written large across the corner of a paper bag.

> *Dear Nellie,*
>
> *I had to go to school. I'll get back as soon after four as I can. You can heet the fride potatoes, and there are some eggs.*
>
> *Louie*

Suddenly the tears blurred into her eyes at the thought of the little disappointed sister yet taking care for her in her absence. Dear little Louie! How hard it must have been for her! And she remembered the sigh she had heard from the kitchen a little while ago. Well, she was thankful she had been awakened right away and not allowed to go on in her selfish indifference. She glanced at the clock. It was a quarter to nine. She had lost a lot of time mooning over her own troubles. She had but seven hours in which to work wonders before anyone returned. She must go to work at once.

Chapter 4

A hasty survey of the pantry showed a scant supply of materials. There was flour and sugar and half a basket of potatoes. Some cans of tomatoes and corn, a paper bag of dried beans, another of rice, two eggs in a bowl, and a dish of discouraged-looking fried potatoes with burnt edges completed the count. A small bit of butter on a plate and the end of a baker's loaf of bread had evidently been left on the dining room table for her. There were a good many things needed from the store, and she began to write them down on the other side of her sister's note. A further investigation revealed half a bottle of milk that had soured. Cornelia's face brightened. That would make a wonderful gingerbread, and she wrote down "molasses, soda, brown sugar, baking powder" on her list.

It wasn't as if Cornelia hadn't spent the first sixteen years of her life at home with her mother, for she knew how to cook and manage quite well before she went away to school; only of course she hadn't done a thing at it since she left home, and like most girls she thought she hated the very idea of kitchen work.

"Now, where do they buy things?" she wondered aloud to the clock as if it were alive. "I shall have to find out. I suppose if I take a basket and go far enough, I shall come to a store. If I don't, I can ask somebody."

She ran upstairs and got her hat and coat, and patted her pocketbook happily. At least she was not penniless and did not have to wait until her father came home for what she wanted to get; for she had almost all of the last money her mother had sent before her illness. It had been sent for new spring clothes, and Cornelia had been so busy she had not had time to buy them. It sent a glad thrill through her heart now, strangely mingled with a pang at the things that she had planned and that now would not be hers. Yet after all, the pang did not last, for already her mind was taken up with the new interests and needs of home, and she was genuinely glad that she had the money still unspent.

Down the dull little street she sped, thinking of all she had to do in the house before the family came home, trying not to feel the desolation of the night before as she passed the commonplace houses and saw what kind of neighborhood she had come to live in, trying not to realize that almost every house showed neglect or poverty of some kind. Well, what of it? If she did live in a neighborhood that was utterly uncongenial, she could at least make their little home more comfortable. She knew she could. She could feel the ability for it tingling to her very fingertips, and she smiled as she hurried on to the next corner, where the gleam of a trolley track gave hint of a possible business street. She paused at the corner and looked each way, a pretty picture of girlhood, balancing daintily on her neat little feet and looking quite out of place in that neighborhood. Some of her new neighbors eyed her from behind their Nottingham lace curtains and their blue paper shades and wondered unsympathetically where she came from and how she had strayed there, and a young matron in a dirty silver-lace nightcap with fluttering pink and blue ribbons came out with her market basket and gave a cool, calculating stare, so far in another world that she did not mind being caught at it.

The nightcap was almost too much for Cornelia, bobbing around the fat, red face of the frowsy woman, but the market basket gave her a hint, and she gracefully fell in behind her fellow shopper and presently arrived at a market.

About this time Mrs. Maxwell and her son sat in the hotel dining room downtown, eating their breakfast. A telegram had just been laid beside the son's plate, and he looked up from reading it with a troubled brow.

"I'm afraid I'm going to have to upset our plans again," he said. "I'm awfully sorry, Mother, but Brown is coming on from Boston expecting to meet me at noon, and I guess there's nothing to do but wait until the two o'clock train. Shall you mind very much?"

"Not at all," said his mother, smiling. "Why should I mind? I came on to be with you. Does it matter whether I'm in Philadelphia or Washington?"

"Is there anything you would like to do this morning? Any shopping? Or would you like to drive about a bit?"

She shook her head.

"I can shop at home. I came here to be with you."

"Then let's drive," he decided with a loving smile. "Where would you like to go? Anything you want to see?"

"No—or wait. Yes, there is. I've a notion I'd like to drive past the house where that little girl I met on the train lives. I'd like to see exactly what she's up against with her firm little chin and her clear, wise eyes and her artistic ways."

"At it again, aren't you, Mother? Always falling in love and chasing after your object. You're worse than a young man in his teens." He smiled understandingly. "All right. We'll hunt her up, Mother, only we shan't have much time to stop, for I have to be here sharp at twelve thirty. Do you know where she lives?"

"Yes, I have her address here," said his mother, searching in her silver bag for the card on which Cornelia had written it. "But I don't want to stop. It wouldn't do. She would think me intruding."

The young man took the address and ordered a taxicab, and five minutes after Cornelia entered the door of her home with her arms full of bundles from the market and grocery, a taxicab crawled slowly by the house, and two pairs of eyes eagerly scanned the high, narrow, weather-stained building, with its number over the front door the only really distinct thing about it.

"The poor child!" murmured the lady.

"Well, she sure is up against it!" growled the son, sitting back with an air of not looking but taking it all in out of the tail end of his eye the way young men can do.

"And she wants to be an interior decorator!" said the mother, turning from her last look out the little window behind.

"She's got some task this time, I'll say!" answered the son. "It may show up more promisingly from the interior, but I doubt it. And you say she's been to college? Dwight Hall, didn't you say, where Dorothy Mayo graduated? Some comedown! It's a hard world. Well, Mother, I guess we've got to get back or I'll miss my appointment," and he gave the chauffeur directions to turn about.

More rapidly they passed this time, but the eyes of the woman took in all the details: the blank sidewall where windows ought to have abounded; the shallow third story obviously with space for only one room; the lowly neighbors; the dirty, noisy children in the street. She thought of the girl's lovely refined face and sighed.

"One might, of course, do a great deal of good in such a neighborhood. It is an opportunity," she murmured thoughtfully.

Her son looked amused.

"I imagine she'll confine her attention to the interior of her own home if she does anything at all. I'm afraid if I came home from college to a place like that, I'd beat it, mother mine."

His mother looked up with a trusting smile.

"You wouldn't, though!" she said sunnily and added thoughtfully, "And she won't either. She had a true face. Sometime I'm coming back to see how it came out."

Meantime, Cornelia in the kitchen started the fire up brightly, put on the teakettle, and began to concoct a soft gingerbread with the aid of the nice thick sour milk. When it was in the oven, she hunted out her mother's old worn bread raiser, greased the squeaking handle with butter, and started some bread. She remembered how everybody in the family loved Mother's homemade bread, and if there was one thing above another in which she had excelled as a little girl in the kitchen, it was in making bread. Somehow it did not seem as though things were on a right basis until she had some bread on the way. As she crumbled the yeast cake into a sauce dish and put it a-soak, she began to hum a little tune, yet her mind was so preoccupied with what she had to do that she scarcely remembered it was the theme of the music that ran all through the college play. College life had somehow receded for the present, and in place of costumes and drapery she was considering what she ought to make and bake in order to have the pantry and refrigerator well stocked, and how soon she might with a clear conscience go upstairs and start clearing up Carey's bedroom. She couldn't settle rightly to anything until that awful mess was straightened out. The consciousness of the disorder up there in the third story was like a bruise that had been given her, which made itself more and more felt as the minutes passed.

When the cover was put down tight on the bread-raiser, Cornelia looked about her.

"I really ought to clean this kitchen first," she said thoughtfully, speaking aloud as if she and herself were having it out about the work. "There aren't enough dishes unpacked for the family to eat comfortably, but there's not room on those shelves for them if they were unpacked."

So, with a glance at the rapidly rising gingerbread that let out a whiff of delicious aroma, she mounted on a chair and began to clear off the top shelves of the dresser. It seemed as if there had been no system whatever in placing things. Bottles of shoe polish, a hammer, a box of gingersnaps, a can of putty, and several old neckties were settled in between glass sauce dishes and the electric iron. She kept coming on little necessities. With small ceremony she swept them all down to an orderly row on the floor on the least-used side of the room, and with soap, hot water, and a scrubbing brush went at the shelves. It didn't take long, of course, but she put a great deal of energy into the work and began to feel actually happy as she smelled the clean soapsuds and saw what a difference it made in the shabby, paintless shelves to get rid of the dirt.

"Now, we've at least got a spot to put things!" she announced as she took the gingerbread tins out of the oven and with great satisfaction noted that she had not forgotten how to make gingerbread in the interval of her college days.

The gingerbread reminded her that she had as yet had no breakfast, but she would not mar the velvet beauty of those fragrant loaves of gingerbread by cutting one now. She cut off a slice of the dry end of a loaf and buttered it. She was surprised to find how good it tasted as she ate it going about her work, picking up what dishes on the floor belonged back on the shelves, and washing and arranging them. Later, if there was time, she would unpack more dishes, but she must get up to Carey's room. It was like leaving something dead about uncovered, to know that that room looked so above her head.

It was twelve o'clock when she at last got permission of herself to go upstairs, and she carried with her broom, mop, soap, scrubbing brush, and plenty of hot water and old cloths. She paused at the door of the front room long enough to rummage in the bureau drawers and get out an old allover gingham apron of her mother's, which she donned before ascending to the third floor.

In the doorway of her brother's room she stood appalled once more, scarcely knowing where to begin. Then, putting down her brushes and pails in the hall, she started in at the doorway, picking up the first things that came in her way. Clothes first. She sorted them out quickly, hanging the good things on the railing of the stairs, the worn and soiled ones in piles on the floor, ready for the laundry, the ragman, and the mending basket. When the garments were all out, she turned back, and the room seemed to be just as full and just as messy as it had been before. She began again, this time gleaning the newspapers and magazines. That made quite a hole in the floor space. Next she dragged the twisted blankets off the mattress and threw them down the stairs. Somehow they must be washed or aired or replaced before that bed would be fit to sleep in. After a thoughtful moment of looking over the banisters at them, she descended and carried them all to the little backyard, where she hung them on a short line that had been stretched from the fence to the house. They made a sorry sight, but she would have to leave them till later. The sun and air would help. There wasn't much sun, and there was still a sharp tang of rain in the air; it had been raining at intervals all the morning.

Well, if it rained on them, they certainly needed it, and anyhow it was too late in the day for her to try to wash any of them. She must do the best she could this first day.

Thus she reasoned as she frowningly surveyed the grimy blankets, her eyes lingering on a scorched place near the top of one. Suddenly her expression changed. "You've just *got* to be washed!" she said firmly, and snatching the blankets from the line, rushed in to arrange for large quantities of hot water, cleared off the stationary tubs and dumped in the blankets, shaved up the only bar of soap she could find, and then went rummaging in the front room while the water was heating. Of course all this took strength, but she was not realizing how weary she was growing. Her mettle was up, and she was working on her nerve. It was a mercy with all she had before her that she was well and strong, and fresh from gymnasium and basketball training. It would take all her strength before she was done.

She emerged from the parlor twenty minutes later triumphant, with a number of things that she was sure would be needed. She went to work at the blankets with vigor, rubbing and pulling away at the scorched place until it was almost obliterated. *Did Carey smoke in his sleep*, she wondered, *or did he have guests that did*? How dreadful that Carey had come to this, and she away at college improving herself and complacently expecting to make her mark in the world!

The blankets were drying on the line in half an hour more, and she glanced at the clock. A whole hour had gone, and she must hasten. She sped back upstairs and went to work again, dragging out the furniture to the hall, picking up books and magazines from the floor, till the room was stark and empty except for cigarette buds. She surveyed them in disgust and then assailed the room with brushes, brooms, and mop. She threw the windows wide open and swept the wall down vigorously. Before her onslaught dust and ashes disappeared, and even the dismal wallpaper took on a brighter hue.

"It's got to come off and be repapered or painted some pretty, soft, pastel shade," she threatened in an undertone to herself as she surveyed the room after soap and water had done their best on floor, woodwork, and windows. She was looking at the bleary wallpaper with a troubled frown.

Of course she couldn't do everything in a day, but Carey's room must be clean and inviting before she would be satisfied. No wonder he stayed out late nights, or didn't come home at all, perhaps, with such a room as that. There ought to be more windows, too. What a pity the builder had been so stingy with them! It was a dark, ugly hole, and there was no need for it, for the room occupied the whole end and could have had openings on three sides and been delightful.

Suddenly she began to feel a great weariness stealing over her and tears coming into her eyes. She was overwhelmed with all that was before her. She sat down on the upper stair and looked about her discouragedly. All these things to be put somewhere! And time going so fast! Then she remembered her bread and with an exclamation rushed down to put it into the pans.

It had risen almost to the top of the bread raiser, and with a mental apology for her forgetfulness she hastened to mold it out into loaves and put it into the greased tins. When it was neatly tucked up under a bit of old linen she had found in the sideboard drawer, she began to prepare the meat for dinner and put it on to cook—a beautiful big pot roast. She deftly seared it with an onion in a hot frying pan and put it to simmer in boiling water with the rinsings of the browned pan, being careful to recall all her mother's early instruction on the subject. She could remember that pot roast was always a favorite dish at home, and she herself had been longing for a taste of real home-cooked pot roast ever since she had been away.

She fixed the fire carefully so that the meat would simmer just enough and not boil too hard and make it tough, and gave a despairing glance at the clock. How fast the minutes flew! She ought to go back upstairs, but it was a quarter to three, and she wanted to get the table set for dinner before she left so that the dining room would have a pleasant look to the children when they came home. She was quite breathless and excited over their coming. She felt as if she would be almost embarrassed before them after the conversation she had overheard in the morning.

So she attacked the dining room with broom and duster, wiped off the windowpanes and straightened the shade, swept away a mass of miscellaneous articles from the clock shelf, cleared off the sideboard, hunted out a clean old linen cover, polished the mirror, and found a clean tablecloth. But the tablecloth had a great hole in it, and fifteen valuable minutes were wasted in finding a patch and setting it hastily in place with a needle and thread that also had to be hunted for. Then some of the dishes had to be washed before they were fit for use, as they were covered with dust from packing. And all together it was five minutes to four before Cornelia finally had that table set to her satisfaction and could stand back for a brief minute and take it in with tired but shining eyes. Would they notice the difference and be a little glad that she had come? They had taken her for a lazy snob in the morning. Would they feel any better about it now?

And the table did look pretty. It was set as a table should be set, with dishes and glasses and silver in the correct places and napkins neatly folded, and in the center was a small pot of pink primroses in full bloom. For it would not have been Cornelia if there had not been a bit of decoration about somewhere, and it was like Cornelia when she went out to market and thought of meat and bread and milk and butter and all the other necessities, to think also of that bit of brightness and refinement and go into a small flower shop she was passing to get this pretty primrose.

Then in panic the weary big sister brought out one loaf of gingerbread, cut several generous slices, left it on the sideboard in a welcome attitude, and fled upstairs to finish Carey's room.

Five minutes later, as she was struggling with the bedsprings, trying to bring them into conjunction with the headboard, she heard their hurrying feet, and leaning from the window, called, "Children! Come up here a minute and help me."

"I can't," shouted Harry with a frown. "I got a job afternoons, and I gotta hustle. I'm late a'ready, and I have to change my clo'es!" And he vanished inside the door.

"I have to go to the store for things for dinner!" reproved the young sister stiffly, and vanished also.

Cornelia felt suddenly in her weariness like sitting down on the floor in a fit of hysterical laughter or tears. Would they never forgive her? She dropped on the floor with her head wearily back against the window and closed her eyes. She had meant to tell them about the gingerbread, but they had been in such a hurry, and somehow the spirit seemed gone out of her surprise.

Downstairs it was very still. The children had been halted at the entrance by the appetizing odor of cooking.

"Sniff!"

"Oh, gee!" said Harry. "It smells like Mother was home."

Louise stalked hurriedly to the dining room door.

"Harry Copley, just look here! Now, what did I tell you about college girls?"

Harry came and stood entranced.

"Oh, gee!" he murmured. "Isn't that just great? Oh, say, Lou Copley, just gaze on that sideboard! I'll tell the world this is some day!" And he strode to the sideboard and stopped all further speech by more than a mouthful of the fragrant gingercake.

The little housewife took swift steps to the kitchen door and sniffed. She took in the row of plump bread tins almost ready to go into the oven, the gently bubbling kettle with its fragrant steam, and the shining dresser with its neat rows of dishes that she had never been able to find, and then she whirled on her astonished brother.

"Harry Copley! You answered her real mean! You go upstairs and apologize quick! And then you beat it and change your clothes and get to work. I'll help her. We're going to work *together* after this, she and I." And seizing a large slice of gingerbread in her passing, she flew up the stairs to find her sister.

Chapter 5

They appeared in the doorway suddenly, after a sound like loco-motives rushing up the stairs, and surrounded her where she sat, after one astonished pause at the doorway staring around the unfamiliar room. They smothered her with hugs and kisses and demanded to know how she got so much done and what she wanted of them anyway, and they smeared her with gingerbread and made her glad; and then just as suddenly, Harry disappeared with the floating explanation trailing back after him:

"Oh, gee! I gotta beat it."

A few rustling movements in his own little closet of a room, and he was back attired in an old Boy Scout uniform and cram-ming down the last bite of his gingerbread.

"Anything I can do before I go? Oh, here!" as he saw his sisters about to put the bed together. "That won't take a second! Say, you girls don't know how to do that. Lemme."

And, surprising to state, he pushed them aside and whacked the bed together in no time, slatted on the mattress with his sturdy young arms, and was gone down through the dining room and out into the street with another huge slice of gingerbread in his hands.

Cornelia straightened her tired shoulders and looked at the subdued bed wonderingly. How handily he had done it! How strong he was! It was amazing.

Louise stood looking about with shining eyes.

"Say, Nellie, it looks lovely here, so clean and nice. I never thought it could be done; it looked so awful! I wanted to do something, and I know Mother felt fierce about not fixing his room before she left, but I just couldn't get time."

"Of course you couldn't dear!" said Cornelia, suddenly realizing how wise and brave this little sister had been. "You've been wonderful to do anything. Why didn't they send for me before, Louie? Tell me, how long had you been in this house before Mother was taken sick?"

"Why, only a day. She fainted, you know, trying to carry that marble bureau top upstairs, and fell down."

"Oh! My dear!"

The two sisters stood with their arms about each other mingling their tears for a moment, and somehow as she stood there, Cornelia felt as if the years melted away, the college years while she had been absent, and brought her back heart and soul to her home and her loved ones again.

"But Louie, dear, what has become of the best furniture? Did they have to rent the old house furnished? I can't find Mother's mahogany or the parlor things, anything but the piano."

The color rolled up into the little girl's face, and she dropped her eyes. "Oh no, Nellie. They went long ago," she said, "before we even moved to the State Street house."

"The State Street house?"

"Why, yes, Father sold the Glenside house just after you went to college. You knew that, didn't you? And then we moved to an old yellow house farther toward the city. But it was pulled down to make room for a factory; and I was glad, for it was horrid, and a long walk to school. And then we went to a brick row down near the factory, and it was convenient for Father, but—"

"Factory? Father? What do you mean, dear? Has Father gone into business for himself? He was a bookkeeper at Dudley and Warner's when I left."

"Oh, but he lost that a long, long time ago, after he was sick so long."

"Father sick? Louie! And I not told?"

"Why, I didn't know they hadn't told you. Maybe Mother wouldn't like it—"

"Tell me everything, dear. How long was Father sick?"

"About a year. He lost his position and then wasn't able to do anything for ever so long; and when he got out of the hospital, he hunted and hunted, and there wasn't anything for him. He got one good job, but they said he had to dress better, and he lost that."

Cornelia sank down on the floor again and buried her face in her hands.

"O Louie! And I was wearing nice clothes and doing nothing to help! Oh, why didn't Mother let me know?"

"Oh, Mother kept saying she thought she could manage, and it was Father's dream you should get your education," quoted the little girl with dreamy eyes and the memory of many sacrifices sweetly upon her.

"Go on, Louie, what next?"

"Oh, nothing much. Mother sold the furniture to an 'antique' woman that was hunting old things, and that paid for Father's medicine, and they said they wouldn't touch the money they had put in the bank for your college; and then Father got the place at the factory. It's kind of hard work, I guess, but it's good pay, and Father thought he'd manage to let you finish, only Mother gave out, and then everything went to pieces."

The small, red lips puckered bravely, and suddenly the child threw her arms around her sister's neck and cried out, sobbing, "Oh, I'm so glad you've come!" and Cornelia wrapped her close to her heart.

Into the midst of this touching scene there stole a sweetly pungent odor of meat boiling dry, and suddenly Cornelia and Louise smelled it at the same instant and flew for the stairs.

"I guess it's not really burned yet," said wise Louise. "It doesn't smell that way," she said comfortingly. "My, it makes me hungry!"

"And oh, my bread!" exclaimed Cornelia as she rounded the top of the next flight. "It ought to go into the oven. It will get too light." They rescued the meat not at all hurt but just lusciously browned and most appetizing, and then they put the bread into the oven and turned their attention to potatoes and waffles.

"I'm going to make some maple syrup," said Cornelia. "It's better homemade. I bought a bottle of maple flavoring this morning. We used to make maple fudge with it, and it's good."

"Isn't this great?" exclaimed the little girl, watching the bubbling sugar and water. "Won't Father be glad?"

"But Louie, where is Carey?" asked Cornelia suddenly.

The little girl's face grew dark.

"He's off!" she said shortly. "I guess he didn't come home at all last night. Father worries a lot about him, and Mother did, too, but he's been worse since Mother was sick. He hardly ever comes in till after midnight, and then he smokes and smokes. Oh, it makes me sick! I told Harry if he grew up that way I'd never speak to him. And Harry says if he ever does, he gives me leave to turn him down. Oh, Carey acts like a nut! I don't see how he can, when he knows how Father has to work and everything. He just won't get a position anywhere. He wants to have a good time. He plays ball, and he rides around in a rich fellow's car, and he has a girl! Oh, he's the *limit*."

Cornelia felt her heart sinking.

"What kind of a girl, Louie?"

"Oh, a girl with flour on her face, and an awful tight skirt; and when she goes out evenings, she wears her back bare way down almost to her waist. I saw her in a concert at our church, and she was dressed that way there, and folks were all looking at her and saying it wasn't nice. She dances, too, and kicks, with lots of skirts and ruffles and things, made of chiffon; and she makes eyes at boys; and I know a girl at school that says she saw her smoking cigarettes at a restaurant once. You see it isn't much use to fix up Carey's room when he does things like that. He doesn't deserve it."

Cornelia looked aghast.

"Oh, but we must, Louie! We must all the more then. And perhaps the girl isn't so bad if we knew her, and—and tried to help her. Some girls are awfully silly at a certain age, dear."

"Well, you oughta see her. Harry knows, and he thinks she's the limit. He says the boys all talk about her. She wears makeup, too, and big black earrings down on her shoulders sometimes, and she wears her hair just like the pictures of the devil!"

Cornelia had to laugh at the earnest, fierce little face, and the laugh broke the tension somewhat.

"Well, dearie, we'll have to find a way to coax Carey back to us," she said soothingly, even while her heart was sinking. "He's our brother, you know, and we love him, and it would break Mother's heart."

"Oh yes," said Louise, not noticing her sister's face. "We hadn't any side windows at all there; the houses were close up, and there were very unpleasant people all around. It wasn't at all a good neighborhood. Carey hated it. He wouldn't come home for days and days. He said it wasn't fit for pigs."

"Where did he go? Where has he gone now, do you suppose?"

"Oh, off with the boys somewhere. Sometimes to their houses. Sometimes they take trips around. One of them has a car. His father's rich. But I don't like him. His name's Brand Barlock. He drives wherever he likes. They went to Washington once and were gone a week. Mother never slept a wink those nights, just sat at the front window and watched after we went to bed. I know, for I woke up and found her so several times. He might've gone to Baltimore now. There's a game down that way sometime soon. I guess it was last night. Harry heard 'em talking about it. They go with the gang of fellows that used to play on our high school team when Carey was in school."

"School?" Cornelia caught at the word hopefully. "Perhaps it's only fun, then, Louie. Maybe, it's nothing really bad."

"No. They're pretty tough," sighed the wise child. "Harry knows. He hears the boys talk."

"Well, dear, we'll have to forget it now, anyway, and get to work. We must fix Carey's room so he can sleep there tonight if he does come back, and we must have supper ready when Father gets home."

The child brightened. "Won't they be surprised?" she said with a happy light in her eyes. "What do you want me to do? Shall I peel the potatoes?"

"Yes, do, and have plenty. We'll mash them, shall we? I found the potato-masher in the bottom of a barrel in the parlor, so I don't believe you've been using it lately."

"That's right. We had all we could do to bake them or boil them whole," said Louise. "You bake the bread, and I'll get things away upstairs and make Carey's bed."

"Are there any clean sheets? I didn't know where to look."

"No, there's only one pair, and I kept them for you next week."

"We can't keep anything for me, duckie dear," said Cornelia, laughing. "Carey's got to have clean sheets this very night. I have a hunch he's coming home, and I want that room to be ready. That's the first step in getting him back to us, you know."

"Oh, well, all right," said the little sister. "They are in the lower drawer of our bureau. How good that bread smells! My, it was nice of you to make it! And how dear the dining room table looks with that little flower in the middle. Some girls' sisters would have thought that was unnecessary. They would have made us wait for pretty things. But you didn't, did you? I guess that's what makes you an interior decorator, isn't it? Father and Mother are awfully proud of you. They talked about it most every night before Carey got to going away, how you would be a great artist someday and all that. And, my! It most killed them to have to call you home."

Louise chattered on, revealing many a household tragedy, until Cornelia was cut to the heart and wanted to drop down and cry, only she had too much at stake to give up now.

They went upstairs presently with the clean sheets and the blankets that had almost miraculously got themselves dry owing to a bright sun and a strong west wind that had arrived soon after they were put out, and they had a beautiful time making that bed. Carey wouldn't know himself in such a bed. Then they hunted out a bureau scarf, and they went through the tousled drawers of the chiffonier and bureau and put things in order, laying out a pile of things that needed mending or washing, and making the room look cheery and bright.

"It ought to have something pretty like a flower here, too," sighed Louise, taking a final glance around as Cornelia folded the old down quilt in a self-respecting puff at the foot of the bed and gave another pat to the clean white pillow. "I know!" said Louise, suddenly flitting downstairs to her own room and hurrying back again with a small oval easel picture of her mother, dusting it carefully with her handkerchief as she came. "There! Won't that look better?"

"Indeed it will," said her sister, her eyes filling with tears as she looked into the loving eyes of the dear mother from whom she had been separated so long. "And perhaps it will do Carey good to look into his mother's eyes when he comes home, who knows?"

So they went down together to put the finishing touches to the supper and to talk of many things. Louise even got around to the play and the costume she was going to try to make, and Cornelia delighted her heart by saying she was sure she had just the very costume in her trunk, one that she wore in a college play herself, and she would help her make it over to fit.

Everything was ready for supper at last, and it was time within three minutes for Father's car to arrive. Harry would likely meet him at the corner and come with him. Cornelia was taking up the pot roast and telling Louise about beating the mashed potatoes to make them lighter. The waffle iron had been found under the piano stool in the parlor and was sizzling hot and well greased awaiting the fluffy batter. The hot maple syrup was on the table and everything exactly ready. Suddenly they heard a noisy automobile thunder up to the front of the house and pause, a clatter of voices and the car thundered on again. Footsteps up the walk, and the front door banged open and shut; feet stamped up the stairs, while a faint breath of cigarette smoke trailed out and penetrated into the kitchen to mingle with the fragrance of the dinner. The two cooks stopped and looked at each other understandingly.

"He's come," said the eyes of the little sister.

"We must make him very welcome," answered the eyes of

the big sister, so tired she could hardly hold her young shoulders straight.

"Maybe he won't stay," whispered Louise softly a minute later. "Sometimes he doesn't; he might have a date."

"Here's hoping," said Cornelia cheerfully, as she dabbed the batter into the irons for the first waffle. "You'll have to contrive to catch him if he tries to go away, Lou."

"I wonder what he thinks of his room," giggled the little sister. "I guess maybe he thought he'd made a mistake and got into the wrong house."

It was all very still upstairs. There were not even any footsteps going around, not for what seemed like several minutes, then slowly the footsteps came down the stairs again, hesitating, paused at the second flight, and came on until they reached the open dining room door.

Carey stood there gazing at the table as Louise came in bearing the dish of potatoes, and Cornelia followed her with the platter of meat, both earnestly intent and flushed with their work; and just at that moment, before the girls had looked up, the front door opened, and in came the father, with Harry whistling happily behind him.

"Oh, gee!" he cried, stopping his whistling. "Don't that supper smell good? Here's hoping there's plenty of it."

It was at that instant that Cornelia looked up, and her eyes met the eyes of her handsome, reckless-looking brother, astonishment, bewilderment, shame, delight, and embarrassment struggling in his face.

Chapter 6

"Nell!"

There was genuine delight in the boy's tone as he came forward to greet her, shyly, perhaps, and with a bit of shamed hesitancy because he could not but remember that the family had probably told her all about him, and she would of course disapprove of him as much as they did.

But Cornelia, with the steaming gravy boat in one hand and a pile of hot plates in the other, turned a warm, rosy cheek up to him, her eyes still intent on putting down the dishes without spilling the treacherous gravy on the clean tablecloth.

"It's great to see you again, Carey," she said heartily, trying to make the situation as casual as possible. "Sorry to seem brief, but I have something luscious on the stove, and I'm afraid it'll burn. Sit down quick, won't you—and be ready to eat it while it's hot? We'll talk afterward. I want to have a good look at you and see if you've grown more than I have."

Her voice trailed off into the kitchen cheerily, and not in the least as though she had been palpitating between hope and fear about him all the afternoon and working herself to a frazzle getting his room ready.

She returned almost immediately with the first plate of golden-brown waffles and stole a furtive glance at him from the kitchen doorway. He had not yet seated himself, although the others were bustling joyously and noisily into their chairs. He was still standing thoughtfully, staring around the dining room and at the table. As she approached, he gave her a furtive, sweeping look, then dropped his lashes and slid into his chair, a half frown beginning to grow on his brow. He looked as if he were expecting the next question to be: "Why weren't you here last night? Where were you? Don't you know you were rude?" but none of those questions were voiced. His father did clear his throat and glance up at him gravely, but Louise with quick instinct began to chatter about the syrup that Cornelia had made. His attention was turned aside, and the tense expression of his face relaxed as he looked around the pleasant table and noticed the happy faces. "It hasn't looked this way since your mother went away," said the father with a deep sigh. "How good that bread looks! Real homemade bread again! What a difference that makes!" And he reached out and took a slice as if it were something merely to look at and feel.

"I'll say! That looks unbelievable!" Carey volunteered, taking a slice himself and passing the plate. "Some smell, this dinner!" he added, drawing in a long, deep breath. "Seems like living again."

His father's tired eyes rested on him sadly, contemplatively. He opened his lips to speak, but Cornelia slid into her chair and said, "Now, Father, we're ready," and he bowed his head and murmured a low, sad little grace. So Carey was saved again from a much-deserved reproof. Cornelia couldn't help being glad, and Louise looked at her with a knowing gleam in her eye as she raised her head and broke into a brilliant smile. Louise had bitter knowledge of what it meant to have Carey reproved at a meal. There was always a scene, ending with no Carey.

"Yes, and," began Louise swiftly as soon as the "Amen" was concluded, "there's waffles *and* gingerbread! Think of that! And Nellie had time to fix up your bedroom, Kay. Did you go up there?"

"I should say I did! Nell, you're a peach! I never meant to have it looking that way when you came home. I sure am ashamed you had to dig that stuff all out. Some junk I had there. I meant to take a day off and clean house pretty soon."

"Well, now you can help me with some of the other rooms, instead," his sister replied, smiling, and hastened back to turn her waffles.

"I sure will!" said Carey heartily. "When do you want me? Tomorrow morning? Nothing in the way of my working all day if you say the word. We used to make a pretty good team, Nell, you and I. Think we could accomplish a lot in a day."

"Yes, Carey hasn't any job to hinder him doing what he pleases," put in Harry with a bitter young sneer. "I'd've had it all done by myself long ago if I hadn't had a job after school!"

"Yes, you young brag!" began Carey with a deep scowl. "You think you're it and *then* some!"

"It would seem as if you might have given a little time, Carey," began his father almost crossly, with a look about his mouth of restraining less mild things that he might have said.

Louise looked apprehensively at her sister.

"Oh, well," put in Cornelia quickly, "you couldn't be expected to know what to do, any of you, till your big sister got home. You've all done wonderfully well, I think, to get as much done as you have; and I only blame you, every one of you, especially Father dear, for not sending for me sooner. It was really—well, criminal, you know, Daddy, to keep me in expensive luxury and ignorance that way.

But I'm not going to scold you here before folks. We'll have that out after they've all gone to bed, won't we? We're going to have nothing but pleasant sayings at this supper table. It's a kind of reunion, you know, after so many years. Just think, we haven't all been together for—how long is it?—Four years? Doesn't that seem really awful? When I think of it, I realize how terribly selfish I have been. I didn't realize it in college because I was having such a good time, but I have been selfish and lazy and absolutely thoughtless. I hope you'll all forgive me."

Carey lifted wondering eyes, and his scowl faded while he studied his pretty sister's guileless face thoughtfully. The attention was diverted from him, and his anger was cooling, but somehow he began to feel deep in his soul that it was really he that had been selfish. All their scolding and nagging hadn't made him in the least conscious of it, but this new, old, dear, pretty sister taking the blame on herself seemed to throw a new light on his own doings. Of course, it was merely momentary and made no very deep impression, but still the idea had come and would never be quite driven away again.

The supper was a success from every point of view. The pot roast was as tender as cheese, the mashed potatoes melted under the gravy like snow before the summer sun and were enjoyed with audible praise, and the waffles sizzled and baked and disappeared, and more took their places, until at last the batter was all gone.

"Well, I couldn't hold another one," said Carey, "but they certainly were jim-dandies. Say, you haven't forgotten how to cook, Nell!" And he cast a look of deep admiration toward his sister.

Cornelia, so tired she could hardly get up out of her chair after she dropped into it, lifted a bravely smiling face and realized that she had scored a point. Carey had liked the supper and was over his grouch. The first night had been ushered in greatly. She was just wondering whether she dared suggest that he help wash the dishes when he suddenly jerked out his watch, glanced at it, and shoved his chair back noisily.

"Gee! I've gotta beat it," he said hurriedly as he strode to the hall door. "I've gotta date!" And before the family had drawn the one quick, startled, aghast breath of disappointment and tried to think of some way to detain him or find out where he was going or when he was coming back, he had slammed the front door behind him.

The father had an ashen-gray, helpless look; Louise's mouth drooped at the corners, and there were tears in her eyes as she held up her head bravely and carried a pile of plates out to the kitchen; while Harry with an ugly sneer on his young lips shoved his chair back, noisily murmuring, "Aw, gee! Gotta date! Always gotta date! When I grow up, I'll see if I always have to have a date!" Then he snatched an armful of dishes and strode to the kitchen, grumbling in an undertone all the way.

Cornelia cast a quick, apprehensive look at her father and said cheerily, "Oh, never mind. Of course young men have dates, and when you've promised, you know it isn't easy to change. Come, let's get these dishes out of the way quickly, and then we can sit down and talk. It's great to all be together again, isn't it? Father, dear, how long do you suppose it will be before Mother is well? Have you had a letter today?"

The father beamed at her again, and putting his hand in his pocket, drew out an official-looking envelope.

"Yes," he said wistfully. "That is, a note from the nurse with the report. Of course she is not allowed to write. She just sends her love, that's all, and says she's getting well as fast as possible. She seems to be gaining a little. Here's the report."

They all gathered around it, studying the little white, mysterious paper that was to tell them how the dear mother was getting on, and then turned away little wiser. Suddenly Harry, noticing the sag of Cornelia's shoulder as she stood holding on to the back of her father's chair, turned with a swift motion and gathered her into his strong young arms like a bear. Before she could protest, he bore her over to the old, lumpy couch, where he deposited her with a gruff gentleness.

"There you are!" he puffed commandingly. "You lie there, and Lou and I will do the dishes. You're exhausted, and you don't know enough to know it."

"Nonsense!" said Cornelia, laughing and trying to rise. "I'm used to playing basketball and hockey and doing all sorts of stunts. It won't hurt me to get a little tired. I'm going to wash those dishes, and you can wipe them."

"No, you're not. I say she's not, Lou, is she?" and he held her down with his rough young force.

"Certainly not," said Louise grown-uply appearing with her hands full of knives and forks. "It's our turn now. She thinks we don't know how to wash dishes. Harry Copley, you just oughta see all she's done by herself upstairs, cleaning Carey's room and washing blankets and all, besides making bread and gingerbread and everything. Come on upstairs and see. No, we won't go yet till the dishes are done. 'Cause Nellie would work while we were gone. Daddy, you just sit there and talk to her, and don't let her get up while we clean up. Then we'll take you upstairs."

So Cornelia lay still at last on the lumpy couch and rested, realizing that she was exhausted and feeling well repaid for her hard work by the loving light in the children's eyes and her father's tender glance.

The thought of Carey hung in the back of her mind and troubled her now and then, but she remembered that he had promised to help her in the morning, and somehow that comforted her. She succeeded in keeping the rest of the family so interested in her tales of college life that they did not remember their troubles.

When the dishes were done, Cornelia told Louise how to set some buckwheat cakes for morning.

"I saw they were selling buckwheat cheap in the store," she explained, "and so I got some. It will soon be too warm to eat buckwheat cakes, and I'm just crazy to taste them again. I haven't had a decent one since I left home."

"Carey just loves 'em," said Louise thoughtfully.

"Aw, he won't get up in time to get any," sneered Harry.

"He might if he knew we were going to have 'em," said Louise.

"Let's write him a note and leave it up on his bureau," said Cornelia brightly. "That'll be fun. Let's make it in poetry. Where's a pencil and a big piece of paper?"

"I've got some colored crayons," suggested Harry.

So Cornelia scribbled a minute and produced the following, which Harry proudly copied in large, clear letters on a piece of wrapping paper:

The Copley's breakfast's buckwheat cakes,
With maple syrup, too;
They're light and tender, sweet and brown,
The kind you needn't chew.
So, Carey, rise at early dawn,
And put your vesture on,
And come to breakfast in good time,
Or they will all be gone!

Louise danced up and down as she read it.

"O Nellie, Nellie, that's real poetry!" she declared. "And aren't we having a good time?"

"I should say we are!" declared Harry, beginning to make a large flourishing capital T with green and brown crayons. "Talk about dates!" he said contemptuously. "If a fella has got a good home, he oughta stay in it!"

"O Nellie, it's so good to have you home!" sighed Louise suddenly snuggling down into her sister's tired arms. "I'm so glad your college is done!"

And all at once Cornelia realized that she, too, was glad. Here she had been nearly all this afternoon and evening having a first-rate, beautiful time getting tired with hard work but enjoying it just as much as if she had been working over the junior play. It came to her with a sudden start that just at this hour they were having one of the almost last rehearsals—without her! For a second it gave her a pang; and then she realized that she really and truly was just as much interested in getting Carey's room fixed up and making a cheerful, beautiful living room someday for the family to gather in, and in having good times to win back Carey, as ever she had been in making costumes for the girls and making the play a success by means of her delightful scenery. For was she not, after all, about to plan the scenery for the play of life in the Copley family? Who should say but there would be as much tragedy and comedy and romance in the Copley play as ever there had been at Dwight Hall? Well, time would tell, and somehow the last twenty-four hours had put her on a different plane and enabled her to look down at her college life from a new angle. What had done it? Her knowledge of how her father and mother had struggled and sacrificed? The dearness of her young brother and sister in their sturdy, honest desire to be helpful and to love her and look up to her? Or was it her longing to hold and help the young brother who had been her chum and companion in the days before she had gone to college? At least, she could truly say in her heart that she was glad she was here tonight, and she was not nearly so dismayed at the dreary house and the sordid surroundings as she had been twenty-four hours before, for now she knew that it only spelled her opportunity, as that lovely lady on the train had suggested, and she was eager to be up and at it in the morning.

They all went up together to the third story presently and stood in the swept and garnished front room, Mr. Copley going over to the bureau and touching with a tender movement of caress the picture of his wife that stood there and then looking toward the empty white bed with a wistful anxiety. Cornelia could almost read the words of his heart, and into her own there entered the burden of her brother, and she knew she would never rest in her own selfish ease again until she felt sure that Carey was all right.

She crept into bed beside Louise at last, almost too weary to pull up the covers, and let the little girl snuggle thankfully into her arms.

"You're almost—almost like my dear muvver," murmured Louise sleepily, nosing into her neck and settling down on her sister's arm with a sigh of content; and Cornelia thought how sweet it was to have a little sister to love and be loved by and wondered how it was that she had dreaded having her for a roommate.

Then, too weary to think any longer, she fell asleep.

Hours afterward, it seemed, she was awakened by a stumbling footstep up the stairs, halting and fumbling about in the hall and then going on, stumbling again, up to the third story. She heard a low muttering, too, and it frightened her. Had Carey been drinking? A strange, rank smell of cigarette smoke—and more—drifted into the door, which had been left ajar, and a cold frenzy took hold of her heart. Carey had been drinking! She felt sure. A moment more, and she heard light footsteps from the little hall bedroom above and Harry's indignant young voice remonstrating, the sounds of a brief struggle, the thud of a heavy body on the bedsprings above, and then Harry's voice coming clearly down the stairs in disgust as he pattered back to his hard little cot.

"Ow! You great big fish, you! You oughta be ashamed of yourself!"

It was hours after that that Cornelia finally fell asleep again, and during those hours she found herself praying involuntarily, praying and pleading: *Oh God, help me to help Carey. Don't let Carey be a drunkard. Don't let him be wild and bad! Help him to want to be good and right. Help him to be a man. Oh God, help me to do something about it!*

Chapter 7

The first thing of which Cornelia was conscious in the morning was a scuffle overhead. Louise was sitting up, rubbing her eyes and looking apprehensively toward the ceiling, and the sounds grew louder and more vigorous, with now and then a heavy thud, like a booted foot dropping inertly to the floor.

Cornelia sat up also and listened.

"It's Harry, trying to wake Carey up!" whispered Louise knowingly. "Harry's mad. I guess Carey came in late again and didn't undress. He does that way sometimes when he's tired."

"Yes?" said Cornelia with a shiver of understanding. "Yes, I heard him come in."

"Oh, did you?" Louise turned a searching glance on her sister and then looked away with a sober little sigh. "Something ought to be done about that kid before Mother gets home," she said maturely. "It'll kill Mother."

"Something shall be done. There! Don't look so sorrowful, dear. Carey is young, and I'm sure we can do something if we all try with all our souls. I'm so glad I came home. Mother ought not to have been bearing that alone. Come, let's get up." She snatched her blue robe and dashed to the foot of the stairs.

"Harry! Harry!" she called softly. "Never mind. Let him sleep."

Harry appeared angrily at the head of the stairs, his own outfit only half completed, his hair sticking all ways.

"Great, lazy dummy!" he was saying. "He never undressed at all!"

"Hush, dear! Don't wake him. It will be better in every way if he gets his sleep out."

"But he hasn't seen the poetry at all," wailed the disappointed boy. "I held it in front of his face, and he wouldn't open his eyes. I washed his face for him, too, and he wouldn't get up."

"Well, never mind, dear. Let him alone. I'll save him some cakes after you are gone."

"Yes, coddle him, the great, lazy baby! That's what's the matter with him; he's too big a baby, selfish, *selfish*! That's what he is."

"Sh-sh, dear! Never mind! You can't do anything when a person is as sleepy as that, and it's no use trying. Come. Let's have breakfast. I'll be down as soon as you will." And Cornelia smiled brightly above her aching heart and hurried into her own clothes.

"Cakes! Cakes!" said Louise happily. "Won't it be great? Oh, I just can hardly wait for them. I'm sorry Carey isn't awake."

"Never mind, dear, it will all come out straight pretty soon, and we mustn't expect to succeed right away."

So she cheered them on their way and made the morning meal a success, steadily keeping her father's thoughts from the absent boy upstairs until he had to run to catch his car. She put up a delightful lunch for Harry and Louise, with dates and cheese in some of the sandwiches and nuts and lettuce in others, and a big piece of gingerbread and an orange apiece.

"It's just like having Mother again," said Louise fervently as she kissed her sister good-bye and ran to catch Harry, who was already halfway to the corner.

Cornelia held the thought of those words in her heart and cherished them over against the words she had heard from her young brother and sister the day before, and it comforted her. She watched them until they were out of sight, and then with a sigh climbed the stairs to Carey's room. But Carey was locked in a heavy slumber, with a flushed face and heavy breathing. She pinned up a paper to keep out the light, threw the down quilt over him, and opened the window wide. Then she tiptoed away and left him. There was no use doing anything now. The fumes of liquor were still about him, and the heavy breath of cigarettes. She felt a deep horror and disgust in her soul as she thought about her brother and tried to work out a plan for saving him as she went about clearing off the breakfast table and washing the dishes.

There was plenty of meat for dinner that night and lots of gravy left. She would need to think only about vegetables and a dessert. Chocolate blancmange would be good. She would make it at once and set it on the ice. Then, when the milkman came, she must remember to get a small bottle of cream to eat with it. By and by she would run down to the store and get a few carrots and a stalk of celery, and stew them together. That made a good combination. No, that wouldn't do, either, too much sweetness, carrots and blancmange. A can of tomatoes cooked with two onions and a little celery would be better. That she could put on in the middle of the afternoon; there was plenty of pancake batter left for Carey and herself for lunch. She fixed the griddle far back on the range and set the batter in the refrigerator. Then she went with swift steps to the disordered front room.

She went to work unpacking the boxes and setting things in order in the hall and the dining room. She discovered many needed kitchen utensils and some more dishes, and these she washed and put away. It was discouraging work, and somehow she did not seem to have accomplished much when at eleven o'clock she straightened up from a deep packing box from which she had removed the last article and looked about her. Piles of things everywhere and not a spot to walk anywhere! When would she ever get done? A great weariness from her overwork of the day before was upon her, and she wanted to sit down in the midst of the heaps and cry. It was just then in her weakness that the thought of college came upon her, college with its clean orderliness, its regular places for things, its delightful circle of companions, its interesting work, never any burden or hurry or worry.

Just at this hour the classes were filing into the halls and going to new work. If she were back there, she would be entering her psychology class and looking at the blackboard for the announcement of the day's work assigned to each member of the class. Instead of that here she was in the midst of an unending task, hopeless and weary and frightfully discouraged. A tear of self-pity began to steal out, and she might have been weeping in a minute more if she had not been suddenly arrested in her thoughts by sounds overhead, far away and slight, but nevertheless unmistakable.

She wiped her eyes, and went out into the hall, softly listening. Yes, undoubtedly Carey had wakened at last. She could hear the bedsprings rattle and hear his feet moving lightly on the bare floor, as if he might be sitting up with his elbows on his knees and his face in his hands. Her instinct told her that he would not be very happy when he awoke. She could imagine how disgusted he must be with himself; for Carey had a conscience, and he could not but know that what he was doing was wrong. She could remember how good and helpful a boy he used to be, always thoughtful for his mother. It did not seem possible that he had completely changed.

She could hear him moving slowly about now, a few steps and stopping a long time. Perhaps he had found the poetry on the bureau, although she reflected that it was altogether likely that Harry in his wrath might have cast it under the bed or anywhere it happened. Well, she had better be getting the griddle hot.

She hurried into the kitchen and pulled the griddle forward over the fire, opened the drafts, and began to get the table in order for an early lunch. She glanced at the clock. It was half past eleven. She would have everything ready the minute he came down. She could still hear him stirring around. He had come down to the bathroom, and the sound of his razor strop whirred faintly. Well, that was a good sign. He was going to fix up a little before coming down. She put the last touches to her table, set the plates to warm, put on the syrup, and made the coffee. Then she took a broom and went back to the front room to wait until he came down.

Oh, that front room! It seemed drearier than ever as she attempted to make a little path in the wilderness.

She was trying to drag a big packing box out into the hall when Carey finally came down, looking wholly a gentleman except for a deep scowl on his brow. He came at once to her assistance, somewhat gruffly, but quite efficiently.

"What on earth are you trying to do, Nell?" he asked. "Don't you know that's too heavy for a girl to move? I told you. I'd help. Why didn't you wait for me?"

Cornelia, feeling a strange excitement upon her, looked up brightly and tried to ignore the fact that he ought to have come down several hours before.

"Well, there's so much to be done," she said. "I certainly am glad to see you, though. But suppose we have lunch first. I'm hungry as a bear, and see, it's five minutes to twelve. Can you eat now?"

"Oh, anytime!" he said indifferently. "What is it you want

done, anyway? This room's a mess. Some dump, the whole house! It makes me disgusted."

He stood with his hands in his pockets, surveying the desolate scene and voicing Cornelia's own thought of a few moments before. But it was Cornelia's forte to rise to an occasion when everyone else was disheartened. She put on a cheery smile.

"Just you wait, brother, till I get through. I've plans for that room, and it won't be so bad when it gets cleaned and fixed a little. Suppose you take those boxes down to the cellar, and those pictures and tubs, and the old trunk and chest out to the shed room beyond the kitchen, while I scramble some eggs and settle the coffee. Everything else is ready. Then after lunch we'll get to work. I shall need your help to turn the piano around and open those boxes of books. Why do you suppose they put the bookcase face against the wall, with the piano in front of it? Seems to me that was dumb."

"All movers are dumb!" declared Carey with a sweep of his arm, as if he would include the whole world. But he went to work vigorously and carried out the things with a whirl, and Cornelia perceived she must rush to have a plate of cakes before he was done with his assigned task.

"Aw, gee! You saved me some cakes!" he said with a grin of delight when they sat down at the table. "I oughta've got up for breakfast. But I was too tired. We took a joy ride last night down to Baltimore. I saw your poetry. It was great. Who wrote it? You of course."

"We wanted you to be sure to get up, but of course you must have been sleepy riding all that way in the wind. It must have been great, though. It was a full moon last night, wasn't it?" said his sister, ignoring the horror that the thought of the "joy ride" gave her.

"It sure was," said the boy, brightening at the memory. "The fellas put ether in the gas, and she certainly did hum. We just went whizzing. It was a jim-dandy car, twelve-cylinder, some chariot! B'longs to a fella named Brand Barlock. He's a prince, that boy is! Has thousands of dollars to spend as he pleases; and you'd never know he had a cent, he's so big-hearted. Love him like a brother. Why, he'd let me take that car anywhere, and not mind; and it cost some money, that car did, this year's racing model! Gee, but she's a winner. Goes like a streak of greased lightning."

Cornelia suppressed her apprehension over the possibilities of accident both physical and financial, and bloomed with interest. Of what use would it be to reprove her brother for taking such chances? It would only make him angry and turn him against her. She would see whether she could win him back to the old friendship, and then there might come a time when her advice would reach him. At present it would be useless.

"It must be great to have a fine car," she said eagerly. "I love to ride. There were two or three girls at college who had cars and used to take us out sometimes, but of course that didn't happen very often."

"I'll borrow Brand's car and take you sometime," he said eagerly. "He wouldn't mind."

"Oh, Carey! No, you mustn't do that!" she cried in alarm. "At least"—as she saw his frown of displeasure—"not till I know him, you know. I shouldn't at all like to ride in a car whose owner I didn't know. You must bring him here when we get all fixed up, and I'll meet him. Then perhaps he'll ask me to go along, too, sometime, although I'm not sure I'd like to go like a streak of lightning. Still, I've never tried it, and you know I never used to be afraid of things."

"Sure, you're all right, Nell. But I'd never bring Brand to this dump! He's a rich man's son, I tell you, and lives in a swell neighborhood."

"Doesn't he know where you live?"

Carey shrugged his shoulders.

"Oh yes, he drives around and honks the horn for me and brings me home again, but I wouldn't ask him in—"

"Wait, I say, till we get it fixed up. You know, I'm an interior decorator! Oh, I wish there was just a fireplace! It makes such a cozy, cheerful place."

"I could build one if I had the stuff," declared Carey, interested. "What kind do you want? But then, everything costs so darned much. If I only had a job!"

"Oh, you'll get a job, of course," said his sister sympathetically, tying to reconcile his troubled look with what the children had said about his indifference toward work. "Where did you work last?"

The color rolled in a slow, dull wave over Carey's restless young face, and a look of sullen hopelessness came into his handsome eyes.

"Oh, I haven't had anything regular since I left school. I—you see—that is—oh, hang it all! I can't get anything worthwhile. I've been doing some tinkering down at the garage. I could work steady there, but Dad makes it so hot for me when I do that I have to do it on the sly. He says it's just a lazy job, hanging round with the fellas getting rides. He don't know anything about it. It's real man's work, I tell you, hard work at that; and I'm learning all about machinery. Why, Nell, there isn't a fella at the garage can tell as quick as I can what's the matter with a car. Bob sends for me to find out after he's worked half a day, and I can tell right off the bat when I hear the engine go what's wrong."

Cornelia watched his eyes sparkle as he talked and perceived that when he spoke of machinery he was in his element. He loved it. He loved it as she loved the idea of her chosen profession.

That being the case, he ought to be encouraged.

"Why, I should think it was a good thing to stick at it while you are looking around for something better," she said slowly, wondering whether her father would blame her for going against his advice. "I should think maybe it will prepare you for something else in the line of machinery. What is there big and really worthwhile that you'd like to get into if you could? Of course, you wouldn't want to be just a mender of cars all your life."

His face took on a firm, manly look, and his eyes grew alert and earnest.

"Of course not!" he said crisply. "Father thinks I would, and I can't make him see it any other way. He's just plain disappointed in me, that's all." The young man's tone took on a bitter tinge. "But I know it will be a step to something. Why, there's all sorts of big companies now that make and sell machines, and if you understand all about machinery, you stand a better chance for getting in to be business manager someday. There's tanks and oil wells and tractors and a lot of things. Of course I couldn't jump into a thing like that at the start. Dad thinks I could. He thinks if I had any pep at all I could just walk up to the president of some big company and say, 'Here I am; take me,' and he'd do it, just like that. But—for one thing, look at me! Do I look like a businessman?" He stood back and lifted his arms with a dramatic gesture, pointing toward his shabby clothing.

"And then another thing, I've got to get experience first. If I only had a pull somewhere, but—"

"I'll talk to Father," said Cornelia soothingly. She looked at him thoughtfully. "You ought to earn enough for a new suit right away, of course, and have it ready—keep it nice, I mean, so that when a good opportunity offers, you will be suitably dressed to apply for it. Suppose I talk to Father? I'll do it tonight. Meantime, you help me here a day or two, and then you go back to that garage and work for a week or two and earn money enough for your suit and what other things you need, and keep your eye open for something better all the while."

"That's the talk!" said Carey joyfully. "Now you're shouting! You put some heart in a fella. Gee, I'm glad you're home. It's been awful without Mother. It was bad enough the last few months when she was sick, but it was some dump when she went away entirely."

"Yes, I know," said the sister sympathetically, reflecting that it would be wiser not to suggest that he might have helped to make the mother sick by his careless life. "Well, we must get things fixed up nice and pleasant for her when she gets back and try to keep her well and happy the rest of her life."

"That's right!" said Carey with a sudden deep note in his voice that came from the heart and gave Cornelia a bit of encouragement.

"I think I could clean that suit up a little for you and make it look better—"

Carey looked down at himself doubtfully.

"It's pretty bad," he said. "And it costs a lot to have it cleaned and pressed. I tried last week to do something, but we couldn't find the irons."

"I found them yesterday," said Cornelia brightly. "We'll see what we can do this evening if you can be at home."

"Oh, this evening. . ." said Carey doubtfully.

"Yes, we can't spare the time till then, because this house has got to be put in order." She gave him a swift, anxious glance and a winning smile. "If you have another engagement, break it for once. There's so much to be done, dear, and we do need you terribly. Tell that Brand friend of yours that you're busy for a few days, and you'll make it up by inviting him to a fudge party when we get settled."

"Oh, gee! Could we?" said Carey half doubtful, half pleased. "Well, all right! I'll do my best. Now, what do you want done with this old junk?"

"Those go on in the back shed, over by the tubs. Take that out in the yard and burn it, and this pile goes upstairs. Just put it in the upper hall, and I'll attend to it later. My! What a difference it makes to get a little space clear!"

They worked steadily all the afternoon, Carey proving himself as willing as herself.

They washed the windows and the floor and swept down the walls of the parlor and hall.

"Ugly old wallpaper!" said Cornelia, eyeing it spitefully. "That's got to come off if I have to do it myself and have bare walls."

"Why, that's easy!" said Carey. "Give me an old rag!" And he began to slop the water on and scrape with an old case knife.

"Well, that's delightful!" said Cornelia with relief. "I didn't know it would be so easy. We'll do a little at a time until it is done, and then we'll either paper it ourselves or paint it. I do wish we could manage to get a fireplace."

"Well, maybe we can find some stone cheap where they're hauling it away. Harry'll know someplace likely; he gets around with that grocery wagon. You know I helped a stonemason last summer for a while. Mother hated it, though, so I quit, but I learned a lot about mixing cement and how to lay it on. I know about the drafts, too. I bet I could make as good a fireplace as the next one. Gee! I wish I knew where to get some stone or brick."

"Stone would be best," said Cornelia. "It would make a lovely chimney mantel, but I suppose you couldn't be so elaborate as making a mantel!"

"Sure, I could! But it would take some stone to do all that."

"I know where there's a lot of stone!" They turned around

83

surprised, and there stood Harry in the doorway with Louise just behind him, looking in with delighted faces at the newly cleaned room and the hardworking elder brother.

"Where?" Carey wheeled around eagerly.

"Down on the dump. It was brought there yesterday, a whole lot of it, several cartloads. Came from a place where they have been taking down an old wall, and they had no place to put it, I guess. Anyhow, it's there."

"I'll go see if there's enough," said Carey, flashing out of the door and up the street.

He was back in a minute with a big stone in his hand.

"It's just cellar stone," he said deprecatingly, "but there's plenty."

"Humph!" said Louise maturely. "Well, I never thought I'd be glad I lived near that old dump! Do you mean we're going to have a real fireplace, Carey?"

"That's the idea, kid, and I guess I can make good. But how are we going to get that stone here?"

"There's the express-wagon," said Louise thoughtfully. "Harry has to work, but I could haul some."

"You!" said Carey contemptuously. "Do you suppose I'd let a *girl* haul stone for me? No, I'll go borrow a truck. I know a fella has one, and it's almost quitting time. I know he'll lend it to me; and if he does, I'll work until I get those stones all landed, or like as not somebody else will get their eye on them. Stones like that cost a lot nowadays, even if they are only cellar stones."

"Cellar stones are lovely," said Cornelia delightedly. "They have a lot of iron in them and make very artistic houses. I heard a big architect say that once in a lecture at college."

"Well, there's nothing like being satisfied with what you have to have," said Carey. "Here, Nell, you look out for the rest of that baseboard; I'm off to borrow a truck. Next time you see me I'll be riding a load of stone!"

"I'll come down at six o'clock and help you load!" shouted Harry from the third story, where he was rapidly changing into his working clothes.

"All right, kid, that's the stuff. Nell will save us some supper, and we'll work till dark."

"It won't be dark," said Louise sagely. "It's moonlight tonight."

"That's right, too," said Carey as he seized his hat and dashed out of the house.

Chapter 8

"You've got him to work!" said Louise joyously, looking at her sister with shining eyes.

"I didn't do it," said Cornelia, smiling. "He came of his own accord and seems awfully interested."

"Well, it's because you're here, of course; that makes all the difference in the world."

"Thank you, Louie," said her sister, stooping to kiss the warm cheek lovingly.

"Now," said Louise, pulling off her clean middy blouse and starting upstairs, "what do you want me to do first?"

"Well, I thought maybe you'd like to dust these books and put them in the bookcase, dear. Then they'll be out of our way."

Louise was rapidly buttoning herself into her old gingham work dress when Cornelia came hurriedly from the kitchen and called up the stairs, a note of dismay in her voice.

"Louie, I don't suppose you happen to know who owns this house, do you? It's just occurred to me we'll have to ask permission to build a fireplace, and that may upset the whole thing. Maybe the owner won't want an amateur to build a fireplace in his house."

"Oh, that's all right," shouted Louise happily, appearing at the stair head. "Father owns it. It was the only thing he had left after he lost his money."

"Father owns it?" said Cornelia incredulously. "How strange! A house like this! When did he buy it?"

"He didn't buy it. He signed a note for a poor man, and then the man died and never paid the money, and Father had to take the house."

"Oh!" said Cornelia thoughtfully, seeing more tragedy in the family history and feeling a sudden great tenderness for the father who had borne so many disappointments and yet kept sweet and strong. "Well, then, anyhow we can do as we please with it," she added happily. "I'm awfully glad. I guess we shan't have to ask permission. Father'll like it all right."

"Well, I rather guess he will, especially if it keeps Carey busy a little while," said Louise.

They worked rapidly and happily together, and soon the books were in orderly rows in the bookcase.

Cornelia had found a bundle of old curtains in one of the boxes, and now she brought them out and began to measure the windows.

"The lace curtains all wore out, and Mother threw them away," volunteered Louise sadly.

"Never mind. I've found a lot of pretty good scrim ones here, and I'm going to wash them and stencil a pattern of wild birds across them," said Cornelia. "They'll do for the bedrooms, anyway. The windows are the same size all over the house, aren't they? I have some beautiful patterns for stenciling up in my trunk that I made for some of the girls' curtains at college."

"How perfectly dear!" said Louise. "Can't I go up and find them?"

"Yes, they are in the green box just under the tray. I wish we had a couple more windows in this room; it is so dark. If I were a carpenter for a little while I would knock out that partition into the hall and saw out two windows, one each side of the fireplace over there," said Cornelia, motioning toward the blank sidewalls where already her mind had reared a lovely stone fireplace.

"There's a carpenter lives next door," said Louise thoughtfully. "He goes to work every morning at seven o'clock, but I suppose he would charge a lot."

"I wonder," said Cornelia. "We'll have to think about that." And she stood off in the hall and began to look around with her eyelashes drawn down like curtains through which she was sharply watching a thought that had appeared on her mental horizon.

On the whole it was a very exciting evening, and a happy one also. When Harry and his father came home, there were two loads of stone already neatly piled inside the little yard, and Carey was just flourishing up to the door with a loud honk of the horn on his borrowed truck, bringing a third load. Harry had of course told his father the new plans, and the father had been rather dubious about such a scheme.

"He'll just begin it and then go off and leave a mess around," he had told Harry with a sigh.

But, when he saw the eager light on his eldest son's face, he took heart of hope. Carey was so lithe and alert, worked with so much precision, strength, and purpose, and seemed so intent on what he was doing. Perhaps, after all, something good would come of it, although he looked with an anxious eye at the borrowed car and wondered what he would do if Carey should break it and be liable for its price.

Harry turned to and helped with the unloading, and both were persuaded to come in barely for five minutes' bit at the good dinner that was already on the table. They dispatched it with eagerness and little ceremony and were off for another load, asking to have their pudding saved until they returned, as every minute must count before dark, and they had no time for pudding just now.

When the boys were away again, Cornelia began to talk with her father about Carey. She told him a little of their talk that morning and persuaded him not to say anything for a while to stop Carey from working at the garage until he had earned enough to buy some new clothes and get a little start. The father reluctantly consented, although he declared it would not do any good, for Carey would spend every cent he earned on his wild young friends, and if he bought any clothes, they would be evening clothes. He had seen before how it worked. Nevertheless, although he spoke discouragedly, Cornelia knew that he would stand by her in her attempt to help Carey back to respectability, and she went about clearing off the supper table with a lighter heart.

After supper she saw to it that there was plenty of hot water for baths when the boys got through their work, and she got out an old flannel shirt and a pair of Carey's trousers and set a patch and mended a tear and put them in order for work. Then she had the ironing board and a basin and soap ready for cleaning his other clothes when he came in. Carey-like, he had gone to haul all that stone in the only suit he had to wear for good. She sighed as she thought what a task was before her. For something inside Carey needed taking out and adjusting before Carey would ever be a dependable, practical member of the family. Nevertheless, she was proud of him as she listened to the thud of each load and glanced out of the front window at the ever-increasing pile of stones that now ran over the tiny front yard and was encroaching on the path that led to the back door.

"Gotta get 'em all, or somebody else'll get onto it and take 'em," declared Harry when he came in for a drink, his face and hands black and a happy, manly look around his mouth and eyes.

It was ten o'clock when the last load was dumped, by the light of all the lamps in the house brought out into the yard, and it was more than an hour later before the boys got back from returning the truck to its owner. They were tired and dirty almost beyond recognition but happier than they had been for many a day, and glad of the bit of a feast that their sister had set out for them, and of the hot baths.

"Well, if we don't have a fireplace now, it won't be my fault!" declared Harry, mopping a warm red face with a handkerchief that had seen better days. "Gee! We certainly did work. Carey can work, too, when he tries, I'll say." And there was a note of admiration in his voice for his elder brother, which was not missed by either the brother or the watching sisters. Everybody slept well that night, and they were all so weary that they came near to oversleeping the next morning.

It was after the children had gone to school and Carey was off getting lime and sand and cement for his work that Cornelia went out into the backyard to hang up the curtains that she had just washed, and turning toward the line, she encountered a pair of curious eyes under the ruffle of a pretty calico nightcap whose owner was standing on the neighboring back porch, the one to the left, where Louise had said the carpenter lived.

"Good morning!" said the other woman briskly, as if she had a perfect right to be intimate. "You all ain't going to build, are you? I see all them stones come last night, and I couldn't make out what in life you all was going to do with 'em, lessen you was goin' to pull down and build out."

Cornelia had a foolish little hesitancy in responding to this lively overture, for her instinct was to look down upon people who lived in so poor a neighborhood, but she reflected quickly that she was living there herself, and perhaps these people didn't like it any better than she did. Why should she look down upon them? So she looked up with a pleasant smile, if a trifle belated.

"Oh, good morning. No, we're only going to have a fireplace. I wish we were going to build; the house isn't arranged at all the way I should like it, and it's such fun to have things made the way you want them, don't you think?"

"Yes," said the neighbor, eyeing her curiously. "I s'pose it is. I never have tried it. My husband's a carpenter, and of course he don't have time to make things for me. It's like the shoemaker's children goin' barefoot, as the sayin' is. I was going to say that, if you all was buildin', my husband, being a carpenter, might be handy for you. He takes contracts sometimes."

"Oh, does he?" Cornelia's color rose brightly. "I certainly wish we could afford to have some work done. There are two windows I need badly and a partition I want down, but I can't do it now. Perhaps later, when Mother gets home from the hospital and we're not under such heavy expense, we can manage it."

The neighbor eyed her thoughtfully.

"Be nice if you could have 'em done when she got back," she suggested. "Your mother looked to be an awful sweet woman. I saw her when she come here first, and I said to my husband, I said, 'Jim, them's nice people. It does one good to have a woman like that livin' next door; she's so ladylike and pretty, don't you know, and so kinda sweet.' I was awful sorry when I heard she had to go to the hospital. Say, she certainly did look white when they took her away. My, but ain't she fortunate she's got a daughter old enough to fill her place? You been to college, ain't you? My, but that's fine!

Well, say, I'll tell Jim about it. Mebbe he could do your work for you nights if you wasn't in a hurry, and then it wouldn't come so high, you know. It would be nice if you could get it all fixed up for your ma when she comes back. Jim wouldn't mind when you paid him, you know. I'll tell him to come in and look it over when he gets in this afternoon, anyhow."

"Oh!" said Cornelia, taking a quick breath of astonishment. "Oh, really I couldn't believe you more. Of course, I might manage part of what I want if it didn't cost too much, but I've heard all building is very high now."

She was making a lightning calculation and thinking of the money she had brought back from college. Would it—could she? Ought she? It would be so nice if she dared!

"That's all right. You're a neighbor, and Jim wouldn't mind doing a good turn. He'd make it as cheap as he could. It won't cost nothing for him to look it over, anyhow. I'll tell him when he comes back. My goodness! I smell that bread burning. Excuse me, I must go in."

And the neighbor vanished, leaving Cornelia bewildered and a trifle upset and immediately certain that she ought not to allow the woman to send in her husband. Well, she would think it over and run in later to tell her it was impossible. That was clearly the only thing to do.

So she hurried back to put on the irons, for her curtains would soon be dry enough to iron, and she wanted to get them stenciled and up as soon as possible; the windows looked so bare and staring, especially up in Carey's room.

Chapter 9

Carey came back and worked all the morning in the cellar at the foundation for his fireplace, occasionally coming up to measure and talk learnedly about drafts and the like. Cornelia was very happy seeing him at it, whether a fireplace ever resulted or not. It was enough that he was interested and eager over it. And while she was waiting for her irons to heat, she sat down and wrote a bright little letter to her mother, telling how Carey was helping her put the house in order, although she carefully refrained from mentioning a fireplace, for she was still dubious about whether it would be a success. But late in the afternoon, after the lunch was cleared away, the dinner well started, and the beautifully laundered curtains spread out on the dining room couch ready for decoration, Carey called her down to the cellar and proudly showed her a large, neat, square section of masonry arising from the cellar floor beneath the parlor to the height of almost her shoulders and having its foundation down at proper depth for safety so he told her.

"My! How you've worked, Carey! I think it's wonderful you've accomplished so much in such a short time."

"Aw! That's nothing!" said Carey, exuding delight at her praise. "I coulda done more if I hadn't had to go after the stuff. But say, Nell, I promised Pat I'd come around and help him with a big truck this afternoon, and I guess I better go now or I won't get home in time for supper. Pat owes me five dollars anyhow, and I need it to pay for the stuff I bought this morning. I told the fella I'd bring it round this afternoon."

Cornelia thought of her hoarded money and opened her lips to offer some of it then thought better of it. It would be good for Carey to take some of the responsibility and earn the money to beautify the house. He would be more interested in getting a job. So she smiled assent and told him to hurry and be sure to be back in time for supper, for she was going to have veal potpie, and it had to be eaten as soon as it was done or it would fall.

Carey went away whistling, and Cornelia sat down to her stenciling.

She had done a great deal of this work at college, often making quite a bit of money at it, so it was swift work, and soon she had a pair of curtains finished and pinned one up to the window to get the effect. She was just getting down from the stepladder when she heard a knock at the door, and wondering, she hurried to open it.

There stood a tall, bronzed man with a red face, very blue eyes, and a pleasant smile, and it suddenly came over her that this must be "Jim," and she had forgotten to tell his wife not to send him over.

"My wife said you wanted me to come over and see about some work you wanted done," he said, pulling off his cap and stepping in. "I thought I'd just run right in before dark, if you didn't mind work clothes."

"Oh no," said Cornelia, looking worried, "of course not. But really, I'm afraid I didn't make it plain to your wife; I haven't any idea of doing anything now—that is, I don't suppose it would be possible—I haven't any money and won't have for a while."

"That's all right," said the man, looking around the house alertly. "It don't cost nothing to estimate. I just love to estimate. What was it you was calculating to do when you do build over?"

"Oh!" said Cornelia, abashed. "I don't know that I had really thought it all out, but this house is so cramped and ugly I was just wishing I could take down this partition and throw the parlor and hall all into one. Do you think the ceiling would stand that? I suppose it's a foolish idea, for I don't know a thing about building, but this would really make a very pretty room if the hall wasn't cut off this way."

The man stepped into the doorway and looked up, eyeing the ceiling speculatively, with his mouth open.

"Why, yes, you *could* do that," he drawled. "It's a pretty long span, but you could do it. You'd have to use a coupla colyooms to brace her up, but that's done—unless you used a I beam. That you could do."

"An I beam! What's an I beam?" asked Cornelia, interested.

"Why, it's an iron beam running along underneath. You might be able to get her under out of sight, but most likely you'd have to have her below the ceiling. You could box her in, and you could make some more of 'em and have a beamed ceiling if you want."

"Oh, a beamed ceiling! But that would be expensive. How much does an I beam cost?"

"Oh, I should say a matter of fifteen or eighteen dollars fer one that long," said the man, letting his eyes rove back and forth over the ceiling as if in search of a possible foot or two more of length concealed somewhere.

"Oh!" said Cornelia again wistfully. "And would it cost much to put it in?" She was trying to think just how much of that money was lying in her drawer upstairs.

"Well, not so much if I did it evenings. That would make a mighty nice room out of it, as you say. I'd be willing to let you have the stuff it took at cost, and I might be able to get a secondhand I beam. Come to think, there is one down to the shop a man ordered and then done 'ithout. I might get it for you as low as five dollars if it would be long enough."

He took out his foot rule and began to measure, and Cornelia drew her breath quickly. It seemed too good to be true! If she only could make over that room before her mother got home!

"What else was it you was calculatin' to do?" the man asked, looking up suddenly from the paper on which he had set down the measurement. "I'll look at that there I beam in the morning when I go down to the shop. I believe she's long enough. Was there anything else?"

"Well, my brother is trying to build a stone fireplace over on that blank wall opposite, and I was wishing I had a window on each side; the room is so dark. But I guess we would have to wait for that, even if we did this. Windows are expensive, aren't they?"

"Well, some; and then again they ain't, if you get a secondhanded one. Sometimes people change their minds and have a different kind of winder after one's made, and then it's left on the boss's hands, and he's glad to get rid of it at cost. Got a lot of winders all sizes layin' round over there. Get 'em cheap, I guess. Say, you'd oughta have a coupla them di'mon'-pane winders, just smallish ones, over there each side your chimney."

He cast his eye around back to the hall and pointed uncertainly toward the long blank space of dull brown, faded wallpaper.

"Then you need a bay there," he said interestedly. "Say them bays now do make a pretty spot in a room. Got one where I was workin' yesterday, just sets right outa the room 'bout the height of a table, like a little room; has three winders to it, and the woman has cute little curtains to 'em, and ferns and a birdcage. Say, that would make your room real pleasant-like."

"It certainly would," said Cornelia, her eyes shining, and a wistful sigh creeping to her lips. "But I guess it won't be pos—"

"Say! You got some real nice curtains to your winders. I like them birds flying."

Then he caught a glimpse of the table over which Cornelia had spread the curtain on which she was working. He saw the three birds already finished and the brush and paints and patterns lying there, and then he glanced back at her in astonishment.

"Say, you don't mean to say you're *makin'* them birds on them curtains! My! Ain't that interesting? How do you do it? Make one, and lemme see."

Cornelia obligingly sat down and made two birds in flight while the carpenter watched every movement and exclaimed admiringly. It would not have been Cornelia if she had not imagined at that instant how her college friends would laugh if they could see her now, but she smiled to herself as she pleasantly showed him all the tricks of her small craft.

"Well," he said as she finished the second bird, "now ain't that great? I never supposed anyone could do a thing like that. I supposed it was done by machinery somehow. Say, I hope you won't take no offense, but would you be willing to do something like that fer pay? Your saying you couldn't afford them winders made me think of it. I'd like mighty well to get some curtains for my wife for all over the house, and if you could do some kind of a fancy pattern on 'em—you and she could talk it over and fix that—I'd be willin' to trade off your work fer mine. She'd tell her friends, too, and you could get other orders. I think it would pay."

Cornelia's cheeks grew rosy, but she held up her spirited little head and tried to be sensible about it. This wasn't exactly what she had expected, of course, to get her first order from a common workingman, but then, what difference? It was a real order and would bring her and the family what they needed: more windows, more light, more room. Why not? And, if her dream of uplifting and beautifying homes had been a true ideal, why, here was her opportunity. Everybody began in a small way, and it really was wonderful to have opportunity, even so humble as this, open up right at the beginning. She caught her breath and tried to think. Of course everybody began everything in a small way at first.

"Well," she said, hesitating, "I think perhaps I could. That is really my business, you know, interior decorating. I mean to do it on a large scale someday."

"You don't say!" said the man, looking at her admiringly. "I know women is getting into business a lot these days. But I ain't never heard of that—what do you call it—interior decorating? You don't mean wallpaper and painting? 'Cause I could introduce you to my boss. He builds a lot of houses."

"Well, yes," said Cornelia, trying not to laugh. "My business is after the house is all built. I select wallpapers and curtains and tell them what furniture to get or how to arrange what furniture they have so it will look well in a room. I've been studying along those lines in college; it's artistic work, you know."

"I see!" said the man, looking at her with narrowing, speculative eyes. "Good idea, real good idea! Like to have someone arrange my house. Tell us what to buy. We're laying out to get some new furniture, either a parlor suite or a dining room, though my wife's got her heart set on a new bedroom outfit, and I don't know which'll come off first. Guess I'll send her in to talk it over with you. I like them little birds real well. Where you goin' to put 'em? Here?" He looked at the two long front windows.

"No, these are going up on the third floor in my brother's room, the front room. I'm going to make that all blue and white, and these bluebirds will make it look cheerful."

"H'm! I guess when Nannie sees 'em she'll be strong fer the bedroom set and let the other rooms go a spell till we can afford it."

"Why not paint your old bedroom set and have it decorated like your curtains and save the money for some good furniture downstairs? They are using painted furniture a lot now for bedrooms."

He stared at her eagerly.

"There, now, see? I told you you were going to be real useful to me. You've saved me the price of a bedroom set a'ready. It's a bargain. You do the decorating, and I'll do the carpentering. I'll see about them winders and let you know tomorrow afternoon."

When he had gone, Cornelia stood in the middle of her dreary little parlor and looked around with startled eyes. Here she had contracted to have windows put in and the partition taken down and promised to go into business herself right away. What would her father say to it all?

But she could see Harry and Louise coming down the street, and she hurried into the kitchen to prepare the dessert for dinner, for it was getting late for what she had planned.

The children came bursting into the kitchen, eager to see how much Carey had accomplished, and clattered down to the cellar and up again, their hands full of cookies their sister had baked, their eyes happy; and somehow home and life looked good to Cornelia. This was the great day at college when the play on which she had spent so much time and thought was to come off, and she had expected to have a hard time bearing the thought of all that was going on and she not in it; but she never once thought of it all day until just as her head was touching the pillow that night, and then she was so sleepy that it only came as a floating thought of some far-off period of her existence in which she now had no part. She was wholly and entirely interested just now in her home and what she was going to do for the neighborhood. She had not told her father yet about the carpenter and his propositions. She wanted to have something more definite to tell, perhaps to surprise her family with, if possible, so she had merely asked him casually if he objected to her making little inexpensive changes in the house, things that she could manage herself, and he had joyously told her to do what she liked and pull the walls down if she wanted to, only so she got things fixed to please her.

Chapter 10

Cornelia awoke with a great zeal for the work upon her. She had dreamed of a living room that would lift the whole house out of the sordid neighborhood and make it a place of delight. She had thought out some built-in seats with lockers where many of the odds and ends could be stowed; she had planned to paint the old, cheap dining room furniture a wonderful deep-cream enamel and decorate it like some of the expensive sets in the stores; so would she treat the old bedroom sets that were not of real wood. The set in Carey's room was old walnut and valuable. A little oil would bring it back to its rich-brown beauty. The set in her mother's room was a cheap one; and that she would paint gray with decorations of little pink buds and trailing vines. The set in her own room should be ivory-white with sepia shadows. She would go somewhere and learn how to put on wallpaper, or find a man who would do it very cheaply, and little by little the old house should be made over. Cheap felt-paper of pale gray or pearl or cream for the bedrooms, and corn-color for the living room. She wasn't sure what she would do with the dining room yet till she had the furniture painted, perhaps paint the walls white and tack little moldings in patterns around for panels outlined in green. Green! That was the color for the dining room, with a fern dish for the center of the table and a grass rug under the table. White curtains with green stenciling! That was it! And Carey's room should be painted white, walls and ceiling and all. She would set him at it as soon as he finished the fireplace, and then she would stencil little birds, or a more conventional pattern, around the top of the walls for a border, in the same blue as the curtains. That would be a room to which he could bring home his friends. A picture or two, well chosen—she had the *Lone Wolf* in her trunk done in steel-blues, the very thing for one—and an unbleached muslin bedspread and pillow and roll also stenciled in blue. That would make a beautiful room. Then the bathroom, of course, must be all white, heavy white enamel. She saw where her money would go now, in pots of paint and brushes, and the work would take days, weeks, but it would be beautiful. She could see her dream before her and was happy.

She went downstairs and found the fire out. That made delay. It was her own fault, of course; she had forgotten to look after it the last thing at night, and also everybody else had forgotten. Her father had gone to bed early with a headache. He usually looked after the fire. Carey ought to have thought of it, but Carey never thought of anything but himself and his own immediate plans unless his interest was held. Cornelia found on looking for it in her haste that her stock of patience had run low, and added to this she had a stiff shoulder from washing windows, and Harry had a bad toothache and had to hurry away to the dentist's. Carey didn't get up at all when he was called, and Louise and Cornelia had a rough time of it making some coffee for their father over the gas flame. There was no time to wait for the fire, for Father must catch his car at the regular time, whether he had breakfast or not. When Louise had gone off to school, and Harry, returning smelling of cloves and creosote, had also been fed and comforted and sent off with an excuse to his teacher, Cornelia wanted to sit down and cry. Suddenly the whole thing seemed a house of cards. The sordid neighborhood became more sordid than ever, the house too dingy and hopeless for words, all her plans tawdry and cheap and useless. Why try, when the result to be attained at best would be but a makeshift of poverty?

To add to her misery, the morning mail brought letters of condolence from her classmates because she could not be with them at the play, and bits of news about how this and that were going wrong because she wasn't there, and who was trying to take her place and bungling things.

Suddenly Cornelia put her head down on the dining room table in the midst of the breakfast clutter and cried. She felt sorrier and sorrier for herself. Carey upstairs, great, big, lazy fellow, sleeping and letting her make the fire and do the work and carry the burden. He ought to be out hunting a job and helping to fill the family purse. He ought to be up and at his fireplace. She felt like going up and shaking him and telling him just how despicable he was. And she wished she could shut up the house and go off all day somewhere and have a good time. She was tired, and she loathed the thought of washing windows and scouring the floor and getting meals. Even stenciling curtains had lost its charm.

She became ashamed of herself presently, remembering her mother and how many years she had done all these things and more. She dried her eyes and began to clear off the table. She had barely finished when she had a visitation from the woman next door, who came beaming in to see the curtains her husband had told her about and to ask whether Cornelia minded her having bluebirds on some of her curtains if she put them on the other side of the house. Somehow the woman's eagerness to have her home made over into an artistic one melted away some of Cornelia's gloom, and she was able to rise to the occasion and talk with her neighbor almost as enthusiastically as if she had been really interested. Perhaps she was interested; she wasn't sure. Anyway, it was going to be fun to get rid of ugly things in that woman's house and substitute simple, pretty ones. When Mrs. Barkley got up to go, Cornelia thought she heard faint movements up in the third story and took heart. When she opened the door to let her neighbor out, promising to run in sometime within a day or two and look over the rooms, the sun shot out from behind a grim cloud and flooded the damp street with glory, and Cornelia began to feel better.

Carey came down whistling, and twinkling with good humor, and she hadn't the heart to give him the reprimand he richly deserved. She smiled a good morning, and he went at the kitchen range with a good will.

They had an early lunch and breakfast together, and Carey went to work at his stonework once more.

It was a trifle after two o'clock when Brand Barlock arrived on the scene.

Carey was down in the cellar picking up the last stones and poking them through the opening he had cut in the parlor floor. He was making such a racket that he did not hear the insistent *honk! honk!* of the horn. But Cornelia, polishing off the front window where some of the wet paper of the day before had stuck, did hear, and she looked out at the expensive car with a sinking heart. That must be Brand Barlock! But surely, *surely*, Carey wouldn't go off now in the midst of his work, when he was so anxious to finish!

After several almost insolent honks of the horn, and imperious looks houseward, a boy in the backseat got out, received some brief instruction from the handsome youth who was the driver, and came and knocked at the door.

"Kay here?" asked the boy. "Oh!" Seeing Cornelia, he dragged off his cap perfunctorily.

The boy had a pleasant face, though weak, and Cornelia smiled. If this was one of Carey's friends, she would know him sometime, and she must make a good impression upon him. She wanted the boys to come and see Carey rather than to always be carrying him off.

"Why, yes, he's here," said Cornelia. "But he's awfully busy. We're getting settled, you know. Could I give him a message?"

"Why, oh yes! Tell him Brand Barlock wants him. Tell him he wants him right away quick, please. Brand's in an awful hurry."

If he had said, "The president of the United States is here and wants to see Carey," he could not have given the order more loftily.

Cornelia turned doubtfully. She wanted to resent this imperious tone, but perhaps Carey wouldn't like it, and after all, boys were— well, just boys. When they were at that age, they likely thought they were it.

"I'll tell him," she said pleasantly. "Won't you step in? We don't look very nice here yet, but we hope to be ready to offer more hospitality to our friends soon."

The boy looked at her as if he was surprised to find her human. "Naw, thanks. I'll stay here," he replied, and tapped his foot impatiently. She gathered that Carey's family meant nothing at all and less than nothing to this uninteresting youth, but she turned and went swiftly through the hall and the dining room and down the cellar stairs rather than to call Carey through the opening in the floor. Carey might not care to see these friends of his in present attire.

"Gosh!" said Carey, looking down at his disheveled self when she had told him. "Well, I s'pose I've got to go up. Can't keep Brand waiting. Oh, gee! I thought I'd get this up through the floor today."

"But, Carey," cried his sister, putting out a detaining hand, "can't I explain to him what you're doing? Surely he will understand that you are busy and can't come. Can't I ask him to come down to you if he must see you now? If he sees what you are doing, you won't look so bad."

He stopped short in the cellar and looked at her witheringly.

"Ask Brand Barlock to come down *here*? Well, I should say *not*!"

"Why not?" she asked with unconscious scorn. "Is he as grand as all that? Who on earth is he, anyway?"

But Carey was gone, taking the stairs three steps at a time. He was out at the car when his sister got back to her window, staying only a minute, and then tearing back and up the two flights of stairs to his room, while the car waited in front in grave importance. The sounds above stairs indicated that Carey was dressing hastily. The water gushed in the bathroom in full force, and splashing, slamming doors, dropping shoes, hurrying footsteps, succeeded one another. The jamming of a bureau drawer, the dropping of a hairbrush, told his worried sister that Carey was "dressing up" and going somewhere.

Cornelia climbed the stairs to remonstrate but was prevented with a snort before she spoke.

"Oh, doggone that collar button! That's always the way when I'm in a hurry."

"Carey, are you—you're not—" she stopped to gather breath and began again. "Carey, is there anything I can do to help you?"

"Only just get out of my way—*please*!" he roared as he tore past her down the stairs to the bathroom again and began to strop his razor furiously.

She came downstairs slowly, trying to think what to do. Calamity of unnamed proportions loomed ahead, and she felt she must prevent it somehow. She paused in the hall.

"Carey, is anything the matter?" she asked anxiously.

"There you are again, doggone it! Now you've made me cut myself, and I haven't another collar. No, of course there isn't anything the matter. I'm just in a hurry, can't you *see*? They're waiting for me!"

"Well, but why are you so cross?"

"Aw! I'm not cross. I'm just nervous. Now, just look at that collar! It's just like all my luck."

"I think your laundry came this morning," volunteered his sister.

"Well! Why didn't you say so? Where is it?"

"Look here, Carey," she said with fire in her eyes, "you have no need to be a bear, and if you want me to get your collar, you'll have to speak decently, or I won't have anything more to do with you."

There was silence in the bathroom for the space of half a second, then an obviously controlled voice said, "Pardon me, Nell. I'm almost cr–r–azy. Can't you see?"

"Why, yes!" said his sister significantly and went swiftly downstairs for the package of laundry.

Carey was elaborately polite when she presented it, but he refrained, boy-like, from telling her that he was going after a job he had heard about, which would have made the whole affair perfectly reasonable to her. *What business is it of hers?* he reasoned. *And then suppose I didn't get it?*

So he stormed from the house like a whirlwind, leaving no word of when he would return, and Cornelia was too much on her dignity to ask him. She stood at the window, watching him out of sight, the quick tears springing into her eyes. What a boisterous, happy bunch they were, all of them, piling into the car, which started even before they were in. What a noise the car made, as if it, too, had partaken of the spirit of its owner and went roaring through the world with a daredevil blare and throb of a converted fire engine just to attract attention and show the world they didn't care! Her cheeks grew hot with shame over it, and for some strange reason her imagination conjured up a possible day in the future when that fair lady, her fellow traveler of the other day, with her handsome son should perhaps come to call upon her. How terrible to have it happen when her brother would go roaring away from the house in this wild fashion! Oh, how had Carey ever grown into such a person? So impossible a combination!

She came and stood beside the yawning hole in the parlor floor. How hard he had worked. How much in earnest he had been! And then at a snap of the finger from this young lord of creation he had dropped it all and fled on some fool whim or other, who knew?

She felt sick and utterly tired, and as if she could not go on with her own work. She had just dropped into a chair and covered her face with her hands when there came a knock at the door. For an instant she meditated not noticing it, but thinking better of it, hastily brushed her hand across her wet eyes and hurried to answer the knock.

It was the carpenter, tall and smiling, with a kit of tools and a big window frame on a wheelbarrow just behind him.

"Well, I brought one along fer you to see," he said, stooping to lift the frame and bring it in. "They said you could have 'em for two and a half apiece, and I thought that was reasonable. Now, where was it you wanted 'em? There's four or five available. You can take as many as you want and leave the rest, and there's a bay like I was telling you. He says he'll make it five 'cause he wants to get it out of the way. It has these here di'mon' panes. It's real pretty like."

Cornelia had stood back aghast at the sight of the window frame, but when she heard the price, she opened the door wide and forgot all her troubles for the moment.

"Oh, how wonderful!" she said, her eyes shining. "Come in. Could you—you couldn't—put it in *now?*"

"Why, yes, that's what I come fer, if you want it done. 'Course I don't want to force it on you, but I thought you could tell if it would do. We quit early today, 'count of being all done at one place and not wanting to begin another till Monday 'cause the stuff ain't come yet, so I just thought to me I'd bring my tools and work all day tomorrow and Saturday—course that's a half, but then— And if you wanted, I'd go at this job right off. I oughta be able to get this winder in by dark. Of course, that's working after union hours, but this here don't count, being right next door to home, you know; it's kind of a favor to a neighbor, see? I brought the sash and all; it's standing just outside, against the house. Now, you want these one each side the fireplace, don't you?"

Cornelia drew a deep breath of daring and said, "Yes!" And then suddenly was glad—just a little—that Carey had been called away. Now she could surprise the whole family.

With her heart in her mouth she stood by the open parlor door and watched a great hole arrive in the blank wall, and then with a breath of relief turned and sped quickly upstairs to make up for lost time and to put the rooms there in order. It would soon be time for the children to come home from school. How surprised they would be! She knew she could count on both of them to be delighted, but she wished it had been possible for that window to be in before they arrived; it would be such fun to surprise them with it. Then she glanced out the window and saw a little girl coming in the gate, and she hurried down to the door to see what was wanted.

"Why," began the small maiden, "your sister Lou said to tell you she and Harry won't be home till late. She said they had to practice that play for the entertainment. She said you needn't to worry. She said to tell you Harry had telephoned to the store, and it's all right."

"Oh, thank you!" said Cornelia with a pleased smile. Now there would be something done to show them when the children got home. How nice that the rehearsal should happen today! She had almost forgotten her disappointment about Carey in her desire to surprise the family.

The man went right to work, and she would see in five minutes that he was interested and was no laggard. In half an hour they had located the window, and he had half of the opening sawed out. Cornelia went back to the kitchen to get some neglected cooking underway, and when she returned, he was fitting the window frame. She looked around the little room with delight. What a difference it was going to make to have light and air from that side! She slipped happily back to her work again, and the sound of the saw and hammer was like music to her soul. There was no longer any doubt whether she ought to have waited. Now and then the thought of Carey hurt through her brain like a sting of something sharp, but she soothed herself by making custard pies for supper. Carey liked custard pies, and while she was making them it seemed easier to believe he would return in time for the evening meal.

At a quarter to six the carpenter went home. He had finished putting in the window, and he had marked out the place for the other one. He had also ripped off the baseboards on the parlor side of the wall that was to come down and had taken off the trim of the door frame. It began to look like business. He promised to come in the morning and bring the I beam and the other window. As he had to go to his boss's shop for them, she had no fear he would arrive before her family were away. So with a gleeful glance at the new window Cornelia carefully closed the parlor door and turned the key in the lock, putting it into her pocket. If the family questioned, she would say that she thought it safer to keep it locked, lest someone might forget in the dark and fall into that open fireplace hole. Then, hugging her secret to her heart, she hurried back to get her dinner ready to serve.

The children came tumbling joyously into the side door, both talking at once about the play and demanding to know how much Carey had gotten done on the fireplace, and their father smiling behind, interested in all—but Carey had not come yet!

Chapter 11

The children found out at once that Carey had gone with Brand, and a gloom settled over the little household. Cornelia had no trouble in keeping them out of the parlor; they did not want to go in. Even Harry seemed oppressed and broke out every few minutes while he ate his supper with, "Aw, gee! If I was a fella!"

Cornelia suddenly roused to break the gloom that had fallen upon them. She looked at her younger brother with a cheery smile.

"Well, you will be someday. You are already, you know, really."

Harry looked up proudly and met her appreciation with a glow.

"I think," said Cornelia thoughtfully, "that this would be a nice night to clean the kitchen, if you all could help."

"Clean the kitchen!" They looked up unenthusiastically.

"Why, I thought you cleaned that the first day. It looked awfully nice," said Louise. Somehow kitchens seemed uninteresting places.

"Oh, but not really clean," said Cornelia, taking a deep breath and trying to get courage for the evening, for she was already weary enough to rest, but she must do something to take the family's mind off Carey and that locked parlor door if she wanted her plans to succeed.

"I want to paint it all white, walls and ceiling and woodwork, and then I want to paint the floor gray and put that waterproof varnish on it so it will wash up easily. Those boards are very hard to keep clean the way they are and show every grease spot. Did you ever paint, Harry?"

"Oh sure. I painted the porch down at the grocery, and the henhouse, and all around the windowsills for Mrs. Brannon. I can paint. Got any brushes?"

"Yes, I got one for each of us the other day and a can of paint to be ready when there was time. Then, Father, I wonder if you couldn't put up some brackets and fix those old marbles for me."

"Marbles?"

"Yes, those old marbles that came off the washstand and bureau that fell to pieces. They are out in the back shed, and I want one of them out on the dresser, screwed on, you know, so I can use it for a molding board, and the other two, the back and top of the old washstand, put up on brackets for shelves in the kitchen near the sink. They'll save buying oilcloth and be lovely to work on and simply delightful to clean."

"Why, I guess I can fix them. There's an old marble-topped table around somewhere, too."

"I know. I'm going to paint the woodwork white and get some ball-bearing casters for it and use it in the kitchen to work on. Then I can wheel it around where I need it, over by the sink when I'm washing dishes, over by the stove to hold the bowl of batter when I'm baking cakes."

"Say, that'll be great!" cried Louise. "Oh! I never realized a kitchen could be pretty. Why, I'd like to wash dishes in a place like that—all white! Say, Nellie, is that a part of interior decorating? Kitchens?"

"Surely!" smiled the sister. "We want to make it pleasant where we have to work the most. Now let's get these dishes out of the way first, and then you children put on your oldest clothes, something that won't be hurt with the paint, and we'll go to work."

"You ought to have one of those 'lectric dishwashers, Nell," said Harry energetically, getting up with a pile of dishes and starting toward the kitchen. "They got one down to the store on exhibition. Say, it's great! You just stick 'em in, and they come out all washed and dried. I'll buy you one someday when I get ahead a little."

"Do," said Cornelia warmly, smiling. "That would be wonderful!"

And so in the bustle and eagerness the disappointment over Carey was somewhat forgotten. They all worked away happily together until ten o'clock, painting and pounding and scrubbing, and when they finally put up the brushes and went to bed, the kitchen was in a fair way toward reconstruction. The window frames had lost their grimy, years-old green paint under a first coat of white; the doors had been sandpapered and primed; the sidewalls had been patched with plaster-of-paris and received a coat of shellac. Everything began to look clean and hopeful.

"Aw, gee! Carey don't know what he's missin'," mourned Harry as he climbed reluctantly up the stairs, not wanting to leave till he had finished all the first coat and was persuaded to bed by his sister only on the ground that he wouldn't want to get up in the morning.

For three days Carey stayed away without a sign, and for two evenings Cornelia kept her family interested in the kitchen so that they did not notice the locked parlor door.

It was a bit hard on Cornelia. She worked steadily all day then worked again all the evening and lay awake most of the night worrying about her brother. She was beginning to get dark circles under her eyes, and her father looked at her anxiously and asked her whether she didn't think she was doing too much. But she managed to smile cheerfully and keep a brave front. She knew by the weary little wrinkles around his eyes that he, too, was lying awake nights worrying about Carey. But the kitchen was beginning to take on the look of a lily and was rapidly becoming a spot where the family loved to go and gaze around, so transforming is a little white paint.

Later on the second afternoon, Cornelia went to a telephone booth and looked among the Bs for Barlock. When she had found it, she called up the one with the initials R. B., taking a chance between that and Peter, Mary, Silas, and J.J., and trembling put in her nickel and waited. It was a young girl's voice, fresh and snappy, that answered her, for she had called the residence and not the business office, and she tried to control her voice and answer calmly as she asked whether Mr. Brand Barlock was at home. The girl's voice at the other end was a trifle haughty as she answered, "No, he's motored down to Baltimore. I don't know when he'll be home. Maybe two or three days. Who is this?"

"Oh," said Cornelia a trifle relieved, "then I'll call again," and hung up the receiver in the face of the repeated question, "Who is this?" Her cheeks were glowing as she emerged from the telephone booth and hastened out to the street as if she were afraid someone would chase her. That was likely Brand Barlock's sister on the telephone, and Cornelia had appeared to her like a bold girl calling up her brother and then retreating without giving her name, but it had been the only way. At least she knew this much: that Brand also was still away. Carey was likely safe; that is, probably nothing had happened to his body, though there was no telling what had happened to his soul on such a wild trip with such companions.

But the third day the carpenter took down the parlor partition, and turned the hall and parlor into one, and Cornelia could no longer conceal the interesting changes that had been going on within the old front room.

There was a fine big window on each side of the big fireplace hole, with a box window seat under it, and the little "bay" had been put into the long, dark wall of the hallway, with a row of three diamond-paned windows opening just over the staircase. Cornelia had managed to conceal the first bay window, which had been put in the second day, by means of an old curtain tacked across the wall. But, when the third night came, there stood the big new room with all its windows, a place of great possibilities.

"Now," said the carpenter as he stood back and surveyed his finished task, "there's just two more things I'd like to see you do to this room. You need to break that there staircase with a landin' about four steps up. You got plenty a' room this side yer dining room door, an''twould jest strike them three winders fer the landin'. They got a half circle an' two long, narrer side winders down to the shop would jest fit around that there front door. If you say the word, I'll put 'em in tomorra. I jest about could do it in a day. But I'd like to turn them stairs around. I certainly would."

So, with fear and trembling Cornelia told him to go ahead. He assured her she needn't worry about the pay, that his mother-in-law and his two cousins' wives all wanted curtains, and it began to look as if she would be stenciling birds the rest of her natural life, so she had no fear but she would be able to pay him sometime. She was getting five dollars a set for her curtains and felt quite independent. Perhaps, after all, she would be an interior decorator someday, even if this was a day of small things, scrim curtains instead of rich fabrics and rare hangings.

That night, when the children came home, they discovered the changes in the front part of the house, of course, and their sister found them standing in awe on the stairs looking around them as if they had suddenly stepped into a place of enchantment.

"Oh, Nellie, Nellie, how did you do it?" they cried when they saw her. "Isn't this great? Isn't it wonderful?" And then, with a look at the yawning cavity in the floor where the fireplace was to be, "Oh, what will Carey say? Why doesn't he come home?"

And that night after they were all in bed, Carey came.

Even the children heard the car drive up to the door, and the whole shabby house seemed to be straining every alert nerve to him.

Carey came whistling a jazzy little tune up the path and with a careless happy-go-lucky swag, not at all like the prodigal son that he was, with the whole family in a long three days' agony over him. It was almost virtuous, that whistle and the way he subdued it as he unlocked the dining room door and groped his way through the dark to where the foot of the stairs used to be. They heard him strike a match, and then, as if they had all been down there to watch him, they could visualize his amazed face as he stood in the little halo of the match and looked around him at the strange room and the strange staircase, with a turn in the stairs and only one rail up yet, and a platform. They heard him strike another match, and then they heard his footsteps and more matches as he walked around looking. Cornelia knew when he spotted the bay window and the seats under the two windows by the fireplace. She heard the gentle thud of the top as he opened it and closed it again. She heard the soft whistle of approval and drew a long breath of relief. At least he was interested.

She knew that the little sister heard, too, and was following Carey's every movement, for she felt the quick grip of the little hand on her shoulder and the soft, tense breath against her cheek, and somehow it gave her courage and strength. With all the family united in loving anxiety for him.

Afterward she thought about it and wondered at herself, and resolved to pray regularly again, even if just to pray for Carey. It was so necessary that Carey be saved and made a good man. It was necessary just for their mother's sake, and it must be done before she came home, or she would be likely to get sick again worrying about him.

Carey came slowly up the stairs and went to his room. The family listened to his movements overhead, listened for his shoes to fall and then to the creak of the springs as he at last got into bed. Listened longer as the springs continued to creak while Carey rolled around, settling himself—thinking, perhaps?—and then at last when all was quiet, they slept.

It was well for Carey that a night intervened between his homecoming and the meeting with his family. The sharp words that swelled in the heart of each of them, and would surely have arisen to the lips of them, would not have been pleasant for him to hear. They might have been beneficial; they undoubtedly would have been true; but it is exceedingly doubtful whether in his present state of mind he would have endured them graciously. He had had a good time, and he had come home. He was in no mood for fault-finding. The sight of the unfinished fireplace in the wide desolation of the renovated and enlarged room had given him a good-sized pang of remorse, which was in a fair way to stay with him for a day or so. Sharp words would most certainly have dispelled it instantly and put him on the defensive. To blame as he undoubtedly was, he preferred to blame himself rather than to have his family do so; and the fact that he arose before light, before any of the others were even awake, and descended to the cellar quietly to pursue his interrupted work proved that he had begun to apprehend the likelihood of blame and wished to forestall it.

It was Harry who awoke first, feeling rather than hearing the dull thuds of the silent worker in the cellar. Hastily dressing, he stole down in wonder and delight and was so well pleased with what he saw and with the most unusually cordial greeting from his elder brother that he remained to help and not to blame. When Louise came down, followed almost immediately by Cornelia, and found the two brothers working so affably, with a whole row of stones reared in the parlor, they gave one another a swift, understanding glance and greeted their brothers collectively and joyously as if nothing had happened for the last four days.

Carey rattled off jokes and worked away like a beaver, keeping them all in roars of laughter; and the father, waking late from his troubled sleep, heard the festive sound and hurried down, relieved that the cloud of gloom had lifted from his home. He had had it in mind to give Carey a regular dressing down when he returned. Words fitly framed for such a proceeding had been forming red hot in his worried mind all night. But the sight of his four children in gales of laughter over some silly story Carey had told, and the sight of the clock hastening on to the moment of his car, restrained him, and perhaps it was just as well. Cornelia hurried him into his place and gave him his breakfast, chattering all the time about the rooms and the changes and so kept his mind busy. At last they all got away without a word of reproof to Carey, and Cornelia was left to wonder whether she ought to open the subject.

All the morning they worked eagerly together, finding personal conversation impossible because of the presence of the carpenter. At lunch time, however, Carey, having been most courteous and apologetic, seemed to feel his time had come. Or perhaps he appreciated his sister's silence. At any rate, he remarked quite casually that he had been out for a job in Baltimore and hadn't got it. Worse luck! Missed the man he went to see by half an hour but had a dandy time.

Cornelia took the news quietly, thoughtfully, and presently raised her eyes.

"Carey, dear, next time you go, wouldn't you be good enough to tell us where you are going and how long you expect to be gone? You've given us all an extremely anxious time, you know."

She managed to make her voice quiet and matter-of-fact, without the least bit of fault-finding, for a black cloud hovered almost imperceptibly over the handsome young brows across the table, and she had no mind to spoil the pleasant atmosphere that had surrounded them all the morning.

"The idea!" said Carey, excited at once. "Why should I do that? I'm not a baby, am I? I'm a *man*, ain't I? I guess I can go as far as I like and stay as long as I like, can't I?"

"Yes, you can, of course," soothed his sister. "But, if you really are a man, you've noticed how gray and worn Father looks. How sick he looks! He's been through a lot, you know, and he can't help thinking that maybe something else dreadful is coming. He has to worry for himself and Mother, too, you know. Because just now everything is very critical on Mother's account. I know you wouldn't want to worry Mother, and you wouldn't want to worry Father, either, if you just stopped to think."

"Well, but how absurd! A trip down to Baltimore that any fella would take. You aren't such a goose as to worry over that, are you?"

"Of course it is a bit silly," admitted the sister. "But I must confess I lay awake several hours every night myself. You re-member you had just got done telling me what a wild driver that Brand Barlock is and how he put ether in the mixture. And one can't help knowing there are hundreds of terrible automobile accidents every day. They might happen even to a *man*, you know, and then—well, we *love* you, Carey, you know."

"Oh, gosh! Well, I didn't know you were that sort of a goose. I know of course Mother—but then she isn't here."

"Well, when it comes down to it, Carey, I guess we all care about as much as Mother." She smiled at him through a sudden mist of tears that all unexpectedly welled into her eyes. "And you know it was quite sudden, and well, if you had just thought to telephone, you know, to say you would be gone several days."

"Aw, gee! Well, I suppose I might have done that. I will next time. Sure, Nell, I'll try to remember. It was wrong of me not to say anything, but I figured that if I didn't get it, no one would be the wiser."

"Well, I guess you can't cheat your family." She smiled again, ignoring the mist in her eyes. "We're a kind of gang together. Isn't that what you call it? And what affects one affects all. Why, even little Louie cried herself to sleep in my arms last night because she thought maybe you had been killed."

"Aw! Gee!"

Carey got up swiftly and went over to the window, where he gazed out past the neighbor's blank wall until he had control of himself; then he turned with one of his lightning smiles.

"All right, Nell. I'll give you the tip next time. I'm sorry I had to stay so long, but I waited for the man. See?"

"Well, Carey, I suppose you thought that was the right thing to do, but I've been wondering since you've been talking whether there isn't something good for you in all this big city where we live without going away to Baltimore."

"I'd like to see it," gloomily answered the boy, with a sudden grim look in his eyes. "I've tried everything I heard of."

"Well, it will come," said his sister brightly. "Come, let's get this house finished first, and then we'll be ready for the big position you're going to have. Next week, you know, you've got to go back to the garage and earn that suit. You need it badly."

Carey caught her suddenly and gave her a bear hug and then spun her around the room till she was dizzy; and so, happily, they went back to their work, Cornelia wondering whether she had done right to pass the matter off so lightly. But brother, as he worked away at his stones silently, was thinking more seriously on the error of his ways than he had thought for four years past.

Chapter 12

It was several weeks before the Copley house was finished. Even then there were cushions to make out of old pieces brightened up by the stitches of embroidery or appliqué work of leaves cut from bits of old velvet. There were rugs to braid out of all the old rags the house afforded, and there were endless curtains to wash and hem and hemstitch and stencil and put up. All the family united to make the work as perfect a thing of the kind as could be accomplished. Every evening was spent in painting or papering, or rubbing down some bit of old furniture to make it more presentable, and gradually the house began to assume form and loveliness.

Paint, white paint, had done a great deal toward making another place of the dreary little house. The kitchen was spotless white enamel everywhere, and enough old marble slabs had been discovered to cover the kitchen table and the top of the kitchen dresser and to put up shelves around the sink and under the windows. Mr. Copley brought home some ball-bearing casters for the kitchen table and spent an evening putting them on so it would move easily to any part of the kitchen needed. Cornelia and

Louise rejoiced in scrubbing the smooth white surfaces that were going to be so convenient and so easily kept clean. Even the old kitchen chairs had been painted white and enameled, and Cornelia discovered by chance one day that a wet sponge was a wonderful thing to keep the white paint clean; so thereafter Louise spent five minutes after dinner every evening going about with her wet sponge, rubbing off any chance fingermarks of the day before and putting the gleaming kitchen in order for the next day.

The dining room had gradually become a place of rest and refreshment for the eyes as well as for the palate. Soft green was the prevailing color of furniture and floor, with an old grass rug scrubbed back to almost its original color. The old couch was repaired and covered with pretty cretonne in greens and grays, with plenty of pillows covered with the same material. The curtains were white with a green border of stenciling. The dingy old paper had been scraped from the walls, which had been painted with many coats of white, and a pretty green border had been stenciled at the ceiling. The carpenter had found an old plate rail down in the shop, which, painted white, made a different place of the whole thing, with a few bits of Mother's rare old china rightly placed; two Wedgwood plates in dull yellow, another of bright green; a big old Blue Willow ware plate; and some quaint cups hung on brass hooks under a little white shelf. One couldn't ask for a pleasanter dining room than that. It dawned upon the family anew and joyously every time any one of them entered the room and made them a little better and a little brighter because it spoke "home" so softly and sweetly and comfortingly.

"Mother won't know the place!" said Louise, standing back to survey it happily after putting the sideboard in perfect order with a clean linen cover. "She won't know her own things, will she? Won't it be great when she comes?"

But the living room was the crown of all: wide and pleasant with many windows, with its stone fireplace and wide mantel, adorned with a quaint old pair of brass candlesticks that had belonged to the grandmother; the walls covered with pale yellow felt-paper like soft sunshine; the floor planed down to the natural wood, oiled and treated with shellac; and the old woolen rugs in two tones of gray, which used to be bedroom rugs when Cornelia was a baby, washed and spread about in comfortable places; it no more resembled the stuffy, dark little place they used to call a "parlor" than day resembles night. Soft white sheer curtains veiled the windows everywhere, with overcurtains of yellow cotton crêpe, and the sunshine seemed to have taken up its abode in that room even on dark days when there was no sun to be seen. It was as if it had stayed behind from the last sunshiny day, so bright and cheerful was the glow.

The little "bay" was simply overflowing with ferns the children had brought from the woods, set in superfluous yellow and gray bowls from the kitchen accumulation. Harry ran extra errands after hours and saved enough to buy the yellowest, throatiest canary the city afforded, in a big wicker cage to hang in the window.

Cretonne covers in soft gray tones covered the shabby old chairs and couch, and Carey and his father spent hours with pumice stone and oil, polishing away at the piano, the bookcase, and the one small mahogany table that was left, while Cornelia did wonderful things in the way of artistic shades for little electric lamps that Carey rigged up in odd, unexpected corners, made out of all sorts of unusual things: an old pewter sugar bowl, this with a shade of silver lace lined with yellow, a relic of some college costume; a tall gray jug with odd blue Chinese figures on it that had been among the kitchen junk for years, this with a dull blue shade; a bright yellow vase with a butterfly-yellow shade; and a fat green jar with willow basketwork around it on which Cornelia put a shade of soft green with some old brown lace over it.

The room was really wonderful when it was done, with two or three pictures hung in just the right spots and some photographs and magazines thrown comfortably about. Really one could not imagine a pleasanter or more artistic room, not if one had thousands to spend. The first evening it was all complete the family just sat down and enjoyed themselves in it, talking over each achievement of cushion or curtain or wall as a great connoisseur might have looked over his newly acquired collection and gloated over each specimen with delight.

Carey's delight in it all was especially noticeable. He hovered around, getting new points of view and changing the arrangement of a chair or a table, whistling wildly and gleefully, a new Carey to them all. For the whole evening he did not offer to go out, just hung around, talking, singing snatches of popular songs, breaking into a clumsy two-finger "rag" on the piano now and then, and finally ending up with a good sing with Cornelia at the piano. It was curious, but it was a fact that this was the first time Cornelia had had time since her homecoming to sit down and play for them, and it seemed like a revelation to all. They had not realized how well she could play, for she had been studying music part of the time in college. Also no one had realized how well Carey could sing. Perhaps he had never had half a chance with a good accompaniment before. At any rate, it was very plain that he liked it and would sing as long as anyone would play for him.

And the father liked it, too. Oh, *how* he liked it! He took off his glasses, put his head back on the new cretonne cushion, closed his eyes, and just enjoyed it. Now and then he would open his eyes and watch the flicker of the fire in the new fireplace, look from the one to the other of his children, sigh, and say, "I wish your mother were here now," and again, "We must write Mother about all this. How she will enjoy it!"

Then right into the midst of this domestic scene there entered callers.

Carey was singing when the knock came and did not hear them, or else he would most surely have disappeared. It was a way Carey had. But the knock came twice before Louise heard it and slipped to the door, letting in the strangers, who stood listening at the door, motioning to her to wait until the song was finished.

Then Mr. Copley saw them and arose to come forward. Carey, feeling some commotion, turned, and the song stopped like a shot, a frown of defiance beginning to grow between his brows.

The strangers were a man and a woman and a young girl a little older than Louise and younger than Cornelia, and one could see at a glance that they were cultured, refined people, though they were quietly, simply dressed. Carey, in his gray flannel shirt open at the neck and the old trousers in which he had assisted in the last rites of putting the room in perfect order, looked down at himself in dismay and backed suddenly around the end of the piano as far out of sight as possible, meeting the intruders with a glare of disapproval. Cornelia was the last to stop playing and look around, but by that time the lady had spoken.

"Oh, please don't stop! We want to hear the rest of the song. What a beautiful tenor voice!"

Cornelia arose to her duties as hostess and came forward, but the man by this time was introducing himself.

"I hope we haven't intruded, brother." He grasped Mr. Copley's welcoming hand. "I'm just the minister at the little church around your corner here, and we thought we'd like to get acquainted with our new neighbors. My name is Kendall, and this is my wife and my daughter, Grace. I brought the whole family along because I understood you had some daughters."

"You're very welcome," said Mr. Copley with dignity that marked him a gentleman everywhere. "This is my daughter Cornelia; this is Louise, and Harry; and"—with an almost frightened glance toward the end of the piano, lest he might already have vanished—"this is my son Carey."

There was something almost proud in the way he spoke Carey's name, and Cornelia had a sudden revelation of what Carey, the eldest son, must mean to his father in spite of all his sharpness to the boy. Of course Carey must have been a big disappointment the last few months.

Carey, thus cornered, instead of bolting, as his family half expected of him, came forward with an unexpected grace of manner and acknowledged the introduction, his eyes resting interestedly on the face of Grace Kendall.

"I'm not very presentable," he said. "But, as I can't seem to get out without being seen, I guess you'll have to make the best of me."

Grace Kendall's eyes were merry and pleasant.

"Please don't mind us," she said. "You look very nice. You look as if you had been playing tennis."

"Nothing so interesting as that," said Carey. "Just plain work. We're still tinkering around this house, getting settled, you know."

"There's always such a lot to do when you move, isn't there? But what a lovely spot you've made of it!" She turned and looked about her. "Why, I shouldn't know it was the same house. What a lot you have done to it! This room looks so big! How did you get the space? You've changed the partitions, haven't you? I used to come here to visit a little lame boy, and it was such a tiny little front room; and now this is spacious! And that wonderful fireplace! Isn't it beautiful?"

"Yes," put in Mr. Copley, as the whole group seemed absorbed in gazing around them at the lovely room. "My son did that. He built it all himself."

Carey looked up in surprise, with a flush of pleasure at his father's tone of pride, and then his eyes came back to the girl's face all sparkling with eager admiration.

"You don't mean you did it yourself? How perfectly wonderful! That darling mantel! And the way the chimney curves up to the ceiling! It has charming lines! Oh, Father, can't you coax him to come over and build one for us?"

"Sure! I'll build you one!" said Carey graciously, as though he kept stone fireplaces in his vest pocket. "Start tomorrow if you can get the stone."

"Oh, great! Just hear that, Father! We're going to have a fireplace! Now, don't you let him off. Did you design it, Mr. Copley?"

Carey lifted embarrassed eyes to his elder sister's face and met her look of loving pride and flushed happily.

"Why, no, I guess my sister Nell's to blame for that. She suggested it first and worked it out mostly," he said.

"Indeed, you did it all yourself, Carey," said Cornelia. "I only wanted it, and Carey did the rest."

"Yes, Gracie, that's where you're lacking," said the minister laughingly. "You haven't any brother to carry out your every wish. Only a busy old father, who doesn't know how."

"My father's all right!" said the daughter loyally. And Carey, with a swift, appraising glance, decided that he certainly looked it and that for a minister it certainly was surprising. He had a faint passing wonder what this man's church might be like. Then they settled down in groups to talk: Carey beside the minister's daughter, Cornelia beside the minister's wife, and Mr. Copley with the minister, while Harry and Louise sat down together in the window seat to watch them all.

"Doesn't Carey look handsome?" whispered the little girl, with her eyes on her elder brother. "My, but I guess he's mad he didn't put on his other shirt."

"I should say! Serves him right," said Harry caustically, yet with a light of pride in his eyes. "Say, she's some bird, isn't she? Better'n that little chicken we saw him have out last Saturday!"

"Oh, Harry! You mustn't call *any* girl a chicken. You know what Mother would say."

"Well, she *was* a chicken, wasn't she?"

"I think I'd rather call her a—a fool!" said Louise expressively.

"Call her what you like, only don't call her at all!" said the boy. "Say, doesn't our sister look great though?"

So they sat quietly whispering, picking up bits of the conversation and thinking their wise young thoughts.

Mr. Copley's face looked rested and happy.

"My! I wish my wife were at home," he said wistfully. "You know she's been very sick, and she's away getting a rest. But we hope she'll soon be back with us before many months now. How she would enjoy it to have you run in like this! She's a great church woman, and she felt it, coming away from the church we have always attended over on the other side of town—"

Then the talk drifted to the little church around the corner and to its various organizations and activities.

"Father'll be after you for the choir," confided the daughter to Carey. "A good tenor is a great find."

"No chance!" said Carey, looking pleased in spite of himself. "I can't sing."

Then they all began to clamor for Carey to sing. And right in the midst of it there was another knock at the door, and in walked the carpenter and his wife.

Carey began to frown, of course, for, although he liked the

carpenter, he felt that he was of another social class from the deli-cate young girl who sat by his side. But when he saw her rise and greet the carpenter's wife as cordially as if she were some fine lady, his frown began to disappear again. This certainly was a peach of a girl, and no mistake. In fact, the whole family was all right. The minister was a prince. Just look at the way he took that carpen-ter by the hand and made him feel at home.

The carpenter, however, didn't seem to be troubled by embar-rassment. He entered right into the conversation comfortably and began to praise Cornelia Copley and her ability as an interior decorator; and before any one knew how it happened the company had started to see the dining room and kitchen.

Nobody realized it, but they were all talking and laughing as if they had known one another for years, and everybody was having a happy time. When they came back to the living room, they insisted that Carey should sing and Cornelia should play for them. Harry and Louise whispered together for a moment then slipped silently back to the kitchen while the music was going on and returned in a few minutes with a tall pitcher of lemonade and a plate of Cornelia's delicious gingerbread. Carey went for plates and acted the host beautifully. It all passed off delightfully, even with the presence of the carpenter, who proved to be a good mixer in spite of his lack of grammar.

Before they went away, the minister had asked the brother and sister to join the choir and come to the Sunday school and young people's society and all the various other functions of the church, and had given a special urgent invitation to the whole family, including the callers, to come to a church reception to be held the coming week. Carey acted as if church receptions and young people's prayer meetings were the joy of his life and agreed in everything that was suggested, declaring, when the door closed behind them, that that girl was "some peach." And the household retired to their various pillows with happy dreams of a circumspect future in which Carey walked the happy way of a wise young man and had friends that one was not ashamed of. And then the very next afternoon, being Saturday, everything was wrecked in one quick happening, and a cloud of gloom fell over the little household.

For it happened that Cornelia and Louise had taken an afternoon off, having arisen quite early and accomplished an incredible amount of Saturday baking and mending and ironing and the like, and had gone down to the stores to choose a much-needed pair of shoes for Louise. The shoes were purchased, also ten cents' worth of chocolates, and they were about to finish the joyful occasion by a visit to a movie when suddenly, walking up Chestnut Street, they came face-to-face with Carey and a girl! Carey, who was supposed to be off that whole afternoon hunting for a job! And *such* a girl!

The most noticeable thing about the girl was the whiteness of her nose and the rosiness of a certain outlined portion of her cheeks. As she drew nearer, one also noticed her cap-like arrangement of hair that was obviously stained henna and bobbed quite furiously under a dashing hat of jade-green feathers. Her feet were fat, with fat overhanging flesh-colored silken ankles, quite transparent as to the silk, and were strapped in with many little buckles to a very sharp toe and a tall little stilt of a heel. Her skirt was like one leg of a pantaloon, so tight it was, and very short, so that the fat, silken ankles became most prominent; and her dainty gait reminded one of a Bach fugue. She wore an objectionable and conspicuous tunic, much beaded with short sleeves and very low neck, for the street.

A scrubby little fur flung across the back of her neck completed her outfit, unless one counted the string of big white beads that hung around her neck to her waist and the many rings that adorned her otherwise bare hands. She was chewing gum, rhythmically and industriously, and giggling up into Carey's face with a silly, sickening grin that made the heart of Cornelia turn sick with disgust.

As she drew nearer, a pair of delicately penciled stationary eyebrows, higher than nature usually places them, emphasized the whole effect; and the startling red of the girl's lips seemed to fascinate the gaze they were coming nearer. They were almost near enough to touch each other, and Carey—Carey was looking down at the girl—he had drawn her arm within his own, and he had not seen his sister.

Suddenly, without any warning, Cornelia felt the angry tears starting to her eyes, and with a quick movement she drew Louise to a milliner's window they were passing and stood, trembling in every nerve, while Carey and the girl passed by.

Chapter 13

$\mathcal{L}$ouise had given her sister one swift, comprehending look and stood quietly enough looking into the window, but her real glance was sideways, watching Carey and the girl.

"That's the one! That's the chicken, Nellie!" she whispered. "Now, isn't she a chicken? Don't you think Harry is right? Turn around and watch her. They've gone ahead so far they'll never see us now. Look! Just see her waddle! See her toddle! Aren't those shoes the limit? And her fat legs inching along like that! I think she's *disgusting*! How can my brother not be ashamed to be seen with her? And down here on Chestnut Street, too, where he might meet *anybody*! Think if that Grace Kendall should come along and see him! She'd never speak to him again. Oh, Nellie, isn't she *dreadful*?"

"Hush, dear! Somebody will hear you. Yes, she's pretty awful."

"But, Nellie, can't we do something about it? Can't Carey be ordered not to go with a thing like that anymore? Why, even the girls in my school are talking about them. They call her my brother's *girl*! Nellie, aren't you going to *do* anything about it? Aren't you going to tell Father and have it stopped?"

"Hush, darling! Yes, I'm going to do something—but I don't know what yet. I don't know what there is to do."

She tried to smile with her lips in a tremble, and looking down, she saw that tears were rolling down the little sister's cheeks.

"Darling! Don't do that!" she cried, roused out of her own distress. "Here, take my handkerchief and brighten up a little. You mustn't cry here. People will think something dreadful has happened to you."

"They can't think any worse than it is," murmured Louise, snubbing off a sob with the proffered handkerchief. "To have my nice, handsome big brother be a big *fool* like that! Oh, I'd like to *kill* that girl! I would! I'd like to choke her!"

"Louie! Stop! This is awful!" cried Cornelia, horrified. "You mustn't talk that way about anybody, no matter how much of a fool she is. Perhaps there's another side to it. Perhaps Carey is just as much to blame. Perhaps the girl doesn't know any better. Maybe she has no mother to teach her. Maybe Carey is sorry for her."

"He—didn't look sorry; he looked glad!" murmured the little girl, trying to bring her emotions into control. "And anyhow I can't help hating her. Even if she hasn't got a mother. She doesn't need to dip her face in a flour barrel like that and make eyes at my brother."

"Listen, Louie." Cornelia's voice was very quiet, and she felt a sudden strength come to her from the need to help the little girl. "Dear, it won't do any good to hate her; it will only do you harm and mix us up so we can't think straight. Besides, it's wicked to hate anybody. Suppose you stop being so excited and let us put some good common sense into his thing. There must be a way to work it out. If it's wrong for Carey to go with her, there will be a way somehow to make him see it. Until Carey sees it himself, there isn't a bit of use in our tying to stop his going with her. He probably has got to the place where rouge and powder are attractive to him, or else perhaps there is more to the girl than just the outside. At any rate, we've got to find out what it is about her that attracts our brother. And, Louie, do you know I've a notion that there's nobody but God can help us in this thing? Mother used to say that, you know, when any big trouble came. And several times lately when I've been worried about things, I've said, 'Oh God, help me,' and things have seemed to straighten out right away. Suppose you and I try that tonight."

Louise looked up through her tears and smiled.

"You're an awfully dear sister, Nellie. I'm glad you came home." And she squeezed her sister's hand tenderly.

"Thank you, lovey. I'm glad I came, too, and you're rather dear yourself, you know, Lou. I think we'll come through somehow. Now, shall we go into this movie?"

"I don't believe I feel much like it, do you, Nellie?" said the little girl hesitatingly and studying a picture on the billboard outside the theater. "Look! That's one of those pictures with cabaret stuff in it that Daddy doesn't like us to see. I don't want to go in. Those girls in that picture make me think of her."

"I'll tell you what. Let's go home and get a good dinner for Carey and the rest, and perhaps we can think of a way to keep him home tonight and have a good time."

So home they went and got the dinner and waited half an hour after the usual time, but no Carey appeared that night until long after the midnight hour had struck. When at last he came tiptoeing up the creaking stairs, trying not to arouse anybody in the house, his two sisters lay hand in hand listening and both praying, "Oh God, show us how to keep Carey away from that girl and make him a good man."

⁓

Carey slept late on Sunday morning and came down cross, declining utterly to go to church. Cornelia and Louise went off alone sorrowfully. Carey had lounged off in the direction of the drugstore, and the father had a headache and decided to nurse it up, lest it keep him away from work on the morrow. Harry volunteered to stay home and get dinner.

The sermon was about prayer, very simple and interesting. Cornelia did not remember having listened to many sermons in her life. Somehow this one seemed unique and struck right home to her need and experience. The preacher said that many people prayed and did not receive because they had failed to meet the conditions of answered prayer. Even Louise sat up and listened with earnest eyes and flushed cheeks. Here was something she felt would help the Copley family if they could only get hold of the secret of it. Mother prayed, and Mother had great faith in prayer, but none of the rest of them had ever specialized along those lines. Unless perhaps Father did, quiet Father, with all his burdens and disappointments.

These thoughts flitted through the minds of the two daughters as they sat listening intently, reaching out for the help they needed. The preacher said that there were many promises in the Bible concerning prayer but always with a condition. The first was faith. One must believe that God hears and will answer. The second was will-surrender. One must be ready to let God answer the prayer in *His* way and to leave that way to Him, believing that He will do what is best. Then one must pray with a free heart, out of which hate and sin have been cast; and he quoted the verse: "If thou bring thy gift to the altar, and there rememberest that thy brother hath ought against thee; leave there thy gift before the altar, and go thy way; first be reconciled to thy brother, and then come and offer thy gift."

Louise cast a fleeting, questioning glance toward her sister. Did that mean that she must forgive that hateful, bold Dodd girl? But the speaker went on:

There were gifts for which one may ask with a definite assurance of receiving if one comes asking with all their heart, namely, the forgiveness of sin, the strength to resist temptation, the gift of the Holy Spirit. And one may always be sure that it is God's will that other souls should be saved, and so we can pray always for others' salvation, knowing that we are not asking amiss.

But there is a condition in which it is the privilege of every child of God to live, in which one may be sure of receiving what one asks, "If ye abide in me, and my words abide in you, ye shall ask what ye will, and it shall be done unto you."

The two sisters listened most carefully to the simple, clear description of the life that is hidden with Christ in God, the life that lets Christ live instead of trying to please self, and that studies daily the Word of God and keeps the Word constantly in mind. And the preacher spoke with confidence about answers to prayer for daily needs, as if he had known great experience in receiving.

On their way home Louise, walking along with her eyes on the sidewalk, asked shyly, "Nellie, do you s'pose that's all true, what he preached about?"

"Why, yes—of course," said the elder sister, hesitating, scarcely knowing where her words were leading her. "Why, certainly," she added with belated conviction and a sense that, if it were so, she had placed herself in a very foolish position, for she had never lived as if she had believed it, and the little sister must know that.

"Well, then," with the quick conclusion of childhood, "why do we worry? Why don't we do it?"

"We—could," said her sister thoughtfully. "I don't know why we never did. I guess we never thought about it. Shall we try it?"

"It won't do to *try* it," said the matter-of-fact little girl, "because he said we had to believe it, you know. And trying is holding on with one hand and watching to see. We've got to walk out with both feet and trust. I'm going to!"

"Well, so will I," said Cornelia slowly, her voice low and almost embarrassed. It seemed a strange topic to be talking about so familiarly with a little girl, her little stranger-sister, but she could not let the child get ahead of her. She could not dash the bright spirit of faith.

"That's nice," said Louise with satisfaction. "I'll tell Harry, too. I guess he will; boys are so funny. I wish he'd been in church. But say, Nellie, we can be happy now, can't we? We don't need to worry about Carey anymore; we can just pray about it, and it will all come out right."

Cornelia smiled and squeezed the little hand nestling in hers.

"I guess that's what we're expected to do," she said thoughtfully.

"Yes, and I think God'll show you what to do about that— that—chicken girl, too, don't you, if you ask Him?"

"I guess He will."

The whole family, of course excepting Carey, who telephoned that he wouldn't be home till late, went to church that night and lingered to be introduced to some of the church people by the cordial minister, who had come down to the door to detain them. They finally went home cheered in heart both by the earnest spiritual service and by the warm Christian fellowship that had been offered them.

That night as Louise nestled into her pillow, she whispered, "Nellie, have you been shown yet? I mean anything about Carey and that girl."

Cornelia drew the little girl into her arms and laid her lips against the warm, soft cheek.

"I'm not quite sure, dear," she answered. "I've been thinking. Perhaps it will seem strange to you, but I've almost come to think perhaps we ought to get to know her."

"Oh–h–h!" Louise said doubtfully. "Do you really think so? But she's—why, she's just *awful*, sister!"

"I know, dear, and I'm not sure yet. But you see we can't do a thing till we really get acquainted with her. She may be simply silly and not know any better. She may not have any mother or something, and perhaps we could help her, and then, if we get acquainted with her, we would perhaps be able to make Carey see somehow. Or else we might help her to be—different."

"Oh–h! But how could we get acquainted with her?"

"Well, I don't know. We'd have to think that up. Do you know her name?"

"Yes, it's Clytie Amabel Dodd. They call her Clytie, and it makes me sick the way they say it. She—she smokes cigarettes, Nellie!"

"She does!" exclaimed Cornelia. "Are you sure, dear? How do you know?"

"Well, Hazel Applegate says she saw her on the street smoking with a lot of boys."

There was a long pause, and the little girl almost thought her sister was asleep; then Cornelia asked, "Do you know where she lives?"

"No, but I guess Harry does. He gets around a lot delivering groceries, you know. Anyway, if he doesn't, he can find out."

"Well, I'll have to think about it some more—and—pray, too."

"Nellie."

"Yes, dear?"

"Nellie, you know that verse the minister said this morning about if two of you agree to pray for anything, you know; why couldn't you and I do that?"

Cornelia pressed the little fingers close. Then it was all very quiet, and presently the two slept.

The next afternoon, while they were getting dinner and working about in the kitchen, the older sister suddenly asked, "When is Carey's birthday? Isn't it this week? The twenty-fifth, isn't it?"

"Yes," said Louise gravely. "It's Thursday. Are you going to do anything? Oh Nellie!" Louise cried in consternation. "You're *not* going to invite that girl *then*?"

"I don't know," said Cornelia. "I know it wouldn't be very pleasant for us, but I thought perhaps it would be a good excuse. There isn't really any other that I know of."

The little girl was silent for a moment.

"Wouldn't it make her think we thought— I mean, wouldn't she get a notion we liked— That is, wouldn't she be awfully set up—and think we wanted her to go with Carey?"

"I'm sure I don't know, dear, and I don't suppose that part of it really matters if we just get this thing sifted down and find out what we've got to do. We simply can't say anything about her to Carey till we've somehow come in contact with her in his presence, or he will think we've been snooping about watching him, and he will just be angry and go with her all the more."

"I know," sighed the little girl.

"If we have her here," went on the older sister thoughtfully, "we'll at least know what they both are doing; and, if she doesn't act nicely, we'll have some ground to influence Carey."

"Yes," answered the little girl with another sigh. "Have you thought, Nellie, perhaps he won't like it?"

"Yes, I've thought that, too, but I guess it won't really matter much. It may do good, you know."

"But he might not come home to supper that night. Or he might get real mad and get up and leave while she's here."

"Well, I don't see that that would really do any harm. I guess we've got to try something, and this seems kind of a plain way to go. If Mother were here, it would be better. Mother would know how to give dignity to the occasion. But I guess for Mother's sake I've go to do something to either improve her or get rid of her before Mother comes home. It would kill Mother."

"Yes, I know. What do you suppose Father'll say?"

"Well, I don't believe I'll tell Father, either, only that I'm going to have a girl here to supper. It would only worry him if he knew she went with Carey, and you can always depend on Father to be polite, you know, to anybody."

"Yes," said Louise soberly. "He'll be polite, but—he won't like her, and she can't help knowing it, no matter how thick-skinned she is; but maybe it'll do her good. Only I'm afraid Carey'll be mad and say something to Father or something."

"No, I don't think he will, not before a girl. Not before any girl. Not if I know Carey. He may say things afterward, but we'll have to be willing to stand that. And besides, what can he say? Aren't we polite to one of his friends? We're not supposed to know anything about her. When it comes down to facts, little sister, we don't really *know* anything about her except that she dresses in a loud way, chews gum, and talks too loud on the street. The other things you have only heard, and you can't be sure they are true unless you see them yourself, or someone you trust perfectly has seen them. I know she may get a notion in her head that Carey is crazy about her if we single her out and invite her alone, but I've about decided it's the only way. Anyhow, she's let herself in for things of that sort by getting herself talked about. I believe we've got to do something quite radical and either kill or cure this trouble. I've thought about asking that Brand fellow, too, and maybe someone else, some other girl. But who would it be?"

Louise thought a moment, then she clutched her sister's hand eagerly.

"Nellie! The very thing! Invite Grace Kendall! She would make them all fit in beautifully. I'd hate awfully to have her know our Carey went with that Clytie thing, but I guess there isn't any other way, and somehow I think a minister's daughter ought to understand, don't you? And help?"

Cornelia was still struggling with her pride.

"Yes," she said thoughtfully. "I guess you're right, little sister. Grace Kendall would understand—and help. I think God must have given you that idea. We'll invite Clytie and Brand and Grace Kendall and then trust God to show us how to make them all have a good time without suspecting what it's all about. We'll just tell Carey that he must come home early because we have a birthday cake and a surprise for him—make him promise to be there, you know; and then we'll take him into the living room, and they'll be there waiting. If he thinks it strange and says anything about it afterward, we'll tell him we invited all the people we knew were his friends, and we couldn't ask him about it beforehand because it had to be a surprise party. Now, little sister, I think you've solved the problem with your bright idea, and we can decide on that."

Chapter 14

They had the hardest time with Harry when they confided to him their plans and asked for his assistance. It took a great deal of argument and much tact to make him believe that anything good might come out of inviting "that chicken," as he persisted in calling Carey's lastest admiration. He had little less scorn for Brand Barlock, but when he heard that Grace Kendall was to be included in the list of guests, he succumbed.

"Aw, gee! It's a rotten shame to mix her up with that gang, but if she'll come, it'll be some party. Gee! Yes, I'll take your invites round, but you better find out if the minister's girl will come before you get any of the others."

The sisters decided that Harry's advice was wise, and after the children had gone to school and the morning work was done up, Cornelia took her walk to market around by the way of the minister's house and proffered her request.

"I'm not at all sure you'll like the company," she said with a deprecatory smile. "They are some young people Carey got to know last winter, and I want to get acquainted with them and see if they are the right kind. I thought maybe you'd be willing to help make it a success."

That was all the explanation she gave, but the other girl's face warmed sympathetically, and she seemed to understand everything.

"Oh, I'd love to come. Shall I bring some games? We have a table tennis that is a lot of fun; you use it on the dining room table, you know. And there are several other games that we enjoy playing here when we have a jolly crowd. Suppose I bring my violin over and we have some music, too. I'll bring some popular songs; we have a bunch for when the boys come in from the church."

When Cornelia started home, she felt quite cheerful about her party. Grace Kendall seemed to be a hostess in herself. She offered to come around and help get ready, and the two girls had grown quite chummy. Cornelia hummed a little song and quite forgot that across the miles of distance her classmates were this day preparing for the elaborate program that had long been anticipated for their class-day exercises. Somehow college days and their doings had come to seem almost childish beside the real things of every day. This party, for instance. How crude and homemade it was all to be! Yet it stood for so much, and it seemed as if momentous decisions depended upon its results.

She stopped in an art shop on her way back and studied little menu cards and favors, purchasing a roll of pink crêpe paper, some green and yellow tissue paper, wire, and cardboard. As soon as she had finished the dessert for dinner she hurried to get out scissors, paste, pencils, and went eagerly to her dainty work. Before Louise and Harry came home from school she had fashioned eight dainty little candy baskets covered with ruffled pink paper, and on each slender threadlike pink handle there nodded a lovely curly pink rose with a leaf and a bud, all made of paper, with their little green wire stems twining around the pink basket. Eight little bluebirds, with their claws and tails so balanced that they would hover on the rim of a water glass and bearing in their bills a tiny place card, also lay on the table beside the baskets, the product of Cornelia's skillful brush and colors. The children went into ecstasies over them, and even Harry began to warm to the affair.

"I guess *she'll* see we're fashionable all right," he swaggered scornfully. "I guess she'll see she's got to go some to be good enough to speak to our Carey. Say, what did the Kendall girl say? Is she coming? Say, she's a peach, isn't she? I knew she'd be game all right. Did you tell her 'bout the other one? You oughta. She might not like it."

"I told her as much as was necessary. You needn't worry about her; she's pure gold."

"You're talking!" said the boy gruffly and went whistling upstairs to change his clothes. But Louise stood still, enraptured before the little paper baskets and birds. Suddenly she turned a radiant face to her sister, and in a voice that was almost expressive of awe she said softly:

"But it's going to be real special, isn't it, Nellie? I never knew we could be real special. I never knew you could do things like that. It's like the pictures in the magazines, and it's like Mrs. Van Kirk's luncheon. Hazel and I went there on an errand to get some aprons for the Red Cross for our teacher at school, and we had to wait in the dining room for ten minutes while she hunted them up. The table was all set for a luncheon she was going to give that day, and afterward we saw about it in the paper, and she had baskets and things just like that."

Cornelia stooped and kissed the eager young face tenderly and wondered how she would have borne to be separated all these years from her little sister and brother and not have known how satisfactorily they were growing up.

"What are you going to put into them?" asked the little girl.

"Well, I haven't decided yet," said Cornelia. "Probably salted almonds, don't you think?"

"Oh, but they're awful expensive!"

"Not if you make them, dear. You and I will make them. I've done tons of them at college for feasts. It's easy; just blanch them and brown them in a pan with butter and salt or oil and salt."

"Oh, can you?" More awe in the voice. "And what will we have to eat?"

"Well, I'm not sure yet. We'll have to count the dishes and let that settle some questions. We must have enough to go around, you know, and all alike. I wonder if there are enough bouillon cups. It takes eight, you know—Father, Carey, you, and Harry, three guests and myself. Yes, that's eight. Climb up to the top shelf there, dear, and see if there are enough of Mother's rosebud bouillon cups."

"There are nine and an extra saucer," announced Louise.

"Well, then we'll have some kind of soup, just a little. I think maybe spinach, cream of spinach soup. It's such a pretty color for spring, you know, that pale green, and matches the dining room. It's easy to make and doesn't cost much; and then we can have the spinach for a vegetable with the meat course. Now, let's see, those little clear sherbet glasses, are there enough of those?"

"A whole dozen and seven," announced Louise.

"Then we'll use those at the beginning for a fruit cocktail— orange, grapefruit, banana, and I'll color it pink with a little red raspberry juice. I found a can among the preserves Mother had left over from last winter. It makes a lovely pink, and that will match the baskets."

"Oh, lovely!" exclaimed the little girl ecstatically. "But won't that cost a lot?"

"No, dear, I think not. I'll figure it down pretty close tonight and find out; but it doesn't take much fruit to fill those tiny glasses, and it's mostly show, you know—one grapefruit, a couple of oranges, and bananas, and the rest raspberry juice. Spinach is cheap now, you know; and we can make the body of the soup with a can of condensed milk. We can eat cornmeal mush and beans and things for a few days beforehand to make up."

"I just love fried mush and bean soup."

"You're a ducky! And besides, I'm going to save on the dessert."

"Aren't we going to have ice cream?" Louise's voice showed anxiety.

"Yes, but we'll make it ourselves. I found the freezer out in the back shed under all those carpets yesterday. And we'll have pale-green peppermint sherbet. It's beautiful and costs hardly anything. You just make lemonade and put in a few drops of peppermint and a drop or two of confectioners' green coloring; and it is the prettiest thing you ever laid eyes on. Looks like a dream and tastes—wonderful!"

"Oh!" said Louise, her eyes shining.

"We'll have angel cake for the birthday cake, I think," went on the sister, "with white icing and little pink candles. Eggs are not expensive now, and anyway I found a recipe that says measure the whites, and such big eggs as we get take only nine to a cup. How will that be, angel cake and green sherbet for dessert?"

Louise sat down and folded her hands, her big, expressive eyes growing wide and serious.

"It's going to be a success!" she said solemnly with a grown-up air. "I was afraid she wouldn't be—well—impressed, but she will. It's regular! You wanted her to be impressed, too, didn't you, Nellie?"

Cornelia couldn't help laughing at the solemn question, but she sobered instantly.

"Yes, dear, I guess I did. I wanted her to have respect for

Carey's family and to know that however foolish he may be, there is something, as you say, 'regular' behind him. Because there is, you know, Louise. Father and Mother are 'regular.'"

"They are!" said the little girl.

"It sounds rather strange to try to impress people with fuss and show and food fixed up in fancy styles, but if I can judge anything about that girl, she hasn't reached the stage yet where she can appreciate anything but fuss and fancy and fashion. So we've got to use the things that will appeal to her if we want to reach her at all. If it were just Grace Kendall coming, or even the young man Brand, I would have things very plain and simple. It would be in better taste and more to my liking. But I have a notion, kitten, that if we had everything very simple, that young lady with the fancy name would rather despise us and set out to ride right over us. They talk a great deal nowadays about people's reaction to things, and if I know anything at all about the girl, I feel pretty sure that her reaction to simple, quiet things would be far from what we want. So for this once we'll blossom out and have things as stylish and fancy and formal as possible. I've heard it said that there is nothing so good to take the pride out of an ignorant person as an impressive array of forks and spoons, so we'll try it on Miss Clytie and see if we can bring her near enough to our class to get acquainted with her real self. Now get a pencil and write down the menu and see how it reads."

"But what are you going to have in the middle, Nellie, after the soup? Any meat?"

"Why, surely, round steak, simmered all day with an onion and browned down with thick gravy the way you love it so well; only we'll cut it into small servings like cutlets before we cook it, and nobody will ever dream what it is. Then we'll have new potatoes creamed, with parsley sprinkled over them, and spinach minced, with a hard-boiled egg on top; and for salad we'll make some gelatin molds in the custard cups with shredded cabbage and parsley in it, that on a lettuce leaf will look very pretty; and I'll make the mayonnaise out of the yolks of the eggs from the angel cake. There'll be enough left over to make a gold cake or some custard for the next day besides. Now write the menu. Raspberry fruit cocktail, cream of spinach soup, round-steak cutlets with brown gravy, creamed new potatoes with parsley, spinach, aspic-jelly salad, angel cake, mint sherbet, and coffee. Doesn't that sound good?"

"I should say," answered the little girl with a happy sigh.

"We'll have everything all ready beforehand, so that the serving will be easy," went on the elder sister. "The butter and water and fruit will be on the table. We can fill the soup cups and keep them in the warming oven, and you and Harry can get up quietly, remove the fruit glasses, and bring on the soup cups. You see I've been thinking it all out. I've planned to buy two more wire shelves to fit into the oven. You know there are grooves to move them higher or lower, and I find that if we use the lowest groove for the first, there will be room to set the eight plates in there; and we'll just have everything all served on the plate ready: the little cutlet with gravy, the creamed potatoes, and the spinach. Then, if we light only one burner and turn it low, and perhaps leave the door open a little—I'll have to experiment—I think they will keep hot without getting dry or crusty on the top, just for that little while. The only thing is, you'll have to be tremendously careful not to drop one getting them out. They'll be hot, you know, and you'll have to use a cloth to take them out. Just think if you dropped one, there wouldn't be enough to go around."

Louise giggled and squeezed her sister's hand.

"Oh Nellie, isn't it going to be just packs of fun? I won't drop one, indeed I won't, but if I should, I just know I'd laugh out loud; it would be so funny, all that grand dinner party in there acting stylish, and those potatoes and spinach and meat sitting there on the floor! But don't you worry, if I did drop 'em, I'd pick 'em up again and take that plate for myself. Our kitchen floor's clean, anyway. When do we bring in the salad?"

"Oh, we'll just have that on the kitchen table by the door, ready. And then, while the people are finishing, you and Harry can slip out and get the sherbet dished out. Do you think you two can manage it?"

"Oh, sure! Harry does it at school every time we have an entertainment. The teacher always gets him to do it 'cause he gets it out so nice, and not messy, she says. Shall we cut the cake beforehand, or what?"

"Oh no, the cake will be on the table with the candles lit when we come into the dining room. And when the time comes, Carey will have to blow out the candles and cut his own cake."

And so they planned the pretty festival and almost forgot the unloved cause of it all: poor, silly little Clytie Amabel Dodd.

Cornelia's hardest task was writing the letter of invitation to the guest she dreaded most of all. After tearing up several attempts and struggling with the sentences for half an hour, it was finally finished, and read:

My dear Miss Dodd,

We are having a little surprise for my brother Carey on his birthday next Thursday, the twenty-fifth, and would be very glad if you will come to dinner at six o'clock to meet a few friends. Kindly say nothing to Carey about it, and please let us know if we may expect you.

Looking forward to meeting you, I am,

Very sincerely,
Carey's sister,
Cornelia Copley

After a solemn meeting it was decided to mail this note, and then the three conspirators waited anxiously for two whole days for a reply. When Harry and Louise arrived from school the third day and found no answer yet, anxiety was strong.

"Yes, Harry, you oughta have taken that note yourself, the way Nellie said," declared Louise.

"Not me!" asserted Harry loftily. "Not if that chicken never comes! We don't want her anyway. I guess we can have a party without her!"

But a few minutes later a clattering knock arose on the front door, and a small boy with an all-day sucker in his cheek appeared.

"My sister, she says sure she'll come to your s'prise party," he announced indifferently. "She didn't have no time to write, so I come."

He waited expectantly for a possible reward for his labors. Cornelia smiled, thanked him, said she was glad, and he departed disappointedly. He was always on the lookout for rewards.

"That's Dick Dodd," Louise explained. "He's an awful bad little kid. He put gum in the teacher's hat and hid a bee in her desk. And once she found three caterpillars in her lunch basket, and everybody knew who put them there. He never washes his hands nor has a handkerchief."

The little girl's voice was full of scorn. She was returning to her former dislike of their expected guest with all that pertained to her.

"Well, there's that," said Cornelia smiling. "She's coming, and we know what to expect. Now I think I'll call up the Barlock house and find out when they expect that Brand fellow to be at home. I think I can do that more informally over the phone."

It just happened that Brand Barlock was passing through the house where he was supposed to reside—probably for a change of garments or something to eat or to get his wallet replenished—and he answered the phone himself. Cornelia was amused at the haughty condescension of his tone. One would think she had presumed to invite royalty to her humble abode by the loftiness in which he answered: "Why, yes—I might come, if nothing else turns up. Yes, I'm sure I can make it. Very nice, I'm sure. Anything you'd like to have me bring?"

"Oh no, indeed!" said Cornelia emphatically, her cheeks very red indeed. "It's just a simple home affair, and we thought Carey would enjoy having his friends. You won't mention it to him, of course."

"Aw'right! I'll keep quiet. So long!" and the young lord hung up.

Cornelia emerged from the drugstore telephone booth much upset in spirit and wishing she hadn't invited the young upstart. By the time she reached the outer door, she wished she had never tried to have a party for Carey. But, when she got back to Louise and her shining interest, her common sense had returned, and she set herself to bear the unpleasantness and make those two strange, mismatched guests of hers enjoy themselves in spite of everything, or else make them feel so uncomfortable that they would take themselves forever out of Carey's life.

Steadily forward went the preparations for the party, and at last the birthday morning arrived.

Chapter 15

Arthur Maxwell over his morning grapefruit, buttered toast, and coffee, which he usually had served in his room, began in a leisurely way to open his mail.

There was a thick, enticing letter from his mother, which he laid aside till the last. He and his mother were great pals, and her letters were like a bit of herself, almost as good as talking with her face-to-face. He always enjoyed every word of them.

There were the usual number of business communications, which he tore open and read hurriedly as he came to them, frowning over one, putting another in his pocket to be answered in his office, and then at the very bottom, under a long envelope, which carried a plea for money for his alma mater to help build a new observatory, he came suddenly upon a square, foreign-looking envelope addressed in a dashing, illegible hand and emitting a subtle fragrance of rare flowers, a fragrance that had hovered exquisitely about his senses from the moment the mail had been laid by his plate, reminding him dimly of something sweet and forbidden and half forgotten.

He looked at the letter, half startled, a trifle displeased, and yet greatly stirred. It represented a matter that he was striving to put out of his life, that he thought he had succeeded in overcoming, even almost forgetting. A grim speculative look came into his face. He hesitated before he reached out his hand to pick up the letter and questioned whether he should even open it. Then with a look that showed that he had taken himself well in hand, he picked it up, ran his knife crisply under the flap of the envelope, and read:

> Dear Arthur,
>
> I am passing through Philadelphia tomorrow on my way to Washington and am stopping over for a few hours especially to see you about a matter of grave importance. I feel that you will not be angry at my breaking this absurd silence that you have imposed between us when I tell you that I am in great trouble and need your advice. I remember your promise always to be my friend, and I know you will not refuse to see me now for at least a few minutes.
>
> I am coming down on the two o'clock train from New York and shall go directly to the hotel and await your coming anxiously. I know you will not fail me.
>
> Yours eternally,
> Evadne

The subtle fragrance, the dashing script, the old familiar turn of sentence reached into his consciousness and gripped him for a second in spite of his being on his guard. Something thrilling and tragic seemed to emanate from the very paper in his hand, from the royal purple of the lining of the expensive envelope. For an instant he felt the old lure, the charm, the tragedy of his life that he was seeking to outlive, which he had supposed was already outlived.

In his senior year in college Arthur Maxwell had become acquainted with Evadne Chantry at a house party where both had been guests. They had been thrown together during the two days of their stay, whether by the hostess's planning or at the lady's request is not known, but Arthur, at first not much attracted by her type, found himself growing more and more interested.

Evadne was a slender, dark, sophisticated little thing with dreamy eyes and a naive appeal. His chivalry was challenged, and when it further appeared that she was just from England and was of the old family of Chantrys whom his mother knew and visited, he got down from his distance and capitulated. They became close friends, in spite of the fact that Evadne's ways were not the ways in which he had been brought up, and in which his young manhood had chosen to walk. But he had found himself excusing her. She had not been taught as he had. She had lived abroad where standards were different. She had been in boarding schools and convents and then traveled. He felt she could be brought to change her ways.

It appeared that she was going to be for some time in the city where his college was located, and the friendship ripened rapidly, taking Arthur Maxwell into a social group as utterly foreign to his own as one could imagine, in fact one that he did not really enjoy; yet he went for Evadne's sake.

When he came to the point of telling his mother of the friendship, about which it had been strangely hard to write, he found that it was no easy matter. In the light of her clear eyes there were matters that could not be so easily set aside as his own conscience had been soothed to do. He suddenly realized what a shock it would be to his conservative mother to see Evadne smoking, to watch her in her sinuous attitudes, to know that her son was deeply interested in a young woman who had plucked eyebrows and used lipstick freely. When he came to think of it, some of her clothing might be exceedingly startling to his mother. Yet he believed in his mother so thoroughly that he felt she could be made to understand how much this girl had suffered from lack of a mother and how much she was in need of just such a friend as his mother could be.

When the time arrived that Mrs. Maxwell had to learn these things, her son was even more startled than herself to find out how much she really was shocked at this choice of a girl. The stricken look that came into her eyes the first time they met told him without further words from her lips. In that moment he might be said to have grown up as he suddenly looked upon the girl, whom he thought he loved beyond all women, through the eyes of his mother.

His mother had been wonderful even though she carried the stricken look through the entire meeting. She had perhaps not exactly taken Evadne into her arms quite as he had hoped, but she had been gently sweet and polite. His mother would always be that. She had been quiet, so quiet, and watchful, as if she were gravely considering some threatened catastrophe and meeting it bravely.

Afterward, she had met his eyes with a brave, sad smile, without a hint of rebuke, not a suggestion that he should have told her sooner, only an acceptance of the fact that the girl was here in their lives and must be dealt with fairly. She listened to his story of Evadne's life, considered his suggestion that she might help the girl, and heard how they had met and his reasons for feeling that she was the one and only girl. As he told it all he was conscious of something searching in her sweet, grave eyes that turned a knife in his heart, yet he was full of hope that she would eventually understand and come under Evadne's spell with himself.

Only once she questioned about the girl. How did he know

she belonged to the Chantrys she knew? What relationship did she bear to them? Was she Paul Chantry's sister? Cousin? She did not remember that there had been a daughter.

Evadne had not taken kindly to his mother. She wept when Arthur talked with her alone after their meeting and said she was sure his mother did not love her. But the days passed on, and Mrs. Maxwell kept her own counsel and invited the girl to her home, doing all the little gracious social things that might be expected of her, yet with a heavy heart, till one day when it seemed that an announcement of the engagement should be the next thing in order, there came a letter from England in answer to one Mrs. Maxwell had written, disclaiming any relationship between Evadne and the distinguished old family who were her friends.

This was a matter that Arthur could not ignore when his mother brought it to his notice, and Evadne was asked for an explanation.

Evadne met his questions with haughty contempt and then with angry tears and retired into an offended silence that seemed as impenetrable as a winter fog, from which she presently emerged like a martyr with vague explanations of a distant cousinship that seemed full and sufficient to his gallant, young spirit, till he tried to repeat them to his perceptive mother, and then they did not seem so convincing.

The matter was finally smoothed over, however; and it seemed as if the mother was about to be called upon to set the seal of her approval upon a speedy marriage between the two, when there came a revelation through the medium of an old friend who had met Evadne abroad and asked her quite casually, in the presence of the Maxwells, where her husband was. Explanations followed, of course, and it appeared that Evadne was married already and had left her husband in South Africa without even the formality of a divorce.

Gradually, however, the girl's clever story broke down his indignation at her deception, as she told him sobbingly how lonely she was and how she longed for friendship and something real in life; and it took many days and nights of agonizing thought before the plummet of his soul was able to swing clear and tell him that no matter how lonely she was or who was to blame, or how much or when or why, there was one thing true: if Evadne was married, she was not for him, no, not even if she got a divorce. So much inheritance had he from long lines of Puritan ancestors and from the high, fine teachings of his mother. It was a law of God, and it was right. He was not altogether sure just then that he believed in the God who had let all this tragedy come into his life, but he believed in the law, and he must keep it. He had felt himself grow old in those days while he was coming to that inevitable conclusion that if it was not right for them to love one another, then they must not see one another.

For days, he could not talk about it to his mother, and she spent the hours upon her knees, while he went about stern and white; and Evadne did all in her power to make him see that time had changed and modern ways did not accept those puritan laws anymore, which he was holding forth as final and inexorable. Sin! What was *sin*? There *was* no such thing! *Law*! She laughed. Why keep a law that everyone else was breaking? It was all of a piece with his old-fogy notions about drinking wine and having a good time. He was the dearest in all the world of course, but he was narrow. She held out her lily arms from the sheath-like black velvet gown she had assumed and pleaded with him to come with her, come out into the broad, free air of a big life! She was clever. She had caught most of the modern phrases. She knew how to appeal to the finer things in him, and *almost* she won her point. Almost he wavered for just the fraction of a second and thought,

Perhaps she is right—perhaps I am narrow. Then he lifted his eyes and saw his mother standing in the doorway, being shown in by a blundering servant, his fine patrician mother with her sweet, true eyes, and pure, sorrowful face, and he knew. He knew that Evadne was wrong, and his mother—yes, his mother and he were right. There could be nothing but sin in a love that was stolen—a love that transgressed.

He had gone away then and left his mother to talk to the other woman, and something, somewhere in his manhood had kept him away after that. He had written her fully his final word, with so stern a renunciation that even Evadne knew it was unalterable. He had laid down the law that they must not meet again and had then gone away to another part of the country and established himself in business and tried to forget.

That had been two years ago. Long years, he called it when he thought of them by himself. The haggard look of the gray young face had passed away gradually, and the stern lines had softened as his fine mind and strong body and naturally cheerful spirit came back to normal, but there had been a reserve about him that made people think him a year or two older than he really was and made some women when they met him call him "distinguished." He had passed, in the struggles of his soul, slowly away from the place where he regarded Evadne as a martyr and had come at last to the time when he could look his experience squarely in the face and realize that she had been utterly untrue to all that was fine and womanly and that he was probably saved from a life of sorrow and disappointment. Nevertheless, back in his soul there lingered his pity for her slender beauty, her pretty helplessness. A natural conclusion had come to him that all girls were deceitful; all beautiful women were naturally selfish and untrue. There were no more good, sweet, true girls nowadays as there were when his mother was a girl.

Away from home he drifted out of churchgoing. He immersed himself in business and began to be a brilliant success. He wrote long letters to his mother and enjoyed hers in return, but his letters were not revealing. She sensed his reserves, and when they met she felt his playful gentleness with her was a screen for a bitterness of soul that she hoped and prayed might pass. And it did pass, gradually, until she had almost come to feel that his soul was healed and the tragedy forgotten. More and more she prayed now that someday, when he was ready, he might meet a different kind of girl, one who would make him forget utterly the poor little vampire who had almost ruined his life's happiness. In fact, the last time she had seen him on her recent trip to Philadelphia he had laughingly told her that she needn't worry about him anymore. He was utterly heart whole and happy.

But it is a question, whether, if she had been permitted to look in on him this morning as he read Evadne's letter, she would have felt that his words had been quite true.

He had promised his mother, in those first days after the break with Evadne, that he would not see her nor communicate with her for at least two years. The time was more than past, yet he felt the righteous obligation of his promise still upon him. He knew that he ought not to see Evadne again. He knew that the very sight of her would stir in him the old interest, which he now felt to be of a lower order than the highest of which he was capable. He could see her sitting now, flung back in some bewildering outfit that revealed the delicate, slim lines of her figure, some costly bauble smouldering on the whiteness of her neck that might have graced an Egyptian queen, her hair molded in satin-like folds about her small head, and her slanted eyes half closed, studying him tauntingly as she held her cigarette in her jeweled fingers and considered with what clever personality to bind him next.

The distance of time had shown him that he had been bound, that he had been a fool, and had brought him disillusionment; yet he knew that if he gave it half a chance the enchantment would work again upon him, and he felt contempt for himself that it was so. Yet strangely he found a law within himself that longed again to be enchanted, even while he sneered at the emptiness of it all.

Suppose he should go tonight to meet her—it was tonight. He glanced at the date of the letter to make sure. He could tell almost to a flicker of an eyelash what would happen.

She would meet him as if they had parted but yesterday, and she would ignore all that was passed except that they loved each other. His soul rebelled at the thought of that, for he did not now feel that he loved her any longer. The cleanness of his spirit had put that away. She was not his; she was another's. She was not fit for a real love, even if there had been no barrier. That had been his maturer thought, especially at times when he remembered her deceit. Yet human nature is a subtle thing. Though he resented her thinking that he had continued to care for her, he feared for himself, lest when he saw her he would allow her to think that it was so. And yet he longed to go and see how it would be. He felt curious to try his dearly bought contentment and see if it would hold. Should he go?

His mother would advise against it, of course. But he was a man now. This was his personal responsibility. Whether he should see her or not. All that about her needing advice in trouble was nonsense, of course. There were plenty of people who could advise her. He could send the old family lawyer to her if necessary. Her plea had been well planned to make him come, because she wished to see if he still cared or if he had forgotten her. But yet it might be beneficial for them both for him to go for a few minutes and show her that there was nothing to all the tragedy that they had thought they were living through.

Well—there was plenty of time to decide what to do. She wasn't coming till afternoon—he could go, of course, and take her to the Roof Garden for dinner—or perhaps she would better enjoy one of the quieter places—he knew a little Chinese restaurant that was more her style. However, he would thrash it out during the day. It was getting late and he must hurry to the office. But he must read his mother's letter first, of course. There might be something she wanted done at once. She was staying in the mountains for a little while with her sister who was recovering from a severe illness, and there often was some shopping she wanted him to attend to at once.

He opened the letter, his mind preoccupied with thoughts of Evadne.

The letter was filled with wonderful descriptions of views and people his mother had met, mingled with wise and witty comments on politics and current events. He skimmed it hastily through to the last paragraph, which read:

I came on a lovely clump of maidenhair ferns yesterday in my walk, and I had the gardener at the hotel take them up and box them carefully for me. I want to send them to my little friend, the interior decorator whom I met on the train a few weeks ago. You remember? But after they were all ready to go and I came to look for the address, I remembered that I left it in the little drawer of the desk in your apartment. I have tried my best to rack my brains for a clue to the street and number and can't remember a thing except that her name was Cornelia Copley. I remembered that because of the Copley prints of which we are both so fond. So rather than give up the

*idea or trust to the ferns finding her in that big city with just
her name and no street address, I am sending them to you. I
want you to slip the box into your car and take a run out that
way the very day they come and deliver them for me, please.
I like that little girl, and I want her to have these beautiful
ferns. They will help her decorate her forlorn little house. I
hope you won't consider this a nuisance, Son. But you never do
when I ask a favor, I know. Be sure to do it at once, for the
ferns won't stand it long without water.*

A knock came on the door just then, and the young man looked up
to see the wife of the janitor, who looked after the apartment and
cooked his breakfast, standing in the open door.

"The 'spressman done brung a box, Mr. Maxwell," she said.
"What you want did with it?"

"Oh, it's come! Well, tell him to put it into my car. It ought to
be out at the door waiting by this time; and just sign for it, please,
Hannah. I'm in a hurry this morning. I have an appointment at
half past eight."

Five minutes later, when Maxwell hurried down, he found the
big box on the floor of his car, with feathery fronds reaching out to
the light and blowing delicately in the breeze.

"Well, I should say she did send a few!" he grumbled to
himself. "Trust Mother to do a thing thoroughly! I don't see when
I can possibly manage to deliver these today! I'll have to get away
somehow at lunch time, I suppose. I certainly wish Mother hadn't
chosen this special day to wish one of her pet enthusiasms on me!
She's always hunting out some nice girl! I wish she wouldn't!"

With that he slammed shut the door, threw in the clutch, and
was off, and never thought of those ferns all day long until late in
the afternoon, later than his usual hour for going to his dinner,

when he climbed wearily into the car again. He had had a hard day, with perplexing problems to solve and a disagreeable visiting head to show all over the Philadelphia branch and keep in good humor. There had not been a minute to get away, not even for a bit of a run in the car at noon, for the visitor had a cold and didn't care to ride, so they lunched in the downstairs restaurant and went back to work again all the afternoon. The visitor at last was whirled away in the car of another employee to whose home in the suburbs he had been invited to dinner, and Maxwell with a sigh of relief, and feeling somehow very lonesome and tired, was free at last, free to consider the problem of the evening.

He was just backing out of the garage and turning to see that his wheels had cleared the doorway when his eye caught a gleam of green.

"Oh, doggone those fool ferns!" he said under his breath.

"Now I'll simply *have* to get them off my hands tonight or they'll 'die on me' as the elevator man said his first wife did. Mother didn't know what a nuisance this would be. I haven't a minute to waste on such fool nonsense tonight. I really ought to call up Evadne at once and let her know I'm coming—*if* I am. I wonder if I am. Well, here goes with the ferns first. It won't take long if I can find the dump, and it will give me a few minutes' leisure to decide what I'll do. I haven't had a second all day long. I never saw such a day!"

He sent the car shooting forward on the smooth road, climbing the long grade into the sunset.

Chapter 16

The morning had opened most favorably in the Copley home, with everybody in good spirits. At the breakfast table Cornelia had informed the male portion of the family quite casually that there was to be a birthday supper and they must all come promptly home and dress up for it, and Harry had given a grave wink at Louise that almost convulsed her.

Carey was in charming spirits. When he awoke, he had found two new shirts and two pairs of silk socks by his bedside "with love from Cornelia," and a handkerchief and necktie apiece from each of the children; and he came down with uproarious thanks to greet them. Mr. Copley, thus reminded of the occasion, got up before he had finished his first cup of coffee and went into the living room to the desk. When he came back, he carried a check in his hand made out to Carey.

"There, Son, that's from Mother and me for that new suit you need," he said in a voice warm with feeling. "I meant get around to it last night, but somehow the date slipped me."

And Carey, taken unawares, was almost embarrassed, rising with the check in his hand and his color coming and going like a girl.

"Why, Dad! Really, Dad! You ought not to do this now. I'm an old chump that I haven't earned one long ago. Take it back, Dad. You'll need it for Mother. I'll take the thought just the same."

"No, that's all right, Son. You earn the next one," said the father with a touch on his son's arm almost like a caress.

And so the little party separated with joy on every face and went their separate ways. Carey was still working at the garage. He had been secretly saving up to buy a secondhand automobile that he knew was for sale, excusing the desire by saying it would be good for his mother to ride in when she came home. But now he suddenly saw that his ambition was selfish and that what he must first do was to get a job where he could help his father and pay his board at home. To that end, he resolved to hand twenty-five dollars to Cornelia that very night, if he could get it out of Pat, and start the new year aright, telling her it was board money. He promised most solemnly to be at home in time to "fix up" before supper, and Cornelia went about the day's preparations with a light heart. There seemed a reasonable amount of hope that the young man himself would be likely to be on hand at his own birthday party. Having secured the two most likely sources of other engagements, Clytie and Brand, there didn't seem much else that could happen to upset her plans.

The birthday cake had been a regular angel the way it rose and stayed risen when it got there, and blushed a lovely biscuit brown, and took its icing smoothly. It was even now waiting out of sight in the bread box ready for its candles, which Louise was to add when she returned from school at noon. Both children were coming home at noon, and Harry was not going to the grocery that day.

Cornelia had put the whole house in apple-pie order the day

before, made the cake and the gelatin salad, and had done all the marketing. The day looked easy ahead of her. She set the biscuits and tucked them up in a warm corner, washed the spinach in many waters and left it in its last cold bath getting crisp, with the lettuce in a stone jar doing the same thing. Then she sat down with a silver spoon, a sharp knife, a big yellow bowl, and a basket of fruit to prepare the fruit cocktail.

While she was doing this, Grace Kendall ran in with her arms full of lovely roses that had been sent to her mother that morning. She said her mother wished to share them with the Copleys. Grace put the flowers into water and sat down with another spoon to help. Before long the delicious pink and gold mixture was put away on the ice all ready for night. Grace helped scrape the potatoes and dust the living room then went home promising to be on hand early and help entertain the strange guests. Somehow Grace seemed to understand all about both of them and to be tremendously interested in the whole affair. Cornelia went about her pretty living room putting the last touches everywhere, setting a blue bowl of roses at just the right angle on the table, putting an especially lovely half-open bud in a tall, slender glass on the bookcase, pushing a chair into place, and turning a magazine and a book into inviting positions. She kept thinking how glad she was for this new girlfriend, this girl who, though a little younger, yet seemed to understand so well. She sighed as she touched the roses lovingly and recognized a fleeting impossible wish that her brother might have chosen to be interested in a girl like this one instead of the gum-chewing, ill-bred child with whom he seemed to be pairing off.

The children were so excited when they arrived at noon that she had difficulty in persuading them to eat any lunch. They ate the sandwiches and drank the milk she had set out for them in one swallow, it seemed to her, and then they flew to the tasks that had been assigned to them. Harry brought in armfuls of wood and stowed them neatly away in the big locker by the fireside and built up a beautifully scientific fire ready to light. It was a lovely, warm spring day, but with all the windows open in the evening, a good fire in the fireplace would be quite acceptable and altogether too charming to omit. He swept the hearth and then went out and scrubbed the front steps, swept the front walk, and mowed the little patch of lawn, trimming the edges till it looked like a well-groomed park.

Meantime Louise and her sister set the table with the air of one who decks a bride. It was so nice to use the table full length; to spread the beautifully laundered cloth, Mother's only "best" cloth that was left, treasured from the years of plenty; to set the best china and glass in place; and to make the most of the small stock of nicely polished silver. And then the crystal bowl of roses in the center of each end made such a difference in the glory of the whole thing!

"Wasn't it dear of her to send them!" exclaimed Louise, pulling a great luscious bud over to droop at just the right angle.

Of course the crowning glory of all was the big angel cake with its gleaming white frosting set in the middle of a wreath of roses, with the twenty-one candles in a little pink circle cleverly fastened to the cardboard circle concealed by the rose foliage. It certainly was a pretty thing. The little pink paper baskets filled with delicately browned and salted nuts were placed at each place by the exalted Louise, whose eyes shone as if she were doing the honors at some great festival. And the little birds with their name cards tilted on the rims of the glasses delightfully. The little girl stood back with clasped hands and surveyed it all.

"It's *perfect*!" she said delightedly. "It truly is. And she'll be—

she'll be impressed, won't she, sister?"

There was no question between the two which of their young lady guests they desired to impress. Their eyes met in sympathy. Then Cornelia with a fleeting fear of being misunderstood said, "Yes, dear, I hope she will. But you know it's not that I want to make a show before her. It's that—well, she is the kind of girl who lacks all the formalities and refinements of life, and we have to do a little extra to make her understand. You know formalities are good things sometimes. They are like fences to keep intruders out and hedges to keep in the sacred and beautiful things of life."

Louise went and threw her arms around Cornelia, exclaiming, "Nellie, you are just dear! You are like Mother! You seem to find such pretty things to say to make me understand."

Cornelia stooped and kissed the warm pink cheek, realizing how very dear this little sister was growing and how happy a time they had had getting ready for their party.

Meantime the cutlets were simmering away gently, getting themselves tender and brown, and every dish and platter and spoon and knife was in position for serving. Harry had come in and was cracking ice and getting the freezer ready, and Cornelia mixed the materials for the sherbet. There was an excited half hour while Harry ground away at the freezer, and then the paddle was taken out and everybody had a taste of the delectable green mixture that looked like a dream of spring and tasted "wonderful," the children said.

"Now," said Cornelia, putting the biscuits into the oven and looking at the clock, "it's time to go upstairs and rest a bit and get dressed. There's plenty of hot water, and Harry had better take his bath first while you lie down, Louie. Yes, I want you to rest on the bed at least ten minutes with your eyes shut. It will make a big difference. You are so excited you don't even know you're tired, and you've got a long evening before you. You want to be rested enough to enjoy it. Oh yes, I'm coming up to rest, too, just as soon as I get the water on for the potatoes and spinach. Then we'll rest together; and when Harry gets his bath, we'll get up and begin to dress. Harry, you must polish your shoes and make them look fine. I'm so glad you had your hair cut yesterday. It looks very nice. Now let's go upstairs."

But a sudden gloom had fallen over the face of Louise. In all the planning, strange to say, it had never once occurred to her to think what she herself would wear. Now the old, perplexing problem of the ages swept down upon her darkly.

"But, Cornie, what shall I put on?"

She looked down at her blue-checked gingham and thought of the faded blue challis that had been her best all winter, washed and let down, and made to do because there was no money to buy anything else. It had a great three-cornered tear where it caught on the key of the door last Sunday night, forgotten until now.

Cornelia seemed not to notice her dismay.

"I laid your things out on a chair up in our room," she said pleasantly. "Everything is ready."

"But I—there's a—at least, don't you think I better wash out my collar? It's just awful dirty!"

"Everything's all right, dear," said her sister, bending over to look at the oven flame and be sure it was just high enough to bake the biscuits the right shade of brown. "Run up, and you'll see."

Louise turned and walked slowly up the stairs, considering the possibility of her sister's having mended the tear and washed the collar and deciding not to be disappointed if she had done neither.

"She had a lot to do this morning and couldn't, of course; and I wouldn't want her to. I'll hurry and do it myself," said the loyal little soul. Then she entered the bedroom and stood entranced.

"Oh Harry, Harry! Come quick and see!" she cried to the boy, who was pattering downstairs barefoot in his bathrobe with a bunch of clean garments under his arm. "She's made over her beautiful pink organdie with the lace on it for me! Isn't she *dear*?

Isn't it a darling? And the little black velvet bows! And there's a white apron with lace ruffles for me to wait on the table in, and some of her own white silk stockings, and look at the ducky rosettes on my old pumps! They look like new! Oh! Isn't she the most darling sister in the world?"

"She sure is!" fervently agreed Harry. And Cornelia, halfway up the stairs, stopped suddenly and brushed away two tears that plumped unannounced into her tired eyes. "Gee! That's some dress," went on Harry. "You'll show Clytie, won't you? Glad you got it kid! You deserve it." And Harry bolted into the bathroom after this unusual display of affection and slammed the door after him, while Louise came like a young whirlwind into Cornelia's arms to hug and kiss her.

"And what are you going to wear, Nellie?" the little girl asked anxiously when they were resting together on the bed. "You know you must look just right, because you're the center of it all, the head, kind of, you know—the—the—well—*more* than mother, because you're young and have to look stylish. We've got to have that girl understand you know; and clothes do make such a lot of difference—to a girl like that! I'll tell you a secret if you won't feel bad. I was planning to stay mostly in the kitchen so she wouldn't see my old blue challis. I thought she wouldn't have much opinion of us if Carey's little sister dressed like that at a party. But now, *now* I can come out and have a good time."

"Darling!" Cornelia patted her tenderly on the shoulder. "I'm so sorry you've been troubled about your clothes. I ought to have got at them sooner and not made you worry. I think I'll wear my white rajah silk with the burnt-orange trimmings. I made it after a French model, and I always liked it. It's right to have everything pretty and neat, of course, but I hope I haven't made you too conscious about such things. You know it really doesn't matter about clothes if we look clean and neat and behave well. I think we've been placing too high a value on looks anyway. Of course looks do count a little, but they are, after all, only a trifle beside real worth. And, if we can't impress that girl with our refinement by our actions, why, we can put on all the clothes in the universe, and we won't be able to do it any better."

"I know it," answered the little girl wisely. "Only it is nice to have everything nice this time, because really and truly, Nellie, it's going to be just awful hard to have that girl here. I—I just kind of *hate* her! It seems as if she's going to spoil this whole nice party."

Cornelia had been stifling some such sinking of heart herself as she stood looking at the pretty table and thought of the insignificant little flirt who had brought it all into being, but now she roused to the danger.

"Dearie! We mustn't feel that way! We just mustn't. You know we've been praying, and now we've got to trust. And after all, I don't suppose she is any different from Grace Kendall."

"Oh, but she is, Nellie. How can we forget it? Why do there have to be such girls made? And why do brothers have to have anything to do with them? I just feel so upset when the girls at school talk about her and then look at me. My face always burns."

"There, dear! Now, you mustn't think such things. Just remember that for tonight, at least, she is our guest and we've got to treat her as well as any guest, we ever expect to have. The rest is up to her."

"And to God," breathed the little girl softly and solemnly.

"Yes, dear. Think of that." And she came close and kissed the pink cheek tenderly.

Then Harry came whistling from the bathroom and shot upstairs, leaving a pleasant odor of scented soap and steam behind him; and the two on the bed knew it was time to rise and get to work, for the last round was on in the game, and there was no time to idle.

Chapter 17

Carey came in at a quarter to six, a most unusual thing for him to do, even though he had been implored to do so by both sisters, and a great anxiety rolled from their minds as he went whistling merrily up the stairs and was heard splashing around in the bathroom. He had not been allowed to go into the dining room. Louise had met him at the front door, showed him the glories of her new dress, and piloted him straight to the upper floor, but the general gala atmosphere of the house and the breath of the roses in the living room gave him the sense of festivity. He had not yet recovered from this boyish pleasure of the morning gifts and the unusual tenderness of his father. He had the air of intending to do his part toward making this evening a pleasant one. As he went about dressing elaborately, he resolved not to go out at all but to stay at home the whole evening and try to make himself agreeable to his family, who were going to so much trouble for him. This virtuous resolve gave an exalted ring to the jazzy tune he whistled above the sound of the running water and also served to hide from his ears numerous sounds below stairs.

Grace Kendall arrived and slipped into the kitchen, donned a big apron, and did efficient service arranging the lettuce leaves on the salad plates and turning out the pretty quivering jelly on them. Louise was posted at the front window with wildly throbbing heart and earnest little face, awaiting the guest of anxiety, afraid she would come before Carey got out of the bathroom and safely up into his room, afraid and half hoping she wouldn't come at all, after all—and yet!

Oh! There she was coming right in the gate! Suddenly Louise's feet grew heavy, and for one awful second she knew she couldn't walk to the front door and open it. And Carey—yes, Carey was unlocking the bathroom door. He was going upstairs. Strength returned to her unwilling feet, and she sped to the door and found herself opening it and bowing pleasantly to the overdressed and somewhat embarrassed young woman standing on the steps. Suddenly the sweetness and simplicity of the little pink organdie her sister had made for her enveloped all Louise's shyness and anxiety, and she felt quite able to carry off the situation.

"Come right in," she said sweetly with a tone of real welcome.

Clytie stepped in and stared around curiously, almost furtively. It was evident she had not at all known to what sort of place she was coming and was startled, embarrassed. She was dressed in a vivid turquoise-blue taffeta evening dress composed of myriads of tiny ruffles, a bit of a sash, and silver shoulder straps, the whole being much abbreviated at both ends and but partially concealed under a flimsy evening coat of light tan. Her face had that ghastly coloring of too much powder and makeup. Her hat was a strange creation of henna ostrich feathers hanging out in a cascade behind and looking like a bushy head of red hair. Rings and bracelets glittered and tinkled against a cheap bead handbag, and her gauzy hosiery and showy footwear were entirely in keeping with the full ensemble. But when she stepped into the beautiful living room with its flickering fire, its softly shaded lights, its breath of roses and harmony of color, she seemed somehow as much out of place as a potato bug in a lady's bedroom. Louise had a sudden feeling of compassion for her as the victim of a terrible joke, and she felt afraid of her no longer.

"Will you come upstairs and take off your hat?" she asked sweetly and led the way up to her bedroom, where everything was in dainty order. A single rose in a tiny vase in front of the mirror under a pink-shaded candlelight set the keynote for the whole room.

Clytie stepped awesomely into the pretty room and gazed about fearsomely, almost as if she suspected a trap somewhere, almost as if she felt herself an intruder, yet bold enough to see the experience through to the finish. It wasn't in the least what she had expected of Carey, but it was interesting. She decided they were "highbrows," whatever that was. She took off the elaborate hat and puffed out her hair, bobbed in the latest way and apparently electrified to make every hair separate from every other in a whirl around her head, much like a dandelion gone to seed.

Louise watched her as she primped a moment before the mirror, rubbing her small tilted nose with a bit of a dab from her handbag, touching her eyebrows and lips, and ruffling out her hair a little wilder than before. The little girl was glad that the guest said nothing. Now if she could only get her down into the living room before Carey suspected! Somehow she felt that it would not be well for Carey to know before he came downstairs that the girl was in the house. There was no knowing what Carey might do. So she led the silent guest downstairs and remarked as they reached the safety of the landing, "It's a pleasant evening."

The guest stepped down, took another survey of the astonishingly lovely room, and responded absently, "Yeah! It is!"

"Just sit down, and I will tell my sister you have come," said Louise airily and vanished with relief, her awful duty done.

Cornelia came in at once, followed by Grace, and overwhelmed the young woman with their pleasant welcome. Astonishment and wary alertness were uppermost in the guest's face. She had begun to suspect something somewhere. She was sharp. She knew a girl of this kind would never have chosen her as a guest. Could it be that Carey had demanded it? She resented the presence of this other pretty, quiet girl in a blue organdie with no rouge on her face. Who was she, and what did they have to invite her for? Was she another of Carey's girls? She sat down uncomfortably on the edge of the chair offered her and tried to pull down her inadequate little skirts. Somehow these graceful girls made her feel awkward and out of place.

Cornelia excused herself and went back to the kitchen after a few pleasant words, and Grace Kendall took over the task of entertaining the silent guest, who eyed her sullenly and could not be made to reply more than "yes" or "no" to any question. But Grace had not been born a minister's daughter for nothing, and she was past mistress of all the graces of conversation and of making people feel at their ease. She was presently deep in the story of a certain set of photographs of strange lands that had been gathered by her father in a trip he had taken several years before, and the other girl in spite of herself was getting interested.

It is curious how many little things manage to get across into one's consciousness at a time like this. How, for instance, did Cornelia in the kitchen, taking up the cutlets and placing them on the hot plates, know just the precise instant when Brand Barlock's car drew up before the door and Carey's clear whistle in the third story ceased? She felt it even before the door opened and Louise's excited whisper announced, "He's come, Nellie! Hurry!" And she was even then unbuttoning the big enveloping apron and hurrying forward.

So she met Brand Barlock at the front door with a welcoming

hand outstretched to greet him and a hearty low-voiced, "I'm so glad you could come! Carey doesn't know about it yet, but I expect he'll see your car out of his window. He's upstairs dressing. Come in. Let me take your hat. Mr. Barlock, let me introduce Miss Kendall and Miss Dodd."

Brand Barlock stared. First at Cornelia, swiftly, approvingly, and with an answering smile for her cordial one; then at the lovely room that he entered, and gave a swift, comprehensive survey; and then at the lovely girl in blue who came forward to greet him.

"Pleased to meet you, I'm sure!" he said giving her a direct appraisement, a respectful interest, and shaking her hand quite unnecessarily. He was entirely at ease and altogether accustomed to rapid adjustments to environment—one could see that at once, yet it was also perceptible that he was surprised, and agreeably so. He held Grace Kendall's slim young hand impressively, a trifle longer than was in keeping with polite usage, yet not long enough to be resented; and his eyes made several sentences' progress in acquaintance with her before he took them from her face and let them rest upon Miss Dodd, who had at last risen with some show of interest in life again and come a step or two forward. Then he stared again.

"Oh! Hello, Clytie! You here?" he greeted her carelessly and went and sat down beside Miss Kendall. His tone said that Clytie Dodd was decidedly out of her element, and suddenly under the heavy veneer of white Clytie Dodd grew deeply red. Cornelia with a glance took in all these things, and a wave of sudden compassion swept over her, too, for the girl whom she had thus placed in a trying position. Had she done well? She could not tell. But it was too late now. She must go forward and make it a success. She tried to make it up by smiling at the girl pleasantly.

"Now, if you will just talk a minute or two, I think Carey will be down soon. It is time for Father's car to come, and we'll have dinner at once." Cornelia disappeared through the dining room door again.

Just at that precise moment, Arthur Maxwell slowed up his car at the corner where Mr. Copley's trolley was about to stop and looked perplexedly about him, studying the houses on either side.

"I beg your pardon," he said politely, as Mr. Copley got out of the trolley and crossed the street in front of him. "Could you tell me if there is a family by the name of Copley about here? I seem to have mislaid the address, but my memory of it is that they live somewhere along this block or the next."

"Copley's my name, sir," said Mr. Copley with his genial smile. "What can I do for you?"

"Glad to meet you, Mr. Copley," said Maxwell cordially. "I've had no end of a time finding your house. Thought I could go directly to it but find my memory wasn't so good as I banked on. I must have left the address at home, after all. I've a box there to deliver to your daughter. You have a daughter, haven't you?"

"Why, yes, two of them," said the father, smiling. He liked this pleasant young man with the handsome smile and the expensive car asking after his daughter. This was his idea of the kind of friends he would like his daughters to have if he had the choosing. "I guess you mean Cornelia. I suppose you're somebody she met at college."

"No, nothing so good as that. I can't really claim anything but a secondhand acquaintance. It was my mother who met her on a journey to Philadelphia some months ago. Mother quite fell in love with her, I believe, and she's sent her some ferns, which she asked me to deliver. Suppose you get in, and I'll take you the rest of the way. It is in this block?"

Mr. Copley swung his long limbs into the seat beside the young man. "No, the next block, middle of the block, just at the top of the hill right-hand side," he said. "I remember Cornie speaking of your mother. She was very kind, and Cornie enjoyed her. It certainly is good of her to remember my little girl. Ferns!" He looked back at the box. "She certainly will like those. She's a great one for fixing up the house and putting flowers about and growing things. She'll be pleased to see you. Here's the house, the one with the stone chimney. Yes, that's new, my son built it since Cornie came home. She wanted a fireplace. Now, you'll come right in. Cornie'll want to thank you."

"Thank you," said the young man, lifting out the heavy box. "That won't be necessary. She can thank Mother sometime when she sees her. I'll just put the box here on the porch, shall I?—and not detain your daughter. I really ought to be getting along. I haven't had my dinner yet."

"Oh, then you'll come right in and take dinner with us. The young people will be delighted to have you, I know. Cornie said they were going to have a company supper tonight because it's my son's birthday, twenty-one. I'd like you to meet my son, that is, I'd like him to know you, you know." And the father smiled a confiding smile.

"Oh, but really," Arthur Maxwell began.

But Mr. Copley had a detaining hand upon the young man's arm.

"We couldn't really let you go this way, you know," said the father. "We couldn't think of it. We haven't any very grand hospitality to offer you, but we can't let you go away without being thanked. Cornie!"

Mr. Copley threw wide the door of the living room. "Cornie, here's Mr. Maxwell. He's brought you some ferns, and he's going to stay to dinner with us. Put on another plate."

It was just at this instant that Carey Copley, humming his jazzy tune and fumbling with a refractory cuff link, started down the front stairs and paused in wild dismay.

Chapter 18

Cornelia, alert to make everything pass off smoothly and aware that Carey was coming down the stairs, had slipped off her apron and entered the living room exactly as her father flung open the front door. Now she came forward easily, brightly, as if strange guests flung at her feast at the last moment were a common occurrence in her life, and greeted this tall, handsome stranger.

"The plate's all on," she answered cheerfully, putting out a welcoming hand and meeting a pair of very nice, very curious, wholly interested eyes that for the moment she wasn't aware of ever having seen before. She was aware only of the eight plates back in the oven keeping piping hot, and the eight places at the pretty table, and the awful thing that her father had done to her already incongruous party, and wondering what she should do. Then suddenly she recognized the young man, and a pretty color flew into her cheeks and brightness into her eyes. The room with its strange guests—Grace Kendall trying to interest Brand and Clytie in her lapful of photographs, Carey standing on the stair landing, even her young brother and sister peeping curiously in at the dining room door—fell away, and she put out her hand in real

181

welcome to this stranger. An instant more, and her pulses swept wildly back into frightened array again, and her thoughts bustled around with troubles and fears. What should she do now? How would he ever mix? That awful girl with her face all flour? That noisy Brand with his slang and bold indifference! How could she ever make the party a success, the party over which she had so worked and prayed and hoped? And Carey! Would he vanish out the back door? The birthday candles around the cake were all lit. Harry had lit them as she came in. If Carey should bolt, how could they ever go out into the dining room, into the flicker of those foolish pink candles, and have a birthday dinner without the chief guest?

"Oh, but indeed, I couldn't think of intruding," the young man's words interrupted her anxious thoughts. "I merely dropped in on my way to dinner to leave this box of ferns that my mother sent with very explicit directions to be delivered to you at once before they died. As I'm not much of a florist myself, and as they have already had to wait all day without water, I'm ashamed to say, I wouldn't answer for the consequences if I hadn't got them here tonight. Mother is very particular about having her directions carried out. I hope the ferns will live and be worthy of this most beautiful setting." His glance went appreciatively around the pretty room. "You certainly look cozy here, and I know you're going to have a beautiful time. I won't keep you a minute longer."

There was something wistful in his tone even as he lifted his hat to put it on and began backing out the door. Cornelia's resolve to let him go was fast weakening even before her father spoke up.

"Daughter, Mr. Maxwell has come four miles out of his way to bring those ferns, and it will be late before he gets any dinner. He ought to stay. I told him he was welcome."

Cornelia's cheeks flamed, but a smile came into her eyes.

"We shall be *very* glad to have you stay," she urged gently, "unless—someone else is waiting for you."

A quick flush mounted into the young man's face, and he suddenly felt strangely unwilling to have this perceptive girl think that anyone was waiting for him. He would not like her to know what kind of girl was expecting his coming.

"Oh, it's not that," he managed to say lamely, "but I simply couldn't think of butting into a family party like this." His eyes glanced about questioningly, hesitating at Brand and pausing with a reflective wonder at Clytie in the background.

"But it's not a family party," said Cornelia laughingly. "It's a birthday, and—they don't even know one another very well yet, so won't you come in and be another? We really would be glad to have you, and we'll try to make you feel at home. We're not a bit formal or formidable. Let me introduce my brother Carey. Carey, come here and meet Mr. Maxwell. You remember my telling how nice his mother was to me on the way home from college."

She was talking fast, and the pretty color was in her cheeks. She was aware that the stranger was watching her admiringly. Her heart was thumping and the blood was surging through her ears so that it seemed as though she could not hear anything but her own high-pitched voice, and she wanted nothing so much as to break out crying and run and hide. Would Carey come, or would he—

Carey came, dazed, but polite. He was well dressed and groomed, and he knew it. He had no objection to meeting a pleasant stranger who owned a car like the one he had seen drive up at the door before he had left his room. Carey had a habit of judging a man by his car. The two young men appraised each other pleasantly, and there seemed to be a mutual liking. Then suddenly Brand Barlock, never allowing himself long to be left out of consideration, came noisily over to the group and slapped Carey on the back.

"Hello, old man! Got a birthday, have you?"

"Oh, hello, Brand! Forgot you were here. Saw your car out the window. Meet Mr. Maxwell, Mr. Barlock." And the two acknowledged the introduction.

"My father, Brand."

Mr. Copley spoke graciously to the young man, yet with a degree of dignity, looking him over speculatively. This was not the kind of young man he would choose for his son's friend, yet he regarded him with leniency.

Suddenly Carey turned and saw Grace Kendall.

"Oh, I say, Miss Kendall! This is awfully good of you." He took a step and shook hands with her. "Say, this is a real party, after all, isn't it? A surprise party. Upon my word, I thought Cornelia was kidding me when she said we were going to have a birthday party."

Grace Kendall laughed and clapped her hands, and all the rest followed her example. In the din of laughter and clapping Carey suddenly spotted Clytie glowering back by the fireplace, and a wave of panic swept over his face. He turned startled eyes on his sister and father and stood back while Cornelia introduced their guests to Maxwell and her father. He wondered how she could say "Miss Dodd" so easily, and how she had gotten acquainted with Clytie. His cheeks began to burn. Then she must have seen him that day on Chestnut Street, after all. And Louise had talked, too! And yet his sister's face was sweet and innocent!

Then he became aware that an appeal was being made to him to keep the young stranger to dinner and that the stranger was protesting that he could not thrust himself on a birthday party in this way. Carey roused to the occasion and gave an eager invitation.

"Of course you're going to stay to my party!" But even as he said it he wondered what a man of Maxwell's evident type would think of a girl like Clytie. Oh, if only she weren't here! And Grace

Kendall! What must she think? He stole a look at her, standing there so gracefully in that blue dress like a cloud, talking to Brand. What business did Brand have looking at her like that as if he had known her always? Now Brand would pursue her. Carey could see that Brand liked her. He always pursued a girl he took a notion to. He would take her out riding in that car of his, and—

But everybody was talking now, and Cornelia had called upon him to bring in the box of ferns. She herself had suddenly disappeared into the kitchen and was standing against the closed door, pressing her hand against her forehead and trying to think.

"What shall we do, Louie, dear? What *shall* we do? Father has invited that man." Cornelia found she was trembling; even her lips were trembling so she could hardly speak.

"Do?" said Louise maturely. "We'll go right ahead. We heard it all. Harry has fixed it up that he'll stay out and help. There's plenty of things left over for him to eat, and I'll fix him a plate betweentimes."

"I can fix my own plate," growled Harry happily. "You know I didn't want to sit in there with all those folks any of the time."

"But Harry! It's Carey's party, and you not at it?"

"Sure! I'm at it! I'm *it*! Don't you see? I'm the chauffeur running this car. I'm the chef cooking this dinner! Get out there quick, Cornie, and file those folks into their seats. This soup is getting cold, and they ought to get to work. That's a good guy, and he's got some car, I'll tell the world!"

So Cornelia went back to marshal the party out to the table. Maxwell was turning to leave, saying once more that it was awfully kind of them to ask him, but he could not possibly stay. And just then the dining room door was flung open by Harry, and the whole company stopped and breathed a soft "Ah!" as they saw the pretty candlelit room. Then as one man they went forward and began to search for their places, all except Maxwell who went forward indeed to get a closer glimpse of the pretty table but lingered in the doorway. There was something so wholesome and homelike about the place, something so interesting and free from self-consciousness about the girl, that he was held in spite of himself. He had not realized that there were such girls as this in his day. He was curious to watch her and see if she really was different.

So far Carey had not even spoken to his own special guest, Clytie. Since he had spotted her afar, he had religiously kept his eyes turned away from her vicinity.

It was Grace Kendall who took her by the arm and led her to her seat at the right of the host, for Cornelia had known she could depend upon her father's kindliness to make all go smoothly during the supper, and much as he might dislike the looks of the girl, she felt sure he would be polite and see that she was well taken care of. Brand Barlock was on Clytie's right with Louise next, and she had placed Carey opposite Clytie, not liking to seem to separate them too much and yet not wishing to throw them together too conspicuously. Grace Kendall was on Carey's left, with Harry's place next to her. This would have to be for the stranger and would place him on Cornelia's right, the fitting place for the guest of honor, yet—her cheeks burned. What would he think? Still, he had come unannounced. He had stayed. Let him take the consequences! What did she care what he thought? She would likely never see him again.

Perhaps he was not going to stay, after all. He was lingering still in the doorway but seemed just about to go.

Suddenly from behind her came a low whistle.

"Psst! Psst!"

Harry from behind the kitchen door was signaling violently, forgetting that his white shirtsleeve in his excited gestures was as visible to the rest of the company as to the astonished young man in the opposite doorway about to take a hasty leave.

"Oh, I say! Come 'ere!" Harry whispered, as he beckoned wildly with a hand that unconsciously still grasped a muggy dish towel.

"Are you—calling me?" young Maxwell signaled with his lifted eyebrows.

Harry's response was unmistakable, and the young man slipped past the group who were studying place cards and sliding into chairs and bent his head to the retreating head of the boy.

"I say, don't you *see* I don't want to come in there with all those folks? Be a good sport and stay, 'r I'll have to. I'd rather stay out here and dish ice cream. You go take my chair. That's a good guy."

Maxwell smiled with sudden illumination and lifted his eyes to find that Cornelia had heard the whole affair.

"All right, old man, I'll stay," said the young man. "You win. Perhaps you'll let me come into the kitchen afterward and help clean up."

"Sure!" said Harry joyfully, with the tone of having found a pal. "We'll be glad to have you, won't we Cornie?"

To himself Maxwell said, "It will be just as well to go later to see Evadne. Better, in fact. I don't want her to think I'm too eager. I can have more time to decide what to say to her. This is a good atmosphere in which to decide. Besides, I'm hungry and the dinner smells good. It would be ages before we got settled to eating at the Roof Garden or some cabaret. I'd have to go home and dress."

Then he became aware that Cornelia was speaking to him.

Cornelia's cheeks were red as roses, and there was a look in her laughing eyes as if tears were not far off, but she carried the thing off bravely and declared that those things could be settled later; they really must sit down now or the dinner would be spoiled. So they all sat down, and there was a moment's awkward silence till

Mr. Copley bowed his head and asked a blessing, Clytie and Brand openly staring the while. When it was over, Maxwell discovered the place card with "Harry" on it and gravely deposited it in his vest pocket, saying in a low tone to Cornelia, "I shall make this up to him later."

"You mustn't think you're depriving him," said Cornelia, smiling and lifting her spoon to the luscious cup of iced fruit. "He really has tried in every way he knew short of running away to get out of coming to the table. He knows he has me in a corner now, and he's tremendously pleased, so don't think another thing about it. Suppose you play you're one of our old friends, and then it won't worry you anymore. It's really awfully nice of you to come in this way."

But all the time in her heart she was wondering why, oh, why, did this have to happen just this night when she wanted to devote all her energies to making the other people feel at home, and now she was so distracted she didn't know what she was saying?

However, the other people seemed to be getting along famously. When she glanced up, she saw that her father was talking pleasantly to Clytie, keeping her at least employed with questions to answer about where she lived and how her father was employed and whether she had brothers and sisters. He had just asked, "And what school do you attend? High school, I suppose?" And Cornelia caught a fleeting glance of annoyance on Carey's face as she replied with a giggle, "Oh, my goodness, no! I quit school when I was thirteen. I couldn't stand the place. Too dull for me!"

Chapter 19

Carey turned to Grace eagerly and began to ask about Christian Endeavor. Cornelia wondered at his sudden interest in religious matters and perceived that Brand had been carrying on a lively conversation with Grace across the table, and Carey had cut in. She felt like a person who has jumped into an airplane, somehow started it, and knows nothing of running or stopping it. She had started this thing, and this was what had developed, and now she would have to watch the consequences.

Yet it appeared there was no opportunity to watch the consequences, and much as she so desired. The young man on her right was determined to talk to her. He had drawn Louise into the little circle also, and Louise was smiling shyly and evidently pleased. Cornelia could not help noticing how sweet the little girl looked with the wild-rose color in her cheeks and the little soft tendrils of curls about her face. The organdie dress certainly was attractive, and she must get at it right away and make some more pretty clothes for the dear child.

Then her eyes traveled down the table once more. Brand was laughing uproariously, Clytie was endeavoring to get in on his conversation and divert it to herself, and Carey was looking like a thundercloud and talking very rapidly and eagerly to Grace Kendall. How handsome he looked in his new necktie! How the blue brought out the blue of his eyes! And how dear and good and kindly polite her father looked! Then she noticed with a panic that the fruit cups were nearly empty, and it was time for the soup. Would Harry and Louise be able to make the transfer of dishes without any mishaps? She had not felt nervous about it before till this elegant stranger had appeared on the scene. She knew by his looks that he was used to having everything just so. She remembered his mother's immaculate attire, the wonderful glimpse she had caught of the fittings of her traveling bag, everything silver-mounted and monogrammed. This man would know if the soup was not seasoned just right and the dishes were served at the wrong side.

Perhaps she was a little distraught as Louise slipped silently from her seat and took the empty dishes on her little tray that had stood unseen by the side of her chair.

"What a charming little sister!" said Maxwell.

Cornelia's heart glowed, and she looked up with an appreciative smile.

"She is a darling!" she said earnestly. "I'm just getting to know her again since I came home from college. She was only a baby when I went away."

He looked interestedly at the sweet older sister. "I should imagine that might be a very delightful occupation. I think I would like an opportunity myself to get acquainted with her. And say, suppose you tell me about these other people. Now I'm here, I'd like to know them a little better. I haven't quite got them all placed. Your father I know. We came up together, and it doesn't take long to see he's a real man. I shall enjoy pursuing the acquaintance further if he is willing. But about these others. Are they—relatives? This girl at my right, is she another sister or only a friend?"

"Oh, she is our minister's daughter," answered Cornelia brightly. "She's rather a new friend, because we've only been living in this part of the city a short time, but we like her a lot."

"She looks it," he said heartily. "And the next one is your brother. I like his face. He is—a college boy, perhaps?"

"No, he's only finished high school," Cornelia said with a bit of a sigh. "Mother wanted him to go to college, but he didn't seem to want to, and—well—I suppose the real truth about it was I was in college, and the family couldn't afford to send another. I was blind enough not to know I ought to come home and give the next one a chance. However, Carey—"

She looked at him wistfully, and the young man, intensely alert to her expression, perhaps read a bit of her thoughts.

"College isn't always the only thing," he said quickly. "You, being a college woman, have naturally thought so, I suppose, but upon my word, I think sometimes it's more harm than good to a boy to go to college."

Cornelia gave him a grateful smile, and he saw that this had been one of her pains and mortifications. He liked her more, the more he talked with her. She seemed to have her family so much at heart. He lifted sharp eyes to the young man across the table.

"That's one of his friends, I suppose?"

Cornelia nodded half dubiously.

"He owns the car at the door?"

"Yes." There was a whole volume expressed in her tone.

The sharp eyes looked Brand over a second. "Interesting face," he commented. "Does he belong to the automobile Barlocks?"

"Why, I don't know," said Cornelia. "I've only just come home, you know. He's Carey's friend, that's all I know. I didn't even remember he had the same name as the automobile people."

"And who is the other young woman? She is not—a minister's daughter, too?" he asked with an amused twinkle in his eyes.

Cornelia gave him a quick deprecatory glance. "No," she said, half ashamed. "She is just—an experiment."

"I see," he said gravely, giving Clytie Dodd another intense look.

"You must be like your mother," she said, smiling. "She seemed to me so interested in just people. And she read me like a book. Or perhaps you are a psychologist?"

"You couldn't give me a greater compliment than to tell me I'm like Mother. She's always like that, interested in everybody about her and wondering what circumstances helped to form them as they are."

"It was your mother that gave me the idea of fixing up this old house on nothing." She gave a laughing deprecatory glance about. "I was just awfully unhappy and discouraged at having to leave college and go to a poor little house in a new neighborhood, and she managed to leave with me the suggestion of making it all over in such a way that I could not get away from it."

"You certainly have done wonders," he said with an admiring look about. "That was one reason I was so anxious to stay and look around me, the rooms opened up so charmingly and were such a surprise. You really have made a wonderful place out of it. This room, now, looks as if it might have come out of the hands of some big city decorator, and yet there is a charm and simplicity about it that is wholly in keeping with a quiet home life. I like it awfully. I wish Mother could see it. Were those panels on the walls when you began?"

"Oh no. There was some horrible old faded red wallpaper,

and in some places the plaster was coming off. Carey and I had a lot to do to this wall before we could even paint it. And there were so many layers of paper we thought we never would get it all scraped off."

"You had to do all that?" said the young man appreciatively. "It was good you had a brother to help in such rough, heavy work."

"Yes, Carey has been very much interested. Of course, he hasn't had so much time lately, as he could give only his evenings. He has been working all day. He built the fireplace in the living room, too. I want you to look at that after dinner. I think it is very pretty for an amateur workman."

"He built that fireplace!" exclaimed Maxwell. "Well, he certainly did a great thing! I noticed it at once. It is the charm of the whole room and so artistic in its lines. I love a beautiful fireplace, and I thought that was most unusual. I must look at it again. Your brother must be a genius."

"No, not a genius," said Cornelia. "But he always could make anything he wanted to. He is very clever with tools and machinery and seems to know by instinct how everything is made. When he was a little boy, I remember, he used to take everything in the house apart and put it together again. I shall never forget the day Mother got her new vacuum cleaner and was about to sweep the parlor and was called away to answer a knock at the back door. When she came back Carey had the whole thing apart, strewn all around the room, and Mother sat down in dismay and began to scold him. Then she told him sadly that he must go upstairs to bed for punishment; and he looked up and said, 'Why, Muvver, don't you want me to put it together again first?' And he did. He put it all together so it worked all right and managed to get out of his punishment that time."

Maxwell glanced down the table at the bright, clever face of the young man who was eagerly describing to Grace Kendall an automobile race he had witnessed not long ago.

"That's a great gift!" he commented. "Your brother ought to make a business success in life. What did you say he is doing?"

Cornelia flushed painfully. "That's the sore point," she said. "Carey hasn't anything very good just now, though he has one or two hopeful possibilities in the near future. He is just working in a garage now, getting together all the money he can save to be ready for the right job when it comes along. Father is rather distressed to have him doing such work; he says he is wasting his time. But it is good pay, and I think it is better than doing nothing and just hanging around waiting. Besides, he is crazy about machinery, seems to have a natural instinct for finding out what's the matter with a thing; and of course automobiles—he would rather fuss with one than eat."

"It's not a bad training for some big thing in the future, you know," said Maxwell. "There are lots of jobs today where a practical knowledge of machinery and especially of cars is worth a lot of money. I wouldn't be discouraged about it. He looks like an awfully clever fellow. He'll land the right thing pretty soon. I like his personality. That's another thing that will count in his favor. I want to get acquainted with him after dinner. Say, do you know you have let me in for an awfully interesting evening?"

"Why, that's very nice," said Cornelia, suddenly realizing that she had forgotten to worry about Louise's getting the next course on the table safely; and here it was, hot and inviting, and she sitting back and talking like a guest. What a dear little capable sister she was, and how quietly Harry was keeping the machinery in the kitchen going!

Everybody seemed to be having a nice time, even Clytie Dodd was listening to something her father was telling, something about a young man where he worked who had risked his life to save a friend in danger. Clytie was subdued, that was certain. Something—perhaps the formality of the meal or the impressiveness of the guests—had quieted her voice and suppressed her bold manner. She was not talking much herself, and she was not feeling quite so self-sufficient as when she came. It was most plain that she was quite out of her element in such an atmosphere, but she was a girl who was quick to observe and adjust herself to her environment. This might not be her native atmosphere, but she knew enough to keep quiet and keep her eyes open. Cornelia noticed that she was being left very much to herself so far as the two young men were concerned, and perhaps this had something to do with the subduing influence. Clytie was not a girl who cared for the background very long. She was one who forced herself into the limelight. Was it possible that just a little formality and a few strangers had changed her so completely? Perhaps she was not so bad, after all, as the children had led her to suppose. Just a poor little ignorant child who was trying her untaught hand at vamping. There might even be a way to help her, though Cornelia felt opposed to trying it when Carey was about. She could not yet consider Carey in the light of a companion of his girl without mortification. In all that little circle around the table, her common little painted face shone up as being out of place, unrefined, uncultured, utterly untaught.

More and more as the courses came on the table, Clytie grew silent and impressed, and as the meal drew to its close, Cornelia gained confidence. The dainty salad had been eaten greedily; the delectable ice in its pale green dreamy beauty had come on in due time and brought an exclamation of wonder from the whole company, who demanded to know what it was and tasted it as one might sample a dish of ambrosia, and praised and tasted again.

There was much laughter and fun over the blowing out of the

candles by Carey and the cutting of the angel cake, which also brought a round of applause. Cornelia poured the amber coffee into the little pink cups that looked like seashells, and finally the meal was concluded and the company arose to go into the living room.

Then Clytie came into her own again. It seemed that rising from the formalities of the table had given her back her confidence once more. Seizing hold of Carey's arm as he stood near her, she exclaimed:

"Come on, Kay, let's go have a dance and shake some of this down. I'm full clear up to my eyes. Haven't you got a victrola? Turn it on, do. I'm dying for a dance!"

Chapter 20

By this time they were in the living room and in full view of the whole company. Cornelia was standing in the doorway with Maxwell just behind.

It seemed that Clytie had chosen the moment when her remark would be best heard by everyone, and a horrible silence followed it, as if some deadly explosive had suddenly been flung down in their midst. Maxwell heard a sudden little breathless exclamation from Cornelia. He flung a swift glance around the company. Grace Kendall stood quietly apart. Brand Barlock looked amused with a sharp appraisement of the effect of Clytie's words on everyone present. Carey, caught by the unexpected momentum of the girl's action, was whirled about in spite of himself and recovered his balance angrily, flinging her off.

"What's the matter with you?" he said in a low, muttering tone. Then, trying to recover his politeness in the face of everybody, he added haughtily, "No, we haven't got a victrola, I'm thankful to say!" And he cast a swift, furtive glance at the minister's daughter. What must she think of him for having a girl like that be so bold with him? His face was crimson, and for the first time since he had known Clytie Dodd, he put the question to himself whether she was exactly the kind of girl he wanted for an intimate friend.

The silence in the room was intense. There seemed to be a kind of spell over the onlookers that no one was able to break. Clytie looked defiantly around at them and felt she had the floor.

"Oh, well, be a dummy if you want. You ain't the only pebble on the beach. Come on, Brand. Let's do the shimmy. You can whistle if no one knows how to play." It was plain that she was angry and did not care what she said or did. Carey had turned white and miserable; Cornelia looked ready to drop. Young Maxwell noticed the worn hands of the father clench and his face grow gray and drawn. Mr. Copley gave the impression that he would like above all things to take Clytie in thumb and finger and, holding her at arm's length, eject her from the room as one would get rid of some vulgar little animal that was making an unpleasant scene.

The young man gave one more swift look at the annoyed face of the girl beside him and then stepped forward, noticing as he did so that even Brand was a bit annoyed at the turn affairs had taken. Even he saw that Clytie's suggestion was out of place.

"Miss Dodd," said Maxwell in a clear, commanding voice, with a pleasant smile that at once held Clytie Dodd's attention. She turned to him eagerly, all too evidently expecting he was going to offer to dance with her; and the rest of the little audience stood in breathless waiting. "I'm sure you won't mind if we interrupt you. Miss Copley was just going to play for some singing. You'll join us, of course. I'm sure you have a good voice, and we want everybody. Let's all gather around the piano."

He turned with a swift appeal to Cornelia to bear him out. He had taken a chance, of course. What if Miss Copley did not play? But here was the piano, and there was music scattered about. Somebody must play.

A little breathless gasp went from one to another in visible relief as Cornelia came forward quickly, summoning a wan smile to her lips, trying to steady her fingers to select something from the mass of music on the piano that would meet the present need. Her music did not include many popular favorites—a few that Carey had brought home, that was all. But this if ever was the time to bring it forth. Ah! Here was "Tim Rooney's at the Fightin'." It would do as well as anything, and she placed it on the piano and forced her fingers into the opening chords, not daring to look around the room, wondering what Clytie Dodd was doing now and how she was taking her interruption.

But Maxwell was not idle. She felt his protective presence behind her. He was summoning everyone into the chorus, even the father, and he asked Clytie Dodd whether she didn't sing alto, a challenge that won a giggling acknowledgment from her.

"I thought so," he said. "I can almost always tell when people sing alto. Then come over on this side of the piano with me. I sing bass, and Mr. Copley, are you bass, too? I thought so. Now, you two fellows"—turning to Brand and Carey, who were standing abashed in the background, uncomfortable and half ready to bolt but much impressed by the tactics of the stranger—"it's up to you to sing tenor. You've got to, whether you can or not, you know, because we can't do it, and it's obvious that we have to have four parts. Miss Kendall sings soprano, doesn't she? And Miss Copley. Now, we're off! Give us those chords again, please."

He started off himself with a splendid voice, and even a lame singer found it easy to follow. They all had good voices, and while no one felt exactly like singing after a big dinner, they nevertheless stumbled along bravely and before the second verse was reached were making quite a gallant chorus.

Before they had sung three songs they were quite in the spirit of the thing, and Harry and Louise, emerging from a last delicious dish of sherbet, joined in heartily, lending their young voices vigorously. Clytie proved to have a tolerable voice. It was a bit louder than was necessary, with a nasal twang now and then, but it blended well with the other voices and was not too obvious. Even Mr. Copley seemed to have forgotten the unpleasant happening of a few moments before and was singing as lustily as when he was a young man.

Only Cornelia felt the tense strain of it all. They could not sing always. Sometime it would have to stop, and what would happen then? The wonderful stranger could not always be expected to step in and pilot the little ship of the evening safely past all rocks. He had done wonders, and she would never cease to be grateful to him, but, oh, if he would go home at once as soon as they stopped singing and not be there to witness further vulgarities! Grace Kendall, too. But then Grace understood somewhat. Grace was a minister's daughter. What, oh, *what* could they do next to suppress that awful girl?

Cornelia's head throbbed, and her face grew white and anxious. She cast an occasional glace at Carey, who was singing away vigorously out of the same book with Grace Kendall, and wished she might weave a spell and waft all the rest of the guests away, leaving her brother to the influence of this sweet, natural girl. How could she manage to avert another embarrassing situation? But it seemed as if the brain that had brought out so many lovely changes in a dismal old house, that had planned so carefully every detail of this evening and looked far ahead to results in the lives of her dear ones, had utterly refused to act any longer. Her nerve was shaken, and she could scarcely keep the tears back. Oh, if there were someone to help her! Then her heart took up its newly acquired habit and cried out to God, "Oh God, send me help. What shall I do next?"

As if young Maxwell read her thoughts, he turned at the close of the song and, addressing them all casually, said, "I guess we're about sung out for a while, aren't we? I'm hoarse as a foghorn. Miss Dodd, why don't you teach me how to play this game? I've been looking at it for quite a while, and it fascinates me. I believe I could beat you at it. Suppose we try."

Clytie giggled, quite flattered. It was a feather in her cap to have this handsome stranger paying her marked attention. His car was even finer than Brand Barlock's. Not so sporty, perhaps, but much sweller. And the man was older, besides. It was something wonderful to have made a hit with him. She preened herself, still giggling, and sat down at the table, eyeing with indulgent curiosity the little board with its colored squares and bright carved men.

"I d'no'z I know m'self," she granted, glinting her beringed fingers among the bits of colored wood. "Whaddaya do, anyhow?"

Cornelia, with a flush of gratitude in her face, gave a brief clue to the object of the game, and they were soon deep in the attempt to get their men each into the other's territory first.

Clytie was clever and soon got the idea of the game. She might have grown annoyed with it if she had been playing with some people, but Maxwell could be interesting when he chose to exert himself; and he was choosing just now, studying the caliber of the girl before him and leading her in spite of herself to take a real interest in what she was doing. To tell the truth, Clytie was interested in a man of almost any kind, especially if he was good-looking, but this particular man was a specimen different from any that had ever come into her path in a friendly way before. She had met such men as this only in a business way when she was ordered curtly to write a business letter over again or told she could not hold her position in an office unless she stopped chewing gum and talking so much to the other secretaries. Never had a man of this sort stepped down from his height to be really nice to her, and she was not only astonished, but pleased at it. There was nothing of the personal about his manner, just a nice, pleasant, friendly way of taking it for granted that she liked being talked to and was as good as anybody; and it gave her a new feeling of self-respect that she would never forget, even if she never met the man again.

Cornelia, watching furtively and thankfully from her corner where she was showing Brand Barlock a book of college photographs and explaining some of the college jokes inscribed beneath them, marveled at his patience and skill. She had not known him long, only two hours, but he was so obviously of another world from this girl and yet was making her feel so entirely comfortable and happy, that she felt humiliated and ashamed that she had not been able to do the same for the girl. She had invited her with a real feeling that she might be able to help her somehow—at least, that was what she thought she had for one of her objects—but now she began to suspect that perhaps she had in reality desired to humiliate the girl and put her into such a position that Carey would not want to go with her any longer. The girl had shown that she was unhappy and out of her element, and Cornelia had not helped her to find any possible basis for understanding with those about her. It was all wrong, and she ought to have gone further into things and planned to uplift that girl, even if she didn't want to lift her up to the social plane of her own brother. There might be senses in which Carey wasn't so very much higher than the girl, too. He needed uplifting a lot. Of course, that girl wouldn't help lift him nor he her as things were, but Cornelia had had no right whatever to humble her for the sake of saving her brother.

Maxwell was tactful. He managed to draw Louise and Brand

Barlock into the game after awhile, and when they had grown tired of that, he led them into the dining room, where Carey and Grace had just finished a game of Ping-Pong on the dining room table and insisted that they four-play a set. Brand soon gave up his racket to Harry and drifted into the other room, but it was half past ten when the others came back into the living room, where Grace Kendall was singing some Scotch songs, and sat down to listen.

Cornelia looked at Clytie Dodd in surprise. All the boldness and impudence had melted out of her face, with much of the makeup and powder that had been transferred to her handkerchief during the heated excitement of the game. Her hair had lost its tortured look, and her face was just that of an ordinary happy little girl who had been having a good, healthy time. She felt almost on an equality with the people around her because this nice man had been nice to her. She rather hated that yellow-haired girl in blue who had absorbed the attention of her own two special satellites, but what were they but kids beside this man of the world? She stole a look at his fine, strong face and had perhaps a fleeting vision of what it might be to have a man friend such as he was—and who shall say but a fleeting revelation, too, of what a girl must be to have such a friend? She saw him look across the room to where his young hostess sat, and smile a smile with a kind of mysterious light like signal lights at sea. She looked curiously to where Carey's sister sat and saw with a startled new insight how young and really lovely this girl was, and she sat silent, a little wondering, in rare thoughtfulness.

Grace Kendall finished her song and suddenly whirled around on the piano stool and looked at her watch.

"Oh, my dear!" she said, glancing up at Cornelia. "Do you see what time it is? And I have to be up at half past five tomorrow morning to get Father's breakfast before he goes to New York. I must say, 'Good night,' and hurry right home."

Both Carey and Brand rose and hurried up to her in a confidential way.

"I'll take you—" began Carey.

"My car is right at the door," put in Brand dictatorially. "I'll take you, of course."

Carey looked vexed then met Brand's eyes sheepishly.

"Well, I'll take her, and you can drive," he said. And then suddenly they both looked at Clytie, and their tongues clove to the roofs of their mouths, for Clytie had risen with black brows, her sullen, defiant glance returning.

Then Maxwell stepped forward as if he had heard nothing.

"Miss Dodd, my car is here. I'll be glad to see that you get safely home." And Clytie's face cleared. She sped upstairs to get her wraps.

"Haven't we had a beautiful time?" said Grace Kendall, putting an intimate arm around her as they reached the top of the stairs. "I think they're most charming people. Do you know you have a lovely alto voice? Do you live near here? We'd love to have you in our young people's choir if you don't belong somewhere else."

"Where is it?" asked Clytie casually, half suspiciously. She was surprised that there was no look of rivalry in the face of the girl who had obviously carried off both the younger men from her following, but it seemed as if this strangely sweet girl did not realize that she had done such a thing, did not even seem to have wanted to do it. Clytie suddenly smiled and showed the first glimpse of real simplicity and childlikeness that had been visible that evening. She was little more than a child, anyway, and perhaps would not have gone in her present ways if any other that promised a little pleasure had been opened to her.

"No, I don't b'long nowheres," she giggled. "Not since I was a kid. I useta go ta two er three Sunday schools, but I cut 'em all out after I grew up. Took too much time. I like my Sundays fer fun. That's when you get the most auto rides, you know. But I wouldn't mind singing sometime, mebbe."

When they came downstairs, they were arm in arm and chatting quite pleasantly. Grace had promised to come and see her and take her to Christian Endeavor the next Sunday night and introduce her to the leader of the young people's choir; and Cornelia, waiting to receive her guests' farewell, wondered and was thankful.

They all went out together, talking a bit loudly and hilariously, Clytie's voice now raised in her old shrill, uncultured clang. Maxwell, lingering for a moment in the doorway, spoke to Cornelia.

"I want to thank you for letting me come."

She turned to him with a look of suffering in her eyes. "I don't know what you must think of us," she said in a low tone, "having that impossible girl here! An invited guest!"

He looked down at her, smiling with a hint of tenderness in his look, for he saw that she was very tired.

"I think you are a brave girl," he said earnestly. "And I think your experiment was a success. May I come back for a few minutes and help wash dishes? I'm taking your young brother Harry with me and shall have to bring him back, you know. We'll talk it all over then."

He touched his hat and vanished into the starlit night.

Cornelia flushed, wondering, half dismayed, ready to drop with fatigue, yet strangely elated. She stood a moment in the doorway, looking after the two cars as they whirled away down the street and letting the cool evening breeze blow on her hot forehead, then turned back to the bright, pretty room, somehow soothed and comforted. A thought had come to her. She had prayed for help, and God had sent it—right into the midst of her consternation He had sent that young man to help! And how he had helped! What a tower of strength he had been all the awful evening!

But then Louise fell upon her with joyful exclamations. "It *was* a success, Nellie, wasn't it? A great success! Wasn't he *great*? Wasn't it wonderful that Father should have found him and brought him in? Wasn't it just like an answer, Nellie, don't you think? He kept her away from Carey all the evening, and Carey had a lovely time with Miss Kendall. And Brand said he had a good time, too, and told me he wished you would ask him again. He talked to me a lot while you were talking to the others. He said he'd take us all out in his car sometime if you would go; and he said he thought you were a wonderful sister and a beautiful girl! He did, Nellie, he said it just like that: 'Your sister is a *bee–yew*–ti–ful girl!' And he meant it! And it was true, Nellie. You did look just wonderful. Your cheeks were such a pretty pink, and you didn't have your nose all white like that Clytie. Say, I guess she saw it wasn't nice to be the way she is, don't you think she did? I don't think she liked it the way Carey acted. I guess maybe she'll let him alone some now, and I hope she does. My, I hope she does! I didn't think he liked her being here, either, did you, Nellie? And say, didn't the sherbet look lovely? And the table was the prettiest thing! Miss Kendall said she never saw such a pretty table. She said you were an artist, Nellie. And Mr. Maxwell, he couldn't say enough things about the house. Even that Brand said he wished he had a nice cozy house like this. He said his sister didn't have time to get up birthday parties, or his mother, either; they had to have a whole townful when they had parties, and he just loved it tonight. He said twice he wished you'd ask him again. I guess he means to stick, Nellie. Will you like that?"

"He's not so bad," said Cornelia, patting the little girl's cheek. "I think maybe we can find a way to help him a little if we try. And I think maybe we ought not to feel so hard toward that poor foolish girl, either, dearie. Now, come, kitty dear, you ought to be in bed."

"'Deed, no, Nellie dear. I'm going to see the whole thing through," she chatted, hopping around on the tips of her toes. "We've got to wash the dishes. Harry said that Mr. Maxwell was coming back to help, too. We better get some clean aprons ready."

"Where is Father, Louie? Did he go up to bed?"

"Oh no, he went with Brand and Carey and Miss Kendall. They asked him, and he seemed real pleased. I shouldn't wonder if Brand will come back, too, and help. He asked me if he might. I said I guessed you wouldn't care. I thought if he didn't, maybe he'd carry Carey off for all night or something."

Cornelia stooped and kissed the sweet, anxious little face.

"It's all right, dearie, and I guess everything's all right. Somehow we came out of an awful place tonight, and I guess God means to see us through."

"I know," said the little girl wisely. "When Clytie danced, you mean. That was awful, wasn't it? Father looked—just—sick for a minute, didn't he? Poor Daddy, he didn't understand. And he doesn't like dancing. And I thought for just a minute how awful Mother would feel. She doesn't like it either. And that girl—she was so—awful! But my! I'm glad it's over, aren't you, Nellie? And say! There they come! There's enough sherbet for everybody to have some more. Shall we have it? My, isn't this fun?"

They all came in and frolicked through the dishes, Brand and Maxwell entering into it with spirit. Brand didn't do much helping, but he made a show at it, and he certainly enjoyed the angel cake and sherbet, which was most thoroughly "finished" that night. Even the father came out into the kitchen and watched the fun and talked with Maxwell, who was flourishing a dish towel and polishing glasses as if he had always done it.

Harry and Maxwell grew very chummy, and Maxwell declared that he was under deep obligation to the boy for his supper.

"How about it, Mr. Copley? Will you let this boy take a trip with me sometime pretty soon? I'm to go after Mother in a week or so now, and I'd like mighty well to have his company. I shall probably start next Friday, sometime in the afternoon, and expect to get back Monday sometime. That wouldn't take him out of school many hours, and I think we'd have a first-rate time. Would you like it, son?"

Harry's eager face needed no words to express his joy. His eyes fairly sparkled.

The young man took a business card from his pocket and handed it to Mr. Copley.

"I'm really an utter stranger to you, you know," he said with a smile, "and I can understand how you wouldn't want to trust your boy to a stranger. I shall consider it a favor if you will look me up; ask any of the men in my firm about me. I want you to be sure about me, because I intend to come again if you will let me. I'm not running any risk of losing such perfectly good new friends as you all are, and I want Harry for the trip."

Mr. Copley looked the young man over admiringly.

"Don't you think I can tell a *man* when I see one?" he asked amusedly. "It's generally written on his face, and no one can mistake."

"Thank you," said Maxwell. "That *is* a compliment!"

After the dishes were done, there were the ferns to be unboxed and admired, and it was after midnight when at last the two young men said good night and drove away, each with a hearty assurance that he had had a wonderful time and wanted to come again soon.

When Cornelia went up to her room and took off her apron, out of its pocket fell a letter that she had received that morning and had been too busy to read. She opened it now. It was a brief, rattling message from one of her classmates in college, begging her to put off everything else for a few days and come to a house party with them all. It was to be down at Atlantic City, near enough to home not to make the trip expensive, and they all were crazy to see her again and tell her all about commencement. She smiled reminiscently as she laid it away in her desk drawer and found to her surprise that she had no great desire to go. She knew what the party would be, full of rollicking fun and carefree every minute of it, but somehow her heart and soul were now in her home and the new life that was opening before her. She wanted to finish the house; to make the white kitchen as charming in its way as the other rooms were getting to be; to help Carey plan a front porch he had said he would build with stone pillars; to set out some plants in the yard, finish the bedrooms, and make out a list of new furniture for the carpenter next door to buy. The minister had said he knew of some people who were refurnishing their house and wanted her professional advice. She wanted to stay and work. Mr. Maxwell was coming to take them all motoring some evening, too; and Brand had declared he would bring his sister around to call, and they would go out to ride. Life was opening up full and beautiful. College and its days seemed far away and almost childish. Tomorrow morning she and Grace Kendall were going to make curtains for one of the Sunday school classrooms. Carey had promised to help cut them up. Oh, life wasn't half bad! Even Clytie Amabel Dodd did not loom so formidable as earlier in the evening. She knelt and thanked God.

Chapter 21

When Maxwell finally turned his car cityward it was with the feeling of a naughty boy who had run away from duty and was suddenly confronted by retribution.

He glanced at the clock in the car and noted that the hour was getting very late, and his conscience seized him. Now that he had done the thing, it suddenly seemed atrocious. He had ignored a lady in trouble and gone on a tangent. It wasn't even the excuse of a previous engagement or the plea of old friends. It was utterly unnecessary. He had followed an impulse and accepted an utter stranger's invitation to dinner and then had stayed all the evening and gone back to wash dishes afterward. As he thought it over he felt that either he was crazy or a coward. Was it actually true that he, a man full grown, with a will of his own, was afraid to trust himself for an hour in the company of the woman who had once been supreme in his life? What was he afraid of? Not that he would yield to her wiles after two years' absence; not that he would break his promise to himself and marry her in spite of husbands and laws either moral or judicial. It must be that he was afraid to have his own calm disturbed. He had been through seas of agony and reached a haven of peace where he could endure and even enjoy life, and he was so selfish that he wished to remain within that haven even though it meant a breach of courtesy and an outraging of all his finer instincts.

He forgot that his struggle earlier in the evening had been in an exactly opposite line and that the finer feelings had urged him to remain away from the woman who had once been almost his undoing. However, now that it was almost too late to mend the matter he felt that he ought to have gone. Even if her plea of asking his advice had merely been a trumped-up excuse to bring him to her side, yet was it not the part of a gentleman to go? A true gentleman should never let a lady ask for help in vain. And he had promised always to be her friend. It might be that it had been an ill-advised promise, but a promise was a promise, etc.

By that time he had arrived at his apartment and was dressing hastily. The evening and its simple experiences seemed like a pleasant dream that waking obliterates. It might return later, but now the present was upon him, and he knew Evadne when she was kept waiting. If she had not changed, there was no pleasant meeting in store for him. However, he need not tell her that he had been enjoying himself all the evening and had forgotten how fast time was flying.

Arrived at the hotel he went at once to the desk and asked for the lady. The clerk asked his name and called a bellboy. "Go page Miss Chantry," he said. "She's in the ballroom." Then turning to Maxwell, he said, "She left word you were to wait for her in the reception room over there."

"No, don't page her," said Maxwell sharply. "I'll go and find her myself."

"Oh, all right! Just as you please! Those were her orders."

Maxwell turned toward the elevators, half inclined, after all, not to see her. She had not been in such distress but that she could amuse herself, after all. But that was Evadne, of course. He must expect that. Besides, she was doubtless angry at his delay.

Maxwell got off the gallery floor expecting to find the lady seated in one of the little quiet nooks overlooking the happy throng, but he made the rounds without finding her and paused at the last door to look down on the moving, throbbing, colorful life below.

The orchestra was beating out a popular bit of elevated jazz, and the floor below was like a kaleidoscope as the couples wove their many-colored patterns in and out among each other.

Maxwell watched the dancers idly for a moment. He was not a dancer himself and not particularly interested in it. As he looked, he was suddenly struck with the contrast between this scene and the quiet little home where he had spent the evening. How hard these people were trying to enjoy themselves, and how excited and restless and almost unhappy many of them looked.

A group of ladies seated near the railing quite close to where he stood were discussing one of the couples on the floor.

"She is disgusting," said one. "I wonder who she is? How dare she come to a respectable place and dance in that way?"

His eyes followed their glances, and he easily singled out the two who were under their criticism. The man, a tall, dark, bizarre-looking fellow he knew by sight, with money enough and family irreproachable enough to get away with anything in these days.

But the woman! Why did there seem to be something familiar about her? Sleek black hair wound closely about a small, languid head, lizard-like body inadequately sheathed in gold brocade, sparkle of jewels from lazy, graceful feet.

A break in the throng as someone went off the floor, and the two swept around facing him. The woman looked up and met his eyes. *It was Evadne!*

Something clicked and locked in his soul as if the machinery could not go on any longer without readjustment. He stood staring down at her, a growing wonder in his face, aware that she was looking at him and waving, aware that he was expected to smile. Instead he felt as if he were glaring. Was this the woman for whom he had spent two years of agony and struggle? This little empty-faced creature with a smile upon her painted, selfish mask? As he stood looking at her he was struck with a fleeting notion that she resembled Clytie, poor feather-brained Clytie trying to exploit her own little self in the best way she knew, to play the game of life to her own best advantage. What was the difference between them?

Was it for a woman like this that he had wasted two of the best years out of his young manhood? He used to call her beautiful, but now her face seemed so vapid. Was it just the years that had come between or had she changed, grown coarser, less ethereal? A vision of Cornelia Copley floated in his mind. Why hadn't he known sooner that there was a girl like that somewhere in the world? What a fool he had been!

Evadne had signaled to him and led her partner off the floor. Now they were coming to him. He wished he might vanish somewhere. Why had he come? This girl had no real need of him. She was merely enjoying herself.

"What made you so late?" she challenged merrily. "We've been waiting supper for an age. I met an old friend tonight. Bob, meet Artie Maxwell. Come on, I've had the food served in my suite, and I've ordered lobster Newburg and all the things you used to like."

"I'll answer for the drinks," broke in the one called Bob. "I've sampled them already."

"Sh! Naughty! Naughty! Bob!" hushed Evadne with her finger on her lips. "Artie is a good little boy. He doesn't break the law—" She laughed. "Come on, Artie, I'm nearly starved. I thought you never would get here. Ring for the elevator, Bob, please."

Maxwell's whole being simply froze.

He didn't want to remain, and he didn't like the other man, but he could not ask her point-blank what she wanted of him in the presence of this stranger. He was gravely silent as the elevator carried them to the right floor, and Evadne did the talking. But when the door opened into the apartment and showed a table set for three with flowers and lights and preparations for a feast, he made a stand.

"I can't possibly stay for supper," he declared. "I've dined only a little while ago, and I must leave for New York on business very early in the morning. I only dropped in to explain—"

"Indeed, you are not going to leave in that way!" she flashed upon him angrily. "I told you in my note that I had something very important to tell you."

Maxwell looked at the other man politely. "If we could have just a word together now," he said, turning back to the girl. "I really must get back to my apartment at once. I have important papers to prepare for tomorrow."

The other man turned away toward the table haughtily, with a scornful, "Why certainly," and poured himself a glass from the flask that stood there.

Maxwell turned to the angry girl. "Now, what can I do for you? I shall be very glad to do anything in my power of course." He spoke stiffly as to a stranger. The girl perceived that her power over him was waning. Yet she was too subtle to let him see it.

"I am in deep trouble," she sighed with a quiver of the lips. "But I can't tell it in a moment. It is a long story." Her eyelids fluttered down on her lovely painted cheeks. She knew the line that would touch him most.

"What sort of trouble?" he asked almost gently. He never could bear to see a woman suffer.

She clasped her little jeweled hands together fiercely and bent her head dejectedly.

"I cannot tell you all now," she answered desperately. "You would have to hear the whole before you could understand. Wait until we are alone."

"Is it financial trouble?" he urged after a pause with a gentle persistence in his voice.

"Yes, that—and—*other things*!" Evadne forced a tear to the fringes of her almond lids.

He studied her gravely.

"I'll tell you what I want you to do," he said at last. "I will not be here tomorrow nor possibly for several days, but I would like you to talk with our old family lawyer. He was a friend of my father's and is very wise and kind. Anything you could tell to me you can tell to him. He knows you and will fully understand. I can call him tonight when I get back and explain, and he will be glad to come here and see you I am sure. Or if you prefer you can go to his office."

But Evadne lifted her sleek black head wrathfully, flicked off the tear, flung out her chin, and looked him down with her almond eyes as if from a great height. "Thank you!" she said crisply. "When I want a family lawyer I can get one! And YOU— can—GO!"

She pointed to the door with her jeweled hand imperiously, and Maxwell arose with dignity, his eyes upon her as if he would force himself to see the worst, and went.

"Bob!" said Evadne to the intoxicated man at the table when the elevator door had clanged shut after her onetime beau. "I'm not sure, but I shall come back to Philadelphia after a few days and stay awhile. I wonder if you could keep track of that man for me and tell me just where he goes and what he does. I'll make it worth your while, you know."

"Surely, old dear. I'll be delighted. No trouble at all. I know a private detective who would be tickled to death for the job. What did you say the poor fish's name is? Seemed a harmless sort of chump. Not quite your kind, is he? Come, Vaddie, let's have another drink."

But Evadne's eyes narrowed thoughtfully as she took the glass and drank slowly. She was not one to take lightly any loss.

Out in the night the young man drew a deep breath of the clean air thankfully. It seemed as though he had escaped from something unwholesome and tainted. He was glad that he had the sense to know it, and he thought back again with relief to the happy evening in the simple, natural home.

Chapter 22

Carey had been working quite steadily at the garage and giving money to his father and Cornelia every week. It really made things much easier in the home. Word had come that the mother was steadily progressing toward health, and everybody was much happier. It seemed that Carey was happier, too. He was not away so much at night, which relieved his sister and his father tremendously.

Nothing had been said about Clytie Dodd. Carey had thanked his sister for the party and for taking so much trouble to make a pleasant evening, but he utterly ignored the presence of the girl who had been the cause of the whole affair. It was as if she had not been there. Mr. Copley had asked as he sat down to dinner the next evening after the birthday, "Where did you pick up that strange Dodd girl you had here?" and Cornelia had answered quite casually, as if it didn't matter at all, "Oh, she was just a girl I thought perhaps we ought to know," and slipped back into the kitchen to get the potatoes just as Carey entered the dining room. He must have heard the conversation and heard his father's reply: "Well, I guess she's not quite our sort, is she? I guess we can get along without her, can't we?" He made no comment and began to talk at once eagerly about the new stone porch he was going to build. It appeared that he had discovered a lot of stone that was being dug from the street where they were putting down new paving, and it was to be had for little more than the carting away. Pat would let him have his truck at night, and he was going to bring the first load that very evening. Brand was coming around to help. Brand wanted to have a hand in the building.

Brand appeared soon after, coming breezily out to the dining room without an invitation and sitting down for a piece of lemon pie as if he were a privileged friend of long standing. There was nothing backward about Brand. Yet somehow they all liked him, and Cornelia could see that Carey was pleased that they did. She felt a glow of thankfulness in her heart that it was possible to like one of Carey's friends when the other one was so unspeakably impossible.

Brand took off his coat and put on an old sweater of Carey's, and they went off together after the truck. In a little while they were back with the first load of cobblestones and worked till long after dark, load after load, piling them neatly between the sidewalk and the curb till they had a goodly lot. Brand seemed as interested in that porch as if it were his own. After they took the truck back, Brand came in again and wanted to sing. They sang for nearly an hour, and when he left, Cornelia felt as if they had fully taken over Brand as a part of their little circle. She couldn't help wondering what his society mother and elegant sister would say if they knew where he had spent the last two evenings. Then she reflected that there were much worse places where he might spend them, and probably often did, and she began to take Brand into her thoughts and plans for the future with almost the same anxious care as she gave to Carey. Brand was a nice boy and needed helping. He was too young to spend his time running around with girls like Clytie Dodd and taking joyrides with a happy crowd. She would make their little home a haven where Carey and his friends would at least be safe and happy. She could not give them anything elaborate in the way of entertainment, but there should always be a welcome, plenty of music, and something to eat.

Cornelia could see her father visibly brighten day by day as the week went by, and Carey seemed to stick to his task and spend his evenings at home. Brand had bought a pair of overalls and made blisters on his hands digging for the foundation of the stone porch. And every afternoon Carey came home from the garage at five o'clock and worked away with a will.

At this rate it did not take long for the wall to rise. It was level with the front doorstep now, and Carey had put a plank across and a few stones for steps to go up and down.

It was late on Thursday afternoon, and Carey was hard at work trying to finish the front wall before dark. Brand's racing car was standing by the curb with the engine throbbing, and Brand himself was standing with one foot on the wall talking to Carey.

Cornelia had just come out with a plate of hot gingerbread for them and was standing a moment watching them enjoy it when another car suddenly came down the hill and stopped in the road just in front of Brand's car. A wriggling child in the front seat peered out curiously from beside the driver, and Cornelia had a glimpse of a fretful elderly woman's face in the backseat. Then the door on the driver's side of the car was opened, and someone got out and came around. She hadn't thought of its being Maxwell until he was in full view, and a soft flush came into her cheeks with the welcome light in her eyes.

"Come in and have a piece of hot gingerbread!" she called, holding out the plate.

He came springing up the plank and stood beside her.

"Oh, thank you! Isn't this wonderful?" he said, taking a piece eagerly. "But I'm afraid I must eat and run. I'm taking my boss's aunt and her grandchild down to the train and mustn't delay. I just stopped to say that I'm leaving for the mountains tomorrow afternoon about three o'clock and will stop here for Harry. Do you think that will be too early for him?"

"Oh no, indeed. He can come home from school at noon and be all ready for you. It is wonderful of you to take him. He has talked of nothing else since you were here, and Father and I appreciate your kindness, I'm sure."

"No kindness about it. It will be great to have a kid along. I hate to go anywhere alone. Say, this gingerbread is luscious! No, really I mustn't take another bite. I must go this minute. I've left my engine going, and the lady is inclined to be easily annoyed. I—"

He happened to look up at that moment and saw to his horror that his car had begun to move slowly on down the hill. The child on the front seat had been doing things to the brakes and clutch. She had no idea what she was doing, but she always did things to everything in sight. If it was an electric bulb, she unscrewed it; if it was openable, she opened it; if it was possible to throw anything out of gear, she always could be depended upon to throw it. She was that kind of a child. She once threw a pair of heavy sliding doors off the track and almost down upon her and was saved from an untimely death only by the presence of some elderly rescuer. Had Maxwell known the child, he never would have left her alone in that front seat. She had wriggled herself into the driver's seat, and her fat hands were manipulating the wheel. As the car began to move, she gave a shout of horrid glee. A scream from the woman in the backseat, and Maxwell turned sick with the thought of the possibilities and sprang down the wall toward the street.

But quick as he was, Brand and Carey were ahead of him. At the very first sound, even before the car had been really in motion, Carey looked up over the wall he was building, gave a low whistle, and cried, "Hey there! Brand! Your car! Get a hustle!"

Brand turned and needed not an explanation. He dashed across the intervening space to his own car, sprang to the driver's seat, and was off. Carey, though handicapped by the wall he had to leap over, was scarcely a hair's breadth behind and alighted on the running board after the car had started.

"We've got to catch her before she reaches the corner," he shouted above the noise of the racing engine. "There's a trolley coming around the curve at the foot of the hill, and you can't tell what that kid'll do. It's a cinch she never ran a car before; look at her wabble. She's getting scared now. Look! The fool in the backseat has dragged her away from the wheel! Hey there! Give her plenty of room! Now curve her around, and give me space to jump her!"

Maxwell was running frantically and vainly down the street after his car, which was now going at a wild pace. From either direction on the cross street at the foot of the hill he could see cars speeding along. Who would know that the oncoming car was managed by a child who had never run a car in her life, a child who knew nothing whatever about cars, was too young to know, had never even been accustomed to ride in one, but lived in a little country village where cars were scarce articles? All this he knew because the grandmother had talked much to the youngster on the way down, and the child had said she had never been in a car but once before, but she wished she had one; she knew she could run it.

Horror froze in his veins as he remembered all these little details. He had made running a specialty when he was in college athletics, but now, although his way was downhill, his feet were like lead and his knees weak as water. He saw himself a murderer. Every possible detail of disaster rose and menaced his way as he sped onward, determined to do all in his power for rescue. The blood was pounding through his head so that he could scarcely see or hear. His breath came painfully, and he wondered blindly how long this would last. Then suddenly he saw the long, clean body of the racing car slide down the hill like a glance of light, glide close to the runaway car, then curve away and cross the street just in front of the oncoming trolley. He looked to see his own car smash into the trolley car, but instead it swept around in a steady, clean curve that just cleared the trolley car and veered away to the right. It crossed the car track behind the trolley car and circled around and back up the hill again, a steady hand at the wheel. An instant more and the car stopped before him where he stood in the middle of the road, his face white, his eyes staring, unable to believe that the catastrophe had really been averted. He looked up, and there sat Carey in the driver's seat as coolly as if he had been taking a pleasure trip.

"Shall I turn her around?" asked Carey nonchalantly. "Or do you want to go back to the house?"

"How did you do it?" asked Arthur Maxwell, grasping Carey's grimy hand eagerly. "I didn't see you catch her."

"Oh, just jumped her from Brand's running board. Dead easy. Guess she gave a little start though. That kid ought to be spanked. I guess the lady's pretty badly scared."

The lady and the "kid" were bathed in tears and wrapped in each other's arms in the backseat. The child was experiencing a late repentance, and the grandmother was alternately scolding and babying and in a fair way to make the little criminal feel she had done a smart thing. Maxwell gave them a withering glance and turned to Carey, who had swung out over the door and was standing in the road, looking at the car like a lion tamer who has just subdued a wild creature.

"I shall never forget this, Copley," said Maxwell, grasping his hand once more in the kind of a grip a real man gives to another. "I'll talk about it later when I've taken these people to the train. Meantime accept my thanks for yourself and your friend. You're both princes, and I'll see that everybody knows it."

"Forget it!" chanted Carey and swung himself like a thistle-down to the running board of Brand's car as he swept slowly, scrutinizingly up.

"Got her all right, didn't you, old man?" said Brand admiringly. "Any scratches? You had a mighty close shave!"

"Yep! She's all right. Well, so long, Maxwell. We gotta beat it back to work." And with a great whizzing and banging of joyful celebration the racer shot its way back uphill, and the two jumped out quite casually as if they had been off to get a soda and come back to work again.

Cornelia, white and trembling from the horror of the thing, tried to praise, to question, to exclaim; but failing to make an impression on the two indifferent workers, went upstairs, fell on her knees, and cried. Somewhere in the midst of her tears her crying turned into a prayer of thanksgiving, and she came down with an uplifted look on her face. Now and then as she went about her duties, she stole to the front window and looked out on the two sturdy workers. She could have hugged them both; she was so proud of them—they were so cool, so capable, and so indifferent! Just regular boys!

Maxwell came back that evening. She had somehow known he would. He was filled with gratitude to the two who had so gallantly saved him from a catastrophe, which would have shadowed his whole life. He still shuddered over the thought of what might have happened.

"I will never again leave a child alone in an automobile," he declared. "That girl was a little terror. I never saw one so spoiled and disagreeable in my life. She was determined to be allowed to run the car from the minute she got in, and she annoyed me constantly by playing with the electric buttons and getting her hands constantly on the wheel. I never dreamed she would have the strength to start the car, although she is large and strong for her age. But she has all kinds of nerve and impudence, and I might have known better than to stop here at all when I had such a passenger. Her grandmother is a nervous wreck, but she doesn't blame me, fortunately, although I blame myself decidedly. It is my business to know men, and I should have known that child well enough to realize it was a risk to leave her."

"Kid ought to be spanked!" declared Carey gruffly. "Know what she did? When she saw she was going to run into that car, she lost every bit of nerve and began climbing over the back of the seat. Some kid that! Just bad all through. Any nervy kid I know would have stuck it out and tried to steer her somehow, but that kid had a yellow streak."

"You're right there," declared Maxwell, with watchful eyes upon the young man. "But you had your nerve with you all right, I noticed. When you swung off that running board, it was an even chance you took. If you had missed your calculation by so much as a hair's breadth, you would have been smashed up pretty badly, crushed between the cars, probably."

Carey gave his shoulders a slight shrug.

"It's all in a lifetime," he said lightly. "But, say, that's a peach of a car you've got. Had it long?" And they launched into a lengthy discussion of cars in general and Maxwell's in particular. Cornelia noticed that all the time Maxwell was watching her brother intently. As he got up to leave, he asked casually, "Are you still working with the garage people?"

Carey colored and lifted his chin a trifle haughtily.

"Yes. I—*yes!*" he answered defiantly.

"Stick to it till something better comes along," advised Maxwell. "It isn't a bad line, and you learn a lot about machines that won't do you any harm in the future. You're a good man, and there's a good job waiting for you somewhere." And with that, he said, "Good night."

Mr. Copley came in presently with a late edition of the evening paper. He had been called to the home of his manager, who was ill, on a business consultation. He looked tired but exalted. He spread the paper out on the table under the lamp and called the children.

"See!" he said. "Do you know who that is?"

They all gathered around, and behold there was Carey looking at them from the pages of the *Evening Bulletin*. Carey! Their brother! They stared and stared again.

The picture had him in football garb, with one eye squinting at the sun and a broad grin on his lips. It was Carey two years ago, on the high school football team, but it looked like him still. Beneath from a border looked forth the bold, handsome features of Brand Barlock, and to one side another border held the round, fat, impertinent face of the child who had started the car that afternoon. The article below was headed in large letter:

FOOTBALL HERO SAVES TWO LIVES
Carey Copley Jumps from Moving Car
and Saves Child and Grandmother!

"Now, isn't that the limit? How did that thing get in *there*?" demanded the young hero angrily. "And say! How'd they get my picture? Some little fool reporter went around to school, I suppose.

Wouldn't that make you mad? How'd they find that out I'd like to know? Brand never told, that's one thing sure. Brand knows how to keep his mouth shut. You don't suppose that guy Maxwell would give it to them, do you?"

"He said he was going to see that everybody knew about it," chuckled Louise happily. "I think it oughta be known, don't you, Daddy? When a boy—that is a *man*—does a big thing like saving two lives, I think everybody oughta know how brave he is."

"Nonsense!" said Carey. "You don't know what you're talking about, kid. That wasn't anything to do." But his tone showed that he was pleased at the general attitude of his family. Nevertheless, he slammed around noisily in the dining room, pretending not to hear when his father read aloud the account of the accident in the paper, and went whistling upstairs immediately after. At the top he called down, "Say, I'm mighty glad they were fair to Brand in that article. Brand's a great fellow. I couldn't have done a thing without him and his car. He knew just what to do without being told, and he can drive, I'll say. Brand deserves all they can say of him. He's a good fellow."

Altogether, the household slept joyously that night, and Harry dreamed of going to the mountains in a blimp and flying back tied to the tail of a kite.

When Maxwell came to get Harry the next afternoon, he asked Cornelia one question that made her wonder a little. It seemed almost irrelevant.

"Did your brother ever have anything to do with managing men?" he said, looking thoughtfully at the neat masonry that was growing steadily longer and wider and higher.

"Why—I—hardly know," she replied, laughing. "I've been away so much from home."

"Captain of the basketball team in high school," announced Harry shrewdly. "And captain of a local baseball team they had out the other side of the city last summer. Some team it was, too; licked everything in sight and then some. Carey had 'em all right where he wanted 'em, and when a team treated 'em mean once, Kay just called the fellows off, and they wouldn't play one of 'em till he got a square deal with the ump!"

Harry's eyes sparkled. He made an earnest young advocate.

"Fine! I must hear more about that. I foresee I'm going to have a thrilling trip. There'll be lots to talk about. Well, Miss Copley, we'll bid you good-bye and get on our way. I want to get on well this afternoon in case we have bad weather tomorrow. But it looks clear now. We'll travel late tonight. There ought to be a wonderful moon. I wish you were going along." He gave her a wistful glance, and she flushed with pleasure.

"Thank you," she said appreciatively. "If I were only a little boy with nothing to do!"

"Sister!" protested Harry. "I've lots to do. I guess I work every day after school."

"You're not a little boy, Harry; you're almost a man," answered his sister lovingly. "I wasn't meaning you at all. I said if *I* were a little boy with nothing to do, then I could go along. I meant you could take care of me, see?" She gave a dear little smile at him, and he grinned.

"Aw! Quit yer kiddin'. So long, Cornie! Be back Monday. Take care o' yerself!"

Maxwell's eyes met hers; they laughed together at the boyishness of it, and Maxwell said good-bye and departed. Cornelia, as she went into the house, wondered why the brief conversation had seemed to lighten the monotony of the day so much and then fell to wondering why Maxwell had asked that question about Carey.

Five minutes later the doorbell rang, and when she opened the door, there stood Clytie Dodd, a brilliant red feather surrounding a speck of a hat and her face painted and powdered more wickedly than ever. She was wearing a yellow organdie dress with scallops on the bottom and adornments of colored spheres of cloth attached with black stitches at intervals over the dress. She carried a green parasol airily, and there was a "man" with an incipient and tenderly nursed mustache waiting for her at the gate. She greeted Cornelia profusely and talked very loudly and very fast.

"Is Kay here? I'm just dying to see him and kid him about having his picture in the paper. He always said he'd never get his there. But isn't it great though? Some hero, I'll tell the world! Who was the kid? Anybody belonging to the family? The paper didn't state. Oh, darn! I'm sorry Kay isn't here. I wanted him to meet my friend," she said nodding toward the man at the gate. "We've got a date on for tonight, and we want him and his friend Mr. Barlock. Some girlfriends of mine are coming, and we're going to have a dance and a big meal. It's just the kind of thing Kay likes. When'll he be back? Where is he? At the garage? We stopped there, but Pat said he'd went off with a car for some big-timer. I thought p'r'aps he'd stopped off here to take you on a ride er something. Well, I s'pose I'll have to leave a message. Say, Ed, what time we going to start? Eight? Oh, rats! We oughta start at half past seven. It's a good piece out to that Horseheads Inn I was tellin' you 'bout. We'll start at half past seven. Say, you tell your brother to call me up soon's he gets here. He often phones from the drugstore. Tell him I'll give the details. But in case he don't get me, tell him we'll stop by here for him at half past seven. Tell him not to keep us waiting. I gotta go on now 'cause we gotta tell two other people, a girl and a man. It's awful annoying not having telephones everywhere. I don't know what we'd ever do without ours. S'long! Don't forget to tell Kay!" And she flitted down the steps and out the gate to her "man."

Chapter 23

*T*hat awful girl!

Cornelia shut the door and dropped weakly into a chair. Her punishment was come upon her. She might have known she ought not to meddle with a girl like that, inviting her to the house and making her feel free there, setting the seal of family friendship on an intimacy that never ought to have been between her and the son of the house.

And now what should she do? Should she conceal the message and try to get Carey to go somewhere else with her? Or should she tell him the truth and let him choose his own way? She knew beforehand that any kind of remonstrance from her would be vain. Carey was at the age when he liked to feel that he owned himself and took no advice from anybody unless he asked for it. She was enough of a stranger to him yet to realize that she must go slowly and carefully. It is a pity that more of us cannot keep the polite relation of comparative strangers with our own family; it might tend to better things. It is strange that we do not realize this. The fact is, the best-meaning of us often antagonize the ones we love and send them swiftly toward the very thing we are trying to keep them from doing. The wisdom of serpents and the harmlessness of doves are often forgotten in our scheme of living, and loving consideration of one another is a thing far too rare in even Christian homes today.

Cornelia's honest nature always inclined to telling the truth, the whole truth, and nothing but the truth. She would have liked to go to her brother and give the message straight, knowing that he would decline it, but the fact was, she was not at all sure of him. Clytie's manner implied that this sort of thing had been habitual amusement with him. And Cornelia was not at all sure that Clytie's behavior on the night of the party had made any deep impression against her. Carey was young and liked fun. These young people were ready to show him a good time, and what boy of his age could resist that? If she only knew of some way of getting up a counter-attraction! But what would a mild little fudge party or a walk to the park be beside the hilarity offered by Clytie's program?

Moreover, even if she succeeded in getting Carey away from the house before the wild crowd arrived, Clytie would be sure to tell him afterward, and he would blame the sister for not giving the message. She was sure he would do that even if he did not intend to go. And there was Brand! He was invited, too. Of course Carey would go if Brand did. She wildly reviewed the idea of taking Brand into her confidence and rejected it as not only useless but a thing that would be regarded by Carey as a disloyalty to himself. Her perplexity deepened. Then she suddenly remembered her new source of help, and slipping to her knees beside the big chair in which she had been sitting, she prayed about it.

An outsider would think it a strange coincidence, perhaps. It did not seem so to the weary, perplexed sister that even while she knelt and poured out her worries to her heavenly Father, the answer to her prayer should be on the very doorstep. She rose as the bell pealed through the house once more and opening the door found Grace Kendall standing there. She seemed like an angel from heaven, and Cornelia almost wondered whether she shouldn't tell her troubles to this new friend.

"I've come to ask a favor," Grace said eagerly. "And you're to promise first that you will tell me truly if there is any reason why it isn't convenient to grant it. Now do you promise?"

Cornelia laughingly promised, but before the request was made she heard Carey's step at the side door, and a shadow of anxiety came into her eyes. Carey, not knowing of their visitor, came straight into the living room in search of his sister.

"I couldn't get any more cement tonight. Isn't that a shame?" he said before he saw their guest and then came forward, half abashed, to greet her, apologizing for his rough working garb.

"Please don't apologize," said Grace eagerly. "You look fine. You couldn't work in evening clothes, could you? And wait till you hear what I've come to beg you to do. Are you awfully busy this evening, both of you?"

"Not a thing in the world to do," said Carey eagerly. "I'm at your service. What can I do for you? Anything but sing. I really can't sing well enough to go into a choir."

"Well, I don't want you to sing tonight," said Grace, laughing. "Guess again. Now you're *sure* you haven't any engagement?"

"No, indeed, honor bright," he declared, smiling.

"Well, then I'm going to beg you to do a big favor. You see, Father is asked to speak over at Glen Avon tonight, and he has just discovered that they only have two trains a day, and the evening train will get him there too late for the meeting, so he had to hurry around and try to get someone to take him in a car. We have found the car. It belongs to Mr. Williams, and he is just eager to lend it, but he can't drive it himself, because he had to go to New York at five o'clock. He's rather particular about who drives it, and he said if we could get a good, reliable driver, we were welcome to it. Father knew that you were used to cars; he's watched you driving Mr. Barlock's car sometimes, and he wondered if you would be willing to go and drive us. The car is a great big, roomy one, and we can take as many along as want to go. And I thought perhaps you and the children would like to go, too." She turned to Cornelia and then back to Carey. "You're quite sure there isn't any reason at all why it isn't convenient for you?"

"Perfectly," said Carey, with shining eyes. "I'd rather drive than eat any day in the week. And it will be a dandy trip. The roads over there are like velvet. There's going to be a moon tonight, too! Gee! I'm glad you asked me. When do we start?"

"Why, Father has to be there by eight. How long do you think it will take? We must not run any risk of being late. It is some kind of a convention and Father has charge of the hour from eight to nine. We won't have to stay late, you know, and we can ride a while afterward if we like."

"Great!" said Carey. "I'll bring you home by the way of the river. It'll be peachy that way tonight. Say! This is wonderful! I think we ought to start by half past six or quarter to seven. Cornie can you get through dinner by six thirty? That would be safer."

"Oh, surely," said Cornelia eagerly. "We'll have the dinner on the table the minute Father gets in, five minutes to six, and we'll just stand the dishes and run. Won't it be delightful?"

Then suddenly the thought of Clytie Dodd and her party came back with a twinge of horror. Ought she to tell Carey at once?

Grace Kendall was hurrying away with many thanks and happy exclamations of how glad she was she had made up her mind to come. She could not tell it before Grace, anyway, although perhaps

Carey would have thought she ought.

"What's the matter, Nell?" asked her brother as he came in and shut the door. "Don't you want to go? I should think it would be a good rest for you."

"Oh yes, indeed! I want to go, of course, but I just remembered. Perhaps I should have told you before you promised. Clytie Dodd was here—"

"What?" he looked angry and disgusted.

"She wanted you to go to some ride and dance tonight and get Brand to go, too. She wants you to call her up at once."

"Aw! Forget it! She's always got something on the brain. Call her up. I shan't call her up. She's a little fool, anyway."

He looked half ashamed as he said it. He was perfectly aware that his sister must have seen him all dressed up taking her to a movie several weeks ago.

"But—they're going to stop here for you at half past seven."

"Well, let 'em stop! We'll be gone, won't we? She'll have her trouble for her pains, won't she?" He really was speaking in a very rude tone to his sister, but she could see that he was annoyed and mortified to have to talk with her at all on this subject, and the things he said filled her with a triumphant elation.

"But, Carey, oughtn't you to call her up and tell her you have another engagement? Isn't that the right thing, the manly thing, to do?"

"Oh, bother! You don't understand! Let *me* manage this, please. I guess I know my own business. I tell you she's a—fool!"

Carey slammed upstairs to his room, and she could hear him presently in the bathroom stropping his razor and whistling a merry tune. He had forgotten all about Clytie. Cornelia's hand trembled as she slipped the hot apple pie out of the oven and dusted it with powdered sugar. Then she suddenly straightened up and said out loud, "He answered!"

For a moment the little white kitchen seemed a holy place, as if a presence unseen were there, and her whole being was thrilled with the wonder of it. God, the great God, had listened to her troubled cry and sent His angel in the form of the minister's daughter, who had averted the danger. Other people might doubt and sneer at supposed answers to prayer if they knew the circumstances, perhaps call it a coincidence or a "chance" or a "happening," but she *knew*! There was something more than just the fact that the trouble had been averted. There was that strange spiritual consciousness of God answering her, God coming near and communicating with her, as if their eyes had met across the universe, and He had made her certain of His existence, certain of His interest in her and care for her and her affairs.

It was a little thing, an intangible thing, but it glorified her whole life, the day, the moment, and her work. It was real and something she could never forget. She went swiftly about the last details of the evening meal, had everything on the table absolutely on time, even found a moment to run up to her room, smooth her hair, and put on a fresh blouse. Yet through it all, and on through the beautiful evening, it kept ringing back sweetly in her heart. She had a refuge when things grew too hard for her, a God who cared and would help in time of need. She had not thought that faith was given like that, but it had come and made a different thing entirely of living.

They had a wonderful drive, Grace sitting in the front seat with Carey and carrying on a merry conversation, his father and the minister in the backseat, with Louise and Cornelia in the two little middle seats. For the minister had insisted on the whole family going. So for the first time since Cornelia's return from college, the little house was shut up and dark through the whole evening, and now and again Cornelia's thoughts would turn back and wonder what Clytie thought when she arrived with her gang of pleasure seekers.

But the evening was so wonderful, the moonlight so perfect, the company so congenial, that Cornelia found it hard to harbor unpleasant thoughts and for one evening was carefree and happy. Now and then she thought of her little brother riding afar with young Maxwell and wondered what they were talking about and whether they would all know him any better when he got back with Harry. It was always so revealing to have a member of one's family get really close to everyday living with a person. Then her thoughts would come back to the drifting talk from Grace and Carey in front, and she thought how handsome her brother looked and how at ease driving the car and talking to this sweet, cultured girl. She remembered his accents when he called Clytie Dodd a fool so vehemently and compared them with his face as he walked on Chestnut Street, chewing gum and looking down attentively to his overdressed, ill-behaved companion. Which was the real Carey? And do we all have two people shut up inside ourselves? Or is one the real self and the other a mask?

The service, which they attended for an hour, was intensely interesting and quite new to Cornelia. She had never seen anything like it before. It was a "conference." Nobody said for what, and she did not happen to get hold of a program until they were leaving. Mr. Kendall at the desk seemed like a father among his children, or close friend of them all, and he led their thoughts to the heavenly Father in a most wonderful way, speaking of Him as if He were present always with each one, ready to help in any need, ready to conquer for them. And the thought he left with them at the close of his ten-minute talk was drawn from the verse "My grace is sufficient for thee: for my strength is made perfect in weakness."

Cornelia listened in wonder, and instantly to her mind sprang once more her own experience of the afternoon and a conviction that she was being watched and guarded and led and *loved* by an unseen Power. This sense of God had never come to her before. Religion had been a dreamy, mysterious necessity, the wholly respectable and conventional thing to believe in, of course, and a kind of comfortable assurance for the darkness of the beyond. She had never had any particular tendency to the modern doubts. Her mother's faith and her father's living had been too real for that. And always, when a teacher had voiced some skeptical flippancy, she had turned away with an inner conviction that the teacher did not know, because there was her mother and a feeling that she preferred to stick to the faith of her forefathers. But as far as concerned any particular reason for doing so, or any particular conviction on her own part, she was absolutely without them.

But now suddenly she saw and felt something that had never come to her realization before. She felt as firmly assured of all the vital truths she had been taught as if some mystic curtain had suddenly been rolled back and revealed to her things hidden from mortal eye. She remembered somewhere in the Bible there was a verse, one of her mother's favorites, "He that believeth on the Son of God hath the witness in himself." Was this possibly what it meant? Was "the witness" coming to her because she had put her childhood belief to the test?

She came out of the church with a firm resolve to begin to study her Bible and find out more about this wonderful spirit world that was all about her, and by which perhaps she was guided through her life much more than she had ever dreamed. Her feeling that God was somewhere close and taking personal notice of her and her interests was so strong that she could not ignore it, and yet she regarded it almost shyly, like a bird that has quietly alighted on one's hand and might be frightened away. She did not dare to touch it and lay hold on its wonder firmly, lest it should prove to be a figment of her imagination, but it gave her a deep, new joy for which she found no name. Could it be that she had found Christ? She had heard her mother speak of "finding Christ" and had never had much idea of what it could be. Now a deep conviction grew in her that she was experiencing it herself.

The ride home was one of wondrous beauty, and there was a serene happiness in each heart that made it seem a most unusual occasion, one to look back upon with a thrill of pleasure for many a day. Even Louise seemed to feel it. She nestled close to her sister and watched with wide, happy eyes the fleeting starry darkness, and drew long breaths of spring and ferny sweetness as they passed through some wooded road, and every little while would whisper, "Aren't we having just a wonderful time, Nellie, dear? I wonder if it's as pretty where Harry is now. I wonder if they've stopped for the night yet."

The minister and Mr. Copley were on the two middle seats now, having a deep discussion about whether the world was growing better or worse, and Cornelia was on the backseat with her little sister. The evening seemed like an oasis in the great desert of hard work and worry through which she had been passing for the last few weeks. Just to see Carey there in the front seat talking and smiling to Grace was enough to rest her heart. If she could have heard the earnest little talk about real Christian living they were having, she would have been filled with wonder and awe. Carey talking religion with a young girl! How unbelievable it would have seemed to her! But the purr of the engine sheltered the quiet sentences, and Grace and Carey talked on deep into the heart of life and the simplicity of the Gospel, and Carey expressed shy thoughts that he never would have dreamed before of letting even the angels of heaven guess. His living hadn't always been in accordance with such thoughts or beliefs, but they were there all the time, and this girl, who was a real Christian herself, had called them forth. Perhaps the spirit of the remarkable meeting that they had just attended had helped to make it a fitting time and prepared their minds so that it came about quite naturally. Grace was no insistent evangelist, flinging her message out and demanding an answer. She breathed the fragrance of Christianity in her smile, and her words came involuntarily from a heart that thought much "on these things."

The immediate result of the talk became apparent as they were getting out of the car at the minister's house. Carey was to drive his own people on to their home and then put the car in its garage, two blocks farther up the hill.

As Grace turned to say, "Good night," Carey leaned out and asked, "What time did you say that Christian Endeavor met?"

"Oh yes, seven o'clock!" said the girl eagerly, not at all as if it were a doubtful question whether the young man would come or not. "And don't forget the choir rehearsal. That is Friday evening at our house, you know."

"I'll be there!" said Carey graciously.

Cornelia, too astonished for words that Carey was arranging for all these church functions, easily yielded to the request, and they parted for the night, the sister with a singing in her heart that her brother was getting to be friends with a girl like the minister's daughter. Now surely, surely, he would stop going with the girls like Clytie Dodd. Probably that girl would be offended at the way she had been left without even an apology and would drop Carey now. She sat back with a sigh of relief and dismissed this one burden from her young heart. Could she have known what plots were at that very moment revolving in the vengeful girl's mind and being suggested to her hilarious and willing group of companions amid shouts of laughter, she would not have rested her soul so easily nor enjoyed the wonderful moonlight that glorified even the mean little street where she lived. The devil is not idle when angels throng most around, and Cornelia had yet to learn that a single victory is not a whole battle won. But perhaps if she had known, she would not have had the courage and faith to go forward, and it is well that the step ahead is always just out of sight.

Chapter 24

$\mathcal{F}$or three long, beautiful weeks Cornelia enjoyed her calm, and hope climbed high.

The stone columns of the pretty front porch grew rapidly and began to take on comeliness. Brand endeared himself to them all by his cheerful, steady, patient aid, coming every afternoon attired in overalls and working hard till dark, getting his white hands callous and dirty, cut with the stones, and hard as nails. Once Cornelia had to tie an ugly cut he got when a stone fell on his hand, and he looked at her lovingly and thanked her just like a child. From that time forth she gathered him into her heart with her brothers and sister and began genuinely to like him and be anxious for his welfare. It seemed that his mother and sister were society people and made little over him at home. He had his own companions and went his own way without consulting them, and although he must have had a wonderful mansion of a home, he seemed much to prefer the little cozy house of the Copley's and spent many evenings there as well as days. He seemed to be as much interested in getting the stone porch done as Carey himself, and he often worked away alone when Carey felt he must stay at the garage awhile to get money enough for more stone or more cement and sand. Once or twice Cornelia suspected, from a few words she gathered as the boys were arguing outside the window, that Brand had offered to supply the needed funds rather than have Carey leave to earn them, but she recognized proudly that Carey always declined emphatically such financial assistance.

Now and then Brand would order Carey to "doll up" and would whirl him away in his car to see a man somewhere with the hope of a position, but as yet nothing had come of these various expeditions, although Carey was always hopeful and kept telling about a new "lead," as he called it, with the same joyous assurance of youth.

Brand, too, had been drawn into the young people's choir and took a sudden interest in Sunday night church. Once he went with Cornelia and found the place in the hymnbook for her and sang lustily at her side. The next Sunday he was sitting up in the choir loft beside Carey and acting as if he were one of the chief pillars in that church. It was wonderful how eagerly he grasped a thing that caught his interest. He had a wild, carefree, loving nature and bubbled over with life and recklessness, but he was easily led if anybody chose to give him a little fellowship. It seemed that he led a starved life so far as loving care was concerned, and he accepted eagerly any little favor done for him. Cornelia soon found that he grew pleasantly into the little family group, and even the children accepted and loved him and often depended upon him.

Arthur Maxwell, too, had become an intimate friend of the family circle, and since Harry had come back from his trip to the mountains, he could talk of nothing else but "Mr. Maxwell says this and Mr. Maxwell does that," till the family began gently to poke fun at him about it. Nevertheless, they were well pleased that they had such a friend. He came down one day and took

Cornelia off for the whole afternoon on a wonderful drive in the country. They brought back a great basket of fruit and armfuls of wildflowers and vines. Another day he took her to a nursery where they selected some vines for the front porch, some climbing roses and young hedge plants, which he proceeded to set out for her on their return. Then next day a big box of chocolates was delivered at the door with his card.

But his mother had not been out for her promised visit yet, for she had been called away on a business trip to California the day after she reached home and had decided to remain with her relatives there for a month or six weeks. Cornelia, as she daily beautified her pretty home, kept wondering what Mrs. Maxwell would say to it when she did come. But most of all she wondered about her own mother and what she would say to the glorified old house when she got back to it again.

Great news had been coming from the hospital where the mother was getting well. The nurse said that she grew decidedly better from the day the letter arrived telling how Carey was singing in the church choir and going to Christian Endeavor and building a front porch. The nurse's letter did not show that she laid any greater stress on any one of these occupations than on the others, but Cornelia knew that her mother's heart was rejoicing that the boy had found a place in the church of God where he was interested enough to go to work. In her very next letter she told about the minister's people and described Grace Kendall, telling of Carey's friendship with her. Again the nurse wrote how much good that letter had done the mother, so that she sat up for quite a little while that day without feeling any ill effects from it. Cornelia began to wonder whether Clytie had been at the bottom of some of her mother's trouble and to congratulate herself on the fact that Clytie had been overcome at last.

About this time Maxwell arrived one evening while Carey was putting the finishing touches to the front porch, and instead of coming in as was his custom, he sat down on a pile of floorboards and talked with Carey.

Cornelia, hearing low, earnest voices, stepped quietly to the window and looked out, wondering to see Maxwell talking so earnestly with her brother. She felt proud that the older young man was interested enough in him to linger and talk and wondered whether it might be politics or the last baseball score that was absorbing them. Then she heard Maxwell say, "You'll be there at eight tomorrow morning, will you? He wants to talk with you in his private office before the rush of the day begins."

In a moment more, Maxwell came into the house, bringing with him a great box of gorgeous roses, and in her joy over the roses, arranging them in vases, she forgot to wonder what Maxwell and her brother had been talking about. He might have told her, perhaps, but they were interrupted almost immediately, much to her disappointment, by callers. First, the carpenter next door ran in to say he was building a bungalow in a new suburb for a bride and groom, and the man wanted to furnish the house throughout before he brought his wife home, to surprise her. The bride didn't know he was building but thought they would have to board for a while, and he wanted everything pretty and shipshape for her before she came, so they could go right in and begin to live. He didn't have a lot of money for furnishing, and the carpenter had found out about it and told him about Cornelia. Would she undertake the job on a percentage basis, taking for selecting the things ten percent, say, on what they cost, and charging her usual prices for any work she had to do?

Cornelia at the door facing out into the starlight, flushed with pleasure over the new business opportunity and made arrangements in a happy tone to meet the new householder the next morning, talk plans over with him, and find out what he wanted. The young man in the living room, waiting for her, pretending to turn over the pages of a magazine that lay on the table, was furtively watching her all the while and thinking how fine she was, how enterprising and successful, and yet how sweet! How right his mother had been! He smiled to himself to think how nearly always right his mother was, anyhow, and wondered again, as he had done before, whether his mother had a hidden reason for sending him out with those ferns that first night.

Cornelia returned in a flutter of pleasure and was scarcely seated when there came another summons to the door, and there stood the minister's wife. She came in and met Maxwell, and they had a pleasant little chat. Then Mrs. Kendall revealed her errand. She wanted Cornelia to give a series of talks on what she called "The House Beautiful and Convenient" to the Ladies' Aid Society in the church. She had the course all outlined suggestively, with a place for all the questions that come up in making a house comfortable and attractive, and she wanted Cornelia to keep in mind that many in her audience would be people in very limited circumstances with very little money or time or material at hand to use in making their homes lovely. She said there were many people in their church neighborhood who would be attracted by such a course to come to the church gatherings, and she wanted Cornelia to help. The Ladies' Aid had voted to pay five dollars a lesson for such a course of talks as this and had instructed her to secure someone for it at once, and she knew of no one so well fitted as Cornelia. Would Cornelia consider it for the trifle they could afford to pay? They were going to charge the women twenty-five cents a lesson and hoped to make a little money on the enterprise for the Ladies' Aid. Of course, the pay was small, but with her experience the work ought not to take much time, and she could have the added reward of knowing she was doing a lot of good and probably brightening a lot of homes. Also it would bring her opportunities for other openings of the sort.

"I just wish they could all see this lovely house from top to bottom," she said as she looked around. "It would do them a world of good."

"Why, they could," said Cornelia, smiling. "I suppose I could clear it all up and let them go over it, if you think that would help any. I'd love to do the work if you think I'm able. I never talked in public in my life. I'm not sure I can."

"Oh, this isn't talking in public," said the minister's wife eagerly. "This is just telling people that don't know how, how to do things that you have done yourself. I'm sure you have that gift. I've listened to you talking, and you're wonderfully interesting. But would you consider giving a reception and letting them see how you have made your house lovely? That would be a wonderful addition, and I'm sure the ladies would be delighted to pay extra for that. And we'd all come over and help you clear up afterward, and before, too, if you would let us, although I'm sure you always look in immaculate order for a reception or anything else every time I've ever been here."

When the matter was finally arranged and Mrs. Kendall had left, Carey came in, scrubbed, shaved, neatly attired, and proposed that they have a sing. Maxwell joined in eagerly and sang with all his splendid voice. Then after a time he asked Cornelia to play, and before they realized it, the evening was over. Not until Carey said in his usual way, "Call me at quarter to seven, will you, Nell? And turn on the hot water when you get down; that's a dear," did Cornelia remember her curiosity concerning the conversation between her brother and Maxwell. Carey said nothing about it, and Cornelia was enough of a wise woman not to ask.

But Carey told her the next morning. He was so excited he couldn't keep it to himself.

"Didn't know I was going to be a salesman up at Braithwaite's, did you?" he said quite casually between mouthfuls of breakfast.

Harry paused in his chewing a second and eyed him skeptically.

"Yes, you are *not!*" he remarked scornfully, and went on chewing again.

But Cornelia, eager-eyed, leaned forward. "What do you mean, Carey? Is that a fact?"

"Well, just about," said Carey, enjoying their bewilderment. "Maxwell told me the manager wants to see me this morning. Says he's had his eye on me for three months, been looking up everything about me, and when that picture came out in the paper, he told Maxwell he guessed I'd do. Said they wanted a man that could jump into a situation like that and handle it, a man with nerve, you know, that had his wits about him. It's up to me now to make good. If I do, I get the job all right. It isn't great pay to start, only thirty bucks a week, but it's all kinds of prospects ahead if I make good. Well, so long. Wish me luck." And Carey flung out of the house amid the delighted exclamations of his astonished family.

"Oh God, You have been good to us!" breathed Cornelia's happy soul as she stood by the window, watching Carey's broad shoulders and upright carriage as he hurried down the street to the car. Carey was happy. It fairly radiated even from his back, and he walked as if on air. Cornelia was so glad she could have shouted "Hallelujah!" Now, if he really got this position—and it looked reasonably sure—he was established in a good and promising way, and the family could stop worrying about him.

What a wonderful young man Maxwell was to take all that

trouble for practically a stranger! Her eyes grew dreamy, and her lips softened into a smile as she went over every detail of the evening before, remembering the snatches of talk she had caught and piecing them out with new meaning. She leaned over and laid her face softly among the roses he had brought and drew in a long, sweet breath of their fragrance. And he had been doing this for them all the time and not said a word, lest nothing would come of it. As she thought about it now, she believed he had had the thought about doing something for Carey that first night when he came so unexpectedly to dinner, that dreadful dinner party! How far away and impossible it all seemed now! That terrible girl! What a fool she had been to think it necessary to invite anyone like that to the house! If she had just let things go on and take their natural course, Maxwell would have dropped in that night, and they would have had a pleasant time, and all would have been as it was at present, without the mortification of that memory. Carey with his new ambitions and hopes would surely never now disgrace himself by going again with a girl like that. It had been an unnecessary crucifixion for the whole family.

Yet they never would have known how splendid Maxwell could be in a trying time without her, perhaps. There was always something comforting somewhere. Still, she would like to be rid of the memory of that evening. It brought shame to her cheeks even yet to remember the loud, nasal twang of the cheap voice, the floury face, the low-cut, tight little gown, the air of abandon! Oh! It was awful!

Then her mind went back to the day she returned from college and to the sweet-faced, low-voiced woman who was the mother of this new friend. It hardly seemed as if the two belonged to the same world. What would she think if she ever heard of Clytie? Would the young man ever quite forget her and wipe the memory from his mind so completely that it would never return to shadow those first days of their acquaintance?

Carey returned early in the afternoon with an elastic step and a light of triumph in his face. He had been employed as a salesman in one of the largest firms in the country, a business dealing with tools and machinery and requiring a wide grasp of various engineering branches. He was just in his element. He had been born with the instinct for machinery and mechanics. He loved everything connected with them. Also he was a leader and natural mixer among men. All these things Maxwell later told Cornelia had counted in his favor. The fact that he was not a college man had been the only drawback, but after the accident, and after the manager had had a long, searching talk with him, it had been decided that Carey had natural adaptability and hereditary culture enough to overcome that lack, and they voted to try him. The manager felt that there was good material in him. Maxwell did not tell Cornelia that what he had told the manager concerning her ability and initiative had had much to do with influencing the decision. The manager was a sharp man. He knew a live family when he saw it, and when he heard what Cornelia had accomplished in her little home, he was eager to see the brother. He felt that he also might be a genius! Now if Carey could only make good!

Chapter 25

$\mathcal{I}$t was a wonderful day of June skies and roses. Maxwell had sent a note by special messenger to Cornelia to say that two world tennis champions were to play at the Cricket Club grounds that afternoon and would she like to go? If so, he would call for her at two o'clock.

So Cornelia had baked macaroni and cheese, roasted some apples, and made a chocolate cornstarch pudding. There was cold meat in the refrigerator, and she wrote a note to Louise in case she should be late.

She looked very pretty and slim in her dark blue crêpe de chine dress made over with little pockets to cover where it had to be pieced. She resurrected an old dark blue hat with an attractive brim, re-dyed it, and wreathed it with a row of little pale pink velvet roses. Nobody would ever have guessed that the roses were old ones that had been cleaned and retouched with the paintbrush till they glowed like new ones. She added a string of peculiar Chinese beads that one of the girls at college had given her and looked as chic and pretty as any girl could desire when Maxwell called for her. His eyes showed their admiration as he came up the steps and found her ready, waiting for him, her cheeks flushed a pretty pink, her eyes starry, and little rings of brown hair blowing out here and there about her face.

"That's a nice hat," he said contentedly, his eyes taking in her whole harmonious outfit. "New one, isn't it? At least, I never saw it before." He noted with pleasure that her complexion was not applied.

"A real girl!" he was saying to himself in a kind of inner triumph! "A *real* girl! What a fool I used to be!"

The day was wonderful, and there was a big box of chocolates in the car. Cornelia, listening to her happy heart, found it singing.

They made long strides in friendship as they drove through the city and out to the Cricket Club grounds, and Cornelia's cheeks grew pinker with joy. It seemed as though life were very good indeed to her today.

They drove the car into the grounds, found a good place to park it, and were just about to go to their seats on the grandstand when a young, gimlet-eyed flapper with bobbed hair rushed up crying, "Oh, Arthur Maxwell, won't you please go over to the gym dressing rooms and find Tommy Fergus for me? He promised to meet me here half an hour ago, and I'm nearly dead standing in this sun. I'd go in and sit down, but he has the tickets, and he promised on his honor not to be late. I knew it would be just like this if he tried to play a set before the tournament."

There was nothing for Maxwell to do but introduce the curious-eyed maiden to Cornelia and go on the mission, and the young woman climbed up beside Cornelia and began to chatter.

It appeared that her name was Dotty Chapman, that she was a sort of cousin of Maxwell's, and that she knew everybody and everything that had to do with the Cricket Club. She chattered on like a magpie, telling Cornelia who all the people were that by this time were coming in a stream through the arched gateway. Cornelia found it rather interesting.

"That's Senator Brown's daughter. She won the blue ribbon at the Horse Show last winter. That's her brother—no, not the fat one, the man on the right. He's the famous polo player. And that's Harry Garlow, yes, the tall one. He's a *nut*! You'd die laughing to hear him. There, that girl's the woman champion in tennis this year, and the man with her is Mrs. Carter Rounds' first husband, you remember. They say he's gone on another woman now. There goes Jason Casper's fiancée. Isn't she ugly? I don't see what he sees in her, but she's got stacks of money, so I suppose he doesn't care. Say, do you know Arthur Maxwell's fiancée? I'm dying to meet her. They say she is *simply stunning*. I saw her in the distance dancing at the Roof Garden the other night, but it was only for a second. Somebody pointed her out, I'm not sure I'd know her. They say she is very foreign in her appearance. Have you met her yet? Isn't that her now, just getting out of that big blue car with Bob Channing? I believe it is. Look! Did you ever see such a slim figure? And that dress is darling. They say all her clothes come from abroad and are designed especially for her. The engagement isn't announced yet, you know, but it will be I suppose as soon as Mrs. Maxwell gets home again. Miss Chantry doesn't wish it spoken of even among her most intimate friends until then; she doesn't think it is courteous to her future mother-in-law, that's why she goes around with other men so much. She told my cousin Lucia so. But everybody knows it, of course. You, I suppose you know all about it, too? There he comes! They're going to meet! I wonder how they'll act. Isn't it thrilling. My goodness! Don't they carry it off well; he's hardly stopping to speak. I don't believe she likes it. I wouldn't, would you? Isn't that white crêpe with the scarlet trimmings just entering? But where on earth is Tommy?

He didn't bring him. Oh—why *Tommy*! Is that you? Where on earth have you been? Didn't Mr. Maxwell find you? He's been after you; there he is coming now! What made you keep me waiting so long? I've stood here an hour and simply cooked! What? You meant the *other* gate? Well, what's the difference? Why didn't you say so? Oh, well, don't fuss so, let's go find our seats. What? Oh yes, this is Miss—*Cope*, did you say? Copley? Oh yes! Miss Copley, Mr. Fergus. Thank you so much, Cousin Arthur. Good-bye."

She was gone, vanishing behind the neighboring grandstand, but so was the glory of the day.

Cornelia's face looked strangely white and tired as Maxwell helped her down, and she found her feet unsteady as she walked beside him silently to their seats. There was something strange, the matter with her heart. It kept stopping suddenly and then turning over with a jerk. The sun seemed to have darkened about her, and her feet seemed weighted.

"That girl is a perfect pest," he said frowning, as he helped Cornelia to her seat. "I was just afraid she was going to wish herself on us for the afternoon. She has a habit of doing that, and I didn't mean to have it this time. I was prepared to hire a substitute for the lost Tommy if he didn't materialize. Her mother is a second or third cousin of my grandmother's aunt or something like that, and she is always asking favors."

Cornelia tried to smile and murmur something pleasant, but her lips seemed stiff, and when she looked up she noticed that he was hurriedly scanning the benches on the other side of the rectangle. Following his glance her eyes caught a glimpse of white set off by vivid scarlet. Ah! Then it was true! Her sinking heart put her to sudden shame and revealed herself to herself.

This then had been the secret of her great happiness and of the brightness of the day. She had been presuming on the kindness of this stranger and actually jumping to the conclusion that he was paying her special attention. What folly had been hers! How she had always despised girls who gave their hearts before they were asked, who took too much for granted from a few pleasant little attentions.

Mr. Maxwell had done nothing that any gentleman might not have done for a casual friend of his mother's. When she began to sift the past few weeks in her thoughts, his attentions had mainly been spent on her brothers. A few roses, and this invitation this afternoon. Nothing that any sensible girl would think a thing of. She was a fool, that was all there was of it, an everlasting fool, and now she must rouse herself somehow from this ghastly sinking feeling that had come over her and keep him from reading her very thoughts. He must never suspect her unwomanliness. He must never know how she had misconstrued his kindness. Oh, if she could only get away into the cool and dark for a minute and lie down and close her eyes, she could get hold of herself. But that was out of the question. She must sit here and smile in the sun with the gleam of scarlet across the courts and never, never let him suspect. He was all right, of course he was, all right and fine, and he doubtless thought that she, too, knew all about his fiancée, only he could not speak about it now because the lady had placed her commands upon him for his mother's sake. How nice to honor his mother!

A breath of a sigh escaped her, and she straightened up and tried to look bright and interesting.

"You *are* tired!" he said, turning to look into her eyes. "I don't believe this is going to be a restful thing for you at all. Wouldn't you rather get out of here and just take a ride or something—in the park, perhaps?"

"Oh no *indeed*!" said Cornelia quickly sitting up very straight and trying to shake off the effects of the shock she had suffered. "I've always wanted to see a great tournament, and I've never had the opportunity. Now, tell me all the things I need to know, please, to be an intelligent witness."

He began telling her about the two world-famous men who were to play, about their good points and their week ones, and to give a scientific account on certain kinds of services and returns. And she gave strict attention and asked intelligent questions and was getting on very well, keeping her own private thoughts utterly in the background, when suddenly he said, "Do you see that lady in white just directly opposite us? White with scarlet trimmings. I wish you would look at her a moment. Here, take the binoculars. Sometime I am going to tell you about her."

Cornelia tried to steady her hand as she adjusted the binoculars to her eyes and to steady her lips for a question. "Is she—a—*friend?*"

"I hardly think you'd call it that—*anymore!*" he answered in a curiously hard tone. But Cornelia was too preoccupied to notice.

"Shall we—meet her?" she asked after studying the exquisite doll face across the distance and wondering if it really were as wonderfully perfect up close. Wondering, too, why she seemed to suddenly feel disappointed in the man beside her if this was his choice of a wife.

"I think *not*," he said decidedly, and then a sudden clapping arose, growing, like a swift-moving shower. "There, there they are! The players. That's the Englishman, that big chap; and this man, this is our man. See how supple he is. He has a great reach. Watch him now."

After that there was no more opportunity to talk personalities and Cornelia was glad that she could just sit still and watch, although with her preoccupied mind she might as well have been at home cooking dinner for all she knew about that tournament. The players came and went like little puppets in a show, the ball flew back and forth, and games and sets were played, but she knew no more about it than if she had not been there. Now and then her eyes furtively stole a glance across the way at the scarlet line on the white.

Maxwell had glanced at her curiously several times. Her attitude was one of deep attention. She smiled just as pleasantly when he spoke, but somehow her voice had lost the spring out of it, and he could not help thinking she was weary.

"Let's get out of here before the crowd begins to push," he whispered, as the last set was finished and the antagonists shook hands under fire of the heavy rounds of applause.

He guided her out to the car so quickly that they almost escaped the rush, but just within a few paces of the car they came suddenly upon the voluble Dotty and her escort.

"Oh, Cousin Artie!" cried Dotty eagerly. "I've just been telling Tommy that I knew you would take us over to Overbrook if we could catch you in time. You see, we both have a dinner engagement out to Aunt Myra's, and we've missed the only train that would get us there in time. You won't mind, will you, Miss Cope, Copley, I mean? It isn't far, and you know how cross Aunt Myra gets when any of us are late to an engagement with her, don't you, Artie?"

"Not at all!" answered Cornelia coolly as soon as there was opportunity to speak. "My home is right on the way."

Maxwell accepted the situation with what grace he could. Dotty climbed into the front seat when he opened the door for Cornelia.

"You can sit back there with Miss Copley, Tommy," she laughed back at the other two. "I choose front seat. I just *love* to watch Cousin Arthur drive."

Arthur Maxwell scarcely spoke a word during the whole drive, and Cousin Dotty chattered on in an uninterrupted flow of nothings. Cornelia found herself discussing the game and various plays with a technique newly acquired and being thankful that she did not have to ride alone with Maxwell—not now—not until she had gotten herself in hand. It was all right, of course, and he was perfectly splendid, but she had been a silly little fool, and she had to get things set straight again before she cared to meet him as a friend. Oh, it would be all right, she assured herself minute by minute, only she must just get used to it. She hadn't at all realized how she had been thinking of him, and she was glad that the romance of this afternoon had been destroyed, so that she would not find herself in future weakness lingering over any pleasant phrases or little nothings that would link her soul to disappointment. She wanted to be just plain, matter of fact. A respectable girl going out for an afternoon with a respectable man who was soon to be married to another woman who understood all about it. There was nothing whatever the matter with that situation, and that was the way she must look at it, of course. She must get used to it and gradually make her family understand, too. Not that they had thought anything else yet—of course, but it would be well for them to understand from the start that there was no nonsense about her friendship with Maxwell and that they need not appropriate him in such wholesome manner as they had begun to do. She was a businesswoman, meant to be a businesswoman all her life, and she would probably have lots of nice friendships like this one.

Thus she reasoned in undertone with herself, while she discussed tennis with the bored Tommy and came finally to her own door realizing suddenly that Arthur Maxwell would perhaps not care to have his elegant cousin know from what lowly neighborhoods he selected his friends. But she held her head high as she stood on the pavement to bid them good-bye, and not by the quiver of an eyelash on her flushed cheek did she let them see that she did not like her surroundings.

Arthur Maxwell stepped up to the door with her in spite of his cousin's irritated protest, "Artie, we'll be *late* to Aunt Myra's," and said in a low tone, "This whole afternoon has been spoiled by that poor little idiot, but I'm going to make up for it soon, see if I don't. I'm sorry I have a director's meeting this evening or I'd ask if I might return to dinner, but I'm going to be late as it is when I get those two poor fools to their destination, so I'll have to forego, but suppose I come over Sunday evening and go to church with you? May I? Then afterward, perhaps we'll have a little chance to talk."

Cornelia smiled and assented and hurried up to dash cold water over her hot cheeks and burning eyes and then down to the kitchen where Louise was bustling happily about putting the final touches to the evening meal.

"Oh, Nellie!" she greeted her sister. "Have you got back already? I thought perhaps he'd take you somewhere to dinner. They do, you know. I've read about it. But wasn't he *lovely* to take you to that game. All the boys at school were talking about it, and one of the girls had a ticket to go with her brother. I think it was just *wonderful*. I'm so *glad* you had that nice time! You are so *dear*! Now tell me about it."

And Cornelia told all she could remember about the day and the ride and the wonderful game, told things she had not known she noticed by the wayside, told about Dotty and Tommy, and even gave a hint of a wonderful friend of Mr. Maxwell's who wore a white, soft, silk dress lined with scarlet and carried a gold mesh bag, till Louise's eyes grew large with wonder, though she looked a little grave when she heard about the lady. Cornelia hid her heavy heart under smiles and words and was merrier than usual and very, very tired when she crept at last to bed, where she might not even weep, lest the little sister should know the secret of her foolish heart.

Saturday morning dawned with all its burden and responsibility, a new day full of new cares and the gladness of yesterday gone into graver tints. But Cornelia would not admit to herself that she was unhappy. There was work to do, and she would immerse herself in it and forget. There was no need being a fool always, after one had found out one was. And anyway, she meant to live for her family—her dear family!

Chapter 26

Cornelia had had a brief space of anxiety, lest her brother should begin to feel his own importance and perhaps offend his boss in being entirely too smart in his own conceit. But it soon became apparent that the boss was a big enough man to have impressed Carey and made him a devoted servant. He kept quoting what he said with awe and reverence and showing great delight at being admitted to the inner sanctum and entrusted with important affairs.

Carey was to begin his new work on Monday morning, and all Saturday as he went about doing various little things—pressing his trousers, picking up his laundry, getting his affairs in order to leave all day as other businessmen had to do every day—he kept dropping into the room where his sister was at work on some pretty dresses for Louise and telling with a light in his eyes and a ring of pleasure in his voice what "the boss" had said or done, or how the office was furnished, and how many salesmen and secretaries there were. And he could not say enough about Maxwell.

"That fellow's a prince!" he exclaimed. "D'ye know it? A perfect prince of a man. He might have run in any number of friends, old friends, you know, instead of mentioning me. I can't make out what made him. The boss took me out to lunch with him today at a swell restaurant. Gee! It was great! Lobster salad, café parfait, and all that! Some lunch! Took the best part of a ten-dollar bill to pay for it, too. Oh, boy! It was great! Think of *me*! And he told me how much Maxwell thought of me and how he believed I'd bear it out, and all that. He talked a lot about personal appearance and a pleasant manner and keeping my temper and that line, you know. Gee! It's going to be hard, but it's going to be great. He told me that it was up to me how high I climbed. There wasn't any limit practically if I stuck it out and made good. And believe me, I'm going to stick. I like that guy, and I like the business. Say, Nell, do you think this necktie would clean? I always liked this necktie. And whaddaya think? I've got to wear hard collars. Fierce, isn't it? But I guess I can get used to 'em. Say, where's that old silk shirt of mine? I wonder if you could mend a tear in the sleeve. I'll have to keep dolled up in nice clothes a lot now, and I have to get everything in shape. Imagine it. I've got to take big guys out to lunch myself sometimes and show them the ropes, and all that. Gee! Isn't it wonderful?"

So Cornelia laid aside the rose-colored gingham and the blue-flowered muslin she was making for Louise and mended shirts, ironed neckties, and helped press coats, until Carey expressed himself as altogether pleased with his outfit, and joy bubbled over in the house. That night and all the next day their hearts seemed so light that they were in danger of having their feet lifted off the ground with the joy of it.

Brand came over after lunch as usual and heard the news. He looked a bit sober over it, although he congratulated his friend warmly. But once or twice Cornelia caught him looking wistfully at Carey, as if somehow he had suddenly grown away from him, and she realized that it was the first break in their boyhood life. For Carey was a new Carey since the morning, walking with a spring in his step, giving a command in the tone of one who had authority, making a decision as one who had long been accustomed to being recognized as having a right. He had in a single morning become a man and seemed for the time to have put away childish things. He even declined to take a ride with Brand after dinner, to which Brand had stayed, saying that he had promised to run over to the Kendalls after dinner and try over the music for tomorrow. Ordinarily Brand would have gone along without even being asked, but there was about Carey such a manner of masterfulness and of being aloof and having grave matters to attend to, that the boy hesitated with a wistful, puzzled look; and when Cornelia, half sensing his feeling, said, "Well, Brand, you stay here with me, and we'll go over that music, too," he laughed happily and sat down again, letting Carey go out by himself.

It was altogether plain that Carey didn't even see it. Carey was exalted. His head was in the clouds, and a happy smile played over his face continually.

Brand stayed all the evening till Carey came back at half past ten, still with that happy, exalted smile on his face. And then Brand, with an amused, almost hopeless expression, laughingly bade good night to Cornelia, telling her he'd had "a peach of a time." Just as he was going out the door, he looked back and said soberly, "I might have a job myself next week. Dad wants me to come in the office with him this summer, and I believe I will." Then he went away without any of the usual racket and showing off of his noisy car.

Carey's new dignity carried him to church the next morning and to a special Children's Day service in the afternoon, where he had been asked to usher, and joy still sat on his face when he returned at four o'clock and lolled around the living room, restless and talking of the morrow, now and then telling some trifling incident of the afternoon, humming over a tune that had been sung, and finally asking Cornelia to play and sing with him the music for the evening. It was altogether so unusual to have Carey at home like this all day Sunday and seeming to be happy in it, that Cornelia was excitedly happy herself, and every little while Louise would look at him joyously and say, "Oh Carey, you look so nice in that new suit!"

It was like a regular love feast, and Cornelia began to tell her anxious heart that Carey really was started on the right way. There was no further need to worry about him at all. Perhaps there hadn't ever been. Perhaps it was all only because he hadn't had the right kind of job.

It was just six o'clock. The Copleys had elected to have their Sunday night supper after the evening service, and to that end Cornelia had prepared delectable lettuce, cheese, and date sandwiches and had wrapped them in a damp cloth in the icebox to be ready. There was a fruit salad all ready also, and a maple cake. It would take but a few minutes to make a pot of chocolate, and they would eat around the fire in the living room. Maxwell had promised to come early and go to church with them. Cornelia rather dreaded the ordeal, for she felt sure that Maxwell meant to tell her about the crimson lady. Well, she might as well get it over at once and have him understand that she knew exactly where she stood.

She had gone upstairs to dress and left Carey lying on the couch, looking into the fire, dreamily listening to Louise and Harry playing hymn tunes as duets. She planned to write a letter to her mother early the next morning, giving her a picture of their beautiful Sunday and telling the news about Carey. She was flying around getting dressed for the evening when she heard a car come up to the front and stop. It came quietly, almost stealthily, so it could not be Brand. Could it be that Arthur Maxwell had arrived so soon? She tiptoed into her father's room to look out of the window. If it was Maxwell, she must hurry and go downstairs.

The car was a shabby old affair with a rakish air, and she could not see the face of the man who sat in the driver's seat. A small boy was coming in the gate with a letter in his hand, which he pulled from his pocket, looking up at the house apprehensively. There was something familiar about the slouch of the boy and about the limpness of his unkempt hair as he dragged his cap off and knocked at the door, but she could not place it.

A vague, unnamed apprehension seized her, and her fingers flew fast among the long strands of soft hair, putting them quickly into shape so that she might go down and see what was the matter. Two or three hairpins, which had been in her hand as she hurried to the window, she stuck in anywhere to hold the coils. She hurried to her room, seized her dress, began to slip it on, and flew back to the post of observation at the window. She heard Carey get up and open the door, and she strained to hear what the boy said but could not make out anything but a low mutter. Carey was reading the note. What could it be? Clytie? Oh!

Her heart gave a great leap of terror. It was almost time for Christian Endeavor! But surely, *surely*, Carey would not pay any heed to that girl now. With all the new ambitions and opportunities opening before him!

Carey had made an exclamation and was following the boy rapidly out to the car. Oh! What could he be going to do?

Cornelia fastened the last snap of her dress and fairly flew downstairs, but when she reached the door the car was driving madly off up the hill, and Carey was nowhere in sight. The children were still playing duets and had not noticed.

Cornelia turned back to look into the room again and make sure he was not there, and she saw Carey's new panama hat hanging on the hook back by the staircase where he had put it when he came in from afternoon service. She drew a breath of relief and called, in a lull of the music, "Louie, where is Carey?"

The little girl turned and looked wonderingly at her sister's anxious face.

"Why, he was here just a minute ago, Nellie. What's the matter? I think he went out the front door."

He was gone! Cornelia knew it, and her heart sank with a horrible sickening thud. She went back to the door and looked down the street and then up the hill, where the car was a mere black speck in the distance. Her heart was beating so that it seemed the children must hear it. She tried to think, but all that came was a wild jumble of ideas. The meeting that night! Carey had a short solo in the anthem! Suppose he shouldn't get back! What should she say to Grace? How could his absence possibly be explained? He couldn't—he *wouldn't* do a thing like that, would he? He had gone without his hat; perhaps he expected to return immediately. She was foolish to get so frightened. Carey had been doing so wonderfully all day. He certainly had sense enough not to make a fool of himself now.

But her heart would not be quieted, and she trembled in every fiber. She hurried down the steps and to the sidewalk looking up the hill where the car had just disappeared, and her hand pressed against her heart to steady its fluttering. She did not see Maxwell's car drive up until it stopped, and when she looked at him, a new fear seized her: Maxwell must not know that she was afraid about that girl. He had gone to a lot of trouble for Carey, and he would not like it. It might lose Carey the position. She tried to command a smile, but the white face she turned toward him belied it.

"Is anything the matter?" he asked, stopping his car and jumping out beside her. Then he stooped and picked up something from the pavement at her feet.

"Is this yours? Did you drop it?"

She looked down, took the bit of paper, and her face grew whiter still as she caught the words, "Dear Carey." It must be the note the boy had brought, and suddenly she knew who that boy had been. It was Clytie Dodd's brother!

Chapter 27

For a second everything swam before her eyes, and it seemed as though she could not stand up. Maxwell put out his hand in alarm to steady her.

"Hadn't you better go into the house?" he asked anxiously. "You look ill. Do you feel faint?"

"Oh, I'm all right," she said almost impatiently. "I'm just worried. Maybe there isn't anything the matter, but—it looks very—strange. This must be the note the boy brought."

She began to read the note, which was written in a clear feminine hand on fine note paper:

> Dear Carey,
>
> I came out here to see a Sunday school scholar who is sick, and I am in great trouble. Come to me quick! I'm out at Lamb's Tavern.
>
> Grace

"I don't understand it," faltered Cornelia, looking up at Maxwell helplessly. "She—this! It is signed 'Grace,' and looks as if Grace

Kendall wrote it. I am sure Carey thought so when he went. But—Grace Kendall was at home only a few minutes ago. She called me up to ask me to bring some music she had left here when I come to church. How could she have got out there so soon?"

Maxwell took the note and read it with a glance then turned the paper over and felt its thickness. "Curious they should have such stationery at Lamb's Tavern. Who brought it?"

"A boy. I'm not sure. He looked as if I had seen him before. He might have been—" She hesitated, and the color stole into her cheeks. The trouble was deep in her eyes. "He might have been a boy who came here on an errand once; I wasn't certain. I only saw him from the window."

"You knew him?"

"Why, I had just a suspicion that he might have been that Dodd girl's brother." She lifted pained eyes to meet his.

"I see," he said, his tone warming with sympathy. "Has she any—ah—*further* reason for revenge than what I know?"

"Yes," owned Cornelia. "She sent word to Carey to call her up, and he didn't do it. She had invited him to go on an automobile ride. He didn't go, and we were all away when they must have stopped for him."

"I see. Will you call up Miss Kendall on some pretext or other and find out if she is at her home? Quickly, please." His tone was grave and kindly but wholly businesslike, and Cornelia, feeling that she had found a strong helper, sped into the house on her trembling feet, giving thanks that the telephone had just been put in last week.

Maxwell stood beside her as she called the number, silently waiting.

"Hello. Is that you, Grace? Was it 'Oh, Eyes That Are Weary' that you wanted me to bring? Thank you, yes. I thought so, but

I wanted to make sure. Good-bye."

Maxwell had not waited to hear more than that Miss Kendall was at home. He strode out to his car, and when Cornelia reached the door he had his hand on the starter.

"Oh, you mustn't go alone!" she called. "Let me go with you."

"Not this time," he answered grimly. "You go on to church if I'm not back." He had not waited to finish; the car was moving, but a sturdy flying figure shot out of the door behind Cornelia, over the hedge, and caught on behind. Harry, with little to go by, had sensed what was in the air and meant to be in at the finish. No, of course not— His adored Maxwell should not go alone to any place where Cornelia said "No" in that tone. He would go along.

Louise, white-faced and quiet, with little hands clasped at her throat, stood just behind her sister, watching the car shoot up the hill and out of sight. "Sister, you think—it's that *girl* again—don't you?" she asked softly, looking with awe at the white-faced girl.

"I'm afraid, Louie; I don't know!" said Cornelia, turning with a deep, anxious sigh and dropping into a chair.

"Yes, it must be," said Louise. "And—that was that boy, wasn't it? The same one she sent to say she was coming to the party. My! That was poor! She wasn't very bright to do that, Nellie."

Cornelia did not answer. She had dropped her face into her hands and was trembling.

"Nellie, dear!" cried the little sister, kneeling before her and gathering her sister's head into her young arms. "You mustn't feel that way. God is taking care of us. He helped us before, you know. And He's sent Mr. Maxwell. He's just like an angel, isn't he? Don't you know that verse, 'My God hath sent his angel, and hath shut the lions' mouths'? Mother used to read us that story so often when Harry and I were going to sleep. Let's just kneel down and pray, and pretty soon Carey'll come back all right.

I shouldn't wonder. I know he didn't mean to be away. He promised Grace; and I kind of don't think he likes that other girl so awfully anymore now, do you?"

"No, I think not. But, dear, I'm afraid this is a trick. I'm afraid they mean to keep him away to pay him back."

"Yes, I know," said the wise little sister. "I read that note. You dropped it out of your pocket. Grace Kendall never wrote that. It isn't her writing. She put her name in my birthday book, and she doesn't make her Gs like that. She makes 'em with a long curl to the handle. They thought they were pretty smart, but Carey and Mr. Maxwell'll beat them to it, I'm sure, for they've got our God on their side. I'm glad Harry went, too. Harry's got a lot of sense, and if anything happens, Harry can run back and tell."

"Oh darling!" Cornelia clung to the little girl.

"Well, it might—" said the child. "I'm glad Father isn't here. I hope it's all over before he gets back. Was he coming back before church?"

Cornelia shook her head.

"He's going to stay with Mr. Baker while his wife goes to church."

"Then let's pray now, Nellie."

They knelt together beside the big gray chair in the silence of the twilight, hand in hand, and put up silent prayers, and then they got up and went to the window.

The city had that gentle, haloed look of a chastened child in the afterglow of the sunset, and soft violets and purples were twisting in misty wreaths around the edges of the night. Bells were calling in the distance. A faraway chime could just be heard in tender waves that almost obliterated the melody. The Sabbath hush was in the sky, broken now and again by harsh, rasping voices and laughter as a car sped by on the way home from some pleasure trip. Something hallowed seemed to linger above the little house, and all about was a sweet quiet. The neighbors had for the moment hushed their chatter. Now and again a far-distant twang of a cheap victrola broke out and died away, and then the silence would close around them again. The two sat waiting breathlessly on the pretty front porch that Carey had made, for Carey to come home. But Carey did not come.

By and by the sound of singing voices came distinctly to their ears. It seemed to beat against their hearts and hurt them.

"Nellie, you'll have to go pretty soon. It'll be so hard to explain, you know. And, besides, he might somehow be there. Carey wouldn't stop for a hat. I almost think he's there myself." Louise sounded quite grown up.

"Of course, he might," said Cornelia thoughtfully. "There's always a possibility that we have made a great deal more out of this than the fact merited." She shuddered. She had just drawn her mind back from a fearful abyss of possibilities, and it was hard to get into everyday untragic thought.

"I think we better go, Nellie," said the little girl rising. "Christian 'deavor'll be most out before we can get there now, and she'll think it odd if we don't come after she gave us both those verses to read. You won't like to tell her you were just sitting here on the front porch, doing nothing, because you thought Carey had gone to Lamb's Tavern after her! I think we'd better go. We prayed, and we better trust God and go."

"Perhaps you're right, dearie," said Cornelia, rising reluctantly and giving a wistful glance up the hill into the darkness.

They got ready hurriedly, put the key into its hiding place, and went. Cornelia wrote a little note, and as soon as they got there sent it up with the music to Grace, who was at the piano. It said:

Dear Grace,
Carey was called away for a few minutes, and he must
have been detained longer than he expected. Don't worry; I'm
sure he will do everything in his power to get back in time.

Grace read the note, nodded brightly to the Copleys at the back of the room, and seemed not at all concerned. Cornelia, glad of the shelter of a secluded seat under the gallery, bent her head and prayed continually. Little Louise, bright-eyed, with glowing cheeks, sat alertly up, and watched the door; but no Carey came.

They slipped out into the darkness after the meeting was out and walked around the corner where they could see their own house, but it seemed silent and dark as they had left it, and they turned sadly back and went into the church.

The choir had gathered when Cornelia got back, and she slipped into the last vacant seat by the stairs and was glad that it was almost hidden from the view of the congregation. It seemed to her that the anxiety of her heart must be written large across her face.

Louise, quiet as a mouse all by herself down in a backseat by the door, watched—and prayed. No one came in at the two big doors that she did not see. Maxwell and Harry had not come back yet. The cool evening air came in at the open window and blew the little feather in the pretty hat Cornelia had made for her. She felt a strand of her own hair moving against her cheek. There was honeysuckle outside somewhere on somebody's front porch across the street or in the little park nearby. The breath of it was very sweet, but Louise thought she never as long as she lived, even if that were a great many years, would smell the breath of honeysuckle without thinking of this night. And yet the sounds outside were just like the sounds on any other Sunday night; the music and the lights in the church were the same; the people looked just as if nothing were the matter; and Carey had not come! What a strange world it was, everything going on just the same, even when one family was crushed to earth with fear!

Automobiles flew by the church; now and then one stopped. Louise wished she were tall so she could look out and see whether they had come. Her little heart was beating wildly, but there was a serene, peaceful expression on her face. She had resolved to trust God, and she knew He was going to do something about it somehow. But people kept coming in at the door, and hope would dim again.

The service had begun, and in the silence of the opening prayer the two sisters lifted their hearts in tragic petition. Their spirits seemed to cling to each word and make it linger; their souls entered into the song that followed and sang as if their earnest singing would hold off the moment for a little longer.

Cornelia was glad that her seat was so placed that she could not see all the choir. She had given a swift survey as she sat down, and she knew her brother was not there. Now she sat in heaviness of heart and tried to fathom it all! Tried to think what to do next, what to tell her father, whether to tell her father at all; tried not to think of the letter she would not write the next day to her mother; tried just to hold her spirit steady, trusting, not hoping, but trusting, right through the prayer, the song, the Bible reading. Now and again a frightful thought of danger shot through her heart, and a wonder about Maxwell. Lamb's Tavern—what kind of a place was it? The very name "Tavern" sounded questionable. And Harry! He ought not to have gone, of course, but she had not seen him in time to stop him. Brave, dear Harry! A man already.

And yet he knew he ought not to go! But the man in him had to. She understood.

Suddenly she found a tear stealing slowly down her cheek, and she sat up very straight and casually slid a finger up to its source and stopped it. This must not happen again. No one must know her trouble. How wonderful it was that she should have been able to get this little sheltered spot, the only spot in the whole choir loft that was absolutely out of sight by the winding stairs down into the choir room behind! She would not be seen until she had to stand up with the rest of the choir to sing, and then she would step in behind the rest and be out of sight again. She wondered what Grace would do about Carey's solo and decided that she had probably asked someone else to take it. She cast a quick glance over the group of tenors, but she did not know any of them well enough to be sure whether there was a soloist present. She had been at only two rehearsals so far and was not acquainted with them all yet. She was not afraid that the music would go wrong, for she had great faith that Grace at the organ would easily be able to fill the vacancy in some way; she only felt the deep mortification that Carey, the first time he had been asked to sing in this notably conspicuous way, had failed her, and for such a reason! It was terrible, and it was perplexing. It was not like Carey to be fooled by a note. And didn't Carey know that little Dodd boy? If he had been going to the Dodd house at all, wouldn't he know the brother? Why didn't he see through the trick? He was quick as a flash. He was not dumb and slow like some people.

The contralto solo had begun. It was a sweet and tender thing, with low, deep tones like a cello, but they beat upon the tired girl's heart and threatened to break down her studied composure. A hymn followed and the reading of another Bible selection: "All we like sheep have gone astray; we have turned every one to his way;

and the Lord hath laid on him the iniquity of us all." She felt as if all the iniquity of her brother Carey were laid upon her heart, and a dim wonder came to her whether the Lord was bearing a like burden for her. She had never felt much sense of personal sin herself before. The thought lingered through the pain and wound in and out through her tired brain during the offertory and prayer that followed, and at last came the anthem. The opening chords were sounding. The choir was rising. She stumbled to her feet and for the first time saw the audience before her, this congregation that was to have heard Carey sing his tenor solo. It was a goodly audience, for Mr. Kendall touched the popular heart and drew people out at night as well as in the morning, and she felt anew the pang of disappointment. She glanced swiftly over the lifted faces and saw little Louise, white and shrinking, sitting by herself, and saw beyond her at the open door two figures just entering, Maxwell and Harry, looking a trifle white and hurried and glancing anxiously around the audience. Then she opened her mouth and tried to sing, to do her little part among the sopranos in the chorus, but no sound seemed to come. All she could think of now was *Carey is not here!* beating over and over like a refrain in her brain: *Carey has not come! Carey has not come!*

Chapter 28

Carey had lost no time when he read that note of appeal signed "Grace." It was not his way to hesitate in an emergency, but he did not leave good judgment behind him when he swung himself into the already moving car that had come for him. He could think on the way, and he was taking no chances.

It was quite natural that Grace Kendall should have gone to see a sick pupil after Sunday school. It was not natural that any pupil would have lived out as far as Lamb's Tavern; yet there were a hundred and one ways she might have gone there against her plans. He could question the messenger on the way and lose no time about it, nor excite the curiosity of his family. That had perhaps been one of Carey's greatest cares all his life, amounting sometimes almost to a vice, to keep his family from finding out anything little or great connected with himself or anybody else. He had a code, and by that code all things not immediately concerning people were "none of their business." His natural caution now caused him to get away from his house at once and excite no suspicion of danger. Grace had written to him rather than to her father with evident intention—if she had written at all, a question he had at once recognized but not as yet settled—and it was easy to guess that she did not wish to worry her parents unnecessarily. He was inclined to be greatly elated that she had chosen him for her helper rather than some older acquaintance, and this was probably the moving factor in prompting him to act at once.

He would not have been the boy he was if he had not seen all these points at the first flash. The only thing he did not see and would not recognize was any danger to himself. He had always felt he could ably take care of himself, and he intended to do so now. Moreover, he expected and intended to return in time to go to that Christian Endeavor meeting.

He glanced at his watch as he dropped into the seat and immediately sat forward and prepared to investigate the situation. But the boy who had brought the note and who had seemingly scuttled around to get into the front seat from the other side of the car, had disappeared, and a glance backward at the rapidly disappearing landscape gave no hint of his whereabouts. That was strange. He had evidently intended to go along. He had said, "Come on!" and hurried toward the car. Who *was* that kid, anyway? Where had he seen him?

For what had been a revealing fact to Cornelia, and would have greatly changed the view of things, was entirely unknown to Carey. Clytie Dodd kept her family in the background as much as possible and to that end met her "gentlemen friends" in parks or at soda fountains or by the wayside casually. She had a regular arrangement with a certain corner drugstore whereby telephone messages would reach her and bring her to the phone whenever she was at home; but her friends seldom came to her house and never met her family. She had a hardworking, sensible father and an overworked, fretful, tempestuous mother, and a swarm of little wild, outrageous brothers and sisters, none of whom approved of her high social aspirations. She found it healthier in every way to keep her domestic and social lives utterly apart; consequently Carey had never seen Sam Dodd, or his eyes might have instantly been opened. Sam was very useful to his sister on occasion when well primed with one of her hard-earned quarters and could, if there were special inducement, even exercise a bit of detective ability. Sam knew how to disappear off the face of the earth, and he had done it thoroughly this time.

Carey leaned forward and questioned the driver. "What's the matter? Anything serious?"

But the driver sat unmoved, staring ahead and making his car go slamming along, regardless of ruts or bumps, at a tremendous rate of speed. Carey did not object to the speed. He wanted to get back. He tried again, touching the man on the shoulder and shouting his question. The man turned after a second nudge and stared resentfully but appeared to be deaf.

Carey shouted a third time, and then the man gave evidence of being also dumb; but after a fourth attempt he gave forth the brief word: "I dunno. Lady jes' hired me."

The man did not look so stupid as he sounded, and Carey made several attempts to get further information, even to ask for a description of the lady who had sent him; but he answered either "I dunno" or "Yep, I gezzo," and Carey finally gave up. He dived into his pocket for the note once more, having a desire to study the handwriting of the young woman for whom he had newly acquired an admiration. It didn't seem real, that expedition. As he thought of it, it didn't seem like that quiet, modest girl to send for a comparative stranger to help her in distress. It seemed more like Clytie. But that note had not been Clytie's writing. Clytie affected a large, round, vertical hand like a young schoolchild, crude and unfinished. This letter had been delicately written by a finished hand on thick cream stationery. Where was that note? He was sure he had put it in his pocket.

But a search of every pocket revealed nothing, and he sat back and tried to think the thing out, tried to imagine what possible situation had brought Grace Kendall where she would send for him to help her. Wait! Was it Grace Kendall? Grace, Grace. Was there any other Grace among the circle of friends? No, no one that claimed sufficient acquaintance to write a note like that. It certainly was strange. But they were out in the open country now, and speeding. The farmhouses were few and far apart. It was growing dusky; Carey could just see the hands of his watch, and he was getting nervous. Once he almost thought of shaking the driver and insisting on his turning around, for it had come over him that he should have left word with Miss Kendall's people or called up before he left home. It wasn't his way at all to do such a thing. But still, with a girl like that—and, if anything serious was the matter, her father might not like it that he had taken it upon himself. As the car sped on through the radiant dusk, it seemed more and more strange that Grace Kendall after the afternoon service should have come way out here to visit a sick Sunday-school scholar, and his misgivings grew. Then suddenly at a crossroad just ahead an automobile appeared, standing by the roadside just at the crossings with no lights on. It seemed strange, no lights at that time of night. If it was an accident, they would have the lights on. It was still three-quarters of a mile to the Tavern. Perhaps someone had broken down and gone on for help. No, there was a man standing in the road, looking toward them. He was holding up his hand, and the driver was slowing down. Carey frowned. He had no time to waste. "We can't stop to help them now," he shouted. "Tell them we'll come back in a few minutes and bring someone to fix them up. I've got to get back right away. I've gotta date."

But the man paid no more heed to him than if he had been a june bug, and the car stopped at the crossroads.

Carey leaned out and shouted, "What's the matter? I haven't time to stop now. We'll send help back to you," but the driver turned and motioned him to get out.

"She's in there. The lady's in that car," he said. "Better get out here. I ain't goin' no farther, anyhow. I'm going home by the crossroads. They'll get you back," motioning to the other car.

Carey, astonished, hardly knowing what to think, sprang out to investigate, and the driver threw in his clutch and was off down the crossroad at once. Carey took a step toward the darkened car, calling, "Miss Kendall!" And a man with a cap drawn down over his eyes stepped out of the shadow and threw open the car door.

"Just step inside. You'll find the lady in the backseat," he said in a gruff voice that yet sounded vaguely familiar. Carey could dimly see a white face leaning against the curtain. He came near anxiously and peered in, with one foot on the running board.

"Is that you, Grace?" he said gently, not knowing he was using that intimate name unbidden. She must have been hurt. And who was this man?

"Get in, get in, we've got to get her back," said the man gruffly, giving Carey an unexpected shove that hurled him to the car floor beside the lady. Before he recovered his balance, the car door was slammed shut, and suddenly from all sides came peals of raucous laughter. Surrounding the car, swarming into it, came the laughers. In the midst of his bewilderment the car started.

"Well, I guess anyhow we put one over on you this time, Kay Copley!"

It was the clarion voice of Clytie Amabel Dodd that sounded high and mocking above the chug of the motor as the struggling, laughing company untangled themselves from one another and settled into their seats abruptly with the jerk of starting. Carey found himself drawn suddenly and forcibly to the backseat between two girls, one of them being the amiable Clytie.

In sudden rage he drew himself up again and faced the girl in the dim light.

"Let me out of here!" he demanded. "I'm on my way to help someone who's in trouble, and I'm in a hurry to get back."

He reached out to the door and unfastened it, attempting to climb over Clytie's feet, which were an intentional barricade.

"Aw, set down, you big dummy, you," yelled Clytie, giving him a shove back with a muscular young arm. "This ain't no Sunday school crowd, you bet yer life. An' the girl that wrote that note is setting right 'longside of you over there. My sister Grace! Grace *Dodd*. Make you acquainted. Now set down, and see if you can ac' like a little man. We're off for the best meal ever and a big night. Comb your hair and keep your shirt on, and get a hustle on that grouch. We're going to have the time of our life, and you're going along."

Carey was quiet, stern and quiet. The coarse words of the girl tore their way through his newly awakened soul and made him sick. The thought that he had ever deliberately, of his own accord, gone anywhere in the company of this girl was repulsive. Shame passed over him and bathed him in a cleansing flood for a moment, and as he felt its waters at their height over his head, he seemed to see the face of Grace Kendall, fine and sweet and far away, lost to him forever. Then a flash of memory brought her look as she had thanked him for taking the solo that night and said she knew he would make a success of it, and his soul rose in rebellion. He would keep faith with her. In spite of all of them he would get back.

He lifted his head and called commandingly, "Stop this car! I've got to get back to the city. I've got an engagement."

The answer was a loud jeer of laughter.

"Aw! Yeah! We know watcher engagement is, and you ain't going to no Chrisshun 'deavor t'night. Pretty little Gracie'll have to keep on lookin' fer you, but she won't see you t'night."

Carey was very angry. He thought he knew now how men felt that wanted to kill someone. Clytie was a girl, and he couldn't strike her, but she had exceeded all a woman's privileges. He gripped her arm roughly and pushed her back into the seat, threw himself between the two unidentified ones in the middle seat, and projected his body upon the man who was driving, seizing the wheel and attempting to turn the car around. The driver was taken unexpectedly, and the car almost ran into the fence, one wheel lurching down into the ditch. The girls set up a horrible screaming. The car was stopped just in time, and a terrific fight began in the front seat.

"Now, just for this, Carey Copley, we'll get you dead drunk and take you back to your old Chrisshun 'deavor. That's what we were going to do, anyway, only we weren't going to tell you beforehand— get you dead drunk and take you back to your little baby-faced, yella-haired Gracie-girl. *Then* I guess she'd have anything more to do with you? I guess anyhow *not!*"

Clytie's voice rang out loud and clear above the din, followed by the crash of glass as somebody smashed against the windshield. This was what Maxwell heard as he stole noiselessly upon the dark car, running down a slight grade with his engine shut off. He stopped his car not far away and dropped silently to the ground while Harry, like a smaller shadow, dropped from the back, stole around the other side of the car, and hid in the shadows next to the fence.

"What was that?" warned Clytie suddenly. "Grace, didn't you hear something? Say, boys, we oughta be gettin' on. Somebody'll be onto our taking this car and come after us, then it'll be good night for us. Don't fool with that kid any longer. Give him a knockout and stow him down in the bottom of the car. We can bring him to when we get to a safe place. Hurry now. Let's beat it!"

Harry, watching alertly, saw Maxwell spring suddenly on the other side, and stealing close with the velvet tread of a cat, he sprang to the running board on his side and jumping, flung his arms tightly around the neck of the front-seat man next him, hanging back with his fingers locked around the fellow's throat and dragging his whole lusty young weight to the ground. There was nothing for his man to do but follow, struggling, spluttering, and trying to grasp something, till he sprawled at length upon the grass, unable, for the moment, in his bewilderment to determine just what had hold of him.

Maxwell on his side had gripped the driver and pulled him out, not altogether sure but it might be Carey, but knowing that the best he could do was to get someone before the car started again. The unexpectedness of the attack from the outside wrought confusion and panic in the car and gave Maxwell a moment's advantage.

Carey was meanwhile fighting blindly like a wild man, his special antagonist being the man in the middle seat, and when he found himself suddenly relieved of the two in the front seat, he seemed to gain an almost superhuman power for the instant. Dragging and pushing, he succeeded in throwing his man out of the car upon the ground. Then before anyone knew what was happening, and amid the frightened screams of the three girls, Carey climbed over into the front seat, and not knowing that a friend was at hand, threw in the clutch and started the car, whirling it recklessly round in the road, almost upsetting it, and shot away up the road toward the city at a terrible rate of speed, leaving Maxwell with three men on his hands and no knowledge of Harry's presence.

The man that Carey had thrown out of the car lay crumpled in a heap, unconscious. He had broken his ankle and would make no trouble for a while. Maxwell was not even conscious of his presence as he grappled with the driver and finally succeeded in getting him down with hands pinioned and his knee on the man's chest. Maxwell was an expert wrestler and knew all the tricks, which was more than could be said of the boy who had been driving the car, but Maxwell was by no means in training, and he found himself badly winded and bruised. Lifting his head there in the darkness and wondering what he was to do with his man now he had him down, he discovered the silent form in the road but a step away. Startled, he looked about, and suddenly a gruff young voice came pluckily to him from across the ditch.

"All right, Max. I can hold this man awhile now. I've got the muzzle on the back of his neck."

The form on the bank beside Harry suddenly ceased to struggle and lay grimly still. Maxwell, astonished, but quick to take Harry's lead, called back, "All right, sir. You haven't got an extra rope about you, have you, man?"

"Use yer necktie, Max," called back the boy nonchalantly. "That's what I'm doing. There's good strong straps under the seat in the car to make it sure. Saw 'em last week when you and I were fixing the car."

And actually Harry, with the cold butt of his old jackknife realistically placed at the base of his captive's brain, was tying his man's hands behind him with his best blue silk necktie that Cornelia had given him the day before. It seemed a terrible waste to him; but his handkerchief was in the other side pocket, and he didn't dare risk taking that knife in the other hand to get at it.

It happened that the boy that Harry had attacked in the dark was a visitor to the city, very young and very green indeed, and the others had promised to show him a good time and teach him what life in the city meant. He was horribly frightened and already shaking like a leaf with a vision of jail and the confusion of his honorable family back in the country. The cold steel on the back of his neck subdued him instantly and fully. He had no idea that his captor was but a slip of a boy. The darkness had come down completely there in the shadow of a grove of maples, and a cricket rasping out a sudden note in the ditch below made him jump in terror. Harry, with immense scorn for the "big dummy" who allowed himself to be tied so easily, drew the knots fast and hard, wondering meanwhile whether Cornie could iron out the necktie again. Then, feeling a little easier about moving, he changed hands and got possession of his Sunday handkerchief and proceeded to tie the young fellow's ankles together. After which he slid casually down the bank, hustled over to the car, got the straps, and brought them to Maxwell, who was having his hands full trying to tie the driver's wrists with his big white handkerchief.

Gravely they made the fellow secure, searched him for any possible weapons, and put him into the backseat of the car.

Next they picked up the quiet fellow on the ground, made his hands fast, and put him into the backseat of the car.

"It's no use trying to bring him," advised Harry gruffly. "No water; and besides, we can't waste the time. He's just knocked out, I guess, anyhow, like they do in football."

But when they went for Harry's man, they found no trace of him. Somehow he had managed to roll down the bank into the ditch and hid himself, or perhaps he had worked off his fetters and run away.

"Aw, gee!" said Harry, reluctantly turning toward the car. "I s'pose we gotta let him go, but that was my best new necktie."

"Oh, that's all right," said Maxwell almost relieved. "There's more neckties where that came from, and I think we better get this man back to a doctor."

Back they drove like lightning to the city, with Harry keeping watch over the prisoners, one sullen and one silent, and took them straight to the police station with a promise to return with more details in a short time. Then they drove rapidly to the church, Maxwell anxious to be sure that Carey was all right and bent on relieving Cornelia's mind.

They entered the church just as the choir stood up for the anthem, and Cornelia's white, anxious face looked out at the end of the top row of sopranos. Maxwell's eyes sought hers a second then searched rapidly through the lines of tenor and bass, but Carey had not come yet. Where was Carey?

Chapter 29

It was very still in the church as the opening chords of the anthem were struck. The anthems were always appreciated by the congregation. Since Grace Kendall had been organist and choir master there was always something new and pleasing, and no one knew beforehand just who might be going to sing a solo that day. Sometimes Grace Kendall herself sang, although but rarely. People loved to hear her sing. Her voice was sweet and well cultivated, and she seemed to have the power of getting her words across to one's soul that few others possessed.

Cornelia, as her lips formed the words of the opening chorus, wondered idly, almost apathetically, whether Grace would take the tenor solo this time. She could, of course, but Cornelia dreaded it like a blow that was coming swiftly to her. It seemed the knell of her brother's self-respect. He had failed her right at the start, and of course no one would ever ask him to sing again; and equally of course he would be ashamed and never want to go to that church again. Her heart was so heavy that she had no sense of the triumph and beauty of the chorus as it burst forth in the fresh young voices about her, voices that were not heavy like her own with a sense of agony and defeat.

"I am Alpha and Omega, the beginning and the ending, saith the Lord."

It was, of course, a big thing for an amateur volunteer choir to attempt, but in its way it was well done. Grace Kendall seemed to have a natural feeling for expression, and she had developed a wonderful talent for bringing out some voices and suppressing others. Moreover, she trained for weeks on a composition before she was willing to produce it. This particular one had been in waiting some time until a tenor soloist fit for the part should be available. Carey had seemed to fit right in. Grace had told Cornelia this the night before, which made the humiliation all the harder now. Cornelia's voice stopped entirely on "the beginning," and never got to "the ending" at all. Something seemed to shut right up in her throat and make sound impossible. She wished she could sink down through the floor and hide away out of sight somewhere. Of course, the audience did not know that her brother was to have sung in this particular anthem, but all the choir knew it, and they must be wondering. Surely they had noticed his absence. She was thankful that her seat kept her a trifle apart from the rest and that she was practically a stranger, so that no one would be likely to ask where he was. If she could only get through this anthem somehow, making her lips move till the end, and sit down! The church seemed stifling. The breath of the roses around the pulpit came sickeningly sweet.

It was almost time for the solo. Another page, another line! At least she would not look around. If anybody noticed her, they would think she knew all about what was going to happen next. They would perhaps think that Carey had been called away—as, indeed, he had. She caught at the words "called away." That was what she would have to say when they asked her after service, called away suddenly. Oh! And such a calling! Would Grace ever speak to him again? Would they be able to keep it from her that that detestable Clytie had been at the bottom of it all? It wouldn't be so bad if Grace had never met her. Oh, why had Cornelia been so crazy as to invite them together? Now! *Now! Another note!*

Into the silence of the climax of the chorus there came a clear, sweet tenor voice, just behind Cornelia, so close it startled her and almost made her lose her self-control, so sweet and resonant and full of feeling that at first she hardly recognized that she had ever heard it before.

"Holy, holy, holy, Lord God of Hosts!"

Carey!

Her trembling senses took it in with thrill after thrill of wonder and delight. It was really Carey, her brother, singing like that! Carey, standing on the top step of the little stairway winding up from the choir room, close beside the organ. Carey with his hair rumpled wildly, his coat sleeve half ripped out, a tear in the knee of his trousers, a white face with long black streaks across it, a cut on his chin, and his eyes blue-black with the intensity of the moment, but a smile like a cherub's on his lips. He was singing as he had never sung before, as no one knew he could sing, as he had not thought he could sing himself—singing as one who had come "out of great tribulation," as the choir had just sung a moment before, a triumphant, tender, marvelous strain.

"Gee!" breathed Harry back by the door, in awe, under his breath, and the soul of Maxwell was lifted and thrilled by the song. Little Louise in her seat all alone gripped her small hands in ecstasy and smiled till the tears came. And the father, who had found his friend too ill for his wife to leave him and had stolen into church late by the side door and sat down under the gallery, bowed his head and prayed, his heart filled with one longing: that the boy's mother could have heard him.

Into Cornelia's heart there flooded a tide of strength and joy surpassing anything she had ever known in pride of herself. Her brother, *her brother* was singing like that! He had overcome all obstacles, whatever they might have been, and got there in time! He was there! He had not failed! He was singing like a great singer.

Out at the curbstone beside the church sat huddled in a "borrowed" car with a broken windshield—borrowed without the knowledge of the owner—three girls, frightened, furious, and overwhelmed with wonder. All during that stormy drive to the city they had screamed and reasoned and pommeled their captor in vain. He had paid no more heed to their furor than if they had been three pests sitting behind him. When one of them tried to climb into the front seat beside him, he swept her back with one blind motion and a threat to throw them all out into the road if they didn't stop. They had never seen him like this. They subsided, and he had sat silent, immovable, driving like a madman until with a jerk he suddenly brought up at the church and sprang out, vanishing into the darkness. And now this voice, this wonderful voice, piercing out into the night like the searching of God.

"Holy, holy, holy!" They listened awesomely. This was not the young man they knew, with whom they had rollicked and feasted and reveled. This was a new man. And this—this that he was voicing made them afraid. "Holy, holy!" It was a word that they hated. It seemed to search into their ways from the beginning. It made them aware of their coarseness and their vulgarity. It brought to their minds things that made their cheeks burn and made them think of their mothers and retribution. It reminded them of the borrowed car and the fact that they were alone in it and that even now someone might be out in search of it.

"Holy, holy!" sang the voice. "Lord God of Hosts!" And, as if a searchlight from heaven had been turned upon their silly, weak young faces, they trembled, and one by one clambered out into the shadow silently and slunk away on their little clinking high heels, hurriedly, almost stumbling. They were running away from that voice and from that word, "Holy, holy, holy!" They were gone, and the borrowed car stood there alone. Stood there when the people filed out from the church, still talking about the wonderful new tenor that "Miss Grace" had found; stood there when the janitor locked the door and turned out the lights and went home. Stood there all night, silently, with a hovering watchman in the shadows waiting for someone to come; stood there till morning, when it was reported and taken back to its owner with a handkerchief and a cigarette and a package of chewing gum on its floor to help along the evidence against the two young prisoners who had been brought to the station the night before.

But the young man who had driven the car from the crossroads, and who had held on to his glorious tenor through the closing chorus, rising like a touch of glory over the whole body of singers until the final note had died away exquisitely, had suddenly crumpled into a limp heap and slid down upon the stairs.

Someone slipped around from among the basses and lifted him up; two tenors came to his assistance and bore him to the choir room; and Grace with anxious face slipped from the organ-bench and followed as the sermon text was announced. And no one was the wiser. Cornelia in her secluded seat with her singing heart knew nothing of the commotion.

A doctor was summoned from the congregation and discovered a dislocated shoulder, a broken finger, and a bad cut on the leg that had been bleeding profusely. Carey's shoe was soaked with blood. Carey, coming to, was much mortified over his collapse and looked up anxiously and explained that he had had a slight accident but would be all right in a minute. He didn't know what made him go off like that. Then he promptly went off again.

Maxwell and Harry from their vantage of the doorway had seen the sudden disappearance and hurried round to the choir room. Now Maxwell explained briefly that Carey had "had a little trouble with a couple of roughs who were trying to get away with somebody's car" and must have been rather shaken up by the time he got to the church.

"He sang wonderfully," said Grace in a low tone full of feeling. "I don't believe I ever heard that solo done better even by a professional."

"It certainly was great!" said Maxwell, and Harry slid to the outer door and stood in the darkness, blinking with pride and muttering happily, "Aw, gee!"

Carey came to again presently and insisted on going back for the last hymn and the response after the closing prayer. Carey was a plucky one, and though he was in pain and looked white around his mouth, he slid into his seat up by the organ and did his part with the rest. His hair had been combed and his face washed in the meantime, and Grace had found a thread and needle and put a few stitches in the torn garments, so that the damage was not apparent. Carey received the eager congratulations of the entire choir as they filed past him at the close of service. It was a proud moment for Cornelia, standing on her little niche at the head of the stairs, unable to get out till the crowd had passed. Everyone stopped to tell her how proud she ought to be of her brother, and her cheeks were quite rosy and her eyes starry when she finally slipped away into the choir room to find Maxwell waiting for her, a tender solicitude in his face.

"He's all right," he hastened to explain. "Just a little faint from the loss of blood, but he certainly was plucky to sing that solo with his shoulder out of place. It must have taken a lot of nerve. We've got him fixed up, and he'll soon be all right."

Cornelia's face went white in surprise.

"Was he hurt?" she asked. "Oh, I didn't think there would be danger—not of that kind! It was so kind of you to go after him! It is probably all due to you that he got here at all." She gave him a look that was worth a reward, but he shook his head, smiling wistfully.

"No, I can't claim anything like that," he said. "Carey didn't even know I was there, doesn't know it yet, in fact. He fought the whole thing out for himself and took their car and ran away. It's that nervy little youngest brother of yours that's the brave one. If it hadn't been for Harry, I should have been a mere onlooker."

"Well, I rather guess not!" drawled Harry, appearing suddenly from nobody knew where, with Louise standing excitedly behind him. "You just oughta a seen Max fight! He certainly did give that driver guy his money's worth."

"Oh!" said Cornelia. "Let's get home quick and hear all about it. Where is Carey?"

Carey and Grace were coming down the steps together, and his sister came toward him eagerly.

"Oh, Carey, you're hurt!" she said tenderly. "I hadn't thought—" she stopped suddenly with a half look at Grace.

Carey grinned.

"You needn't mind her," he said sheepishly. "She knows all about it. I 'fessed up!" And he gave Grace a look of understanding that was answered in full kind.

"Wasn't his singing wonderful?" said Grace in an earnest voice with a great light in her eyes. "I kept praying and feeling sure he would come. And just at the last minute, when I'd almost made up my mind I must sing it myself, he came. I just had time to hand him the music before it was time for him to begin. It was simply great of him to sing it like that when he was suffering, and with only that second to prepare himself."

Carey smiled, but a twinge of pain made the smile a ghastly grin, and they hurried him into the car and home, taking Grace Kendall with them for just a few minutes' talk, Maxwell promising to take her home soon. They established Carey on the big couch with cushions under his shoulder, and then Harry could stand it no longer and came out with the story, which he had already told in full detail to Louise outside the choir-room door, giving a full account of Maxwell's part in the fight. It was the first that Carey knew of their presence at the crossroads, and there was much to tell and many questions to answer on all sides. Harry had the floor with entire attention, much to his delight, while he told every detail of the capture of the two and his own tying of the man who got away. Maxwell had his share of honor and praise and in turn told how brave Harry had been, fooling his man with his jackknife for a revolver. Everybody was excited, and everybody was talking at once. Nobody noticed that twice Carey called Grace by her first name; and once Maxwell said "Cornelia" and then talked fast to hide his embarrassment. The father came in and sat quietly listening in the corner, his face filled with pride, gathering the story bit by bit from the broken sentences of the different witnesses, until finally Harry said, "Say, Kay, whaddidya do with that stolen car?"

Carey grinned from his pillows.

"Left her on the road somewhere in front of the church, with the three girls in the backseat."

"Good night!" Harry jumped up importantly. "Kay, do you know that car was stolen? I heard 'em say so. They called it 'borrowed,' but that means they stole it. You might get arrested."

"I should worry!" shrugged Carey, making wry face at the pain his move had cost him. "I'm not in it anymore, am I?"

"But the girls!" said Harry again. "D'you s'pose they're in it yet?"

"Don't worry about those girls, Harry," growled Carey, frowning. "They weren't born yesterday. They'll look out for themselves. And I might as well finish this thing up right here and now and own up that I've been a big fool to ever have anything to do with girls like that. And I'm glad my sister went to work and invited one of 'em here to show me what a fool I have been. I don't mind telling you that I'm going to try to have more sense in future, and say, Nell, haven't you got anything round to eat? I certainly am hungry, and I've got to work tomorrow, remember."

Everybody laughed, and Cornelia and Louise hurried out for the sandwiches and chocolate that had been forgotten in the excitement. But the father got up and went over to his son with a beaming face. Laying his hand on the well shoulder, he said in a proud tone, "I always knew you'd come out right, Carey. I always felt you had a lot of sense. And then your mother was praying for you. I knew you couldn't miss that. I'm proud of you, Son!"

"Thanks, Dad! Guess I don't deserve that, but I'll try to in the future."

But just here Harry created a diversion by saying importantly, "Max, don't you think you oughta call up the police station and tell 'em 'bout that car? Somebody else might steal it, you know."

While Maxwell and Harry were busy at the telephone and Cornelia and Louise were in the kitchen getting the tray ready, Carey and his father and Grace Kendall had a little low-toned talk together around the couch. When Cornelia entered and saw their three heads together in pleasant converse, her heart gave thanks, and Louise close behind her whispered, "Nellie, He *did* answer, didn't He?"

A minute later, as they stood in the living room, Cornelia with the big tray in her hands, Harry whirled around from the telephone and shouted, "Hurrah for our interior decorator!" They all laughed and clapped their hands, and Maxwell hurried to take the tray from her, giving her a look that said so much that she had to drop her lashes to cover the sudden joy that leaped into her face. Just for the instant she forgot the crimson and white lady and was completely happy.

Maxwell deposited the tray on the sideboard and took her hand.

"Come," he said gently. "I have something to say to you that won't wait another minute."

He drew her out on the new porch, behind the Madeira vines that Carey had trained for a shelter while more permanent vines were growing, and there in the shadow they stood, he holding both her hands in a close grasp and looking down into her eyes, which were just beginning to remember.

"Listen," he said tenderly. "They have been saying all sorts of nice things about you, and now I have one more word to add: I love you! Do you mind—dearest?"

He dropped her hands and put his arms softly about her, drawing her gently to him as if he almost feared to touch one so exquisitely precious. Then Cornelia came to life.

"But *the lady!*" she cried in distress, putting out her hands at arm's length and holding herself aloof. "Oh, it is not like you to do a thing like this!"

But he continued to draw her close to himself.

"The lady!" he laughed. "But there is no other lady! The lady is really a vampire that tried to suck my blood. But she is nothing to me now. Didn't I tell you yesterday that she wasn't even a friend?"

"Oh," trembled Cornelia. "I didn't understand." And she

surrendered herself joyously to his arms.

"Well, I want you to understand. It's a miserable tale to have to tell, and I'm ashamed of it, but I want you to know it all. I meant to tell it yesterday, but everything seemed to be against me. How about riding in the park tomorrow afternoon and we'll talk it all out and get it done with forever. And meantime, can you take me on trust? For I love you with all the love a man can give to a woman, and nobody, not even in imagination, ever had the place in my heart that you have taken. Can you love me, dear heart?"

The company in the house missed them after a time and trooped out to find them, even Carey getting up from his cushions against the protest of Grace and coming to the door.

"You know I've got to go to work tomorrow," he explained smiling. "I can't afford to baby myself any longer."

And Cornelia came rosily out from behind the vines and went in for the good nights, her eyes starry with joy.

As they went up the stairs for the night Louise slipped an arm around her sister and whispered happily, "Cornie, I don't believe that red lady is anything at all to Mr. Maxwell, do you?"

Cornelia bent and kissed her sister tenderly and whispered back in a voice that had a ring in it, "No, darling, I *know* she isn't!"

Louise, falling cozily to sleep while her sister arranged her hair for the night, said to her sleepily, "I wonder now, *how* she knows! She didn't seem so sure yesterday. He must have told her about her out on the porch."

Chapter 30

Mr. Copley came up the hill with a spring in his step one evening in late September. Cornelia, glancing out of the window to see whether it was time to put the dishes on the table, caught a glimpse of his tall figure and noticed how erectly he walked and how his shoulders had squared with the old independent lines she remembered in her childhood. It suddenly came over her that Father did not look so tired and worn as he had when she first came home. The lines of worry were not so deeply graven, and his figure did not slump any longer. She was conscious of a glad little thrill of pride in him. Her father was not old. How young he seemed as he sprinted up the hill, almost as Carey might have done!

Cornelia hurried the dinner to the table; pulled the chain of the dining room light, for the darkness was beginning to creep into the edges of the room; adjusted a spray of salvia that had fallen over the side of the glass bowl in the center of the table; and then turned to greet her father. She was reaching her hand to strike the three silver notes of the dinner bell that hung on the wall by the sideboard, but her hand stopped midway, and her eyes were held by the look of utter joy on the face of her father. For the first time it struck her that her father had once been a young man like Carey. He looked young now, and very happy. The spring was still in his step, a great light was in his eyes, and a smile that seemed to warm and brighten everything in the room. When he spoke just to say the commonplace "Good evening" as usual, there was something almost hilarious in his voice. The children turned to look at him curiously, but he seemed not to be aware of it. He sat down quietly enough and began to carve the meat.

"Beefsteak!" he said with satisfaction. "That looks good! I'm hungry tonight."

Cornelia reflected that this was the first time she had heard him speak of being hungry since she came home. She looked curiously at him again, and once more that feeling of wonder at the young look in his eyes touched her. All through the meal, as their parent talked and smiled and told happy little incidents of the day, the children wondered, and finally, when the dessert was almost finished, Carey looked intently at him and ventured, "Dad, you look as if you'd had a raise in your salary."

"Why, I have!" said Mr. Copley, looking at his son smiling. "I'd almost forgotten. Meant to tell you the first thing. By the way Cornelia, I'd like it if you'd get up some kind of a fancy supper tomorrow night. I'd like to bring—ah—an old friend home with me. Have chicken and ice cream and things, and some flowers. You'll know what. You might ask the minister's daughter over, too, and Arthur Maxwell. I'd like them to be here. Can you fix it up for me, daughter?"

Cornelia, bewildered, said, "Yes, of course," and immediately plunged into questions concerning the increase of salary.

When did it happen? Was it much? Was his position higher, and did he have to work any harder?

"Yes, and no," he answered calmly, as if a raised salary were an everyday happening and he were quite apart from it in his thoughts. "I shall have practically the same work but more responsibility. It's a kind of responsibility I like, however, because I know what ought to be done, and they've given me helpers enough to have it done right. The salary will be a thousand dollars a year more, and I suppose, if you should want to go back to college by and by and get your diploma, we could manage it."

"Indeed, no!" interrupted Cornelia with a rising color in her cheeks and an unexplained light in her eyes. "I'm quite well enough off without a diploma, and I'm too deep in business now to go back and get ready for it. What's a diploma, anyway, but a piece of paper? I never realized how trivial, after all, the preparations for a thing are compared to the work itself. Of course, it's all right to get ready for things, but I had practically done most of my preparation at college, anyway. The rest of the year would have been mostly plays and social affairs. The real work was finished. And, when I came home, I was no more ready to go out into the world and do the big things I had dreamed than I was when I entered college. It took life to show me what real work meant and how to develop a life ideal. I truly have got more real good from you dear folks here at home than in all my four years' course together. Though I'm not saying anything against that, either, for of course that was great. But, Father, I'm not sorry I had to come home. These months here in this dear little house with my family have been wonderful, and I wouldn't lose them out of my life for all the college courses in existence."

She was suddenly interrupted by resounding applause from her brothers and sister and smothered with kisses from Louise, who sprang from her seat to throw her arms around her neck.

"We all appreciate what you have done for us and our home,"

said the father with a light in his eyes. "Your mother will tell you how much when she has an opportunity to see what you have done here."

"But, Dad," interrupted Carey, as he saw his father rise and glance at his watch, "aren't you going to tell us about your raise? Gee! That's something that oughtn't to be passed over lightly like a summer rain. How did it happen?"

The father smiled dreamily.

"Another time. I must hurry now. I have an appointment I must keep, and I may not be home till late tonight. Don't wait up for me. It was just a promotion, that's all. You won't forget about the supper tomorrow night, Cornelia, and be sure to get plenty of flowers."

He hurried out, still with that preoccupied air, leaving his children sitting bewildered at the table.

"Well, I'll be hanged! What's Dad got up his sleeve, I'd like to know? I never saw him act like that, did you, Cornie? Just a promotion! That's all! A mere little matter of a thousand more a year! Mere trifle, of course. Tell us the details another time! I say, Cornie, what's up?"

But Cornelia was as puzzled as her brother.

"Perhaps he's going to bring home one of the firm," she said. "We must make the house as fine as possible. Father doesn't have many parties, and we'll make this a really great occasion if we can. Strange he wanted to have others present, though. I wonder if he really ought. Hadn't I better talk it over with him again, Carey? If it's one of the firm, he would think it very odd to have outsiders."

"Grace Kendall isn't an outsider!" blustered up Carey. "No, don't bother Dad about it any further. He told you what he wanted; ask them, of course. Max didn't cut his eyeteeth last year, either; they both know how to keep in the background when it's necessary.

Anything I can do tonight before I go to choir rehearsal to help get ready for tomorrow?"

They bustled about happily, getting the house in matchless order. It was something they had learned to do together beautifully, each taking a task and rushing it through, meanwhile all singing at the top of their lungs some of the hymns that had been sung at the last Sunday's service or a bit of melody they had sung the last time Grace and Maxwell had been over. One voice would boom out from the top of the stairs, where Harry was wiping the dust from the stair railing and steps; another from the living room where Carey was adjusting a curtain pole that had fallen; Cornelia's voice from the kitchen and pantry in a clear, sweet soprano; with Louise's birdlike alto in the dining room, where she was setting the table for breakfast. They were all especially happy that evening somehow. A raise! A thousand more a year! Now Mother could be given more comforts and get well sooner! Now Father would not have to work so late at night going over miserable account books for people, to earn a little extra money.

There was a song in Cornelia's heart as well as on her lips. She was remembering the words of her little brother and sister in that despairing conference she had overheard the first morning after her arrival and comparing them with what had been said to her tonight, and she was thinking how thankful she was for her homecoming just when it had been and how she would not have lost the last five months out of her life just as it had been for worlds.

With tender thoughts and skillful hands, Cornelia prepared the festive dinner the next evening and arranged a profusion of flowers everywhere. A few great luscious chrysanthemums, golden and white, lifting their tall globes in stately beauty from the gray jar in the living room; wild, riotous crimson and yellow and tawny brown, of the outdoor smaller variety, overflowing vases and bowls in the window seats and on the stair landing; a magnificent spray of brilliant maple leaves that Harry brought in from the woods before he went to school gracing the stone chimney above the mantel; and on the dining table, glowing and sweet, a bowl of deep-red roses, with a few exquisite white buds among them, the kind she knew her father liked because her mother loved them. There was nothing ostentatious or showy about the simple arrangement, nothing to make the member of the firm feel that extra thousand dollars would be wasted in show. It was all simple, sweet, homelike, and in good taste.

There was stewed chicken with little biscuits and currant jelly, mashed potatoes, and succotash, and for dessert, ice cream and angel cake. A simple, old-fashioned dinner without olives or salads. She knew that would please her father best, because it was her mother's company dinner. It was the dinner he and Mother had on their wedding trip and would always continue to be the best of eating to his old-fashioned mind. Doubtless the old-fashioned member of the firm would enjoy it for the same reason. So Cornelia hummed a little carol as she went about stirring up the thickening for the gravy, stopping to fasten Louise's pretty sprigged challis dress with the crimson velvet ribbon trimming, and smiling to herself that all was going well. She could hear Carey upstairs getting dressed, and Harry was already stumping downstairs. Everything was all ready. There were five minutes to spare before Father had said he would arrive with his company. Grace had gone up to smooth her hair after being out all the afternoon in the wind, and Maxwell had telephoned that he was on the way and would not delay them.

Then, just as she finished taking up the chicken and went into the living room to be sure Carey hadn't left his coat and hat lying around on the piano or table, as he sometimes did, a taxi drew up at the door.

At first she thought it was Maxwell's car, and her cheeks grew a shade pinker as she drew back to glance out of the window. Then she saw it was her father getting out and in a panic flew back to shut the kitchen door.

"They're coming!" she called softly to the brothers and sister chattering at the head of the stairs.

Pulling down her sleeves and giving a dab to her hair as she went, she hurried back to open the door. But before she could reach it, it was flung open, and there on the threshold of the pretty room stood Mother! A new, well, strong mother, with great happiness in her sweet eyes and the flush of health on her cheeks. And close behind her, looking like a roguish boy, was Father, his eyes fairly dancing with delight.

"Dinner ready?" he called. "Here's our guest, children, and we're both hungry as bears! There, children what do you think of your mother? Doesn't she look *great*?"

He pulled clumsily at the veil over Mrs. Copley's hat, helped her off with her traveling coat, and set her forth in the middle of the room. The children, after a gasp of astonished delight, swarmed about her and fairly took her breath away. And when any one of them became momentarily detached from her, he took up the time in whooping with joy and talking at the top of his lungs.

At last the greeting subsided, and Mother became an object of tender solicitation and care again. They placed her in the biggest chair and brought her a glass of water, looking at her as at something precious that had been unwittingly too roughly handled and might have been harmed. In vain did she assure them that she was well again. They looked at their father for reassurance.

"That's right!" he said. "The doctor says she's as good as new.

She might have come home sooner, but I told him to keep her till she was thoroughly well, and he did. Now children, it's up to you to keep her so."

They swarmed about her again and threatened to have the greetings all over once more, till Cornelia suddenly remembered her place as hostess and straightened up.

"But, Father, the company! When is he coming? And our other guests." She looked cautiously up the stairs to where Grace was discreetly prolonging her hairdressing and lowered her voice.

"It's too bad to have anyone here this first night. Mother will not like to have strangers."

But Mother smiled royally. "No, dear, I'm anxious to meet your friends. Father had told me all about them. It's one of the things that has helped to make me well, knowing that everything was going well with my dear children."

"Oh, Mother!" said Cornelia with a sudden succumbing to the joy of having Mother home once more. "Oh, Mother!" And she knelt beside her mother's chair and threw her arms again around the little mother whom she had been without so long and never knew till now how she had missed.

It was the sound of Maxwell's car at the door and Grace Kendall's lingering step upon the stair that roused her once more into action. Springing to her feet and glancing from the window, her face growing rosy with the sight of Maxwell coming up the walk, she exclaimed, "But father, where is your guest, your friend? I thought you were going to bring him with you."

Father stepped smiling over to Mother's chair and stood with his hand resting softly on her ripply brown hair. "This is my guest—my friend," he said, tenderly looking down at his partner of the years with a wonderful smile, which she answered in kind. "This is the one I asked you to prepare for, and I wanted her to meet our young friends. I wanted her to get an immediate taste of the atmosphere of our home as it now is, as it has been during her absence, thanks to you, Cornelia, our blessed eldest child."

The look he and her mother gave her would have been reward enough for any girl for giving up a dozen college graduations. But, as if that had not been enough for the full and free way in which she had given herself, she lifted her eyes, and there beyond them, standing in the doorway, stood Maxwell with such a look of worshipfulness in his face as he witnessed this girl receiving her due from her family as would have repaid a girl for almost any sacrifice.

Grace Kendall, coming slowly down the stairs into the pretty room, watched it all contentedly. Everything was as it should be. The mother was the kind of mother she had hoped she would be, and she liked the way Carey sat on the arm of her chair with his arm around the back protectingly. But suddenly Carey lifted his eyes and saw Grace, and the light of love swept into them. He sprang up and came to meet her eagerly. Taking her hand as if he were about to present a princess to an audience, he led her to his mother and said, "Mother, meet the most wonderful girl in the world," and laid Grace Kendall's hand in his mother's. Mrs. Copley took Grace's rosy face between her two soft white hands, and reaching up, kissed the sweet girl tenderly amid a little hush of silence that none of the family realized they were perpetrating, until suddenly Father awoke to the young girl's sweet embarrassment, and reaching out a boyish hand to Maxwell, drew him to his wife's chair and said roguishly, "Mother, and now meet the most wonderful man in the world!" And the little silence broke into a joyous tumult while they all went out to the waiting dinner and did full justice to it with a feeling that that evening was just the real beginning of things.

Late that night, as they were going up to bed, Cornelia, lingering for some small preparation for the morning, heard Harry say to his younger sister, "Gee! Lou, it's good to have Mother home again, isn't it? But somehow even she can't take Cornie's place, can she? Didn't Cornie look pretty tonight?"

"She certainly did," responded the little sister eagerly. "And she certainly is great. We can't ever spare her again, can we, Harry?"

"Well, I guess you mighty well better get ready to," said Harry knowingly. "It looks mighty like to me that Max intends us to spare her pretty soon all right, all right."

"Yes, I suppose so," sighed Louise. "But then, that's nice. It isn't like somebody you don't know and love already. She'll always be ours, and he'll be ours, too. Won't it be nice? Don't you hope it's so, Harry?"

And Cornelia's cheeks grew pinker in the kitchen as she remembered words and looks that had passed that evening and turned to her task with a happy smile on her lips.

Chapter 31

It was just one year from the day when she had taken that first journey from west to east and met the pretty college girl on her tearful way home to her soul's trying that Mrs. Maxwell came back from her sojourn in California. The business that had taken her there had prolonged itself, and then unexpectedly the sick sister had telegraphed that she was coming out to spend the winter and wanted her to remain. And because the sister had seemed to be in very great need of her, she had remained.

But now the sister was gaining rapidly, was fully about to be left in the care of a nurse and the many friends with whom she was surrounded, and Mrs. Maxwell had been summoned home for a great event.

As the train halted at the college station and a bevy of girls came chattering round, bidding some comrade good-bye, she thought of the day one year ago when she had been so interested in one girl and wondered whether her instincts concerning her had been true. She was going home to attend that girl's wedding now! That girl so soon to be married to her dear and only son, and since that one brief afternoon together she had never seen that little girl again.

Oh, there had been letters, of course, earnest, loving, welcoming letters on the part of the mother; glad letters expressing joy at her son's choice and picturing the future in glowing colors; shy, sweet, almost apologetic letters on the part of the girl, as if she had presumed in accepting a love so great as that of this son. And the mother had been glad, joyously glad, for was she not the first girl she had ever laid eyes upon whose face looked as if she were sweet, strong, and wise enough for her beloved son's wife?

But now as she neared the place, and the meeting again was close at hand, her heart began to misgive her. What if she had made a mistake? What if this girl was not all those things that she had thought at that first sight? What if Arthur, too, had been deceived, and the girl would turn out to be frivolous, superficial, unlovely in her daily life, unfine in soul and thought? For was she, the mother, not responsible in a large way for this union of the two? Had she not fairly thrown her son into the way of knowing the girl and furthered their first acquaintance in her letters in little subtle ways that she hardly realized at the time but that had come from the longing of her soul to have a daughter just like what she imagined this girl must be?

All the long miles she tortured her soul with these thoughts, and then would come the memory of the sweet, sad, girlish face she had watched a year ago, the strength, the character in the lovely profile of firm little chin and well-set head, the idealism in the clear eyes, and her heart would grow more sure. Then she would pray that all might be well and again take out her son's last letter and read it over, especially the last few paragraphs:

You will love her, mother of mine, for she is just your ideal.
I used to wonder how you were ever going to stand it when

I did fall in love, to find out the girl was not what you had dreamed I should marry. For I honestly thought there were no such girls as you had brought me up to look for. When I went to college and found what modern girls were, I used to pity you sometimes when you found out, too. But Cornelia is all and more than you would want. She goes the whole limit of your desire, I believe, for she is notably a Christian. I speak it very reverently, Mother, because I have found few that are, at least, that are recognizable as such; and generally those have managed to make the fact unpleasant by the belligerent way in which they flaunt it and because of their utter crudeness in every other way. Perhaps that isn't fair, either. I have met a few who seemed genuine and good, but they were mortally shy and never seemed to dare open their mouths. But this girl of mine is rare and fine. She can talk, and she can work, and she can live. She can be bright and cheerful, and she can suffer and strive; but she is a regular girl, and yet she is a Christian. You should hear her lead a Christian Endeavor meeting, striking right home to where everybody lives, and acts, and makes mistakes, and is sorry or forgetful as the case may be. You should hear her pray, leading everybody to the feet of Christ to be forgiven and learn.

Yes, Mother, dear, she has led me there, too; and you have your great wish. I have given myself to your Christ and hers. I feel that He is my Christ now, and I am going to try to live and work for His cause all the rest of my life. For, to tell the truth, Mother, the Christ you lived and the Christ she lived was better than the best thing on earth, and I had to give in. I was a fool that I didn't do it long ago, for I knew in my heart it was all true as you taught me, even though I did get a lot of nonsense against it when I was in college; but when

I saw a young girl with all of life before her giving herself to Christian living this way, it finished me.

So I guess you won't feel badly about the way things turned out. And anyway you must remember you introduced us and sort of wished her on me with those ferns; so you mustn't complain. But I hope you'll love her as much as you do me, and we are just waiting for you to get back for the ceremony, Mother, dear; so don't let anything hinder you by the way, and haste the day! It cannot come too soon.

She had telegraphed in answer to that letter that she would start at once. The day had been set for the wedding and all arrangement made. Then a slight illness of her sister that looked more serious than it really was had delayed her again; and here she was traveling posthaste Philadelphiaward on the very day of the wedding, keeping everybody on the alert, lest she would not get there in time and the ceremony would have to be delayed. All these twelve months had passed, and yet she had not seen the reconstructed little house on the hill.

As she drew nearer the city, and the sun went down in the western sky, her heart began to quiver with excitement, mature, calm mother, even though she was. But she had been a long time away against her will from her only son, and her afternoon with Cornelia had been very brief. Somehow she could not make it seem real that she was really going to Arthur's wedding that night and not going to have an opportunity to meet again the girl he was to marry until she was his wife—and never to have met her people until it was over, a final, a finished fact. She sighed a little wearily and looked toward the evening bars of sunset red and gold, with a wish, as mothers do when hard pressed, that it were all over and she going home at last to rest and a feeling that her time was out.

Then right in the midst of it the brakeman touched her on the shoulder and handed her a telegram, with that unerring instinct for identity that such officials seem to have inborn.

With trembling fingers and a vague presentiment she tore it open and read:

Cornelia and I will meet you at West Philadelphia with a car and take you to her home. Have arranged to have your trunk brought up immediately from Broad Street, so you will have plenty of time to dress. Take it easy, little mother; we love you.

Arthur.

Such a telegram! She sat back relieved, steadied her trembling lips, and smiled. Smiled and read it over again. What a boy to make his bride come to the station to meet her two hours before the ceremony! What a girl to be willing to come!

Suddenly the tears came rushing to her eyes, glad tears mingled with smiles, and she felt enveloped in the love of her children. Her boy and her girl! Think of it! She would have a daughter! And she was a part of them; she was to be in the close home part of the ceremony, the beforehand and the sweet excitement. They were waiting for her and wanting her, and she wasn't just a necessary part of it all because she was the groom's mother; she was to stay his mother and be mother to the girl; and she would perhaps be a sister to the girl's mother, who was also to be her boy's mother. Now for the first time the bitterness was taken out of that thought about Arthur's having another mother, and she was able to see how the two mothers could love him together—if the other one should prove to be the right kind of mother. And it now began to seem as if she must be to have brought up a girl like Cornelia.

At that very moment in the little house on the hill, four

chattering college-girl bridesmaids were bunched together on Cornelia's bed, supposed to be resting before they dressed, while Cornelia, happy-eyed and calm, sat among them for a few minutes' reunion.

"Isn't it awfully strange that you should be the first of the bunch to get married?" burst forth Natalie, the most engaged and engaging of the group. "I thought I was to be the very first myself right after I graduated, and here we've had to put if off three times because Tom lost his position. And Pearl broke her engagement, and Ruth's gone into business, and Jane is up to her eyes in music. It seems strange to have things so different from what we planned, doesn't it? My, how we pitied you, Cornie, that day you had to leave. It seems an awful shame you had to go home then, when such a little time would have given you all that fun to remember. I don't see why such things have to happen anyway. I think it was just horrid you never graduated. I don't see why somebody couldn't have come in here and taken care of things till you got through. It meant so very much to you. You missed so much, you know, that you can never, never make up."

Cornelia from her improvised couch by the window smiled dreamily.

"Yes, but that was the day I met my new mother," she said, almost as if she had forgotten their existence and were speaking to herself. "And she introduced me to Arthur. Probably I would never have seen either of them if I hadn't come home just that day."

A galaxy of eyes turned upon her, searching for romance, and studied her sweet face greedily.

"Don't pity her anymore girls," cried Natalie. "She's dead in love with him and hasn't missed us nor our commencement one little minute. She walked straight into the land of romance that day when she left us and hasn't thought of us since. I wonder she ever remembered to invite us to the wedding. But I'm not surprised either. If he's half as stunning as his picture, he must be a treasure. I'm dying to meet him! What kind of a prune is his mother? I think she must be horrid to demand your presence at the station to meet her two hours before the ceremony. I must say I'd make a fuss at that."

"Oh," said Cornelia, a haughty color coming into her cheeks. "You don't understand. She didn't demand! She doesn't even know. Arthur and I are surprising her. Arthur just sent a telegram to the train for her to get off at the West Philadelphia station. She expected to go on to Broad Street. Oh! She is the dearest mother; wait till you see her."

A tap at the door interrupted her, and Louise entered shyly. "Nellie, dear, I hate to interrupt you, but that man, that Mr. Ragan, has come, and he's so anxious to see you just a minute Mother said I better tell you so you could send him down a message. It's something about the curtains for his house. I think he wants birds on them, or else he doesn't, I don't know which. He's so afraid you've already ordered the material, and he wants it the way you said first, she says."

"That's all right, darling. I think I'll just run down and see him a minute; he's so anxious about his little house, and it will reassure him if I explain about it. Tell him to wait just a minute till I slip on my dress."

A chorus of protests arose from the bed.

"For mercy's sake, Cornie, you're suddenly not going down to see a man on business *now*! What on earth? Did you really get to be an interior decorator, after all? You don't *mean* it! I thought you were just kidding when you wrote about it. What do you mean? They're only poor people. Well, what do you care? You're surely not going on with such things after you're married?"

Cornelia, flinging the masses of her hair into a lovely coil and fastening the snaps of her little blue organdie, smiled again dreamily. "Arthur likes it," she said. "He wants me to go on. You see we both regard it not exactly altogether as a business but as something that is going to help uplift the world. I've done two really big houses, and they've been successful; and I have had good opportunities opening, so that I could really get into a paying business if I chose, I think. But I don't choose. Oh, I may do a fine house now and then if I get the chance, just to keep my hand in, for I enjoy putting rich and beautiful things together in the right way, but what I want is to help poor people do little cheap houses and make them look pretty and comfortable and really artistic. So many don't have pretty homes who would really like them if they only knew how! Now, this man I'm going down to now is just a poor laborer, but he had been saving up his money to make a nice home for his girl, and he heard about me and came to me to help him. I've been having the best fun picking out his things for him. I won't get a great fee out of it; indeed, I hate to take anything, only he wouldn't like that, but it's been great! Arthur and I have been together out to see the little cottage twice and arranged the new chairs for him; and I even made up the beds and showed him how to set the table for their first meal. They are to be married next week, and he's so worried, lest the stuff I ordered for curtains won't get here in time to finish his dining room. But Mother is going to finish them, and Harry and Carey will put them up, and I want to tell him so he will not worry." With a bright smile, Cornelia left them and flew downstairs to her customer.

"Goodness, girls! Did you ever see such a change in anyone? I can't make her out, can you?" cried Jane, sitting up on the foot of the bed and looking after her.

"I should say not!" declared Pearl. "What do you suppose has come over her? I suppose it's being in love or something, although that doesn't generally make a girl do slum work at a busy time like this. But I guess we wasted our pity on her. She said she was coming home to a horrid, poor little house. Did you ever see such a pretty nest of a house in your life? That living room is a dream. I'm crazy to get back to it and look it over again."

"Well, I never thought Cornie Copley would turn out to be that kind of a nut. Think of her going to the station to meet her mother-in-law just before the ceremony! Love certainly is blind. Girls, you needn't ever worry, lest I'll do anything of that kind, not me!" cried Natalie. "That man must be some kind of a nut himself, or else she's been all made over somehow."

Jane tiptoed and shut the door; and then in a whisper she said, "Girls, I want to tell you. I believe it's religion. It's odd, but I believe it is. I heard her talking about praying for somebody down in the hall when I stood up here waiting for my trunk to be unlocked by her brother. She was talking to her little sister, and they seemed to be praying for something or somebody, and she mentioned the church every other breath since we came, and the minister, and—look at there! There's her Bible with her name in it. I opened it and looked, and *he* gave it to her. 'Cornelia from Arthur.' That's what it says. And see that card framed over the table? It's a Christian Endeavor pledge card. I know for I used to belong when I was a child. She's going to have the Christian Endeavor society all at her wedding, too. I heard her say the Christian Endeavor chorus was going to sing the wedding march before they came in, and she talks about the minister's daughter all the time. You may depend on it, it's religion that's the matter with Cornie, not being in love. Cornie's a level-headed girl, and she wouldn't go out of her head this way just for falling in love. When religion gets into the blood it's ten times worse than any falling in love ever. I wonder what her

Arthur thinks of it. Maybe he means to take it out of her when he gets her good and tied."

"Don't!" said Ruth sharply. "You make me sick, Jane. I don't care what it is that has changed Cornie. She's sweet, I know; that's all that's necessary. And, if it's religion, I wish we all had some of it. I know she looks all the time as if she'd seen a vision, and that's what precious few other people do. Come, it's time to take a nap, or we'll look like withered leaves for this evening. Now stop talking! I'm going to sleep."

The passengers in the parlor car glanced at the distinguished-looking lady with the sweet smile and happy eyes and glanced again, and liked to look, there was such joy, such content, such expectancy in her face. More than one, as the train slowed down at West Philadelphia and the porter gathered her baggage and escorted her out, sat up from his velvet chair and stretched his neck to see who was meeting this woman to make her so happy since that telegram had been brought to her. They watched until the train passed on and they could see no more—the tall, handsome young man, who took her in his arms and kissed her, and the lovely girl in blue organdie with a little lace-edged organdie hat drooping about her sweet face, who greeted her as if she loved her. As far as the eye could reach Mrs. Maxwell's fellow passengers watched the little bit of human drama and wondered and tried to figure out who they were and what relation they bore to one another.

"You precious child, you shouldn't have done it!" said Mrs. Maxwell, nestling Cornelia's hand in her own as her son stowed them away in the backseat of the car together and whirled them away to the Copley house. "But it was dear of you, and I shall never forget it!" she said fervently with another squeeze of the hand.

A few moments more and she entered the living room that had

been wrought out with such care and anxiety and gazed about her, delighted.

"I knew you would do it, dear. I knew it! I was sure you could," she whispered with her arm around the girl; and then she went forward with a sigh of relief to meet the sweet mother of the Copleys, who came to greet her. The two mothers looked long into each other's eyes, with hands clasped and intense, loving, searching looks, and then a smile grew on both their faces. Mother Maxwell spoke first with a smile of content.

"I was almost sure you would be like that," she said. "And I'm going to love you a great deal." And Mother Copley, her face placid with a calm that had its source in deep springs of peace, smiled back an answering love.

Then came Father Copley and grasped the other mother's hand and bade her welcome, too; and after that Mother Maxwell was satisfied and went to dress for the wedding.

The four bridesmaids did not see much of Cornelia, after all, for when she came back from her ride, they were all breathlessly manipulating curling irons and powder puffs, tying sashes, and putting on pretty shoes, and no one had time to talk of other things. It seemed to be only Cornelia who was calm at this last minute, who knew where the shoehorn had been put, could find a little gold pin to fasten a refractory ribbon, and had time to fix a drooping wave of hair or adjust a garland of flowers.

It had been Cornelia's wish that her wedding should be very simple and inexpensive, and though the bridesmaids had written many letters persuading and suggesting rainbow hues and dahlia shades, and finally pleading for jades and corals, all was to no effect. Cornelia merely smiled, and wrote back:

I want you all in white, if you please, just simple white organdie, made with a deep hem and little ruffles. And then

*I want you to have each a garland of daisies around your hair
and daisies in your arms.*

"White for bridesmaids!" they cried as one maid. "Who ever
heard of such a thing?"

But the answer came back:

*This isn't going to be a conventional wedding. We're just going
to get married, and we want our dearest friends about us. I
love white, and the daisies will be lovely on it, and do away
with hats. I'm going to wear a veil. I like a veil; but my dress
is white organdie, too, and I'll have white roses.*

And so it was, all natural and sweet like an old-fashioned
country affair and not one convention out of a thousand observed
in the order and form of things.

For the bride herself had decked the church with the aid of
her bridegroom and her brother and Grace Kendall. The lacelike
boughs of tall hemlocks drooped back of the altar and smothered
the pulpit; and against it rose a waving field of daisies with grasses
softly blending. The little field flowers were arranged in concealed
glass jars of water so that they kept fresh and beautiful and were so
massed that they seemed to be growing there. All about the choir
gallery the daisies were massed, a bit of nature transplanted to the
quiet temple. Everyone exclaimed softly on entering the church at
the wonderful effect of the feathery, starry beauty. It was as if a bit
of the out-of-doors world had crept into the sanctuary to grace the
occasion. God's world and God's flowers of the field.

There were not many mighty among the guests. A choice few
of the Maxwell and Copley connection and friends; the rest were
new acquaintances, of all stations in life, all trades and professions,
many humble worshippers in the church whom Cornelia and

Maxwell had come to respect and love.

The two mothers came in together and sat down side by side, attended by Harry and his father. Harry had most strenuously objected to being one of the wedding party when it was suggested. He said he "couldn't see making a monkey of himself, all dolled up, going up the church aisle to music."

Grace Kendall was at the organ, of course, and above the daisy-bordered gallery the Christian Endeavor choir girls all in white, with wreaths of green leaves in their hair, sang the bridal chorus; and from the doors at either side of the front of the church there filed forth the bridesmaids and the ushers. The bridesmaids were led by Louise as maid of honor, with a wreath of daisies among her curls and a garland of daisies trailing down from her left shoulder over the little white organdie that made her look like a young angel. Carey as best man led the ushers, who were four warm friends of Maxwell's, and on either side of the altar they waited, facing toward the front door as Cornelia and Maxwell came arm in arm up the middle aisle together.

It was all quite natural and simple, though the bridesmaids were disappointed at the lack of display and the utter disregard of convention and precedent.

The minister spoke the service impressively and added a few words of his own that put the ceremony quite out of the ordinary, and his prayer seemed to bring God quite near among them, as if He had come especially to bless this union of His children. Mother Maxwell's heart suddenly overflowed with happy tears, and the four bridesmaids glanced furtively and knowingly at one another beneath their garlands of daisies, as if to say, "It is religion, after all, and this is where she got it." And then they began to listen and to wonder for themselves.

After it was over, the bride and the groom turned smilingly

and walked back down the aisle, preceded by Louise and Carey, and followed by the bridesmaids and ushers; and everybody rose and smiled and broke the little hush of breathless attention with a soft murmur of happy approval.

"Such a pretty wedding, so sweet! So dear!" Mother Maxwell could hear them breathing it on every hand as she walked out with Mother Copley.

Then just a chosen few came home to the wedding supper, which had been planned and partly prepared by Cornelia herself; and everybody was talking about the lovely wedding and the quiet, easy way in which everything moved without fuss or hurry or excitement, right and natural and as it all should be when two persons joined hands and walked out together into the new life.

"It is something inside her that makes her different," hazarded a sleepy bridesmaid several hours later, after the others had been quiet a long time and were almost asleep. "But wasn't it lovely? Only field daisies and the grass and old pine trees, but it certainly was a dream even if we didn't get to do much marching. Well, Cornelia Copley always did know how to decorate."

TOMORROW ABOUT
THIS TIME

Chapter 1

Early 1920s

The letter lay on the top of the pile of mail on the old mahogany desk, a square envelope of thick parchment with high, dashing handwriting and faint, subtle fragrance.

The man saw it the instant he entered the room. It gave him a sick dull thrust like an unexpected blow in the pit of his stomach. He had come back to the home of his childhood after hard years to rest, and here was this!

It was from his former wife, Lilla, and no word from her in all the twelve years since their divorce had ever brought anything but disgust and annoyance.

He half turned toward the door with an impulse of retreat but thought better of it and stalked over to the desk, tearing open the envelope roughly as if to have the worst over quickly. It began abruptly, as Lilla would. He could see the white jeweled fingers flying across the page, the half-flippant fling of the pen. Somehow the very tilt of the letters as she had formed them contrived to give the taunting inflection of her voice as he read.

> *Well, Pat, the time is up, and as the court decreed I am sending you your daughter. I hope you haven't forgotten, for it would be rather awkward for the poor thing. I'm going to be married in a few days now and wouldn't know what to do with her. She's fourteen and has your stubbornness, but she's not so bad if you let her have her own way in everything. Don't worry, she's the kind that marries young, and she'll probably take herself off your hands soon. I wish you well of your task.*
>
> *Lilla*

He sat back in the old mahogany chair and steadied his arms on the chair arms. The paper was shaking in his fingers. Something inside of him began to tremble. He had a feeling that it was his soul that was shaking. Like quicksilver along his veins the weakness ran, like quicksands his strength slid away from beneath his groping feet. He had not known that a man in his prime could be so puny, so helpless. Why, all the little particles of his flesh were quivering! His lips were trembling like an old person's. He was like a frail ship being tossed in the trough of great waves. He could not right himself nor get any hold on his self-control. He could not seem to think what it all meant. He tried to read it over again and found the words dancing before his eyes with strange, grotesque amusement at his horror, like the look in Lilla's eyes when she knew she had hit one hard in a sensitive spot.

His daughter!

He had not seen her since she was two years old, and had taken very little notice of her then. His mind had been too much filled with horror and disappointment to notice the well-suppressed infant who spent her days in a nursery at the top of the house when she was not out in the park with her nurse. A memory of ribbons and frills, pink-and-whiteness, and a stolid stare from a pair of alien eyes that were all too much like Lilla's to make any appeal to his fatherhood—that was his child, all he could recall of her. Even her name, he remembered bitterly, had been a matter of contention. *Athalie*, the name of a heathen queen! That had been her mother's whim. She said it was euphonious. Athalie Greeves! And she had enjoyed his horror and distaste. And now this child with the heathen name was coming home to him!

He had looked on her as an infant still. He had not realized in the big, sharp experiences of the life he was living that the years were flying by. It could not be fourteen years! He had heard the judge's decree that the child was to remain with her mother until she reached the age of fourteen years, and was then to pass to the guardianship of her father, but he had thought he would not be living when that came to pass. He had felt that his life was over. He had only to work hard enough and fill every moment with something absorbing, and he would wear out early. But here he was, a young man yet, with honors upon him, and new vistas opening up in his intellectual life in spite of the blighted years behind him; and here was this child of his folly, suddenly grown up and flung upon him, as if his mistakes would not let him go but were determined to drag him back and claim him for their own!

He bowed his head upon his arms and groaned aloud.

Patterson Greeves, brilliant scholar, noted bacteriologist, honored in France for his feats of bravery and his noted discoveries along the line of his chosen profession, which had made it possible to save many lives during the war; late of Siberia where he had spent the time after the signing of the armistice doing reconstruction work and making more noteworthy discoveries in science; had at last come back to his childhood home after many years, hoping to find the rest and quiet he needed in which to write the book for which the scientific world was clamoring, and this had met him on the very doorstep as it were and flung him back into the horror of the tragedy of his younger days.

In his senior year of college, Patterson Greeves had fallen in love with Alice Jarvis, the lovely daughter of the Presbyterian minister in the little college town where he had spent the years of his collegiate work.

Eagerly putting aside the protests of her father and mother, for he was very much in love, and obtaining his failing uncle's reluctant consent, he had married Alice as soon as he graduated, and accepted a flattering offer to teach biology in his alma mater.

They lived with his wife's mother and father, because that was the condition on which the consent for the marriage had been given, for Alice was barely eighteen.

A wonderful, holy, happy time it was, during which heaven seemed to come down to earth and surround them, and the faith of his childhood appeared to be fulfilled through this ideal kind of living, with an exalted belief in all things eternal.

Then had fallen the blow!

Sweet Alice, exquisite, perfect in all he had ever dreamed a wife could be, without a moment's warning, slipped away into the Eternal, leaving a tiny flower of a child behind, but leaving his world dark—forever dark—without hope or God—so he felt.

He had been too stunned to take hold of life, but the sudden death of his uncle, Standish Silver, who had been more than a father to him, called him to action, and he was forced to go back to his childhood home at Silver Sands to settle up the estate, which had all been left to him.

While he was still at Silver Sands his father-in-law had written to ask if he would let them adopt the little girl as their own in place of the daughter whom they had lost. Of course he would always be welcomed as a son, but the grandfather felt he could not risk letting his wife keep the child and grow to love it tenderly if there was danger of its being torn away from them in three or four years and put under the care of a stepmother. The letter had been very gentle, but very firm, quite sensible and convincing. The young father accepted the offer without protest. In his stunned condition he did not care. He had scarcely got to know his child. He shrank from the little morsel of humanity because she seemed to his shocked senses to have been the cause of her mother's death. It was like pressing a sore wound and opening it again. Also he loved his wife's father and mother tenderly and felt that in a measure it was due them that he should make up in every way he could for the daughter they had lost.

So he gave his consent and the papers were signed.

Business matters held him longer than he had expected, but for a time he fully expected to return to his father-in-law's house. A chance call, however, to a much better position in the East, which would make it possible for him to pursue interesting studies in Columbia University and fill his thoughts to the fuller exclusion of his pain, finally swayed him. He accepted the new life somewhat indifferently, almost stolidly, and went his way out of the life of his little child of whom he could not bear even to hear much.

From time to time he had sent generous gifts of money, but he had never gone back, because as the years passed he shrank even more from the scene where he had been so happy.

He had absorbed himself in his studies fiercely until his health began to suffer, and then some of his old college friends who lived in New York got hold of him and insisted that he should go out with them. Before he realized it, he was plunged into a carefree, reckless company of people who appeared to be living for the moment and having a great time out of it. It seemed to satisfy something fierce in him that had been roused by the death of Alice, and he found himself going more and more with them. For one thing, he found common ground among them in that they had cast aside the old beliefs in holy things. It gave him a sort of fierce pleasure to feel that he had identified himself with those who defied God and the Bible and went their willful way. He could not forgive God, if there was a God, for having taken away his wife, and he wanted to pay Him back by unbelief.

They were brilliant men and women, many of those with whom he had come to companion, and they kept his heart busy with their lightness and mirth, so that gradually his sorrow wore away, and he was able to shut the door upon it and take up a kind of contentment in life.

And then he met Lilla!

From the first his judgment had not approved of her. She seemed a desecration to Alice, and he stayed away deliberately from many places where he knew she was to be. But Lilla was a strong personality, as clever in her way as he, and she found that she could use Patterson Greeves to climb to social realms from which her own reckless acts had shut her out. Moreover, Patterson Greeves was attractive, with his scholarly face, his fine physique, his brilliant wit, flashing through a premature sternness that only served to make him the more distinguished. When Lilla found that he not only belonged to a fine old family dating back to Revolutionary times but had a goodly fortune in his own right, she literally laid aside every weight, and for a time, almost "the sin which doth so easily beset," and wove a net for his unsuspecting feet.

Then, all unawares, the lonely, weary, rebellious man walked into the pleasant net. He read with her for hours at a time and found himself enjoying her quaint comments, her quick wit, her little tendernesses. He suddenly realized that his first prejudice had vanished, and he was really enjoying himself in her society.

Lilla was clever. She knew her man from the start. She played to his weaknesses, she fostered his fancies, and she finally broke down one day and told him her troubles. Then somehow he found himself comforting her. From that day on matters moved rapidly. Lilla managed to make him think he was really in love with her. He wondered if perhaps after all the sun was going to shine again for him; and he put the past under lock and key and began to smile again.

He and Lilla were married soon and set up a house in New York, but almost from the start he began to be undeceived. The evenings of reading together suddenly began to openly bore her. Lilla had no notion of settling down to a domestic life. Her husband was only one of many on whom she lavished her smiles, and as soon as she had him safely she began to show her true nature: selfish, untrue, disloyal, mercenary, ambitious.

The revelation did not come all at once. Even after their child was born he still had hope of winning her to a simpler, more practical manner of life. But he found that the child was, in her eyes, only a hindrance to her ambitions and that he was not even that; and when Lilla filled his house with men and women of another world than his, whose tastes and ways were utterly distasteful to him, he began to absent himself more and more from home. This had been made possible by the growing demand for his services as lecturer and adviser in the world of science. So it came about that whenever he received an invitation of this sort he accepted it, until sometimes he would be away lecturing in universities for weeks at a time, or touring the West.

Little Athalie had never meant anything to him but a reproach. Somehow her round, blank stare had always sent his thoughts back to the first little one whom he had given away; and he felt a reproach in spite of the fact that he always reasoned it out within himself that he had done well in so doing.

So, at war with himself, he had grown more and more morose, living to himself whenever he was at home, scarcely ever even a figurehead in his own house at the functions that his wife delighted to give to her own frivolous set. As he grew to understand the true character of his second wife, his mind reverted to his old bitterness against a God—if there was a God—who had thrust this hard fate upon him.

So, bitterly and haughtily, he had lifted his proud head and taken the blows of life without comfort. And now he had come home.

He had arrived in the late afternoon and found the town of Silver Sands much as he left it years ago. There was a new thrifty little stucco station in place of the grimy one of clapboards of the old days, but the old barns and blacksmith shop were there just as he left them, a trifle more weather-beaten and dilapidated but doing a thriving business in automobile tires and truck repairs.

The old stone church where as a child he went to Sunday school and sat beside Aunt Lavinia in the dim pew afterward, with Uncle Standish next to the aisle, and squirmed or slept through a long service, looked just the same, except that the ivy on the tower grew thicker and higher. The graveyard sloping down the hill behind, the Baptist church across the corner—redbrick with aspen trees in front and chalk marks where the children played hopscotch during the week on the brick walk up to the steps—were unchanged. A little farther on he could see the redbrick schoolhouse where he went to school glimmering through the trees, and the old bare playground where he used to play baseball. Here he had somehow bluffed his way into high school and finally prepared for college. He had heard rumors of a new high school up in the new part of town, but the old part where he had lived his young life seemed almost unchanged.

He had gone into the old house expecting to find the chill of the long-closed place about it, but the door had swung open, and the old servant, Joe Quinn, with his wife Molly, the cook, had stood smiling at the end of the hall a little wrinkled and gray, rounder as to form, more bent; and there in the parlor door quite ceremoniously had stood Anne Truesdale, an Englishwoman whom his aunt Lavinia had befriended when her husband died and who had been housekeeper since his aunt's death. Her hair was white, and she had lost her rosy cheeks, but her eyes were bright and her thin form as erect as ever in its black silk and thin white cuffs and collar. She put out a ceremonious hand to welcome the boy she used to chide, with a deference to his years and station that showed her reverence for him.

"Well, Master Pat," she said, using the old name he had not heard for years. "So yer come again. Welcome home! It's right glad we are to see ye!"

For the moment it almost seemed as if he were a boy again, coming home for vacation.

He went up to his room and found it unchanged with the years. He spent a happy moment glancing over the old pictures of high school teams that were framed on his walls. Then he came down to the dining room and sat at the wide table alone eating a supper as similar to those of his childhood as the same cook could make it: stewed chicken with little biscuits, currant jelly from the bushes in the garden, prune jam and cherry delight from the trees he had helped to plant, mashed potatoes as smooth as cream, peas that were incredibly sweet, little white onions smothered in cream, cherry pie that would melt in your mouth for flakiness, and coffee like ambrosia.

Shades of the starving Russians! Was he dreaming? Where was Siberia? Had the war ever been? Was he perhaps a boy again?

But no! Those empty places across the table! That ivy-covered church down the street surrounded by its white gravestones showing in the dusk! A world of horror in France between! Other gravestones, too, and an empty sinful world! Ah! No, he was not a boy again!

He opened the door of the dear old library half expecting to see the kindly face of his Uncle Standish sitting at the desk, and instead there was the letter!

He had come home for rest and peace, and this had met him! He seemed to hear Lilla's mocking laugh ringing clearly through the distant halls as if her spirit had lingered to watch over her letter and enjoy its reception. It was like Lilla to prepare the setting of a musical comedy for anything she had to do. Why couldn't she have written to ask him what he wanted her to do about the child?

His anger rose. Lilla should not make a laughingstock of him in any such way. He glanced at the date of the letter and angrily reached for the telephone.

"Give me Western Union!" he demanded sternly, and dictated his telegram crisply:

ON NO ACCOUNT SEND THE CHILD HERE. WILL MAKE IMMEDIATE ARRANGEMENTS FOR HER ELSEWHERE. LETTER FOLLOWS BY FIRST MAIL. P.S.G.

He hung up the receiver with a click of relief as if he had averted some terrible calamity and sank wearily back in his chair, beads of perspiration standing out on his forehead. It was almost as if he had had a personal encounter with Lilla. Any crossing of swords between them had always left him with a sense of defeat.

He tried to rally and busy himself with the other letters. Two from his publishers demanding copy at once; an invitation from an exclusive scientific society to speak before their next national convention; a call from a western college to occupy the chair of sciences; a proposition from a lecture bureau to place his name on their list in a course of brilliant speakers. He threw them down aimlessly and took up the last letter without glancing at the address. They all seemed so trivial. What was fame to an empty life?

Then he brought back his wandering gaze and read: "Dear Father—"

He started. Not for several years had he read a letter beginning that way. Athalie had never written to him. He had not expected it. She was Lilla's child.

But this was from Alice's child. The writing was so exactly like her girl-mother's that it gave his heart a wrench to look at it. Well, it had not mattered. She did not belong to him—never had. He had given her away. He had always felt her childish little letters full of stilted gratitude, for the gifts he sent were merely perfunctory. Why should she care for him? She could not remember him. He had been rather relieved than otherwise because he had a troubled feeling that they entailed more than a mere check at Christmas and birthdays. And now after several years' silence she had written again! Strange that both his children should have been suddenly thrust upon his notice on this same day! He read on:

I suppose you received the word I sent while you were abroad that Grandfather died of influenza last November right in the midst of his work. Grandmother has been slipping away ever since, though she tried to rally for my sake. But two weeks ago she left me, and now I am alone. I sent a letter to your foreign address, but I saw in the papers today that you had landed and were going to Silver Sands, and a great longing has come over me to see my father once before I go to work. I am not going to be a burden to you. Grandfather had saved enough to keep me comfortably even if I did nothing, but I have also secured a good position with a very good salary for a beginner, and I shall be able to care for myself, I think, without at present touching the money that was left me.

Grandmother said something a few days before she died that has given me courage to write this letter. I have always felt, and especially since you married again, that you did not want me or you would not have given me to Grandmother, and of course I don't want to intrude upon you, although I've always been very proud of you and have read everything I could find in the papers about you. But one day two weeks ago Grandmother said: "Silver"—they always called me Silver, you know, because they wanted to keep the Alice for Mother—"Silver, I've been thinking that perhaps your father might need you now. After I'm gone perhaps you'd better go and see."

So, Father, I'm coming! I hope you won't mind—

Patterson Greeves suddenly dropped the letter and buried his face in his hands with a groan that was half anguish, half anger, at a Fate that had suddenly decided to make him a puppet in the comedy of life. He was like one under mortal anguish. He kicked the heavy desk chair savagely back from under him and strode to the window like a caged animal. Staring out with unseeing eyes at the calm dusk of the evening sky across the meadow, he tried to realize that this was really himself, Patterson Greeves, to whom all this incredible thing was happening. Horrible! Impossible!

He sensed that somewhere deep in his soul was a large engulfing contempt for himself. This was no attitude, of course, for a father to have toward his children. But then they had never really been his children in the strict sense of the word, and nothing had ever been right in his life. Why should *he* try to be? It was all God's fault, if there was a God—taking Alice away! None of these unnatural things would ever have happened if Alice had lived! And now God was trying to force him back to the blackness of his ruined life again after he had in a measure gained a certain hard kind of peace.

He flung his head up defiantly toward the evening sky, as if he would vow that God should make nothing from him by treating him so. He was master of his fate no matter how "charged with punishments the scroll." God! To dare to be a God and yet to treat him so!

Chapter 2

The old Silver place stood back from the street just far enough for privacy and not far enough to seem exclusive.

The General Silver who built it in Revolutionary times had been a democratic soul, and his sons who had followed him were of like mind. The last grandson, Standish Silver, now sleeping in the quiet churchyard just below the bend of the hill, was the friend and counselor of everyone in the village, his home the rendezvous and refuge alike of all classes. Perhaps it was the habit of the house through the long years that had given it that genial attitude, widespread and welcoming as it stood among its trees and old-fashioned shrubs, with the same dignity and gentleness of bearing it had worn in the days when its owners were living within, as if it had a character to maintain in the name of the family, though all its immediate members were gone.

There were many newer houses in Silver Sands that boasted modern architecture and in their ornate and pretentious decorations made claim to be the finest houses in town, but still the old Silver place held its own with dignity and gentle grace, as if it had no need for pretension. Like a strong, handsome old man of high birth, it lifted its distinguished head among all the others of the place. There was something classic about its simple lines, its lofty columns reaching to the roof, its ample windows with wide-drawn snowy curtains giving of old a glimpse of companionable firelight blazing on a generous hearth. It had a homelike, friendly look that drew the eye of a visitor as home draws the soul. It had always been kept in perfect repair, and the well-made bricks of which it was built had been painted every year a clear cream-white, always white with myrtle-green blinds, so that old age had only mellowed it and made the color a part of the material. It had the air of well-preserved age, like an old, old person with beautiful white hair who still cared to keep himself fine and distinguished.

About its feet the myrtle crept, with blue starry blossoms in summer, and lush beds of lilies-of-the-valley, generation after generation of them, clustering, occupied the spaces between the front walk and the end verandas, giving forth their delicate fragrance even as far as the dusty street. A tall wall of old lilacs made a background behind the verandas at each end. A gnarled wisteria draped a pergola at one end while a rich blooming trumpet vine flared at the other, miraculously preserved from the devastation of painters each year. A row of rare peonies bordered the walk down to the box hedge in front, and the grass was fine and velvety, broken here and there by maples, a couple of lacy hemlock trees, and the soft blending plumes of the smoke bush. In the backyard there were roses and honeysuckle, snowballs and bridal wreath, bittersweet vines, mountain-ash trees, and a quaint corner with walks and borders where sweet williams, Johnny-jump-ups, Canterbury bells, and phlox still held sway, with heliotrope, mignonette, and clove pinks cloying the air with their sweetness, and in their midst an old-fashioned sundial marking the marching of the quiet hours. Almost hidden in the rose vines was a rustic arbor of retreat, where one might go to read and be undisturbed except by the birds who dared to nest above it and sing their lullabies unafraid. One would scarcely have dreamed that there was left a spot so sweet, so quaint, so true and peaceful in the rushing world.

Across the road a meadow stretched far down to misty vapors rising from the little stream, whose sand, of a peculiar fine and white variety, suitable for use in manufacturing fine grades of sandpaper, had given to the Silver family its prosperity and helped to give a name to the place started by the first old family—Silver Sands.

The meadow was rimmed with trees, and here and there a group of them broke the smoothness of its green, but for the most part the view was kept open, down across its rippling smoothness of close-cropped grass in summer, or glistening whiteness of deep-laid snow in winter, open down to the gleaming "river" as they sometimes dignified the little stream. And one looked back to the owners of that strip of land with gratitude that they had done this thing for the house and for all who should sojourn there, to give this wide stretch of beauty untouched, with room for souls who had vision to grow.

Down beyond the meadow, off to the right, camouflaged now and again by a random tree or a cropping of rocks, huddled the heterogeneous group of buildings that had come to be known as Frogtown. It was really originally called "the Flats" of Silver Sands, but since the factories had gone up—the iron foundry, the glassworks, the silk mill—and like mushrooms, a swarm of little "overnight houses" filled with a motley population, it had somehow grown into the name of Frogtown, and one felt that if the original Silver, who had owned the land and planned the view across the long misty meadow, could have looked ahead far enough he would have planted a row of tall elms or maples like a wall to shut *in* his view as well as out. For Frogtown in winter lifted stark, grim chimneys of redbrick and belched forth volumes of soft black smoke, which, when it got into the picture, was enough to spoil any view.

But in summer the kindly trees had spread more and more to shut out the ugliness of the dirty little tenements and stark red chimneys, and the tall grass reached up and blended the town till one could almost forget it was there. Especially at evening, one could look out from the windows of the dignified old Silver mansion and see the river winding smoothly like a silver ribbon just beyond the stretch of misty green without a thought of dirty laborers, blazing furnaces, flaring pots of molten glass and metal. It was like a vision of Peaceful Valley in its still natural beauty.

But it was most mysterious just after the sun had set, and the "trailing clouds of glory" left behind were lying in lovely tatters across a field of jade, above the pearly shadows where the river pulsed in dusk, and a single star stood out like a living thing and winked to show the night alive.

For the last fifteen years, since the death of Standish Silver, few had looked at this particular view from the angle of the Silver house for the reason that there had seldom during that period been anyone occupying the house except the three old servants, who lived in the back part and went "front" only to clean and air it. They cared little for views. For this reason it was all the more wonderful that the house had kept its atmosphere of home and its air of alert friendliness, its miracle of distinction from all other houses of the town.

But on this night, after all the years, the old house seemed to smile with content as the evening settled down upon it and nestled among its shrubbery with an air of satisfaction. Back in the inner rooms soft lights began to glow under quiet shades, and there seemed a warmth and life about the place as if it had awoke because the owner had come home.

As Patterson Greeves stood at the window surrounded by this sweetness of the night, this peace of home, his raging soul could not help but feel the calm of it all, the balm, the beauty. The sweet air stole in upon his troubled senses, and his soul cried out for comfort. Why couldn't they have left him in peace to get what inspiration there was in this quiet old spot for the hard work that he had before him?

The spell of the meadow came upon him, the mist stealing up from the river in wreaths till he felt the blue eyes of the violets from their hiding places as if they were greeting him, sensed the folded wings of a butterfly poised for the night on a dandelion, began to gather up and single out and identify all the delicate smells and sounds and stirrings in the meadow that he used to know so long ago. Even without going he seemed to know where a big flat stone could be lifted up to show the scurrying sow bugs surprised from early sleep. His anger began to slip from him, his bitterness of soul to be forgotten. A desire stirred in him to steal out and find the particular tree toad that was chirping above his mates and to watch him. He drank in the night with its clear jade sky, littered with tatters of pink and gold. He answered the wink of the single star, his old friend from boyhood, and then he remembered!

Out there was the meadow and the mist and the silver sand in the starlight, but off down the street in the quiet churchyard were two graves! Out the other way was a dead schoolhouse where other boys played ball and bluffed their way through lessons. He was not a boy. He had no part in this old village life. He had been a fool to come. His life was dead. He had thought he could come to this old refuge for inspiration to write a book that would add to the world's store of wisdom and then pass on—out— Where? How different it all was from what he had dreamed in those happy boyhood days!

Even the old church with its faith in God, in love, in humanity and life, in death and resurrection! What were they now but dead fallacies? Poor Aunt Lavinia with her beautiful trust! How hard she strove to teach him lies! Poor Uncle Standish, clean, kind, loving, severe, but fatherly and Christian—always *Christian*! How far he had gone from all that now! It seemed as different—the life he had been living since Alice died—as a windswept, arid desert of sand in the pitch-dark would be from this living, dusky, mysterious, pulsing meadow under the quiet evening sky. And yet—! Well, he *believed* in the meadow of course, because he *knew* it, had lived with the bugs and butterflies and bits of growing things. If he had only read about it or been taught of it he might perhaps think the earth all arid. He had a passing wish that he might again believe in the old faith that seemed to his world-weary heart like an old couch where one might lie at peace and really rest. But of course that was out of the question. He had eaten of the tree of knowledge, and he could not go back into Eden. Poor credulous Uncle Standish, poor Aunt Lavinia! Strong and fine and good but woefully ignorant and gullible! How little they knew of life! How pleasant to have been like them! And yet, they stagnated in the old town, walking in grooves their forbearers had carved for them, thinking the thoughts that had been taught them. That was not life.

Well, why not? He had seen life. And what had it given him? Dust and ashes! A bitter taste! Responsibilities that galled! Hindrances and disappointments! Two daughters whom he did not know! An empty heart and a jaded soul! Ah! Why live?

Into the middle of his bitter thoughts a crimson stain flared into the luminous gray of the evening sky as if it had been spilled by an impish hand, and almost simultaneously out from the old bell tower in the public square there rang a clang that had never in the years gone by failed to bring his entire being to instant attention. The red flared higher, and down behind the tall chimneys beside the silver beach a little siren set up a shriek that almost drowned out the hurried imperious clang of the firebell. Another instant and the cry went up from young throats down the street, where the voices of play had echoed only a second ago, and following the sound came the gong of the fire engine, the pulsing of the engine motor, the shouts of men, the chime of boys' voices, hurried, excited, dying away in a breath as the hastily formed procession tore away and was lost in the distance, leaving the tree toads to heal over the torn air.

It took Patterson Greeves only an instant to come to life and answer that call that clanged on after the firemen had gone on their way. He stayed not for hat or coat. He flung open the front door, swung wide the white gate, took one step on the road, and vaulted the fence into the meadow. Down through the dear old mysterious meadow he bounded, finding the way as if he were a boy again, his eye on the crimson flare in the sky. Once he struck his foot against a boulder and fell full length, his head swimming, stars vibrating before his eyes, and for an instant he lay still, feeling the cool of the close-cropped grass in his face, the faint mingle of violet and mint wafting gently like an enchantment over him, and an impulse to lie still seized him, to give up the mad race and just stay here quietly. Then the siren screeched out again, and his senses whirled into line. Footsteps were coming *thud, thud* across the sod. He struggled halfway up and a strong young arm braced against him and set him on his feet:

"C'mon!" breathed the boy tersely. "It's *some fire!*"

"Where is it?" puffed the scientist, endeavoring to keep pace with the lithe young bounds.

"Pickle factory!" murmured the youth, taking a little stream with a single leap. "There goes the hook 'n' ladder! We'll beat 'em to it. Job Trotter cert'nly takes his time. I'll bet a hat the minister was running the engine. He certainly can make that little old engine go! Here we are! Down this alley an' turn to yer right—!"

They came suddenly upon the great spectacle of leaping flames ascending to heaven, making the golden markings of the late-departed sun seem dim and far away as if one drew near to the edge of the pit.

The crude framework of the hastily built factory was already writhing in its death throes. The firemen stood out against the brightness like shining black beetles in their wet rubber coats and helmets. The faces of the crowd lit up fearfully with rugged, tense lines and deep shadows. Even the children seemed old and sad in the lurid light. One little toddler fell down and was almost crushed beneath the feet of the crowd as a detachment of firemen turned with their hose to run to another spot farther up the street where fire had just broken out. The air was dense with shouts and curses. Women screamed, and men hurried out of the ramshackle houses bearing bits of furniture. Just a fire. Just an ordinary fire. Thousands of them happening all over the land every day. Nothing in it at all compared to the terror of the war. Yet there was a tang in the air, a stir in the pulses that made Patterson thrill like a boy to the excitement of it. He wondered at himself as he dived to pick up the fallen child and found his young companion had been more agile. The toddler was restored to her mother before her first outcry had fully left her lips.

"Good work, Blink!" commended a fireman with face blackened beyond recognition and a form draped in a dripping coat.

"That's the minister!" breathed the boy in Patterson Greeves's ear and darted off to pounce upon a young bully who was struggling with his baby sister for possession of some household treasures.

Then, as quickly as it had begun, the fire was gone, the homeless families parceled out among their neighbors, the bits of furniture safely disposed of for the night, and the firemen getting ready to depart.

"Ain't you goin' to drive her back?" the boy asked the tall figure standing beside him.

Patterson Greeves warmed to the voice that replied:

"No, son, I'm going back across the fields with you if you don't mind. I want to get quiet under the stars before I sleep, after all this crash."

They tramped through the field together, the three, and there was an air of congeniality from the start as of long friendship. The boy was quiet and grave as if bringing his intelligence up to the honored standard of his friend, and the new man was accepted as naturally as the grass they walked upon or a new star in the sky. There was no introduction. They just began. They were talking about the rotten condition of the homes that had just burned and the rottener condition of the men's minds who were the workers in the industries in Frogtown. The minister said it was the natural outcome of conditions after the war, and it was going to be worse before it was better, but it was going to be better before a fatal climax came, and the scientist put in a word about conditions abroad.

When they had crossed the final fence and stood in the village street once more, Patterson Greeves waved his hand toward the house and said: "You're coming in for a cup of coffee with me," and his tone included the boy cordially.

They went in quite as naturally as if they had been doing it often, and the minister as he laid aside his rubber coat and helmet remarked with a genial smile: "I thought it must be you when I first saw you at the Flats. They told me you were coming home. I'm glad I lost no time in making your acquaintance!"

Blink stuffed his old, grimy cap in his hip pocket and glowed with pride as he watched the two men shake hands with the real hearty handclasp that denotes liking on both sides.

The old servants joyfully responded to the call for coffee and speedily brought a fine old silver tray with delicate Sèvres cups and rare silver service, plates of hastily made sandwiches—pink with wafer-thin slices of sweetbriar ham—more plates of delicate filled cookies, crumby with nuts and raisins. Blink ate and ate again and gloried in the feast, basking in the geniality of the two men, his special particular "finds" in the way of companions. "Gee! It was great!" He wouldn't mind a fire every night!

The coffee cups were empty, and the two men were deep in a discussion of industrial conditions in foreign lands when suddenly, with sharp insistence, the telephone rang out and startled into the conversation. With a frown of annoyance Patterson Greeves finished his sentence and turned to take the receiver.

"Western Union. Telegram for Patterson Greeves!" The words cut across his consciousness and jerked him back into his own troubled life. "Yes?" he breathed sharply.

"Too late! Athalie already on her way. She should reach you tomorrow morning. Signed Lilla."

It seemed to him as he hung up the receiver, a dazed, baffled look upon his face, that he could hear Lilla's mocking laughter ringing out somewhere in the distance. Again she had outwitted him!

Chapter 3

Having diligently inquired what time the night express from the East reached the nearby city, and finding that it was scheduled to arrive fifteen minutes after the early morning train left for Silver Sands and that there was not another local train that could bring his unwelcome daughter before eleven o'clock, Patterson Greeves ate his carefully prepared breakfast with a degree of comfort and lingered over his morning paper.

He had in a long-distance call for the principal of a well-known and exclusive girls' school in New England, and he was quite prepared to take the child there at once without even bringing her to the house. He had already secured by telephone the service of an automobile to take them at once back to the city, that she might be placed on the first train possible for Boston. It only remained to arrange the preliminaries with the principal, who was well known to him. He anticipated no difficulty in entering his daughter even though it was late in the spring, for he knew that it was likely that a personally conducted tour of some sort, or a summer camp, could possibly be arranged through this school. These plans were the result of a night of vigil. So he read his paper at ease with himself and the world. For the moment he had forgotten the possible arrival of his elder daughter.

His breakfast finished, he adjourned to the library to await the long-distance call. The scattered mail on the desk at once recalled Silver and her suggestion that she would like to visit him. He frowned and sat down at the desk, drawing pen and paper toward him. That must be stopped at once. He had no time or the desire to break the strangeness between them at present. In fact his very soul shrank from seeing Alice's child, the more so since he had become so aware of Lilla's child's approach.

He wrote a kind if somewhat brusque note to Silver saying that she had better defer her visit to some indefinite period for the present, as he was suddenly called away on business—his half intention to take Athalie to her school served as excuse for that statement to his dulled conscience—and that he was deeply immersed in important literary work in which he could not be disturbed. It sounded good enough as he read it over, and he felt decidedly pleased with himself for having worded it so tactfully. He resolved to send it by special delivery to make sure that it reached her before she started. And by the way—what was it she said about taking a position? Of course that must not be allowed. He was fully able and willing to support her. And she could not be too old to go to school. He would arrange for that—not in the school where Athalie would be, however! Perhaps she herself would have a preference. He would ask her. He reached his hand for her letter, which lay on the top of the pile where he had dropped it the night before, for both Molly and Anne had been well trained by the former master that the papers on that desk were sacred and never to be touched.

As he drew the letter toward him and his eyes fell again upon those unaccustomed words: "Dear Father," something sad and sweet like a forgotten thrill of tenderness went through him, and the face of his beautiful young wife came up before his vision as it had not come now in years.

But before he could read further, or even realize that he had not finished reading the letter the day before, the telephone rang out sharply in the prolonged shrill that identifies a long-distance call, and he dropped the paper and reached for the receiver.

It was the distant school, and the principal for whom they had been searching; but she did not fall in with Patterson Greeves's plans with readiness, as he had expected, although she at once recognized him. Instead, her voice was anxious and distraught, and she vetoed his arrangements emphatically. An epidemic of measles had broken out in the school in the most virulent form. The school was under strict quarantine, and it was even doubtful, as it was now so late in the spring, whether they would open again until fall. They could not possibly accept his daughter under the circumstances.

In the middle of his dismay there came an excited tapping at the door, following certain disturbing sounds of commotion in the hall, which had not yet been fully analyzed in his consciousness, but which rushed in now to his perturbed mind as if they had been penned up while he telephoned and lost none of their annoyance by the fact that they were now memories.

He called, "Come in," and Anne Truesdale in her immaculate morning dress and stiff white apron and cuffs stood before him, a bright spot of color in her already rosy cheeks and a look of indignant excitement in her dignified blue eyes.

"If you please, Master Pat—" she began hurriedly, with a furtive glance over her shoulder, "there's a strange young woman at the front door—"

"Hello! Daddy Pat!" blared out a hoydenish young voice

348

insolently, and the young woman, who had not remained at the door as ordered, appeared behind the horrified back of the housekeeper.

For Athalie Greeves, never at a loss for a way to carry out her designs and get all the fun there was going, had not waited decorously at the city station for the train that should have brought her to Silver Sands, but had called from his early morning slumbers a onetime lover of her mother whose address she looked up in the telephone book and made him bring her out in his automobile. In his luxurious car he was even now disappearing cityward having an innate conviction that he and her father would not be congenial.

Patterson Greeves swung around sharply, his hand still on the telephone, his mind a startled blank, and stared.

Anne Truesdale stiffened into indignant reproof, her hands clasped tightly at her white-aproned waist, her chin drawn in like a balky horse, her nostrils spread in almost a snort, as the youngest daughter of the house sauntered nonchalantly into the dignified old library and cast a quick, appraising glance around, leveling her gaze on her father with a half-indifferent impudence.

"Bring my luggage right in here, Quinn! Didn't you say your name was Quinn?" she ordered imperiously. "I want to show Dad some things I've brought. Bring them in *here,* I said! Didn't you hear me?"

The old servant hovered anxiously nearby, a pallor in his humble, intelligent face, a troubled eye on his master's form in the dim shadow of the book-lined room. He turned a deprecatory glance on Anne Truesdale as he entered with two bags, a shiny suitcase, a hat box, a tennis racket, and a bag of golf clubs, looking for an unobtrusive corner in which to deposit them and thereby stop the noisy young tongue that seemed to him to be committing irretrievable indignities to the very atmosphere of the beloved old house.

"Take them out, Joe," said Anne Truesdale in her quiet voice of command.

"No, you *shan't* take them out!" screamed Athalie, stamping her heavy young foot indignantly. "I want them here! Put them right down there! *She* has nothing to say about it!"

Joe vacillated from the library to the hall and back again uncertainly and looked pitifully toward his master.

"Put the things in the hall, Joe, and then go out and shut the door!" ordered the master with something in his controlled voice that caused his daughter to look at him with surprise. Joe obeyed, Anne Truesdale thankfully disappeared, and Patterson Greeves found himself in the library alone with his child.

Athalie faced him with a storm in her face.

"I think you are a perfectly horrid old thing!" she declared hysterically with a look in her eyes that at once reminded him of her mother. "I said I wanted those things in here, and *I'm going to have them*! I guess they are *my* things, aren't they?" She faced him a second defiantly and then opened the door swiftly, causing a scuttling sound in the back hall near the kitchen entrance. Vehemently she recovered her property, banging each piece down with unnecessary force and slamming the door shut with a comical grimace of triumph toward the departed servants.

"Now, we're ready to talk!" she declared, with suddenly returning good humor, as she dropped to the edge of a large leather chair and faced her father again.

Patterson Greeves was terribly shaken and furiously angry, yet he realized fully that he had the worst of the argument with this child as he had nearly always had with her mother, and he felt the utter futility of attempting further discipline until he had a better grasp of the situation. As he sat in his uncle's comfortable leather chair, entrenched as it were in this fine old dignified castle, it seemed absurd that a mere child could overthrow him, could so put his courage to flight and torment his quiet world. He turned his attention upon her as he might have turned it upon some new specimen of viper that had crossed his path and become annoying; and once having looked, he stared and studied her again.

There was no denying that Athalie Greeves was pretty so far as the modern world counts prettiness. Some of the girls in her set called her "simply stunning," and the young men of her age called her a "winner." She was fair and fat and fourteen with handsome teeth and large, bold, dark eyes. But the lips around the teeth were too red and the lashes around the eyes overladen. Her fairness had been accentuated to the point of ghastliness, with a hectic point in each cheek that gave her the appearance of an amateur pastel portrait.

She wore a cloth suit of bright tan, absurdly short and narrow for her size. A dashing little jade-green suede hat beaded in black and white sat jauntily on a bushy head of bobbed and extraordinarily electrified black hair, and whatever kind of eyebrows she had possessed had been effectually plucked and obliterated, their substitutes being so finely penciled and so far up under the overshadowing hat brim as to be practically out of the running. She wore flesh-colored silk stockings and tall, unbuckled, flapping galoshes with astrakhan tops, out of which her plump silken ankles rose sturdily. Her father sat and stared at her for a full minute. No biological specimen had ever so startled or puzzled him. Was this then his child? His and Lilla's? How unexpected! How impossible! How terrible!

It wasn't as if she were just Lilla, made young again, pretty and wily and sly, with a delicate feminine charm and an underlying falseness. That was what he had expected. That was what he was prepared for. That he could have endured. But this creature was gross—coarse—openly brazen, almost as if she had reverted to primeval type, and yet—vile thought! He could see all the worst traits of himself stamped upon that plump, painted, young face.

Athalie gave a self-conscious tilt to her head and inquired in a smug voice: "Well, how do you like me?"

The man started, an unconscious moan coming to his lips, and dropped his head into his hands then swung himself up angrily and strode back and forth across the far end of the room, glaring at her as he walked and making no reply. It was obvious that he was forcing himself to study her in detail, and as his eyes dropped to her feet, he paused in front of her and inquired harshly: "Haven't you any—any *hosiery*?"

Perhaps the good attendant angels smothered a hysterical laugh, but Athalie, quite wrought upon in her nerves by this time and not a little hurt, stretched out a plump silken limb indignantly.

"I should like to know what fault you have to find with my stockings," she blazed angrily. "They cost four dollars and a half a pair and are imported, with hand-embroidered—"

He looked down at the smooth silk ankles helplessly.

"You are too stout to wear things like that!" he said coldly and let his glance travel up again to her face. "How did they let you get so stout anyway?"

Her lips trembled for an instant, and real red flared under the powder on her cheek, then she gave her head a haughty toss.

"You aren't very polite, are you? Lilla said I'd find you that way, but I thought maybe you had changed since she saw you. She told me—"

"You needn't bother to mention anything that your mother said about me. I shouldn't care to hear it," he said coldly.

"Well, Lilla's my mother, and if I have come to live with you, I shall mention what I like. You can't stop me!"

There was defiance in the tone and in her glance that swept remindingly toward the pile of luggage at her feet, and he veered away from another encounter.

"Do you always call your mother by her first name? It doesn't sound very respectful."

"Oh, bother respect! Why should I respect her? Certainly, I call her Lilla! I had it in mind to call you Pat, too, if I liked you well enough, but if you keep on like this I'll call you Old Greeves! So there! Oh, heck! This isn't beginning very well—" She pouted. "Let's start over again. Here Pat, let's sit down and be real friendly. Have a cigarette?" and she held out a bright little gold case with a delightfully friendly woman-of-the-world air, much as her mother might have done. As she stood thus poised with the golden bauble held in her exquisitely manicured rose-leaf hands, she seemed the epitome of all that was insolent and sensual to her horrified and disgusted father. He felt like striking her down. He wanted to curse her mother for allowing her to grow up into this, but most of all he felt a loathing for himself that he had made himself responsible for this abnormal specimen of womanhood. Scarcely more than a child and yet wearing the charm of the serpent with ease.

Then suddenly the shades of all the Silvers looking down upon him from the painted canvases on the wall, the sweetly highborn gentlewomen and gentlemen of strong, fine character, seemed to rise in audience on the scene and bring him back to the things he had been taught and had always deep down in his heart believed, no matter how far he had wandered from their practice. And here was this child, scarcely turned toward womanhood, daring to offer her father a cigarette, daring to strike a match pertly and light one for herself, here in this old Silver house, where grandmothers of four generations had been *ladies*, and where dear Aunt Lavinia had taught him his golden texts every Sunday morning—taught him about purity and righteousness. Oh, it was all her sweet, blind innocence—her ignorance of the world, of course, yet sweet and wonderful. And to have this child—*his child*—transgressing the old order in her playful, brazen way! It was too terrible! His child! Flesh of his flesh!

"Athalie!"

"Oh, don't you *smoke*? I thought all real *men* smoked. Lilla said—" she pursed her lips and lifted her cigarette prettily.

"Athalie!" he thundered. "Never mind what your mother said! Don't you dare to smoke in this house! Don't you ever let me see you—"

"Oh, very well! Shall I go outside? Perhaps you'll take a little walk down the street with me—"

The child was angry. There were sparks in her dark eyes. She looked very much like the old Lilla he knew so well. This was not the way to handle her. He was bungling everything. What should he do? He must establish his authority. The court had handed her over to his charge. What a mistake! He should have had her when she was young if he was ever to hope to do anything with her. But he must do *something*. He reached out suddenly and took possession of the cigarette and case before the surprised girl had time to protest.

"Those are not fit things for a young girl to have," he said sternly. "While you are under my protection, it must not happen again. Do you understand?"

She pouted. "You wouldn't talk!"

"I can't talk to you while you look like that," he said with a note of desperation in his voice. "Go upstairs and wash your face. And haven't you got some less outlandish clothes? You look like a circus child. I'm ashamed to look at you!"

He stepped to the wall and rang a bell, while Athalie, after staring at him in utter dismay, burst into sudden and appalling tears. Almost simultaneously Anne Truesdale appeared at the door with a white, frightened face looking from one to the other. Patterson Greeves felt a distinct wish that a portion of the floor might open and swallow him forever, but he endeavored to face the situation like a Silver and a master in his own house.

"This is my daughter Athalie, Mrs. Truesdale, and she wished to wash her face and change her apparel. Will you kindly show her to a room and see that her bags are brought up and that she has everything she needs? I did not expect her to arrive so soon or I would have given you warning. It was my intention to keep her in school—"

"Oh–h–h–h!" moaned Athalie into a scrap of green-and-black bordered handkerchief— "O–hhhhh!"

Anne Truesdale looked at the plump tailored shoulders as she might have looked at a stray cat that she was told to put out of the room and then rose to the occasion. She slid a firm but polite arm around the reluctant guest and drew her from the room, and Patterson Greeves shut the library door and dropped with a groan into his chair, burying his face in his hands and wishing he had never been born. Somehow the sight of his daughter weeping, with her foolish frizzled hair and her fat, flesh-colored silk legs in their flapping galoshes, being led away by "Trudie," as he always used to call the housekeeper, made him suddenly recognize her for what she was. She was a flapper! The most despicable thing known to girlhood, according to his bred and inherited standards. The thing that all the newspapers and magazines held in scorn and dread; the thing that all noted people were writing about and trying to eradicate; the thing they were afraid of and bowed to and let be; and his child was a *flapper*!

Just as, after long and careful study, a new specimen would at last unexpectedly reveal some trait by which he could place it, so now this child had shown her true character.

It was terrible enough to acknowledge; it was easy enough to understand how it had come about. But the thing to consider was what was he going to do about it? How could he do anything? It was too late! And God thought men would believe in Him when He let things like this happen! Somehow all his bitterness of the years seemed to have focused on this one morning. All that he called in scorn the "outraged faith of his childhood" seemed to rise and protest against his fate, proving that he still had some faith lurking in his soul, or else how could he blame a God who did not exist?

He rose and paced his study back and forth, dashing his rumpled hair from his forehead, glaring about on the familiar old room that had always spoken to him of things righteous and orderly, as if in some way it, too, with God, were to blame for what had happened to him. He had taken perhaps three turns back and forth in his wrath and perplexity when he was aware that a light tapping on the door had been going on for perhaps several seconds. He swung to the door and jerked it angrily open. Had that girl finished dressing so soon, before he had thought what to do about her? Well, he would tell her exactly what she was, what a disgrace to a fine old family; what a—mistake—what a—!

In the hall stood Anne Truesdale with a deprecatory air, her fingers working nervously with the corner of her apron, which she held as if to keep her balance. Her beloved Master Pat had turned into an inscrutable old ogre, whom she loved but scarcely dared to brave. She felt assured, in view of the modern young specimen upstairs, that he had reason to be in this mood, and she but adored and feared him the more, after the old-fashioned feminine way, that he had it in him to storm around in this fashion; but she was frightened to death to have to deal with him while it lasted. Behind her, smiling quite assured, and splendid to look upon this morning with the soot washed from his face, and his big body attired fittingly, stood the minister, a book in his hand and a look of pleasant anticipation in his face.

Then Patterson Greeves remembered as in a dream of something far past that he had invited the minister to take a hike with him this morning and afterward to lunch with him. The boy Blink was to have gone along. How fair and innocent the prospect was compared to what had now happened to him! He looked as one who was about to tear his hair out, so helpless and tragic were his eyes.

Chapter 4

Oh! It's you!" There was at least a wistfulness in his tone.

"Good morning!" said the minister. "Am I—? Perhaps our plans are not convenient for you this morning—?"

"Oh!" said Patterson Greeves stupidly, as if he had just remembered.

"You look done out, man! Is anything the matter? Can I help? If not, shouldn't I just leave this book I promised and run along till another time?"

"No. Come in!" said Patterson Greeves with a desperate look in his face. "You're a minister! It's your business to help people in trouble. I'm in the deuce of a mess and no mistake. You can't help me out. Nobody can. But it would afford me some satisfaction to ask you how the devil you can go around preaching the love of God when He allows such satanic curses to fall on men."

Bannard gave him a quick, keen glance, and set his clean-shaven lips in a firm line as he threw his hat on the hall console and stepped inside the door.

Anne Truesdale retreated hastily to the pantry and paused to wipe a frightened tear from her white cheek. The other servants must not suspect what had happened to the master. Was this then the secret of the sadness of his face, that he had forsaken the faith of his fathers and taken to cursing and swearing? It made her shiver even yet to remember how familiarly he had spoken of the devil. Dear old Mr. Standish Silver! It was well he was not present to be grieved! And little pretty Miss Lavinia! If she had heard her darling's voice talking that way about her heavenly Father it would have killed her outright! Just have killed her outright! Oh, it was sad times, and the world growing weary instead of bright. And she so glad only the day before that Master Pat was coming home! Poor Master Pat! She must order waffles for lunch. He was always so fond of them. She must do all in her power to win him back to right living. It must have been that awful war! They said some of the officers were that careless! And of course he'd been a long time away from home. Poor Master Pat! She must pray for him humbly. There was no one else left to do it. That was what Miss Lavinia would have done, crept to her old padded wing chair and knelt long with the shades drawn. So she always did when Master Pat was a boy and did wrong. There was the time when he told his first lie. How she remembered that day. Miss Lavinia ate nothing for a whole twenty-four hours, just fasted and prayed.

She, too, would fast, and would go to Miss Lavinia's room and the old wing chair, and draw the shades and lock the door, and pray for the master! Perhaps then her prayer might be heard and answered. She would ask for the sake of Miss Lavinia and his uncle Silver. They must be beloved of the Lord. It would be terrible to have their nephew come out an unbeliever in these days of unbelief. The family must not be disgraced. But she must not let the servants know what she was doing. They must not find that anything was amiss with the master. Surely the Lord would hear and all might yet be well in spite of the awful young woman that had arrived, apparently to remain.

So she scuttled away to Miss Lavinia's sunny south bedroom and locked the door.

Downstairs, Patterson Greeves gave his guest a chair and began to pour out curses against God.

Bannard listened a moment, head up, a startled, searching, almost pitying look in his eyes, then he rose with an air of decision.

"Look here, Greeves, you can't expect me to sit quietly and listen while you abuse my best Friend! I can't do it!" And he turned sharply toward the door.

Patterson Greeves stared at his guest with surprise and a growing sanity and apology in his eyes.

"I beg your pardon," he said brusquely. "I suppose God must be that to you or you wouldn't be in the business you are. I hadn't realized that there was anybody with an education left on earth that still felt that way, but you look like an honest man. Sit down and tell me how on earth you reconcile this hell we live in with a loving and kindly Supreme Being."

"You don't look as if you are in the mood for a discussion on theology to do you any good now," answered the younger man quietly. "I would rather wait until another time for a talk like that. Is there anything I can do for you, friend, or would you rather I got out of your way just now?"

"No, stay if you don't mind my ravings. I have an idea you'd be a pretty good friend to have and I've been hard hit. The fact is, I suppose I've been a good deal of a fool! I married again. A woman who was utterly selfish and unprincipled. We've been divorced for years. Now suddenly our daughter is thrust back upon me, a decree of the court I'd utterly forgotten! She arrived without warning, and she's the most impossible specimen of young womanhood I've ever come across! If a loving God could ever—! What are you smiling about, man? It's no joke I'm telling you!"

"I was thinking how much you remind me of a man I have been reading about in the Bible. Jehoram is his name. Ever make his acquaintance?"

"Not especially," answered Greeves coldly, with evident annoyance at the digression. "He was one of those old Israeliteish kings, wasn't he?"

"Yes, a king, but he blamed God for the results of his own actions."

"Mm! Yes. I see! But how am I to blame for having a daughter like that? Didn't God make her what she is? Why couldn't she have been the right kind of a girl? How was I to blame for that?"

"You married a woman whom you described as utterly selfish and unprincipled, didn't you? You left the child in her keeping during these first formative years. What else could you expect but that she would be brought up in a way displeasing to yourself?"

The scientist took three impatient turns up and down the room before he attempted to answer.

"Man! How could I know? Such a thing wasn't in my thoughts! I insist it was a dastardly thing to wreak vengeance on me in this way. No, you can't convince me. This thing came from your God—if there is such a being. I've been watching and waiting through the years for a turn in my luck to prove that the God I'd been taught loved me had any thought toward me. But this is too much. Why should I wait any longer? I *know*! God, if there is a God, is a God of hate rather than love."

"Jehoram's exact words," said the minister. "This evil is of the Lord. Why should I wait for the Lord any longer?"

"Exactly!" said Greeves. "Don't you see? Jehoram was a wise man. I respect him."

"But he found he was mistaken, you know. Wait till 'tomorrow about this time' and perhaps you, too, will find it out. God's purposes always work out—"

Patterson Greeves wheeled around and looked sharply at his visitor. "What do you mean, 'tomorrow about this time'?"

"Go read the story of Jehoram and you'll understand. The city was in a state of siege. The people were starving crazed by hunger, were eating their own children, and appealing to the king to settle their demoniacal quarrels. The king was blaming God for it all, and suddenly the prophet appeared and told him that 'tomorrow about this time' there would be plenty to eat and cheap enough for everybody. How do you know but tomorrow about this time God may have relief and joy all planned and on the way?"

Greeves turned away impatiently and began his angry pacing of the room again.

"Oh, that's the kind of idealism you were prating about last night with your dreams that God was working out His purposes for the laboring classes and all that bosh! Excuse me, but I don't believe any such rot any more for the classes or the nations than I do for the individual. Take myself for instance. If I don't send off a letter I just wrote to stop it, by tomorrow about this time I may have a worse mess on my hands than I have now. I tell you your God has it in for me! I didn't tell you I had another daughter, did I? Well, I have, and she's taken it into her head to come here also. Here! Read this letter!"

He picked up Silver's letter and thrust it into the young man's hand. The minister glanced at the clear handwriting, caught the words "Dear Father," and pressed it back upon Greeves.

"I oughtn't to read this!" he said earnestly.

"Yes! Read!" commanded the older man. "I want you to know the situation. Then perhaps you'll understand my position. I'd like to have one person in the town who understands."

Bannard glanced through the lines with apology and deference in his eyes.

"This is no letter to be ashamed of!" he exclaimed as he read. "This girl had a good mother, I'm sure! Or a good grandmother, anyway!"

Greeves stopped suddenly by the window, staring out with unseeing eyes, and his voice was husky with feeling when he spoke after an instant of silence.

"She had the best grandmother in the world, I think—but—her *mother* was *wonderful.*" There was reverence and heartbreak in his tone.

"Ah!" said the minister earnestly. "Then she will be like her mother!"

"I *could not bear it*—if she were like her mother!" breathed the man at the window with a voice almost like a sob and flung himself away from the light, pacing excitedly back to the shadowed end of the room.

"But you say you have written her not to come?" interrupted the minister suddenly, glancing thoughtfully at the letter in his hand. "Why did you do that? I should think from the letter she might be a great help. Why not let her come?"

The father wheeled around sharply again, kicking a corner of the rug that almost tripped him as if it had personality and were interfering with his transit.

"Let her come! Let her come here and meet that other girl? Not on any account. I—*could not bear it*!" Again that tortured wistfulness in his voice like a half sob.

The minister watched him curiously with a sorrowful glance at the letter in his hand.

"I don't quite see—*how you can bear not to*!" he said slowly. "After reading that appeal for your love—!"

"Appeal? What appeal? I don't know what you mean?"

He took the letter hurriedly and dashed himself into his desk chair with a deep sigh, beginning to read with hurried, feverish eyes.

"Man! I didn't read all this before! I was so upset! And then the other girl came!"

There was silence for an instant while he read. Then his eyes lifted with a look of almost fear in them. "Man alive!" he gasped. "She's coming this morning! My letter will be too late!" He picked up the envelope he had so recently addressed and looked at it savagely as if somehow it were to blame. "Too late!" He flung it angrily on the floor, where it slid under the edge of the desk and lay. The tortured man jerked himself out of his chair again and began his walk up and down.

"What shall I do? You're a minister. You ought to know. She's on her way now. She'll be here in a few minutes, and I can't have her. She mustn't meet that other girl! I can't have Alice's child see her! What would you do? Oh, why did God let all this come about?" He wheeled around impatiently and stamped off again. "I'll have to get the other one off to school somewhere, I suppose. You wouldn't be willing to meet that train and say I was called away, would you? Get her to go to a hotel in the city somewhere and wait? I could hire an automobile and take Athalie away. Perhaps there's a school near her old home. Wait! I know a woman on the Hudson—I wonder— Give me long distance, central." He had picked up the phone and began to tap the floor with his foot, glancing anxiously toward the clock that was giving a warning whir before striking. "What time does that train get in, Bannard? Have you a timetable?"

Bannard glanced at the clock.

"Why! You haven't much time," he said in a startled tone. "It gets here at eleven ten. Would you like my car?" He stepped to the window, glanced out, gave a long, low musical whistle, and in a moment Blink appeared, darting up the front walk warily, with eyes on the front window.

The minister leaned out of the window and called: "Blink, can you get my car here from the garage in five minutes? I want to meet that train."

Blink murmured a nonchalant "Sure!" and was gone. The minister turned back to the frantic father, who was foaming angrily at the telephone operator and demanding better service.

"Mr. Greeves," he said placing his hand on the other's arm affectionately, "my car will be here in a moment. I think you had better take it and meet your daughter. It will be embarrassing for her to have to meet a stranger—"

Patterson Greeves shook his head angrily.

"No, no! I can't meet her! I can't help it! She'll have to be embarrassed then. She got up the whole trouble by coming, didn't she? Well, she'll have to take the consequences. I have to stay here and get this other one off somewhere. I'll send her back to her mother if I can't do anything else! I won't be tormented this way. I know. You're thinking this is no way for a father to act, but I'm not a father! I've never had the privileges of a father, and I don't intend to begin now. If my wife had lived it would have been different! But she had to be taken away! Central! Central! Can't you give me long distance?"

Down the long flight of polished mahogany stairs heavy, reluctant footsteps could be heard approaching.

Patterson Greeves hung up the receiver with a click and wheeled around in his chair with an ashen look, listening.

"She's coming now!" he exclaimed nervously. "I'll have to do something. Bannard, if you'd just take that car of yours and go meet that train, I'll be everlastingly obliged to you. If you don't want to do it, let her get here the best way she can. It will give us that much more time. I've got to do something with Athalie at once!" He rose and went anxiously toward the door, opening it a crack and listening.

The steps came on, slowly, and yet more slowly. The minister pitied his new friend from the bottom of his heart, and yet there was a humorous side to the situation. To think of a man of this one's attainments and standing being afraid of a mere girl, afraid of two girls! His own children!

It was a simple matter, of course, to meet a train and tell the girl her father had been occupied for the time. The car slid briskly up to the curb in the street on time to the dot, and the minister turned pleasantly and picked up his hat.

"I'll go. Certainly. What do you wish me to say to her?"

"Oh! Nothing. Anything! You'll have to bring her here, I suppose! Make it as long a trip as possible, won't you? I'll try to clear the coast somehow!" He glanced down at the baggage of his younger daughter with a troubled frown. "There's a carriage here— The servants will— Well, I'll see what can be done. You'd better go quickly, please!" He looked nervously toward the door, and Bannard opened it and hurried out to his car, Athalie entering almost as he left, her eyes upon the departing visitor.

"Who was that stunning-looking man, Dad? Why didn't you introduce me? You could have just as well as not, and I don't want to waste any time getting to know people. It's horribly dull in a new place till you know everybody."

Chapter 5

Athalie entered with nonchalance and no sign of the recent tears. Her face had perhaps been washed and a portion of her makeup removed, but she still had a vivid look and her hair was more startling than ever, now that her rakish hat was removed. It stood out in a fluffy puffball, like a dandelion gone to seed, and gave her an amazing appearance. Her father stared at her with a fascinated horror and was speechless.

She had changed her traveling clothes for an accordion-pleated outfit of soft jade-green silk with an expansive neckline and sleeves that were slit several times from the wrist to shoulder and swung jauntily in festoon-like serpentine curves around her plump pink arms. She had compromised on a pair of black chiffon-silk stockings with openwork lace and black satin sandals with glittering little rhinestone clasps. A plantinum wristwatch and a glitter of jewels attended every movement of her plump pink hands with their pointed seashell fingertips, and a long string of carved ivory beads swung downward from her neck and mingled with the clutter of a clattering, noisy little girdle. No wonder he stared. And she had done all that while he was talking with the minister.

He stared, and her dimples began to come like a reminder of her mother in the old luring way, filling him with pain and anger and something worse than helplessness. Her mother's face was not as full as hers, but the dimples went and came with such familiar play!

"Dad, you needn't think you can keep me shut up away from things," she said archly. "I'm going to know all your men friends and be real chummy with them. The men always like me. I'm like Lilla in that! They bring me stacks of presents and slews of chocolates. I've got a lot of going-away boxes in my trunks. Some of them are real jim-dandies. This watch is a present from Bobs. You know who Bobs is, don't you? Bobs Farrell. He was dead gone on Lilla. He gave me this watch on my last birthday. It's platinum and diamond. Isn't it great? He brought me out in his car this morning or I would have had to wait two hours. When I found out what time this little old train started, I just called up his apartment, and he came right down and got me and took me up to his place for breakfast. He has the darlingest apartment all by himself with a servant to wait on him and the most wonderful meals! And he's going to have a theater party for me some night with a dinner afterward at his apartment. Won't that be simply great? I'm to ask any two girls from school I like, and he will get the men. And by the way, Daddy, I've invited a house party for the first week in June. You don't mind, do you? There are ten of the girls in my class, and I've promised them the time of their life. The fellows will be here only at the weekend. They have to be back at prep Monday morning. Their old school doesn't close for another two weeks after ours."

His most amazing child had rattled on without letup thus far, and this was the first period he had been able to grasp. He hurried to make use of it, meanwhile glancing nervously at the clock. "School!

Yes. School! May I ask why you are not in school yourself?"

"Oh!" she wreathed the dimples coquettishly around her lips. "Why, didn't you know I had been expelled?" She dimpled charmingly as though it were something to be proud of. "I suppose Lilla didn't tell you because she was afraid you'd be shocked, but you might as well know all about it at the start. It saves misunderstandings. You see, we had a pajama party!"

"A pajama party!" cried the horrified father.

"Oh now, Daddy Pat! You needn't pull a long face and make out you never did such things. You know you had jazzy times when you went to school, and you can't be young but once. There isn't anything so terrible in a pajama party! You see the whole trouble was I got caught out on the fire escape in mine and all the rest got away, so I had to be expelled, but it was fun. I don't care. I'd do it all over again just to see how Guzzy Foster—that's the math prof—looked when that ice and salt went down his back. You see it was this way. One of the girls had a box of treats from home, and she happened to tell one of the boys from the military prep that she had it, and he coaxed to get some of the things. So May Beth told him if he and some of his friends would come under the fire escape at exactly midnight she'd drop down a box of cake for them. Well, everything went all right till the party was almost over and the girls had eaten all they could stuff, and they had the box for the boys all packed and I was to go out and throw it down to them because May Beth had an awful cold and her pajamas were just thin silk and she was all of a shiver anyway from eating so much cold ice cream. So I said I didn't mind even if it was cold. I thought it would be fun, and I went out with the box and whistled softly for the boys, and they answered once, and then it was all very still. It was moonlight, and I could see them lined up among the bushes on the campus. I swung the box over the railing and whispered, 'Here she comes,' and just as I did it I somehow caught my toe in the burlap that came off the ice-cream freezer—I had on Tillie Irvin's pink satin slippers with forget-me-nots on them, and she was sore as a boil at me about that, too—and then before I knew what was happening, I somehow hit the ice-cream freezer and knocked it over, and *slosh*! Out went all the sloppy ice and salt water through the iron grating on the fire escape, and I looked down and there was Guzzy Foster—he and his wife have their apartment right under my room, and we thought they were away for the weekend; that's why we chose my room for the party. He was just inside his window with his head stuck out of an old red bathrobe looking up—the old ferret. He was always snooping round to stop any fun that was going—and he caught the whole stream of icy saltwater full in his face and down his old mathematical back, and I hope he gets pneumonia from it. He's the limit! Well, I heard him gasp and splutter and draw in his head, and I heard the boys snicker down in the bushes and scatter out to the street—they got the cake all right. I called one of 'em up on the phone at the station before I left and found out—and I just danced up and down in those pink satin slippers with the forget-me-nots and howled for a minute, it was so funny. And then all of a sudden I realized it had got very still behind me, and I looked in the window and the lights were out. There wasn't a sound of a girl to be heard, and down the hall I could hear hard steps that sounded like Mrs. Foster, so I tried to get in the window, but it was fastened! Babe Heath did that because she thought if the window was locked they wouldn't think to look out. But there I was in thin silk pajamas and the wind blowing up from the river like ice! It was grand skating the next day, so you may know it was pretty fierce! But I stuck it out till she found me, and they expelled me so quick Lilla didn't have a chance to come and see what was the matter. They just sent me home that night chaperoned by Guzzy Foster himself. His name's Augustus Charles, but we call him Guzzy, and I had a horrid, horrid time, so it's up to you to be good to me!"

Patterson Greeves gasped and grasped the arms of the big chair into which he had dropped as Athalie entered, looking at his child in abject helplessness. The distant sound of an approaching train stirred him to nervous action once more.

"I certainly cannot approve of your outrageous conduct," he began, in a tone such as he might have used in his classroom. "It was inexcusable, impossible, indecent! I cannot think how a girl could bring herself to so demean herself. And the first thing you must do will be to write a humble acknowledgment and apology to the principal of the institution and promise that for the future your conduct shall be irreproachable. I will see at once about your reinstatement, and I cannot accept in future any disregard of the rules of the school or of the rules of good breeding."

But the girl broke in with a boisterous laugh: "What's that you say? Me go back to that school? Well, I guess anyhow not. *Not on your life, I don't!* You couldn't *drag* me within sight of the old dump. I'm done with it forever, and I'll tell the world *I'm glad*! Why? Don't you like me? Doesn't this dress suit you any better? I've got some stunners in my trunks. When do you think they will bring them out from the city? Can't we get a car and go after them? I'm just dying to show you some of my things and the big portrait of Lilla she had taken for the general!"

Greeves arose, white and angry.

"Get on your traveling things at once!" he almost shouted. "We are going back to your school. It is impossible for you to stay here. I am a very busy man. I have important work to do." He glanced wildly at his watch and then gave a quick look out of the window as he strode to the bell and touched it, flinging open the hall door and looking up the stairs.

"But I am not going back to school!" declared Athalie with a black look. "I'm going to stay right here! I won't be the least trouble in the world. I'll have my friends, and you can have yours. I'll go my way, and you can go yours. That's the way Lilla and I always did. Only, Daddy Pat, have we got to have that old limb of a housekeeper around? I hate her! I couldn't get on with her a day. I'm sure I'd shock her. She's a pie-faced hypocrite, and you'd better fire her. I'll run the house. I know how! Daddy Pat—may I call you *Pat?*"

"*No!*" thundered the scientist. "You may not. You may say 'Father' if it's necessary to call me anything!" He glared at her. "And you may go to your room at once and stay there until I send for you!" he added suddenly, as he glanced once more out of the window and saw an automobile draw up before the door. Then both of them became aware that Anne Truesdale stood in the open door, her face as white as her starched apron, a look of consternation upon her meek face, and her hands clasped nervously at her belt.

Chapter 6

It had not occurred to the minister until he came within sight of the station and heard the whistle of the approaching train that he had come on a most embarrassing errand.

It had appeared to him as he talked with her father and read her letter that the girl he was about to escort to her home might be anywhere between twelve and fifteen years old. His information concerning Patterson Greeves's history had been vague and incomplete. He looked like a young man for all this experience, and the minister had jumped to the conclusion that both girls were quite young.

But when the train drew up at the station and the only stranger who got out proved to be a lovely young woman dressed with quiet but exquisite taste and with an air of sweet sophistication, he became suddenly aware that the errand he had come upon was one of an exceedingly delicate nature, and he wished with all his soul he had not undertaken it.

She carried a small suitcase in her hand and walked with an air of knowing exactly where she was going. She paused only an instant to glance around her and then went straight to the station waiting room and checked her suitcase. She did it with so much apparent forethought, as if she had been there before and knew exactly what she had to do, that the young man hesitated and looked around for a possible other arrival who might be the girl he had come to meet. But the train snorted and puffed its way slowly into motion and started on, and no other passengers appeared. As she turned away from the checking desk, he came hesitantly up to her, and their eyes met.

She was slight and small with a well-formed head poised alertly and delicate features that gave one the sense of being molded and used by a spirit alive to more than the things of this earth. The impression was so strong that he hesitated, with hat lifted in the very act of introducing himself, to look again with startled directness into a face that was so exactly a counterpart of what he had dreamed a girl someday might be that he had the feeling of having been thrust with appalling unreadiness into her presence.

She had violet eyes with a frank clear glance, hair that curled naturally and frilled about her face, catching the sunbeams, lips that curved sweetly but firmly, and the complexion of a wild rose newly washed in dew. She looked like a spirit flower that yet was entirely able to take care of herself on earth.

"Is this—" he hesitated, remembering that he did not know her name, and finished lamely, "Mr. Greeves's daughter?"

She lifted her eyes with a quick searching look and smiled. "You are not— You could not be—my father."

Bannard smiled. "No, I have not that honor. Your father is—" he hesitated again. Why hadn't he thought up some excuse for the father who was not there? It seemed inexcusable—now that he saw the daughter—not to meet such a daughter! "Your father is— importantly engaged! He has only just arrived himself!"

He felt he was doing better.

"He only had opportunity to read your letter a few minutes ago, and it was impossible for him to get to the train. He asked me to meet you—"

She smiled with a rich, warm welcome for her father's friend, and he felt a glow of comfort.

"My name is Bannard," he finished. "I hope we're to be friends also." He put out his hand, and she took it graciously and thanked him.

He directed her to his car and helped her in then hesitated: "Your baggage? Didn't I see you check a suitcase? Wouldn't you like me to get it?"

A soft rose bloomed out in the girl's cheeks, and her lashes drooped deeply over her cheeks for an instant, then she lifted steady eyes and said: "No. I believe not, thank you. I'm not sure until I see—my father—whether I shall remain or go on to New York this afternoon."

He found himself strangely disturbed over this state of things. He wanted to assure her that of course she must not go on anywhere. This was the place that needed her. But of course he could say nothing. He might not even tell her that her father was in trouble. He had not been given permission to do anything but bring her to her home and that by as long a route as possible.

"We're going by a roundabout way," he explained as he headed his car for a detour quite away from the old Silver place. "There's a bad bit of road they are repairing—" He was thankful that he had happened to notice the men at work on his way down and therefore could truthfully give an explanation to this clear-eyed maiden who it seemed to him must be able to read his embarrassment through the very fabric of his coat.

"Shall we pass the old Presbyterian church?" she asked eagerly, leaning forward and looking around as though it were a spot she knew well by heart but had never seen with her eyes.

"Why, yes, we can," he responded eagerly. "Are you especially interested in that?" And he looked down with a smile and then a wonder at the light in her eyes.

"It is where my father went to church," she answered, as if repeating things she had learned well. "And there is a cemetery where my relatives are buried. I was interested to see it."

He drove the car down a smooth ribbon of a road that curved around with wooded land on one side and mellow fields of rippling green on the other, with a glimpse off at the right of the Silver River and Frogtown factories smothered in pale budding willows against a turquoise sky.

"It is beautiful here, isn't it?" The girl's eyes glowed. She drew in long breaths of the spring air. There were violets at the side of the road, and it came to him how like her eyes they were.

They crossed a stone bridge and headed more directly toward the river, and she exclaimed over the bright winding ribbon of water. Just because he had promised to make the trip long, because he liked to see the wild rose color in the round cheeks glow when she opened her eyes wide at the view, he slowed down the car and checked some minute squeak in the engine. Not that it was important. Not that he did anything about it. Just a pleasant little delay. It seemed to him he was experiencing a charmed privilege that was slipping by all too quickly and that he would grasp as it went. It might not ever come his way again.

On their way again they wound around the clump of beeches and came into the main street of Silver Sands, all shining in the morning sunlight with serene houses on either side in long stretches of green, and new gardens in geometrical lines behind the houses flanked by regiments of beanpoles. A wide straw hat sheltered a lady picking strawberries in the patch of luxuriant vines. The breath of the day was sweet with growing things. The people walked crisply down the pleasant maple-shaded pavements as though the going were enjoyment. The anvil rang out with silver sound from the blacksmith shop as they passed. People began to hail the minister with a glad lighting of eyes, and he was kept busy lifting his hat and waving his hand cheerily. Even the boys in the street greeted him, and then curious, half-jealous eyes turned to study his companion as they swept on their way.

"They all know you," the girl commented. "I'm sure you must live in Silver Sands."

"I do," he responded. "It is a good place to live. My particular corner is just down that next street, the white house with the rose trellis over the door. I board with a blessed old lady whom everybody calls Aunt Katie Barnes. She nearly turns herself out of house and home trying to find new ways of making me comfortable. It is a very friendly community. They take one in heart and soul."

She flashed him an appreciative glance and asked thoughtfully: "Have you known my father long?"

"Well, not so very long—" the minister answered, "that is—you know he has only recently returned, but we are wonderfully good friends considering the short time. I—you—" He hesitated. There was something he wanted to tell her for her reassurance, to answer the question in her eyes that he felt sure she was too loyal to her father to ask, but his lips were sealed. And after all, what was there to say even if they had not been? What reassurance had he himself that the man he had left raving at Fate in the old library would give any sort of an adequate welcome to this pearl of a girl? He felt as if he wanted to tell her that if her father wasn't glad to see her he would take him by the neck and shake him till he was. But one couldn't tell a strange girl things like that about her father.

"This is the Presbyterian church we are coming to now, the one on the left. The main part was built in 1617. Hasn't it nobly simple lines? The stones have weathered to as fine a color as any cathedral in the old world. I love to see it against the sky with the sunset behind it. That spire is a thing of beauty, don't you think? And those doves in the belfry are a continual delight. Do you know Aldrich's bit of a verse, 'And on the belfry sits a dove with purple ripples on her neck?' There goes one now swooping down to the pavement. Did you see the silver flash on her wings? And now we're coming to the part of the cemetery where your ancestors are buried. See that big gray granite column? No, the plain one just beyond. That is the old Silver lot. All the Silvers are lying there. Your grandfather and great-grandfather and their wives in that center plot, and those side plots are for the sons and their wives and children. It was a peculiar arrangement and forethought of the first Silver settler and carried out by each succeeding one in turn. There, those two gray stones are for Standish Silver and his sister Lavinia, the last of the family who bore the Silver name."

"Aunt Lavinia and Uncle Standish. I have their pictures," said the girl softly as if doing homage to their memory. "They brought up my father."

She lifted shy, friendly eyes: "Silver is my name, too. It's an odd name for a girl, isn't it? But I like it. I like to think I'm a Silver, too."

"It is a beautiful name," said the young man, doing homage with his eyes.

"They were a wonderful people from all I hear. I would like to have known them."

And now all too soon they were at the Silver door and he was helping her out of the car.

He found his heart pounding strangely with anticipation for the girl at his side. How would she be received? He felt as if he must stay by her till he was sure, although delicacy dictated that he disappear as soon as his errand was done.

Blink, with nonchalant foresight, was idly flipping pebbles at a toad in the meadow from his perch on the fence, his back to the road. At his feet, attentive to each motion, apparently approving and aiding and abetting the game, barked a big yellow collie. The dog bounded jealously across the road at sight of the car and up to the minister with a wag and a glad grin of recognition then gave a friendly snuff to the girl's hands, looked up, and smiled a dog greeting with open cordiality.

"What a dear dog!" exclaimed the girl. "What a beauty!" She was bending over him with the enthusiasm of a true dog lover, and Blink sauntered idly over and leaned against the car, pleased at her demonstration, eyeing her furtively, appraisingly. "May I introduce his master Barry Lincoln, otherwise 'Blink' to his intimate friends?" said Bannard.

The girl lifted frank eyes to Blink's embarrassed ones and liked him at once. She put out her hand warmly and grasped his rough, shy one as she might have done to an older man, and the boy's heart warmed toward her.

"What a very interesting name!" she said cheerfully, "If I stay here long I am sure I shall try to qualify to use it. Is the dog's name Link?"

The boy grinned.

"He's Buddie," he admitted shyly.

"Well, Buddie, I hope I meet you again," she said, with another flash of warmth in her eyes for the boy whose own were now filled with open admiration. She passed into the white gate, and Blink looked after her with a new stirring in his heart—call it loyalty if you like; Blink had no idea what it was. He lifted his glance to the minister's smile and found the same thing in his friend's eyes, and an unspoken covenant flashed between them to protect her if ever she needed their protection. Blink would have expressed it in words: "She's a good sport." Blink and the dog stood by the car, Buddie wagging his plume of a tail vigorously, and watched the man and the girl go up the flower-boarded walk to the big mullioned door.

From inside the library Patterson Greeves watched the two figures arrive.

Joe Quinn watched from the shelter of the smoke bush close to the lilac hedge where he was digging about the tulip beds, and Molly the cook, having seen the car from her pantry window, had hurried up to the front hall window on pretext of looking for the housekeeper and was gazing down curiously on the two, wondering what next was coming to the old house.

At the extreme dark end of the back hall, Anne Truesdale, in hiding, could glimpse the minister's hat through the side lights of the hall door and a snatch now and then of the lady's feather, and she stood with hand involuntarily on her heart, waiting, not daring to come out till "that huzzy," as she thought of Athalie, had gone upstairs. But Athalie, one foot on the lower step, had turned back to look at her irate father, perfectly aware that he was disturbed by the sight of something out of the window, and herself caught a glimpse of the minister returning. Ah! So that was why she was being sent upstairs! A good-looking young man and she bundled away! This was no part of Miss Athalie's plan of life, so she whirled around on the lowest step and waited also.

Then the fine old knocker reverberated through the long silent house. Patterson Greeves retreated hastily in panic to his library, and Anne Truesdale, chained to duty by an inexorable conscience, was forced to come out and open the door.

The stage was set, and the actors came on as the door was timidly opened by Anne.

Chapter 7

Athalie Greeves came noiselessly forward to the library door, a look of expectancy on her round, pink face, a cat-and-cream expression about her lips. As noiselessly Patterson Greeves forced himself to step to the doorway again, a heavy frown upon his brow, a look of extreme suffering—one would almost have said dread—in his eyes. Anne with frightened eyes peered bravely round the door, and the two on the wide flagging stones of the porch waited, the girl with wistful, eager, yet courageous eyes, ready for either love or renunciation, whichever the indications showed; the minister hovering tall above her, a look almost of defiance on his strong face, an air of championship and protection about him.

Nobody spoke for the first instant, which seemed almost like an eternity. The two girls saw each other first, for Patterson Greeves stood within the library door.

The girl on the steps was dressed in a blue-gray tweed suit, well fitted and tailored, and a trim little soft blue straw hat with a sharp black wing piquantly stabbing the folds of the straw. Her hair was golden in the sunlight and as she stood seemed like a halo around her face. The light of the morning was in her eyes as she peered into the shadows of the hall then suddenly grayed with chill and reserve as she met the eyes of the other girl.

Athalie's plump face grew suddenly hard, her lips drooped, her eyes, glared, her head went slightly forward with a look of stealth and jealousy, and her hand went instinctively out to catch the door frame. Her whole form seemed to crouch with a catlike motion, and green lights danced in her eyes, though they might have been reflected from her dress. The minister lifted amazed eyes and saw her. He put out an involuntary hand of protection toward the girl by his side.

Then Patterson Greeves stepped into the hall sternly, his back to Athalie, and came toward the door. He looked and stopped short, his hands suddenly stretched out and then drawn back to his eyes with a quick hysterical motion as if he would brush a fantasm from his vision. "Alice!" came from his lips in a low, broken tone of agony, as if the torture and mistakes of the years were summed up in the word.

During that instant while he stood with his fingers pressing his eyes Athalie began stealthily to step back and across the hall to the wide arched doorway of the stately old parlor that ran the depth of the house on the other side of the hall from the library. Her eyes, wide and round, were fixed on her father. An instant later, there was only left the swaying of the old silk cord tassel that held the heavy maroon curtains of the doorway.

Then the girl on the doorstep came to vivid life and stepped up quickly toward her father with eager light in her face.

"Father!" She said the word with a world of reverence and stored-up love, tender, caressing sound, so genuine, so wistful, it could not fail to reach the heart of any man who was not utterly dead to his fatherhood. They were clasping hands now, looking earnestly, eagerly into one another's eyes.

Anne Truesdale, behind the door, averting her loyal gaze; the minister with anxious attitude upon the doorstep; the alien daughter behind the heavy curtain, one eye applied to a loophole close to the door frame, were breathless witnesses of the moment. Then Patterson Greeves drew his daughter within the library door with the one word "Come," and closed the door behind them. The minister came to himself, murmuring that he would return or telephone later, and departed. Anne Truesdale closed the front door, and with an anxious glance as she tiptoed by the library door, vanished up the stairs. A soft stirring at the end of the back hall where Molly listened, a cautiously closed latch, and all was still.

Athalie in the big, dim parlor held her breath, listening, peered cautiously, and then drew back and gazed around her with a leisurely air.

The room was wide and very long, with windows heavily curtained in the old-fashioned stately way. The ceilings high, the walls hung with dim old portraits in heavy gilt frames. The floor was covered with heavy velvet carpet, rich and thick in scrolls and roses, bright with care, though the years had passed many times over it. The furniture was rare and old and comfortable, and would have graced many a finer mansion. One or two chairs done in fine handmade tapestry softly faded with the years, tables and cabinets that had come down from the masters in woodwork. A rosewood piano of a make some thirty years back, whose name was still dignified and honored. Athalie stood and gazed around, half contemptuously. The chairs, yes—but the carpet! How funny! She would have to see that it was taken up at once and a hardwood floor—of *course*—this would be a grand room for a dance. She gave an experimental whirl on a cautious toe. Those curtains were gloomy! She slid a sleek hand into a well-camouflaged silken pocket and brought out chocolates to fortify herself. Her mouth comfortingly filled with the creamy velvet of Dutch creams, she started on a tour of inspection, pausing first before an ancestral portrait hanging above a curiously carved sofa with handwrought tapestry upholstery. The picture frame, tarnished with the years, seemed like an open doorway to the past. From it looked out a woman plain of face, smooth of hair, with a carved high black comb towering above her sleek head and bearing a bird on her finger. The eyes were so expressionless and the face so somber that it was impossible not to connect it with a monotonous existence. A woman satisfied with a pet bird! Athalie paused and took in the thought. A lift of her well-rounded shoulders, a contemptuous smile, that was her reaction to the woman of long ago. She meant little to the girl modern in all her thoughts and feelings. There was hardly a shadow of conception of that sheltered, sweet, strong life that had given much to the world in her passing. The girl passed to the portrait of the man in military uniform hanging between the two long front windows, and her jaws paused in their slow rhythmic manipulation of the chocolates to study him a moment. This must be old General Silver. Her mother had told her about him. Not much, only that he had been something—made some great mark in the Civil War, or was it the war before that? Athalie's ideas of history were most vague. She knew only that it was very long ago if one might judge by the old-fashioned haircut, the high collar, the strange insignia, not in the least like a modern soldier. He had bushy eyebrows, from beneath which his piercing eyes looked over her head straight out to some far-seen enemy, keen, cutting, stern— the girl shuddered. There had been that look in the eye of this new-found father of hers, not at all fatherly, not "dadish" as she expressed it to herself, purely official. He was like his ancestor, she decided, as she stood and watched the picture. Disappointing. Quite as Lilla

had said he would be. Hard as stone. Flint in his eye. No yielding
to coaxing. No weakness anywhere that one could probe. Was the
bird lady his wife or daughter? She looked back and studied the first
portrait critically, deciding she must have been his wife. No wonder
she looked as if she had dragged out a drab existence! And yet—she
looked back to the soldier's face. There was a fascination about him
somewhere. What was it? The molding of the firm lips? The arch
of the heavy brow? The curve of the wavy hair, brushed fiercely
forward from either side of the head and focusing over the forehead
in a high standing brush? Well—somehow that made you long
to conquer, to draw a smile to those stern lips, a soft light to the
eyes—it must have been that something that made Lilla marry her
father. It couldn't have all been money or position for Athalie had
heard her mother tell many times of other lovers, far more famed
and wealthy. There was something about her father she had come
to conquer, and she hardened her own willful lips in determination
and passed on to the next wall opposite the bird lady.

A stately dame with soft white hair and a cap looked out from
the next frame with a smile, more human than the others, the
girl felt; her stiff black silk seemed almost to rustle from its frame
with dignity and kindliness, and the painted hands held primly a
wide, gracious fan of rare old lace. And beside this picture hung
the portrait of her husband apparently, a fine old gentleman with
silvered hair, high stock, and courtly manner, fitting mate for the
dear old lady, both portraits so lifelike that Athalie paused almost
abashed for an instant as if someone unexpectedly had entered
the room. It gave her a feeling of unaccustomed awe, these strong,
painted personalities all about her, past history caught and im-
prisoned on the canvas for another age to know intimately. They
looked down at her with kindly gracious eyes, and she turned away
awkwardly, uncomfortable, and swept the room with another glance.

On the back wall Uncle Standish Silver in more modern business garb and his sister Lavinia in her Sunday best silk, long sleeved, high necked, fastened with a great cameo at the throat, and pretty crimped hair drawn back and up from her ears in a knot on top of her shapely head, were too modern to excite her curiosity, too old-fashioned to hold her interest. Her eyes wandered to the frame opposite the side window, half in shadow of the heavy curtain, a picture of a young man, a mere boy he was. She walked the length of the room eagerly to inspect it and stopped in admiration. A boy a little older than herself, only slim and tall, and with eyes—yes with eyes like the soldier—and—yes—*eyes like her father's*! It must be her father when he was a boy!

She stood a long time looking at it with mingled feelings, admiring, jealous, determined, studying him as he had been when almost her age. She felt if she knew him then, she would be more able to understand and influence him now. Finally, with a sigh of impatience, she turned and was about to slip out of the room when she suddenly saw for the first time—how had it escaped her?—the portrait of a young and beautiful woman, fresh, vivid, smiling, from a great oval frame over the white marble mantel. The eyes were wonderful, large, loving, innocent, deeply intelligent, and with a look of life about them that made the girl uneasy. Those eyes seemed suddenly to have been watching her all the time, to have followed her around the room, to be searching her down to the depths of her mean, selfish little soul. They were maddening eyes to a girl like Athalie. They belied every purpose of her life, every standard and ideal dear to her soul, every act of which she was conscious. They were like an angel's eyes come down to earth for judgment.

Slowly, with gathering storm in her own dark eyes, she approached, and the two eyes seemed to meet. Who was this young girl dressed in misty white like a bride, fashioned not so long ago either? And was that a veil on her head? And orange blossoms—a spray? What bride of recent years had a right there, in the center of the great room, the place of honor? It must be—! It *was* her father's first wife! Here in the house where she had come to live! Watching her with searching angel eyes like that! Clean eyes that made her conscious of herself! Assured eyes that claimed their right to be there!

And who was it she resembled? Where had she seen that face before, those true clear eyes?

It suddenly flashed over her, and she trembled from head to toe with rage and ground her teeth in quick fury. *That girl out on the doorstep!* Was that the girl of the portrait? Or had her father married another wife, a young girl like that? Had he *dared* and not let them know? Could he do that? Or—wait! There had been a child. Lilla had always said that it died—but perhaps!

Suddenly, Athalie, in a burst of rage, took a long step toward the portrait, a spring up, and spit out a great mouthful of well-chewed, sticky chocolate straight into the lovely painted face, covering eyes and nose and smiling lips and dripping in ugly brown courses down cheeks and chin. The girl surveyed her work of desecration with satisfaction and a lifted chin and stuck out tongue as any naughty child of three might have done. Then lifting her hands in a hateful defiant gesture, she darted from the room and went lightly upstairs.

In a moment more after rummaging in her suitcase, she came out with a large framed photograph hidden in the folds of her skirt and slipped down to the parlor again, going straight to the mantel and putting her picture directly under the picture of the girl bride.

It was a recent picture of Lilla taken in a tremendously gauzy dressing gown, one of the expensive ones of velvet and chiffon and fur she loved to wear, an intimate picture not meant for public gaze, a bold-eyed, challenging, still beautiful woman, with amazing hair falling over bare shoulders and down upon the silk pillows of her chaise longue, on which she was half reclining. It was framed in an exquisite silver frame and intended for Athalie to show her former husband that he might see how lovely she still remained in spite of his indifference.

Athalie stood back and surveyed with jealous eye the picture smiling defiantly beneath the defaced one, made another grimace of hate and flew up the stairs again to her room, leaving her mother's picture to hold its own with the other portraits of the family.

Chapter 8

Within the quiet library, the father and daughter were coming to their own. The alienation of the years like a great wall of ice was slowly melting between them, and they were groping for phantom ends of heartstrings broken long ago.

He had seated his daughter in one chair and drawn another opposite her. He was unnerved with the events of the night and morning. He seemed to find it hard to control his faculties and adjust himself to the present circumstances. He hardly seemed to hear her voice or the words she was speaking. It was his dead wife's voice that he heard. And there was no reproach in it, but it rebuked him. It rebuked him so that he could scarcely speak.

"I have wanted to see you so long—Father! I have wanted to know—" she was saying.

He groaned as he dropped his head for an instant and put his hands up to his eyes: "You—are—*Alice*!" he said hoarsely.

She smiled. That smile he had loved so well! Was ever man tortured like this man? To have the dead come back in such perfection, yet in another body—and with another soul? "My daughter! My *daughter!*" he tried to say to himself, yet it was only babbling. He could not grasp its meaning. This was Alice come to rebuke him. Alice as when he first knew her.

"They always have called me Silver," she said wistfully. "Grandmother couldn't quite bear to call me Alice. But—I shall be glad to have you call me what you like."

He looked at her as in a dream. He could not think what to say to her. He wanted to reach out and touch that lock of hair that was drooping over her ear, the one with the sunbeam nestled in it, brushing against her cheek, that cheek rounded with the same contour as his lost Alice.

What a fool he had been not to know Alice would leave him her image in her child. How he had given it away, this dear growing vision of the lost one! Given it away without a thought, actually been glad to be rid of the responsibility! And now he had lost it! Lost the right! It was like giving light to a blind man, bread to a dead man, to give her to him now. He could never get to know her after these years. He had carved out his life in a different line, a line where she did not fit. He could never learn to speak her language, nor teach her his. He would not have her learn his. He shuddered at the thought. He could only look at her and watch her as she talked, scarcely hearing anything she said.

Afterward some of her sentences came back, stored up by his subconscious mind perhaps: details of her life, where she had been at school, how she had occupied her time, sweet incidents of the last years of those she loved. He understood enough to be rebuked again, seeing how he had failed in what might have been a pleasant duty toward the beloved of his beloved.

"You are not—*angry*—with me for coming?" she asked at last, lifting her eyes anxiously to his silent, staring face.

A swift contortion like sudden pain darted over his face. It seemed as if he might be trying to smile in unaccustomed lines. It hurt him that she should ask such a thing. He had not thought that would hurt! It hurt him that he could not answer her with the right cordial words! What were the right words? Why could he not get hold of them? What a complex thing this life was anyway that one could go on for years according to a certain plan and standard and then suddenly be confronted by unsuspected emotions that upset the whole universe! He became aware that she was still awaiting an answer, with sorrow gathering in those dear blue eyes.

"Angry? Oh no! Why should I be angry?" he found himself saying in a cold distant tone. It was as if he were dead, trying to call to the living, so strange and far away his own voice seemed to him.

A slow flush rose in her cheeks, and her troubled eyes searched his face for sign of welcome.

He struggled once more for words: "I am glad you have come." The words had not been formed in his intention. He found to his wonder that they were nevertheless true. "I wish you had come before!"

"But you were not here!"

"Of course!" he said foolishly. "Then I wish I had come sooner. I wish I had never gone—from you!"

"Oh, Father, do you really? How many times I have wished that!" The blue eyes were full of wistful eagerness now. It had meant a great deal to her! Why had it? Was that her mother looking at him through her eyes? Was he going stark-staring crazy? It was Alice's look. Alice was looking through those eyes of her daughter as one might look through a window!

He was not gazing at the girl now, only at Alice looking through her eyes. Alice was trying to signal to him, to make him understand something. What was that the lips so like hers were saying?

"When I was a little, little child, Grandmother used to tell me all about you, how you first came to see Mother—" Ah! She called her *Mother*! "How you looked, how you used to sing and play football and baseball, how handsome you were—"

Ah! He had lost the thread for a moment, and now she was speaking of her first little baby thoughts of him, how Grandmother had taught her lisping lips to pray, "Dod bess Favver!" Suddenly the thought of rosy baby fingers around his neck—where had he seen rosy baby fingers? Not Lilla's baby! That had seemed too much a part of Lilla to be pleasant to him. He had never made much or seen much of Lilla's baby. He shuddered at the thought of that other girl upstairs. How should he tell this girl about her?

"I used to wonder how it would be to have a father, a *young* father, like other children, to carry me upstairs at night—Grandfather was dear, but you know he had that accident—oh, didn't you know about that? I was only two years old when it happened. He was knocked down by a heavy truck in trying to cross the city street on his way to Presbytery. He was always lame after that and had to be very careful about lifting. I used to so long to be lifted up and carried in strong arms!"

The man wondered at the exquisite thrill that came to him. After all these years of dreary living, his heart burned out to ashes, that the thought of a little child, *his* little child being carried in his arms should so stir him! The thought of a rosy cheek cuddling in his neck, moist lips dropping furtive kisses, soft breath coming and going against his cheek, golden curls spreading on his shoulder— she would have had golden curls he knew by the curl of the sunshine in the tendrils around her forehead. His baby! *Alice's* baby! Alice's gift to him to comfort him through the lonely years! And *he had let her go*! Was that what the eyes had been trying to signal to him? It was as if Alice stood there behind the windows of her daughter's eyes and held out her baby to him with a smile; and suddenly he understood and reached out the arms of his heart to gather her to his life. Fool that he had been that he had not known it sooner, before the mistakes of his life had thickened around him and made him unfit for caring for her! Suddenly he dropped his face into his hands again and groaned.

"Father! Dear Father! What is it? Did I hurt you somehow?"

"Too late! Too late!" he moaned. "What a fool I have been!"

And there somehow he told her all that she needed to know of the years that had separated them, broken sentences, more pauses than words, tender silences. The grafting process had begun in what had been so long severed.

When Anne Truesdale, after long lingering and listening to the low murmur of voices, finally brought herself to tap on the door and announce lunch, their faces were like the clear shining after rain.

"Come in, Anne!" His voice was more like himself than it had been since his arrival. Anne entered bravely, suppressing her own excitement.

"I'm afraid, Anne, we've been upsetting all your arrangements," he began penitently as he used to do when as a boy he took all the cookies in the cookie jar to feed a hungry horde of boys.

"Don't speak of it, Master Pat. Yer not to apologize to me. This is yer own house. I and the rest are but here to do yer bidding. It is the pleasure of us all to have things as you'll be wanting them." The woman held her hands tightly clasped at her waist and made a low courtesy of respect. The master's face softened with affection.

"Thank you, Trudie," he said, using the old childhood name. Then turning toward the girl he said: "Trudie, this is Alice's child! My daughter—Silver! *Silver—Alice!*"

He turned quickly away, his voice husky with feeling, but wheeled as suddenly back again: "Could she have Aunt Lavinia's room? I'd like to have her there!"

Anne gave the girl one swift, sifting glance and rendered instant homage.

"Indeed she could, Master Pat," she said heartily, satisfaction in her eyes. "And right pleased would Miss Lavinia be to have such a successor. Shall I show the way at once? Lunch is putting on the table."

"Why, I'll only be a moment," said the girl beginning to remove her gloves. "How beautiful to have Aunt Lavinia's room!"

Anne Truesdale stepped back as Silver advanced to the stairs and spoke in a guarded voice: "And what about the young miss upstairs? Must I speak to her to come down?"

The man looked as though she had struck him, and the light of shining went suddenly out of his eyes. "Oh, why! Yes—I suppose you'll have to—tell her to come down, please!" he finished with an attempt at ease, and bracing himself made one of his quick turns and went and stood staring out of the long narrow window that framed the front doorway.

Silver had paused, glancing back, and caught the low words, felt the pain in his voice and the sudden dashing of his spirit. It seemed that a cloud must have just passed over the sun. *The young miss upstairs!* That would be the flapper-looking child she saw when she first entered. Who was she? What right had she here in her father's house?

But Anne Truesdale's black silk was rustling close behind, and Silver mounted the stairs looking with eager eyes around, not seeing the glitter of an evil black eye at the keyhole as she passed down the upper hall.

"This was Miss Lavinia's room," said Anne, swinging wide the paneled mahogany door and revealing quaint rare furniture, rich faded carpet, a glimpse of a pineapple-carved four-poster bed, and the depths of a flowered wing chair by the window, with a little sewing table drawn up and even a work basket with a bit of white linen tidily folded atop.

Anne bustled about, setting straight a chair, patting a pillow, and smoothing a dent out of the wing-chair cushion where she had but just been kneeling. Then she slipped away down the hall and tapped at a door nearer the head of the stairs on the other side.

Silver took off her hat, ran her fingers through her hair, washed her face and hands in the great blue and white china bowl, dried them on a fine linen towel fragrant with rose leaves and exquisitely embroidered with a great *S* at one end. Then she fluffed up her hair a bit more, gave a glance into the mirror and another lingering one around the sweet old room, and went quickly downstairs, arriving just in time to hear Anne's low murmured: "She says she'll not come down. She's not feeling so good," and to see her father's relief at the message.

At the head of the stairs, Athalie with velvet tread had crept to the railing to listen and peer over from the shadows of the upper hall as they went to the old, stately dining room, father and daughter, for their first meal together. As they disappeared and the heavy door closed silently behind them, the girl leaned far over the baluster and made an ugly face ending in a hiss. Then as stealthily as she had come, she crept back to her room, closed the door, locked it, rummaged among her luggage for a five-pound box of chocolates and a novel, and established herself amid pillows on the foot of the big old bed.

Anne Truesdale came up presently with a laden tray of good things, but Athalie, with her face smothered in the pillow and her chocolates and book hid out of sight, declined any sustenance. Anne, pausing thoughtfully in the hall, finally scuttled down the dark, narrow back stairs and whisked the tray out of sight, deciding that the master should not know of this hunger strike yet.

After lunch Silver and her father went back to the library for a time, and their low voices in steady, cheerful conversation were not soothing to the other daughter's nerves. She tiptoed to the open window to see if she could hear any words but found she could not on account of a family of sparrows who were nesting in the honeysuckle below and seemed to have been retained for the purpose of chattering.

About half past two Silver and her father went out together down the street. Athalie watched them from the shelter of the window curtain, frowning and noting the amicable footing on which they seemed to be.

They went to the station and reclaimed the girl's suitcase. On the way back, they stopped at the old church and walked slowly through the graveyard, the father pointing out the names on the white stones of those who would be of interest to her among her unknown kin, the girl's face kindling with tender emotions as she read the records mossy with age. While they were gone, the village delivery man arrived with four immense trunks and three wooden boxes. Athalie arose with alacrity from her bed of pain and superintended their installment in the house.

"You can bring the two wardrobe trunks right in here and unpack them at once," she informed Anne Truesdale haughtily. "I shall need more closet room. I think I'll take that room across the hall. You might put the other two trunks and the boxes there till we get them unpacked. I shall probably use that for my dressing room."

"That is the spare bedroom," said Anne coldly but firmly. "There is a trunk room in the attic where your trunks can be stored." Athalie gave her a withering look, but such looks had no effect on Anne. She went her way and called the faithful servant Joe. He managed an extra hand from the street, to help the delivery man, and Athalie's mammoth trunks were carried slowly up the stairs. Nothing so huge in the way of a trunk had ever entered that house before, and Anne stood aghast as the first one hovered in sight and cast a quick and calculating eye toward the attic stairs. But when she saw how heavy they all were, she changed her mind. They should go no farther until they were unpacked. So the first was placed in the back hall for further consideration, while the remaining three proved to be so enormous that Anne demanded the key, and down in the wide, old front hall Athalie's frivolous possessions were brought to light and carried up in the abashed and indignant arms of the three old-fashioned servants, who looked upon the trifles of lingerie with averted gaze and felt that the daring evening frocks of scarlet and silver and turquoise were little short of blasphemies. They hastened them up to the oblivion of the second floor before the master should return, and Anne stood for a full minute gazing out of the hall window across the sunny meadow and pondering whether she ought not perhaps to have left them all down on the back porch where the boxes had been sent, until the return of the master. Such doings! And for a young girl, too. Four trunks! What would Miss Lavinia have said?

Athalie meanwhile was rummaging among her brilliant clothes, pulling out this and that, deciding what she would wear next after she had sufficiently cowed that hard-hearted father of hers, and finally burrowed her way among silks and organdies to her chocolates and her pillow again, deciding not to put anything away until that objectionable "Anne" person came to do her bidding. She felt she must make it understood from the start that she would be waited upon. Anne wasn't much like her mother's maid, but such as she was, she must be reduced to obedience. Perhaps she could coax her father to let her have a French maid all her own, a young girl about her own age. That would be rather fun.

Chapter 9

While Athalie was thus engaged, her father and Silver were wandering through the quiet graveyard, talking of the past. The man found himself telling his child about his own boyhood, his aunt, his uncle, the old minister, the long, sweet services in the quaint old church. There was no bitterness in his voice now as he spoke of the religion of those who had brought him up. Something softening had come over him. He hardly understood himself.

And then suddenly they had come upon the young minister, stooping over a little newly made grave, working with some violet plants in full bloom, planting them in the mellow soil until the little mound became a lovely bed.

They did not see him until they were almost upon him, and then he rose quickly, his hands covered with dirt, his hat on the back of his head, his dark hair curling in little moist waves around his white forehead, and a light of welcome in his face.

"I'm just fixing up this place a bit before the mother comes," he explained. "It looked so desolate and bare, and this was her only child!"

He stooped again and pressed the earth firmly around the violets, with strong capable fingers, arranging the plants as he talked till the whole little mound was one mass of lovely bloom. Then he rose, dusted the dirt away from his hands, and strolled along with them.

"Would you like a glimpse of the old church?" He flashed a smile at Silver.

"Oh, I would!" she exclaimed eagerly. "Grandmother used to tell me stories of my father's home, all she knew, and she always told about the old church. Mother was here—once—wasn't she?" She looked up shyly at her father who was walking absentmindedly, sadly beside the young people, his hands clasped behind him as if his thoughts were far in the past. He started as she asked the question, and a pain seemed to stab into his eyes like one who is suddenly brought to view something long lost and very dear.

"Yes, yes! Your mother was here! On our wedding trip! We went to church. We sat in the old pew. She wore a little white hat with white flowers on it and a thin blue dress!" It was as if he were musing over a beloved picture. The minister and the girl exchanged swift understanding glances.

"We will go in," said the young man. "I have the key."

He unlocked the old oaken door, and the sunshine poured behind them into the ancient hall, lighting up the well-kept red ingrain carpet and meeting the sunshine that poured down from a stained-glass window above in curious blended, dancing colors like the pattern of some well-remembered hymn sacred to many services held within those holy courts.

Patterson Greeves walked beside the young Alice as he had walked beside her mother up those stairs to the chapel above, so many years ago, and saw again in imagination the eager friends of his youth leaning over the grained oak railing to get the first glimpse of the bride. Felt again the swell of the pride in the girl he had chosen, remembered the look of pleasure in the eyes of his uncle Standish as he met them at the head of the stairs and escorted them down the aisle to the pew, and Alice's smile as she looked up at him. Ah! That he had thought was to be the beginning of life! And only one short year it lasted! They all turned to bitterness and night! Fool that he had been that he had thought anything so heavenly could have lasted on this earth! That he had believed there existed a God who cared for him and planned for him! Ah! Well! Bitterness!

The blood rolled through his veins in a sickly, prickly, smothering wave, and he mopped his brow with his handkerchief and wondered why he had let himself in for this sort of thing after all these years. Why had he come down to the old church so full of memories?

Then he lifted his eyes to his girl who stood in the open doorway of the chapel now, framed in all her girlish beauty against the background of the rich coloring of the church, its jeweled windows casting rich, fantastic lights in a rainbow flood of beauty, glancing away from the cluster of gilt organ pipes, glinting on the gold fringe of the pulpit Bible bookmark, focusing on the blood red of the bright old carpet and beating it into a tessellated aisle of precious gems, mellowing the age-worn woodwork of the square high pews and the carvings of the pulpit and red plush pulpit chairs. There was something in the look of his girl as she stood there against that background with all the heritage of her grandfather's and grandmother's religion behind her that took away the pain again and made him watch her breathlessly and trace out every likeness to the mother who was gone, made him glad that she had come in spite of all the pain. Even glad of the pain, if it brought this vision.

The minister was explaining about the organ. "Not a wonderful organ and a bit old, but one of the good old makes, and with two or three beautiful stops." Did she play? She did. He was sure she did. Wouldn't she try the organ?

"Her mother could play! Oh, she could play!"

Greeves had spoken without intending, but the other two gave no sign that they had seen the emotion in his face.

"Yes, I know," the girl said quietly. "I studied with her teacher for two years. He was an old man, but he was wonderful. After he died, Grandfather sent me away to study for a while."

They lingered nearly an hour in the church, the girl drawing sweet harmonies from the old yellow keys, the minister lingering near, calling for this and that favorite, while Greeves sat long in the old family pew and read without seeing them the old familiar texts twined among the fresco, "THE LORD IS IN HIS HOLY TEMPLE: LET ALL THE EARTH KEEP SILENCE BEFORE HIM." Even now after the years, it sent a certain note of awe through his soul, an echo of the old days when God was real and life a rare vista before him. There were the same old windows. He used to count the medallions in the border when the sermon was unusually long. There was the shepherd and the lambs and the first verse of the Twenty-Third Psalm. There was the storm one, purple clouds driven hard across an iron sky, trees and shrubs bowing before it, and the inscription, "FOR IN THE TIME OF TROUBLE HE SHALL HIDE ME IN HIS PAVILION: IN THE SECRET OF HIS TABERNACLE SHALL HE HIDE ME."

How firmly he used to believe in that when he was a child! How truly he expected to take refuge in that tabernacle if any storm overtook him! And how far he was now from any refuge. What a farce it had been! Beautiful while it lasted. But a farce! He drew himself up with a shudder of disgust at it all, and the tones of the organ caught him as Silver's fingers trailed over the keys while she talked in low tone with the minister:

"Nearer my God to Thee,
    Nearer to Thee—"

It had been Aunt Lavinia's favorite, and it stung its way into his soul in spite of his intention otherwise. He could hear her singing it, evenings in the nursery when she held him on her lap, his earliest remembrance, while her eyes watched the sky grow red and gray and deepen into starry blue, and the look about her mouth told him even in his baby days that there was something sad back somewhere in her life, something that she might have given up, possibly for him.

"Nearer my God to Thee,
  E'en though it be a cross—"

He could hear the gentle murmur of her timid voice in that very pew as he had sat beside her many years. Ah! The tears stung into his eyes unaccountably after all these years. And he? His song had been:

"Farther my God from Thee,
  Farther from Thee—!"

How Aunt Lavinia would have agonized in prayer before her deep old wing chair if she could have known! He had seen her kneeling once like that, in her decorous high-necked, long-sleeved nightdress with the little tatted ruffles round her throat and wrists, her eyes closed, her gentle face illuminated with a wistful joy that had awed him, her lips murmuring softly words of pleading for him: "Oh God, bless our little Pat. Make him grow up a good man, loving God more than all else in life! Make him sorry for his sins! Make him love righteousness and hate wrong—"

The words were indelibly graven on his soul. He had not thought of them in years, but they were there just as sharply discernible as when that day he stole into her room to ask some trivial request for the next day's pleasure and came upon her unawares and stood breathless as in the presence of the Most High, stealing away on tiptoe not to disturb her, lying wakeful in his bed till far into the night! Ah! He turned sharply toward the two, and his voice jarred a discord as he spoke to break the spell of solemnity.

"Come home with us and take dinner, Bannard!"

He had not intended to give that invitation. It had been the furthest from his thoughts only a moment before, but his tongue had spoken without leave. Now that it was given he found ease in the thought of a guest. Why not? He liked the young man. A guest more or less made little difference in the strange makeup of his sudden family. Perhaps it might even help out the embarrassing situation. But he was not prepared for the quick lighting of the young man's face.

"That would be great!" he responded. "But—" and his eyes sought the girl's face for the flicker of a glance, "are you quite sure you want—guests this first evening?"

"Oh yes, come along!" said Greeves impatiently, half sorry now he had asked him, yet determined not to go back on his invitation. And Silver's eyes gave him a pleasant impersonal welcome.

"I'll be there at five o'clock," he said, looking at his watch. "I must meet the little mother out in the cemetery first, and there's an old man who is dying—I must drop in there a few moments. I think I can make it by five. Will that be too soon? There's something I've been wanting to talk over with you ever since I knew you were coming. Will you have a few minutes to spare?"

"Make it by five and we'll have tea in the garden. Silver-Alice, can you make tea?" His tone was a shy attempt at playfulness, but it brought a great light into the girl's eyes as she turned a sparkling face.

"Oh, surely!"

"Then make it five. I acquired a foreign habit of drinking tea in the afternoon while I was over there. We'll have plenty of time for a talk then. We dine at seven." Then suddenly it occurred to him that he had another daughter awaiting him and that the prospect was anything but pleasant, so with an almost brusque manner he left hurriedly. Turning back at the door, he said to the minister: "Oh, by the way, what has become of that young person, Blink, I think you called him? We had an engagement with him this morning, hadn't we? I had completely forgotten it. Do you know where I could find him to make my apologies?"

"He is washing my car at present," laughed the minister. "I shall see him before long and can deliver your message. You needn't worry about Blink. He is very wise for his years."

"Well, suppose you tell him to drop in to dinner at seven. Tell him we'll talk over bait after dinner."

Terrence Bannard's eyes registered appreciation.

"Thank you," he said. "I doubt if he'll come. He's shy and proud among ladies, but he'll appreciate the invitation."

"Oh, that's all right!" said the older man, not in the least realizing that he was getting a large party on his hands but determined to discharge his obligations to the young friend of the evening before. "Tell him to come. I liked him."

They were gone down the maple-shaded street, and the minister stood for an instant in the doorway watching the graceful girl as she walked beside her father, with a look in his eyes that would have brought the spyglasses of his congregation on him if any had been there to tell the tale.

Meanwhile, Athalie, never long content at a time, grew restless with her book, and wriggling out from the finery on the bed, stole to the door and listened. All was quiet downstairs except a distant subdued kitchen sound somewhere off toward the back. That impudent housekeeper was away about her business. Now was Athalie's time to pry.

Removing her shoes and substituting blue satin slippers, she stole cautiously down the hall and tried her father's door, the front room on the same side of the hall with her own but separated by deep closets, one belonging to her room, the other to his.

She stood curiously staring around. It was a boy's room, with college photographs and pennants and lacrosse sticks being its chief adornings. Only a bag filled with toiletries and a locked suitcase gave evidence of the entrance of the owner after the years of absence. Patterson Greeves had been too weary and too perturbed to unpack or make any changes since his arrival the night before. Athalie made very sure that there was nothing among his belongings to give any clue to his present character. She went stealthily from bag to suitcase, even opened bureau drawers, but no picture or letter or anything was brought to light that might be of possible interest, though she conducted her search with the manner and wisdom of a young detective.

Coming out, she closed the door again and stole across the hall to the room that had been Aunt Lavinia's.

Her eyes took in the details sharply, the old-fashioned neatness and comfort, and quiet beauty of the room, and the fact that the other girl had been taken there rather than herself, the front room, that best room in the house, with the big sunny windows to the street and at the side! Jealousy filled her heart, and her full, petulant lips came out in ugly lines. She walked quickly to the bed, snatched Silver's hat and gloves, and flung them across the room behind a chair. She picked up her handbag and went through it carefully, ruthlessly tearing in half and restoring to its silken pocket a small photograph of a woman, the woman whose portrait was downstairs, she felt sure. Then she went over to the closet and flung wide the door. After a moment's survey of two or three shrouded dresses of outdated design that hung there, she gathered them up and flung them on a chair. Then she went back to her own room and selected an armful of her clothes and returning began to hang them on the hooks.

All at once she became aware that someone was near, and turning, her arms still half full of finery, she found herself facing Silver.

Not in the least abashed, she looked her up and down contemptuously a full second before either spoke. Then Athalie asked rudely: "Well! Who are *you*?"

"I beg your pardon," said Silver, hesitating on the threshold, "am I intruding? Have I made a mistake? I was told this was my room—"

"Well it *isn't*," said Athalie roughly. "I'm going to take it myself! I don't like the room that old frump gave me, so I'm moving over here. You can have my room when I get out if you're going to stay overnight. I'm Athalie Greeves, and this is my father's house, so *what I say goes!*"

Silver stood quite still for an instant, the smile frozen on her lips, her eyes taking in the details of this impossible sister, her ears trying to refuse the evidence of the sounds they had heard. Something seemed to flicker and go out in her face; a stricken look flitted over it, succeeded by a sweet dignity and a lifting of her chin that in another might have amounted to haughtiness. Then she said quietly, "I see. Well, I will not trouble you."

She walked over to the other side of the bed, recovered her hat and gloves, took up her handbag, and went out and down the stairs. Athalie did not stop to notice where she went nor care. She went on arranging her garments on the hooks, an ugly expression on her heavy young brow.

Silver passed quietly downstairs and found an unobtrusive resting place for hat and gloves on the table in the depth of the wide hall and then went on to a door that opened to a wide bricked terrace with the garden just below, reached by mossy brick steps set in the sod and edged by crocuses and daffodils. Beyond, a flare of color and the perfume of hyacinths and tulips lured the senses, and the subtle breath of lilies-of-the-valley stole from out of the deep-green border of the terrace. Silver stood for a moment looking out and trying to quiet the excited beating of her heart from the encounter. Trying to think what she ought to do. Wondering why her father had said nothing about this strange inmate of the house. Wondering why she had forgotten to ask him who the girl was she had seen on the stairs when she arrived. Thinking that in all likelihood the attitude of this other girl would make even a visit to her father impossible and grieving at the thought.

Already Molly and Anne Truesdale were bustling around, setting out a leaved table on the terrace, spreading it with fine, old embroidered linen and delicate cups of other days, quaint heavy silver, plates of delectable cookies, and squares of spicy gingerbread. The pleasant garden and the bright show of flowers, the coming guest, and the air of happiness seemed not to belong to her. She felt a sudden loneliness, as if she were intruding, abashed in the presence of the things she could enjoy, appalled by the fact of this other girl in the house. The story then had been true that they had heard—that there had been a child by her father's second marriage. And she must have lived instead of dying as rumor had brought to them. Her father had never written a word about either birth or death to her grandfather and grandmother. She wondered again, why? Her loyal heart refused to admit that her father had been wrong. He was her father. Perhaps there was some excuse. Perhaps there was some explanation.

Sudden tears came at this juncture and threatened to overflow. In a panic she withdrew into the shadows of the hall, lest the servants should see her, and almost ran into her father's arms as he came down toward the door to see if his orders had been understood. He passed a loving arm around her, gently, as if he were almost afraid to touch her, almost shyly, she thought, and he whispered very low: "I'm glad you've come—Silver-Alice!"

Then Anne bustled in to ask some question and Silver slipped back to the library for a moment searching for her handkerchief, and so got control of herself. She came back to walk down the terrace with her father and see the places where he used to play as a child and hear all about the old fountain and the fairy tales he used to make up about it. Walking like that, she almost forgot the sister upstairs who was so ungracious, almost forgot that sometime she would have to speak about her if her father did not speak first.

There was a cloud on her father's brow. She noticed it first as they paused beside the sundial and she traced the line of clear-cut shadow half between the four and five of the quaint old figures. A sundial. How delightful! It was like digging up antiquities. Her heart leaped to the poetry of it. Then she looked up and saw the shadow on the stern, sad face above her. Something was troubling him. What was it? Her presence here? Perhaps he knew how distasteful it was to the girl upstairs, and he did not know what to do. Perhaps it was best for her not to stay at all—perhaps—!

She put out a wistful hand and touched his sleeve. "Father!"

"Yes," he said as if answering the thought of her heart. "There is something I must tell you, child. Come over to the old arbor and let us sit down. It is—unpleasant."

"Is it about—Athalie, Father?" she asked as she turned to follow him.

He stopped and looked at her astonished.

"How did you know? Had anyone sent you word she was coming?" he asked with quick suspicion in his voice. Lilla was quite capable of preparing such a setting for the arrival of her daughter. She seemed to have a sort of demoniacal insight into what would be exquisite torture for him. But Silver shook her head.

"Oh no. But I saw her standing on the stairs behind you when I arrived, and again upstairs just now. She was moving her things into the room where I had taken off my hat. She asked me who I was. I am almost sure she does not like my coming. I think—Father—it isn't quite convenient for you to have me visit you just now. I believe it would be better if I went back tonight and perhaps came again later, in a few years when she is older, or away on a visit or something. I would not like to make you trouble. And it has been wonderful to see you and to talk with you for even this short time. I shall never feel quite alone in the world again now that I know I have a father—*such a father!*"

"Stop!" His voice was choked with consternation, anger, something else that sounded almost like humility! Strange to see that expression sitting unaccustomedly on Patterson Greeves's haughty features.

"Don't say any more things like that, Silver," he said brokenly. "I can't bear them. It is bad enough to have got in such a mess. Bad enough to have a daughter like that! Bad enough to have her come here unannounced—she came only a few minutes before you did—without having you reproach me by flying up and leaving. You *cannot* leave me now, my child! You must stay by and help me. *I need you!*"

"Oh, Father!" She put out a loving hand to his arm again, and he drew her within his embrace and down the path toward the summerhouse.

Athalie saw them, coming to the window of her own room, her arms full of more finery, and she stood and gazed. Suddenly she dropped her armful, and great jealous tears of rage welled into her large, bold eyes. From her handsome full lips a smothered sound almost like a roar of some enraged young animal came and was quickly suppressed. For a moment she watched, then she turned around and began to search wildly among the confusion of clothing on bed and chairs and to hastily dress herself in other attire.

Chapter 10

About this time also, Blink, having received the invitation by word of mouth from the minister and not having declared himself either way about accepting it, repaired to the meadow lot opposite the Silver place and proceeded to fill a large tin can with the choicest bait the town afforded from a private and secret source underneath some old rotting logs that had long furnished him with better angles than any other boy was able to produce. He was not yet sure whether he would go to the party, but he would at least be ready with an offering should the fates, when the time arrived, seem propitious.

Sooner than he had expected, the can was filled, and he lay back on the sweet-smelling turf of the meadow and gazed up at the blue of the sky, watching the tiny, lazy, gauzy clouds that floated slowly, drifting like thistledown. It was easy to feel he was floating on one of them, drifting, too. He often did that. It was his way of reading poetry. He read a great deal of living poetry at that stage of his existence.

Lying so with a clump of blue violets close to his hand and the tinkle of a cowbell not far away, he could drift and think of a great many things that an ordinary boy in the everyday of life wouldn't consider profitable for one of his standing.

Out of the corner of his eye, he saw the minister going in the white gate between the hedges. He thought of the little grave covered with violets and the young mother, a social outcast, with her new sorrow and bewilderment in her face. No one had told him about it. It was one of those things that Blink always knew. Before long he would slip back to the cemetery and water those flowers. It wouldn't be necessary for the minister to bother with that. The flowers would just grow all right, and he could let them off his mind. Blink knew how to relieve him of odd little jobs. The minister was a good sport. If Silas Pettigrew made any more of those pharisaical remarks about the minister letting handsome young women of the street go to some "mother in Israel" when they were in trouble, he would see that he found a way to tell Silas where to get off. Silas wasn't such a saint anyway if he *was* an elder in the church! There was that time when he bought Widow Emmet's house for twenty-five hundred dollars and then discovered the very next day that the railroad would buy it at twelve thousand to complete their new franchise, and he never let the widow in on the deal! Old cottonmouth! Thinking he could put one over on the town and get the minister in trouble with the old tabbies, just because that poor girl—when everybody knew young Sil Pettigrew—but *there*!

He watched with satisfaction as the great door opened with a glimpse of Anne in black silk and sheer collar. He, too, might be received there later in the evening if he so chose. He reflected that "the girl" would be there. It seemed a pleasing circumstance. She liked dogs. She was all right.

Then suddenly his attention was attracted to a motion, a shadow—what was it moving at an upper side window of the house?

Someone was climbing out to the pergola below, a boy it looked like, heavily built with a shock of football hair, knee trousers, and a strange belted kind of jacket.

He sat up stealthily, leaning on one elbow, his young face growing grave as he watched. Now who could that be? Not a burglar, this time of afternoon, sun still up? Still. That wasn't any town figure, none of the boys' shoulders that shape, nor hair. It might be a disguise, but—how pink the face looked, like a Chinese painting on a fan!

Without taking his eyes from the object of his attention, he made ready to take a hasty departure. One hand went out and secured the can of bait. His mind turned over the available hiding places where he might store it safely. How clumsy that guy was! Wasn't much of a climber. What in the world was he doing up there in that house anyway?

Slowly the figure crept to the front of the pergola, glanced cautiously around, peeked back and over the vines as if watching someone, and then dropped heavily down among the myrtle beds. A moment more and Blink saw it rise, jam a curious-looking mushroom hat down over the shock of hair, and come out the gate to the street, with furtive glances back toward the house. The whole attitude of the person showed secrecy and stealth. Once outside the gate, it turned toward the direction of the town and walked rapidly with a free stride despite its stocky build.

Blink rose from his bed of green and lost no time in following. The can of bait was deposited in the hollow of a tree a few feet from the street, and Blink was over the fence and making good time in an instant. The stranger was still in sight, had passed the first cross street, and was almost to the drugstore. Blink fell into an easy stride and reached the garage diagonally across from the drugstore just as the figure paused, one foot on the step, one hand on the latch, and looked up and down the street. He had a full view of her face.

Good night! It was a *girl*! A girl in knickers! They passed through the town sometimes, girls like that, out on walks with men Sundays and holidays, but there were none indigenous to the soil of Silver Sands. It was not *done*! And look at her face! Fell in the flour barrel! Painted like an image! Good night! Did a girl think she was nice looking that way, he would like to know? And coming from the Silver house! How was it possible? Blink did not use the word *incongruous*, but it was the way he felt. For one awful second, he experienced deep and horrible disappointment. *The girl.* She liked dogs, but she was like that! Then instantly the thing was impossible. No, she hadn't been a fat thing like that. She wasn't the same one. But who was she? Some interloper? How did she get there without his knowing? Did the family know? What did she have to do with them? Oughtn't something to be done about it?

Since he had been able to walk alone, Blink had been a self-constituted member of the police force of Silver Sands. He belonged to a clan who seldom said what they meant, seldom talked but in parables, and kept their eyes open. Many a wrong had been righted and a petty criminal saved through their ministrations to become a worthy citizen after due chastisement and discipline. They reserved the right to use their own judgment, and on occasion had been known to evade the law for their own wise and worthy reasons, to save an underlying principle that in their opinion would be lost if the law had its course. The strangest part of it all was that the outcome usually would seem to warrant the venture, and occasionally the chief of police himself had been known to wink at some open break on the part of the boy because he had come to have utter faith in his working principle. Blink had been known to search out the criminal and the facts in some mystery more than once where others had failed to get a clue, and the chief always felt it well to keep in with Blink. He took him with him now and again when a raid on some lawbreaker was imminent. He had faith in Blink's intuition.

Blink himself had unerring faith in his own judgment. It was to him like a clear magnifying glass that had been given to him at birth, which showed up Truth, and he couldn't see why other people didn't exercise the same faculty. They all must have the same thing if they only used it.

Athalie, seeing nothing else down the principal business street more attractive than the drugstore, opened the door and went in. Blink leaned up against the show window of the garage in front of a large poster of a new kind of tire, looked idly up and down the street, and saw every move the strange girl made.

She looked around the store with that curious appraising glance she gave to everything the first time of seeing and then turned into one of the two telephone booths that huddled by the corner window, close to the entrance door. She took the front one facing the door and seemed to be looking through the book for a number. When she had lifted the receiver, Blink, without seeming to have been looking that way, sauntered thoughtfully across the street and entered the drugstore most casually, taking one full, impersonal look at the girl's face as he passed. No, it was not *the* girl. He had been pretty sure before, but he was glad to *know*.

And this one was pretty enough, if she hadn't worn so much ghastly makeup and such funny eyebrows, almost as if she wanted you to see she didn't have them in the right place. She had big, brilliant white teeth, with those vivid red lips like the clowns in the circus, and she had a hard, bold look in her eyes. When he entered, she was talking and laughing boisterously. She could be heard all over the store, if there had been anyone around to hear but stupid Sam Hutchins, the soda clerk.

Blink stalked over to the counter and threw down a nickel for a package of Life Savers, and then as if he had had no other purpose in entering, he sauntered straight to the other telephone booth and shut himself in to a careful inspection of the *W's* in the telephone directory. Not that he wanted anyone with a name beginning with *W*. It was just the first page he happened to open.

Clear and distinct came the voice from the booth ahead: "Now *Bobs*! You don't mean you didn't know my voice! Well, I'll say that's a slam! I'm off you for life! Oh! Really? Awwww—Bobbbbs! Now, that's awfully *darling* of you!"

Blink was disgusted. Just one of these foolish Janes. He had heard them talk before, only why did they want to dress like a man, and why should one of them climb out of a second story window in the Silver house? He slammed the book shut and called up the captain of a neighboring baseball team in the next township. He was disgusted with himself for caring. He would listen no more. It was likely some odd visitor. But one thing was settled: he was not going to the Silver house that night. Not with so many girls around. He couldn't stand girls!

"Is that you, kid? Oh, isn't he? Well, call him, won't you? I'll wait. This is Blink. *I* said it."

Boom! came the girl's voice into the silence. "Well, you've got to come and get me, Bobs. You said you would if I sent for you. I'm having a horrid time. No, I haven't gone down to dinner. I didn't have any success at all. If it hadn't been for your five-pounder, I'd have starved. Yes, been on a hunger strike. But honestly, Bobs, it's no use. I simply can't stick it out! I shall die. Can't you come down this evening and take a ride? No, he'd never find out. I've gone to my room with a sick headache, see? He expected to hear nothing more from me till morning. I've shocked him so hard he would be glad if he never had to see me anymore. I'll make him sit up and take notice yet. I promised Lilla I would, and I mean to keep my word. But Bobs, you've simply got to stand by or I shan't survive.

Aw, come on, Bobs! I've found a way to get in the window. We can stay as late as we like. Nobody will ever find out. I can shimmy up the pergola. Oh, sure! I useta do it in gym. . . . Aw, *why* Bobs? . . . I think you're *too mean*! . . . Well, then, how about t'morra? . . . You won't stand me up? . . . Well, if you do, all right for you! . . . Where will I meet you? . . . Why, I'm down at the drugstore now. Couldn't you come here? . . . Aw, why? . . . I don't see. What do I care for these country simps! Let 'em tell Dad! I'll have the fun first, won't I? Leave it to me. I'll get away with it. . . . What is it you're afraid of, you poor fish? Your reputation? Well, I like that! I didn't know you had any! . . . All right, Bobs. I'll come. Where did you say it is? Walk over the bridge at the other end of the village? . . . Yes. . . Woods? On the right-hand side? . . . I didn't get that. Oh, you want me to walk in a little way from the road, out of sight? . . . I see. Yes, sure. All right, I'll be there, Bobs. Four o'clock sharp! But don't you be late or fail me. If you do, I'll never speak to you again, Bobs. And I'll tell Lilla how mean you were. No. I'll tell her you said she was getting *old*. That'll get her goat! Then she won't speak to you either! . . . All right, Bobs. I'll be there!"

The receiver hung up with a click, and the girl adjourned to the soda counter where she tried various flavors and chatted affably with Sam Hutchins in a lofty, patronizing tone, telling him how to prepare the special concoctions they used to get at school. She made out quite a respectable lunch, what with the sponge cake they kept in a glass showcase and several chocolate ice cream sundaes. Certainly enough to keep the breath of life in her plump well-cared-for body until the next morning, and then she left and stalked on down the street to the end of the village and crossed the bridge. Blink went across to the garage, borrowed a motorcycle, and took a breezy turn that way himself. He felt that this young adventuress needed a chaperone. She came from the house of a man he liked, and loyalty to his friends, even his very new friends, was one of Blink's specialties. He felt instinctively that Patterson Greeves would not like a guest of his, whoever she might be, to be sailing through the open countryside alone in such an outfit at the hour when the workmen from the quarry half a mile below the town would be coming home.

So he chortled noisily by her on his wheezy steed and sailed on down the road, arranging to have something the matter with the cycle about the time she turned off the road toward the woods, which made it necessary for him to dismount and get down in the road to examine it.

Athalie did not stay in the woods very long. Nature unadorned never had much attraction for her. She entered a narrow winding path, followed it to a log within the thick grove, and sat down. But solitude never appealed to Athalie either, and after a moment's investigation, she came back to the road again and pursued a monotonous way back to the village.

"Fat thing!" reflected Blink contemptuously, jogging along behind at a sickly pace for one of his ambitions. Whenever he came too near, he had to stop and examine his engine again, but in time the two arrived in the neighborhood of the drugstore. Athalie went in, purchased some salted almonds, and went on to her father's house. Blink returned his motorcycle and took a back way to the meadow, arriving in plenty of time to watch the lady mount the pergola and enter her window once more.

The incident finished, Blink sat for some minutes turning it over in his mind, decided there was something here that needed further investigation and that he must accept the invitation to the house and see what he might see, although he could not bring himself to go through the agony of a dinner with *girls*. To this end, he picked himself up from the ground, retrieved his can of bait, and took the shortest way to his home, where he began a thorough search for a clean shirt.

Athalie, having regained the stronghold of her room, was about to return to her task of moving her clothes to the front-room closet when suddenly the sound of a tinkling spoon against a thin china cup and a ripple of soft laughter, with an undertone of heavier merriment, sent her flying to her window.

For an instant, her face took on the wild look of a young savage as she gazed down at the pretty tea table set out on the terrace below; the plate of thin bread and butter, so tempting to her bonbon-jaded appetite; the orange marmalade like drops of amber; the dainty dish of sugar cookies, thin and attractive in clover-leaf form. The whiff of orange pekoe wafted up as Silver passed her father his cup. Tea on the terrace, and she not even told! And there was that stunning-looking man again! Who was he? Did that other girl think she would take possession of him, too, as well as her father, and the house, and the best room, and everything? Well, they would find out! She was going down at once. She would show that stuck-up girl!

Athalie turned from the window after a moment more and began to fly around with catlike tread, dropping off garments and sliding into others, searching wildly amid the mass of finery for the thing she wanted. It was a coral crepe dress she finally chose, with a low-cut bodice of silver cloth and startling touches of black velvet fastened with jeweled buckles.

She worked frantically over her complexion and brushed out her permed waves until they looked like an electric sign. A platinum chain like a breath of air about her plump white neck held a single jewel like a drop of dew. In her ears were long jet earrings, giving her a more brazen expression than ever. Her large pink arms were bare as she stood before the mirror, turning this way and that on the high heels of her little silver shoes into which her plump feet seemed to be fairly forced. She was well pleased with herself. Probably this wasn't exactly the right kind of outfit, according to social rules, for that early hour in the day, but at least it was effective, and that was all she really cared about. She felt that she could afford to be a law unto herself.

As she took her final glimpse and tiptoed toward the door, she seemed like some great bright bird with a large part of its gaudy plumage plucked away. The floating coral and silver fabric was inadequate. "Naked" was what Anne Truesdale expressed to herself as she stood in frozen horror behind the pantry door with a plate of fresh cookies and watched the bright apparition move out of the door to the terrace and stand a moment. "The very devil of a smile on her lips" as Tom who was watching behind the lilacs afterward told his wife, Molly.

Then Patterson Greeves, with his cup halfway to his lips and a look of comfort and relaxation on his brow, suddenly looked up and stared. They all looked up and saw her. Athalie came forward, her eyes fixed straight on the minister, her most coaxing spoiled-baby look on her pink face.

Chapter 11

$\mathcal{I}f$ a cavern had opened beneath his feet revealing dead men's bones, Patterson Greeves could not have been more shaken. He was white with consternation as he faced his astounding daughter and trembled.

"I hope you haven't eaten everything up," she said airily, coming forward. "I'm simply dying of starvation. Why don't you introduce me, Dad?"

She stood facing the young man, her bare pink shoulders turned toward her stepsister utterly ignoring her, her whole forward young personality flaunting itself at Man in the concrete, this man in particular, the kind of an appeal that a woman of her mother's sort always used with a good man to disarm his disapproval. Greeves recognized instantly Lilla's arts and ways with himself, and pain and rage shot through his heart. Why had he not understood it then? Why had he let himself be fooled? Would this young man be fooled, too? He glanced anxiously toward his guest and saw that the minister's eyes were meeting Silver's in a quick look of understanding as if the two had joined forces to protect him against the humiliation his daughter was bringing upon him. Ah! So might the memory of Silver's mother have protected him if he had not been too upset and bitter to let it! Fool! Fool! Was he destined to go always from this time seeing nothing but his folly, his everlasting folly that was bringing with it retribution now? Athalie, his daughter, seemed to him an embodiment of his own sins, come back after years to torment him. Was this what hell meant? The old-fashioned hell that nobody believed in anymore?

He was still standing, shaken and trembling, his cup in his hand, but nobody was paying any attention to him. He gradually realized this and was glad. They were trying to help him. Silver had poured a cup of tea and held it out to her sister, but Athalie ignored it, as if it were a ghost she did not see, and reaching out poured another for herself.

"Isn't there any lemon?" she asked looking the table over. "Quinn, bring some lemon. I never take cream. Why don't you pass the cakes, Mr. Man?" She was addressing the minister with a freedom that made Silver turn her eyes away in pain for her father's embarrassment. But the young man handed the plate of cookies with a gentle, impersonal dignity that seemed to take the edge from the girl's audacity and put her down in the class of a child who knew no better than to take the center of attention.

"Gracious but you're a grouch!" commented Athalie cheerfully, looking straight into his eyes with her bold black ones. "Won't you smile anymore just because we haven't been introduced? You must excuse Dad, he seems to be—"

But just then her father stepped forward haughtily and took the cup from the girl's hand.

"Athalie, you are not properly dressed to be out here. Go upstairs and put on—a—a—*sweater* or something," he ended helplessly. "It is chilly—"

But the girl burst forth in a ripple of hoydenish laughter: "A sweater with an evening dress? Oh, Dad! You certainly have been out of the world. Don't worry about me. I'm never cold. I'll take another cake, Quinn."

Patterson Greeves's face hardened into a set helpless look. He was one whom men had always obeyed. This mere girl defied him openly, and something somewhere in his moral armor was so weak that he could not meet her and conquer her. His lips shut sternly, and his voice was like icicles.

"Then I will go further and say that your dress is unseemly and out of taste. What may have seemed to you fitting among girls of your school is not in keeping with our quiet home life in this village. We do not wear evening dress on ordinary days, and you will oblige me by finishing your tea in your room and then changing into something less flimsy, that has sleeves and a—a—*neck* to it. Something more—*adequate*. Let me introduce to you your"—he hesitated—"my eldest daughter, Silver. She is older than you are. She will be able to advise you about your apparel. I commend you to her friendship. She is—ah—your sister, of course, you know."

Silver knew instantly that her father had touched the wrong chord. Athalie's impudent chin went up, her eyebrows—what there was left of them—went up, her full cupid's bow of an upper lip went up, and the sharp red corners were drawn quickly and contemptuously down in a smirk of hate. She did not look at Silver. She did not acknowledge the introduction. Her big black eyes were fixed on her father who had already turned his back, having manlike cast his burden upon womankind and was moving off toward the door with a relieved note in his voice.

"Come, Bannard, let's go into the library and have our talk. It grows chilly out here already. The spring sun has not much warmth yet."

"Thanks! I don't need any advice from anyone about my clothes! I generally wear what I like!" Athalie hurled after him, her shoulders lifted irately. But he was already inside and did not choose to hear further defiance. He hurried toward the library door and drew chairs in front of the fireplace where a fire was already laid.

"Sit here, Bannard. I'm sorry and ashamed that you should have seen my family under these trying circumstances. What would you do with a girl like that? What are young people coming to? Wasn't I right in saying she was impossible?"

Out on the terrace, Athalie whirled around so that her back was turned to Silver. So she stood facing the glow of hyacinths and tulips, herself the most flaring tulip of them all, and drank her tea in leisurely manner, helped herself to more cake and another cup of tea, and utterly ignored the presence of the other girl.

Silver, after watching her a moment, stepped over toward her.

"Listen!" she said firmly. "You might as well cut that out. It's just as hard for me as it is for you. He's my father just as much as yours, you know. He *was my father first*! We're sisters, you know. We can't help that—"

Athalie whirled on her with her eyes blazing. "We're not *sisters*!" She stamped her foot. "I'll never call you my sister. You've no business here! I know all about *you*! My father *gave you away*, and you're *adopted*! You're the same as dead! You have no right to turn up and spoil my life! And you needn't think you can get his money either. I'm his natural heir! The court—"

"Stop!" cried Silver suddenly white with anger. "As if *money* had anything to do with it!"

"Shut up!" flashed Athalie. "I'll say what I please. And you needn't pretend you're so awfully saintly. I know your kind, you mealymouthed hypocrite! You can't put one over on me. You're in for the money as well as anybody. Now, I'll give you one day to get out and stay out, and if you don't do it, I'll make *hell* for you, do you understand? And I know how to do it when I try! You're not going to stick around here and spoil my plans! And if you go and tell Dad, *you'll be sorry*, that's all I've got to say!"

She jerked the little gold case out of a silken hiding place among the folds of her skirt, lit a cigarette insolently, and flung the lighted match full into the face of the other girl, turning with another whirl, and marching down the garden path with her cigarette tilted in her contemptuous red lips, her gaudy outfit looking as out of place in the quiet garden among the spring blossoms as a painted lily in the woods.

Silver jerked back from the flaring match just in time to escape the flame, gazed in consternation for an instant after the plump, arrogant figure of the other girl, and then throwing her head back, she sent a clear ringing laugh after her sister. Athalie paused in her majestic progress to turn and stare angrily, but Silver had gone into the house.

Anne Truesdale slipped a ready arm around her as she entered the shadow of the hall. "Yer not to mind, my sweetie, what a huzzy like that says. She'll not be here long, I'm thinking. The master was telephoning the morn' something about a school for her. He'll be soon sending her kiting, the little upstart."

"Oh, thank you, Mrs. Truesdale," quivered Silver. "I'm sorry you had to overhear this disgraceful conversation. I thought I could get her to see things in a different way, but I see it was very unwise to speak at all. She wasn't in the right mood—"

"I doubt if she has any right moods, my dearie. She's a little sinner, that girl is. I've read about 'em in the newspaper. Look at her now, puffing away like a man, the impertinent chit. Disgracing her father and his respectable house! The sooner she gets out of this respectable town the better for all concerned. Her mother must be one of the devil's own to bring up a girl like that. Now come upstairs, my dearie, and I'll help you to dress and fix yer hair. Yer trunks haven't come yet, but that doesn't matter, the master doesn't care for things to be formal."

"Oh, but Mrs. Truesdale—"

"Call me Anne, Miss Silver, I like it better. It's what yer father always calls me."

"Oh, Anne, I thank you, but I must get ready and go away. Couldn't you help me to go at once before my father hears anything about it? It would only distress him to know the reason. You could just tell him that I felt that I must go for the present, and that perhaps someday I will come back if he wants me—or he can come to see me. I didn't really intend staying when I came. I have a position, and I ought to begin my work right away this week. Can you find out how soon there is a train back to the city and help me to get away quietly before she comes in? I haven't anything to pack. My suitcase hasn't been opened yet—"

"Indeed no, my dearie!" said Anne firmly. "I'll not help ye to any such fool doings. Yer not to go away at all. And my master would half kill me if he found me a party to any such thing. Besides, can't ye see he needs ye just now? He's beside hisself with grief and shame over that young thing. Do ye think it's a joke fer a man to come back from a far land and find a thing like that is a child o' his? You'll stay right where ye are, my sweet lady, and help that distracted father o' yours back into sanity. Besides, he's got company, and he's depending on you to help entertain with him this night. He told me to open the old piano and light a fire in the drawing room. He's looking forward to hearing ye sing, I'm thinking, and yer not to disappoint him. He's been a much-disappointed man already, and it's not good fer him."

She drew Silver up the stairs to the bedroom where she had first taken her and then gazed around with a growing fury in her strong old face.

"The young *viper*!" she exclaimed under her breath. "I'll teach her to upset orders! The master's orders, too!"

Before Silver could stop her, she had seized an armful of silks and lingerie from the bed where Athalie had deposited them in her last trip and rushed across the hall, throwing them in a heap on the floor of the room she had given Athalie, and was back for another.

"But you mustn't!" cried Silver. "It will only make her angrier. Let her have the room she wants. I don't care where I am put. If I stay at all, one room will do as well as another."

"Indeed no!" said Anne with fire in her eye. "Do you think I'm going to have the sacred room of the dear mistress profaned by a little devil like her? The master would in no wise allow her to enter here. He considers his aunt's room as a holy place, and it shows where he feels you belong that he gave orders you should be put in here. Now, my dear, you just sit down while I empty this closet in the blink of an eye, and then I'll help you unpack your suitcase."

"But Anne, I'm sure Athalie will blame this on me. She came in while I was up here and told me she wanted this room and I could go into the other one."

"Did she, indeed! The limb of Satan! Well, I'll see that she understands you had nothing to do with it. I'm still housekeeper here, I hope, and the master is still master! I'm not thinking he'll take her impudence long." She seized another armful ruthlessly and marched it across the hall, and in a brief space of time the closet was again cleared.

"And look at the dear lady's best black silk!" she crooned suddenly discovering the garments that Athalie had flung from their hooks to the floor. "It's a desecration, it certainly is! If Miss Lavinia had lived to see the day that a huzzy like that that flaunts her nakedness before the gentlemen and tries to drag her womanhood in the dust by smoking the vile cigarettes like a man!" Anne drew her breath in a sob of grief and humiliation. "I'm thinking she's what they call in the newspapers a 'flopper'! And I never thought when I read about their like that we'd be having a real-live flopper here in this blessed house the day! Aw! It's a sorry day in the old house that's always been that respectable!"

All the time she was babbling away in her intense voice her fingers were flying, making the room right once more. She straightened the cover of the little sewing table that had been twisted awry, pulled the winged chair back to its place, picked up a wisp of fabric that had floated under the bed, and even produced a duster and wiped down the walls and shelves of the closet, shaking as it were the very dust from the alien garments out of the sacred chamber.

Silver stood at the front window looking out across the field with troubled eyes, trying to think out the horrible situation. She was convinced that she ought not to have come, that she had followed her heart rather than her good judgment, and probably a bit selfishly and determinedly, too, coming unannounced. She had wanted to forestall any attempt on the part of her father to refuse to see her. She had wanted him so, and now, see!

It took no very great stretch of imagination for her to realize that this other girl was in greater need of a father than she herself, much greater! No matter how fatherless or lonely she would be, she would never be tempted to go down a wrong path or do anything to disgrace the family. She had been too well grounded in the things of righteousness for that. She was established. But this other girl was all too apparently self-willed, lawless, ungoverned, like a wild little craft set sail upon a stormy sea without a rudder and liable to wreck not only herself but any others that happened in her path.

Silver was accustomed to look on life in this way, to think of what would be good for others as well as herself. Her conscience had been well trained and was in good working order. If she became convinced that she ought to go, no argument would keep her there. She had a duty toward life to perform, and her highest aim was to perform it right. She was as utterly different from the other daughter as two human souls could well be. And how could there ever be harmony in such an ill-assorted household?

Into the middle of her thoughts came a summons from her father. Would she come down to the library and talk something over with himself and his guest as soon as she was ready for dinner?

Anne nodded approval. That settled it. She must hurry and get ready. Had she another dress, or did she wish just to wear her suit?

Silver realized that this was no time to discuss when her father had a guest, hastily shook out of her suitcase a little silk crepe dress that fell around her like the soft shadows of evening, the color of twilight with gleams of silver in the fastenings that reminded one of the afterglow in the sunset sky and set off her delicate complexion and the gold of her hair, making her eyes starry. The little cloud of worry on her brow only brought out the sweet thoughtfulness and made her more like her mother as she entered the library a few minutes later. Her father could scarcely take his eyes from her face. The wonder of it that Alice's face and form had come back in the person of her child! The sorrow of it that he had not had the patience to wait for this and enjoy the privilege of seeing it grow! The selfishness of himself!

Bannard had a work down among the foreigners of Frogtown. He had a plan for a school for them that they might learn English and be fit to apply for citizenship. He wanted a class in cooking and sewing for the mothers, and meetings where they might learn American ways and how to care for their children and make their homes sanitary and attractive. He wanted a meeting place for them and some men and women with tact and love of humanity to come down and help him. He had been waiting for Professor Greeves to arrive, feeling that he would be the very one to help him get the educational department started. There was a small room over a grocery they could have for the present. It was lighted with lamps and heated by a small box stove, but warm weather was coming; they could even meet out of doors somewhere down by the river.

"Why not build a hall, a gymnasium or something of the sort, with accommodation for all the different classes? It oughtn't to cost much. It wouldn't have to be elaborate. I'll look after the financial part. I'd be glad to give something to a work like that."

"Oh, Father! Can you do that?" Silver's eyes were large with wonder and joy. Money had not been in overabundance in the little parsonage where the Jarvises lived. Greeves looked sharply, keenly at his daughter. Was it possible that there had been any lack in her life that money might have supplied? He had sent presents now and then, a hundred dollars or so. Why had it never occurred to him to send more? His own child never having a real part in his abundant worldly possessions. He began to see more and more how wrong he had been to separate himself from her. And yet, how sweet and unspoiled she was! That other one, Athalie, had had an abundant income stipulated by the court, and see what she had become! Perhaps it had been better for Silver to have been brought up without riches. That was the way her dear mother had been reared. Ah, but it all shut him out of her life, and he had had the right to be in it and had thrown it away! Well, he would make up for it now all he could, but he could not go back and gather from the years the precious experiences that were gone forever.

They talked until the silver-tongued gong sounded through the house for dinner, and then, still quite absorbed in their topic, they went out to the dining room, forgetting that there was anything in the world except beautiful plans for the uplifting of others. And there, like an arrogant young goddess stood Athalie, still in her silver and coral undress as she had been in the garden, with only the addition of a wide coral-colored ribbon, the kind her girlfriends called a "headache band" drawn firmly over her forehead from the little sketchy uplifted eyebrows to the crown of her head, the ends concealed in some mysterious way under the shock of outlandish hair somewhere in the neighborhood of where her ears ought to be. She had arrived unbidden on the scene the moment the dinner gong sounded and stood like an apparition, belligerent and sullen behind a chair at the foot of the table, eyeing her father defiantly.

There had been a pleased smile on his face as he entered, his hand just touching Silver's arm caressingly, but when he saw her he stopped short, and a stern, angry look came into his eyes. It was not a baffled look as Athalie had counted on. She felt that he had weakened during that scene on the terrace, and she could dare anything, but she saw a light in his eyes that boded no good for the one who disobeyed his orders. His eyes gave one full glance at the bare arms and neck, the low, tight silver bodice with it straps of tiny coral roses, the flimsy fabric, and his lips set sternly, then he looked away and ignored her presence. This was not the time for further demonstration. He was a gentleman. He would deal with her later. Yet all through the meal as he spoke to the others, his voice was harsh, restrained. They could see that he was very angry. His attitude perhaps awed the girl, or else she was very hungry, for she said not a word except to demand second helpings of everything from the servants. For the rest of the meal, she maintained a sullen silence, her eyes on her plate, only now and then raising them in a blank stare of amazement at Bannard when he spoke of his church and his work with earnest enthusiasm. She had never met anyone like him before. Also, she was angry that he ignored her so utterly, giving his entire attention to Silver and her father.

Everyone was glad when the meal was concluded. It had been

a particularly trying time to Silver. And as they rose from the table, the master of the house said almost sternly: "Now we will go into the drawing room and have some music." His eyes dwelt on Silver lovingly, but something in the tone told Athalie that she was excluded from the company. As he stepped back to let the ladies pass through the door, Bannard caught a look of hate on the face of Athalie that almost startled him in one so young. Yet she did not slip away as he had supposed she would after the snub she had received at the table. She followed, slowly, almost stealthily toward the heavy crimson curtains of the wide doorway, as if she had some evil intent in her going.

Old Joe had built a fire in the fireplace, and the flames flickered and leaped rosily on the white marble mantel, making shadows and fitful lights on the high ceiling as they entered and giving a look to the lifelike paintings on the wall as if the owners were there awaiting them. They stepped within, and then Greeves touched the switch and flooded the room with light. Old Standish Silver had been a progressive man, and the house had been wired as soon as electricity for lighting had come to Silver Sands. It flared up garishly now and brought the sleeping portraits to life, and instinctively all eyes were raised to the painting over the mantel, where special lights had been placed to show it to advantage.

Joe Quinn had been mending the fire and was just backing away; Anne Truesdale was hovering uneasily beside the curtain, wondering how she could extract the fly from the ointment. The minister and Silver stood inside the doorway at one side, with Athalie still defiant just behind them, when Patterson Greeves stepped within and looked up. They all looked up, and breath was suspended. For there rose the lovely face of Alice Jarvis within her gilded frame, smeared and disfigured with chocolate, covering the sweet lips, dripping down the curve of cheek and chin grotesquely! And there below with bold, sensuous challenge, exulted the pictured eyes of Lilla!

Chapter 12

There was a tense moment during which all eyes were fastened with a horrible fascination on the desecrated picture. Then Patterson Greeves's army officer voice rang out like cut steel: "Who did that?"

His face had grown so white that it frightened Silver to look at him. Athalie instinctively withdrew to the shelter of the curtain. He stood looking around on the group, slowly from one face to another, beginning with old Joe, who had halted midway to the door and was ashy under his weather-tanned skin, answering back his master's severe gaze with grave, frightened eyes.

"I dunno, sir. I ain't seen it, sir, before, sir! It was that dark when I come in to light the fire. I didn't look up, sir!"

The look passed on, steadily, unflinchingly, recognizing the sympathy in the eyes of Bannard and Silver only by a quiver of the set upper lip. He read the face of Anne Truesdale like a book. It said in every quiver of indignant lip and fiery eye that she was not to blame, though she could tell him where to search for the culprit and only awaited a word from him to turn the tide of retribution as it certainly ought to be turned. So his eyes came to rest upon the daring, unsorry face of his younger daughter, peering out eerily as if relishing the dénouement of her escapade.

No one dared turn and look at her. It would seem that look of her father's must have scorched her soul, so full it was of outraged pride and love and sanctity. She must have learned from it at once how deep her arrow had gone in his soul, how much he had cared for that woman in the golden frame. How impossible it had been for him ever to care for her own mother like that. How really futile in the light of that look her mission in the house had become. Yet part spirit of his spirit, she dared him back with a glance as steady, as haughty, even while she trembled visibly at what she had invoked. It was as though she had been the embodiment of all his mistakes and sins come to mock him. So their eyes clashed, and the man with one final thrust of judgment and condemnation in the flash of his eye, turned back once more to the profaned picture.

It was then for the first time that he saw the portrait beneath it, set out in the clear detail of perfect photography, as beautiful yet sensuous, as dauntless, as abandoned in every line of supple body and smiling face as the daughter whose hand had placed her there.

A low exclamation of horror burst from his lips, and he strode forward, white with anger, and struck it full in the faithless smiling face till the glass shivered in fine fragments on the white of the marble below and the blood ran down in drops from his hand.

He was beside himself with fury now, and snatching the picture, frame and all, he dashed it to the hearth and ground it beneath his heel.

Then out from behind the heavy curtain, with a wild cry like a young tigress, darted Athalie and flung herself upon him, beating him back with her hands and screaming out: "Stop! Stop! You shall not! That is Lilla! That is my mother! Ohhh!" And her cries were like the torn heart of an infuriated creature who had never been controlled.

She pushed him away and, crouching low with raining tears, gathered up the fragments of the picture and clasped them to her chest. Then standing, she faced her father, a glare of hate in her black glittering eyes, and looked him down even as he had looked at her, and all who witnessed could not but see a resemblance to him in her eyes and attitude.

"You murderer!" she hissed between her red lips. She ground her teeth audibly and repeated, "You murderer!" And then she suddenly reached out with one hand and seized a large triangle of glass that still remained on the edge of the marble shelf and hurled it with all her force straight into the face of the wonderful painting above her, where it cut a deep jagged gash between the lovely eyes and fell in a thousand pieces below.

As the glass slithered through the canvas, Athalie gave a scream like a lost soul and darted from the room, almost knocking over the white and frightened Truesdale in her flight, and tore up the stairway to her room, slamming the door with a thunderous sound behind her and flinging herself with wild weeping on her bed.

Meantime Blink had arrived at the front door with his offering of worms and had rung several times before Molly, who thought Joe and Anne were busy in the drawing room with the fire and lights, had slipped to the door and let him in, asking him to wait in the front hall until the housekeeper came to show him where to go. Blink had stood by the door, his cap in his hand, and been a most unwilling witness to the whole awful scene, with its climax of flying coral gauzes, pink flesh, and silver shoes hurrying up the distant staircase. He stood for an instant uncertain what to do and then with innate courtesy stepped to the door of the darkened library where only a dying fire flickered on the hearth, and slipped inside. At least in here, they would think he had not heard. He dropped silently into one of the great leather chairs at the farther end of the room and tried to think what it all might mean and what connection it had with the girl who had climbed out the second-story window and telephoned to a man in the city.

It was most silent in the big drawing room after Athalie left. No one dared hardly to breathe. Patterson Greeves stood white and dazed, gazing up at the injured picture with a stricken look on his face, as if he had suddenly seen a loved one put to death. For an instant, he looked in silence, then uncertainly he put up his hands and rubbed them across his eyes as if he were not seeing right. It was as if the mutilated eyes of the picture were accusing him. He turned a pleading, pitiful look on the group standing about him, and with a moan he suddenly dropped into a chair, burying his face in his hands and relapsing into an awful silence.

"Dontee, dontee, Master Pat, dearie!" crooned Anne Truesdale, in her sorrow forgetting the presence of the others and relapsing into his childhood's vernacular. "She's only a naughty child! She didn't mean—she doesn't know!"

A great shudder passed over the man's body, and the woman gave a frightened look toward the other two and retreated.

Bannard stepped forward.

"Get that washed off the picture, can't you?" he whispered. "And sweep up the glass?" Anne Truesdale vanished, glad to have something tangible to do.

Bannard stepped to his host's side and put a firm hand on his shoulder.

"Come, Greeves, don't lose your nerve. This isn't nearly as bad as it seems! It really isn't, you know. The woman was right. She's only a naughty ungoverned child. And besides, you've another little girl to think about—"

Greeves raised his eyes to the sorrowful girl in the doorway, and

Silver crept to her father's side and knelt, slipping her arm within his and putting her face close to his.

"I'm afraid this is all my fault, Father," she said with a catch in her voice. "I ought not to have come. I knew as soon as I saw her. It hurt her, you know, to have me here. She wanted your love for herself—"

The man stirred uneasily and lifted his head, drawing his arm around her.

"Don't say that again!" he commanded sternly. "She is worse than nothing to me! Never can be or could be!"

Anne had come in with soft cloths and a basin of warm water followed by Joe with a stepladder, brush, and dustpan. They tiptoed in silently, as if to a place where a murder had been committed. They did their work swiftly and well and withdrew. The master of the house remained with his head down, resting on one hand, the other arm still encircling his daughter. Bannard stood a little to one side thoughtfully until the servants were gone. Then he raised his eyes to the picture.

"Come, Greeves," he said with relief in his voice. "It's not so bad at all. I'm sure it can be fixed. They mend those things so you'd never know, and it isn't as if the artist were dead. You can have him touch it up himself—"

Patterson Greeves rose shaking, his arm still about his daughter, who slipped up from his knees and stood beside him. The father gazed agonizingly up at the picture, tears blurring into his eyes.

"The little devil!" he murmured. "That's what she is! A little hellcat!"

"Oh, I wouldn't talk that way, friend!" Bannard's hearty voice was like a breeze from a windswept meadow driving the unpleasant atmosphere away from the room. "Nothing gained by that. Try to understand what has made her like this."

"Do you mean to say I'm to blame for her devilishness?" Greeves demanded excitedly.

"I wasn't saying who was to blame, my friend. I was merely suggesting that you might look further into the matter before you feel in utter despair. The mother is responsible for a lot, I should say, but your problem is not who is to blame, but what can you do about it."

"I shall send her away at once, either to some school where she will be made to behave, or else back, back to the mother who made her what she is." The man's tone was hard, unforgiving, uncompromising. "I shall *make* her take her back. Money will do it!"

"Then you *would* be to blame!" flashed Bannard. "What, would you give her no opportunity *ever*? Would you force her to remain what she is?"

"I would get her out of my sight forever."

"Isn't that just where you made your mistake before? Pardon me. I realize that I know nothing about the matter. It is only a suggestion."

"You do think I'm responsible for having a child like that!"

"Well, isn't a father responsible? Isn't that what God meant he should be?"

Silver had moved away from her father and was standing by the mantel looking up at the pictured eyes of her mother, her eyes full of wistfulness. Her father began a restless striding up and down the room, answering nothing, now and then tossing back his head in an impatient way he had. At last he wheeled around and faced Bannard.

"I cannot think there is any fairness in that," he said harshly and took another turn across the room. Then coming back with more of a grip upon himself, he said: "But I have made enough of a scene today. I had hoped you were to be my friend. If you stand this test, you will indeed be a friend. I must work this thing out by myself. Let us forget it if you can and endeavor to glean a little friendship at least from the evening. We came in here to have some music, and I have exhibited a family skeleton instead. Let us close the door on it for the night and do something else. My daughter, after all this are you equal to giving us a little music?"

The girl forced a smile and came quickly toward the piano. "Anything that will please you, Father," she said with an attempt at brightness.

Bannard opened the old grand piano and drew out the creaking stool with the haircloth cushion, and as Silver seated herself, it suddenly came over her that here she was in the old ancestral home, sitting at the piano where others who were gone had often sat bringing sweet strains from the old instrument. It thrilled her to realize that she was really here at last in the home she had so long dreamed about. She touched the keys tenderly, and there came forth a sound as if she had caressed them. Her father settled down in the old tapestry chair and shaded his eyes with his hand, watching her graceful outline of head and neck and shoulders and the sweeping curve of the young body as it swayed gently to the music.

Over in the library, Blink nestled back in the big chair and closed his eyes to let the music sweep over his soul, while the fire burned low and fell in bright sparkles among the ashes, and a long, young angleworm from the can in his lap struggled up and out and over draping itself in an arabesque, perhaps in some modern attempt to interpret the music.

Upstairs in the bed in a tumbled heap of coral and silver, Athalie clasped the bits of her mother's broken picture to what heart she had and wept and wailed, "Oh, Lilla! Lilla! Lilla! Why did you send me here?"

But not even Anne Truesdale, white and anxious down in the back hall, listening for developments and trembling with weariness, heard.

Chapter 13

$\mathcal{D}$iagonally across the street, about two hundred yards from the Silver place, next to the meadow, whose white picket fence bordered and whose old brindle-colored cow thrived on the meadow, stood a small brick cottage, somewhat Tudor style in architecture, low and thatchy, with moss on the roof and sunk deep in the thick green turf. It had a swing gate with an iron weight on a chain to make it latch, and a lilac bush leaning so low that the visitor had to duck his head to enter.

The inhabitants were all female, and they looked on the cow and the old yellow cats as their protectors. They were called the "Vandemeeter girls," though the mother and the ancient grand-mother were still of the company. There were three elderly spinsters, Maria, Cordelia, and Henrietta. There was also a niece, daughter of a fourth sister long since dead, who rejoiced in the name of Pristina Appleby. Pristina was "thirty-five if she was a day" according to Ellen Follinsbee, the Silver Sands dressmaker who always wore pins in her mouth and kept the other corner open to pass on pleasant conversation.

Pristina was tall and thin and spent much time studying the fashion magazines and sending for all the articles in the advertisement pages. She sang in the choir, and her voice was still good though a trifle shrill on the high notes. She held her book with elbows stiffened and always opened her mouth round and wide, and she took care to have a fresh change of clothes and always got a new hat four times a year. She felt it was due to her position as first soprano, although it was not a paying job, and frequently required much sacrifice of necessities to keep it. They were a progressive family and took several family magazines besides a church paper and the Silver Sands *Bulletin*. Pristina belonged to a literary club entitled the Honey Gatherers and sipped knowledge early and late. She had recently been appointed to write a paper on some modern author and had chosen Patterson Greeves, "our noted townsman" as the first sentence stated, and waded through volumes of technical works and thoroughly mastered the terms of bacteriologists in order to do her subject justice. Maria and Henrietta had not approved. They thought the choice of a divorced man, especially as he was reported to be returning to his native town to live, not a delicate thing for a young girl to do. Cordelia maintained that it was a part of the strange times they were living in and added: "Look at the flappers!"

"Well, I never supposed we'd have a flapper in our family," said Grandma sadly. "The Vandemeeters were always respectable. Poor, but always respectable."

"Now, Ma, who says Pristina ain't respectable?" bristled Mother, appearing in the kitchen door with a bread pan in one hand and a lump of lard in the other. "Pristina has her life to live, ain't she? I guess she's got to think of that."

They all looked at Pristina standing tall and straight, her abundant brown locks piled high in a coil on the crown of her head, a little too much of her slim white ears showing, a faint natural flush in the hollows under her high cheekbones, the neck of her brown dress guarding the hollow of her throat, and her bony arms encased in full-length bell sleeves. She wore sensible high-heeled shoes (with the addition of tan spats in winter), and her dresses were never higher than eight inches from the ground, even at the highest watermark of short dresses. Yet she seemed to them most modern. They could not have been more worried if she had taken to chewing gum. She was the kind of woman you would make for a good stepmother of eight. Conscientious and willing to take what was left.

"That's all right, Pristina. Write your paper the way you want. You have to follow your own bent," said Mother.

And Pristina wrote her paper.

Grandma and the three girls talked it over once when Mother was preparing hotcakes for breakfast.

"You don't suppose Pristina is getting ideas about Pat Greeves, do you?" suggested Cordelia.

"Gracious!" said Grandma, dropping her knitting. "What put that into your head?"

"Oh, nothing—only she's so anxious to write that paper and all. And it wouldn't be strange. She's young, you know."

"Well, I should hope she'd have sense enough not to think of marrying a divorced man. That wouldn't be respectable! And she a church singer!" This from Maria.

"Patterson Greeves isn't so young anymore, you'll kindly remember!" said Henrietta, pursing her lips. Patterson Greeves had been a senior in high school with Henrietta. They might all remember that he gave her a bouquet of jacqueminot roses when she graduated.

"That's nothing!" said Cordelia. "Old men always pick out young girls."

"He's not *old*!" said Henrietta.

"You just said he wasn't *young*. Oh well! I only suggested it. I shouldn't like to see Pristina get ideas. That man has lived *abroad*. And he's lived in *New York*. He's no fit mate for a girl like Pristina. But then, I don't suppose he'd look at her. Only as I say, I hope she doesn't get ideas."

"We've always been respectable," said Grandma. "It's likely Pristina knows that. She's rather respectable herself. You remember how she wouldn't let that young drugstore clerk hold her hand. Blood will tell generally. I wouldn't worry."

But after the paper had been read before the Honey Gatherers, Mrs. Arden Philips, the wife of the postmaster, dropped in with some cross-stitch embroidery doilies for her new hardwood table and casually asked: "Henrietta never kept up her acquaintance with Pat Greeves, did she?"

Mrs. Arden Philips used to be Ruby Hathaway of the same class in high school.

"Henrietta?" said Cordelia looking sharply at that sister.

"Henrietta!" exclaimed Maria contemptuously, as if Henrietta had somehow endeavored to outclass her sisters.

"Mercy, no!" said Henrietta. "Why, Ruby, he's a married man, very much married. What makes you ask that? It's years since I've heard a word of him."

"Well, I told Julia Ellen so. After Pristina read that paper there was a great to-do about it, how she got to know so much about him, and then Julia Ellen and Jane Harris both remembered that he was sweet on Henrietta once, and we thought maybe—although Arden said he never noticed any foreign letters coming. Well, Henrietta, how did Pristina come to find out so much about Pat Greeves anyhow? All that about his books on bugs and how he came to be called to those colleges and everything. I'm sure Miss Lavinia Silver never told anything. She was so closemouthed. She always just smiled and said something pleasant, and you came away knowing no more than when you went."

"She got it out of some sort of an encyclopedia," said Grandma indignantly. "It began with Bi, I forget the name of it. She took it out of the library. It had a lot of other great men in it. She read it all aloud to us. And then she sent for his book to the city and studied that a lot. It wasn't very interesting. I tried to read it one day, but it had a lot of words I never saw before. Pristina said they were names of animals and bugs that lived before the foundation of the world or thereabout. I'm sure I don't know. But Pristina is real smart. She believes in patronizing home talent. I thought it was a bright idea myself, telling people about him before he came back to live here."

"Why yes, of course!" said Mrs. Arden Philips, looking sharply at Grandma. "That's what *I* said, but then people will talk, you know. But if I were Pristina, I wouldn't mind in the least. It'll all blow over, and Pristina's reputation can stand a little whisper now and then, I guess. But say, wouldn't it be interesting, thinking back to how he used to like Henrietta, if he should make up to Pristina sometime? Quite romantic, I say. Aunt and niece, you know. It might be."

"Nonsense! He's too old!" said Henrietta sharply.

"Besides, he's divorced!" said Maria with pursed lips.

"Yes, of course," said the visitor. "But they do say in the city, that doesn't count so much, and besides, he's lived in the city so long he probably doesn't know the difference. It isn't as if he'd lived here always and kept Silver Sands's standards. I heard the new school superintendent say the other day it was standards counted. And he can't help his standards, can he?"

"We've always been respectable!" said Grandma sharply. "And I hope we'll always stay *so*. Pristina has standards if Standish Silver's nephew *has* lost his! Ruby, did your grandmother send you that recipe for strawberry preserves? My daughter was wishing she could get it."

"Yes, I have it. I'll copy it off for you. Well, I must be going. We're having the minister to supper tonight. I only just dropped in to satisfy myself that I had told the truth to Julia Ellen. I never like to sleep on a lie. I was real sure Pristina hadn't been corresponding with him."

There was silence in the room while Maria went to the door with the visitor and until she had reached the picket gate and the iron weight had swung back and clicked against the chain as it always did when the gate shut after anyone. Then Grandma's pursed lips relaxed and her needles began to click.

"Cat!" said Henrietta. "She always was jealous about those roses!"

That happened three months before Patterson Greeves came home. Nothing more was said in the Vandemeeter home about the matter, but whenever Anne Truesdale opened and aired the front rooms, or stuck pillows out of the windows in the sunshine for a few minutes, "the girls" took occasion to glance over and wonder. And when at last the signs of a more thorough housecleaning than had gone on in years became unmistakable, Grandma had her padded rocking chair moved to the side window where she could watch the house all day long. She declared the light was poor at the front window where she had been accustomed to sit. When the news of the imminent arrival went out officially, Pristina went up to town and bought her new spring hat. It would not do to look shabby on the first Sunday of the noted man's arrival. After that the Vandemeeters were in a state of continual twitter, making errands to the front window on the slightest possible excuse and always glancing out across.

"I declare it looks good to see the house alive again," said Mother. "I can almost think I see Miss Lavinia's white hair at the window over there. My! If she were only back!"

"It's a good thing she's not!" said Grandma somberly. "It couldn't mean anything else but suffering to have her nephew come home divorced!"

"Well, I don't know about that, Mother," said her white-haired daughter. "There's some women you're better divorced from. You know even the Bible says that!"

"Well, why did he marry her then? That's what I'd like to know. A boy brought up the way he was, why *did he marry her*? Oh, you can't tell me. He just went and got into the nasty ways of the world, the flesh, and devil! That's what's the matter. If he'd just come to his hometown and taken a good, sweet girl he'd known all his life—"

"There now, Mother, for mercy's sake, don't say that. Somebody might think you meant one of ours!"

The curtains were in use at every side window of the Vandemeeter house the night that Patterson Greeves came home. Henrietta at her chamber window high in the peak of the roof noted the gray hair crisply short beneath his soft hat and the slight stoop in his shoulders, and said to herself quite softly: "Goodness! Do I look as old as that?"

They watched the house quite carefully until the lights from the side windows announced the dinner hour in the house across the way, and then they retired to their own belated meal. While they were eating it, Henrietta on a visit to the kitchen for hot water for Grandma's tea spied the red glow in the sky and called them all to the back kitchen window, or else they would have seen their neighbor vault the fence and sprint down the meadow to the fire.

But the next morning they were up early and keeping tabs from every window spryly.

When the big racing car drew up in front of the house and Athalie got out, they were fairly paralyzed with astonishment.

"Perhaps he isn't divorced after all," said Mother in a mollified voice.

"Yes, he is," insisted Pristina. "I read it to you from the biographical encyclopedia. A book like that, that's in all the libraries, wouldn't make a mistake."

"Well, maybe he's married again," said Cordelia. "That's what they do nowadays!"

"I don't believe he *would!* Not with his bringing up!" said Mother. "*He couldn't!*"

"Well, the law allows it!" snapped Maria. "That's why I'm glad I can vote. There ought to be laws!"

"Well, who is she then?" asked Grandma petulantly.

"She's young," announced Pristina, who had the best eyes for far seeing. "And her cheeks are awfully red."

"She's wearing *makeup!*" said Maria. "That's the kind! Maybe she's—"

"Maria!" said her mother and eyed Pristina. "You shouldn't say such things."

"I didn't say anything, Mother. I was going to say maybe she is just some friend of his wife's. Or maybe she is a secretary. Writers have secretaries. I've read about them."

"I should think it would be more proper to have a male secretary!" said Grandma. "There's no excuse for a man having a girl always around him. If he does a thing like that I should think it was plain nobody ought to welcome him."

"Well, she's taking an awful while saying good-bye to the man that brought her!" declared Cordelia. "Perhaps he's her father. He looks old enough to be. He's held her hand all this time. Why, she's only a child. Look, she's got short hair!"

"That's bobbed!" said Pristina in disdain. "I should think you'd know that, Aunt Cordelia. Plenty of the young girls in Silver Sands have had their hair bobbed."

"Oh yes, bobbed. Oh yes, young girls! But not like that!"

"There goes the minister in!" announced Henrietta a little later. "I wonder why? He's not the kind that todies to rich people."

"He would think he owed respect to the relative of so prominent a former member of his church," suggested Mother. "The Silver family really gave the money to build that church, you know. Gave the lot anyway."

"I hope the minister is not going to countenance divorce," said Grandma with a troubled look out the window over her spectacles.

"He preached against it two weeks ago," contributed Pristina, her hands clasped on the window fastening, her chin on her hands.

"Perhaps he doesn't know about Patterson Greeves," said Maria. "Somebody ought to have told him."

"He's coming out again. Perhaps Mr. Greeves wouldn't see him. There's his car. That rowdy Lincoln boy driving it again. What the minister sees in him!" announced Cordelia. "See, he's hurrying. I wonder what's the matter."

"Perhaps he's just found out," suggested Grandma.

Speculation ran rife, and the watchers hovered not far from the windows, doing extra dusting in the front sitting room to keep near. It was almost like the time when the circus rented the meadow for a week and they could watch the rhinoceros and giraffe go to bed at night. None of them really admitted they were watching until suddenly the minister's car drew up in front of the Silver house.

"He's back!" said Pristina, glued to the window. "And there's another woman—no, girl, with him!"

"It looks as if there might be going to be a wedding!" declared Maria primly. "I declare some men are the biggest fools! You'd think after two experiences he'd be satisfied. Oh, men! Men! Men! I've no patience with them."

"Well, I certainly don't think much of a woman that comes to his house to get married!" said Pristina. "I wonder our minister has anything to do with it."

"A woman that will marry a divorced man, too," sighed Grandma.

"Well, I wonder which one it is, the first one or this one?" questioned Pristina. "They both look awfully young. Perhaps they don't know a thing about him."

"And neither do you," said Mother. "Pristina, why don't you take that cake over that you baked for the sewing circle tomorrow? You've plenty of time to make another before the circle, and anyhow, now you've found out Stella Squires has made a chocolate cake, it would be better for you to make some other kind, say marble cake or a coconut. If they're going to have a wedding, it would be nice of the neighbors to help out a little."

"I think I'll find out whether there is a wedding or not first," said Pristina with a toss of her head. "We'll *eat* the chocolate cake ourselves. I'm going to cut a big piece now."

Pristina was like that sometimes. And when she was, the aunts looked at her in a hopeless sort of way and kept still. They called it the "Appleby" in her.

All day long they kept their watch on the house. When Silver and her father came out to walk after lunch, they huddled anxiously at the window and commented. This was the bride probably, and the other one—who was the other one? Bridesmaid or secretary? It was hard to decide.

While they were still discussing it, Athalie's trunks arrived and brought them all to the window again.

"Upon my word, there must be more coming!" said Pristina from her window. "Look at the trunks. They surely wouldn't have more than one apiece."

"A bride might have two," suggested Mother.

"Yes. You know New York! They're very extravagant livers!" declared Maria who had had the advantage of a week in New York when she was sixteen and had been going on the strength of it ever since and claiming obeisance from her family from it.

"Well, even so. Count them. One, two, three, four! Are those other boxes? They must have books in them. They probably belong to Mr. Greeves. But the girl that came first had her baggage with her. She wouldn't need a trunk."

"Well, there's one apiece and one other besides the boxes," said Henrietta. "A man wouldn't want a trunk, would he? Not if he carried his books in boxes. What would a man find to put in a trunk?"

"His clothes, of course," said Cordelia sharply.

"But a man has so few clothes. Just a suit or two. It seems as if he could hardly fill a trunk with those. Perhaps he brought home relics from the war. If he did, I certainly do hope we get a chance to see them."

"Perhaps sometime if they're away, Mrs. Truesdale will ask you in quietly to see them," suggested Mother.

"Those trunks are enormous! See, Grandma, they had to get Hank Lawson to help carry that one in. I think that's scandalous!" This from Maria.

The shades of night settled down and left them still wondering.

"There's a light in Miss Lavinia's room. It's strange they'd let anybody be put in there!"

"Maybe he took that room himself!" suggested Grandma.

Arden Philips and his wife ran in on their way to a committee meeting at the town hall, something about a supper to be given in the firehouse as soon as the first strawberries were ripe. They settled into the window seats and asked everything that had happened all day. Arden contributed the fact that a great pile of mail had come for Mr. Greeves and among them three from New York City.

"Whatever became of that child of Pat Greeves?" asked Mrs. Philips, loosening her silk wrap and throwing it back to adjust a long string of green beads slung around her scrawny neck and looping down below her waist! "Did it live? Boy, wasn't it?"

She was a tiny, wiry little woman with bright beads of eyes and the quick restless motions of a bird. She perched on the edge of her chair and looked quickly from one to another as she talked.

"Girl," said Grandma pursing her lips and looking over her spectacles. "It was a girl. He gave it to its mother's parents. I heard they didn't have much to do with one another."

"Well, I should think not!" said Ruby Philips. "A man that would marry again!" Mrs. Philips didn't believe in second marriages.

"And then get divorced!" reminded Grandma.

"Well, poor thing. I hope she hasn't suffered from her father's sins," said Maria righteously.

"Now Maria," reproved Mother, "you're going a little far. You don't really *know* that her father sinned."

"Well, he got divorced, didn't he?"

"Yes, but Maria, he might uv *had* to—you know, it isn't *always* the *men's* fault."

"It's pretty generally the men's fault, I guess," declared Maria, tossing her chin. "I thank goodness I never got tied up to one."

"Well, Maria, I don't think you're very polite to Arden," said Mrs. Arden, rising with a flame in each cheek.

"Oh, Arden's Arden of course. Besides, he's my third cousin. And present company is always excepted, you know," laughed Maria sharply.

Mrs. Arden drew her cape around her briskly and stepped toward the door. There was still a stiffness in her voice. She pursed her thin lips as if her mouth shut with a drawstring like a bag of marbles.

"Well, I must say I don't like insinuations, even when it's a joke," she said coldly. "Come Arden, we'll be late to that meeting. You'd think if there *was* a wedding he'd invite someone from the town, just for old time's sake, wouldn't you? Of course the minister; but he's a comparative stranger, and he *has* to have him. Well, I suppose we'll know sometime. Good night."

Arden, drab and homely with blue eyes and light eyelashes, followed her obediently out with an air of getting in the way of his own feet. She tripped along down the walk like a sparrow, and Arden loped behind, a long-limbed, disproportionate man who never seemed to be quite inhabiting all the room in his garments. They crossed the street and passed the Silver house, looking closely and walking slowly. The streetlights twinkled over their heads as they passed.

Before long a shadow passed along the street, with something low trailing after, but there was no sound of footsteps, though Grandma had her window open a trifle. A moment later the front door of the Silver house opened, letting out a stream of light, and shut again before they could see who had gone in. There seemed to be a dog around. He howled once from near the Silver gate.

At ten o'clock someone came out, perhaps two. It almost seemed like a group. Was one the minister? Was that a dog or only a speck in the eyes that had strained so long through the darkness?

Lights appeared upstairs across the street, went out, and the Silver house remained a white shape against the velvet blue of the night sky. Little stars blinked distantly, and the tree toads sang uninterruptedly in the meadow and down by the brook. Grandma was snoring gently in her downstairs bedroom, and Pristina lay in her narrow bed up in the roof bedroom and wondered why life had seemed to pass her by.

Chapter 14

To the right of the Silver house and almost directly across from Vandemeeter's stood a neat gray house with wide verandas and white trimmings. There were tall trees of great age in front of the place that gave it a retired look, and the fine lace curtains at the front windows were always immaculate. The fence was gray with square, fat gateposts, and a row of blue and yellow and white crocuses were picketed on either side of the gravel path. It was one of those places that you always feel you can depend on, and the people who lived in it were the same way.

Joshua Truman was the Silver Sands banker, and the fact that the whole neighborhood called him Josh, and that he had a hearty handshake and a smile for everybody, in no way detracted from his dignity. He seemed to have been an honest banker and beloved by everybody. He had shaggy overhanging gray eyebrows, but they hid a twinkle in the mild blue eyes. Mrs. Truman was plain with sweet eyes, wore her hair in close satin ripples above her ears as she had done ever since she was married, and always kept a neat brown silk with touches of velvet trimmings for her best dress. She was president of the missionary society in the Presbyterian church. There were two children, David, a lump of activity aged ten, and Mary, a tall lank girl of fifteen with a heavy braid of yellow hair down her back and big dreamy eyes.

"I think Patterson Greeves has come back," Mrs. Truman announced at the breakfast table next morning. "I didn't notice anyone coming in, but Hetty says she saw some trunks arrive. I thought perhaps you'd want to run in and see if there is anything we can do—"

"Oh, why, yes of course," said the banker heartily. "I forgot to speak about it, those men coming in and staying so long after supper last night. He did come. I met the minister, and he told me. It seems he has brought his two daughters home. One is about Mary's age. I think she had better arrange to run in today sometime and show a little attention, perhaps offer to take the girl to school or something just to make her feel at home."

"Oh, Mother!" said Mary in dismay. "I can't call on a strange girl! *You go*."

"Is his—? Did he—? Well—what about his wife, Joshua? Isn't he—*married* now?"

"Oh, well—no—I believe not. That is—" he glanced at the children, "I should think that was all the more reason why we should show some courtesy to those motherless girls."

"Yes, of course," said his wife with a look of relief that the matter was settled. "Certainly, Mary, you run in after school this afternoon and visit. You can take some of our strawberries and a bunch of daffodils and just run in without any formality."

"Oh, Mother!" said Mary aghast. "I promised Roberta I'd play duets with her this afternoon."

"Well, take Roberta along," said her mother crisply. "The Moffats were always good friends of the Silvers."

"Yes, certainly," spoke up the father. "Get some of the other girls to go, too. It will be a pleasant thing for a stranger to feel that she is welcomed into a community the first day. Talk to some of the girls and make it *work*, Mary."

"All right," said Mary reluctantly, with a speculative glance over at the Silver house, which she could see from her place at the table. "I might ask her to go to Christian Endeavor," she suggested. "We girls are on the Lookout committee. We all promised to try and get some new members. What's her name?"

"Well, that I didn't discover. I guess it's up to you to find out, daughter," said her father with a pat on her shoulder as he got up and went to kiss his wife good-bye for the morning.

"Do I have to dress up, Mother?" asked Mary, still thinking of her prospective visit. "I don't mind going if I can wear my school dress, but I hate to waste the time dolling up. Besides, I always feel so embarrassed in my best clothes."

"I don't think it will be necessary to dress up," said her mother with a quick inspection of the neat blue gingham with its sheer white ruffles and the crisp dark blue hair ribbon that tied the heavy braid of hair. "Little girls don't have to bother about their clothes. She'll probably like you far better if you go just as you come from school. Be sure your hands are clean of course."

Mary brightened and went off to school quite full of her plans for the afternoon. Her grade was in the old brick schoolhouse up beyond the Truman house. She did not pass the Silver place. She would have been surprised to know that the girl she was proposing to visit was still in bed asleep. Mary had been up for two hours, had practiced an hour and a half, and helped her mother get the breakfast on the table because Hetty, the maid of all work, had a lame foot and was being spared. Mary glanced back at the Silver place and felt a warm spot around her heart. It was going to be nice to have a girlfriend living there. They could go to school together. Living next door she naturally would be "best friend." The Silver place would be an awfully nice house to have a Christian Endeavor social in sometime. Would Mr. Greeves be willing? She would suggest this to the girls. This would make them eager to go and see her. She could hear the first bell ringing as she hurried along. She started to run to have more time to talk before school began. Her eyes were bright with the new idea when she entered the schoolyard. She decided that she would ask the new girl over to make fudge that evening if all went well.

On the other side of the Silver mansion, the side where Athalie's room faced, there was an old brown wooden house. It hadn't been painted in years and was not likely to be painted in years to come if it lasted so long. It was built in the days of scrollwork and rejoiced in a cupola, lofty and square, with alternate lights of red and blue and yellow glass bordering a large clear one, two on each side. The front gable was ornamented with a fretwork of ancient wood, faded brown like the rest, which had somehow, either in a storm or in consequences of the mending of the roof, become detached from the ridgepole on one side and fallen out of plumb. The result was rakish, like a woman with her bonnet on cockeyed. The windows of the house were gothic and latticed, and the doors all sagged. The Weldons lived there, and they sagged, too. Uri Weldon usually did his sagging down in the lobby of the one hotel, sunk deep in a worn-out leather chair with his heels above his head on another and a large sagging cigar in one corner of his mouth. He kept up the hallucination that he was thus conducting business, which consisted in trying to get someone to patent some of his inventions, but his business sagged, too, and never came to anything. Lizette Weldon, his wife, was spare with little black gimlet eyes. When she walked, she was the shape of rain in a driving storm, but nothing ever escaped her vision whichever way she was going. The property was theirs for life, entailed so that they could not sell it and would pass to a nephew now residing in China when they no longer had need for it. They had been there for years, however, and seemed likely to outlast the nephew in China. Gentle Aunt Lavinia had had her trials with Lizette, and young Patterson Greeves owed many a sound thrashing to her sharp eyes and ready tongue.

A long stretch of ill-kept wire grass constituted the lawn in front of the Weldons, ending abruptly in a row of somber pine trees behind which the house retired as if aware of its hopeless shabbiness. Had it not been for these pines the whole place would have been a sorry contrast to the well-kept Silver estate. There was something shielding, almost dignifying, in the pines.

But the side windows had no row of pines and looked across a clear space straight to the side of the Silver house; and Athalie's window presented a liberal view for any interested eye.

On the first afternoon of Athalie's arrival, Lizette was mounting the stairs for her daily nap when she happened to notice a curious figure climbing from the window. Having been occupied in the kitchen during the morning, she was as yet unaware of the arrivals, although she had seen a light in the front room the night before, but the shades were drawn almost immediately, and the light remained only about five minutes, so she thought nothing of it. But this was startling.

Lizette hurried to get an old pair of binoculars, which she kept handy and with which she had often settled uncertainties in the neighborhood in times past, and brought it to bear upon the object of her interest. She applied the binoculars to her eyes and screwed them hastily into focus then withdrew them and stared with her naked eyes.

"Oh, my!" she said aloud. "Ain't that awful!" She lifted the binoculars once more and gazed. "Pants!" she exclaimed wildly, a kind of triumph in her tone, "Well, now I guess they're coming down a peg! What would the old Silvers say to that! A girl in pants! Of course the papers advertise them, but the Silvers never were that kind. And look at her hair! My soul! How does she get it to stay out so. Ain't it redickilus! Where's she going? My good father's! If she isn't going to climb down! Well, that beats everything! Who is she?"

Lizette hurried down the stairs and rushed to the front window to get a closer view between the pines, then noting the stranger's general direction toward the town, she hastened to the telephone, calling up a friend who lived farther down the street.

"That you, Miz Hoskins? Well, go to your front window and see that girl in pants coming down the street. She just climbed down off the old Silver pergola out the side bedroom window. Hurry, and I'll hold the phone."

Mrs. Hoskins had a hot loaf of bread in a pan, holding it with a wet towel in one hand when she picked up the receiver, but she hurried to the window, hot pan and all. There succeeded a pause during the passing of Athalie, then steps and a voice.

"My, ain't that scandalous? And all those young boys down around town! Not that I mind the pants so much if everybody wore 'em. It's sensible, you know. But the way she walks and all. And her face. Did you see how it was made up? Why those girls that sang at the minstrel show weren't half so coarse looking. And the air of her. You said she came from Silvers? Well, I guess there's going to be some doings there from all I hear. My husband took the express over with the trunks. Say, you oughta have seen those trunks. Seven of 'em I think there was, and not one could be lifted without four men. Just to think such goings on in this respectable town!"

"But who is she?"

"Dear knows! John says she might be most anybody. You know Patterson Greeves got a divorce! Maybe she's his secretary. That's the way they do things nowadays. Isn't it the limit? Say, I smell my other loaf of bread burning. Excuse me a minute, please. You hold the wire. I want to ask you about what happened at the sewing circle the other day. I'll be back in a minute."

Mrs. Weldon took no nap that afternoon. She was too excited. She felt it her bound duty to keep a watch and find out if there were "doings" going on in the old house and if she ought to do something about it. What else should a good neighbor do when the respectable dwelling of an old neighbor was threatened with modernism?

The hedge was too high for her to see the terrace and the scene in the garden, but later when Athalie, having cried out her brief wrath, dressed herself in a bright little pair of pajamas with lace ruffles around the ankles and having turned on all the lights proceeded to practice a little dancing in front of the window, Lizette was there, binoculars and all, with her fat husband behind her staring over his spectacles and laughing coarsely in her ear. This was a good joke, a good joke to tell down at the hotel. Those religious Silvers come to this!

The next morning when she slipped through the garden and under the back fence across the lots to the garden of Aunt Katie Barne's neat little place on the side street where the minister boarded, to get a cup of sour milk, she paused with her apron over her head and said:

"Oh, have you heard what's happened over at the Silver place? They do say Pat Greeves has come back and brought a *woman* along! I've been told she was his secretary or typewriter or something. But she's very ordinary. I saw her go by myself, and I was shocked!

Painted and powdered, her hair all kind of wild, the strangest hat, and *pants*, mind you, in the middle of the afternoon! I feel so sorry for poor Miss Lavinia. She set such store by that boy! But it never pays to bring up other people's children, does it? I can remember how she used to sit out there in the garden by the hour playing with him and reading to him. A waste of time, I say—but aren't you surprised that he should do this? It seems as if he might have managed to stay respectable even if he is divorced."

Aunt Katie looked up from the potatoes she was frying for the minister's breakfast and smiled. "Oh, didn't you know who that was? It's one of his daughters. He has two, but this must have been the younger one. She's only a child, fourteen, I think Mr. Bannard said, and she's been off at boarding school—I suppose you must expect some craziness from little girls nowadays; there is so much more freedom in the world, especially in New York. But isn't it nice Mr. Greeves has two daughters to keep him from being lonely? The other one is a little older. Her name is Silver. Mr. Bannard says she is the perfect picture of her mother's portrait hanging over the mantel in the drawing room. Do you remember it, that lovely Sargent painting?"

"No," said Lizette, coldly eyeing her adversary. "I don't go over there. That Mrs. Truesdale doesn't show herself very friendly. I think she takes on airs. *Daughters*, you think then? Are you *quite sure?* Well, I suppose the minister ought to know." She surrendered the bit of scandal reluctantly. "It certainly is strange we never heard of them before. Daughters! Well, he better keep a little control of them then. One of 'em was having carryings on in her room last night, I'll tell you! Dancing, that's what she was doing, in her underwear! A great big girl like a full-grown woman, and all her shades up! I never did approve of those pajamas for men even. And when a woman takes up with such outlandish fashions, it's time she was stopped by law, I say."

"Well," said Aunt Katie soothingly, "we don't all have the same taste in dress, you know—"

"Dress!" sniffed Mrs. Weldon. "*Undress*, I should say! However, as you say, it takes all kinds to make a world. Well, I just ran over to see if you could let me have a cup of sour milk. Mine got too sour, and I had to throw it out."

Aunt Katie always seemed to have whatever was needed by anyone, and the sour milk was immediately forthcoming.

There being no further excuse for lingering, the neighbor lingered anyway.

"The minister told you! So he's been over to the Silver place *already*! He's a good deal younger than Pat Greeves. He must be nearer the age of one of the daughters. Curious he should run after a man like that right off the first day! I thought he set up not to be a tody-er, but I suppose they're all alike. They know which side their bread is buttered when a rich man comes along."

"Oh, they met at the fire down at Frogtown night before last. Mr. Greeves ran across the meadow as soon as he heard the alarm and got into the thick of it helping with the best of them. Then they came home together and took to each other right away. It's going to be grand having the old Silver place open again, young people in it, and folks going back and forth visiting." Aunt Katie's face was innocent as a lamb. The guest eyed her keenly but could detect no hidden sign that Aunt Katie realized she had ignored the criticism.

"Oh, well, if you take it that way of course. Some might feel they wanted to wait and be sure all was as it should be. But time will tell. Well, I must run home and stir up my batter cakes. Uri'll be waiting."

Down at the firehouse where Uri spent much of his time when he was not sitting in the lobby of the hotel, it was discussed that morning.

There was always a knot of conversation around the firehouse door even in early morning. It was just across from the blacksmith's shop and the hotel, and "handy-by" from the market and post office. When any frequenters came down to the business portion of Silver Sands, morning, noon, or night, they always dropped around for a minute, or an hour, to wait for whatever errand had brought them to mature, it might be the mail to be distributed, the horseshoe to be set, or the drummer to arrive at the hotel for their appointment with him and there paused for a bit of gossip. It was a distributing agency for the private affairs of the town and now and then the outlying districts. It was the country club for the so-inclined of the town and stood in place of golf for the men who did not aspire to athletics. The good old fire engine was athletic enough for them, and between fires they stood around and polished it and worshipped it and told tales of their own valor.

Uri Weldon hastened early to the rendezvous that morning with an air of mysterious importance and felt gravely the responsibility of so choice a bit of news as he carried.

Back in the dim shadows of a windowless room under the stairs where the oiling and polishing rags were kept, a tramp awoke at the first scraping of the first armchair on the cement floor. Awoke to the dismal necessity of another day and the immediate problem of getting out of his hiding place before he was discovered. His hairy, dirty face appeared weirdly in brief relief at the doorway as Uri Weldon settled back with his feet on an old soapbox and his pipe tilted at the right angle for conversation. Ted Loundes and Flip Haines lounged up to the doorway and leaning up against the door frame, one on either side of the door, were like a couple of bronze figures personifying Ease and Relaxation.

Uri Weldon started in on his tale with many an embellishment, interrupted by loud haw haws on the part of the younger men. The tramp frowned and ventured another look, scouting for a back exit and finding none. The tale went on. The tramp was not interested. He could not help hearing, but he paid no attention till Ted, helping himself to a log sliver from the batten door behind him and cautiously picking his teeth remarked: "I hear that guy Greeves has a pile of dough."

Uri Weldon nodded importantly. "Well, yes, he's got a pile. Them Silvers was always well off. Course they owned the beach and the sand business, and all that ground the fact'ries were built on, and then the right of way where the railroad went, and stocks, and so on. But now, you know, a lot of land they had somewhere out in Oklahoma has begun to produce oil. They say the money is rolling in from that. And besides all that, he writes books! Everybody knows they charge a high price for books. It always beat me how they got it. Just a little paper and ink, and words—just *words*! And getting paid for it! They tell me he's written a book about *bugs* that they charge three dollars and seventy-five cents for, and the people in the colleges are buying 'em like hotcakes! It beats me how with all that learning they can be so easily fooled! But so it is, and Pat Greeves is profiting by it. Well, I suppose his pretty little brats of daughters will inherit a coupla millions apiece or more when he kicks off. Seems odd though. You boys don't remember, but Pat Greeves and I used to be in a fight in school pretty near every day when we was kids— Hi, there boys! Look up the street there! I bet that's her coming down this way now!"

Uri's feet and the front legs of his chair came down to the cement pavement with a crash simultaneously, and the two younger men came about-face with alertness and looked in the direction of Uri's finger.

"Gosh!" exclaimed Flip. "She's some winner, isn't she?"

All three men with casual manner sauntered eagerly nearer the street and the tramp, peered earnestly out, stealing across the open space with catlike celerity, then drifting hastily behind the firehouse paused to make his own observation. This then was the daughter of the rich oil magnate who wrote books about bugs.

He had once been a city tramp, and he flattered himself he knew style when he saw it. The cut of a garment, the hang of a fold that indicated quality, the deep-blue flash of a jewel, the peculiar dash of the whole makeup that spoke of lavish expense. The tramp watched and listened to the comments of his companions unaware of his very existence and thought within himself how he might turn this accident of knowledge to his own good. But when the three friends returned to their former positions in the doorway of the firehouse, the tramp had melted away like the shadows and was seen no more.

Chapter 15

$\mathcal{P}$atterson Greeves had not slept at all the night before. His mind was wrought to so high a pitch that it seemed as if he never would sleep again. Silver's music had not soothed him; instead it had brought his heart sorrow with the memories that came trooping, flooding, threatening his self-control. Her touch was so like her mother's, her selections, many of them Alice's own favorites. It seemed as he sat there with half-closed eyes watching her that it must be Alice. It could be no other.

At last the girl herself had seemed to feel the strain she was putting on her father, and whirling around on the piano stool, she declared she had played enough for the first night.

It was then the minister roused from his delight in the music, realizing that it was time for him to take his departure and leave this father and daughter to settle their own situation by themselves. He expressed his pleasure in the music and his hope that he might hear it again, more and often, and said his good-byes.

"Just a moment, Bannard," said Greeves as they neared the

front door. "I'll get that book for you I was speaking of. I saw it this morning in its old place on the shelf—if you don't mind taking it with you."

They stepped into the library and turned up the light. There sat Blink, sound asleep, with a draping of angleworms all around the rim of his tomato can, and one bolder than the rest strewn out across his knee.

Roused, he declared he had not been asleep but had been enjoying the fire and the music, merely waiting till they were through to present his gift. Trust Blink to be equal to a situation. Nevertheless, he grinned at his worms and, gathering them up, flashed a joke at them that brought a little breath of mirth into the tense atmosphere of the evening and made everybody feel better.

When Blink and the minister had left, Silver and her father sat before the fire hand in hand, half shyly for a few minutes, and talked.

If the music had not helped Patterson Greeves to solve the difficulties, it had at least made the situation clearer to his daughter.

"Father," she said shyly, almost hesitantly, "don't you think perhaps if you will have a quiet talk with Athalie in the morning it might help? I've been thinking about it. She's probably as excited as we all are. It must be hard for her, too. I think perhaps if she understood, you might be able to make it easier for her. I was trying to think how I would feel if I were in her place—she was terribly excited and hurt—you could see that—"

They talked for some time, and when Silver finally went to her room, Patterson Greeves turned out the light, and in the dying firelight, he paced the room for hours, back and forth.

In the small hours of the night, Anne Truesdale, from her anxious chamber off the back hall, heard him come softly up the stairs to his room, but when she went in the morning to put his room to rights, the bed had not been slept in. There was only a deep dent in the coverlet where folded arms and a head must have rested as of one on bended knees. But Patterson Greeves had no one left to pray to, unless it might have been his dead wife, Alice, or his sweet departed Aunt Lavinia, for he did not believe in a God. And if there had been a God, he was angry with Him for bringing all this horrible thing to pass upon him.

But when morning dawned, even before Anne Truesdale had been down to open the shutters and tidy up the rooms, he was back in the library again, pacing back and forth. And as soon as ever it would have done any good to call, he was trying to telephone long distance to his divorced wife. He had decided that Athalie must go back to Lilla. He would make it worth her while.

He made a pretense of eating some breakfast with Silver—no sound had as yet been heard from Athalie's room, and none in the family were disposed to disturb her—but it was plain that he was nervous and overwrought, and the slightest sound made him start and listen for the telephone.

When the call came at last, he hurried to the library only to be informed that Mrs. Greeves had sailed for Europe the day before to be gone indefinitely.

He hung up the receiver and stared around the room with that dazed expression he had worn the day when he first knew that Athalie was coming to him. And again there sounded in his ear the ring of that derisive laughter, echoing along the halls of his soul with taunting sweetness. Lilla had won out again. It was as if she had tossed her daughter over into his keeping and put the sea between them, so that he was not able to send her back, not even able to bribe Lilla with money to take her unwelcome child to her heart again.

After a few moments, he rose and gravely walked to the window. The stun of the blow was subsiding, and he was beginning to take it in for the first time that this impossible child was his irretrievably to keep and to care for from this time forward and that he could not rid himself of the duty. For the first time he was taking it in, and some of the things he had flung out in his first bitterness of soul in talking with the minister the night before came back to him as great truths that he had uttered. He was responsible for the child, responsible for what she had become. He could not shirk any longer what he had tried to shirk for life. He must face it now. There was not distance enough in the whole universe to put his responsibility away from him. It would follow him like a shadow wherever he went, whatever he did.

How could he ever write again with this horror hanging over him? Well, what difference did it make to anyone whether he ever wrote again? What difference did anything make to him?

Gradually, however, the business habits of his life settled upon his mind, and he began to come at the question more sanely, more seriously, and to really try to think what he could do and what he should say to this strange, unloving, unlovable girl.

Perhaps the thought of Silver with the Alice-eyes writing some letters up in Aunt Lavinia's room, a sweet, strong, sane presence, helped to keep him from the insane desperation that had come upon him the day before. At any rate, his tortured mind finally thought out a way, made a semblance of a plan, of what he should say to Athalie and how he should say it.

Thinking more coolly now, he could see that he had antagonized her. She was like Lilla. That was plain. Strange that both his children should be like their mothers entirely—and yet—no, he could see some things in Athalie exactly like himself. That being the case, perhaps he could understand her a little better if he would come at her in the way he would like to be approached himself, reasonably, gently, firmly, but pleasantly. Subconsciously he had known that yesterday, but it had seemed too much like yielding to an outrageous imposition to treat her in any way but imperiously. Well, that was all wrong, of course, from her standpoint. He had simply antagonized her. It would be of no sort of use to try to control her until he had some hold upon her. He had shown his utter disapproval of her, her dress, her appearance, her habits, from the start. Could he possibly retrieve the past and begin again? Well, it was up to him to try. He could not rid himself of her by making her hate him, though he had no real desire to win her love. Still, he must try something. He could easily see now it would be useless to send her to any school against her will in this state of mind. She would only disgrace him and be back on his hands in a worse condition than before. He must do his duty somehow, whatever a father's duty was. Somehow he had never thought before, till Silver looked at him with Alice's eyes, what a duty of a father might be.

So he rang the bell for Anne and asked her to say to Miss Athalie that he would like to see her in the library as soon as she had finished her breakfast.

Athalie took her time.

She bathed herself leisurely; toying with her perfumes, she washed her face many times in very hot water and only powdered it lightly, giving a becoming touch of shadow under her eyes as from much weeping and no lipstick at all to her full mouth. It took quite awhile to get just the right atmosphere, for it was difficult to make the healthy Athalie look as if she were going into a decline.

She really was trying to please her father. She chose a little dashing frock of dark blue wool with a great creamy white wool collar curiously rolled around her shoulders and a daring scarlet sash of crimson silk with fringe that hung several inches below the hem. She even put on black silk stockings, thin they were and extremely lacy, but black, and completed by little fairy patent leather shoes with straps intricately fastened to look like ancient Greek foot attire. A black velvet band around her forehead completed her outfit, and she descended slowly, casually, to the dining room and rang the bell imperiously.

It was Molly who brought a tray with ample food, but she rang again and sent for more and pursued the even tenor of a prolonged breakfast with satisfaction, until Patterson Greeves awaiting her in the library was almost at the limit of his patience and his newly assumed gentleness and could barely keep his resolves from leaping out the door and escaping him altogether.

But at last, after lingering in the garden a moment to gather a flaunting red tulip and stick it in her dress where it flared against the white of the collar, she sallied into the library without waiting to knock and gave her father a cool "Good morning," quite as if he might have been the naughty child and she the casual parent, with many, many greater interests than just parenthood.

Following out his resolves with a visible effort, he wheeled over a comfortable chair for her to sit down where the light would fall full on her face and he might study her as they talked. She watched him sharply and then turned and stood with her back to him looking out the window.

"Come here and sit down, Athalie," he said. "I want to have a little talk with you."

"Fire ahead, Pat," she said nonchalantly. "I'd rather stand here and look out."

What could a father do under those circumstances? What *would* a father do? His blood boiled. His temper arose and clamored for satisfaction. He was no father of course, but how could he be? Here was this impish child of his defying him again, making it practically impossible for him to exercise the self-control and gentleness he had intended. It was as if she suspected his scheme and was blocking it. How could he have a heart-to-heart talk with a broad blue and white back, a blur against the sunshine of the morning? How was he to make her understand that he meant to do his best by her, do all that was best for her whether it was hard for him or not, if she stood like that and ignored him? He ought to give her a good whipping. That was what she deserved. It was barbarous of course, but she was a little barbarian, and nothing else would probably reach her. Nevertheless—he glanced around and summoned his new resolves that were just sliding out the door, grappled them to his side, and began:

"Athalie, my child," he began, realizing that it was necessary for his own good that he recognize the relation openly. He cleared his throat, "I—ha—"

"Aw, cut the comedy, Pat! What's eating you? Spit it out! I know I'm in for the deuce of a time, but if you're going to preach a sermon, you'll have to do it without me. This is too gorgeous a morning to be shut up in the house. Say, Pat, don't you ever play golf? What say if you and I go to some country club around here and have a game and then take lunch? Let's have a ripping old time together and get acquainted, and after that if you haven't got it all out of your system yet, I'll agree to listen."

For an instant, the astounded father gazed at the face of his cock-sure amazing daughter and wavered, almost considering whether he could accept this high-handed proposal. Perhaps if he had, this story might have been a different one in many details, who can tell? But Patterson Greeves's sole contact with youth since he passed out of that class himself had been in the classroom or on the battlefield, in both of which places he had been the dictator, able to put his victim through instant discipline if he did not obey in every particular; where a mere black mark on a report card or spoken word to an under officer meant that the delinquent would be dealt with speedily and thoroughly, and where respect and obedience were the foundation of breath itself, and nothing else was to be tolerated.

And now, while flesh shrank from the encounter before him, and his whole soul cried out for respect, and the open air relaxed conscience and a chance to get things into some natural order again, his puritan inheritance and his whole training demanded respect and obedience, and the moment passed. The scene of the night before rose in his mind's eye, and his blood boiled. He was again in the position of an outraged parent struggling for self-control while he read the Ten Commandants to a naughty child.

And perhaps it was as well, for Athalie knew how to take advantage of the least opportunity, and she *had* to learn *sometime* that law was law.

The silence was growing very tense. Athalie, quick to note his every phase of attitude toward her, so sure of him when she finished her wheedling sentence, began to grow uneasy as his gaze continued, staring, stern and displeased.

"Athalie," he spoke at last, and his words were like icicles, "I can go nowhere, do nothing, until I have had an understanding with you."

A sullen cloud settled down over the girl's face.

"Sit down." He pointed to the chair. Athalie hesitated a second, then with her sullen eyes like smoldering fires fixed on him, seemed to think best to obey, but she sat down tentatively, with one foot slid slightly behind her in readiness to rise again if he offended her. Her lips were pouted angrily. She shrugged her shoulders with a bored attitude as if she were but humoring him for the moment.

The speech he had framed through the long hours of the night deserted him now when he most needed it. Strangely it did not seem to fit. He struggled to find the phrases, cutting ones, intended to show her her place and keep her in it, an ultimatum that would put things on a proper basis. But the whole thing was gone, and nothing but his own helplessness was upon him.

Then something Silver had said the night before about talking gently, reasonably, came to him. A sense of the room and its hallowed memories filled him. It was as if those who had loved him and cared for him in his earlier years might be hovering around unseen waiting to help him through this trying time. He dropped his forehead on his hand for a moment almost humbly, and then lifting his eyes, he tried to tell the girl what was in his heart. None of the sentences he had planned were there. Many of the words he spoke he would not have wished to say to her; it was condescending too much to one who had treated him and his so lightly.

"Athalie," he said, and his voice sounded now gentler, with that certain something that always brings attention, "you and I are not in a very pleasant position. Perhaps it may be as hard for you as for me; I do not know. I may not have seemed to you very kind nor sympathetic when you arrived. I certainly did not welcome you. I was utterly unprepared for your arrival, as your mother must have known and intended that I should be. I do not intend to speak of her nor the past any more than is necessary; and there must of course be a great many things that you do not understand about our peculiar situation. We shall just have to put away the past and try to build up a relationship from the beginning. In order to do that, there are one or two things that must be clearly understood.

"In the first place, we belong to an old and respectable family with many traditions that must be honored and standards that must be upheld. We owe it to the past."

He studied her blank, sullen face for a moment wondering if she understood. He struggled to make his words plainer. "There are certain customs and laws of society that we have always maintained. I cannot have my daughter transgressing these things. Our women have always been good and pure and have never sought to imitate men nor to flaunt their personalities or their persons. They have always been modest, quiet, sweet women, dressing unobtrusively, becomingly, and in a modest way. I cannot countenance the way you speak, the flippant, pert, rude disrespect both to me and to the old house servants who have been with us so long that they are an integral part of the family. I cannot countenance your mannish ways, nor your cigarette smoking, nor your revealing dresses. I like sweet, modest girls, and if you and I are to get on at all together, you must drop these ways and try to be a good girl."

Athalie's eyes smoldered furiously, and her lips curled in contempt. "I suppose that other girl just suits you!" she stormed. "Little simp!"

"Silver seems a very modest, sweet girl," he assented, wondering what he ought to say about the way she had treated the picture last night.

"Well, I *hate* her!" said Athalie in low, hard tones. "I HATE HER! And you sound to me awfully what they call at school 'mid-Victorian.' "

Patterson Greeves began to realize that he was not getting on very well. He looked at his hopeless offspring and longed to vanish out of her sight forever, caring not where or how his soul was disposed, so he might finally escape the problem of her. But something in his puritan conscience refused to let him slide away from the issue. He must face and conquer it. He had slid out of his situation with Lilla by letting it take its course—or had he? Was she not even now as poignant and tangible an element in his life as though he were struggling to live his daily life by her side? It passed through his mind that perhaps nothing was quite ever shoved aside or slid out of. Perhaps we always had to reckon with everything we did, sooner or later—sooner *and* later. That was a question of life that might be worth looking into, might make a good subject for an article for a magazine—what strange thoughts form themselves beneath the surface when we are in the middle of a tense and trying time! Patterson Greeves brushed the thoughts away impatiently and sat up. He must get these things said that he had resolved to say.

"It makes no difference what I sound like," crisped the father, "nor by what names your school friends choose to call things. I am telling you certain facts that must be acted upon by you as long as you are under my care. They are the only basis upon which you and I can have any dealings whatever. You cannot carry things with a high hand, ignore everybody else, and overturn systems. You are not the ruler here, and you must understand it from the beginning."

He paused and eyed her, but she gave no sign, just let her smoldering eyes rest on him sullenly, unflinchingly, the slow contempt in the upper lip continuing to grow.

"Those things being thoroughly understood and complied with on your part willingly," he went on hurriedly, determined not to give her an opportunity to demur, "I am entirely willing to talk over your future with you and try to arrange, as far as is possible and best for you, to make such plans as will be agreeable to you. As to the school you will attend, I shall be glad to send for catalogs and let you have a part in the selection of your—"

She raised her hand imperiously.

"Stop right there!" she demanded sharply. "If you're banking on me being a good little girl and going to school, you might as well understand that I won't! I came here to live with you. The court said I was to be under your care, and here I'm going to stay. If you try to send me away anywhere, I'll simply run away and make you more trouble. I'd drown myself before I'd go to another boarding school. I've lived in boarding schools all my life, and I'm *done* with them! You can't shut me off that way, for it can't be done!"

A glance into her eyes showed that she fully meant every word she said, and something in her tone reminded her stubborn father that she had inherited his power of sticking to a decision. Remembering last evening, it seemed fully likely that she would carry out any threat that she might choose to make. He shuddered inwardly and began to weaken.

"Of course, if I found that you were entirely submissive and obedient, it might be possible to arrange a school not far away—"

Athalie arose abruptly.

"Is that all you have to say to me?" she asked in a businesslike tone. "Because I've got some letters to write."

"Athalie, sit down," he thundered, entirely unnerved, feeling that his work was all undone again.

"Not when you speak to me in that tone," said the girl, shrugging her shoulders and raising her chin. "I suppose you call that kind of talk up to the standards of your respectable family."

The crimson swept over her white, sensitive face. Her voice was so perfectly like Lilla's, the reply so entirely what she would have given.

"I beg your pardon, Athalie. It was not. I am very much upset this morning. I will endeavor to control my voice. Will you kindly be seated? Now, I want to ask whether you are going to be willing to be subject to my authority. If not, I must begin to take immediate steps to place you where you will be looked after in the right way. I cannot have such scenes recurring. I may as well say I *will* not have them. I am a busy man with important work to do, and this is utterly upsetting. Will you be a good girl and try to do right?"

His child regarded him coolly. "I don't know whether I will or not," she answered calmly. "It depends on how you behave. If you let me have my own way and have a good time, I presume I shall— depends on what you call good. I don't intend to be goody-goody. But if you try to bully me, you'll wish you hadn't, that's all. That's what I told Lilla when I left her. I said, 'Lilla, he may have bullied you, but he's not going to bully me. It isn't being done.'"

A sudden startled wonder came to him as she spoke of her mother that made him forget to listen to the arrogant ending of her sentence.

"Athalie," he said, suddenly changing the subject, "are you aware that your mother has sailed for Europe?"

The girl gave him a look as if he had unexpectedly stabbed her, and her eyes filled up with tears, her lips trembled. She struggled for an instant with a sob, gave a slight nod of assent with her chin, and broke down with a heartrending little cry, sinking her head on her arms, her whole gaudily attired body shaking with suppressed sobs, as if the thought was too deep for sound.

Patterson Greeves stared at her for a moment, uncomprehending, unable to meet this amazing phase of his most mysterious daughter, resenting her change of combat as if she had broken some rule of the game. She was not being true to type. How could he meet such an antagonist? Lilla used to cry prettily, pettedly, outrageously, to order, when she found all other weapons useless; but this was grief, genuine, deep, terrible. The grief of an uncontrolled nature. Grief of the kind he always had felt in his own troubles. Was it possible that something in his heart was stirring toward her, yearning? No. This child of Lilla's deserved all she was getting—ah! but child of himself, too. Could it be possible that Lilla loved the child? If so, why had she sent her away from her? It seemed impossible that Lilla could love anything but herself. Could it be possible that the child loved Lilla? She did not seem like a loving child. But those sobs were not angry; they were hurt, stricken cries. Had Lilla been unkind to the girl? His sense of justice roused toward her. He put out a vague hand and touched her shoulder.

"Athalie, haven't you had a—*happy*—life? Hasn't your mother been good to you?" he asked hesitatingly.

She lifted a tear-stained face from behind which fires flashed in her eyes and shook his groping hand off.

"That's none of your business," she said. "You never tried to make it any happier, did you?"

The father sat and saw a few more of his shortcomings marched out before him in the open and swallowed hard on the sight. He, Patterson Greeves, of a respected family, had contrived to do some of the most contemptible things a man can do on earth! It was unbelievable, and yet he was beginning to believe it.

He stared at her a moment with that dazed expression coming again. It dazes most souls to really look in their own eyes and see how different they are from their fancied selves. Then he drew a deep sigh and rose, going to the window to stare out across the meadow.

"No. I don't suppose I ever did," he said reluctantly at last. The sobs ceased as suddenly as they had begun. There ensued a prolonged silence. Then the father added as though to himself: "I had no intention of overlooking any duty; I simply did not realize."

Finally, the girl raised her head and in quite a controlled voice said, "That's all right, Pat, I'm here now. Forget it! We aren't getting anywhere, and I'm going up and wash my face. If you change your mind about that golf, just send me word."

She was at the door when he wheeled around and said hesitatingly, "There's one thing, Athalie. I wish you wouldn't call me Pat. I don't like it. It sounds disrespectful. It makes me ashamed. I—"

"All right, Dad, since you ask it that way, I won't. But I like you a lot more when you're Pat. It seems to make you more homey and understandable. Well, so long! You know where to find me!" and she flashed away like a bright-throated, naughty blue jay.

The father sat down in a chair and covered his face with his hands. The interview for which he had been all night preparing was over, and he had gone nowhere. Nothing had been accomplished, except that perhaps he himself had weakened. A sense of his own forgotten responsibility and a certain wistful turn of her voice had undone him. How was he ever to do anything with his unmanageable child?

The door suddenly opened without warning, and Athalie's head flashed in again. "I just wanted to say, Dad, that if you take that other girl along, you needn't count me in. She and I are two people. I hate her. So don't go to bunching us up, for it won't work, and don't give me any more of that line about getting advice from her about clothes, see? I won't stand for it, that's all. If you want me to live up to your standards, you've got to live up to mine! Understand?"

She was gone. And if she had suddenly hurled a leaden weight on her father's heart, the world could not have turned darker or his heart been heavier. How was such a state of things ever to work out?

A soft knock on the door broke in on these thoughts, and Silver stepped inside the room dressed in coat and hat and gloves, with her suitcase in her hand.

Chapter 16

Whenever Silver came into his vision, again she gave her father a start, her appearance was so much like his lost Alice.

There was something exquisite and spiritlike in her face that rested and soothed him. It was curious that the word *blessed* flitted through his mind when he thought of how she made him feel. He lifted a troubled face to greet her now, and a sick dismay stole over him as he saw the suitcase in her hand.

She put it down and came quickly over to him, her lips smiling although her eyes were grave. Her voice had a lilt of sorrow in it though she tried to make it cheerful.

"Father, I've thought it all out in the night," she said, perching on the arm of his chair and putting her arm softly around his neck—just as her mother used to sit and touch his hair lightly with her fingers. He had not thought of it in a long, long time.

"You see, I've sort of promised this man that I would take this position, and he has held it for me already for several days while I was getting packed up. I feel that I ought to go back right away and get to work."

She was talking rapidly, trying to stem the tide of emotion she evidently felt, and the stricken look on his face made it no easier.

"I didn't tell you this morning at breakfast because I didn't want you to be disturbed by any other question till you had had your talk with Athalie. It wasn't fair to her. But I saw her just now as she came upstairs, and I feel sure you have come to some understanding.

"Now Father, dear, please don't try to change me." She took the hand that he put out in protest and held it close. "Listen to me. It isn't at all the way you are thinking. I'm not being driven away or anything. I am simply going away because I feel that is my duty. No, you're not to talk, please, till I'm through. Listen, Father, Athalie is younger than I am, and she needs you more. You must get acquainted with her and teach her to love you. She hasn't ever had anybody real to love her, I am sure, and I have, you know. And it isn't as though I didn't have you, too. It's quite, quite different from what it was before I came. I have a father now, and I know he loves me. And we can write to each other, and that will be wonderful! And I'll have someone to advise me—"

"Stop!" cried Patterson Greeves, springing to his feet, his tortured nerves refusing to hear more. "Stop! Don't speak of it again! I tell you I have withstood enough. You shall not go away, Silver, my Silver-Alice! I need you! I want you! You remember your grandmother told you to find out if I needed you. Well, *I do*! God knows I do! Do you suppose for an instant I would let the welfare of that other strange child come between us? She is nothing to me, never can be. Her mother was a viper, and she is going to be just like her! I will send her—"

Suddenly both of them became aware of the opening of the door, and there on the threshold stood Athalie, attired in giddy sports clothes with a golf club in her hand, but the bright smile with which she had entered had died on her lips, and her face was white as death, her eyes like two blazing coals.

For an instant she stood there facing her father, her eyes wide with sorrow, consternation, something terrible and inscrutable. Then she turned with a quick glance of hate toward Silver and exclaimed, "Oh, heck!"

The slam with which she emphasized her exit from the door reverberated through the house like thunder as she stormed upstairs again. Anne Truesdale hurried in from the back hall with her apron wrapped around her hands and over her heart and stood like an old gray squirrel, her head on one side perking her ears, watching, listening. But Athalie's sobs were smothered in the pillow, for the hurt had gone deep, deep!

The two left in the library white and shaken looked at one another.

Silver's eyes said sadly, *Father, don't you see I must go?*

But the man's lips spoke the answer: "It would be impossible, Silver. I could not endure her."

It was an hour before they arrived at a compromise. Silver was to remain for a time, was to send for her trunk and to be allowed to follow her own course about keeping out of Athalie's way, on condition that the father was to make an honest effort to win Athalie to a better way of behavior and to try to cultivate a little love between them, though that Patterson Greeves declared was an impossibility.

To this end he had agreed to keep his feelings in the background and try to show Athalie a good time, that being the thing that seemed to be uppermost in her mind and the most likely to make her amenable to reason.

When Silver left him to go back to her room, it was with the satisfaction of seeing Anne Truesdale precede her up the stairs to tap at Athalie's door with the message that her father was now ready to go with her to the golf links if she would come down at once.

How had the slip of a girl learned to wind one round her finger? Just as her mother used to do. Always able to make one see the sensible, sane thing to do, always willing to give up herself and stand in the background while someone else was being helped. Oh, why, why could that mother not have lived? He wondered all these things as he waited for the other daughter to present herself, half hoping she would declare not to go.

Athalie came slowly down with a gloomy air. Her eyes looked heavy and her mouth slouched at the corners. She carried her bag of clubs slung over her shoulder, and she had taken care to wear a bright skirt in place of the knickers that she would have chosen, obviously trying to please him if he had but known it, trying to respect that vague respectable family standard of which he had spoken.

"Pristina!" called Grandma from the sitting room. "Come here quick and tell me which one this is."

Pristina hurried from the kitchen where she was making cake, a flour sifter in her hand.

"That's number one," said Pristina assuredly. "She was the fat one with the painted face. I wonder why the other one didn't go, too. They are going to play golf."

"Seems to me that's rather frivolous to begin with—golf," said Grandma. "Seems as if for a man of his years he ought to be getting settled and getting out his work. If he's really so great as they say, writing books and all, why don't he write 'em? I have no patience with people trying to keep from growing up. Golf! Humph!" sniffed Grandma.

"All great people do it nowadays, Grandma," assured Pristina. "They talk in the magazines about it's keeping you in shape."

"Shape! Fiddlesticks! If he'd get out and do a little digging in his own garden, it would keep him in shape enough. What was that, Pristina, that your uncle Ned said the last time he came down from New York? It was something very fitting about this golf."

"Oh, Uncle said he had no time for knocking a pill around a ten-acre lot. But Grandma, that wasn't original. I've heard it since and read it in the joke column."

"Very likely they got it from your uncle Edward," said Grandma reprovingly. "You have a way of discounting your relatives that is very disappointing, Pristina. Your own family are as good as any you'll find anywhere. Don't go yet, Pristina. Who is that coming up from the post office? She's met them. Perhaps she'll be coming here. She'll be able to tell us something, and then we shall know what to think. I declare it's very embarrassing not knowing what to think nor how to act."

"That's Lizette Weldon, Grandma, and she's bringing back the cup of yeast she borrowed last week. I see a cup in her hand."

Lizette had seen Greeves and his daughter start out.

"My soul!" said Lizette and hastened to grab her brown cape and get the cup of yeast that she might not miss this great opportunity. She met them as they were passing the gate. *Yes, that's the one! My, ain't she coarse!* she commented inwardly. *Now, does he think he's going to pretend he don't know me? Well, I rather guess not.* "Good morning, Mr. Greeves. We're pleased to see the old house lighted up." *There, now,* she thought to herself. *That'll make that fat thing understand that I saw her last night, and perhaps she'll be more careful when she cuts up her antics.*

Patterson Greeves, startled into recognition, lifted a belated hat. "Oh yes, good morning. It is a long time since it was. Thank you. I hope you are quite well!"

He didn't know me from the man in the moon, she thought to herself as she hastened up the street with the yeast. *What a man! I don't wonder she divorced him. Mercy, but that girl is fat! And her clothes looked like my patchwork quilt with the rising sun pattern. I wonder he lets her go out that way. He knows what's expected in this town, he lived here long enough, goodness knows. But perhaps he doesn't care what we think.*

Pristina hastened to the door. Ordinarily Lizette was not overly welcomed, but a common cause does a great deal to bring folks down to a common level.

"Well, what do you think of Patterson Greeves's daughters?" she asked almost before she had her breath from coming up the steps.

"Daughters?" chorused the Vandemeeter girls, all present but Harriet who was hastening down from the third story as fast as possible, having left a pillow in midair as she was making the bed, when she heard Lizette's voice at the front door.

"*Daughters!*" reiterated Lizette, sitting down complacently with the cup of yeast still in hand. "Sort of startling, ain't it? I never heard of them before, did you? Strange that Mrs. Truesdale or someone never let it out, but land! She's as closemouthed as Miss Lavinia Silver was, every bit, and a thousand times more aristocratic. Well, I met one of 'em face-to-face, and I don't think much of her. She's fat and coarse and dresses outlandish. I was just thinking on my way down she looked as if she had on my rising sun bed quilt, all odd stripes and stitches over her skirt and sweater."

"Daughters!" echoed the Vandemeeters again and looked at one another. "We must tell Arden's wife!"

"What's her name?" asked Pristina.

"Well, he didn't name her when he introduced her," evaded Lizette. "Perhaps that's the fashion now. But the fact is I don't believe he remembered my name, although he pretended he was awful pleased to see me."

"Well—it's only natural—after all these years—" said Mother comfortably.

"No 'tain't natural, you know 'tain't. Why, I've spanked him for stealing my cherries!"

"That's probably the reason," said Pristina. "One can't be dignified in the face of a spanking. How old is that girl anyway?"

"Well, I hardly know, Pristina. She looked older, an' younger, 'n she oughta be. I couldn't quite describe it. Kind of as if she was an old woman that hadn't growed up, or a baby that had lived a hundred years. One thing I know, she had smut under her eyes, and them lips never grew red like that. It ain't natur'."

"Is she the oldest or the youngest?" asked Mother, biting off her thread and holding up her needle to the light.

Well, 'deed I can't really tell you, Mis Vandemeeter, but I shud judge she might be the youngest. But then I ain't seen the other, so you can't tell. This one wears pants, regular pants like the boys, if that'll tell you anything. But laws! The other one may, too, for all I know. She keeps herself mighty close."

"She went out with Pat—with her father, I mean—yesterday afternoon," contributed Harriet. "She looked to me like a real modest-appearing girl. She has pink cheeks, not too pink, and light hair, a real girl. I liked her looks."

"I'm sure I don't see how you could tell at that distance, Aunt Harriet," said Pristina coldly.

"Well, her dress seemed quiet," defended Harriet.

"Well, they may wear dresses that scream for all me," said Pristina crossly. "I'm going back to my angel cake."

Lizette's languidly alert eyes followed her mournfully, and when the click of the flour sifter could be heard, she lowered her voice somberly: "Wasn't Pristina rather interested in Mr. Greeves at one time?"

"Mercy, no!" clamored Mother so audibly that her voice could be heard in the kitchen. "Pristina was a babe in arms when he went away from here. Just because she did her duty by honoring a fellow citizen in her essay at the club, everybody has jumped to the conclusion that she's in love with him. I wish to pity's sake you'd turn your attention to someone else, Lizette, and not carry gossip around about my child."

"Well, now Lucy, I certainly think you'll have to take that back. I don't know what you mean. I only asked a simple question, didn't I? And I don't originate all the questions in this town, do I? If I give you a little hint of what's passing, isn't that only kindness?"

Mrs. Vandemeeter pursed her lips around a pin and looked angry.

"Well, all I've got to say," said Lizette rising offendedly, "is, if you don't ever find any worse things said about you than I say, you can count yourself well off. There's your yeast. Don't trouble to get up. I've got to run right back. I thought you'd be interested to know, but of course if you're not, I'll keep the rest to myself. Good-bye."

She shut the door with a slam and swished down the front walk.

"Cat!" said Pristina from behind the pantry door.

"There, now Lucy, I'm afraid you've done it. She'll tell something a great deal worse. It never does to make an enemy mad, especially if she's got a tongue. 'Let sleeping dogs lie,' the saying is, and it's very true," said Grandma. "Something about it being better to have even a dog your friend, too, what is it? Don't any of you know? It bothers me so to have something like that I can't remember. Now I shall lie awake all night tonight thinking of that, and it will worry me like anything that you gave her a chance to talk about Pristina, Lucy. She'll talk; I know she will."

"Let her talk!" said Mother with her head in the air. "I guess Pristina can stand it. Pristina's a lady."

"Well," said Pristina, "I'd like to know what those girls are named. You can tell a whole lot by names."

"You'll know soon enough," said Grandma. "Get back to your

cake. I wonder if Arden's wife knows about their being daughters! Well, I must say, it's a relief to know they're daughters. The neighborhood has always been so respectable."

Athalie was a different creature on the golf course—alert, strong, skillful, full of eagerness—like a boy. She whistled and talked slang and patronized her father till he began to feel like a small boy himself, and all the time as he walked silently from point to point studying his amazing child, he was seeing himself in all her actions and then seeing Lilla in her waywardness between and realizing more and more that he was responsible for this strange, tantalizing creature. Part of the time also he was wondering why he had been persuaded to come out on the golf course with this child of whom he disapproved, whom he did not want to be with, and why he was trying with all his might to control his temper and make her have a good time. It was all Silver's doing. "Silver-Alice!" he said it over and over to himself. "Silver-Alice! Silver-Alice! Silver-Alice!" And the name sounded sweet to his soul. Why had he not known what sweetness there was in fatherhood?

On the way home, it almost appeared from something Athalie said that she had been trying to make him have a pleasant time. He felt strangely touched and chagrined. Not that he liked to have her put herself out for him. It went against the grain to find her doing such a thing. But the justice in his soul cried out for her due. He found himself promising that the morning should be repeated and then groaning within himself over the interruption to his life this was going to be.

But when they reached the house and Anne told him that the minister had called up to ask if they would like to take a drive that afternoon, he found himself entirely willing to be interrupted still further.

There was a struggle in his mind about taking Athalie along on the drive. He felt she would be a disturbing element. But when he asked her finally if she would like to go, she asked suspiciously: "Is *she* going?" And when he answered in the affirmative, she shrugged her shoulders and said, "Thank you, no. I told you how I felt about that. You can't expect me to come when you take her."

He was relieved. It made things easier. He felt sure Bannard would be even more pleased.

Silver, too, was relieved. He could see that. Yet there was a cloud in her eyes, a weight, a weight on her heart. Her conscience was overactive. It troubled her that there should be enmity between her father's daughter and herself.

But the day was gorgeous, one of those caressing days in spring when June seems to have anticipated herself and Earth's tuning has begun. Little warm scents flitted about and tiny melodies of living creatures moving: the whir of a bee's wings, the grumble as he worked, the stir of things growing, budding, blossoming, grass blades like rockets shooting everywhere, sharp emerald sounds broadcasting only to those whose ears attuned to their pitch, a meadowlark's note, high, clear above it all.

And then the three seemed so congenial. There was so much to see and talk about, so much in which all were interested.

Bannard was the guide, Greeves the historian, Silver the audience, eager, questioning.

They started up the road past the schoolhouse where Greeves had been a student, out the old Pike, across the covered bridge and curving back of the village along the beach of silver beside the sparkling stream, down toward Frogtown. Bannard wanted to show them his mission and to point out a good location for the proposed building.

They drew up in front of a row of old stone hovels crazily

jostling each other facing the road and the creek. Bannard pointed to a vacant lot not far away, and he and Greeves were discussing whether it would be better farther up the hill. Silver sat watching the children playing on the path, dirty little things, yet beautiful beneath the dirt. Wonderful starry black eyes set in faces that might have been the models for some of the angel faces in the paintings of great masters, tumbled curls, and rosy cheeks, tiny earrings glittering sharply under the dirt and tousle, little bodies scantily clad, little savages unaware of their soil and nakedness. Clamoring, fighting, throwing mud, the older girls carrying babies too large sized for their backs, the younger babies huddled to watch the automobile.

A woman hurried out from one of the houses, a curious three-corner shawl of bright colors thrown over her head and folded back like a headdress. She had an air of excitement. Bannard called to her: "Good morning, Nuncie, all well at your house?"

"Oh, it's the maister!" cried the woman, her voice full of agitation, her dark-lined face working with emotion. "It's the baby, little Mary, Angelo's Mary. Vary seek. I go for the doctor. He come two times yesterday. I tink she got the pneumonias. She turn all black. Her heart stop—"

Before the account was finished, Bannard was out of the car. "Will you excuse me a moment?" he said hurriedly. "I must go in and see. This is the beautiful baby I told you about," he finished, looking at Silver.

"Oh, please let me come, too. Perhaps there is something I can do. I have had a course in nursing."

"Come then," said Bannard and hurried into the house without knocking.

Greeves put out his hand to stop her, but Silver was gone before he realized. Pneumonia! Didn't the child know that was contagious? What did Bannard mean by letting her go? Suppose she should catch it and die, now when he had just got her, leave him as her mother had done! He shuddered and sprang out of the car, resolved to bring her back again into the clean air and sunshine, away from germs and contamination. What was the use of being a specialist on germs if one couldn't save one's own from danger? So he stumbled up the steps and into a deserted room.

There was no squalor nor dirt. The walls were discolored with age and use, and the bare floor was worn in hollows by many feet, but both were clean as soap and water could make them. He looked around. There was nothing in the room but a cookstove neatly blacked with a pot of stew simmering away, a wooden table covered with oilcloth, two chairs, and an old sofa with lumpy springs. A painted dresser held a few cheap dishes, some spoons and forks, and a pair of crude steps shallow almost as a ladder led up through an open door, winding out of sight. He could just see the flash of Silver's gray-blue tweed skirt as she disappeared up those impossible stairs.

"Silver!" he called, and then without knowing it, "Alice!" But no one answered him. The sound of the factory nearby kept up a monotonous clatter in regular rhythm, and there were subdued voices overhead. He stepped to the door and looked up. Such stairs! He never had seen their like. They were like carvings in a sheer wall. They went winding up in the shallow space like pictured stairs, like the stairs in a nightmare. How did anybody ever climb them? Didn't Bannard know any better than to let a girl go up a place like that? He put a tentative foot on the first step and perceived that it was hollowed out in bowl shape by many feet that had gone before. He groped with his hand to the wall that seemed to advance and slap him in the face. He lifted another foot to another step and went winding and groping up in the dark and uncertainty. A woman appeared at the head of the stairs weeping. She had wonderful dark hair, and her eyes were piteous.

"I have come for my daughter. She ought not to be in here," he shouted at her. The woman chattered some jargon at him that had a tang of French, or was it Italian? But he could understand nothing but the words "doctor" and "little ba-bee" and then more tears. She passed beyond his sight.

He lifted himself another step and yet another and stood head and shoulders in a room light and clean with whitewash, a large framed picture of the painted Christ on the cross hung on the wall opposite him over the head of a big brass bed made up with white sheets trimmed with hand-knit lace. And on the clean pillow lay a little face, the most beautiful baby face Greeves had ever looked upon. Short black curls tumbled on the pillow, long curling lashes dark upon the rounded cheek, beautiful baby lips gasping for breath, treacherous blue shadows deepening around the eyes and nose.

"These windows ought to be up if it's pneumonia," Bannard explained in a whisper. He stretched out a strong arm and threw up both windows. Silver was leaning over the baby feeling her forehead, touching the pulse of the little, fluttering, restless hand.

"She ought to have oxygen, Mr. Bannard. Can't you get some quick?" Silver looked up.

"I'll get it," said the minister. "Can you stay here till I come?"

She nodded. "Quick!" She was down on her knees beside the bed, putting the spoon that the mother handed her to the little tight-shut lips.

"She ought not to be here!" repeated Greeves wildly, but Bannard swept him along down the stairs with a strong arm.

"Greeves, just run over to that grocery and ring up Doctor Carr. Tell him I said to come instantly to Angelo's house. I must go for oxygen. You stand by till I come. I'll be back in five minutes."

Before the dazed professor of bacteriology knew what was happening or could put in a protest, Bannard's car had given a lurch and darted down the road, and Greeves found himself walking across that squalid street, entering the grimy, unsanitary grocery and asking if he might telephone for the doctor. It reminded him of France. But it was very different from sitting in an office and telling other officers where to go and what to do. He had done reconstruction work, yes, by proxy. It was not the same. He had been an executive. But this was close contact. He hurried back with the idea of carrying Silver bodily out of the infected air and found himself once more standing at the top of those ladderlike stairs in that white airy room, gazing at the little blackening face, listening to the gasping of the baby, the mother's tears, and his daughter's voice praying in low, gentle tones:

"Oh, Jesus, You know how this mother loves her baby. Come and help us if it be Your will. Save this little darling's life. For Jesus' sake, we ask it." And the mother bowed and crossed herself, hushing her sobs.

Someone brushed roughly by Greeves on the stairs, almost upsetting his balance. To think these people lived every day on stairs like this. Incredible! A tall man, young, splendidly built came quickly to the bed and knelt on the other side from the mother and Silver. And he took the little fluttering hand in his big rough one. His face was tender, and there were tears raining down his cheeks, but he paid no attention to them. "Poppie come, Mary, Poppie come! You hear Poppie, Mary? Poppie come home from his work to stay with Mary!"

Greeves stood and gazed transfixed at the face of the rough man before him, transformed by love, tender and sweet with fatherhood! So this was what it meant to be a father!

This was the way he would have felt if he had let himself! This was what he threw away carelessly when he took himself out of the reach of his first little child and brought another carelessly into the world to leave to any fate that came her way.

"Let Poppie hold it, Mary. Let Poppie hold it!" The strong hand grasped the weak, restless fingers, and the little hand relaxed. For an instant, the great dark eyes opened wide in recognition of the beloved face, and the dark head that had kept up its restless motion back and forth from side to side on the pillow rested. The parched lips that had murmured hoarsely "No! No! No!" were quieted. Then the blessed oxygen in the hands of Silver and Bannard reached her nostrils, and she drew a long deep breath. The gasping ceased little by little, and another breath came. A sigh of relief. The fluttering lids drooped, and the long lashes lay on the white cheeks again. A restful natural sleep was coming to the little one.

The doctor came in quietly, and laid a practiced finger on the fluttering pulse. The child started and opened her eyes once more. Her glance rested on the doctor in frightened question then turned to the father and was content, dropping off to sleep again. The doctor nodded to Silver in answer to some question about the oxygen, opened his case, and prepared some drops that he handed to Angelo. The father took it and held it to the little lips with as much skill as one trained to such service could have rendered. Greeves stood there watching him with almost jealous eyes, seeing as in a vista a long line of tender services he might have rendered had his heart been right to his own. Where did this rough, untaught man learn such angelic gentleness? Here in this bare little house with an environment of the plainest necessities, the father had fenced in a little piece of the kingdom of heaven for his child. Greeves suddenly realized that he was envying this rough, untaught working man. With all his knowledge and culture, he had missed the blessedness of living that this other man had found, and even his sorrow was sacred because of the love that was between him and his child.

Bannard had gone out again and now returned, bringing with him the district nurse. She quietly took things in her capable hands, and the minister's group was no longer needed.

As he stumbled shakily toward the treacherous stair, Greeves caught hold of the crude railing and gave one more glance back at the big brass bed with the exquisitely knitted white spread and the tiny white face framed in dark curls on the big pillow. The Madonna mother was standing at the head on one side, the tender father kneeling at the other, tears raining unchecked down their sorrowful faces, and the face of the painted Christ overhead looked on with yearning eyes. It was a sight he never would forget.

He felt his way down the dark chute, for it was little else, groping with his feet for shallow steps, and stumbled out into the sunshine, silent and thoughtful. He forgot how it was that he came to go into that house of sorrow, forgot that he had let his child stay as long as she was needed, forgot the words of criticism he had prepared for Bannard for letting her go into the infectious atmosphere. For the first time in years, he had become a part of a great suffering universe. He forgot his own individuality and his grievances, and his heart was throbbing with sorrow for another.

Meantime Athalie, at home, was dressing elaborately for her evening with Bobs in the city.

Chapter 17

$\mathcal{D}$own the street from the direction of the schoolhouse proceeded a merry group of girls, stopping at their various respective houses on the way to leave books and lunch boxes, and tidy up hair and hands and face. Laughing and chattering, they came on with a sudden hush of awe as they approached the Silver gate, so long an unopened portal to young people.

Mary Truman and Roberta Moffat went first by reason of Mary's having been the instigator of the function. Mary's heavy braid of bright, long hair had needed little tidying. It ended in a massive wave of gold below the crisp dark blue ribbon and frilled in little golden tendrils about her face. Mary wore no hat to rumple the smoothness of the ripples from the delicate line of parting on her crown. She scorned hats, except for Sunday.

Her neat blue-and-white checked gingham dress was just low enough to show the white of her throat above the sheer collar that matched the rolled-back cuffs and pockets banded with the gingham. The whole school thought that Mary Truman was always well dressed.

Those little gingham bindings on the organdy pockets, for instance, marked the line between the banker's daughter and other girls whose mothers had not the time to bother with such details.

Roberta Moffat was short and fat, attired in a pink chambray dress whose hem had visibly been "let down" and whose yoke had faded to a nice dependable flesh tint, but her round pleasant face was always wreathed with smiles. She had a glitter of white even teeth and a pair of nice black eyes above the little pug nose that was covered with freckles. Always copying Mary as far as her limited means allowed, she wore no hat, gathered her scant locks into a pigtail, and acquired a habit of tossing back the straight locks that would keep falling over her eyes where the hair wasn't quite long enough from a defunct bang to catch into the confining pink ribbon that held the pigtail. The ribbon was washed and dyed and showed signs of droop but had been retied and stuck out bravely for the occasion.

"I guess she'll be glad when she sees somebody coming to call on her so soon, don't you, Mary?" whispered Roberta with a soft giggle.

"I should think she ought to," said Mary seriously. "I certainly am glad you are all with me, girls. Just think how I'd feel now if I were alone!" And she squeezed Roberta's plump elbow lovingly.

Emily Bragg was tall, and her sleek brown hair had been bobbed, not for purposes of style however. The top was longer than the rest and fastened at the side with a barrette that gave her the look of an old-fashioned china doll with painted hair all made up hard. She wore a straight, little, one-piece frock of brown denim with characters worked around the edges in red yarn. On her head was a boy's brown wool cap, one of her brother Tom's, and the big shell-rimmed glasses that sheltered her merry eyes and gave her the look of a good-natured boy. She climbed trees and fences, could whistle as well as any of her brothers, and everybody liked her, but she wasn't a beauty. She was just behind Mary and Roberta, walking arm in arm with Carol Hamilton, a slight little fairy with pink cheeks and short golden curls who always dressed in pale blue and was adored because she was so pretty.

Della McBride was much taller than the rest, wore her long brown braids in a coronet around her head, and had big dark blue eyes with long lashes. The seriousness of her face was somewhat accentuated by a retreating chin. She was wearing a middy blouse and a dark blue skirt, and her companion, Vera Morse, a quiet girl with pale eyes and her hair "done up" and brought in sleek loops over her ears, wore a white shirtwaist left over from last year and a brown wool skirt. She carried a brown straw sailor hat in her hand and talked in a low, sweet voice.

They were a wholesome group as they fluttered up to the steps and sounded the old brass knocker, their subdued chatter like the chirps of a bunch of sparrows on the garden wall.

Anne Truesdale let them into the house and seated them in the drawing room dubiously. Such a circumstance had not happened since the days of Miss Lavinia, six whole callers at once in the old house! Then with deep reluctance, only goaded by an indubitable conscience, she mounted the stairs and tapped at Athalie's door.

"Oh, come in," drawled that young woman affably. "I'll let you fasten this dress. I can't seem to reach around there anymore. I was just about to ring for you. It fastens up the back under that drapery."

Anne paused in dismay and surveyed the young woman but made no move to investigate the hooks in question.

"There are some young persons down in the drawing room came to call on you," she announced severely, as if it were a reward far too good for the girl before her but must be handed over for honesty's sake.

Athalie swung around and faced her. "Come to see *me*? What are they? Men?"

"Of course not!" reproved Anne. "They're little girls."

"*Little girls!*" scoffed Athalie, taking up a powder puff and giving a touch to her nose. "Well, you can tell them to go to thunder! I'm busy. I hate little girls."

Anne gasped and tried to begin again, with fearful vision of what it would be if this strange freak of a girl refused to go down.

"Indeed, Miss Athalie, they're quite grown-up little girls. They're some of them older than yourself, and they're the daughters of the best people in this town. Your father'll be quite angry if you don't see them."

Athalie surveyed her coldly. She remembered that she was trying to please her father as far as it was compatible with her own plans.

"Very well," she said coldly. "I'll be down after a while and look them over, but I never had much time for girls, unless they have some pep, and I don't fancy they have in this little old town. Are you going to fasten those hooks for me or not?"

"Oh, Miss Athalie," said Anne disapprovingly. "You'll never wear that dress downstairs at this time of the day! The whole village would be scandalized, and your father would be disgraced. The young ladies would not understand it, I am sure. It's not at all the custom to dress in that style in the afternoon."

Athalie was attired in a startling outfit of scarlet satin and tulle, set off by long clattering strings of enormous jet beads and pendant hoops of jet with long fringes dangling from her ears. Her hair stood out in a perfect thistledown fluff; scarlet stockings of sheerest silk and tiny high-heeled red leather shoes with intricate straps adorned her plump feet. Her face and arms and neck, of which there was much in evidence, were powdered to a degree of whiteness that reminded Anne Truesdale of a Bible phrase about whited sepulchres. Indeed, she was a startling vision as she stood there imperiously waiting for Anne to fasten her scant shoulder drapery and looked years older than she was. But when Anne finished her protest and made no move to assist her ladyship, a storm arose on the whited face, and the red kid shoes stamped in rage.

"Thank you," she said grandly. "I'm not in the habit of accepting advice from the servants about what I shall wear. You can go! I'll get along without your assistance. I see I shall have to ask my father for a French maid. Go! I said, *go*!"

Anne went.

When she reached the door she paused.

"You'll be down at once, Miss Athalie, please! It's not considered good breeding to keep young ladies waiting."

"Shut the door!" stormed Athalie. "I'll be down when I like and not before."

Then in quite a leisurely manner she dabbed more powder on her nose, struggled with the refractory hooks until she conquered them, tilted a bit of a hat of scarlet straw and ribbon atop her fluff of hair, brought it well down over her eyes, jerked it aslant until the dangling cluster of overgrown cherries with which it was adorned hung well over one cheek. She surveyed herself in the glass complacently, posed imperiously, then took up a pair of long black gloves and an evening coat of black satin with a collar of white fur and slowly descended the stairs.

Down in the drawing room the waiting girls were having a grand time. They had been little children when last they remembered coming to that dim, shrouded room to call on dear Miss Lavinia, whom each one of them had loved. They went quietly about looking at the portraits and whispering at first, giving bits of memoirs that were family traditions in their homes. Gradually they settled down to await their hostess's coming.

"We ought to have told Mrs. Truesdale not to have her dress up," said Mary. "We should have said we've just come from school."

"Oh, well, what's the difference? She'll come pretty soon," said Roberta. "I like to sit in this big room and wait. Won't it be a grand place to have the Christian Endeavor social? My! I hope she asks us. We could toast marshmallows at that fire, and there's room for a long line of chairs for Going-to-Jerusalem. The boys always like that so they can roughhouse."

"Maybe Mr. Greeves might not like roughhousing," suggested Della. "He's a very great writer, my father says."

"Oh, we'll get Father to invite him over that night so he won't hear it," said Mary happily. "Father can always fix people so they don't mind things."

"Well, I'm sure I don't think it's very polite of her keeping us waiting so long. There won't be any time to take her walking nor show her the schoolhouse before supper if she doesn't hurry."

"Maybe she was taking a bath," suggested practical Emily Bragg. "You know, you couldn't come down all soapy."

The girls giggled.

"Shh!" said Mary. "I think she's coming."

"I wonder what grade she'll be in," whispered Carol.

"Sshhh!" said Roberta. "There she is! Oooohhh!"

Athalie flashed on their vision between the curtains and stood, one hand holding back the heavy curtain, her evening cloak still on her arm, and looked them over half contemptuously. They had never seen anything like it before, not even in the movies. Silver Sands was rather careful what films came to town. Mrs. Truman headed a committee of patrons who assisted the managers in making their selections.

At last Athalie broke the stillness, which was growing fairly electric: "I'm Miss Greeves!" she announced. "Did you want to see me?"

The girls might have been said to huddle in a group, feeling suddenly that in numbers was strength. Mary as leader and instigator of the expedition gave a frightened glance behind her and stepped bravely up as her father would have done if he had been there.

"We've come to call," she said pleasantly, watching the twinkling earrings with curious fascination. "Mother thought you might be lonesome—"

"Very kind, I'm sure," responded Athalie insolently. "I was just going out, but it's early. I can spare a few minutes."

She flung her cloak and gloves on a chair and sat down, her scarlet tulle skirt flaming around her. She sat with the pose of a society lady, her body flung rather than seated upon the chair. The girls were deeply impressed, all but Emily Bragg who wanted to laugh.

"We don't have to stay," said Emily. "Girls, let's go over to Mary's and make the fudge if she's busy."

"We just came in because we thought you might be lonely," repeated Mary again, deeply embarrassed.

"Oh, I'm never lonely," flipped Athalie. "Besides, I have hosts of friends who'll soon be here to see me from N'York. I'm going to have a house party next week, sixteen in all, eight girls and eight men!"

"Men?" echoed Roberta wonderingly.

"Yes, eight men. Of course it's awfully hard to get them this time of year when it's so near time for exams, but they'll be here for the weekends."

"Oh, you mean examinations," said Della seriously.

"We thought perhaps you'd like to join our Christian Endeavor society," braved Mary. "It's awfully interesting."

"I don't imagine so. What is it? A dancing club?" queried Athalie indifferently.

"Oh no!" said Mary, two red spots appearing on her pretty cheeks. She felt she wasn't getting on very well somehow. "It's just our young people's society. We have lots of good times. Picnics and socials, and we play games, and then we have our meeting Sundays—"

"What kind of games? Bridge? Five hundred? Or do you go in for athletics? I don't suppose you play golf?"

"Bridge? Oh no, not bridge!" said Vera.

"Nor five hundred," said Della. "Just games."

"My father plays golf," said Carol. "I've tried it, but I don't care much for it. It's too slow. I like tennis better. We have tennis courts at the school."

"Are you going to start school right away? We've been wondering what grade you'd be in."

"I? School? Oh, I'm done with school! Dad tried to talk school to me when I first arrived, but I let him understand he couldn't make anything on that line. I'm certainly sick of school. Of course we had piles of fun at the last one, pajama parties every night and screams of times. The boys from the prep weren't far away, and they were always onto us when any of us got a box, so they'd come over under our windows and we'd throw down cake, and they'd tie boxes of candy and cigarettes on the strings we let down, and notes, oh, say! Those boys were the limit! There was always something new. But what bored me was the teachers! They didn't seem to remember that they had ever been young, and they kept at us continually, nagged us about our lessons and exams—it made me hot! They were getting paid for us being there! I don't see what more they wanted."

Silence, prolonged and heavy, ensued. The girls looked at one another, awe stricken for the father whose daughter had so little daughterly respect. They all had fathers whom they obeyed, fathers who were trusted, tried companions. It didn't quite go down. Athalie realized she had struck a wrong note. She liked to shock people, but when it came to being looked down upon, she didn't quite like it. Neither did she understand the look of awe and disapproval on their young faces. Emily Bragg began to giggle as if somehow she were some sort of show. The others darted quieting glances of rebuke.

Athalie felt she must break the silent disapproval. She hated them for not admiring her. She got up with a swagger and whipped out her cigarette case.

"Oh, excuse me, girls, do you smoke? Have a cigarette." She passed the gold trinket to Mary.

Mary seemed to turn pale. She got up and took a step toward the curtained doorway.

"I think we must be going," she said coldly.

"Oh, don't you smoke? Not *any* of you? How tiresome! Then I'll order tea. Truesdale!" She lifted her voice. "Tea for the ladies!"

Anne appeared instantaneously, as though she had not been far away, her face white with emotion.

The girls eyed one another uncertainly. They wanted to get away. They did not any of them drink tea. It was not allowed in most of their homes at their age unless they were ill. They didn't like it.

But the tea tray appeared as if by magic, and behold, Anne had provided lemonade as well as tea! And there were heaping plates of angel cake and chocolate cake. No one ever caught the servants in that house napping. They were always on the job and always anticipating every possible contingency. Molly was even then in the pantry concocting another cake to take the place of those for dessert that evening along with strawberries.

Athalie had lighted a cigarette and taken a few puffs at it delicately as the tea tray was brought in. Now she poured herself a cup of tea and drank it with several pieces of cake while Anne was serving the girls.

Mary, with her plate in her hand, looked up to find Athalie's eyes upon her with amused contempt. Her heart cried out to get away and weep on her mother's shoulder. She never had felt so utterly outraged in the whole of her happy, protected life. It seemed as if the very foundations of her clean, beautiful world had been torn away and flung to the four winds. "I hate her! *I hate her!*" her heart kept saying over to herself.

"I thought you were going to ask her over to your house tonight to make fudge," suggested Roberta in a loud whisper, and Mary, lifting her eyes, perceived that Athalie had overheard.

"We were going to make fudge tonight at our house," said Mary, thus prodded. "I live next door. Would you like to come? We'll have a lot of fun."

"Any men coming?" asked Athalie speculatively.

"Men?" queried Mary half puzzled. "My father—"

"She means the boys," said Emily Bragg. "My goodness!" She giggled.

"Our high school boys will be there," said Mary truthfully, hoping Athalie couldn't read it in her eyes how much she did not want her.

"Boys?" said Athalie. "Awfully young, I suppose? Well, I'm sorry, but I can't make it tonight. I expect to spend the evening at the roof garden in the city, maybe a cabaret or two afterward. I shan't be home till quite late. Sorry—some other time perhaps. Now, I'll have to ask you to excuse me. It's getting late. So glad you called. Good-bye."

She gathered up cloak and gloves and marched grandly out of the room, down the hall, and out the front door just as Anne Truesdale appeared with another plate of cookies to supplement the rapidly disappearing cake. She had intended to leave word with Anne Truesdale that she had gone to bed with a sick headache and did not wish to be disturbed for dinner and then to descend to the street by way of the pergola, but the temptation to sail grandly out before these girls was too great, and she followed her impulse. There would be a way out of it all after she had had her fun, and the momentary vision of Anne, startled, her mouth dropped open as she watched her leave, did not worry her at all as she adjusted her long cloak and sailed jauntily down the street.

Over at Vandemeeter's, every eye was watching, as they had been since the schoolgirls entered. It made a pleasant little stir in the monotony of the day to feel that festivity going on. It recalled days when they themselves, arrayed in best silks, new hats, and fresh gloves had accepted Miss Lavinia's sweet, friendly invitations and felt above the common lot for a few brief hours. Ever since Arden's wife had run in in the morning to tell them that the girls had planned to go, they had gone about their work with a pleasant anticipation. They felt in a way concerned and thought highly of the Trumans for having suggested the call, for was not this a public recognition? And if departed spirits were permitted a glimpse now and then of their old homes, would not Miss Lavinia be pleased that the town had honored her beloved boy's family? They felt the Trumans had done the proper thing and were glad they belonged to a town that knew what to do in a trying situation. Glad, too, that the question of accepting Patterson Greeves or not into good, regular standing in the town had been settled so satisfactorily by the Trumans. No one ever questioned what the Trumans did.

But when the scarlet lady with her flapping coat of black and white suddenly emerged from the old front door and sallied down the front walk and with such an air, they gazed in amazement with bated breath, and no one dared whisper till she was out of sight. Then all with one consent, they drew back from their several windows and looked at one another as if facing some awful thought.

"*Who* was she?"

It was Mother, her rugged face almost white with a kind of social fright, who broke the silence and voiced the wonder of them all.

Pristina whirled back to the window and in a hard little voice answered: "It was *her*! The fat one! The one *they went to call on*!"

"Oh, my *soul*! said Mother, stooping to pick up a pin and unable to find it in her excitement. "Oh, my soul and body! Why, that's an insult."

Maria licked her lips with the tip of her tongue with the motion a man used to whet a scythe. "Now I wonder what'll happen!" she said, a hard glitter in her eyes, as if she rather enjoyed the prospect. Maria was one of those who, having failed in gaining many of the joys of this life, was not content to see others receiving them. Not that she was unkindly when it came right down to actions—only in a little cattish way with her tongue and the expression of her face.

They were watching the Silver house so hard that they failed to notice the minister's car until it drew up in front of the gate. Mother strained her eyes anxiously.

"Well, anyhow, I'm glad it wasn't that one. She seems to be real sweet."

"Now, Mother, you always jump to such hasty conclusions," said Maria. "I'm sure I don't see how you can tell whether she's sweet or not at this distance."

Pristina said thoughtfully: "She's sitting in the front seat with the minister!"

"Yes," said Maria caustically. "Seems to me it's a little soon to begin that."

"Maybe he began it," said Harriet sympathetically.

"Not he!" said Maria. "He wouldn't have to! It beats me what the girls nowadays have done with their modesty!"

"Well, where did modesty bring us?" laughed Cordelia.

"Cordelia Vandemeeter! I'm surprised!" rebuked Maria.

Then Silver and her father and the minister got out and went up to the house, and the front door closed again. And what had become of the high school girls at tea?

Chapter 18

℗arry Lincoln was helping Sam Fitch to build a fence for his chicken run. The Fitch place stood up and back from the street on a slight elevation among a grove of light maples. The chicken run was higher up the hill to one side and commanded a wide view of the road winding round to the bridge and over into the woods. It was the last house on the street as you went toward Frogtown from the south end of Silver Sands.

Barry had just pounded his thumb trying to straighten a stubborn nail and had thrown down the hammer and stuck the throbbing thumb in his mouth when the flash of a scarlet hat and the flutter of scarlet tulle came into sight down the road. For an instant, he stared in astonishment, for such a sight was not native to Silver Sands, and Barry knew everybody that lived there, by sight at least. Then something familiar in the swagger of the plump figure struck him and he drew his brows in a frown and turned a quick look at Sam.

Sam was down on his hands and knees with his back to the street nailing wire to the base. He would not be likely to see her.

Barry stooped and picked up his hammer and began a tremendous pounding on the corner post, straightening another nail, his weather eye to the road, unheeding the blood that was streaming from his bruised thumb.

At just the right instant as Athalie passed behind the group of tall cedars and was for a few seconds lost to view, he threw down his hammer with an exclamation and called to Sam in an imperative voice: "Oh, I say, Sam, run to the house quick and get me a rag to do up this blamed thing. It's bleedin' like the deuce!"

Sam, accustomed to obey Barry, his baseball idol, dropped his own hammer instantly and with a sympathetic glance toward his wounded companion steamed toward the house without delay. When he returned with the required rag and a bottle of arnica, Athalie was well across the bridge.

A tumult of thoughts was running through Barry's brain, foremeost among them the telephone conversation he had overheard the day before. Vaguely in the background the sudden flash of coral and silver skirt and little shiny shoes and the tempest of words he had heard in the Silver hall the evening before, with the stormy sobs, lasting long after the music had begun. How much responsibility had he, Barry Lincoln, for their strange specimen of womanhood who wore pants and made appointments over the telephone to meet men from the city, agreeing to stay till all hours of the night? Barry Lincoln's code was a simple one, but it had an old-fashioned twist to its ideas of womanhood. His mother was a sweet-faced, sad-eyed little widow who wore plain black dresses and did her hair smoothly except for the satiny crinkle of it around the edges of her forehead. She had given him the habit of a clean mind in the midst of a wicked and perverse world, and he somehow patterned his ideas of girls and what they should be on a picture of his mother taken just before she was married, when the light of joy was in her face and her eyes were like reflections of the kingdom of heaven. Barry knew a whole lot more about the world than his mother had ever told him, but he had kept his clean habit of mind, and any deviation from it on the part of a woman, especially a young woman, gave him always a feeling of nausea. However, this was something no one would ever have guessed. Barry was one who didn't tell his thoughts among men.

So, now, when he saw this poor little daughter of Eve making her way toward the path of temptation, he was not interested. But the memory of a haunted look in her father's eyes the night before and the good comradeship he had offered on the evening of the fire, together with the lingering fragrance of cookies, now laid upon Barry's conscience a duty toward his fellowman. If this girl was really going on an immoral trip that might bring pain and shame to his friend, ought he not in all loyalty to that friend to do something about it?

Out of the corner of his eye, he watched the scarlet flash as it followed along the line of the road, crossed the bridge, left the road, and crept up the hill toward the woods. He sat down on the doorstep and kept Sam's back to the hillside until the scarlet hat and the dark cloak disappeared into the woods and only glimmered unnoticeably among the young leaves as it went farther and farther away from the road. At last his mind was made up.

"Doggone it, Sam, now that hand's goin' to be no good today. Wha'd I have to pound that for? Clumsy! Say, Sam, les finish this t'morra. What'dya say we take a day off and go see if we can find Beazley? He ought to be back home from his aunt's by this time, and it isn't much of a run over to the Corners. Say, you go get the roadster and run her over to the Pike, an' I'll skip across to the creek where I was yesterday morning and see if I can find my knife. I'll meet you up by the old camp entrance in about fifteen minutes. But if it's half an hour or longer, you stick, for I'll be there! Beat it now, and don't talk, Sam. Remember to keep yer mouth shut!"

Sam hurried away with a light of eagerness in his eyes, and Barry rose and took long strides across the fields toward a spot in the landscape a quarter of a mile to the north where Athalie had entered the woods. As he disappeared among the undergrowth, he cast a speculative eye to the distant road, but no one was to be seen as yet.

Now the "roadster" above mentioned was as much a part of Barry Lincoln's existence as his dog or his fishing rod or anything but his mother. It was called the "roadster" by courtesy because it could get over the road so rapidly, but there was nothing about it that would have suggested that name in the modern acceptation of the term. It was ancient and worn and stripped of everything that it could be stripped of and still be. It consisted merely of its throbbing loyal heart, its four wheels, and enough timber and metal to keep them from flying apart when they went catapulting through space. However Barry and whomever he elected to take with him as a companion managed to stick on and always come home alive was a continual wonder in Silver Sands. People told Mrs. Lincoln that they didn't see how she stood it having her son go off in that awful thing, that it wasn't safe and it wasn't Christian, and he always looked as if he were going to destruction and was glad of it, that they should think it would affect his morality, a boy like that to own an infernal machine. He was in daily danger of becoming a murderer!

And besides, how could they *afford* to keep it?

When they twisted on that prying look and said that about affording—it was usually the people for whom she did plain sewing that said it—Barry's mother always crinkled up her lips into a smile that let little gold lights into her brown eyes and made her look like Barry, and answered always quite pleasantly: "Oh, the old roadster is one of the family. We couldn't live without that. Barry never has killed anybody yet. I hope he never will." And she never even reminded them how he had saved a girl's life once with it, running after an automobile that had got out of her control, nor how he rushed Tad Moffat to the hospital in the city in time to save his hand, the time he got it caught in the reaper.

But if you had asked the boys of the town about the old roadster, they would have told you that Barry made it "out of pieces of nothin' of the junk heap behind the garage" and that its chief characteristic was that it could "go like the devil."

It was this same go-devil that Sam climbed into, as it stood waiting under its oilcloth lean-to beside the Lincoln cottage, and presently shot out of the yard and around the creek road toward the Pike, a proud lad that Barry had selected him to run his car.

Barry himself had rustled across the creek by a route well known to himself and stolen up to a favorite rendezvous of his own near an old tree under which he often sat by the hour fishing, looking down from his perch on a rock into the limpid stream below or swinging up in the trusty branches above, from limb to limb till he reached a point where all the woods was an open book and himself enveloped in foliage.

It was to this point of vantage that he now hastened, silently, stealthily, as only such as he knew how to go. The tree was the tallest in all the region round about. Looking east from its height, he could see the Flats of Frogtown with the gleaming water and Silver Sands shining in the late afternoon sun. Between him and the Flats wound the smooth white ribbon of a road, and far as he could see a black speck sped like a spider down its thread. He watched it an instant, and then his eyes scanned the hillside below him, down through the trees. Yes, there was a gleam of scarlet. Her hat. She had thrown it on the ground and was sitting on the log. Her scarlet dress was spread around her radiantly like a splash of vermilion in the spring newness of green. She seemed like some great scarlet tanager waiting for its mate. Yet when she lifted her face to look up at the strangeness of her surroundings, her bare neck and arms, her painted lips and penciled brows, the white, white, whiteness of her face seemed out of place there in the holy quiet of nature's temple, a parody on a living soul, stark and shameless in a setting of God's things as they are. Something of this thought perhaps entered the boy's mind as he saw her first, half startled to realize how near he was to her meeting place, half tempted to slide quietly down and slip away before she discovered him.

Yet her waiting, listening attitude held him. She was evidently expecting someone. If the guy she had phoned up should turn out to be an all-right fellow, why, then he would just make a quiet getaway and join Sam, and no one the wiser. If, on the other hand, he should turn out to be one of these fresh rotters from the city, he could let him know where to get off and see that no harm came to that silly little simp down there, just for the sake of her father who was a good old sport.

Presently Barry turned his eyes westward and noted the "roadster" darting along like a small black bug as if it had the speed of a thousand-legger. He watched it to the pike and knew when it passed behind the old red barn that Sam would be waiting there for him should it be ten minutes or ten hours. Then he glanced to the south and saw the other car, coming at full speed down toward the bridge. Now, if he was right, this would be his city man. There were two other cars coming, Eli Ward's old gray limousine that he bought for two hundred and fifty dollars and fixed up himself, and the grocery delivery truck, speeding recklessly back from the afternoon rounds. But this was a strange car he saw at a glance, and presently it came to a halt just below the group of chestnut trees, and a head came out and looked around. The car jerked on a few feet farther, and the man got out looking around him uncertainly. He measured the distance from the bridge with his eye and began an ascent at random, looking this way and that, furtively. As he came on, there were places where the branches were thin and his face was in full view. Barry studied him curiously. He was tall and thickset, with a heavy jowl and a tiny black moustache over his full red lips. He had taken off his hat and was mopping his face. The climb seemed to be hard on him. As he looked up once, the boy was astonished to see that he was not young and that there were bags under his eyes, puffy places that belonged to a high liver.

He's old enough to be her grandfather! thought Barry disgustedly. *What a doggone little fool!*

Athalie arose and balanced on the log with outspread arms, and the man cautiously approached, a hungry bestial glint in his eye that the boy in the tree resented.

"He's rotten!" said the boy to himself. "Gosh! What'll I do about this? Her father oughta keep her in! Gee!"

The man was upbraiding Athalie for coming in such a noticeable dress. "Are you sure nobody saw you come?" he asked her in a surly tone, smoothing the plumpness of her bare arms with his well-groomed hand as he talked. "It won't do to have your dad get onto us," he added. "You've got to be careful, you know."

Athalie pouted, and the man talked to her in a low rumble. Barry could not hear many words. He wished he were well out of that tree and back making a chicken run. He wished he had never gone to that fire in Frogtown nor met the new Silver man, nor taken his old worms to him! What a mess! What did folks want to be fools for?

The word *divorce* floated up once, and then something about the state line. He heard Athalie protest that she must go home and get on a white dress, but the man insisted that he could not wait—it was now or never. What on earth did it all mean? The state line was miles to the south. Premonition filled his chest. That man certainly was a rotter. He wished he could get down and punch his head, but it didn't seem to be advisable at the moment. He didn't know enough about things to interfere. Maybe the man just wanted to take her back to her mother. Her mother was divorced from her father. *Sure*, that was it. Some conspiracy to get her away to her mother again. Well, why worry? Wouldn't that be a good thing for Mr. Greeves? From all he had heard the night before, all the gossip that had been going around the town that day, he would not expect his new friend to be deeply grieved at his daughter's disappearance. And yet—he didn't like that man's face! Of course, he might be her uncle or something coming after her. But anyhow, he didn't like the way the man felt her wrist. It wasn't nice. Gosh, she was just a kid! Just a foolish little kid. Gosh! He'd like to punch that man's head even if he *was* her uncle!

While he was thinking these things, the two below him suddenly got up and began to move down toward the road. The man made the girl put on her cloak and turn the white fur inside, out of sight. He made her hold up her scarlet dress so it wouldn't show below the black and tuck her red hat under the cloak, and then he pointed down the road to where a clump of bushes was embowered with wild honeysuckle close to the roadside, making a complete refuge, and the girl hurried off and crept under it. The man waited, hidden in the grove till the bread wagon passed by, and then went down to where he had parked his car.

A little way up the hill in a shelter of laurel bushes, a tramp looked out with greedy eyes like an old bird of prey and watched the girl.

Barry waited only long enough to see the man turn around, drive to the honeysuckle arbor, and stop. Then he began quickly to slide down the tree. As he reached the ground, he heard the purr of the engine starting again, and his feet hardly touched the sod as he sprang away along the ridge above the creek to where a log spanned the water. Across like a bird in flight and up the opposite bank he ran. Now this field, and the roadster waited for him. "Over!" he shouted to Sam as he came panting up the hill and vaulted the fence. "We gotta hurry! Took me longer 'n I expected."

"Got'cher knife?" queried Sam as he moved over and gave Barry the wheel.

"Yep," said Barry pulling his knife out of his pocket for a brief glimpse and started his engine.

"Say, which way you going, Blink? You don't wanta turn round. I turned here on purpose. You said you were going after Beazley."

"That's all right, Sam. We gotta make the state line now before another guy gets there. You sit tight."

Sam perceived that Blink had had one of his inspirations. This was an expedition! He settled his lank length on the airy structure of his seat and prepared to enjoy himself. Sam had pale blue eyes under golden lashes, carroty straight hair that stuck up like bristles, a gaunt mouth, and cheeks peppered with freckles. He remembered contentedly that his mother was making apple dumplings for supper when he went in for the arnica. He glanced at Blink's hand and noticed that the rag had disappeared. A smudge of blood on the finger was all that remained of the accident.

"Have any trouble findin' yer knife, Blink?"

"Nope."

The roadster was going like a bullet through the air now; its four wheels scarcely seemed to travel the earth. They had rounded the top of the hill and curved down into the lower thoroughfare. Far ahead on the road another car like a speck appeared and disappeared. Barry eyed it steadily as he shot ahead, the speck in the distance growing visibly larger mile by mile. He let the roadster out a trifle more and watched the distance grimly. Was this his man? He didn't want to waste time.

Sam pulled his hat over his eyes and flipped up his collar with a lank hand. His teeth were chattering.

"Gee! Blink, this is—grrr–reat!" He gulped and held on tight, a trifle pale under the freckles.

Barry shot ahead silently. Was that a glint of scarlet fluttering out the side of the car or only a budded maple branch by the road?

At last they were within hailing distance, and Barry let down his speed a trifle. He didn't want to pass before the crossroad, now half a mile ahead. Strange he saw no sign of anyone on the backseat of that car, and only one head appeared at the front. If that was his man, what had he done with the girl? If it wasn't his man, it was a pity to waste any more time and lose the trail. He began to cast about in his mind where his quarry could have gone if this was not the right car and to plan for instant action in case he found out his mistake.

The car ahead did not turn off at the crossroads, and three minutes later Barry shot ahead. As he passed the other car, he was sure he caught a glimpse of something red like a big ball suddenly dropping down out of sight in the backseat.

"Watch that car, Sam!" he ordered grimly.

Sam fixed his pale eye on a bit of mirror fastened in midair over the engine, but the car seemed to be coming on steadily enough.

"Watch if there's more than one person in it."

Sam shifted the gum between his teeth and gave himself to more concentrated effort.

"Thought I saw something move in the backseat," he said at length. "There it went again. Mighta been mistaken though."

Barry thought he saw it, too. He suddenly ground his brakes on and sprang off to kneel before his engine.

"Nut loose," he explained to the astonished Sam who had been nearly thrown to the ground by the sudden halt. He wasn't quite sure which car Blink meant "the nut" traveled in.

Barry's car was well into the road. A passing vehicle must turn out if it went by. Barry reclined by a wheel, apparently deeply absorbed. At the very instant, however, when the other car was about to curve by him, he was as by a miracle upright on his feet in the middle of the remaining road space, with one arm raised in distress. The oncoming driver had either to stop or submit to being a murderer. As the man ground on his brakes and jerked to a violent stop, he let out an ugly oath, but Barry, unconcerned, asked nonchalantly: "Len' me a wrench?"

"No!" said the man shortly. "Mine's lost! Get out of my way!"

Barry lifted his cap from his curls politely and grinned.

"Thank you!" he said with his eye on the backseat and stepped out of the way. The car shot ahead, but Barry had seen what he was after, a big black eye peering up over the door of the car, covered by a traveling blanket that seemed exceedingly alive. A flash of a white arm and a dash of scarlet showed against the darkness of the backseat as the car swept by, and Barry was satisfied. He was on the right track.

"What's eatin' you, Barry? The wrench's in its place under the cushion." Sam eyed him puzzled. It wasn't like Barry to forget anything.

"Oh, it is?" said Barry innocently, swinging up on his seat. "Pile in, boy, we gotta hurry."

Sam scrambled back into place again as the roadster leaped forward. The other car was some distance ahead now. Barry seemed to have lost interest in it. Sam couldn't make him out. Somehow Sam never could quite make out Barry. He said so to the boys once, and Ben Holden told him it was because he hadn't any sense of humor, but that troubled Sam still more, because what did a sense of humor have to do with understanding a person who was perfectly grave and serious?

Whenever they came near a crossroad or a village, Barry sped up. Sam kept hoping he would stop and buy something to eat. He kept remembering those apple dumplings. The sun was getting lower and lower. A dank little breath swept up from the valley, full of sleepy violets and drowsy bees humming. The birds were calling good night. Sam's legs were long for the space allowed in the roadster. He grew uneasy.

"Say, what time do you expect to get home for supper?" he questioned, shifting a little and putting his hand under his knee surreptitiously to ease the stiffness.

"Don't expect!" said Barry crisply. "If you do, you might get disappointed. Hungry, Sam? Let you out on the road anywhere you say, if you like."

"Oh no," said Sam detecting displeasure in his idol's voice. "Oh no, no, I'm just enjoying this, havin' the time of my young life. Gee, it's great. Only I was wondering what your plans were."

"That depends," said Barry and said no more. With shut lips, the two whizzed through the country, watching a little black speck ahead that grew dimmer and dimmer as the light of the sun failed.

Then suddenly it seemed quite dark. The other car was only a place of blackness in the darkness; one could not be sure if it was there or only had been. There were lights ahead. They were nearing a town. The roadster reached the top of a hill leading down into the main street among dwellings. A little trolley like a toy plied to and fro with childish bells and lights. A church bell rang with a sweet, wholesome call to prayer. Cottages appeared. A child under a light with a green porcelain shade looking at a book. A family in the dining room eating their supper. Pleasant thought. Dumplings, apple dumplings with plenty of goo! Ummmmm! Sam looked wistfully back.

The other car at the foot of the hill, turning into the main street, stopped for an instant by the trolley. Barry made time and arrived in its immediate vicinity as it started on again. Barry slowed up. He let several cars and trucks and foot passengers get between him and the open road. Sam eyed him wonderingly. The other car had gone on. Sam hadn't noticed it particularly.

Barry saw it slow up in front of a drugstore, and immediately he ran his car down a side street by the blank side of a real estate office closed for the night and sprang out.

"Watch me, Sam! Keep yer eyes peeled," he said to his astonished vassal. "If I don't come back soon, you folla. I gotta get that car and its contents back to Silver Sands t'night! See? But mind you keep yer mouth shut."

He was gone in the darkness, and Sam, whirling dazedly round on his unsteady seat, saw him vanishing round the car that was parked in front of the drugstore. An instant more and he heard the door on the driving side slam and the engine begin to purr.

"By gosh!" Sam said and unfolded himself to his full height on the curb. "He's a nut if there ever was one," said Sam to the roadster aloud.

The other car was moving! It was passing out of sight! Blink was nowhere to be seen. Sam must move, too, if he was not to lose him. Sam clambered to his task with sudden panic and threw in the clutch.

"By gosh!" he exclaimed, but the roadster was already going so fast that his words fell backward on the curb unheard in the darkness. Sam had already assumed his new importance. Apple dumplings were forgotten for the time. He had to get that roadster home or he'd hear about it all the rest of his mortal days. Besides, he knew his mother would keep plenty of dumplings warm for him on the back of the stove. He made out a dim outline of a car in the darkness ahead and followed, being madly aware of an excited man on the pavement behind him shouting and waving his arms.

Chapter 19

Anne Truesdale, bringing another plate of angel cake that had been put aside for the master, saw the minister's car through the front window and, urging the plate upon Roberta, hastened to the door to meet them.

It was Greeves who was walking ahead, and she put up her hands as if in prayer and almost curtsied in her agony, her words tumbling out in true old-country style: "Oh, Master Pat, I'd not be troublin' ye, but the young ladies is in there, and ye'll have to tell me what ye want done. I've fed 'em an' fed 'em everything there is left in the house, tryin' to keep 'em from realizin' they've been insulted, an' now you'll just have to do something about it. It'll be a scandal in the neighborhood in five minutes after I let them be going, for Emily Bragg has an awful tongue in her head, an' she lives next door to Arden Philips's wife."

"Why, Anne, what's the matter? Try not to be excited. Tell me, what has happened? Who is in the house?"

"It's the young ladies, the daughters of yer uncle's old friends.

Mary Truman next door and Roberta Moffat and them, six of them, nice girls as ever was, come to call on your daughters. And Miss Athalie first kept them waitin', an' then she come down all in a red party dress with that bare a neck and no sleeves at all and a little red hat like a red hen atop her and then monstrous cherries a dangling—"

Anne was almost sobbing as she talked and was unaware that Bannard and Silver had come up and were standing behind her.

"Never mind, Anne," said Greeves soothingly. "It can't be so very bad. You say they're only little girls."

"'Igh school girls, sir, an' comin' on young ladies. Oh, but you don't know sir, it was werry bad, werry bad indeed, sir. She come in an' called herself Miss Greeves, and she offered them her smoking box, an' then she orders tea an' walks out that imperious you'd think she was a queen, sayin' as how 'twas late an' she had a engagement to go to in the city an' see a carabay on a roof, sir, whatever that may be, sir. An' she's gone—an' I don't know what to do with 'em. It'll be all over town before the night, Master Pat—"

"Is there somebody in there to call, did you say, Mrs. Truesdale?" interrupted Silver suddenly. "Why, I'll go right in!"

Silver ran up the steps and into the hall, flinging off her hat in her transit and dropping it on the hall table, tossing her gloves after it. She entered the drawing room where the embarrassed girls were huddled together, trying to get rid of napkins, eating furtive pieces of cake from the plate on the edge of the tea tray, and planning a hasty exit before any more stupefying and insulting daughters were presented to their indignant gaze.

"Oh, how lovely of you all to run over so soon!" exclaimed Silver, ruffling up her hair with a merry attempt at smoothing it. "Now, tell me who you are. I'm Silver Greeves, I suppose you know—or perhaps you don't. Call me Silver, please. I'll feel more at home.

And what's your name? Mary Truman. Oh, you live next door, don't you? Father was telling me about you this morning at breakfast. We'll be friends, won't we? Now you introduce the rest."

She had them all chattering together in a moment more, and they hadn't an idea she was a day older than any of them. She was small and slender and had a smile like sunshine. They liked her at once and forgot their grievances. They began to tell her as one girl about their school and their Christian Endeavor and their fudge party, and she entered into it all eagerly. Christian Endeavor? Of course she would join. She had been in Christian Endeavor at home. Fudge? She loved it. Of course she would come!

Bannard stood for a moment in the doorway where he had followed to see if he could help out in the trying situation, which he had easily sensed from the few words he had caught of Anne's excited recital, and behold, this wonderful little girl had everything in the hollow of her hand. Then one of the girls looked up, Emily Bragg it was, and giggled.

"Oh yes, the boys are invited," beamed Mary Truman. "They don't know it yet, but I'm going to call them up on the phone. Say, Mr. Bannard, will you see Barry Lincoln? I'd like to ask him, but they haven't any phone."

"Yes. I'll tell Barry," promised the minister, and then Anne Truesdale, with suspiciously red eyes, bustled in and began pouring tea for the minister and Greeves. Silver jumped up, and taking her father's arm, drew him around the group, making him acquainted with each one, and the girls marveled that she remembered their names so well. When they finally broke up and started home to get ready for their fudge party, Silver walked with them down to the gate, an arm around Mary and Roberta, her head turned backward to smile over her shoulder at the other three who were fairly tied in a knot to get closer to her, and so they took their adoring leave at the front gate to the great edification of the Vandemeeters, who felt that their heads were fairly reeling with the exciting program of the day.

"I declare, if this goes on," said Mother, mopping her weary brow with her apron, "I shan't get half my work done. I do hope things will settle down pretty soon."

Over at the Silver mansion, Anne Truesdale was gathering the scattered tea things and trying to plan for the evening meal, which had been robbed of several articles of its menu. Greeves stood in the front hall talking with Bannard and watching Silver come brightly up the path, both men thinking how wonderfully she had turned the situation.

"You have no cause to worry about *her*," said Bannard with a touch of reverence in his tone.

"I should say not," said Greeves. "She's—she's—like her mother!"

"Didn't I tell you," said Bannard with a twinkle in his eye, "that tomorrow about this time you'd begin to see God's way taking shape?"

Greeves's face turned sharply toward him, a heavy shadow crossing his brow. "Don't talk to me about God's way!" he said harshly. "I've seen too much of that. What about my other girl?" And a spasm of anger went like white lightning over his features.

"That will work out, too," said Bannard reverently. "Give God His way and see."

"Don't!" said Greeves sharply. "What about that man down at the Flats, that father! I can't get him out of my head, Bannard. That's cruelty to make that little one suffer so. It's cruelty to take her away from a father and mother like that. She isn't going to live, is she?"

"She has a chance, the doctor says. It depends a lot upon the nursing. The father and mother are wonders, but they don't know how."

"Do you know of a trained nurse you can get, Bannard? I'd gladly pay for one! Couldn't we telephone to the city for one? Two, if necessary. I'd like to see that child saved. Bannard, if there's anything that money can do, you'll let me help out? I'd like to make that much amends for the mess I've made of my life."

Bannard cast him a quick, appreciative look. "Thank you," he said. "That means a lot. There'll be plenty of chances for that sort of thing. But in this case it isn't so much a question of money as love. It would be hard to find a regular trained nurse that would fit into that household. You saw how primitive everything was. It would have to be somebody who could love to make the service possible. I'm going down now for Mrs. Lincoln. I think she'll spend the night there. She's done such things before. She knows how to love."

After Bannard was gone, a shadow of care seemed to drop upon Greeves's face, even while he was closing the front door, as he remembered his younger daughter. Now his was the disagreeable task of finding out all about what she had done and dealing with her. How sickening the thought! All the advantage he had gained, or thought he had gained, in the morning would be gone with the first word. His soul shrank from the contest. He was angry and disheartened. How was he to reach her and make her understand that at least she must refrain from outward disrespect to him and his family or she could not remain under his roof? What was the secret of her strange nature that made her willing to do these astonishing things? He hurried back to the drawing room where he could hear Anne's excited voice relating over again to Silver the chief points of Athalie's offense. He could see how, to Anne, what had been done was almost the unpardonable sin. To keep the honor and respect of the village was certainly among the first articles of Anne's creed. With a deep sigh, he pushed back the curtain and listened.

"I wouldn't bother about it, Anne," Silver was saying. "Athalie probably hasn't an idea how disagreeable she appeared. She is in a different atmosphere from any she has ever been in before, and it isn't really her fault, perhaps, that she acts so. I don't think the girls will say much about it. We are going over next door tonight, and we'll just have a good time and make them forget about the other. After a little when Athalie gets acquainted and gets to know the ways of Silver Sands, she will want to make them like her. I'm sure she will. Just now she's rather strange and upset in all her ideas—"

"That's all very well, Silver," put in the father, "but Athalie can't publicly disgrace us. And she has openly disobeyed me it seems about the cigarettes. I can't have that—in this house!"

"She's been brought up seeing it I suppose—"

"Oh—yes!" said her father with a look of remembrance sweeping over his face. "Of course she's seen it every day. It's her standard. But she's got to learn that it isn't mine!"

"When she learns to love you, Father, maybe that will make a difference," suggested Silver shyly.

The father's face was hard.

"I doubt if she knows how to love anyone but herself," he said bitterly. "It was the way with her mother. Anne, will you tell Miss Athalie to come down at once to the library?"

Anne was mopping up her eyes. She seemed to take Athalie's misdeeds as a personal offense. Sacredly all these years she had guarded the honor of the family, and now to have it trampled underfoot by a stranger in one short afternoon was too much. Anne could not put it easily aside. It was an outrage, like having bad boys tear up the tulip beds after Joe had newly trimmed them, or scarring the family Bible. Anne could not get over it. She came sniffling back from the pantry door with a handful of dirty dishes and her cheeks red and angry looking. When she was excited, her cheeks always turned fire red.

"But she's not here!" she affirmed indignantly. "Didn't I tell ye she's away down the street like a big red peacock. I would have stopped her if I could, but she'll not mind the likes of me."

"She went out?" queried Greeves startled. "I didn't understand you before. I thought you said she went up to her room. Are you quite sure? Perhaps she's returned and slipped up the back way."

"I'm that sure, but I'll go see, Master Pat," sniffed Anne and hurried up the stairs.

In a moment, she was back again.

"She's not upstairs, Master Pat. And you should see her room! It's like a hurricane. There's frocks and shoes just where she's dropped them and stockings all over the place. It's scandalous. If there should be a fire—"

But Greeves was already on his way to the front door.

"I'll go out and find her," he said in a low tone to Silver, grabbed his hat from the rack, and was gone.

An hour later, he came back with an anxious look on his face.

"Is she back yet?" he asked Silver who had been hovering from window to window trying to think of a way out of the dilemma for her father, wondering if perhaps Athalie hadn't run away back to her mother, considering once more whether she ought not to go away herself and so remove one stumbling block from this wayward sister's path.

"I met a woman—she lives next door—Weldon, Lizzie Weldon, I think her name is. She said she saw Athalie go down the street toward the post office. She was standing at the gate, she said, and watched her out of sight. She's one of those hawks who knows everybody's business. I used to hate her when I was a boy. She evidently wanted to find out where Athalie had gone. It isn't hell enough to have these things happening, but we have to have a lot of vultures around picking at the bones!"

"Well, never mind, Father. I shouldn't feel too bad about it. It isn't your fault, and things'll come right after a while—"

"So you believe that, too!" he said eyeing her keenly. "Well, I must say, I don't. They've never come right for me yet. The thing I'm afraid of is they may confuse you with Athalie. I wouldn't have a breath of scandal touch you, my Silver-Alice." He came and touched his lips tenderly to her forehead. She lifted clear eyes to meet his look.

"Why, I wouldn't be afraid of that, Father. It isn't possible."

"What makes you so sure?" he asked. "You don't know what old carrion crows inhabit a village like this till they once get scent of a bit of a scandal. Why, even really good women, women who live otherwise a right life, will snatch up such a thing and rush about carrying it from house to house till there isn't a tatter left of somebody's reputation."

Silver still looked untroubled and shook her head. "It can't be," she insisted. "There's a promise, don't you know? Listen! 'No weapon that is formed against thee shall prosper; and every tongue that shall rise against thee in judgment thou shalt condemn. This is the heritage of the servants of the Lord.'"

He looked at her as a man looks at a beloved woman who has just uttered some sweet fallacy concerning which he does not wish to undeceive her. His eyes grew tender with admiration and yearning.

"You are like your mother," he said with a strange embarrassment in his voice. "If only—" and then he stalked to the window and stood looking out for a long, long time.

Dinner was late that night while Molly made shortcake for the strawberries, but when they sat down, Athalie had not yet arrived.

"It's very strange!" said Greeves looking at his watch anxiously, and he went himself to Athalie's door and switched on the light to make sure she was not hidden somewhere to evade them all.

He made Anne tell over again what she had heard.

"She said it would be that late," insisted Anne, "and she was going to the roof garden and a carabay! I'm sure that was what she said, *carabay!*"

Greeves looked thoughtful. What was it Athalie had said about somebody in the city bringing her out the first day? Giving her presents, going to give her a theater party? Surely the child couldn't have gone in town to meet him without leaving any word. It was absurd. Nevertheless, he kept bringing out his watch and looking at it nervously.

Silver, too, seemed worried.

"Perhaps we better not go to that little party tonight, Father, unless Athalie comes in before it is time for us to start."

"No, that would be foolish," he said. "Of course you must go. We will both go. Truman was an old friend of mine. I'd like to see him. She will come in before long of course. She is doubtless hiding not far away just for a freak. She is a strange child. I do not understand her."

But at eight o'clock Athalie had not arrived.

"There is no use fretting over it," said her father as he walked restlessly up and down, realizing that he was more angry with her than worried. Why should he worry about a child whom he neither wanted nor loved? And yet for that very reason something in him rose and prodded his conscience. Why didn't he care?

He went to the telephone and called up Bannard.

"That you, Bannard? Say, that strange child of mine is still at large. Have you any way of finding out whether she took a train to town this afternoon, without exciting interest on the part of the whole countryside? Good. I thought you could. I suppose it is foolish to worry. She certainly seems able to look after herself, but somehow I feel responsible. Darned responsible! Thanks. Yes, we're going over. See you in a few minutes."

Greeves and his daughter went to the neighbor's and Bannard

went out to find Barry, but Barry was not to be found. His mother had gone to the Flats for the night to care for the Italian baby, and there was no sign that Barry had been home at all. Bannard sauntered down to the station and inquired of the agent who was just closing up whether he could remember if Mr. Perry went to the city on the four o'clock train, and the agent said no, there wasn't a soul who'd gone on that train. It was late, and he had to hang around waiting to give the engineer a message. There never was much travel in the afternoon—only one man and a boy took the six o'clock train, and the seven didn't even stop. It only stopped in Silver Sands for flagging anyway, unless there was somebody to get off.

He sauntered into the drugstore and bought a toothbrush, taking plenty of time in the selection, and the soda clerk was relating a tale about the "jane who took two chocolate fizzes and a banana split that afternoon. Some red bird!"

He dropped in at the firehouse to ask the chief if the first of the month would suit the fire company to have their annual service in the church and, keeping his ears open, gathered another straw or two more of evidence.

"An ankle like a square piano!" Uri Weldon was saying with his coarse laugh.

"I wonder she didn't scare the birds!" said another. "Some bathin' suit for a country walk!" Then the front legs of the respective chairs came down reluctantly, and the men straightened up to greet Bannard gravely. Everybody liked Bannard. There was nowhere in the town he might not go, nowhere that he would be unwelcome. Young though he was, he had that Pauline trait of being all things to all men, though it must be owned that the men at the firehouse were all just a trifle afraid every time he came that he was somehow going to save some of them and take them away from all that life held dear. They had no doubt in their minds but that he could "save" them if he once got them in his clutches.

Slowly progressing up the street, stopping at Mrs. Hoskins to inquire if her nephew in the city had received the letter of introduction he had procured for him, he learned incidentally, as he had thought he would, that Athalie Greeves had passed there that afternoon about half past four "in a scandalous rig," had gone to the drugstore—"and it's the second time, Mr. Bannard, the second time in two days, and all those young boys always hanging around the drugstore"—had gone on from the drugstore down the village street as far as she could see from the gate and passed out of sight without returning.

"And I threw my apern over my head and ran out to look," added the good woman, showing that she always did her duty by whoever passed, that nothing should be missing out of the general report of the day.

"And I think her father ought to look after her better'n that, don't you, Mr. Bannard? A young girl like that! And a stranger in town. Folks might misunderstand her. Don't you think it's strange we never heard that he had any daughters before?"

Bannard finally reached the Truman's, but he had little to tell Greeves about his daughter, except that she had not gone on either train to the city and that she had been seen walking down the village street and had bought a soda at the drugstore.

"I wouldn't be in the least alarmed, though," he added in a low tone. "There really isn't anything much can happen in the town. They're a friendly lot, even the pryingest of them. She'll probably turn up at home before long."

Just at that moment, the dining room door opened and in came the next act of the charade that was in progress, led by Silver who seemed to be the prime mover in every feature of the evening. The girls simply surrounded her and adored her from the start. Bannard watched her, and his eyes lit up with that strange wonder he had felt when first he saw her the day before. A wonderful girl! A real unspoiled girl in the modern world. He thought of how she had gone into that sorrowing home in the afternoon and entered into the need; and now here she was the center of all this merriment, and just as much at home, and just as self-forgetful.

It was remarkable that part she was taking in the act, playing her delicate features into the contortion of a haughty woman of the world. She was talented! But of course she would be. With such a father! And that spirituelle look must have come from the mother. He remembered the exquisite painted face.

Then eager voices claimed him to come and join the group for the next word, and he was drawn away to the other room.

"Oh, have you heard how the baby is?" a low, vibrant voice asked as he passed her in the hall.

So she hadn't forgotten! She was in all this, a part of it, but she had thoughts for the anxious home.

"She is holding her own," he said. "I took Barry's mother down there a little while ago. She will stay all night. You don't know Barry's mother yet. She is a strong arm to lean upon, a cool hand on a fevered brow. She knows how to do things without seeming to, and she loves people."

"Oh, that is good!" said Silver. "Tomorrow I will go and take her place awhile if I may."

"It will not be necessary," he said, looking his thanks, "but—you may if your father does not object."

"Object?" she looked surprised. "Oh, he could not object to that. Of course I will go."

The company clamored for Silver, and she was swept laughingly into the other room, but the minister felt that somehow between them a bond had been established that was very good to think upon.

Only two days and he felt this way about her! But she was an unusual girl. Then he heard her ringing laugh, smiled into the eyes of the boys who were pummeling to tell him them the best way to act the word "penitentiary," and plunged into the matter before him.

At half past ten they all went home, most of the company being of high school age and not allowed late hours. The half-past was a special dispensation on account of its being Friday night and no lessons tomorrow. The minister walked down the street with Greeves and his daughter and stepped in a moment to learn if the prodigal had returned or if his further services as detective would be required.

They found Anne Truesdale sitting in the dark drawing room watching the street. She would not have owned to anybody, least of all her master, that she was praying for "that huzzy," but she was. Somehow Anne's sense of justice wouldn't allow her to let even a girl like that be wandering along in the world in the darkening night without even a prayer to guide her. She deserved all she might get, but, oh, think of the disgrace of it all in the town. Anne didn't know that she really cared more for the disgrace in the town than she did for the young girl's soul in the dark.

But there! See how all our motives are mixed! Anne was praying for her! That was something gained. Anne had begun to feel her responsibility, and leaven of that kind always works. It may take time on a cold day, but it always works at last.

When the three discovered that the missing one was still absent, they stood and looked at one another in dismay, with that helpless air that always says, *What is there that I can do next?*

Then sharply into the silence of their anxiety there rippled out the insistent ring of the telephone.

Greeves hurried into the library to answer it, and the others stood breathless, listening to his voice: "Hello!"

It was a man's voice that answered: "I want to speak to Miss Athalie Greeves."

"Who *is* this?" asked Athalie Greeves's father sternly.

"Well, who are *you*?" The voice was insolent.

"I am Athalie's father, and I insist upon knowing to whom I am speaking."

"I'm one of her mother's friends. You wouldn't know me. Call Athalie. She'll tell you who I am. I want to speak to her!"

"It will be necessary for you to explain to me first."

"Why? Isn't she there?"

"What is your business with her, sir?"

"Is she there or not?" said the ugly voice.

"She is *not*," said the father coldly.

"Oh, well, I'll call up again!" said the voice, and immediately the line was cut off.

Patterson Greeves turned toward the two who stood in the doorway and looked with a helpless dazed expression for a moment then hung up the receiver with a troubled air.

"That is very strange!" he said. "Somehow I get the impression that that man knew Athalie was away—or was trying to find out—"

"It is strange," said Bannard. He made no pretense of not having heard. The voice on the telephone had been loud enough to be heard out in the hall. "I wish Barry were here. I'll go out and look for him. If she isn't heard from by the time I get back, we'll begin to do something. Don't get frightened. It's probably only some schoolgirl prank. Barry will very likely be able to find out where she has gone. He's a regular ferret. I never saw a boy like him."

Meantime, Barry, out in the night, was having troubles of his own.

Chapter 20

When Barry Lincoln left Sam in the side street with the roadster and darted across the trolley track and around the back of the stranger's car, the big man with the heavy moustache was visible in the brightly lit drugstore talking with the clerk at the back of the store. He was handing out some money and lighting a big black cigar at the taper on the desk.

Barry drew himself up for one glimpse and saw that the girl was now seated in the front, left hand, away from the curb.

He swept the street either way with a quick glance, saw no one coming in his immediate vicinity, gave another glance to the man in the drugstore, and made a dash for the door of the driver's seat.

Barry had grown up as it were in the garage, that is, he had spent every available minute there since he was a small child, hovering over every car that came within its doorway, watching the men at work, as he grew older, helping with the repairs himself, and finally becoming so expert that they were always ready to give him a job on Saturdays and half holidays and often even sent for him to help them discover what made the trouble in some stubborn engine or carburetor. There was no car rolling that Barry didn't know by name and sight and wasn't able to describe its characteristics and comparative worth. He was a judge of cars as some men are a judge of their fellowmen. Also, he had a way with cars. When he put his hand to a wheel, it obeyed him. He was a perfect, natural driver, knowing how to get the best out of every piece of machinery.

And now as he slid into the driver's seat with the owner only a few feet away, a strange unwarned girl beside him, a strange unfriendly town around him, a dark unknown way ahead, it was not a strange unknown mechanism to which he put his hand. He had known that car as a man recognizes his friend even when he was up in the tree some hours before and saw it coming down the road.

The girl was evidently startled, but Barry, his face turned half away from her, threw in the clutch and was off in a whirl.

"Why, Bobs! You scared me!" cried Athalie. "I didn't see you come out; I thought I was watching you light a cigar. It must have been another man who looked just like you. Did you get the chocolates? Hand them over quick! I'm simply dying of starvation."

Barry began to fumble in his pocket silently with one hand. He brought out a package, half a bar of milk chocolate, and dropped it into her lap. His eye was ahead. He had no time to waste. The owner of the car would be out in a second and raise a rumpus. He whirled around the first corner he came to and fled down a dark side street, passed two blocks, a third that went perceptibly downhill, and darted into an old covered wooden bridge.

It was pitch-dark in there except for their own lights. The noise of the engine echoed and reverberated like an infernal machine.

The girl was leaning forward looking at the package. An instant more and they roared out of the bridge into the quiet starlight.

"Why, Bobs! I think you're horrid! Was that all you bought for me? And it's not even a whole bar!" She flung it disgustedly on the floor of the car and looked up angrily. "Do you call that a *joke*?" she asked with a curling lip, and then suddenly she saw his face and was transfixed with horror. For an instant, she held her breath, her eyes growing wilder and wider with fright, then she let out one of the most bloodcurdling screams Barry had ever heard.

Just at that second, there lumbered into view the lights of a big gasoline truck that was hurrying to the end of its long day's journey. One instant they saw it, the next they were in its very embrace. Barry curled out of the road just in time and back into it again, while Athalie screamed some more.

They shot into a black road overarched with tall forest trees. The smell of the new earth leaped up to Barry's taut senses with a soothing touch. The road as far as his lights reached ahead was empty. His woodman's sense told him there was no one near. But how far in the night had that scream reached? What straggler might have heard it and sent a warning? There! She was beginning it again! He must stop it somehow. A sudden thought came to him. He groped in the pocket of the door by his side. There ought to be one there, in a car like this! A man of that sort would carry one. Yes, there it was! His fingers grasped the cool metal, found their way with confidence, and drew it out.

"Bobs! Bobs!" screamed Athalie. The echoes rang through the woods on either side as they raced along. She was leaving the trail behind them for any straggler to report their whereabouts. This must not go on.

Suddenly the dull gleam of the revolver flashed in front of her face.

"Cut that out!' said the boy sternly.

Athalie opened her mouth to scream again and instead dropped her jaw just as the scream was about to be uttered. She turned wide, horrified eyes to her captor and sat white and still in her seat, cringing away from the weapon.

"Now," said Barry, still holding the revolver in one hand, "you might as well understand that you aren't in any danger whatever if you keep your mouth shut, but if you yodel again like that, I'll knock you cold. Do you get me?"

Athalie's eyes acknowledged that she understood. She cringed still farther away from the revolver, and he lowered it, keeping it still in his hand however. The woods flew by in one long, sweet avenue of spring night. Barry settled to his wheel, eyes to the front, with a mind to the back, and a sort of sixth sense keeping tabs on the girl by his side. He could see that the revolver had frightened her terribly. Her face was too much powdered to admit of its turning pale, but there was a sagging droop around her lips and eyelids that showed her whole spirit stricken with fear. She gathered her cloak closer about her and shivered. Her big, dark eyes never left his face except now and then to glance fearfully out as if wondering what were the possibilities of jumping overboard. Barry began to feel sorry for her.

"Nothing but a little kid," he said to himself. "A foolish little kid!"

Two miles farther on they turned into the highway, and Barry slowed down a bit. There were two cars ahead—he could see their taillights—but nothing coming behind. He turned to the right in the general direction of Silver Sands and then looked at the girl.

"You needn't be afraid," he said half contemptuously, half gently. "I'm not going to hurt you."

"I'm not afraid," said Athalie, some of the old spirit returning.

"Oh!" said the boy. "All right! I thought you were!" They speeded on again in silence. Presently Athalie spoke. Her voice showed returning temper. "What are you going to do with me?"

"Going to take you home to your father!" said Barry.

The young woman sat up suddenly. This then was no highwayman.

This was some meddler in her business. He knew her father. He had somehow trailed her and recognized her. She was furious.

"But I don't choose to go home," she said indignantly.

"That doesn't cut any ice," said Barry crisply. "You're getting there pretty fast all right."

Athalie turned on him angrily. "Look here," she said fiercely, "I'm not going to stand this another minute. Do you know what a terrible thing you're doing? You'll probably be put in prison for life for it. But if you'll turn right around now and take me back to my friend, I'll tell him you just made a mistake. You didn't try to steal the car at all."

"Thank you," said Barry, a grim shadow of a smile flickering across his face in the darkness. "I'm not worrying about that just now."

"But you've *got* to take me back," said Athalie, almost on the verge of tears. "I'm on my way to be *married*!"

"Not tonight!" said Barry grimly.

"Well, I guess I'm not going to be stopped by a kid like you!" burst out Athalie. She suddenly rose with all her might and flung herself on the wheel, and Athalie had some weight and grip when she chose to use them.

Barry, utterly unprepared for this onslaught, ground on the brakes and put forth all his strength, trying to keep the wavering car from climbing a tree while he was bringing it to a standstill, but he managed to keep his head.

It was a sharp, brief struggle, for Athalie's muscles were untrained, and in a moment more, Barry was holding her firmly with both hands, and she had ceased to struggle. He had not again brought the revolver into play. He hated dramatic effects when physical force would do as well.

But he could not stay there all night and hold her down. He cast about for some way of making her hold still. There was a handkerchief in his pocket. He managed to get hold of it, and crossing her hands, bound them together. Her cloak had fallen off, revealing the flimsy dress and the long fringed ends of a satin sash tied around her waist. He pulled at it and found that it came loose. With this he bound her across the shoulders and down to the waist.

"You're cold!" he remarked as he saw her shiver. "And that flimsy coat is no good. Here, put this sweater on."

He pulled off his own sweater and pulled it down over her head. She started to scream again, but he put his hand over her mouth and when she was quiet remarked very gently, "I hate awfully to treat a girl this way, but I'll have to gag you if you try that line again," and she knew by his tone that he meant it. "I don't think you'd like gagging."

Athalie began to cry.

"I'm sorry," said Barry remorsefully, "but you can't be trusted."

He was down on his knees now fastening her ankles together with a bit of old rope he had found in his pocket.

"But I'm on my way to be *married*," sobbed out the indignant child. "You're spoiling my *life*—" She was weeping uncontrollably now.

"Excuse me," he said quietly, "I guess I'll have to use my necktie for a gag." And he began unconcernedly to take off his necktie. "I can't have all this noise."

Athalie stopped short.

"I won't cry," she said shortly, "but won't you just listen to reason? Would you like it if you were going to get married, to be interfered with this way?"

"Say, kid," he said gently, "you talk sense, and I'll help you. You know, you aren't old enough to get married yet. And I say, did you know what kind of a rotter you were going off with?"

Athalie's eyes fairly blazed.

"He's nothing of the sort!" she retorted. "I've known him for years. He's perfectly darling! He's my mother's friend."

"Is that all?" said Barry witheringly. "I thought you were going to say your grandmother's."

"I think you're perfectly horrid!" said Athalie, shrugging what was left of her shoulders and drawing as far away from him as she could. "You think you're smart!"

"Look here, kid! There's no use quarreling with the only friend you've got just now. I'm telling you facts. Can't you listen to reason? That man's a rotter. I know his kind. If he's your mother's friend, so much the worse. He knew he wasn't doing the square thing taking a kid like you off that way at night. What kind of a rep would you have had, will you tell me, when you got back, I'd like to know?"

"I wasn't coming back," sobbed Athalie softly. "I told you—I—was ggg–g–oing to be m–m–married!"

"Yes, in a pig's eye you were! If that man ever married you, kid, I'd eat my hat. He hadn't any more idea of marrying you than I have, and that's flat! This isn't a very nice way to talk to a girl, I know, but when you won't listen to sense, why, you've gotta be shown."

"He was going to buy me—a—st–st–string of real pearls!" wept Athalie, suddenly remembering, "and we were going to have a turkey dinner! I'm—ju–s–t—st–ar–r–r–ved!"

Barry shrugged down behind his wheel disgustedly.

"You look as if you had meat enough on you to stand it awhile!" he said contemptuously. "I thought you were a girl, not a baby!"

Athalie held in the sob on a high note and surveyed him angrily. "You are the most—*disagreeable* boy!" she shouted.

"I didn't state my opinion of you yet. But you certainly aren't my idea of agreeable."

"I didn't ask you your opinion."

"Say, look here," said Barry, "let's cut this out. This isn't getting us anywhere. What I want is for you to see some sense before I get you home. Your father's kind of a friend of mine, and I'd hate like the deuce to have all this get out about you in the town. You see, whatever you think of this rotter you were going off with, the little old town would know fast enough what he was, if any of 'em knew you were off in the night with him. You can't kid the town!"

"I haven't the slightest desire to bother with your little old town," said Athalie loftily. "It may go to the devil for all I care!"

Barry was silent with disgust for a moment.

"Well, if it does," he said slowly, "it will carry you on a pointed stick ahead of it, and like as not they'll try out the point of the stick on your father first. You can't kid the devil!"

There was a long pause. The night was very still. They had not passed a car for some time. The lights in the sleeping villages in the valley below them were nearly all gone out; moist, dank air rushed up in wreaths and struck them lightly in the face as they passed. The sudden breath of an apricot tree in bloom drenched the darkness. Over in the east, toward which they were hurrying, a silver light was lifting beyond the horizon, and in reflection a little thread of a river leaped out from the darkness where it had been sleeping in winding curves among the dark of plumy willows.

"I *hate* you!" said Athalie suddenly. "You called me names! You're a vulgar boy!"

"What names did I call you, kid?" Barry's voice was gentle.

"You called me fat in a very coarse way!"

"Well, you're not exactly emaciated, are you?" He gave her a friendly grin in the darkness.

"I hate you!" reiterated Athalie again. "And I want to get out and walk!"

"Anything to please you!" said Barry, quickly bringing the car to a full stop and reaching over to throw open the door by her side.

Athalie was surprised to be taken so literally, but she made an instant move to get out, and then realizing that her ankles were tied, she subsided again.

"Oh, excuse me," said Barry, and stooping unfastened the cord on her ankles and sat back again.

"Are you going to untie my hands?" she asked imperiously.

"Oh no, I guess not," said Barry easily. "You don't walk on your hands, do you?"

She cast him a furious look and bounced out of the car, walking off very rapidly down the road with her shoulders stiff and indignant.

Barry sat back and watched her. She went on swiftly till she came to the bend of the road, and then she looked back half fearfully. The car was still and dark as if Barry had settled for a nap. The road ahead wound into a dark wood, and the trees were casting weird shadows across the roadway. But no one should call her bluff. She would go on and show him. She stumbled forward on her little high-heeled shoes, almost falling as she ran fearfully toward the darkness of the wooded road. Then suddenly on her horrified sense came the distant sound of a motor in the opposite direction, and a long, thin forecasting of light shot out with a blind glare ahead. Another car was coming! And it was far into the nighttime! And she alone on the road with her arms tied! Horrible fear seized upon her and rooted her to the ground. Then with a mighty effort, she gathered her ebbing strength and turning fled.

Chapter 21

In the first few yards, her right shoe flew off and lay at the side of the road, but she waited not for shoes. Her silken-clad foot went over the rough, stony highway with the fleetness of a rabbit. She darted to the side of the car and panted: "Let me get in, quick! Quick! There's another car coming!"

Barry leaned over and pulled her up, cast a quick glance to the oncoming lights, started his motor, and dashed along at full speed just in time to pass swiftly as if he had come from a distance, and then when the passing car was out of sight remarked pleasantly, "Have a nice walk?"

"Don't!" said Athalie, shuddering. He looked at her furtively. The tears were coursing down her cheeks, but she was not making any sound.

"Look here, kid, I'm sorry!" he said pleasantly. "Let's call this off. You're all in! And say! I'm going to untie your hands. I know I can trust you not to make any more trouble. We're almost home now, kid. Only a matter of about four miles, and we'll run through the town as still as oil and get you home and nobody any the wiser. But before we get there, you've got to make a pact to can that rotter or I'll have to make a clean breast of the whole thing to your father, how you phoned him, and how you met him in the woods, and what he said to you and all—"

Athalie turned an amazed face toward him now, smeared with powder and tears, and lit by the newly risen moon.

"You know?"

"Yep! Know it all! Saw you climb out your window and go to the drugstore. Was in the next booth and heard every word you phoned. Wasn't ten feet away from you in the woods. I tell you, you can't kid this town."

Athalie looked aghast.

"No, you don't need to worry. Nobody else knows yet, and I don't intend they shall if you agree to can that man. Is it a bargain?"

There was a long pause, during which Athalie sniffed quietly, then she murmured, "My father—he'll half kill me—"

"No, he won't! He'll be much more likely to kill the man. But perhaps we can fix that up, too. You leave it to me. Now, lean over here, and let's get those knots untied."

"I didn't say I would yet!" said Athalie with a catch of rebellion in her breath.

"No, but you're going to," said Barry pleasantly. "You're not yella."

Barry worked away at the satin sash, talking meanwhile.

"Say, kid, you know you'll forget all this when you get acquainted in town and begin to have good times. What you need is to get into high school and play basketball. You'd need to train a little of course, but you'd make a great player. I watched you as you went up the road, and you've got the build all right. Say, some of the girls on our team are peachy players, but you could beat 'em all at it if you'd try. If I was you, I'd begin to train tomorra. Cut out those sundaes and sodas and chocolates, and don't be everlastingly eating cake and fudge. You'll never make a player unless you. . ."

It was surprising how their attitudes toward one another had changed. Athalie wiped up her smeary face and began to take an interest in life. She even smiled once at a joke Barry made about the moon. She was rather quiet and almost humble.

Barry grew almost voluble. He described in detail several notable athletic features of the past that had put their high school in a class with several large prep schools in the state. He opened up on the prospects for the season's baseball games, admitting reluctantly on inquiry that he was their team's captain and coach.

Suddenly the brow of the hill they were climbing was reached, and there before them lay the plain of Silver Sands, with the belching chimneys of Frogtown glaring against the night, and off to the left the steeple of the Presbyterian church shining in the moonlight. It was very still down there where the houses slept, and the few drowsy lights kept vigil. Barry cast it a loyal glance and brought the car to a standstill.

"Look, kid," he said with something commanding in his young voice, "that's our town, down there! Doesn't she look great with her feet to the river and her head on the hills? She's a crackerjack little old town if you treat her right, and no mistake. See that white spot over there behind the trees? That's the pillars on the old Silver house. It's a prince of a house, and the people that lived in it have always been princes. My mother says the whole country round has always looked up to the Silvers. They've always been *real*! Do you get me? It's a great thing to belong to a family like that!"

Athalie turned her large eyes on him wonderingly, and suddenly some of her father's sentences of the morning came to her, sentences about gentlemen and ladies and respectable standards, and their meaning went home on the shaft of Barry's simple arrow.

Barry was never one to explain a joke or a sermon. He let it rest and passed to another line of thought.

"We're going around on the beach road," explained Barry, "and come in the lane just below your house. We'll stop at Aunt Katie's where the minister boards and slip through the back hedge. Then there won't be a whole lot for anyone to see and hear. Anybody might drive up to the minister's door any time of night and nobody think anything of it. If Aunt Katie sees us, she'll keep her mouth shut. She's a peach, she is. If you ever need a friend, tip up to her, kid. Now, before we go on, I'll trouble you for the name and address of that rotter!"

"What are you going to do?" asked Athalie in an alarmed voice.

"Got to return this car, haven't I?"

"Oh, why yes, I suppose so. But—he'll be awfully angry! You might get arrested, you know!"

"Watch me!" said Barry lightly. "Now I'll trouble you for that address."

"I don't remember the address," said Athalie. "I went there in a taxicab. It's somewhere in a big apartment house. I got it out of the telephone book."

"What's his name then? You haven't forgotten that, have you?" asked Barry, eyeing her suspiciously. "Is Bobs the first or last part of it?"

Athalie cast a startled glance at him.

"Farrell, Robert Farrell," she answered meekly.

"That's all right," said Barry. "I'll look him up."

Barry started the car again, and they were silent as they sped along for some minutes. Then Athalie asked in a scared voice, "What are you going to tell my father?"

"Nothing much, unless I have to," said Barry easily. "If you can that man, he doesn't need to know anything about it, but if I find you haven't played square, he'll know the whole thing in about three minutes. It's entirely up to you."

Athalie looked frightened.

"I won't phone him anymore—nor write to him!" she said at length. "But I can't be sure what he'll do."

"I don't think he'll bother you anymore after I get through with him," said Barry airily.

Athalie cast him another frightened glance. "You'd better be careful—" she warned. "He's got an awful temper."

"So I should judge," said Barry. "I'm glad you're out of his clutches."

The car slid along the Silver beach quietly as fine machinery can be made to go. Past the belching furnaces with the night shift in sleeveless shirts moving picturesquely past the light in the rosy dusk of the big structures; past the ruins of the pickle factory and the darkened windows of the rows of little houses; past the house with the lighted upper window where little Mary and Barry's mother struggled with death the long hours through, and the stricken father and mother knelt each side of the bed and prayed; past the darkened cannery and the silk factory and the buildings of the Sand Company, across the side tracks and the railroad; over the bridge that spanned a small tributary stream; and winding the back way into Silver Sands, down Sweetbriar Lane to Aunt Katie's upper front window as Barry helped Athalie out of the car. Barry looked up as they passed in the gate and gave a soft, low whistle like the chirp of a bird. But it was Aunt Katie's voice, not the minister's, that spoke in a low tone from an open side window:

"Is that you, Barry?"

"Sure," growled Barry cheerfully.

"Oh, you have found her!" said the voice again, "I am *glad*!" And there was something so vibrant and pleased about it that it thrilled

Athalie. No one had ever been glad like that about her before. She had always been considered a nuisance, something to be appeased and gotten rid of as quickly as possible. She warmed to a voice like that and looked up wistfully. It almost seemed to her that she ought to say thank you. She had scarcely ever felt that thanking impulse before in all her wild young life.

"Sure I found her!" said Barry. "Mist'r Bannard over t'th'house?"

"Why, yes, he's just gone back again. He said he and Mr. Greeves were going to the city to hunt for her. You better hurry."

"Aw'right. G'night!" And Barry led the way rapidly around the side porch, down through the garden, and over the back fence. Athalie was stumbling painfully along the plowed ground with one little high-heeled shoe and one silken-clad, sorry foot. As she struggled up on the fence, Barry saw it.

"Say, kid, when did you lose your shoe?" he asked solicitously.

"Up there on the road when I was running," said the girl with a catch in her breath, and looking up he saw that she was suffering and that there were tears on her face.

"You poor kid!" he said gently and, stooping, picked her up and carried her all the way up through the garden to the brick terrace at the back hall door. There he set her down gently and tapped at the door.

"I wonder what time it is by moonlight," he said glancing down at the sundial. "It must be a good piece into tomorrow already. My timepiece got kicked across the room the other day by mistake, so I have to get along without it."

Athalie stood shivering, a sorry little figure in her tattered scarlet dress, with her smeary face, her hat jammed over one ear, and one torn silk stocking; but a faint semblance of a wistful smile went over her face as she watched the nice big boy beside her. How strong he had been, and how tender! It gave her that thankful feeling again.

How strange! And yet how like a ruffian he had treated her out on the road and made her come home! Her mingled feelings held in check by the very salutary possibility that she was about to meet with a well-deserved punishment from the stranger-parent inside the door were overwhelming enough without any addition. But when hurrying footsteps came down the hall and Anne Truesdale's face, red with weeping, appeared as she opened the door, Athalie suddenly remembered her exit from the house that afternoon and realized that there were many scores for her to settle and shrank back behind her protector.

Greeves and Bannard came quickly down the hall, and at the top of the stairs there was a soft stirring and the flutter of a blue bathrobe as Silver leaned over the banister by her door to listen.

Barry stepped inside and lifted his old cap respectfully. He was in his shirtsleeves, and his face looked tired and haggard but had a cheerful grin.

"She got lost, Mr. Greeves, and took the wrong road. I happened along and brought her back. Sorry we had to be so late, but it was a good piece away. She's about all in, so you better put her to bed. No thanks, I can't stay. I got a borrowed car over in the lane I gotta return. Oh, well, I don't care if I do have some cookies."

They plied him with plates of cake and cups of coffee and took the attention entirely away from Athalie, and the girl thankfully slipped upstairs. Then she remembered the sweater she was still wearing and slipped it off quickly, paused to put on another shoe that lay in her way, flung her cloak about her, and stole down again.

She had almost a shy look on her face as she brought the sweater over to where Barry stood by the dining room table swallowing down hot coffee and talking to the minister about the baseball prospects.

Both the minister and Greeves looked at her in surprise. Somehow, with the makeup washed off, even in dirty streaks she looked more human, and less bold and bizarre.

Barry looked up with one of his brilliant smiles that he gave rarely and took the sweater.

"I'm afraid you were cold!" said Athalie most unexpectedly to herself. It hadn't occurred to her to think of anyone but herself until that instant.

"Oh, that's all right, kid!" he said, setting down his coffee cup and struggling into his sweater with a couple of motions. "Glad I had it along. Hope you feel all right in the morning."

Athalie retired, feeling for perhaps the first time in her life that she was forgiven and given another chance. Somehow all her escapades up to this time, with nurses, governesses, teachers, and parents, had ended in enmity and a bitter feeling of spite. She went upstairs slowly, wondering what it was about this boy that made her feel like a happy little child. She ought to hate him. He had baffled her and ruled her as no one had ever done before, and he was only a kid like herself, and yet she had a sort of awe for him, and interest in him, a pleasure in his smile. She took off her red tatters pondering this, forgetful entirely of her bridegroom that was to have been.

While Barry was stowing away the sandwiches and cake and coffee that Anne Truesdale seemed always to be able to produce without a moment's warning, Greeves and Bannard withdrew to the hall. The father looked worn and haggard. He cast an anxious eye up the stairs and said in a low voice: "Bannard, I can't thank you enough for sticking by through this. It seems strange, but this is getting me worse than anything that has ever come to me. I need some advice. I need some help. How on earth am I ever to teach that unruly child?"

"You need God, Greeves! I mean it! Kneel down and pray. That will do you more good than any advice that anyone could possibly give you."

"Don't get on your hobbyhorse again tonight, Bannard. I'm in no mood for trifling. I've got to give that girl some kind of a lesson—"

"She looked to me as if she had learned her lesson pretty thoroughly," said Bannard. "I wonder where Barry found her. I thought he must be out on one of his specials. That boy certainly is a wonder!"

"Yes, I am deeply grateful. What are his circumstances? Can I reward him?"

"Give him your friendship. That's all he would ever take. He's proud as Lucifer, but he's loving as they make 'em."

"Yes, I liked him the first time I met him. I'd like to know more about where he found her."

"Well, perhaps she'll tell you. I doubt if he ever will. He's a man of few words where it concerns anything he has done. But I wasn't trifling, Greeves. I meant what I said. There is nothing in the wide universe would open up this situation and show you the right way like getting down on your knees and getting back to God, and when you get there, that 'tomorrow' I was telling you about will be about to dawn."

"Ready, Barry? I'll walk along with you. Good night, Greeves. I'm glad your vigil is at an end!"

They went out the terrace door and walked silently down the garden, two dark shadows among the growing things. Even if Lizette Weldon had been awake, she would not have noticed them for the hedge was tall, and they kept close in its shadow.

Silently the two, as those who understand one another, passed over the fence and through Aunt Katie's little garden, around the side of the house to the front gate.

"Anything I need to know, partner?" asked Bannard affectionately.

Barry considered. "I guess not tonight, sir." He looked up with a smile.

"Have to go far with that car?"

"Quite a piece."

"Your mother is down at the Flats with a sick child tonight."

"Aw'right! I'll be back before she is. G'night!"

Barry slid into the car noiselessly, and as quietly as a car can go, that one backed out of the lane to the beachway and sped away into the night. He did not immediately take to the city highway however. There was something he had to do first. About an hour later he turned into the highway a mile or so above Silver Sands and made high speed to the city. In his hip pocket under his sweater reposed a muddy little shoe.

The minister had slipped into his door and extinguished the light at once, going softly upstairs in the dark. From behind Aunt Katie's door, there came a question: "Was it all right?"

"All right, Aunt Katie. Your prayers brought us through!"

About half an hour later, Lizette, who had fallen asleep on watch, woke up and scanned both her windows, but neither Aunt Katie's nor the Silver mansion showed any signs of light, yet she had been sure she heard an automobile somewhere in her dreams. For Anne Truesdale, faithful even to a "daring huzzy," prepared a hot bath for Athalie and a tray of good things for her to eat, but she had been careful to hang a black shawl behind the drawn shade of the window looking toward the Weldon house.

The eastern sky was paling into dawn as Barry drove into the outskirts of the city and began his search for an open telephone booth. He found presently an obscure little hotel and had no trouble in discovering Robert Farrell's name. He purchased a sheet of paper and an envelope and, standing by the desk, wrote a brief and characteristic letter:

Mr. Robert Farrell,
Redwood Apartments,

 Dear sir: This is to notify you that you are not to have any
further communication with Miss Greeves. The police force
of Silver County is on to you and is watching every move you
make, and if the investigation of your past that is being made
brings any further criminal developments, we will make Silver
County too hot to hold you. If this warning of the police of
Silver Sands is not obeyed, Mr. Greeves will stop at nothing to
prosecute you to the limit.

Signed,
B. Link, member of police force, Silver Sands

With this letter duly addressed and sealed, Barry made his way to the
Redwood Apartments and rang up the man in Farrell's apartment. To
him, when he finally appeared yawning, Barry handed over the letter
and the car, and touching his hat politely disappeared, running like
a deer to the station as soon as he had passed the corner and arriving
just in time to catch the milk truck for Silver Sands.

Chapter 22

The only possible condition under which you are free to remain in this town and in my house is that you hereafter conduct yourself as a lady in every way!"

This was the ultimatum that Patterson Greeves, after a night of vigil, flung out upon his subdued and waiting daughter sometime along in the middle of the morning when she chose to come down to a languid breakfast.

Silver had gone early to the Flats with the minister, and Anne Truesdale was out doing marketing. They had the house to themselves. The father girded up his soul and went to the talk before him. It had to come sooner or later.

Athalie regarded him composedly for a moment before responding. "Well," said she, "with Lilla on the high seas and my money mostly gone, I suppose I'll have to make a try. I won't go to school. What is it you want me to do? Go to church and Sunday school?"

Now, nothing was further from Patterson Greeves's intention than to attend divine service of any sort or to make his family do so, but in that instant it flashed across his consciousness that that was the very thing that would have to be done if Athalie was to remain in the town and live as a member of the old Silver family should, in good and regular standing. Athalie could not associate with the young people of the town and expect to be comfortable among them unless she did as they did, unless she did as the traditions of the family laid down. For himself he would probably have ignored what people thought and have shut himself in with his books and his few friends and let the town go hang. But here he was preaching the standard of his old family and insisting upon its being kept high, and in his heart not planning to do so himself. He saw the inconsistency at once and knew also that the thing she had suggested was the very influence that would readjust her abnormal young soul, if anything could do it. If religion was good for anything, it ought to be good for that. In fact, there was somewhere hidden away in his own soul the belief not yet extinct that religion did do things to souls when it really got a chance! Also, there was Bannard. He had some sense if he was a minister. She wouldn't likely get much nonsense hearing him. And there was Silver! Of course Silver would want to go to church. Somehow he shrank from letting Silver know how far he had strayed from the religion of her mother and her mother's people. All this passed through his mind in the lifting of an eye. He was accustomed to control his face and cover it with a mask among men. He scarcely seemed to hesitate as he replied.

"Yes. Certainly. Of course you will go to church and Sunday school."

"Oh, heck!" said Athalie, a kind of hunted look coming into her eyes as she flounced around and stared out of the window.

Greeves watched her painfully, trying to adjust his own thoughts to this unexpected turn. He would have to go to church himself probably to enforce this. He felt like echoing her exclamation. What was he letting himself in for? Well, if it got too strenuous, he could always send her away to camp when he found the right place. Then, too, he would have to be courteous to Bannard. He had been awfully decent last night, knowing just the thing to be done, and not making a great fuss about it as some would have done, and making everything public. Yes, of course he would have to go to church occasionally. Tomorrow was the Sabbath. He would have to go then to start things right. Then after that perhaps he could manage to be away a good deal Sundays, run down to the shore or make a visit to New York or Boston—any excuse would do. He would have to go a good deal anyway to consult libraries.

"Well," said Athalie as suddenly, whirling back as she had turned away. "What else? I'm game."

Her fixed gaze was rather disconcerting. He couldn't help admiring the way she took it. There was something rather interesting about her in spite of all her devilishness. Where did she get that?

"There are three things that I shall require," he said following out the plan he had formed during the night. Poor soul, he had gone such a little way in this matter of fatherhood and discipline. He thought it could all be enumerated under three headings.

Athalie watched him attentively.

"Obedience—"

Athalie winced.

"Who do I have to obey? Not that red-faced servant woman! Not that other girl!"

Her father faltered.

"Because I *won't*! That's *flat*!"

"They would fall under the next point," temporized Patterson Greeves, "which is courtesy."

"Oh, you mean I've got to be *polite*! All right. I suppose I can. What next?"

"Modesty!" finished the father with a sudden realization that his list was pitifully short, and she was dismissing them all and making it shorter.

"Well, what do you mean by that?"

"I mean that I do not like the way you dress or behave. You constantly call attention to yourself, to your person. It is probably not your fault that you are somewhat stout, although I have understood there are diets that will regulate that sort of thing, but it is your fault when you dress in loud and noticeable colors and strange styles, or when you expose your flesh to view."

Athalie's brow drew down.

She glanced down at her dashing little blouse of orange crochet over a flannel skirt of orange and black stripes. Her plump pink arms showed through the knitted mesh, and the brilliant scarf she was wearing jauntily across one shoulder revealed much fat neck. A flush of disappointment rolled up her carefully unpowdered cheek. She had really tried to look pleasing for that interview. According to her standard, she looked nice.

"I've worn the only things I have," she said sullenly. "I'm sure I don't know how to please you."

Something in the wistfulness of her tone appealed to him. He cast about how to answer her.

"Suppose you go up and spread out what you have, and I'll come and look at your things. If you haven't got the proper clothes we'll have to go and buy some."

A glint of interest shone in Athalie's eyes.

"I'll go up and spread them out," she said eagerly. "It won't take me long. There's really some quite spiffy ones."

He almost groaned aloud as she disappeared like a bright, saucy butterfly. How was he to make her understand that it was their very "spiffiness" that made the trouble?

In a few minutes, he heard her calling, and he goaded himself up the stairs, trying to prepare to be very diplomatic and gentle and firm.

Athalie stood by the door, her face radiant, and behind her on the bed lay shining masses of silks and satins and velvets in gaudy array, and all around the room were hangers on which hung limp effigies of herself done in all colors of the rainbow, the vintage of Lilla's cast-off frocks, made over for her neglected daughter.

Athalie led him around the room, beginning with what she considered the sober ones and going on to the dressier affairs. He went from one to the other with growing bewilderment and pain, and when he had finished, he stood back in dismay and began at the beginning again. He could not find one thing that filled his idea of what a young girl should wear. Once he thought he had discovered it in a simple-looking brown outfit with a gleam of brilliant green, which Athalie had hung behind the door as if she had forgotten it or did not want it inspected because it was too dull. He took the hanger down and began to examine it.

"Now this," he said with a tone of growing satisfaction and picking up a corner of the long tunic that was bound in tailored fashion, "this seems—why, what is this? Trousers?"

"Yes, those are the knickerbockers," said Athalie. "I used to like that a lot, but I'm sort of tired of it. However, if you like it, I'll put it on. I thought maybe—but I'll put it on!"

She seized the hanger and slipped into the bathroom, returning in a brief space of time with the garment on. Patterson Greeves drew a long breath. She seemed to be clothed properly for the fist time. The lines were straight, the color was dark, her form did not appear so sensuous.

"Now that—" he began, "step out from behind the bed and let me see."

Athalie stepped out and walked.

"Why, what is that? Is it torn? Is it ripped? Why, how short it is!"

"No, those are open all the way up to the waist. That is the knickerbockers underneath. Haven't you been used to the knickerbockers suits? They're all the craze at school. I had one of the first that came out. I just made Lilla get it, or rather I bought it myself and sent the bill to her and told her I'd tell a friend of hers something she didn't want told if she didn't pay it—"

Athalie's tongue was rattling on eagerly, but Athalie's father was sick at heart. As she strode about the room, whirling in front of the long mirror on the old-fashioned bureau, her stout legs were revealed clad in green trousers that finished in a tailored cuff below the knee, and a full eight inches above this, brown tunic flopped and flared, making her a grotesque figure, neither man nor maid. A fashion that might have been tolerated or even fancied on a slender little child but was revolting on a girl of Athalie's age and build.

"Take it off," ordered the discouraged parent. "Haven't you anything decent at all?"

Athalie stopped, dismayed, and retreated half frightened into the other room. When she came out again, she was wearing the little orange dress, and she looked lonesome and unhappy.

Her father wheeled around from the window where he had been looking unseeingly into the garden—it was strange how the only relief from things sometimes is to look out the window and get a wider vision—and eyed her perplexedly.

"We'll have to go to town and do some shopping. I think it would be best to take your sister along—"

"She's *not* my sister! And I won't go if you take her! I thought you understood that!"

"That's not obedience, Athalie!"

The girl looked down stormily. "Well, then if you force her on me, I won't obey. I don't see why you want her along. She can't pick out my clothes! I wouldn't wear a rag she selected. You ask her if she would like what I chose for her."

The father reflected that that was probably true. Silver would certainly not look right in any of Athalie's clothes.

"Well, then we'll take the housekeeper," he temporized.

"That frumpy thing!" said Athalie.

"Well, who would you suggest?" He looked desperately at his daughter and wondered why a creature of so young an age should be able to perpetrate so much trouble and get away with it.

Athalie dimpled into a charming smile. "I don't see why you and I couldn't go just together. It's you that's to be suited, isn't it? And me that's to do the wearing? Well, then, what has anybody else to do with it?"

"I'm not at all certain that I—"

"Oh, if you don't know what you want—" began Athalie with a toss of her head.

"Very well," said her father with swift decision. "Get ready at once. I'll phone for a car. Can you be ready in half an hour?" He looked at his watch.

"Yes," she said brightly, casting a selective eye around her wardrobe.

"But what will you wear?" he asked, uneasily looking around trying to find something that would do. "I don't see anything here that is suitable."

Athalie pouted.

"Perhaps we'd better wait, and I'll telephone for something to be sent out on approval, a blue serge suit or something," he suggested helplessly.

Athalie darkened. "I've got an old tweed thing in the trunk. I hate it, but maybe you'd like it."

"Let me see it."

She pawed in her trunk a moment and fished out a brown tweed coat and skirt. He took it up and examined it, his face clearing.

"Now, that's what I call a nice, neat, sensible dress for a girl," he said. "Is it all whole? There aren't any slits or anything in it? Well, put that on, and some kind of a hat that doesn't look too fast, and dark stockings and gloves. And—Athalie, wash your face! *Wash* it, I mean!"

Athalie waited until he had closed the door and then she materialized her thought of him behind his back in a very forceful expression. Having thus unburdened her soul, she set about dressing hastily and, when she came downstairs, seemed to him quite presentable in her trim brown coat and skirt. The skirt was shorter and narrower than he would have desired, but it would have to do for the present, and she wore a small, neat hat of brown straw from which she had just extracted some kind of an ornament in feathers that resembled a burning bush. It was drawn down over her forehead till she looked quite demure, and her feet were quietly encased in brown stockings and tan oxfords with low heels and rubber soles. She wore gloves, and her whole aspect seemed to have changed. Looking on her now, her father wondered perhaps if it might not be possible sometime to even—well—rather like her.

That morning's shopping was an experience Patterson Greeves will never be likely to forget. He felt as if he were leading a wild young coyote by a chain, which might at any moment give way in his hand and let chaos loose in the stores. The number of things that Athalie picked out and her father disapproved were too numerous to mention. Sometimes they found a saleswoman who sided with the girl and took it upon herself to advise the father, and then Greeves went to another store. Again they fell to the hands of a prim, sharp woman who called Athalie "dearie" and patronized her, and the girl simply refused to try on or look at a thing under her guidance.

In his pocket, Patterson Greeves carried a brief memorandum, the result of a secret interview with Anne Truesdale, which he from time to time consulted anxiously as if it were a talisman that would somehow guide him through the mazes of this expedition. It read:

> *Four or five heavy gingham dresses for school.*
> *Two sprigged muslins for afternoons.*
> *A nice white dress for evening socials.*
> *A dark blue silk for best.*
> *Two serviceable blue serges made sailor style.*

Athalie had two methods. One was to go into ecstasies over something she liked, talk about its simplicity and its classic lines, and how sweet and quiet it was. The other was to walk off out of the department entirely and be found looking drearily out of a window when she saw her father's eye on something that did not interest her.

On the whole she worked things pretty well and came off with four wash silks, which, by the aid of the saleswoman, she had persuaded her father were now taking the place of ginghams, several crèpe de chines, a couple of linens, and a one-piece serge that cost twice as much as any dress she had ever owned before. If she was going to have to be severe and plain, by all means let it be on the severity of elegant simplicity. After a sumptuous repast at an irreproachable tearoom at which she ordered everything on the menu that captured her fancy—from lobster salad to café frappe— she carried her exhausted parent home triumphantly and spent the afternoon making little alterations in her purchases. He had selected them himself, hadn't he? Well, then he couldn't possibly find fault with anything about them. He would never know what she had done to them.

Life settled down quietly. Patterson Greeves got out some of his notes and began to put his papers away in the desk. Silver had sent word that she was spending the day at the Flats. There was nothing to hurt or annoy. He reflected that both Lizette Weldon and several of the Vandemeeters had appeared at their front windows or gates when he and Athalie had driven away and again when they returned. Surely Athalie's escapade would be forgotten if all went on in the conventional manner. Surely he might relax a little now.

From the region of the kitchen, there floated from time to time spicy, suggestive odors.

And the next day was the Sabbath.

Chapter 23

Mary Truman called for Athalie Greeves to take her to Sunday school.

Mary did not want to go. She had told all the girls at the school picnic the day before that she didn't intend to do it. She had cried for two hours and begged both father and mother to let her off, but they had insisted, and so with her neat blue serge suit and her blue straw sailor hat, her hair tied with a fresh ribbon, and her hands and feet encased in simple girlish fittings, she reluctantly swung the Greeves's gate open and slowly made her way up the path.

It was early. The first bell had only begun to ring. Mrs. Truman had insisted that she must give the stranger plenty of time to get ready. She had also, unknown to her daughter, telephoned Mr. Greeves that Mary was coming.

Patterson Greeves, having come down to breakfast in much better frame of mind than since he had returned to Silver Sands, had forgotten entirely that it was the Sabbath day or that there was such a thing as Sunday school to be dealt with. Indeed, left to himself he might have been persuaded to forget it altogether for this time, but when Mrs. Truman offered an escort, he jumped at it eagerly, and Athalie heard herself promised as a new scholar in the class with "that frumpy little Truman girl."

However, Athalie was going to be a good sport. When her father turned from the telephone and informed her that she must get ready for Sunday school, she looked up with just a flicker of a gasp and stared, but that was all. Quite like a lady, she arose from the table and went to her room. When she came down dressed in her brown tweed suit, gloves, hat, and shoes as she had dressed the day before for her trip to the city, her father looked her over almost with approval, and when he saw her go down the path beside Mary Truman, he sighed with relief. Perhaps she was going to be amenable to reason after all.

Mindful of her triple promise to her father, Athalie was quite polite, but in a lofty way, like a lion condescending to walk with a lamb.

"So kind of you to come for me," she said haughtily. "I never went to Sunday school before in my life. What do they do?"

"You—never went—to *Sunday school?*" Mary paused in horrified astonishment. "Why! Where have you lived? Didn't they *have* any Sunday school?"

"Why, I really don't know. I never inquired. Perhaps they had, but nobody said anything about it. I'm curious to see it! Is it as dull as day school?"

"Oh, day school isn't dull! We have lovely times. Silver Sands is said to have the best school in Silver County. We have the darlingest teachers! And debating society! And contests and athletics! Oh, it's great! I feel dreadfully when I'm sick and have to miss a day. I haven't missed a day now in two years, not since I had the measles."

"Dear me!" said Athalie. "I should think you'd be bored to death!

Do all those girls you brought to see me go to Sunday school?"

"Oh yes, of course. Everybody goes to Sunday school in Silver Sands. Most of them go to our church. Only Emily Bragg—she's a Methodist, but they have a nice Sunday school, too, only not so large. I was allowed to go with her once when she was going to speak on Children's Day. We have a lovely teacher. Her name's Pristina Appleby. She lives right across the street from you. She tells us very interesting things about the pyramids and the tablets they've dug up and things like that, you know. Sometimes she brings us pictures to help understand the lesson."

"Lesson? Do you have lessons? Mercy! I hate lessons."

"Oh, you won't hate this," laughed Mary. "She just talks. We call her Miss Prissie!"

"Oh! And this Miss Pussy! Is she an old maid?"

"Miss *Prissie*, I said. No, oh no, she isn't an old maid. Her aunts are that. She has three aunts and a grandmother and a great-grandmother, and they all live together in that brick house across the street from you."

"Oh! I hadn't noticed. Then she's a young girl."

"Well, not exactly young. She's not as young as your sister. I think *she's* lovely. We girls are all crazy about her. I'm so sorry you couldn't have come to the fudge party the other night. We had such fun. Your sister was wonderful! She started all the games—"

Athalie's face darkened, but she kept her stiffly polite manner, a trifle more haughty perhaps.

"Yes, it was a pity!" she drawled. "Is this your church? What are they ringing that bell for?"

"Why, for Sunday school."

"Oh! I thought somebody might be dead! I've read of that! You never can tell what curious thing they may do in a strange place, you know."

Mary started to giggle and then looked at her questioningly and grew red instead. Was this rude girl trying to make fun of her again?

"Especially in the country," added Athalie.

Mary said no more. Other girls and boys were standing around the entrance as they went up the path. Athalie stared at everyone as if she had come to a show and that was what was expected of her. Bannard came down the street from the other direction and lifted his hat gravely to Athalie. She dimpled and smiled.

"So he goes to Sunday school, too!" she remarked complacently.

"Why, yes of course," said Mary somewhat shortly. "He's the minister. Why shouldn't he come?" She was getting tired of the publicity of escorting this strange girl. She wished Sunday school were well over.

Athalie was much entertained all through Sunday school. She stared at everybody's clothes, kept her eyes wide open during prayer, watching the contortion of the superintendent's lips as he prayed. The other girls, dully devout, stole curious glances at her between their fingers. Her conduct of the day before had been carefully discussed at the dinner tables and a general taboo placed upon her as far as an associate for daughters was concerned. To find her in Sunday school was therefore a surprise. The more so as a rumor had been started by Pristina Appleby's essay at the club that Patterson Greeves was one of the new thinkers and had left the faith of his fathers to wander in dangerous speculations.

But when Sunday school was out, there was Patterson Greeves coming up the walk with Silver by his side, her sweet face smiling to everyone, her smile almost like a ray of sunshine, her eyes as blue as the dress she wore, and the little hat with its black feather. Athalie stood by the door with Mary Truman and watched them approach, noted her father's fine presence with pride, heard the whispered remarks about him, then heard, "Isn't she sweet!" and saw that all eyes were directed toward Silver. The sullen fires came back to her eyes. She looked around like a hunted thing and for an instant thought of bolting straight through the graveyard. Then her father's grave glance was upon her pleasantly, and her face lit up. He was not displeased with her then. She experienced a sudden surprised pleasure in it. Fiercely did she desire to belong to someone, to have someone care for her, to be able to please. All her life she had met with impatience and curbing. This father she had come determined to win to herself or die in the attempt. Deeply had she longed for a home and parents like other girls and had not had them. Perhaps she had, down deep in her heart, the thought that maybe somehow she might draw hers together. All her young life she had showered upon her selfish mother a degree of devotion, one might almost say adoration such as few real mothers get, and it had only returned upon itself in bitterness. The mother had regarded her lightly, tolerantly, cheerfully, yet if that mother had asked of her any sacrifice, no matter how great, the fierce young soul would have given it, gladly, freely. So now Athalie regarded her father with eyes of pride and of possession.

Another face just then picked itself out from the throng of churchgoers, a young face, strong and manly, vaguely familiar. He was standing under the willow tree near the gravestones, bare headed, cleanly shaven, neat and trim in a much brushed suit, talking to a group of other boys. Presently they sauntered over toward the steps, nodding to the girls who came by, calling out a pleasant word. Mary Truman stepped down below Athalie and spoke.

"Why, hello, Barry. Where were you Friday night? Didn't Mr. Bannard give you my invitation to the fudge party?"

Barry turned quickly and pleasantly. "Sorry, Mary, I didn't get home till late. Had an errand that kept me. Hear you had a great time. Save some fudge for me?"

Then he lifted his eyes and recognized Athalie. He did not speak. It was rather a lighting of the eyes, a pleasant understanding that gave her heart that warm glow, and she knew him for her captor of the midnight ride. After that Athalie was satisfied to stay and see this thing called church through to the finish.

Oh, she had been to church before of course. At school those things were compulsory. But there was something about this church, like a big family gathering of people who all liked each other and enjoyed being there, that was new to the girl. She stared around and wondered at it. Funny old women in strange bonnets, coats that were antique of cut; a few of recognized culture and education, though that counted very little as yet with Athalie; one or two with stylish clothes. She watched the Vandemeeter tribe file into the pew, Grandma first, slowly with a cane, Mother just behind, Henrietta helping Grandma, Maria in the same black broadcloth coat and black felt hat with the coque feather band she had worn for the last seven years. Maria was never one to put on summer clothes until summer was really there. Harriet and Cordelia with pink velvet roses wreathed around their last year's dyed straws. She eyed them curiously. Each a replica of the other in a different stage of life. What tiresome people. How did they endure life? She noted Grandma's bent head, Mother's closed eyes, the squarely folded handkerchiefs, the little tremble of the feathered bonnet when Henrietta handed Grandma the hymnbook. Everything was strange and unusual to Athalie. She wondered why such common people want to *be*, why they seemed to take an *interest* in being. Why did her father stay in a place like this when there were cities where things were going on, wild, merry life for which she thirsted?

She was surprised to see Barry sitting in the back row of the choir. How strange for a boy like that to be willing to waste his time this way!

Suddenly Bannard's voice arrested her attention. He was telling a story, though he seemed to have a small leather book open in his hand as if he was about to read. He painted a picture with his words. She forgot the sunny church with its bright carpet and unfashionable congregation. She was seeing a walled city in a strange land, under a blazing sky with hungry faces looking out from little slits of windows in towers and turrets, and an army camped around on every hand. They had been there days and days and had starved out the stronghold. The people were reduced to eating loathsome things. An ass's head, something that would not be thought of as food at another time, sold for about forty dollars, coarse chickpeas were selling at a prohibitive price. Even the king and his court were starving.

The king was walking on the wall, visiting his sentries. You could see his face, lined with anxiety, as he shaded his eyes and looked out across the sea of enemies' tents. There was no sign of discouragement on the part of that enemy. They had come to stay until the city surrendered. They knew it would not be long. They had spies who had discovered its state. They were well supplied with food themselves and had nothing to do but eat and drink and make merry until they had worn out the resources of the people and there was nothing left for them but to surrender. The king sighed and passed on; as he went, someone reached out and caught his robe with clawlike hands, a woman from the doorstep of one of the little hovels on the wall. There were deep hollows under her eyes and in her cheeks. She looked more like a skeleton than a woman. "Help!" she cried. "Help, my lord, O king!"

The king drew away impatiently. So many cried for help, and what could he do? "Curse you!" he said impatiently. "With every barn floor bare and every winepress empty, what can I do?" And he turned as if to pass on. But the woman continued her strange, weird cry and began a terrible story. Another woman appeared, crouching frightened against the doorway.

"This woman promised if I would kill my baby boy yesterday and cook and eat him that she would kill hers today, but we ate my son yesterday, and now she has hid hers today. I pray you, O king, speak to her. Make her give up her son that she has hid."

Athalie's eyes were wide with horror. She had never heard a story like that.

The speaker depicted the horror on the face of the king as he listened to the tale and watched the faces of the hunger-crazed women, realized that he was powerless to aid, that things could only grow worse rather than better, that the Lord in whom he had put at least a little of his trust had apparently deserted him, and then he laid hold on his kingly robe and tore it.

Like a crowd of children, the listening congregation attended, not an eye looked dreamy, not a brain was planning out tomorrow's work nor calculating the sum of yesterday's mistakes. The Bible lived and breathed before them as Bannard spoke. They saw that king reach down and tear his robe as he passed on; they were among those who looked beneath and saw the sackcloth next to his skin, oriental symbol of humiliation, of repentance, of prayer. They caught a glimpse of King Jehoram's past, his mother the wicked queen Jezebel, his father of whom it was written, "There was none like unto Ahab, which did sell himself to work wickedness in the sight of the Lord."

One saw that Jehoram was not quite so bad as his father and mother. He put away the image of Baal that his father had set up for worship to please his mother, but he worked evil in the sight of the Lord.

The king on the wall in the torn robe, with the sackcloth showing beneath, suddenly turned and swore a terrible oath that he would have the head of God's prophet that day, the prophet who had been promising day after day that God would deliver them from the enemy; and now they were come to the great extremity and God was not helping. Why should he wait for God any longer?

The king walked to his palace and sent a messenger to the little house where Elisha lived. One saw the soldier from the palace hurry along with sword in hand down the narrow streets of odd, flat-topped oriental houses, and Elisha sitting quietly in his door talking to some of the old men and suddenly lifting his eye to his servant and saying in a quiet voice: "The king is sending a soldier to behead me. Shut the door and lock it. The king will be here presently. Keep the soldier out till he comes."

The hurrying feet, the hastily shut door, the altercation. Athalie sat breathless with glowing eyes of wonder. The impudent air of the king as he came, the parley: "Behold, this evil is of the Lord; what should I wait for the Lord any longer?" And Elisha's quiet voice answering, "Hear ye the word of the Lord. This time is up! Tomorrow about this time shall a measure of fine white flour be sold at less than prewar prices."

"Ha!" the laugh of the servant on whom the king leans. "If God were opening windows in heaven just now this might be!"

The quiet rebuke: "You shall see it but not eat thereof."

Night drops quickly, suddenly in that eastern land. Twilight on the white parched city where skulking shadows pass on the wall and huddled human beings sleep and forget for a little while their sufferings. The king in his palace asleep. No faith whatever in what Elisha promised. Twilight outside the wall in the little leper village, four lepers waiting at the gate, starving, talking it over. Shall they throw themselves on the mercy of the enemy, beg something to eat? "If they kill us, we shall but die anyway!" The hesitant approach, peering like white ghosts into the first tent, the pause, the eager going forward. No one there! The table spread. They snatch the food and devour it, and move on to the next, suddenly are struck with the silence throughout the great camp. The hurrying investigation then the hastening back to the city to tell, the waking of the unbelieving king, the five men sent to verify the story, the garments strewn in the way as the enemy fled, the rejoicing, the crowding out of the city to spoil tents of the enemy, crushing out the life of the astonished servant who had laughed the day before! The wonderful reason of the enemy's flight, that the Lord had caused a sound of horses to be heard by them!

Athalie looked around the church to see if anybody was really believing it. Where did they get a strange story like that? The Lord! *The Lord!* How strange that sounded, as if the Lord was a real person! Did her father believe that? She glanced at him as he sat with stern listening attitude, his gloved hands on his knee. She couldn't tell whether he was astonished at it or not. She listened again. The minister was talking now about world problems. He said the world was waiting today as then for the Lord to deliver them from a state of siege into which their own sin and folly had placed them, and blaming God that He did not come. They were tired of wearing sackcloth and ready to do murder. When all the time God's wonderful tomorrow was waiting, just over the way, waiting for them to reach the limit of their own possibilities that God might show His power and grace. He said that the troubles of the world would never be solved and peace never come until Christ came into human hearts, and that all these things pointed to a time close at hand when some tomorrow about this time Christ Himself was coming back to relieve His own forever from a state of siege.

Athalie never took her eyes from the face of the speaker during this closing talk. She had never heard anything like it in her life before. It made realities out of what had been vague mythical stories, like fairy tales, before. Was there really a Jesus Christ then? He died, didn't He, long ago? On a cross? What did they mean, *coming again*?

She was silent and thoughtful all that day. Her father looked at her relieved. She wandered around the house, played a few little jazzy tunes on the piano—which scandalized the Vandemeeters and Lizette, who both made it a point to listen intently for any sign of a hymn tune—then drifted away to her room and her fast-disappearing stock of chocolates and literature.

Silver had gone to the mission school at the Flats. The house was silent all the afternoon, with a Sabbath stillness Athalie had never known before. Sabbath meant nothing to her but a merrier day than usual, the focus of the merriment of the week.

Mary Truman, still under parental pressure, called for her to go to Christian Endeavor that evening, and because Athalie saw nothing else to do, and her father and Silver were talking in the library before the fire, she went. She wondered if the strange boy would be there. Barry. What a nice name!

He was there. He passed her a hymnbook and looked pleased when she came into the bright little chapel room where they met. He sang in a quartet, growling a nice low bass. She watched him wonderingly, remembering how he had held her like a vise when she tried to get the wheel away from him. Remembering how gently he had lifted her and carried her.

It seemed a strange meeting. The girls and boys spoke, just like a frat meeting at school, only they said odd things. They referred to the sermon of that morning as if they were altogether familiar with the story of that siege. They spoke of Mr. Bannard as if he were a brother and comrade. Mr. Bannard was there among them, just like one of them. It was rather interesting, only it was embarrassing when they prayed. She didn't know what to do with her eyes, so she watched them all.

That boy Barry gave an announcement about a committee

meeting after service. Two others jumped up and spoke about socials that were being planned. They all seemed so eager and friendly. Athalie felt lonely and outside everything.

When they went in the church again, there was Silver sitting with her father. Mary asked her politely to come in their seat, and she went. She did not want to sit beside Silver again.

Mr. Bannard spoke about the coming of Christ. He made it plain that He was really coming, and that some people, good people presumably, for Athalie did not understand that language about "believers," were to be taken away and the world would wonder where they had gone. Athalie looked over at Silver. She thought Silver would be one that would be taken away. Well, that would be good. She hated good people, and she would be left with her father. It was reasonably sure a noted man of the world like her father wouldn't be taken away from earth like that. He didn't have that spirit-look that Silver wore as a garment. It frightened her a little— this talk about the Son of God coming back to earth. She hoped on second thought that it wouldn't come till she was old, very old, and didn't care about living anymore. It stayed with her after she got home, and when she went to bed and thought of Lilla in a little boat on the great ocean, she cried a few tears sorrowfully. Lilla was the only god she had ever had.

On the whole, she was rather docile about going to school the next morning when her father suggested that she enter high school and finish out the spring term. She remembered what Barry had said about athletics and resolved not to eat any more chocolates for a week after this last box was gone.

So she polished her nails to a delicate point and took herself languidly to school to see how she liked it. She was astonished to see how little impression she made on the wholesome atmosphere of high school. The teacher, a placid-faced elderly woman with a firm chin, said to be the finest school principal in the county, smiled at her pleasantly and put her in the front seat directly in front of the desk. None of the boys gave her a glance, except Barry who showed mere recognition. The girls she had met smiled politely and went on with study. Whenever she looked up, she was met with that pleasant challenge of a smile. There was absolutely no opportunity to get away with anything unless one first crossed that friendly smile, and Athalie wasn't just exactly ready to do that yet until she had tried things out. There had not been too many smiles in her life. She took the book that was handed to her to read, until the principal should have time to examine her and place her in the classes where she fit, and was surprised to find it was an interesting novel. The teacher explained it was the book the English class was reading for review and discussion that week.

Her father glanced into the study hall half an hour later, after an inspection of the building led by an old friend who was the Latin teacher, and saw her absorbed in the book. He went home with a sigh of relief, comforted.

But that very night Athalie wrote eleven invitations to six boys and five girls for a house party that weekend and mailed them early in the morning before she went to school. But that no one in her family knew.

Chapter 24

The tramp had found work as a laborer in the glass factory through the efforts of some of the good Presbyterian women whose woodpiles had been supplying his breakfasts and dinners for some time. He worked feebly and with great effort and managed to maintain his role of semi-elderly invalid who was doing his best.

He was working with a gang of other men shoveling sand into a cart when Silver Greeves came by with a basket of broth and oranges and a lovely dolly for the little Mary who was now on the high road to recovery.

The tramp paused in the monotony of his service. He put in regularly one shovelful to the other men's two. He always paused longest for interruptions and rested his weary back. The other men paused also and watched the progress of the lithe girl as she stepped down the roughly cobbled path and entered the cottage.

"That's that girl from the Silver family," said one of the men. "Take notice of her? She's been comin' down to that wop's house every day. She's been takin' care of the sick kid."

"Well, they'd oughta do things like that. They got plenty, ain't they? Don't we keep 'em in cash with our labor? They couldn't sell this sand if we didn't shovel it, could they? She'd make a pretty hand shovelin' sand, now, wouldn't she? How would she live if we didn't shovel her sand fer her, I ask you?"

"Oh, they got plenty else 'thout sand. Anymore. They got stacks and stacks of money. I heard they got sompin' like a million fer the railroad right of way. She'd oughta take notice of the poor folks. I guess that family wasn't named Silver fer nothin'."

The tramp gazed steadily at the door where Silver had disappeared and began to turn around what he heard in his cunning old brain. He let his companions heave five shovelfuls before he started in again at a rapidly diminishing sandpile, and his face wore a thoughtful look. Whenever he stopped to rest, he eyed the house where Silver had entered. When she finally came out, lingering on the doorstep to talk with the smiling dark-eyed mother, he took another break and studied the scene carefully, talking in details of dress and height and coloring. Then his cunning eyes dropped to his task again and lifted for an instant to meet hers only when Silver passed opposite him, as she smiled and greeted them all in a friendly way.

"Some gurrul!" remarked a short burly man with red curls and a brogue. "The master must be proud o' her. I guess he'd not take all his millions for the likes of her!"

"Yes, she's a fine lady! But it'll take plenty of millions to keep her in all she'll want," grouched the other man.

"Well, what's a lady!" said the tramp as he lifted another shovelful of sand.

Down by the bridge Silver met Bannard and lingered there to watch the little fishes darting in the stream. She had much to tell him of the condition of some of the families she had visited. Sam was bringing his wife over from Italy, and Carmen was having trouble getting his citizenship papers. Something about his questionnaire during the war. He had not understood enough English to make out what they were asking him, and he couldn't write it himself, so some absurd mistake had been made. Could he see the county judge and straighten it out?

Bannard finally turned and walked back with her through Sweetbriar Lane, into Aunt Katie's for a moment to get a taste of the honey cakes she was baking, and so on through the hedge into the sweet old Silver garden. They lingered talking beside the sundial, tracing the quaint figures on its face, watching the slow, sure march of the sun from point to point.

There was powdered gold in the air and sunshine, powdered fire shimmering over the tulip bed. The birds sang with joyous abandon as though they would split their throats. Greeves looked out of his window from his work, and his heart was at rest. That was a nice fellow. A bit wrong in his head knowledge and his beliefs but all right in his heart and living. And after all, if one could believe in the old legends, they were a wonderful safeguard. Far be it for him to disturb such saintly faith. He would be careful what he said about unbelief. It almost seemed as if what the minister had said had been true. Things had settled down into a pleasanter way. The siege was lifting, but of course God had nothing to do with it. It was merely the adjusting of all elements to the environment. It was sound philosophy anyway, to be patient and wait for things to adjust themselves. Then he went back to his preface, which he was writing with great care.

"If the present advance of science—" How was it he had meant to phrase that sentence?

And down in the garden the two had sauntered into the summerhouse and were telling each other about their early life. It is a beautiful stage of friendship when two who admire one another reach that point. It is the building of a foundation for something deeper and truer.

Well for them that the garden was located behind the house, with tall hedges surrounding, and that neither the Weldons nor Vandemeeters could penetrate, and only the kindly eye of Aunt Katie knew where they were, or the whole town would have been agog. They found so much to talk about that the minister forgot to go back to the Flats until the lunch bell rang in the Silver house, and then he made his sudden apologies and departed hastily over the fence. Silver went in with flushed cheeks and bright eyes thinking how wonderfully life was opening out for her who had been only such a short time before bereft and alone.

Athalie came home from school quite pleasant and tractable. She had an armful of books, and she seemed interested in them. Her father looked the books over and talked with her a little about them, gave her a few hints how to concentrate on studying, and went away to his library again entirely satisfied that he was doing the father-part as well as could be expected. Perhaps after he got used to it it wouldn't be so bad after all.

Meantime Athalie up in her room was working with needle and thread and scissors to transform several of her new frocks for Friday evening, while her books lay in a heap on the floor not to be touched until the next morning, and her thoughts were wandering in daydreams.

About half a mile below the bridge at the lower end of Silver Sands, to the left of the road where it curves around to go to Frogtown, there rises a little hill. On its top, set in a thick grove of maples, birches, and oaks with plenty of undergrowth, there stands a little one-roomed hut. It had been built of field stones a long time ago, when the grove was a big woods of sugar maples, perhaps for a shelter at sugaring time. There was a fireplace at one end, a little prisonlike window, and a sagging wooden door. The window was boarded up, and the door had stood ajar for years. The boys of the town used to use it for a rendezvous but had long since deserted it for newer quarters below the bridge where some enterprising seniors in high school had built a camp among the pines.

The tramp had sighted this empty dwelling, and after watching it for several days and sampling its hospitality at night, he took up his abode there, repaired the door, unnoticeably, left the window boarded up, and built his meager fires at night when no one would see the smoke. There was plenty of wood around for the taking.

The floor was the bare earth, and in one corner a pile of leaves and moss made a bed, with an old blanket he had taken from somebody's clothesline down in the village. In a big packing box that he had found behind the cannery quite early one morning, he kept his frugal stores: eggs, butter, bread, tobacco, half a ham, and a big black bottle. The top of the box served as his table.

Here he crept at evening when his shoveling was done, taking care to arrive by a circuitous route and to close the door before lighting his bit of a candle. Here at evening he sat with his pipe and pondered many a scheme or went over and over the various mistakes and failures of his life, which had landed him in confinement within stone walls for a time, and searched how he might carry something through yet again.

That same night he crept to his lair and sat on the sheltered side looking away toward the village thinking. Through its nest of trees, he could see the white pillars of the Silver house standing as it did at the top of the street, lifting its head just a trifle above the other houses. As the twilight deepened and darkness gave opportunity for Sin to walk abroad unrecognized, he loitered down the hill and crept by unused paths into the town where he had a few patrons who kept their little odd jobs for him at night. They talked about him in their sewing circle and said he was a self-respecting man, and one had given him a shirt and one some pairs of much darned socks, and they talked about helping him to find a place to board where he could look after the furnace for his keep when winter came on. Drab he was as he walked along in the shadow side of the moonlit street, and drab he faded into space when he came to a high hedge. Carefully he stole around the old Silver place, and felt out the garden paths, and peered in cautiously at all the windows. He studied the lines of Patterson Greeves's thoughtful face as he sat at his desk working on that preface, and judged it cannily with the eye of a specialist. He put his ugly mask to the very pane of glass beside Silver's head as she sat reading in the big easy chair at the other end of the library. He cautiously searched the darkened drawing room with a pocket flashlight, and he took in the dining room, especially the silver on the sideboard, while Anne and Molly were setting the table for the next morning's breakfast. The kitchen was not so easy, but he managed it while Joe and Molly and Anne sat eating their dinner.

"I thought I saw a face at the window, Joe. Go out and see if someone is looking for you," said Anne in her calm voice, and Joe shoved back his chair noisily and went out but came back presently and reported that Anne was "seein' things."

"It must be the young huzzy upstairs is gettin' on yer nerves, Anne."

"The young lady's all right the last two days," said Anne complacently. Athalie's church going and willingness to go to school had done much toward mollifying Anne. "And *I saw* a face at the window. It was likely Jock Miller brought back that sickle you lent him. I'm

581

not so old that I can't tell a face at the window when I see it."

Back in the lilac bushes among the lilies-of-the-valley a drab shape huddled, listened, and presently shrunk away, puzzling. That wasn't the young lady he saw pass the firehouse that day. Were there two?

For the rest of that week, life settled down into the grooves of what a well-regulated family life should be, and Patterson Greeves took heart and plunged into his book. Athalie had been regular at school, late only once, and seemed to be giving actual attention to her studies. She professed to be deeply interested in education for the first time in her life and took her books upstairs to her room immediately after dinner at night. Her father began to hope that perhaps she had inherited his love of study. Several times she came to him with some question about her lessons. Usually some unusual question. She was sharp as a needle. Would he ever learn to be proud of her?

Friday morning as Athalie was about to start for school she stepped into the dining room where Anne was crumbing the table preparatory to taking off the breakfast cloth and said loftily: "Oh, Truesdale! Have plenty of cake ready this afternoon. I'm bringing guests."

"There's always plenty of cake in the house," said Anne stiffly. She wasn't sure she cared for being called Truesdale. Of course it was English, but she had an inkling that in this case it was intended for patronage.

"I mean—*lots*!" said Athalie. "There'll be about twelve of us altogether."

"There's always cake enough in the house for twenty if need be!" Anne froze.

"They'll all be here for dinner, I think," added Athalie as she closed the door and ran down the steps. "I told Dad about it."

Now it happened that "Dad" had gone to the city on the seven o'clock train to consult a book in the library.

"It's strange he said nothing to me about it. He's always that particular about making trouble," said Anne as she reported the invasion to Molly.

"Aw, that's all right, Anne," said Molly cheerfully. "You'd oughta be glad she's going to be friendly with the townspeople. We'll just get up a real dinner, Anne. He seems real satisfied with the way she's took to school."

"Yes," agreed Anne grudgingly, "but I'd a been better satisfied if the master had a spoke to me hisself."

The house was always spic-and-span. Anne saw to it that there were flowers in the vases and the best doilies as if for a company of ladies.

"Because them children has eyes and tongues in their heads," she explained to Molly who came in to consult her as to whether she should make hard sauce or boiled sauce for the bread pudding that was destined for lunch.

Athalie telephoned at noon that she was not coming home for lunch.

"She'll be taking it with some of the girls!" Anne said happily. "It's nice to think of her gettin' in and bein' like other girls. Mebbe she'll get rid of her strange hair and eyebrows someday. I think she might be passable lookin' if she didn't dress so strange! Now them dresses he bought her. They looked real simple, but when she gets um on they somehow look diffrunt. But I'm sorry she didn't come home, I wanted to ask her more about who's coming? How'll we know to set the table?"

"Oh, there'll be time when she comes! Half past three is plenty." So they set about the delightful task of getting up a young dinner party again in the old house, which had not happened since Master Pat's twenty-first birthday.

It was nearing three o'clock when a taxi from the city drew up at the door causing great sensation over at the Vandemeeter's. They could not figure out who this might be.

A young woman got out and paid the driver, preceding him up the walk to the house as he carried two armfuls of luggage.

"She's all tails around her feet," said Grandma Vandemeeter, "and I can see myself without any glasses that she's got a painted face even if she has got a mosquito netting over her hat."

"This is Marcella Mason," announced the stranger as Anne opened the door. "I suppose you're expecting me. I'll just have my bags carried up to my room at once. I'm frightfully dusty. Hot water, please. I suppose you have plenty of it here in the country? If not, please heat it at once. I'm accustomed to a hot bath."

A silver dollar, skillfully manipulated, slid into Anne's astonished hand and out again to the floor quicker than it went in. She stepped back indignantly, with blazing cheeks and snapping eyes.

"Is that your money, miss? You dropped it!" she said crisply.

"Why, that's your tip!" laughed the girl. "Don't you want it?"

"Tip?" repeated Anne with her chin aloft. "Tip? I don't understand you. You'd best pick it up, miss, or it'll get lost. You can step this way." She led the way up the wide stair, thinking rapidly. It was not a possibility that this upstart should occupy one of the best rooms. Anne led her down the back hall to a little bedroom off the sewing room where a seamstress sometimes stayed. Neat and trim it was with a single iron bed, a bit of a bureau, and a stationary washstand. The Silver house was not behind the times in the matter of conveniences.

"You can put your things down on the chair," said Anne indifferently.

The stranger advanced and surveyed the room. "Oh, I'm afraid this room won't do for me!" She looked around. "No mirror. And don't you have private baths? What other rooms have you? I came first to make my choice. This seems to be a large house."

"This is the only one, miss. You can take it or leave it, as you like. I'm busy just now. You'll have to excuse me. Miss Athalie will be home from school in a short while."

"School! You don't mean to tell me she goes to school! That's rich! She swore she'd never enter a schoolroom again!"

Anne gave her a withering glance and departed with indignation.

"You should see the huzzy!" she told Molly. "Rings on her fingers and jewels on her toes. And the impertinence of her! Offering me money like a porter in a hotel. Well, I wonder what the master'll be saying now!"

"The master just called up while you was upstairs. He says he may miss the first train and not to wait for him, to go right on and have dinner. I guess he thought he'd like to get out of the fuss of it."

"Well, I shouldn't wonder! I wish Miss Athalie were here. Miss Silver hasn't got back from the Flats yet, has she? She's a good girl. She would go see to that thing upstairs. Keep watch for her comin', and tell me. I'll warn her afore she goes up the stairs."

But Silver was helping an Italian woman to make a little dress for her baby and did not come home until five o'clock. Before that time, many things had happened.

Before Athalie arrived, the three o'clock train had come in and a troop of young people—shouting, laughing, hooting at every person they passed, criticizing the houses, jeering at the stores—came pouring down the street. Their baggage followed in Hoskin's delivery truck, with two men on behind to help and observe. The girls were attired in the most striking outfits and lolled on the boys' arms, pulled off each other's hats and threw them into the street, and in

585

general conducted themselves with great indiscretion. The villagers came to their front windows in astonishment and deep disapproval, and one woman even telephoned for the police who happened to be away from his headquarters at that moment.

They stormed up on the Silver's front veranda like a hurricane, having inquired of everyone they met where "Greeves" lived, and while they awaited the answer to their continuous and imperious knocking, two girls and a young man had a skirmish in the yard, incidentally breaking off three of Joe's most cherished hyacinth blooms.

Then down the stairs with boisterous laughter tripped the young woman who had arrived in a taxi and opened the door before the scandalized Anne could get farther than the pantry.

"Oh, boy! I guess I put one over on you this time!" screamed the girl.

The horde swarmed in, slinging caps and handbags in every direction.

"Here's Marcy! I say, that isn't fair, Marcy! You got the best room! You always do."

"Come on up and take your choice. There's not so awful many as I thought there'd be. The old prune that showed me up gave me a sort of servant's room, but I got rid of her and went around till I found what I wanted. I take the left-hand front, and I've got my door locked so you needn't try to get in. I'll take Maebeth with me and nobody else. There's plenty of room. I've been everywhere. You two girls better take that other front room. There's somebody's things in there, but you should worry. Possession is how many points? I forget. Violet better go with Athe. Her things are in that second door. Say, boys, did you bring the booze? Plenty of it? Isn't that great. We'll have a real time! You boys better go up to the third story. There's five big rooms up there! Come on, Beth, let's hurry and get dressed before Ath comes. She goes to school! Isn't that the limit? She must have some old grouch of a governor! Don't say anything. His clothes must be in this closet, and I'm going down to dinner in *his dress suit!*"

"Oh, Marcy! Do you *dare*, Marcy?"

"My soul!" said Anne Truesdale. "What'll we do? Do you think maybe I better send for the minister? Oh, I wish you had told me Master Pat was on the phone."

"But you didn't know it then."

"Well, no, but I coulda told him about there being company."

"Well, you didn't. I guess that harum-scarum'll be home pretty soon. There she comes now, running! I'd give her a piece of my mind, I certainly would!"

Chapter 25

But before Anne could get into the hall, Athalie had stormed up the stairs and there ensued such greetings as made the old house sound like a vaudeville show behind the scenes. The girls in various stages of disarray opened doors to call to her; the boys issued from a cloud of cigarette smoke on the third floor by way of the old mahogany stair rail and came shooting into their midst amid howls and screams and pretended running to cover. Anne hurried up to do something about it and resembled an old hen running from the person who was trying to catch it while she clucked at her young to get out of the way. But she made no impression whatever on the young people until suddenly a great stalwart youth discovered her in his way and stooping over said, "Here, Auntie, what are you doing here?" and picking her up like a child, ran fleetly down the stairs with her in his arms, depositing her on the table in the hall and vanishing up again in three strides.

Anne, when she recovered her breath, crept fearsomely into the pantry white and spent, her dignity drooping like a broken feather, and while she stood panting, her hand on her heart, her back against

588

the swing door, a gentle hand pushed it, and Silver's voice said: "It's only me, Anne. What is the matter upstairs?"

"It's a 'ouse party!" sobbed Anne, and buried her face in Silver's neck. "They've took the master's room, and Miss Lavinia's. I don't know what the master'll say when he comes. And your things! They maul everything they lay their hands on, Miss Silver. Oh, I oughta have prevented this! I oughta! I oughta! I'm no housekeeper at all to let this come behind his back. I'm getting old! I'm no good anymore—"

"There, there, Anne, don't feel so badly. There isn't any harm done. They are only a parcel of kids out having a good time, and it's gone to their heads. Don't worry. Father won't blame you. It's Athalie, I suppose. Let's try to see what we can do to make everything move off quietly. How long are they going to stay? Just for dinner?"

"I don't know. I don't know! She said a 'ouse party, that first one that come. How long does that last? As long as the 'ouse stays together, I'm thinking, and that'll not be long if they carry on as they have been goin'. They've slid down my nice polished stair rails, and there'll be scratches on everything. And I've kept it all so nice all the years! Oh, dear, oh dear!"

"Never mind, Anne, it won't be half so bad as it seems. Cheer up, and get dinner ready. Are you going to try to have tea?"

"Deary knows! Miss Athalie ordered cake made before she left this morning. And me a-thinkin' she was that good a girl to please her father an' invite the neighbor's children home from school to have a good time an' make 'em forget how she treated 'em Saturday afternoon!"

"Well, never mind. I'll go upstairs and see if I can't stop that noise."

Silver went, but her arrival proved no more than if she had been a fly on the wall. The girls and boys were having a scuffle in the hall, and one girl's dress was half pulled off of her. They did not even glance at Silver as she hurried by them to take refuge in her room and think what she ought to do. But two other girls were in there attired in lacy lingerie, and one was smoking a cigarette.

"I beg your pardon," she said pleasantly. "I think someone has made a mistake. This room is occupied. If you will let me help you gather up your things, I will show you to another room."

Silver did this, not because she was so disturbed at having her room taken as because Anne had felt so strongly about Miss Lavinia's sacred chamber being desecrated.

The girls simply stared. "Who are you?" asked the girl who was powdering her face at the glass.

"I am Miss Greeves. Athalie's sister. You must be her school friends."

"Oh, I know who you are. You're that baby that was given away. Your name isn't Greeves at all. It's Jarvis. Ath told us all about you. You needn't bother about us; she put us here, and we'd rather stay. You can take your own things out if you want to." The girl turned back to the mirror with an air of having dismissed her. Silver reflected for an instant. What chance had she to maintain her rights against such insolence? She would frustrate her desire of quieting the company and getting control of things if she was not a perfect lady. She was amazed that girls could say such things. There must be a whole school of them, bred in the same atmosphere.

The color had fluttered into her face at the insulting words, but her sense of humor came to her assistance, and as once before she had foiled insolence by her silvery laugh, so now she let it out again until the visiting girls turned and stared. They even grew a little red. They had intended to make her angry, and now she laughed!

With a quick turn, Silver went out of the room and closed the door.

"Boys!" she said, placing a firm hand on the arm of the scuffling gentleman nearest her, "I know where there's some awfully good cake.

If you'll follow me and be perfectly quiet about it, I'll get it for you!"

Instantly every boy of the six was surrounding her and clamoring with all his might, even attempting to lift her off her feet and carry her down the stairs.

But there was something about Silver when she chose to be like that that awed every boy in the vicinity. Her spirit face suddenly could become grave and stern, with a power of command that arrested the attention and demanded respect.

"No, you've got to be perfectly quiet!" she said smilingly. "The spell won't work unless you do! No quiet, no cake!"

Athalie had forgotten when she summoned all these gorgeous young hoodlums to dissipate her gloom and informed them well about her unbeloved sister, that Silver was a girl and that a boy will "fall for anything" sometimes, as she said with a shrug that very evening. To the amazement of the other girls, the boys became tame at once, and Silver led them all off quietly down the stairs and to the drawing room where she rang the bell and said in low tone: "Anne, dear, would you bring that cake now?"

The "Anne dear" got it. Anne brought the cake in bountiful supply, and Silver, improving the brief and shining hour, got all their names and made quite a little ceremony learning them so she would remember.

The boys were quite pleased with her, and she held them there with talk about things boys like. Dogs and athletics and national games. She had seen some big ones. She talked familiarly about some of the fraternities they longed to be called to join, she spoke of college, and with just that rare flattery of smile and camaraderie that touches a boy of seventeen and brings him to her feet, she sat on a low divan and chatted with them, bringing burst after burst of gruff laughter and winning them thoroughly as her friends.

In the middle of an exciting recital of how a famous baseball team got ahead of an opposing team that was employing unfair measures to win the game, they all became aware of a hostile presence standing on the stairs.

Athalie had come down in gorgeous array in a short dress of gold tissue strapped over the shoulders and down the skirt in floating panels with peacock feathers. Around her forehead was bound a band of green and blue sequins, and the gold tissue of which her stockings were composed was so exceedingly sheer as to give the effect of bare skin above the tiny jeweled gold shoes. Nobody would have bought such an outfit for a young girl, but Lilla had been regal in it once upon a time, and the long pendulum earrings that dangled from the ears of her daughter and gave her such an Egyptian-princess effect had been especially designed in jewels to match the costume for some great occasion. It might be possible that Lilla on the high seas knew nothing of the whereabouts of some of her most-valued possessions. Athalie had helped herself as she chose before her departure.

But Athalie's face was marked with disdain, jealousy, and hate in startling lines. Silver rose quickly with a smile that faded as she saw the girl's fixed look as if she were not there at all. Athalie was determined to ignore her among these her friends. How could she put up any kind of a front against that? And yet she must for her father's sake, and keep things within bounds if possible until his return. It occurred to her that she might telephone Bannard and ask him to dinner. He would help her and know what to do, but supposing anything unforeseen should occur, anything out of the conventional order that should get out, it might not be good that the minister should be known to have been there. She had been brought up to think of those things. She had not been a minister's granddaughter for nothing. Therefore she shut her firm young lips and determined to fight it out alone.

She was wearing a crêpe de chine dress of soft gray the right tint to bring out the pink in her cheeks and the gold in her hair and lashes. It was simple of line and girded with a sash, itself heavily fringed and knotted at one side hanging a little below the deep hem of her skirt. She wore no jewelry, and the elbow sleeves and round neck were without decoration. It was scarcely a dinner gown for a formal affair, yet she could not have changed if she wished since the invasion of her room, and she would not if she could. There were more important things at hand.

Her sister's attitude plainly dismissed her, but she rose and deliberately turned her conversation to one of the boys nearest her, ignoring the look, and finally Athalie spoke, as one speaks to an inferior: "You don't need to eat with us, Alice Jarvis. It will make an uneven number. We have just men enough to go around."

"Oh, that's all right," said Silver with a careless smile, "Father'll be here pretty soon, you know," and went on talking to the admiring boy, although her heart was beating wildly and she wished herself far away from this scene of dissension and frivolity.

"Oh, very well. Suit yourself!" said Athalie with her haughtiest voice and began to devote herself to the entire group and attract them all from Silver.

Silver slipped out of the room and went back upstairs. If she could keep the bunches of girls and boys apart till dinner was ready, it might help. She went from room to room offering help. Had they all the towels they needed? Could she help them with their dresses or play ladies' maid in any way? Would they like ice water? Her insistent, pleasant service met with no response except silence. They whispered behind her back and exchanged glances. She saw that the way ahead was to be most unpleasant, but she went steadily on ignoring the meaning of their attitude. She was the pleasant elder sister waiting on her younger sister's guests.

But she had committed what was to them an unpardonable sin. She had taken their devoted admirers away from them and interested them herself. That could never be forgiven.

Silver was very tired when at last the scene changed to the dinner table. She had placed herself at the head and was there as they came into the room, acting the part of hostess. Athalie stopped and looked furiously at her but finally decided to get her revenge some other way and, leaving the other end seat unoccupied, proceeded to seat her guests to suit her own purposes.

The chairs were all filled but one.

"Marcy! Where are you? You sit at the corner next to Dad's seat. Hurry. I'm starved."

Marcella Mason, who had just ripped downstairs and was entering from the hall, paused a moment, lifting up a monocle on a long silk cord.

"Good evening, gents and women!" she saluted elegantly. "So glad you all could come!"

Every eye turned toward the doorway, and then a shout arose, gradually growing into a roar.

"Marcy! Marcy! Look at Marcy!"

For Marcella Mason was attired in Patterson Greeves's full dress suit—broad white shirtfront, patent leather shoes, and all—and looked the very personification of impudence and daring.

Silver and Anne Truesdale had agreed before dinner was served that whatever happened they would keep their composure and not look shocked nor horrified. Poor Anne Truesdale scuttled hurriedly into the pantry. This was too much for her. Silver struggled with her irritation and mastered a grave little smile. It was rude of course, impudent, but only a prank, after all. It was not for her to deal with a thing like this. Her father would be here pretty soon. Oh, that he might arrive at once!

From the start, the hilarity was uproarious. Several times bits of bread went whizzing back and forth across the table that had for years seen gathered around it grave and dignified and honored men and women. Anne trembled for the delicate long-stemmed glasses in which the delicious fruit nectar was served.

The dinner progressed through a rich cream soup, roast chicken with vegetables, homemade ice cream with crushed strawberries, and great plates of delectable cake.

The little cups of black coffee were being served when Athalie reached under her chair and brought out a lacquered box, which she passed around. Cigarettes! Strange Silver had not thought that might happen! And the guests were all taking them, girls, too, and lighting them. Little curls of smoke rose delicately in the stately dining room, and six little flappers pursed their painted lips and blew six more wreaths of smoke into the air.

Silver took her coffee cup and toyed with it thoughtfully. What would her father say to this? She was not quite sure whether the time had come for her to take a stand or not. But when at a signal from Athalie one of the boys rose and, stepping out of the room, brought back two tall bottles of dark liquid, then she knew her time had come. He had pulled out the cork and was filling an empty glass by one of the girl's plates. The fumes of the liquor rose hotly to her sensitive nostrils. What chance had she against so many? Her face was white and stern like a spirit as she rose from her chair and faced them. "Stop!" she commanded to the astonished boy who held the bottle. "Joe, will you remove these bottles at once? And Anne, will you kindly take that tray and gather up the cigarettes and throw them out? My father does not allow such things to go on in his house nor around his table!" she said, addressing the company in a clear ringing voice. "If you want to smoke and drink, you must go elsewhere!"

Then Athalie rose suddenly with her glass of water in her hand and flung its contents at her sister.

"Shut up!" she said roughly. "It's none of your business what we do. This is my party, and I'm the *daughter* in this house."

"*Athalie!* What does all this mean?"

Patterson Greeves was standing in the doorway, his hat still on his head, his hands still cluttered with packages of books as he had come in, his face stern with anger.

Chapter 26

$\mathcal{T}$he entire company turned in startled surprise, and Anne and Joe scuttled furtively over to stand by him. They had been plainly frightened by a situation that they knew they could not control.

"Oh, Dad, is that you? I didn't hear you come in. I'm glad you've arrived. It was naughty of you to be late the first night of my house party," broke forth Athalie nonchalantly. "Come and let me introduce you to my guests."

Patterson Greeves made no move to go forward. He handed his packages to the attendant Joe and took off his hat and gloves, still standing where he had first appeared, still looking the company over, person by person, his eyes growing sterner, his mouth more displeased.

"I do not understand," he said, coming forward inquiringly, giving a searching glance into each impudent face, guest by guest.

"Let me have that bottle, please!" He took the big bottle from the unresisting hand of the once-arrogant youth and lifted it near to his nose.

"Where did you get this liquor, may I ask? I'm afraid somebody has been breaking the laws of the land. I shall have to put you all under arrest until we investigate. Joe, will you kindly call up the chief of police?" The entire company of would-be revelers rose in consternation and looked to right and left for a place of exit, but Anne Truesdale, her cheeks flaming an angry crimson, her eyes like two sword points, barred the way of the pantry, and the angry householder and his ancient servant stood in the wide doorway leading to the hall. They began to steal furtively behind one another and sidle toward the pantry, fancying Anne less formidable than their inhospitable host.

"Why, Dad! I think you're horrid!" broke forth Athalie, her lips trembling. "Why, *Dad*!"

"Be still, Athalie! You may go to your room! You have broken all three of your promises. I have nothing more to say to you at present. You know what the consequence was to be."

"But, Dad—"

"Leave the room!"

And Athalie actually left it.

The moment was awful. Even Silver felt sorry for them.

"Now, ladies and gentlemen, while we are waiting for the officer, let me get your names and addresses," said Patterson Greeves, his classroom tone upon him as he brought out pencil and notebook. "Your name, sir?" He turned to the first white-faced boy, the one who had held the bottle as he entered.

The boy lifted a face from which the fun had fled and tried to brazen it out.

"Oh cert, my name's Brett Hanwood. Hamilton Prep pitcher, you know."

Straight around the table he went writing down carefully the addresses, asking a searching question now and again. When he reached Marcella Mason, he eyed her curiously for an instant, felt the sleeve of her coat, a flicker of amusement passing over his otherwise grave face, and said, "And this—ah—gentleman?"

Marcella winced.

"This completes the list, I think."

Patterson Greeves lifted his pencil and counted, "Four ladies and seven—" his eye was on Marcella— "men! The ladies of course we will not hold accountable. And now, as it is not convenient for me to entertain guests tonight, they will be returned to their homes or their schools as the case may be. The men"—again he glanced at Marcella—"will await the officer's verdict. Doubtless they will be held till the trial, or possibly let out on bail if they can furnish sufficient evidence. The state is laying stress on this matter of prohibition just now, and—"

"Oh!" gasped Marcella and collapsed in sobs.

"Now," said Greeves, "if you four young ladies will just go into the library, I will call up your school and arrange for your return."

"Oh—h–h–h!" murmured the girls in a panic.

Just then the officer was brought in by Joe, and Greeves explained to him in a low tone. Then he turned back to his frightened victims. "You four girls may come into the library now."

The girls huddled in a mass and followed him. The sound of hasty feet scuttling after, and Marcella arrived red and teary.

"I—I—I'm a girl, too!"

"Oh," said Greeves surveying her through his glasses, "curious specimen, I must say. Man and girl! Well, well! Which school do you attend?"

Marcella bore the sarcasm meekly and tried to hide her borrowed plumage behind the other girls. They made a curious group in their wild young flapper frocks with their plump, bare shoulders shivering in the shadows of the big old room while they waited for Patterson

Greeves to get long distance. They glanced mutely into one another's eyes and thought of the school records already against them.

"Is this Briardale School for Girls? Is this the principal? Let me speak to the principal, please. I have five young ladies here in my house who claim to belong to your school. They have been attempting to have a hooch party during my absence. Can you tell me where they are supposed to be tonight? Shall I return them to you? Their names are—"

He consulted his paper and read off the names. The girls stood and shivered as if he were striking them.

"I beg your pardon. Did you say Miss Mason was at home at the bedside of her sick mother? Yes? And this Violet? Her sister is being married? Oh! I see!" His eyes dwelt mercilessly on the trembling Violet. "Having her eyes examined? I see. And the other one? Oh, she was taken sick and was sent home? I see. Then would you prefer that I return these young ladies to their various homes—"

"Oh no, no!" broke in Marcella. "My father would half kill me! I'd rather go back to school."

"Mine would take my next month's allowance away, and it's spent already," wept Violet then hushed to hear what was being said on the telephone.

"You say this Violet lives in our neighboring city? And Miss Mason in a suburb? Where? Oh, Hazelbrook. Yes, I know it quite well. I'm not sure, but her father is an old friend of mine. Walter Mason? That's the one. Very well, then. I quite agree with you that these two should go to their homes. I will personally escort them there at once. The other two you would prefer to have return to the school tonight? Just how far is that from the junction? I see. No, there is no train out of here until ten o'clock. That would miss connection. I think it would be better to get an automobile. Yes, I have a reliable man and his wife, old trusted servants. I can send them in their care.

Oh, that's all right. I'm only glad to get it all so easily arranged. They will be there tonight. It may be late. I may be delayed in finding a car, but they will arrive, don't worry. Thank you! Good night!"

The girls were trembling and furious, but looking in his determined face, they saw they had no way of escape. Especially did Marcella quail as she looked down at her borrowed garments and thought of her father's face when he should hear the report of his old friend.

Patterson Greeves hung up the receiver, rang for Anne Truesdale, and said: "Now, young ladies, you will go upstairs in charge of Mrs. Truesdale and find your belongings. We shall be ready to start in twenty minutes."

He herded them to the stairs and went into the dining room to consult with the chief of police, who had the bottle of liquor in his hand and was asking keen questions with eyes that were used to reading human countenances and penetrating human masks.

After a brief consultation between the two men, the uncomfortable boys were called into the library and subjected to a telephone conversation much like that which the girls had passed through, except that it was decided by the headmaster of the school that the boys should be returned in a body under police escort and that their fathers should be at once summoned from their various homes. The boys looked even more hunted than the girls had done. They perhaps had more reason to fear both parental and scholastic discipline.

The boys were marched out of the house at once with hastily packed suitcases and sober looks on their faces. A grocery truck was requisitioned. The boys piled in, and six men, two of them regular police aides, the other four pressed into service from the firehouse with hastily improvised uniforms, climbed in after them, a man to a boy. There was no escape.

The guards hugely enjoyed the occasion. They were getting a

night's excitement and a long ride free. It would be something to talk about at the firehouse for many a day. Uri Weldon had been the first one to volunteer. He had no time even to telephone to Lizette before leaving. But then Lizette was not one to worry about him.

In a quarter of an hour, an automobile arrived and two unhappy maidens with handkerchiefs to their eyes stole out and crept into the backseat. Molly, in a flannel petticoat and an extra sweater under her long winter coat, climbed fearfully in between them, and Joe took the front seat beside the driver. They moved off hurriedly through the night, and presently Patterson Greeves and two silent, angry frightened girls emerged from the house and walked down the street to the ten o'clock train for the city.

"Well, they're all getting away early!" sighed Mother Vandemeeter. "Now we can go to bed in peace. I was afraid they were going to have a dance, and that would have been so out of place in the old Silver house. I just couldn't have gone to sleep for thinking."

"I don't know as they could have gone much later!" said Grandma, getting stiffly up from her padded rocking chair and tottering toward her downstairs bedroom door. "This is the last train, isn't it?"

Said Pristina up at her top bedroom window: "Now! I wonder which one he is taking to the train!"

Silver and Anne Truesdale busied themselves in putting the house to rights and gathering up the debris of the brief onslaught of the enemy.

"Them old stemmed fruit cups was one of Miss Lavinia's best prized set," Anne mourned. "To think one shoulda got broke tonight fer them little fools. I almost just used the old sauce dishes, and then I thought the master might not like it!"

"Never mind, Anne. What difference does a glass or two less make? They're gone. They might have broken more if they had stayed longer. It looked to me as if they were out to break more than fruit glasses."

"Yes!" said Anne. "My soul! So that's that!"

Five hours later, Patterson Greeves, dismissing the car that had brought him back from the city, walked up from the post office corner where he had got out and let himself silently into the house. Anne, released from her vigil, turned over and murmured drowsily to herself again: "So that's *that!*"

In the wee small hours of the morning, with the east paling into pink, the only two who had got any enjoyment out of the affair, Molly and Joe on their way home from their long pilgrimage, sitting in the backseat holding hands and never saying a word, were having a second honeymoon. Their first automobile ride! An all-night affair. They were sore and stiff with the long ride, next day. But what did it matter? They had something to remember to their dying day. They might have other rides, doubtless would when Patterson Greeves got time from parenting to buy a car of his own, but never would any be like that first one, where the moonlight lay like thin sheets of silver over the springtime world.

Chapter 27

Sometimes a storm will settle the atmosphere, for a time, and it seemed as though Patterson Greeves's summary dismissal of the house party had really subdued Athalie and made life bearable and even almost pleasant at times in the Silver house.

There had been a stormy scene the next morning between Athalie and her father, but his brief experience in dealing with the young hoodlums the night before had seemed to give him confidence. He laid down the law in no uncertain manner to the young woman, who went through various stages of rebellion to argument then pleading and finally surrender.

"But I told you about that house party when I first arrived, and you never said a word. You had no right to come in and raise a row afterward," had been her opening sentence of the interview, spoken with stormy eyes.

She left the library with downcast countenance and a promise to apologize to Silver for her insolence of the night before, a condition of her further remaining in the house.

"Although I hate her just as much as ever and always shall!" she added as she was about to close the door behind her.

Her father thought it as well to let this sentiment go unanswered, and Athalie went up to Silver's door, walked in without knocking, and announced, "My father sent me to apologize." Having said it, she slammed the door after her and departed, leaving Silver no opportunity to reply.

Thus matters had settled into a semblance of amity between them. The conversation at the table consisted in animated talk between Silver and her father and absolute silence on the part of Athalie whenever her sister was present. The two girls walked their separate ways as much as if they were in separate spheres. Silver made one or two unsuccessful attempts to bridge over this chasm between them and finally settled down to forget it and be happy.

Silver was living a rich and beautiful life, entering into the church work of the new community with zest and rare tact, already beloved by everyone, and spoken of often as being like her great-aunt Lavinia.

The minister was a frequent visitor at the house, going often on hikes and fishing trips with Greeves, and spending long hours in discussions on political, scientific, and on rare occasions, religious subjects; and often Silver was a third member of the party on these occasions. But the minister was a busy man and did not make his visits to Silver's house too noticeable. It was fortunate for him that Aunt Katie's back fence joined the Silver garden and that the high hedge made passing possible without calling the attention of the neighbors, for Silver Sands was very jealous of their minister and would never let him pay more attention to one family or individual without an equal amount somewhere else. Much of his friendship with Silver and her father was carried on in the evening or morning when they had taken a trek to the woods and come upon the minister, also sometimes when there was no school, with the addition of Blink and his dog.

Athalie had begun to take a real if rather puzzled interest in high school. At first she had attempted to become a leader, had even offered to furnish cigarettes and teach the girls to smoke, telling them they were far behind the times, but this resulted in an instant aloofness on the part of the girls of the better class, Emily Bragg being the only one who really accepted the offer and attached herself to Athalie like a leech.

This was not part of Athalie's plan. She retired from the field as leader and studied the situation for a few days. She began slowly to perceive that she would never be accepted nor welcomed as long as she lifted her own standards. She must accept the standards of Silver Sands or count herself as an outsider forever.

Experimentally she made an attack on the boys and found to her amazement that they, too, had standards. They might not be exactly the same as their sisters', and there were few among them who were ready surreptitiously to meet her halfway and laugh with her, yet on the whole, she was losing rather than gaining in influence. Because for some unaccountable reason, even the boys seemed to feel that she was unclassing herself. She sat down to ponder and decided that it was the old-fashioned town and that it was hopeless. Whereupon she brushed her hair a long time one day and began to curl the ends under and teach it to be "put up." She ceased even the surreptitious application of cosmetics applied on the way to school, since her father's distinct command had put an end to a careful makeup before her own mirror. Her eyebrows began to grow in their legitimate place, with a strange likeness to Patterson Greeves's, and altogether she took on a more wholesome look in every way.

Saturday mornings, at Silver's suggestion, Patterson Greeves made it a point to be at home and to take Athalie to the country club for a round of golf. Even when she grew closer with her schoolmates and found some of her amusement in their Saturday picnics and little round of simple parties, she never failed to accept his invitations for golf with alacrity. At such times there were flashes of something like real affection in her eyes, although he was usually too preoccupied to notice her. Indeed, he would often have forgotten the engagement if Silver had not reminded him.

Greeves had sought to induce Athalie to eat more wholesome food. He had hunted out a diet menu and urged it upon her, and in some degree she had acquiesced, though he found her often with surreptitious boxes of candy, or taking more cake at tea than the law allowed. It was not until Barry again wielded his influence that she really got at it and began to show a loss in weight.

It was one Saturday morning that she had at last decided to try her father on the subject of knickers. She came down nonchalantly arrayed in them and announced herself ready for the country club. Her father looked up from a page he was correcting with an annoyed frown upon his brow. He had forgotten that it was Saturday and was exceedingly anxious to finish the theme he was at work upon. He took her in, knickers and all, and laid down his papers with a stern look on his face.

"You'll have to go by yourself if you're going to wear those things!" he said sharply. "It's strange you don't know what a figure you cut in them. You're too stout for any such getup!"

Athalie, cut to the heart as she always was when her figure was criticized, turned with a shrug and a flip and an "Oh, very well!" and flung out of the room.

Her father settled back to his writing again, thinking that probably she had gone to change, but as she did not return he became absorbed once more and forgot all about it.

Athalie meantime, had stamped out of the front door, down the street, and was making her way swiftly to the old log in the woods, the only refuge she knew outside the house where she would probably meet no one and would be free to cry her heart out and wonder what had become of Lilla. She had not had word from Lilla since they parted.

She was sitting on the log weeping with long quivering sobs when suddenly she felt a hand on her shoulder, and looking up she saw that Barry was sitting beside her.

"What's the matter, kid? Has anything happened? Anyone been treating you mean?"

She lifted eyes that were brimming with tears, and there was something childish and almost sweet about her helpless young despair.

"You poor kid," he said again. "What's the matter?"

He fished a moment in all his pockets then brought out from the breast pocket of his brown flannel shirt a neatly folded clean handkerchief.

"I thought I had a blotter," he remarked and, moving up gently, proceeded to wipe the tears from her eyes.

In a moment, he had her smiling through her tears with his bright remarks.

"Oh, there's nothing much the matter," said the girl, relapsing into her despondency. "I guess I'm only mad. Dad called me fat, and I hate it! He said he wouldn't go with me in my knickers. He said I looked awful!"

Barry surveyed the garments in question.

"Does make you look sort of wide," he admitted. "Must be a lot easier to walk in than skirts though. I like 'em. Why don't you get thinner, kid? It's easy. I can tell you what to eat. We tried it one year when we wanted to run. Listen. I'll write it down for you."

"I hate spinach!" remarked Athalie coldly.

"Oh, well, that doesn't cut any ice, kid! When you get skinny, you'll be glad. Try a month and get weighed and see what a difference it makes."

They talked for some time, and Athalie finally agreed to try it. Then they drifted into more personal talk, and Barry said he wished she'd come and see his mother sometime.

Athalie told him about her mother being off in Europe somewhere. She spoke drearily, and the boy read much between the lines that she did not dream she was telling. He was quick to read the heart hunger and yearning in her voice. There was much that was comforting in his cheery tone and the way he talked of common things. Athalie soon sat up and began to smile. Somehow the world looked brighter and life more possible even without chocolates. Barry said again he wished she would come and see his mother, and this time she said she would and almost thought perhaps she meant it. It would be interesting to see what kind of a mother Barry had.

Then suddenly the boy stood up quite sharply as if he had only just thought about it.

"But I oughtn't to let you stay here," he said. "Your father might not like it. Why don't you go home and put on the togs he likes. It won't take long. Wait till you get skinny and then wear these again."

"They won't fit me," giggled Athalie. She was growing quite lighthearted.

"Come on over this way. I'll show you a shortcut home, and you won't need to pass the firehouse. There's always a lot of crows there waiting to pick the flesh off your bones."

"Maybe that would be quicker than dieting," laughed Athalie brightly.

"You bet it would!" said Barry. "We won't try that way this time. They'd make remarks if an angel flew by. Now come on down by the creek. It's pretty there. Have you ever seen the rapids? Not very rapid, but it takes some strength to get a canoe up 'em. Some day we'll get your sister and take a canoe jaunt."

But at that, Athalie's brow darkened, and her chin went up. "I don't think she'd care to go," she said stiffly. "She's all taken up with doing things down in that Frogtown place."

"Oh, wouldn't she?" Barry's voice was disappointed. Athalie looked at him jealously. The sun seemed to have grown gray. Her loneliness had settled down again.

Barry was tactful for one so young. He saw that for some reason she did not want the sister. He turned the subject immediately to the day and the beauties about them.

"There's a squirrel up in that tree that throws nuts down on me when I'm fishing sometimes," he said. "Do you like to fish? Why don't you come along with your father? He and the minister often come up here. Your sister was along last time."

Ah! It was the sister! Athalie stiffened perceptibly.

"There he goes now, look!"

Athalie looked up while the boy talked, pointing out the squirrel nest, telling how the squirrels stored their nuts, how they often ran up the tree with a mouthful of leaves to stuff in their nest for a bed.

"See that branch of scarlet leaves up there?" exclaimed the boy suddenly. "It's early for them to turn red, but aren't they peachy? Shall I get them for you?"

He was off up the tree in no time, nimble as a squirrel himself, up, up, and up, till the girl watching felt dizzy for him, then out on a hazardous limb and whipping his knife from his pocket. Presently down came the splendid branch, fluttering like thousands of scarlet blossoms, and fell at her feet.

She stooped and picked it up wonderingly. It was almost the first time in her life she had gathered trophies from the woods, the first time any boy had presented her with anything so glorious and so wild.

Barry was down again in a second as if it had been nothing to climb like that, and was walking beside her telling her about the scarlet maples in the fall. Then all at once he turned and pointed.

"Now, you go across that meadow. When you get to the corner of the board fence, turn to the right next to the pasture and go straight ahead of you, and nobody will get a chance to see who you are before you are at home. I won't go with you. It will be better not. Those Vandemeeters have eyes all over the house. Here! Do you want this junk?"

Athalie, with her arms full of the gorgeous leaves, made her way slowly across the sod of the pasture and around the corner of the fence, thinking over all that had happened, wondering why the boy didn't come all the way with her, why he minded those old Vandemeeters, getting a thought of his reasons into her soul, comparing them with all her father had said, resolving to try again, and saying over as she entered her own gate, "Spinach! Spinach! How I hate it!"

The spring deepened into summer and school had closed. Athalie felt lost. Her father was immersed in his book and had little time for golf. Mary Truman and her mother and brother had gone away to the mountains for a month; several of the other girls were visiting relatives in the country or at the seashore, or taking little trips. She had to stay around the house and garden. Always there was Silver everywhere in the way. She did not get any nearer to Silver.

Barry came one day and took Silver away in the minister's car to see a sick child two miles out of town. The minister had sent for her to come and bring some broth. They all came home together with a sheaf of goldenrod and got out with much laughter and chatter. Athalie from the upper window watched them. There was a look in Bannard's eyes as he helped Silver from a car that made her suddenly feel all alone in the world. Barry, too! He came in after them carrying flowers. Silver had a heap of velvet moss in her hands dotted with scarlet berries. She was carrying it carefully. The minister put out his hand to catch a falling spray of the vine where the berries grew. Barry was close, with deep admiration in his face. He answered something Silver said and flashed his beautiful smile. Silver on the step above him broke a tiny spray of goldenrod from the armful he had just handed her and, stooping, fastened it in his button-hole. She could not hear the byplay of words that went with the act; she could only see the flush of pleasure on Barry's face, the tender smile on Bannard's, Silver's look of utter joy and content. A pang of jealousy like none she had ever felt before shot through her undisciplined heart. Her face was almost distorted with hate, and the red-hot tears went coursing down her face so that she could not see Barry and the minister as they went back to the car. They had not asked for her. They had not either of them suggested that she go along. If Barry had done so when he came for Silver, she would have gone. This once she would have gone, if just to keep Silver from riding in the front seat with Barry. But Barry had not asked it. Barry had not cared about anything except just to make her safe for her father's sake, and to make her get thin so her father would be pleased. Nobody cared for her!

Her young, lonely soul raged fiercely within, going over and over the doleful situation, until she scarcely knew what she was doing, and suddenly a gentle hand touched her on the shoulder.

"Athalie, dear! You are crying! Is there anything I can do to help you?"

It was Silver in her white dress with her arms full of goldenrod, come softly up the stairs on the rubber-shod feet and finding Athalie still at the hall window.

Athalie turned in a fury of anger to be caught this way and shook off the gentle hand.

"Don't you dare touch me!" she hissed. "I *hate* you!"

"Athalie!"

"Yes, *Athalie!*" mocked the angry girl. "You mealymouthed hypocrite! You liar! You thief! That's it! You are a *thief!*"

"Athalie, what has got into you?" asked Silver in dismay. "What on earth can you mean? What have I done to annoy you?"

Athalie had not been in such a fury since the night she spoiled the painting. She was simply blind with rage.

"Done! Done!" she screamed. "It isn't enough that you stole my father away. Stole him! Stole him! You had no right to him! He gave you away, and you had your home, and you had people that loved you! You had a grandfather and grandmother. I never had any grandfather or grandmother or anybody. My mother never loved me!" Her tone was growing higher and more excited. The pent-up anguish of the weeks was breaking out in a flood. Silver lifted up a hand and tried to make her listen, but she rushed on in a torrent of words.

"She went away and left me to come here alone. She hasn't written to me. She doesn't love me. And I came here to find a father. I would have made him love me. Yes, I could, if you hadn't poked your nose in and got ahead of me. You had no right. He had given you up. You thought just because you had that old Silver name—"

"Athalie!" said Silver compassionately, but Athalie was beyond hearing.

"Don't speak to me. *I hate you!*" she raved on. "It wasn't enough that you stole my father, and the house, and are trying to get the money and Mr. Bannard, but you have to steal my only friend!"

Her head went down on the window frame and she sobbed aloud.

"What do you mean, Athalie? I haven't stolen any friend away from you!" said Silver in a puzzled, indignant voice.

"Yes, you have. You've stolen Barry. He was nice to me. He brought me back when I was going to run away and get married!"

"Athalie!"

"Oh, you needn't 'Athalie' me! I guess I could have done it if I wanted to, and now I wish I had. I would have got out of this old hole anyway. Isn't Mr. Bannard enough for you? Why can't you let Barry alone? You pretend to be so loving and all, calling me *dear* and all that mush, and yet you spoil every nice time I try to have. It was you who spoiled my house party! You can't deny that! And you're at the bottom of my having to wear frumpy old-fashioned clothes. If you hadn't come here dressed like a mouse, my father wouldn't have known the difference. He just wants me to dress like you, and I won't! So there! But I won't stand your making eyes at everybody that likes me either. Look how you did when I had the house party! Carried all the boys off downstairs and flirted with them. Got every one of them crazy about you. Oh, but the girls were furious about that."

Under the torrent of words that she could not stop, Silver suddenly collapsed into a chair and dropped her face into her hands.

"Oh yes! That makes you ashamed, doesn't it? You don't like it put like that. Well, why can't you marry somebody and get away? I've been waiting and waiting for you and Mr. Bannard to get things fixed up so you would get out of the house and let me have a real home for once in my life."

Silver lifted a white face and listened sternly.

"Athalie! Stop! You mustn't say such things. They are disgraceful. The neighbors will hear!"

"I don't care if they do! I hope they will!"

"Athalie, if you will stop, I will go away!"

"Well, go, go! Why don't you go then? You don't mean it at all; you know you don't. You intend to stay right here and spoil my life. I'm here to try and get my father to marry my mother over again. She didn't know it, but I've always wanted to do that. I've always wanted a home like other girls and a real father and mother! And then when

I got here, I found you! What good do you suppose it would do me to get my father to see my mother again while you were here? She wouldn't come here with you! She would hate you, too, worse than I do. She would smile and do something terrible to you. That's Lilla! But she would never come here with you here! Oh, I shall never have a real home nor anybody that loves me!" She suddenly broke away from the window with a wild sob and darted toward the door of her own room.

Silver turned, putting out her arms to try and stop her.

"Athalie! Let me speak! I will go! I did not understand before."

But Athalie broke away fiercely.

"Well, *go* then!" she shouted, and slammed her door so that it reverberated through the house like thunder.

Down in the kitchen, Anne Truesdale and Molly stopped working and looked at one another anxiously.

"It's Miss Athalie got one of her tantrums again!" said Molly in an awed whisper.

"Well, the master's coming home early tonight, praise be!" said Anne, and tiptoed to the door to listen. But all was still upstairs.

Silver was in her room with the door shut, kneeling beside her bed.

Chapter 28

The tramp was not working that afternoon. He was recovering from a three-day vacation he had taken in the city following the weekly payday. He sat in the door a long time looking down toward the village and hating the world. He always took it out in hating the world when he was out of sorts. He had a settled conviction that the world owed him a living.

He looked as usual toward the Silver house with jealous eyes and began to calculate, as he had often done before, how many millions they must have and what he could do if he had only a small portion of their wealth. And as before he began to work at a plan that had for a long time been maturing in his brain. He had worked it out link by link till he had all the details perfect up to a certain point. There he always had to stop. He never could quite get beyond that missing link. He always thought if he could just think a little harder it would come to him, that missing link, but as yet it had not come.

And now he felt sick and sore from the three days' debauch, and the fire was out, and there wasn't a bit of food in his lair, neither was there wood to cook any food if he had any.

He stirred his stiffened limbs and got himself to his feet shivering from sheer revolt against life. He knew that the afternoon was waning and that he must go soon to get wood or there would be no way to get supper, and supper he must have if he was to go work in the morning. And to work he must go if he were to live longer, because his last cent was spent and bacon cost money. They were not trusting tramps for bacon and tea in Silver Sands.

So down the mountain he trudged, gathering wood slowly in little heaps by the way to be gathered up on his return trip. He must go trim that hedge of Truman's, and that would bring him enough for sugar and butter and all that he needed that night. Then on his return he would gather up the wood and have a little comfort out of life. Strange that with such a life he could still gather comfort from it.

It was ten minutes to five when he returned with his sugar and bacon and cheese. He hadn't cut the hedge very well, but Mrs. Truman had been having a missionary meeting and hadn't come out to see. She had sent the money out to him before he had quite finished, and he lost no time in getting down to the store. His inner man required immediate refreshment.

So he sat down in a sheltered spot not far from the road to eat a snack to stay him before he should gather up his wood. And suddenly his slow jaws lagged and moved slower, and his little eyes peered cunningly between the bushes, and his ears pricked up and listened, for down the road in the distance he saw the missing link in the well-forged chain of his plans approaching, and with eager caution and much peering he stowed away his bundles under the leaves and moved down to a more convenient position nearer the road where he could watch and be ready for the right moment.

Silver had risen from her knees with a face in which sorrow and purpose were having their way. She went straight to her desk and, drawing pen and paper toward her, began to write rapidly:

Dear Athalie:

I have been praying ever since I came that you and I might learn to love one another and be real sisters. I have always wanted a sister. But I see that I was mistaken and that cannot be. So I am going away at once to show you that I really wanted to love you. I haven't wanted to hurt you in any way, nor to steal Father or anybody or anything away from you. You said a good many things in your excitement that hurt me, but perhaps you won't remember them when you get calmer. I want you to know that I forgive you and want you to be happy. As you say, I have had a happy home, and you haven't. Besides, I am the older and ought to go if one of us must, so it is all right. Only if I go, Athalie, please make Father happy. He is lonely, too. And I shall always pray that God will give you joy.

Sincerely,
Silver

She folded it and wrote "Athalie" across the back then drew more paper toward her and began again. This one was harder to write. It began:

Dear Father:

Something has happened since you went to the city this morning that has made me know that it is not right for me to stay with you any longer. Not now, anyway. You know how sorry I am about it, but I feel this is the only thing to do, so I am going to do it quickly before you return. That will be easier for us both. I have not time to tell you all it has meant to be with you, to know I have a father, and to be sure I have your love. I shall be rich in that knowledge always now wherever I am, but I feel that Athalie needs you more than I do and that you never can be everything to each other while I stay. You will see it this way, too, after a little and know that I did right. Perhaps someday it will be right for me to come back, and then I shall return with joy. Now I am going away, and I am not going to tell you where just yet, for I am not quite sure of my plans, but as soon as I am located, I will send for my trunk, which I will leave packed and ready, and then perhaps you will write and tell me you forgive me for going away without seeing you. I just felt that I couldn't quite bear the good-bye, precious Father! I love you. Don't feel bad. Love Athalie.

Silver-Alice

Silver paused a moment to wipe away the tears that would gather in her eyes as she wrote the words that meant so much to her, then she began another note:

My dear Mr. Bannard:

I am writing in great haste and dismay to let you know that I cannot fulfill my promise to go with you to the orchestra concert in the city tomorrow because I find that I must suddenly go away. It is a deep disappointment to me, for I had looked forward to the pleasure eagerly. I cannot tell you what pleasure I have found in our work among the little children on the Flats, nor how disappointed I am that I shall not be able to carry out our plans for this winter. I am not sure how long I shall have to stay. It may be quite awhile. It is hard for me to have to go, and go this suddenly without bidding my new friends good-bye, but I know I am right in going at once.

I thank you for what your friendship and your sermons have meant to me while I was here, and I hope that someday I may have the pleasure of seeing you again.

Very sincerely,
Silver Greeves

This letter she sealed, addressed, and stamped, and put in her pocket. Then she rose and quickly folded her garments from the closet, laying them in her trunk, and opened drawers and boxes and stowed everything away swiftly. There was not very much, for she had not brought a great deal when she came. In her little suitcase she put the few things of immediate necessity, locking her trunk, put on her hat and a long silk wrap over her simple dark china silk frock, and taking her suitcase, slipped across the hall with her letters. Her father's she laid on his bureau where he would be sure to see it as soon as he came in, and Athalie's she slipped softly under her door. It was all still in the hall when she went down. She longed to speak to Anne and Molly before she left but knew she might upset all her plans if she did. So she went swiftly out the door.

"Well, now, where's she going?" announced Grandma from her window. "A suitcase in her hand, too! And this time of day!"

"Maybe she's taking her suit down to the cleaners," suggested Pristina.

"They would send for it if she phoned," said Harriet.

"Well, she's pretty independent. She doesn't take any rich folks' airs on herself," said Cornelia. "I wonder why they never go together. They're not so far apart in age."

When Silver reached the station, she found that the next train to the city did not stop at Silver Sands; being an express, its only stop was at the junction two miles below.

Looking at her watch, she found that there was plenty of time to walk it. She knew the way well, for she had driven there several times with Mr. Bannard. She mailed her letter to Bannard at the station and took the backstreet for several blocks to avoid the center of the town, as she did not care to be noticed in this sudden flight.

When she came to the last cross street, she turned into the main road again and crossed the bridge. She hoped with all her heart that Bannard would not happen to be out in his car and come across her. She felt she could not bear that. But if he did, she would just have to tell him how things were. She somehow felt sure she could make him understand.

But nobody came along to disturb the afternoon peace. The white road stretched like a ribbon ahead under arching trees, and the crickets sang under the browning goldenrod, a cicada grated out his raucous voice, the wild asters, white and pink and blue and yellow, nodded in the soft breeze with their first opening clusters of stars, and yellow butterflies whirled dreamily, lighting in the dusty grass by the roadside. It was beautiful and still. It looked so dear. She could not believe she was going away from it all, out into the world alone. Her soul cried out to return, to destroy her notes and unlock her trunk and try to make some other finish to this day that had begun so gorgeously and was ending so sorrowfully. But something drove her feet forward, and she passed on around the curve of the road till Silver Sands and the way to the Flats were out of sight and the tears blinded her eyes so that she could not see ahead.

"Good-bye, dear home!" she whispered softly to herself. And then just ahead of her, an old man hurried, hobbling into the road, and waved his hand.

"Oh, lady, lady! I'm so glad you come by. There's a little child up there in that shanty dying, I'm feered. It fell over the rocks an' broke its leg, an' done somepin' to its insides, I guess, an' I'm runnin' to get the doctor. Won't you just go up there lady and stay with the baby till I git back? I shan't be five minutes. I just canta bear to leave it all alone."

Silver looked at her watch and glanced up the hill. There was plenty of time if the man hurried, even if it took him ten minutes, for the train did not leave the junction till ten minutes of five, and it was just as well that she should not get there till train time, lest someone might see her.

"Yes," she said, "but hurry! I must make my train." Then she turned and began swiftly to climb the hill while the old man began to run stiffly down the road.

The hill was steeper than she thought and the suitcase heavy, but she managed to reach the little hovel in very good time, and stepping inside, rubbed her eyes to get the sunshine out, for the room seemed very dark. She put down her suitcase and began groping across to find that child, pausing a moment to get used to the dark, when suddenly she felt the door shut behind her with a slam and something like a key turning in a lock.

In horror she rushed back, almost falling over her suitcase, and groped for the knob, but there was none. The door was fast, and when she pounded on it, there were only hollow reverberations. It was so still in the little place that it did not seem possible that there could be anyone else in the room, even a dying child. Perhaps it was dead already. She felt so alone. Her heart was beating wildly. She tried to tell herself that of course the door had blown shut, and a night latch had fastened it, but a night latch usually opened from the inside. It must be she would be able to find a knob when she grew calmer and could see better. She groped back to the door and tried once more but with no better success. The door seemed smooth all over and fitted close. There was no crack for light to come in. Was that a step outside? No, she must have been mistaken. And yet—how strange! She had seen the man run down the road! But the child! She ought to be attending to it! Could it be that she had got into the wrong place? Were there two buildings on the hill? Should she cry out for assistance? It was not far from the road. Someone would be passing soon. Surely there was no need for her to be frightened. The old man would soon return with the doctor, and then she would be set free.

She remembered her little pocket flashlight that she always carried in her handbag. She tried to find it and at last located it and touched the switch. The ray of light revealed the bare stone walls, the crude box, and huddled leaves, the empty fireplace, the frying pan and cup, and a crust of dry bread. There was no child anywhere.

She examined the window carefully and found it firmly sealed. There seemed to be no implement with which she might attempt to break it open. She swept the room with the light and saw no possible way to get out. Her heart was fluttering so that her breath was labored.

"Help me, O Christ! Steady me! Show me a way to get out of here before it is too late!" she prayed. Then she advanced to the fireplace and turned the flashlight upward. The rough sooty stones loomed above her in irregular knobs, jogging out here and there, and above them, in the brilliancy of the speck of light, a branch of a tree, thick with leaves, waved backward and forward.

"There is always a way up," came the words in memory from some famous story or sermon, she could not tell which, but it thrilled her soul. It was not far to the branch. Could she make it, up the slippery, cobbled way? Was the space big enough? Could she get her suitcase out, too? She measured the distance with her eye, noted the stones that stuck out. Would they support her? But how could she climb with a suitcase? Yet she must have it if possible. There was a bolt of blue ribbon in her suitcase, a whole ten yards. Was it strong enough to hold the suitcase if she tied the other end around her waist and then pulled it up after her? And supposing she made the top of the chimney, could she climb down without breaking her neck? Well, it would be better there, out in God's open, than shut in the dark place where no one could see or hear her, and perhaps she could climb the tree. As for the suitcase, she would do her best and then let it go if she had to. But she must get out of here before that man returned if he was the instigator of some intention against her. If it was only some mistake of a dead bolt she must find the child. It even now might be crying with fear. She must work fast in any case.

She hurried back to her suitcase, searched for the ribbon, tied one end firmly to the handle, the other round her waist. She put her purse inside the neck of her dress, turned her wrap inside out and tied it firmly over her head and shoulders to protect hat and dress as much as possible, and flashlight in hand began her perilous climb. It was a narrow place to squeeze through. She put her suitcase up a couple of feet and rested it on a leg, supporting it with one hand as she climbed, setting a foot here on a projecting stone, putting a hand there in a crevice where the crumbling plaster gave way before her touch. Slowly, painfully, stopping for breath, cautious because one wrong move might undo all, she crept on. Once she missed her footing and the stone rolled down leaving her with only one foot on a loose stone, and once the suitcase slipped off suddenly jerking the ribbon around her waist and almost bringing her down with it, but she caught herself in time and, clinging to the wall, prayed, "Help me! Help me! O Christ, give me strength! Give me steadiness!"

It was like those dreams that come sometimes, where we find ourselves crawling through an endless tunnel that grows smaller and smaller, and finally our strength gives out and we collapse and are stuck. Two or three times she thought she could not go on and closed her eyes to rest. She couldn't look up because the dust and soot filled her eyes, so on and on she crept, coming to one place so small she could just get her head through and was sure she couldn't go farther but finally managed to wriggle through, with the dead weight of the suitcase dangling after, hitting again the wall and bumping, impending her upward way. Perhaps, after all, she would have to cut the ribbon and let it drop.

"Help! Help! O Christ—" and the blessed breath of air struck her face, and light, real sunlight, blinded her eyes. She was out! She caught a firmer hold, and just then the little flashlight slipped away! She caught at it and almost lost her own hold but could not get it. She heard it knock its way to the bottom of the hearth. Well, what did it matter? She would not need it now. Then she pulled herself free from the encasing wall and was out, head and shoulders above the little hut.

She paused to rest and look around. No, there was no sign of any other building. No sound of a crying child. What did it mean? Down below she could see the road, and there was no pedestrian on it. An automobile swept by going very fast, but it was not the doctor's car. Fear clutched her by the throat. She must get away at once.

She writhed herself up out of the chimney. It proved to be a mere knob above the low-sloping roof. She had a struggle with her suitcase and almost gave it up once but finally brought it out, crushed at one side and badly scratched but still intact, and then it was a comparatively easy thing to slide cautiously down the roof and drop carefully to the ground.

She was free! But she was trembling so that for a moment she could not move. Her hands and face were scratched and sooty, and her arms were bruised and sore. She looked up at the blue sky and her heart said quickly in a burst of joy, *Oh, thank You, Christ!*

Then new strength seemed to come, and breath, and she flew away down the hill on the side where the undergrowth was comparatively light, got into the highway and the sunshine, and saw that she was not pursued, gradually grew steadier, and began to straighten her garments, wipe off the soot, and give more thanks to God. There was a long strip torn out of her crêpe de chine dress from hem to waist, an inch or two wide and left somewhere behind in that chimney, but what did that matter? She was free. Her shoes were scratched and dusty and not fit for a lady to take a journey anywhere in, but that was a small matter. One glove was split from wrist to finger and the other entirely gone, but what were gloves in a lifetime! She was on the road, some road. It did not look familiar, and perhaps coming down this side of the hillside, she had missed her way, but there would be a train sometime, somewhere, and she would find it. God had set her free, and now she knew she had done right in coming away. God had helped her on and not let her be hindered to make a lot of trouble for everybody. She would be able to get to her destination and write back in due time to set her father's mind at rest. Then all would be well.

Half an hour's walk brought her to a small hamlet, but it was not the junction. She had missed her way and missed her train, but they told her that a trolley line passed half a mile below, and the cars ran every half hour. They would take her to her destination in less than two hours, and what did it matter? She lifted up her tired head and went forward.

Chapter 29

$\mathcal{G}$reeves came home an hour earlier than he had planned, with it in mind to take the young people all into town to a concert that he had unexpectedly discovered. He stepped into the pantry and told Anne to have dinner ready by quarter to six if possible and then up to his room to wash his hands and make one or two changes in his attire.

No one seemed to be around though the doors of both the girls' rooms were closed. They were probably dressing for dinner or resting. There was time enough. He would not disturb them for another half hour. He stepped to his bureau, and there lay Silver's letter. He read it quickly with a fear at his heart, and then again. Then tearing down to the library wildly, he picked up the telephone and called up the station. No, Miss Greeves had not taken a train from there. She had come in and asked about the train, but when she found the next one only stopped at the junction, she had gone out again. No, they had not noticed which way she went. They were busy with some freight, and they couldn't stop to watch every female that came into that station anyhow; they were busy men, they were.

Patterson Greeves slammed the receiver and stared at the wall. What was he to do next? She had taken a car to the city probably. He called up the garage. No, they had not even seen her. Bannard? Perhaps Bannard had taken her. He would find out if Aunt Katie knew.

But as he picked up the receiver to phone, Bannard himself walked into the room, having been let in by Anne, an open letter in his hand, his face white and questioning.

"Has something happened, Greeves? I just found this in the post office. Has Sil—has Miss Greeves gone back to her former home? What's the matter?"

Patterson Greeves turned a white, anxious face to the minister. "Upon my soul, Bannard, I don't know what's the matter! I just got this myself," and he handed over his letter. "I suppose it's another outbreak of that other devilish child of mine!"

"Perhaps Anne will know."

He rang and Anne appeared.

"Did Silver say anything about going out, Anne?"

"No, Master Pat. I think she's in her room! I heard her there a little while back."

"She's not in her room, Anne. She's gone!"

"Gone, Master Pat! Gone! Oh, that can't be! Why, it's not over an hour since she called to me something about a package she'd left in my room, a collar she promised to give me."

"Well, she's gone. Did anything happen, Anne? Anything especially out of the way?"

"Miss Athalie," Anne had her hand over her heart. "I heard her crying and carrying on in one of her tantrums," she said anxiously.

"That's it! I thought so! Silver has gone because she thinks Athalie would be happier with her out of the house. She wanted to go once before, and I wouldn't let her. Oh, my God!"

"Oh, Master Pat, don't be a-swearin' now, please. She was that sweet a Christian. Surely she'll come back."

"Why, certainly," said Bannard eagerly. "We must find her and bring her back. *I* will find her. Let me phone for Barry to bring my car. He can take his car, too. It can't surely take long to find her. She can't have gone far in this short time. What time did you say she spoke to you, Anne?"

Suddenly they all became aware of Athalie standing in the door, her face stained with tears and white with recent emotion. A letter in her hand, a frightened look in her eyes.

"Is—Silver—here?" she asked in a scared little voice as she looked around the room.

Athalie had been growing taller lately and had really lost a good deal of flesh. And now as she stood and watched them all, as if she had heard what had been going on, she looked fairly fragile. Her father turned on her with fury in his eyes.

"No, your sister is not here. You have driven her away, you little devil! Get out of my sight. I never want to look on your face again!"

With an awful cry like the tearing of soul from body, a continued cry that screeched through the house as the scream of a moving locomotive through the night, Athalie regarded her father for an instant and then, turning, tore up the stairs screaming as she went. She flung herself with a mighty thud upon her bed and went into raving hysterics, but nobody paid the slightest attention to her. Bannard and Greeves had gone out of the house to meet the car, and Anne Truesdale was doing some telephoning for which the master had left orders, a message to Silver's lawyer, another to the city station where she was to be paged, a discreet word to the chief of police.

Barry met the two men half a block from the house and, waiting only for a brief explanation of what he was wanted to do, went down the street on a dead run after his own car. The Silver house grew silent as the dead everywhere except in Athalie's room, where loud cries and sobs continued to ring out, until Grandma called, "Come here, Pristina, don't you hear something strange? It sounds like some animal in distress."

Lizette Weldon hurried up the five stairs to her bay window landing and turned her head from side to side to try each ear and identify the voice. An hour later, Aunt Katie, unable to stand it any longer, quietly slipped through the hedge with her smelling salts and asked Anne Truesdale, who was slamming things around in the dining room with pursed, angry lips and streaming eyes, if she might go up.

"Please yerself!" said Anne, jerking a chair into place. "She's not worth it, the nasty little tyke! Let her cry herself sick if she wants. She and I are two people!"

So Aunt Katie went up with her smelling salts and talked kindly in a low, soothing tone, but Athalie knocked the bottle across the room and took on more wildly than ever, and finally Aunt Katie departed with a sigh, saying to Anne in the kitchen as she went out, "The poor thing! The poor willful thing!"

The weeping kept steadily on for an hour longer. Then Anne's patience gave out, and she went up with a glass of ice water and threw it in Athalie's face, but the girl only strangled and choked and cried on the harder, so Anne went down, half frightened, and wondered if she ought not to call the doctor.

But at last the sounds died away, and Lizette and the Vandemeeters were able to get a little rest. It was growing very late, but Greeves and Bannard had not returned. Anne sent Molly and Joe to bed with instructions not to undress but be ready for any call, and herself put out the lights and took up her watch by the front drawing room window. Once she thought she saw a face peering round the lilac bush, but she knew it must be her eyes after all the excitement, so she put the thought away. Before long she dozed off, and the town slept.

When the morning dawned and the sun finally penetrated the lilacs and shot into the drawing room window, Anne Truesdale sat up and blinked.

"I must have dozed off," she said shamedly to herself. "I wonder if the master has come. I'll just slip up and see if that tyke is asleep."

But when she reached Athalie's room, there was nobody on the bed. With a growing fear, she hurried from room to room, thinking perhaps she had changed her bed as once before, but found no sign of her, and on the pillow in her father's room was a little blistered note, dramatically left open, written large:

> *Dear Dad: I've gone to find my sister. I won't come back*
> *without her. I'm sorry. Athalie.*

When Greeves read that a few minutes later, having come in with Bannard after an all-night fruitless search, he sank his haggard face in his hands and dropped into the nearest chair.

"My God! What have I done to deserve this?"

"Dearie, dearie," said Anne to Molly, "he's swearin' again. I guess mebbe there's a pair of 'em. Mebbe she mightn't to be so much to blame after all, takin' after him as she does."

In the library, the tray of breakfast that Anne had brought stood untouched.

"What shall I do, Bannard? What shall I do? I have lost them both—"

"I tell you, man, you must pray! If you ever prayed, you must pray now. Get down on your knees quick and tell the Lord you're a sinner. He's the only One can straighten this out."

And Patterson Greeves dropped down on his knees and prayed, "Lord, I have sinned! I have sinned against Thee and against both my children. It is right I should be punished, but don't let them suffer. Oh Lord, forgive and help and save!"

And while he prayed, the telephone rang. Bannard answered it.

"Is that you, Father?" a sweet voice called that thrilled him with its familiarity.

"Oh, Silver, is that you? Are you all right?" said Bannard, his whole soul in his voice, and did not notice that he had called her by her dear name.

"Yes, your father is here. We have searched all night for you. Your father is quite broken by anxiety. Is Athalie with you? Yes, she's gone. She apparently went sometime in the night. She left a note saying she had gone to find you and would not come home without you."

"Oh, the dear child! I'll come right home. I just got the message Father phoned to the lawyer. I'm sorry I've caused so much trouble."

"Where are you now? The city? Good. There's a train in a few minutes that doesn't come through. You take it, and I'll meet you at the junction with the car."

Barry had come in while the conversation was going on, and he turned a startled face to Anne in the doorway.

"Athalie gone?" he asked. "Aw, *gee!*"

Anne handed him the note that Greeves had dropped on the floor. He read it with softening eyes then turned to Anne and said in a low tone: "Say, you get me a shoe or something of hers. I've got the dog here. He's good on following a scent. I'll see what I can do."

Anne obeyed, and Barry departed with instructions for Anne to tell Bannard when he had finished telephoning.

Greeves was still on his knees, his face buried in his hands. Bannard stepped over and put his hand on the man's shoulder.

"Silver is found," he said gently. "She's coming right home on the next train. I'm to meet her at the junction. Will you go with me?"

He had forgotten for the moment that Athalie was gone.

Greeves roused and stood up, his face white and deeply marked. There were tears on his cheeks.

"I must go and find my other girl," he said hurriedly. "My poor wronged child!"

Chapter 30

It was growing light enough to see the way around her room when Athalie Greeves, dressing in whatever garments she found lying around the room, and not stopping even to wash her poor swollen face, climbed softly from her window and swung herself down the pergola trellis and to the ground.

She hadn't an idea of where she was going or what she was going to do. Her one thought was to find her sister. It had come to her in the long sobbing hours of the night that that was one thing she could do before she died to atone for all her misdeeds. She could find and give Silver back to her father and so show him that she was going to die.

This strange, wild emptiness that filled her being, this utter weakness and collapse was unlike anything she ever remembered before, except once when she was a very little child with the measles and had cried herself to sleep because Lilla was afraid to kiss her good night. Lilla had gone to a party and left her with the nurse. Lilla was afraid of catching the measles.

She stumbled down the gray morning street like a wraith in her rubber-soled shoes. There was only one way to go, the way she had always gone on her pilgrimages, out through the town, the long sleeping, silent street, and down the empty road to the bridge. She was a little afraid of the sound of the water under the bridge in the dark that way, but what did it matter? She would be dead pretty soon, and there would be plenty of things down there to be afraid of. This one thing she must do. Perhaps if she could get to the city, she might find Silver somehow. She hadn't an idea what a walk to the city would mean. And there were no trains so early.

So she walked on through the lifting night into the gray of the morning hardly able to see out of her swollen eyes, drawing each breath like a sob, stumbling and hurting her feet, crying out with the pain without knowing it.

She did not notice two shadowy figures a little way up the hill in the bushes nor hear a suddenly hushed whisper. She was walking as in a dream with only one thought in mind: to find Silver.

Suddenly as she swerved unsteadily around the curve of the road, something large and solid and soft like a bag of sand seemed to come from somewhere up in the air and struck her on the side of the head. She crumpled like a lily and went down in the road, with everything growing suddenly dark again around her.

When she roused again, she was lying on a hard place like the ground, only with stone walls all around her and a match flaring in her face. She saw two ugly faces above her, one old and lined, with grayish hair and sagging features, the other round and hairy and wicked looking, and she heard the old one say: "It ain't her at all. It's the other one!"

"I've come to find my sister," she piped up feebly and then was gone again.

A long time after, she seemed to see the two men sitting by a box with about an inch of flaring candle between them, and one was writing with a stump of pencil.

"Say they must put the money under the stone and go away back up to town and stay there or the girl won't ever turn up. Say that, Jerry, and better make it twelve, it's no use havin' all the trouble without some returns. Seein' we missed out on the other gal, make it twelve thousand. Not a cent less."

Later they stumbled out together, and a rush of air brought a breath to her lips. She heard one say to the other as they went out: "It beats me, Jerry, where the other one went. She must a ben a spirit, fer I had her shut in an' padlocked, and not a stone is touched. Nobody couldn't a come an' let her out, fer the lock wasn't hurt. I don't know what to make of it."

Far off a dog was barking. It made her think of cool water with little darting fins and a bank with mosses on it. Nuts falling down and red branches. A dog barking, coming nearer. Rushing feet, a heavy body falling. The dog barking wildly. Sounds of a struggling down the hillside and then a wild, piercing whistle sweet as thrushes. Where had she heard that whistle before? Ah! Now she knew. The day they went to the baseball game, and Barry—it was Barry! If she only could call, perhaps Barry would help her find Silver, but the sound stuck in her throat and came out a sob. There it was again, that sweet whistle, and the sound of an automobile horn down on the road. Voices. Someone coming on. Voices again!

"Mr. Bannard, come and help me tie up this guy. It's the old tramp that's been going around for several weeks. Got a handkerchief? Sure, that'll do. Here, you hold his hands. Buddie's got the other fellow by the seat of the pants. I guess he'll keep all right. They were sneaking round here looking mighty suspicious. I wanta see what they've got in that hut. Chief has been looking for a hooch still 'round these parts. It might be in there!"

Oh, why couldn't she cry out? They would go away pretty soon. There. The dog was coming nearer. He seemed to be just outside the wall. "Buddie, Buddie!"

Ah! The air again! The door had been broken open! She opened her eyes, gave a long, shuddering sob, and closed them again. It didn't seem to matter now that they had come. She hadn't found Silver, and she heard her father's voice! She had failed!

And then she heard Silver's voice. Was she maybe in heaven? No, heaven was not built of stone walls, she was sure. She struggled with her eyelids once more and looked. It was Silver, looking down with that sweet smile. With all the power that was left in her body, she summoned her will and crept to her sister's feet. It seemed a long way, though it really was only an inch or two, and she laid her tired hands around Silver's feet and pressed her hot lips to Silver's little dusty shoes. Then she slipped off again, this time she thought for good.

Till she suddenly heard Barry's voice. He was down on his knees beside her with an old tin cup of water.

"Say, kid, drink this; it'll do you good. And say, kid, brace up; you'll make it yet!" Then she looked up, and they were smiling, just as if they loved her, and her father took her hand and smoothed it. Why, he didn't hate her anymore! The hate was all gone everywhere, just love left, and she was happy.

They left the tramp and his friend in the hut with the padlock securely fastened and carried Athalie down to the car. She wasn't sure but that she was dead and they were taking her to her funeral, but she was happy, so happy. Barry and the minister had made a chair and were carrying her down the hillside, while her father held her hand and Silver carried her feet gently, under her arm. It all seemed so wonderful.

They put her in the car and drove her home and laid her on a couch in the library while they all stood around talking, asking her questions that she couldn't answer. Barry was telephoning to the chief of police, and the minister was talking to Silver with that light in his eyes. Her father was holding her hand and looking at her and saying, "Dear little girl!" Just like that! "Dear little girl!"

It was all just what she had dreamed a home would be.

Then Bannard: "Well, I guess we'll go home now. You all need to get a good sleep, and then, well, 'tomorrow about this time,' let's celebrate."

Greeves looked up and smiled.

"That's all right, Bannard, we'll do it, but I'd just like to begin now by saying that after this I belong to the Lord, soul and body. I have been a poor, miserable sinner living for myself and railing out that there wasn't any God, but He answered my prayer when I was in distress, and now I mean to live for Him and for my children the rest of my days, so help me the God that I have blasphemed!"

Anne Truesdale, listening nearby, said aloud to her soul: "It's come, it's come, it's come! Th' verra windows of heaven is open. Praise be!"

CRIMSON ROSES

Chapter 1

1920s

Eastern United States

The room was very still except for the ticking of the little clock, which stood on the table in the hall and seemed to Marion Warren to be tolling out the seconds one by one.

She sat by her father's bedside, where she had been all day, only rising to give him his medicine or to tiptoe into the hall to answer some question of her sister-in-law's or to speak to the doctor before he went out.

The doctor had been there three times since morning. He had come in the last time without being sent for. Marion felt sure that he knew the end was not far off, although he had not definitely said so. As she looked at the gray shadows in the beloved face, her own heart told her that her dear father had not much longer now to stay.

She would not call him back if she could to the suffering he had endured for the last two years, following an accident at his factory. She knew he desired to be through with it. He had often spoken about how good it would be to feel that the suffering was all over. Yet she had hoped against hope that he might be cured and given back to her. She had nursed him so gladly, and loved her task, even when sometimes her head ached and her back ached and her slender arms ached and her flesh fairly cried out for rest. Her father was almost her idol. He and she had always understood one another and had had the same dreams and ambitions. He had encouraged her in taking more time for reading and study than her more practical mother had thought wise. He had talked with her of life and what we were put on this earth to do. He had hunted out books to please and interest her. She had read aloud to him for hours at a time, and they had discussed what she read. And after her mother died he had been both mother and father to her. How was she going to live without her father?

She had known, of course, since he was first taken ill that there was a possibility that he might not get well.

But he had been so cheery and hopeful always, never complaining, never taking it as a foregone conclusion that he was out of active life forever, and always saying at night: "Well, daughter, I feel a little better tonight, I think. Perhaps the doctor will let me sit up in the morning. Wouldn't that be great?"

Yet he had also lived and talked as if he might always be going to heaven tomorrow. Once he had said, "Well, I'm satisfied to live to be a very old man if the Lord wills, or to go right now whenever He calls."

These memories went pacing before the thoughts of the girl like weird shadows as she sat waiting in the darkened room, watching the dear white face. She had had no sleep since the night before last when her father had grown suddenly so very much worse. At intervals she wondered whether she were not perhaps a little light-headed now.

Marion's brother, Tom, was sitting at the foot of the bed by the open hall door. He had been sitting there for an hour and a half. Occasionally he cleared his throat with a rasping sound. She knew he must be suffering, of course, yet somehow she felt that she alone was the one who was being bereaved. Tom was older and was not what he called "sentimental." He had never understood the deep attachment between Marion and her father. He sometimes had called it partiality, but the girl always knew her father had not been partial. He loved Tom deeply. Yet he had never been able to make a friend and comrade of his practical, cheery, and somewhat impatient son. The son never had time to read and talk with his father. He had always had some scheme on hand to which he must rush off. He was like his bustling, practical mother, who even in her last illness had kept the details of the house and neighborhood in mind and sent others on continual errands to see this and that carried out as she planned. It was just a difference in temperament, perhaps. Marion wondered idly if Tom was thinking now how he might have made his father happier by being with him more. Tom loved their father, of course.

But Tom sat silently, dutifully, and now and then changed his position or cleared his throat. He seemed so self-possessed.

Marion was glad that he sat there. She would not have liked to have the responsibility alone. Tom had always been kind when it occurred to him. It did not always occur to him.

Jennie was there, too, Tom's wife. She did not sit down but hovered in and out. Marion wished she would either go or stay. It somehow seemed like an interruption to have her so uneasy. It was just another thing to bear to hear her soft slipping around in felt slippers, calling Tom to the door to ask about some matter of household need, asking in a whisper if there had been any change yet. Marion shuddered inwardly. It seemed somehow as if Jennie would be eager for the change to come. As if there were no sacredness to her in their father's dying. Yet that father had been exceedingly kind to Jennie. He had always treated her as if she were his own.

It was during one of these visits of Jennie to the sickroom that there seemed to come a change over the shadows on the white face. Jennie had breathed a syllable, emphasizing it as it came, as some people will always make vocal a self-evident fact. Marion wanted to cry out, "Oh, keep still, won't you, *please!*" but she held her lips closed tight and drew a deeper breath, trying to pray for strength.

The doctor was coming in. They could hear the street door open and close softly. The latch had been left off that he might come in when he wished. Marion looked up with relief. Ah! The doctor! Now, if there was anything to do, it would be done!

The doctor noted the change instantly. Marion could understand by the grave look on his face that it was serious business. He stepped silently to the bedside and laid practiced fingers on the frail wrist.

It was at that moment that the pale lips moved and the eyelids opened and her father looked at her.

Her hands were in his cold one instantly, and she thought she felt a faint pressure of the frail fingers.

"Bye, little girl!" he said faintly. "I have to leave you!" The eyelids closed, and she thought that he was gone, but he roused again and spoke in a clearer voice.

"You'll have your home here—Tom will see to all that. He'll understand—" The voice trailed off into silence.

Tom roused himself huskily and tried to speak, as if he were talking to one very far away.

"S' all right, Dad. I'll look after Marion. Don't you worry."

The sick man smiled.

"Of course!" he gasped, his breath nearly gone. "Good-bye!" His eyes searched the room.

"Jennie, too, and the children!"

But Jennie had slipped away suddenly.

Perhaps she had gone to her room to cry. Perhaps Jennie was fond of Father in her way after all, thought Marion.

But Jennie had not gone to cry. Jennie was stealing stealthily down the stairs, slipping like a ghost into the little den that had belonged to her father-in-law, where his big rolltop desk stood and his old desk chair, the walls lined with books. She closed the door carefully, snapped on the light, and pulled down the shade, then looked furtively around. It was not the first time that Jennie had visited that room.

Since her father-in-law had been ill, and Marion closely held in his service, she had managed to make herself thoroughly familiar with every corner of the house. She was not going in search of something. She knew exactly what she was after.

She took out a key from her pocket and went over to the desk. The key had been in her pocket for a week. She had found it while putting away things in her father-in-law's closet. It had been on a key ring with other keys. She had taken it off of the ring one day when Marion was downstairs preparing some food for the invalid while he was asleep.

Jennie opened the right-hand lower drawer of the desk and moved some account books over. Then she took out a tin box from the back end of the drawer. She fit the key into the lock and opened the box. Breathlessly she turned over the neat envelopes carefully labeled DEED OF THE HOUSE, TAX RECEIPTS, WATER TAX, and the like, till she came to the envelope labeled MY WILL.

Jennie took this out, quickly put the rest back, locked the box, returned it to the drawer from which she had taken it, replaced the books, and closed the drawer. Then she picked up the envelope and held it in her hand for an instant, an almost frightened look in her eyes, as if she were weighing the possibilities of what she was about to do. She did not open the envelope and read the will, for she had already done that a week ago. Every word and syllable of the neatly written document was graven on her soul, and she had spent nights of waking, going over and over the brief paragraphs indignantly. The old man had no right to discriminate between his children. He had no right to leave the house entirely to Marion. If there *were* no will—that is, if no will were *found*, why, the law would divide the property. Tom would look after Marion, of course, in any case. But Tom should have the right to decide things. He should not be hindered with a girl's whims. She could not see that what she was about to do was in any way wrong. No harm would come to her sister-in-law. In any case, she would be cared for. It would simply smooth out things for Tom. And it was perfectly right.

Having shut her thin lips firmly over this decision, she opened the upper right-hand drawer, pulled it entirely out, and laid it on the desk. Then she reached far in and laid the envelope containing the will carefully at the back of the opening, replacing the drawer and shutting it firmly again, even turning the key that was in the lock.

Having done this, she snapped out the light and groped her way to the door, unlocking it and stealing back into the hall. She listened an instant and then glided up the stairs as silently as she had come down, a nervous satisfaction in her face.

She appeared in the doorway an instant too late to hear the last kindly word from her father-in-law. The doctor had raised his head from bending over to watch, and Marion was turning away with her hands to her throat and a look of exalted sorrow on her face. Marion was so strange! Why didn't she cry? Jennie began to cry. It was hardly decent not to cry, Jennie thought. And Marion pretended to think so much of her father! Probably, though, she was worn out and really glad it was over. It was perfectly natural for a girl not to enjoy taking care of an old, sick man for so long. Two years! It had been two years since Father took sick! Well it was over, thank goodness, at last! Jennie buried her face in her handkerchief and sobbed gently.

Marion wished again that Jennie would keep still. Their last minutes, and the precious spirit just taken its flight! It seemed a desecration!

The doctor and Tom were talking in low tones in the hall now, and Marion turned back for one last, precious look. But even that look had to be interrupted by Jennie, who came with an air of doing her duty and stood at the other side of the bed.

"Poor old soul! He's at rest at last!" she said with a sniff and a dab at her eyes with her handkerchief. "And you, Marion, you haven't any call to blame yourself for anything. You certainly have been faithful!" This by way of offering sympathy.

It was piously said, but somehow the unusual praise from her sister-in-law grated on her just now. It was as if she were putting it in to exonerate herself as well.

Oh, please, please keep still! shouted Marion's soul silently. But Marion's lips answered nothing. She still wore that exalted look. After all, what did anything like this matter now? Let Jennie voice her meaning-less chatter. She need not pay attention. She was try-ing to follow the flight of the dear spirit who had gone from her. She had not yet faced the life without him that was to be hers now that he was gone. She still had the feeling upon her that for his sake she must be brave and quiet. She must not desecrate the place by even a tear.

All through the trying days that followed until the worn-out body was laid to rest beside the partner of his youth in the peaceful cemetery outside the city, Marion had to endure the constant attentions of her sister-in-law. Jennie was always bringing her a cup of tea and begging her to lie down. Jennie wanted to know if she would like her to come into her room and sleep lest she would be lonely. Jennie disciplined the children for making a noise and told them their Aunt Marion didn't feel well. Jennie became passionate in her vigilance until after the funeral was over. Marion was glad beyond words to be allowed at last to go to her own room alone and lock the door. To be alone with her sorrow seemed the greatest luxury that could now be given her.

And while she knelt beside her bed in the room that had been hers during her father's illness—because it was next to his and she could leave the door open and listen for his call in the night—her brother, Tom, was down in the den going over his father's papers.

Tom was a big, pleasant-faced man with an easygoing nature. He would not for the world hurt anybody, much less his own sister. He intended with all his heart to take care of her all her life if that was her need and her desire. He had not a thought otherwise. Yet when he began the search among those papers of his father, it could not be denied that he hoped matters were so left that he would have full charge of the property without any complications. He had certain plans in the back of his head that an uncomplicated will would greatly facilitate. He and Jennie had often talked about these plans, and Jennie had urged him to speak to his father about it someday while there was time. But Tom did not like to seem interested; and, too, there was something about his father, perhaps a kind of dignity that he did not understand, that made Tom embarrassed at the thought of broaching the subject of money. So Tom had never said a word to his father about the property.

Once or twice Tom's father had dropped a word to the effect that if anything happened to him, Tom was to look after his sister, and Tom had always agreed, but there had never been anything definite spoken regarding the house or what money was left or even the life insurance. And Tom had never broken through the silence.

During that last afternoon when he had sat in the sickroom, tilted back against the wall in the shadows, clearing his throat now and then, he had been thinking about this. He had been wondering if, for all their sakes, he ought to try and rouse his father and find out just what he had done, how he had left things. But Marion had stayed so close to the bedside, and somehow he could not bring himself to speak about it with Marion there. There was something about Marion's attitude that forbade any such thing.

But after his father had spoken to them about the house and about Marion, and said that he would understand, Tom had been uneasy. Perhaps after all his father had complicated things by putting Marion into the will in such a way that he would continually have to ask her advice and get her to sign papers and be always consulting her. He hoped against hope that his father had not been so foolish. Poor Father! He had always been so visionary. That was the word Tom could remember hearing his mother call his father. Visionary. She had said once that if father hadn't been so visionary they might all have been rich by this time, and Tom had decided then and there that he would profit by his father's mistakes and not be visionary.

But although Tom was a little worried, and thought about it quite often, he would not open the desk or try to find out anything about matters until his father was laid to rest. It did not seem fitting and right. Tom had his own ideas of what was the decent thing to do.

He waited until his sister had gone to her room and had had time to get to sleep, too, before he went to the den. It wasn't in the least necessary for Marion to have to worry about business. She was a woman. To his way of thinking, women should not be bothered about business affairs; they only complicated matters. He always tried to make Jennie understand that, too. Sometimes he talked things over with her, of course, as she was his wife, but when it came to the actual business, he felt that he was the head of the family.

So he had told Jennie to go to bed, as he had some papers to look over and might not go up for an hour or so yet, and he took himself to his father's desk, armed with his father's keys.

But Jennie was not so easily put off as Tom thought.

Jennie crept to her bed with an anxious heart. She had put the little key back on the bunch with the other keys and felt that no one in the world would ever find out that she had had it, but yet she could not sleep. She could not help lying there and listening for Tom.

Jennie did not feel that she had done anything actually wrong. Of course not, her strange little conscience told her briskly. Why, she might easily have destroyed that will and nobody been any the wiser. But Jennie felt most virtuous that she had not. Of course she would not do a thing like that! It would have been a crime in a way, even though its destruction was a good thing for all concerned. But to put it away carefully was another thing. The will was there. It was like giving Providence one more chance to save the day. If anything ever came up to make it necessary, it could be found, of course. Why worry about it? It was safely and innocently lying where there was little likelihood of its ever being found, at least not till long after everything had been satisfactorily settled. And Marion wouldn't make a fuss after a thing was done anyway. Suppose, for instance, Tom sold the old house and put the money into another one out in the country. Jennie loved the country. But Marion was strange sometimes. She took strong attachments, and one of them was this old house. She might make a lot of trouble when Tom tried to sell it if she owned it outright, as that will stated. It was perfect idiocy for Father ever to have done that anyway. It wasn't right for a man to make a distinction between his children, and when he did it, he ought to be overruled.

So Jennie lay awake two hours until Tom came to bed, wondering, anxious, and beginning to be really troubled about what she had done. Suppose Tom should somehow find it out! She would never hear the last of it. Tom was so overconscientious! Well—but of course he wouldn't find it out!

And then Tom came tiptoeing in and knocked over a book that had been left on the bedside table, and Jennie pretended to wake up and ask what he had been doing. She yawned and tried to act indifferent, but her hands and feet were like ice, and she felt that her voice was not natural.

Tom, however, did not notice. He was too much engrossed in his own affairs.

"You awake, Jennie? Strange thing! I've been looking through Dad's papers, and I can't find a sign of a will. I was sure he made one. He always spoke as if he had."

"Mmmmm!" mumbled Jennie sleepily. "Will that make any trouble? Can't you get hold of the property?"

"Oh yes, get the property all right. Sort of makes things easier. The law divides things equally. But of course I'll look after the whole thing in any event.

Marion doesn't know anything about business. Gosh, I didn't know it was so late! Let's get to sleep. I'm dead tired. Got a hard day tomorrow, too!" And Tom turned over and was soon sound asleep.

Chapter 2

"This house ought to have a thorough cleaning," announced Jennie, coming downstairs a few days after the funeral. "It hasn't been cleaned right since Father has been sick. I couldn't really do it alone, and of course I'll get at it this morning. It'll do you good to pull out of the glooms and get to work."

Marion reflected in her heart that it was not exactly lack of work from which she had been suffering, but she assented readily enough. She had not been able to do much housework for the last five years, and it probably had been hard on Jennie. So she put on an old dress and went meekly to work, washing windows vigorously, going through closets and drawers and trunks, putting away and giving away things of her father and mother. That was hard work. It took the strength right out of her to feel that these material things, which had belonged to them and been, as it were, a part of them, were useless now. They would never need them anymore.

Of course most of her mother's things had long ago been disposed of, but there were her father's clothes and the special things that had belonged to his invalidism. It was hard to put them away forever. Yet Jennie demanded that they be sent to a hospital.

"That bed table and the electric fan and the little electric heater and the hot water heater. They give me the creeps to look at them. It isn't good to have such reminders around, Marion. You want to get away from everything that belonged to the sickroom. I for one want to forget sickness and death for a while and have a little good time living."

Marion felt that Jennie was a bit heartless in the way she talked about it, but she realized that it would be better to put the things where they would be doing someone some good, so she packed them tenderly away and sent them to a poor, little, new hospital in which her church was interested, and sighed as she took down the soft curtains from the invalid's windows and washed the windows and set them wide, realizing that the sunshine would not hurt tired eyes in that room anymore and could be let in freely without hindrance.

"Would you mind if Tom and I were to take Father's room now?" asked Jennie the next day. "Then Bobby and the baby could have the room you've been occupying, and you can go back to the room you used to have before we came. It would change things around a little and not seem so gloomy in the house, don't you think?"

The house didn't seem gloomy to Marion the way it was, and she felt it rather sudden to tear up her father's room and give it to another use, but of course it was sensible and better in every way for the children to be next to their father and mother. So she said she didn't mind, and they set to work moving furniture and changing things from one closet to another.

And after all, Marion rather enjoyed getting back to her old sunny room at the back of the house, with the bay window her father had built for her, her own little bookcase full of books, and her own pretty furniture her father and she had picked out years before. It brought sweet and tender memories and made her feel that life was a little more tolerable now. She could retire to her own pleasant room and try to feel like her little-girl self again, lonely and sad, of course, but still at home in the room that her father had made for her just after her mother had died—the sunniest, prettiest room in the house, she felt. It was a wonder that Jennie didn't like it. Still, of course, she wanted to have the children nearer, and where they had been sleeping in the guest room was too far away for comfort. Now Nannie could come down from the small, third-story room and take the room her brothers had been occupying. It was better all around. But yet, she felt a lingering wistfulness about that front room where the invalid had lain so long. It was hard to feel its door shut and to know it did not belong to her anymore. It seemed as if Jennie was so anxious to wipe out all memory of her father.

But Jennie gave Marion very little time to meditate over these things. She seemed restlessly eager to keep something going all the time. At breakfast one morning she said to Marion, "Marion, I don't see why you don't get out and see your friends now. There's nothing to hinder. Have a little company in and make the place lively. It will do you good. It's been so gloomy all the time Father was sick. Let's have some life now. Don't you want to ask some friends in to dinner or lunch or something?"

Marion roused from her sad thoughts to smile.

"Why, I guess not, Jennie. I don't know who I'd ask, I'm sure. Nearly all my old school friends are married or gone away or interested in their own affairs. I really haven't seen any of them for so long they would think it odd if I hunted them out now. I never did go out much, you know. When I was in school, I was too busy, and after Mother got sick, I had no time."

"Well, you're too young to get that way. You'll be an old maid before you know it. Tom, don't you think Marion ought to get out more?"

"Why, if she wants to," said Tom good-naturedly.

"Marion always was kind of quiet."

"Now, Tom, that's no way to talk. You know Marion ought to get out among young folks and have good times. She's been confined too long."

But the tears suddenly came into Marion's eyes, and her lip quivered.

"Don't, please, Jennie!" she protested. "I wasn't confined. I loved to be with Father."

"Oh, of course," said Jennie sharply. "We all know you were a good daughter and all that. You certainly deserve a lot of praise. But you owe it to yourself to go out more now. It isn't right. Shut up in a city house. If only we lived out in the country, now it would be different."

Marion didn't quite see why the country would be any better, but she tried to answer pleasantly.

"Well, Jennie, I am going back to take my old Sunday school class if they still need me. I had thought of that."

"Oh, a Sunday school class!" sniffed Jennie. "Well, if that pleases you, of course. But I should think you'd want to get in with some nice young folks again. My land! This house is as silent as the tomb! Why, I had lots of friends in Port Harris before we came here to be with you. They would run in every day, and we'd telephone a lot in between. They do that in the country or in a small town. But in a city nobody comes near you. They aren't friendly."

"I suppose you are lonely, Jennie," said Marion apologetically. "I hadn't realized it. I have been so occupied ever since you came."

"Oh, I'm never lonely," said Jennie, tossing her head. "I'm thinking of you. I could be alone with my house and my children from morning to night and never mind it. It's you I'm worrying about."

Marion looked at her sister-in-law in mild surprise. It was so new for Jennie to care what became of her. Jennie had manifested very little interest in her during the years she had been living with them. What had gotten into Jennie?

When they came to clean the den, Jennie insisted upon doing it herself, saying she thought it would be too hard for Marion yet awhile; it would remind her of her father too much. Marion tried to protest, but when she got up the next morning she found that Jennie had arisen before her and finished cleaning the room entirely, so that there was nothing left for Marion to do in there. She stood for a moment looking around the bare room with its book-lined walls, its desk and worn old chair, and the little upholstered chair where she used to sit by her father's side and study her lessons in the dear old days when he was well and she was still in school. Then she dropped into the desk chair with her head down on the desk and cried for a minute.

A wish came into her heart that she might have

her house to herself for a little while. Just a little while. Of course it was nice of Jennie to be willing to come there and do the work all these years while there had been sickness. Of course Jennie had given up things to come. She had come a long way from her own father and mother, who lived up in Vermont, and she had not liked the city very well. But oh, if she just wouldn't take things into her own hands quite so much and try to make her sister do everything she thought she ought. If she only hadn't come into this sacred room and done the cleaning! It seemed to Marion that the spirit of the room had been hurt by such unsympathetic touches as Jennie would have given.

But that was silly of course! So Marion raised her head and wiped her eyes and summoned a smile to go out and help Nannie wash the breakfast dishes. But somehow day after day the strange, hurt feeling grew in her heart that all the precious things of her soul life were being desecrated by Jennie. Yet Jennie was doing it out of kindness to her. If only there were some way to let Jennie know without hurting her feelings. Marion was gentle and shy and couldn't bear to hurt people's feelings.

Marion went to church the next Sunday. She had always loved to go to church, but it had been so long since she had been able to leave her father and go that it seemed strange now to her to be sitting alone in the old seat where she and father had sat.

She had dreaded this and had even ventured to suggest to Tom that perhaps he would go with her. Jennie had declined most decidedly. She couldn't leave the baby. But Tom said he had to see a man who had some property for sale, and he wanted to find out about it. So she had to come alone.

But it was good to be there again, after all, in spite of loneliness, and she had a feeling that her father would be pleased she had gone.

The minister came down and spoke to her kindly. He asked if she would come back to her old Sunday school class again. One of the ladies came over and asked her if she would come out to the Mite Society social and help wait on the folks; they had so much trouble getting girls to come and be waitresses.

Marion agreed to come, although she shrank tremendously from it. But it was something she could do, of course, and she felt she ought not to refuse. Jennie was most enthusiastic about it and offered to go with her, but when the evening came, Jennie had a cold, and so she had to go alone.

As she entered the big Sunday school room where the social was to be held, she had an instant of hesitation. It seemed to her she could not go through a long evening all alone with strangers. She had always been a shy girl, and her five years of service caring for Mother and then Father had made her still more so. She was at home among books, not humans. If her books could have come alive and been present at that gathering, how gladly would she have walked in and conversed with their characters, one by one, thrilled by the thought of meeting those she knew so well. But a lot of people frightened her. She liked to be on the outside of things and watch. She loved to weave stories to herself about people, but to have to move among them and make conversation was terrible. She had purposely come late to avoid having to sit and talk a long while with someone while people were gathering.

But a group of merry girls was coming in behind her, and she hated to have them stare at her, so she hurried in and took off her coat and hat in the ladies' parlor, which was already well decorated with hats and wraps.

The bevy of eager girls entered just as she turned to go out, shouting and laughing, pretty in bright-colored dresses, combing their bobbed locks, some of them even dabbing on lipstick, holding up their tiny hand mirrors and teasing one another loudly in a new kind of slang that Marion did not in the least understand. They were very young girls, of course, but some of the things they were saying were shocking. Could it be that girls, nice girls, girls who belonged to the church and Sunday school, talked like that nowadays?

She shrank away from them and went into the main room.

For a moment, she was dazed before the clamor of tongues and the medley of pretty dresses. Someone was playing the piano, and everybody seemed trying to talk as loud as possible to be heard above it. She felt somehow a stranger and an alien.

She began to look about for someone she knew.

Off at the other side of the room was a group of young people, three of them old schoolmates of Marion's. Mechanically she made her way toward them, half hoping they might welcome her to their midst. There was Isabel Cresson. She used to help Isabel with her algebra and geometry problems in school. She had never been especially intimate with her, but at least she was not a stranger.

But when she arrived at the corner where the young people had established themselves, she was not met with friendliness. Anna Reese and Betty Byson bowed to her, but Isabel Cresson only stared.

"Oh, why you're Marion Warren, aren't you?" she said with a condescending lift of her eyebrows. "How are you? It's been ages since I've seen you. I thought you must have moved away."

Marion tried to explain that her father had been ill and she had not been able to be out, but Isabel was not listening. She had merely swept Marion with a disconcerting glance, which made her suddenly aware that her dress was out of date and her shoes were shabby, and then turned her eyes back to the young men with whom she had been talking when Marion arrived.

Marion mechanically finished her sentence about her father's recent death, feeling most uncomfortable and wishing she had not explained at all. Isabel turned her glance back toward her long enough to say, "Oh, too bad. I'm sorry, I'm sure," and then got up and moved across to the other side of the circle to speak to one of the young men. She did not suggest introducing Marion to the young men. No one made any attempt to move or include her in their circle. Marion dropped down in a chair just behind them, too hurt and bewildered to get herself away from them immediately.

The girls and men chattered on for some minutes, ignoring her utterly. Once she heard Isabel say, with a light laugh in response to something one of the men had said, "Yes, one meets so many common people at a church affair, don't you think? I've coaxed Uncle Rad to let us go to some more exclusive church, out in a suburb you know, or uptown, but he doesn't see it. He was born and brought up in this church, and nothing will do but we've all got to come. I've quit, however. I simply can't stand the affairs they have here constantly. I only came tonight because I was asked to sing. Say, Ed, did you hear that Jefferson Lyman is home? That's another reason I came. They say he is coming here tonight just for old times' sake. I don't much believe it, but I took the chance."

"And who is Jefferson Lyman?" asked the young man, who was evidently a newcomer in town.

"Oh, mercy, don't you know Jeff? Why, he's an old sweetheart of mine. We used to be crazy about each other when we were kids. Walked back and forth to school together and all that. Jeff's been abroad for five or six years, and they say he's tremendously sophisticated. I'm just dying to see him."

"But who is he? Does he live around here? Not one of *the* Lymans, from the Lyman firm?"

"Sure, boy!" said Isabel. "He's the Lyman himself, all there is left. Didn't you know it? His father and his uncle are both dead. That's why he's come home. He's to be the head of the firm now. He's young, too, for such a position. But he's been abroad a lot. That makes a difference. I'm simply crazy to see him and renew our acquaintance. Yes, he went abroad for the war, of course—was in aviation, won a lot of medals and things—and then he stayed over there, looking after the firm's interests part of the time, traveling and studying. He's a great bookworm, you know. But he's stunningly handsome, if he hasn't changed, and he's no-end rich. My soul! He owns the whole business, and it's been going ever since the ark, hasn't it? He's got a house in town right on the Avenue with a picture gallery in it; that house next to the Masonic Club, yes, that's it, and an estate out beyond the township line on a hillside where you can see for miles, and a whole flock of automobiles and an army of servants and a seashore place up in New England with a wonderful garden right out on the beach almost, among the rocks. Oh, it's perfectly darling. We motored past it last summer on our trip. I'd adore to live in it!"

"Gracious!" said Betty Bryson. "If he's got all that, why does he come to a church social? I'm sure I wouldn't bother to if I had all that."

"Well, perhaps he won't come," said Isabel. "I'm sure I wouldn't either. But they say he's interested in the church because his father helped to found it, and he always comes when he's home and there's anything unusual going on. You know this is the minister's twenty-fifth anniversary, and there's just a chance he may come. I should think he'd be disillusioned, though, wouldn't you? All these common people. Why some of them aren't even dressed up decently!" Isabel lowered her voice and cast a covert glance about.

Marion somehow felt she was looking at her. She rose suddenly and made her swift way toward the kitchen. She would look up the woman who had asked her to come and say she would have to go home, that she was not feeling well or something. She simply could not go around among those dressed-up girls. She would drop something, surely, feeling like this. Oh, why had she been led to come to a scene like this? Why did they have things of this sort anyway? There was no worship in it, and what else could people want of it? How terrible those girls had been. Cruel and terrible. And Isabel Cresson, how she had changed and coarsened. Her lips and cheeks were painted. What a difference it made in her. She used to be a pretty girl with lovely golden, curly hair, and now it was all cut off, close, like a boy's. That might be pretty on some people, perhaps, but Isabel looked too big and old for it.

Marion's pale cheeks were flushed now and her tired eyes bright with distress. She had never had quite such an experience as this, being turned down by an old schoolmate. One who had been under obligation to her, too, in the old days. What was the trouble? Wasn't she dressed right?

She glanced down at her plain brown dress, made in the fashion of two years ago. It was still fresh and good, but of course the fashion was behind the times. Why hadn't she realized that she needed to furbish up her wardrobe before going out into the world? She must attend to that before she went anywhere, even to church again. But what kind of people were they all to look down on an old acquaintance just because she was oddly dressed? She had been shut away from the world so long that she had gotten far away from the sense of worldliness. How odd it was that just dress made so much difference. And what a silly she was. Was she going to cry right there in the church before all those people? Oh, Jennie and Tom had been all wrong! She was not fit to go out anywhere. She was all tired out and needed to stay at home and rest and just be quiet.

She was edging her way through the merry crowds toward the church kitchen now, hoping to make her excuses and get away, when the minister loomed in her way and greeted her with a royal smile and his wife put a comforting arm around her and began talking in a low tone, saying dear things about her father, telling her just how she had felt when her father was taken away. The tight lines of suffering around Marion's delicate lips relaxed a little, and she began to look almost happy. Then with a swoop, Mrs. Shuttle, the chairman of the entertainment committee, arrived.

"Well, here you are at last, Marion Warren!" she exclaimed in a loud voice that made Marion shrink. "We've been looking all over the place for you. We want you terribly in the kitchen right away. The woman we hired to wash dishes hasn't come yet. She's always late nowadays. She's got a little baby and can't leave early, and we find the Christian Endeavor used the glasses and ice cream plates at their last social and just left them in the closet dirty! Isn't that the limit? Something ought to be done about that. And see, we're almost ready to serve and not enough ice cream plates or glasses. You wouldn't mind washing a few for us, would you, Marion? I told them I thought you wouldn't. We're almost wild back there in the kitchen. Come on!"

So Marion vanished into the kitchen and was presently established at the church sink washing dishes. Of course she could wash dishes. She had done that all her life. It was much less embarrassing than being out there in the other room being made to feel as if she came out of the ark. Yes, she was glad to wash dishes. She would rather wash dishes than serve. Much! Oh, much! This was what she said when it was discovered that the woman with the little baby did not arrive at all and that many more dishes besides the glasses and ice cream plates would have to be washed before the evening was over.

So Marion stayed in the kitchen and washed dishes the rest of the evening and rejoiced that she was not called upon to go back into the big room and be looked at. Never, never, never would she come to anything again till she made sure she was dressed just right! And never would she come at all just for pleasure.

Marion did not even eat any ice cream. The thought of it was revolting to her. She felt cold and hot and wanted to cry, but she washed dishes faithfully all the evening and smiled when each new trayful was landed on the table beside her and did not groan or complain and was rewarded at the end by commendation from Mrs. Shuttle.

"Oh, Marion, you've been just wonderful! I can't thank you enough! You love to wash dishes, don't you? You make dish washing a fine art, don't you? Now, you really do! I wish you would come every time and help us. We'll remember you when we get in a pinch again."

"It's a small thing to do," said Marion, trying not to let her voice sound weary.

"And will you really come and help us again?"

"Why, surely," said Marion, "if you need me," and resolved if she did, that she would enter by the back door and not go at all into the main room. It was all well enough to serve the Lord in the church by washing dishes if she was needed, but there was no law at all either moral or spiritual to compel her to force herself on the church socially. She would never do it again.

So Marion went home at half past eleven, having wiped and set up the last hundred glasses and spoons herself, and let herself in at the front door with her latchkey, and hoped that Jennie had gone to bed.

But Jennie was very much awake. She called down from the head of the stairs.

"Mercy! What kept you so late? Did you have a good time? You must have, to stay so long. Did anyone come home with you?"

"I was washing dishes," said Marion wearily. "No, I didn't have an especially good time. I stayed because the dishes had to be washed. No, no one came home with me. The janitor offered to, but I told him it wasn't necessary."

"Well, I certainly wouldn't have stayed," said Jennie indignantly. "What do they think you are? A servant? I wouldn't go to that church anymore if I were you. There are other churches. Anyway, perhaps we're not going to stay here much longer. Tom's heard of a farm for sale up in New England. He's taking the New York express tomorrow at six. We'll have to get breakfast by five. You better get right up to bed or you won't wake up. I can't be depended on to do much, you know, because the baby is sure to wake up and cry."

Marion stood in the hall where she had been when Jennie called to her and stared at the pattern of the wallpaper dazedly as she heard Jennie shut her door with a click and snap off her light. So that was the next thing that she was going to be confronted by, was it? They were going to try to go away. They wanted to sell the house and go away from the only spot on earth that was dear to her!

She went over and sat down on the lower step of the stairs and put her face down in her hands and thought how she was tired and sick of it all, and how wonderful it would be if she could just slip away and go where her father had gone.

After a few minutes, she got up sadly, locked the front door, turned out the light, and went up to her room. After taking off her hat and coat, she dropped upon her knees by her bed and let her heart cry out to God.

"Oh, God! What am I going to do? How am I going to bear it? Won't you take care of me?"

Praying thus, she fell asleep upon her knees, and woke hours later, stiff and chilly, to creep under the covers shivering and go to sleep again, with a dull, vague realization that she must get up pretty soon and get breakfast for Tom.

Chapter 3

The light had been turned out in the kitchen to save electricity while they ate supper, and Marion Warren did not turn it on when she slipped away from the table with her hands full of dishes. She did not wish to have anyone see the trouble in her face. By the light that came through the open door, she scraped the dishes quietly and filled her dishpans without much noise, that she might hear what her brother was saying.

Tom Warren was a large man with heavy movements and a voice to correspond. His sister had no difficulty in hearing it above the subdued clatter of the dishes.

He had arrived home but an hour before from the trip to Vermont, where he had gone to look at a farm that was for sale at a low price. The days of his absence had been a time of anxiety for his sister and of eager expectations for his wife. Jennie was hovering around him now, interrupting him occasionally with a chirp of assent as she helped to clear off the table. She resembled a sparrow whose mate has just brought home a new twig for the nest.

Tom talked on in his large, complacent voice. He was immensely pleased with his "find." The farm was all and more than it had professed to be. The house was in good repair, the location charming and healthful, the land rich and under a good degree of cultivation, with a convenient market for its produce. He had all but said that he would take it.

"A grand place for the babies to play," he said. "No one will have to stop work to cart them out into the street for the air. No brick walls, no dust, no noise. You and Marion will have nothing to interrupt you from morning till night. The nearest neighbor is half a mile away, and it's two miles to the village. That needn't bother us any; we'll have a car, of course, and when the children get old enough to go to school, Marion here can teach them all they need to know. She's always been crazy to teach. How about that, Marion?" he asked, raising his voice unnecessarily. "It isn't every family that has a schoolmarm all ready-made."

But Marion did not answer. The gentle clatter of the spoons in the dishpan might have drowned out his question. He did not stop to see.

The girl in the darkened kitchen caught her breath in a half-sobbing sigh, and the tears came into her eyes; but she kept her peace and went on with her task.

"I'm going to see Matthews in the morning," went on Tom joyously. "If he sticks to his offer about buying this house, I'll accept it and bind the bargain for the farm tomorrow. Then how soon do you two ladies think you can get ready to move? If Matthews buys this house, he's likely to want possession at once."

Marion gasped and drew her hands from the dishwater suddenly. She hesitated for an instant then appeared like a ghost at the dining room door, her wet hands clasped, her delicate face looking ghastly white against the dark background of the kitchen.

"Tom!" she said in an agonized voice. "Tom!"

Tom wheeled about his chair and faced her, startled from his contented planning.

"Tom! You're not going to sell this house! The house that Father worked so hard to buy and to pay off the mortgage! Our home! My—my home! Tom, you know what Father said."

The last words were almost a cry of distress.

Tom frowned uneasily. Jennie's face grew red with anger.

"That's just like you, Marion Warren!" she burst out hotly. "Three little children that you profess to love, your own nephews and niece, languishing in the crowded city air and needing the lovely country and a chance to play on the green grass, and you letting a mere sentimental notion for a little old house stand in the way of their life, perhaps!"

Jennie's eyes flashed sparks of steel as gray eyes can do sometimes. Marion shrank from their glance, her very soul quivering with their misunderstanding of her.

"Oh, now Marion," began Tom's smooth tones, "that's all nonsense about Father's slaving to pay for this house. Sentimental nonsense," he added, catching at his wife's adjective. "He worked hard, of course. All men with a family do. I work hard myself. But you know perfectly well that Father wouldn't have hung on to this particular house just because he had worked hard to pay for it if he had a good chance to better himself. It isn't throwing it away to change it into something better, and this is a great opportunity. As for its being your home, why, you'll have a home with us wherever we go; so you needn't get up any such foolish ideas as that. The farm'll be your home as much as this is in three months' time. Don't be a fool."

He said it kindly in his elder-brother way; but Marion's face grew whiter, and she stood looking at him as if she could not believe what he had said. Her great dark eyes made him uncomfortable. He turned from her and went to wind the clock.

"Come, hurry up, Jennie," he said with a yawn.

"Let's get to sleep. I'm about played out. It's been a hard day, and I must get up early in the morning to catch Matthews before he goes to the store."

Marion dropped silently back into the kitchen and finished her dishes. Jennie came in presently and turned on the light with an energetic click, looking suspiciously at the silent figure wringing out the dish towels; but Marion's face was turned from her, and she could not see whether or not there were traces of tears upon it. Marion hung up the dish towels on the little rack beside the range and went silently upstairs.

Jennie listened until she heard the door of Marion's room close; then she went back to her husband.

"Do you think she'll make trouble about selling this house?" she asked anxiously.

"Trouble? Pooh! She'll not make trouble," he said in his complacent voice that always soothed his wife. "She'll have her little cry over giving it up, but she'll be all right in the morning."

"But doesn't she own half of it?" queried the wife sharply. "Hasn't she a right by law to object?"

"Yes, she owns half of it, but she'll never object. Why, she'd give me her head if I told her she ought to," said the husband, laughing.

"She might give you her head," said Jennie with a toss of her own, "but she's got a terrible will of her own sometimes, and I've an idea she's got it on the brain to go to teachers' school, yet."

"Nonsense!" said her husband ponderously. "She's too old! Why, she's almost twenty-three."

"Well, you'll see!"

"Well, *you'll* see. I guess my sister has some sense! Come, let's shut up shop."

Marion locked her bedroom door and went straight to her white bed, kneeling beside it and burying her face in the pillow.

"O Father, Father," she whispered, "what shall I do? How can I bear it?"

Long after the house was silent, she knelt there trying to think. By and by she crept over to her back window, and, sitting in her willow chair, rested her cheek against the window frame. The spring air stole in and fanned her cheeks and blew the tendrils of damp hair away from her temples soothingly, like a tender hand.

The Warren home was a pleasant redbrick house with white marble trimmings and marble steps. It was in a nice, respectable neighborhood, with plain, well-to-do neighbors and neat backyards meeting on a cement-paved alleyway. In a few weeks now, these backyards would be carpeted with well-kept turf and borders of pretty flowers. Her own crocuses and hyacinths and daffodils that her beloved father had taught her to care for were even now beginning to peep through the earth. Her window had always framed for her a pleasant world of sights and sounds that were comfortable and prosperous. She loved to watch and compare the growing things in the green backyards, or to enjoy their clean white covering in winter; and she knew every varying phase of cloud or clearness in the bit of sky overhead. She looked up now; a broken moon beamed kindly down between dark, tattered clouds.

Within, the room was a white haven of rest. The simple enamel bed with brass trimmings, the white bureau and washstand, the willow chair, the plain muslin curtains, and the gray rugs with pink borders had all been the gift of her loving father. They represented sacrifice and extra night work after the wearisome day's toil was completed; and some had been acquired under protest of the more practical mother, who felt that the money might have been displayed to better advantage in the parlor.

Marion loved her white room. It seemed an inner shrine to fortify her soul against the trials and disappointments of life. And the bit of window view of flying cloud and neat yards and brick rows was a part of it all. The whole was linked eternally with precious memories of her dear father. And her brother was planning to take them all away! It was appalling!

It was not that she did not appreciate pure air and green grass and unlimited sky. She, more than the rest of the family, had the artist eye to see the beauties of nature. But the change meant to her a giving up of her life ambitions, a cutting herself off from the great world of education. Ever since her childhood, she had longed for a fine education and contact with the world of art and culture. She and her father had planned that she should be a teacher, and to that end she had taken great care with all her studies. Her mother had felt that she had had quite enough of school when she graduated from the high school, but her father encouraged her to take up the teachers' course. But five long years of nursing had broken in upon her fondest hopes. She realized that it was rather late for her to think of going back to teachers' school and completing her course. Quietly, patiently, she had relinquished the idea. Nevertheless, she had hoped to be able to do something else in the world that would bring her into contact with the things she most longed to see and hear and know. And the city was the only place where she could hope for that.

There were lectures, free libraries, great music, and sometimes exhibitions of wonderful pictures. She felt instinctively that there was still opportunity for her to acquire a certain amount of true education and mental culture; and she knew in her inmost soul that it was not to be found in that Vermont farmhouse, where the days would follow one another in a monotonous succession of homely household duties, enlivened by Jennie's pleasant shallow chatter. Jennie's idea of life was to keep one's house spotless and then to sit down with her sewing in the afternoon and enjoy it. She could not understand what more Marion wanted.

That might be all very well for Jennie. It would be Jennie's house and Jennie's children. Jennie cared for no more. It was certainly commendable in her. She was a good wife and mother. But Marion, even though she owned a part of the house, could not seem to feel that she really belonged there since her father's death. It was as though the home had passed into other hands.

Jennie had taken command in the house years ago, when Marion's mother first fell ill, and had always treated Marion as if she were a child who ought to do whatever she was told. There had been nothing else to do at that time but to put Jennie in command. It had been good of Jennie to be willing to give up her own home and come to help them out. Marion had always recognized that and tried patiently to do whatever Jennie asked in the ceaseless round of duties, relieving Jennie whenever it had been possible.

But now she felt that the time had come when she could no longer go on as an underservant, stifling the life that was in her for no reason at all. If it had been necessary for Tom's sake, or even for Jennie's or for the children's good, in any way, she would never have faltered. But here was no reason for anyone's sake why it was necessary for her to go on working in her brother's household, almost as if she were a sort of dependent. Half of the property, of course, belonged to her. And Tom had been doing a good business. He had money in the bank aside from what his father had left. If Tom went to farming, he would make that pay, too. He was an active, successful man. He could afford to hire a servant if Jennie wanted one. And Nannie was old enough to help a good deal. She often cared for the baby when her mother was busy.

Of course, if they had stayed on here at the old home, Marion would have felt that for a time, while the baby was so young, she ought to give all the help she could to Jennie. But Jennie seemed to talk as if this state of things was to go on forever. Marion knew now that it could not. It must not.

When Tom had first heard of the farm in Vermont and began to talk about going to see it, Marion had hoped against hope that the farm would not please him. But now, as she lay awake through the long night and thought it all out, she knew that she had been sure all the time that Tom would want to sell this house and buy that farm. And she knew that back in her consciousness she had been just as sure then as she was now that she was never going to be willing to go to Vermont with them.

She felt it would be like being smothered both mentally and spiritually, out in the country, away from all opportunities, with no books except the few she owned, no lectures or courses of study open to her, few chance meetings with helpful people, not even a church within walking distance. Marion's church life, quiet and unobtrusive though it had been, was very dear to her—the church of her father and mother, the church of her childhood. The prospect looked utterly dreary to her. And yet, if she refused, what was she to do? Demand her part of the money and buy another house, a smaller one? And try to keep house all by herself? That would be dreary, lonely, but peaceful perhaps. But Tom would not be able to purchase his farm unless he had all the money that came from the sale of this house, and Tom would be bitter about it. Jennie would, anyway. Jennie's people lived in New England. She had always longed to go back.

For the first time since her father's death, Marion considered seriously the matter of her inheritance.

Tom had said there was no will and seemed to consider that it meant that they had all things in common. That might be all very well while they remained in the old home, but if they separated what ought she to do about it? Demand her share? Of course her father had intended that she should have her part.

Almost his last words had been about the home. Poor Father, he would not have liked Tom to sell the house. He had loved it as much as she did. But surely she had some right in things. What ought she to do about it?

She had willingly signed all the papers Tom had brought to her at the time the estate was settled up, and asked no questions. She had been too sorrowful to care. Tom would, of course, do the right thing. Naturally, Tom would be terribly upset if she asked for money. He wanted to put everything into that farm. Also, he would think that Marion ought to stay with them and be taken care of. She did not like to stand in the way of his desires. Perhaps if she made no trouble about the sale of the house, if she quietly gave up her share, he would the more readily agree to her staying in the city. In fact, after her long vigil she began to see clearly that if she could not bring herself to go with the family to the country, it was plainly her duty to give up her share of the property. This was not, of course, according to her father's plan for her, but it seemed the only way without coming to an open clash with Jennie and hurting her brother irretrievably. If she gave up her claim, surely there was nothing left for Tom to say. She had a right to live her own life and do the things her father had planned for her to do.

Of course, she reflected, it would be a great deal harder to accomplish anything in the way of education without money. She would have to earn her living, and that would leave little time for study. But there would be a way. She was sure there would be a way for her to be independent. It was the only thing possible. It would be equivalent to mental and spiritual death to live her life out with Jennie. They had not a thought in common. She must get out and away and breathe the free air. She must live out some of the longings of her soul, or she would die of stagnation. Life was not merely a round of household duties spiced with gossip and blame. Why, Tom and Jennie scarcely ever even went to church. Sunday was like every other day to them, a day to get more done. They wondered at her that she cared to waste her time in teaching a Sunday school class and why she was interested in a church that brought her no social life.

If they had stayed in the dear old home where all her precious memories clung, she might have endured it, but since they were going to a strange place, it was far better she should leave them. And she was conscience-free, surely, if she gave up her share of the property. If Father had left a will, it would have been different, perhaps, but since he had not done so, it was better to say nothing about it. Just let it all go. There would be some way. She would not ask for a penny.

Marion came down early the next morning and got breakfast. There were dark rings under her eyes, and her lips were white; but otherwise she wore the same quiet calm that had been on her face during the patient years of serving her mother and father.

Jennie eyed her sharply and drew a breath of relief that there was no sign of rebellion on the sweet, sad face.

Tom came in with his boisterous "Good morning" and appeared to have forgotten all about the little out-break of the night before. He ate his breakfast hastily and hurried off to find Matthews.

Marion washed the breakfast dishes as usual. Jennie was impatient with her that she did not talk. It seemed sullen and ugly of her. Jennie wanted to bubble over about the prospect of the farm and was annoyed that she could not. She did not understand Marion's attitude of quiet resignation. Jennie had never cared for red-brick with marble trimmings. She had lived in a suburb before she was married and had ideas about a single house and a Dutch hall, but a Vermont farmhouse might have possibilities of spaciousness beyond even a Dutch hall.

Tom came home at noon in high glee. Matthews had paid a hundred dollars down to bind the bargain. He was to pay the remainder in ten days and wanted possession at the end of the month.

Marion said nothing but wore a white, pained look as if she had braced herself to receive this blow and would not wince. Jennie and Tom stole furtive glances at her but made no reference to her words of the evening before.

Marion ate but little lunch and hurried through the dishes afterward. Jennie watched her uncertainly. At last she said, "Marion, what if you and I take down the curtains and wash them this afternoon? We can't begin too soon to get packed. A month isn't long."

"I'm sorry," said Marion gently as she washed her hands and hung up her apron, "but I have to go out this afternoon. I'll try to help tomorrow morning."

Then she went up to her room, leaving Jennie vexed and mystified and worried. What in the world could Marion have to go out for? Why did she have to be so terribly closemouthed? She was acting very strange indeed, Jennie decided. Maybe she was going to make trouble after all. Tom was always so cocky about everything. He ought to have had a good talk with his sister and let her get her grouch out of her system. This silent gentleness was dangerous.

She watched behind the parlor curtains and saw Marion signal a trolley going downtown, and went back to her work with uneasiness. She wished Tom would come back. He ought to know Marion had gone out.

Half an hour later, Marion entered the imposing building of a great trust company down in the city and timidly approached the clerk behind the steel-grated window, frightened at her own nerve, so that her voice fluttered as she asked for the president of the great company.

"Mr. Radnor is very busy today," said the brusque young clerk, eyeing her doubtfully, noting her shyness and shabbiness, and growing haughtier. "He has a meeting of the board of directors at three o'clock, and it is a quarter to three now. I doubt if he can see you this afternoon."

"Oh," said Marion with a quick little movement of her hand to her fluttering throat. "Oh, I won't keep him but a moment. If you would just tell him my name and ask him if I can see him just for a word—it won't take long."

The clerk hesitated but wrote down her name and gave it to a messenger, who departed through a great mahogany door into the inner regions. Marion stood palpitating. Now, if he shouldn't be able to see her today, she would have to come again, and there was so little time! Each day counted for a lot. And when Jennie got started at tearing up the house, it would be next to impossible to get away without explaining, and that would be fatal to her intentions. She felt her only chance for success was to keep her plans to herself until they had matured. Tom would surely find some way to frustrate them unless she did.

But suddenly the messenger returned through the heavy door and nodded to the clerk, who turned with a more respectful look and informed Marion that Mr. Radnor would see her for a moment if she would be brief.

Now it happened that the president of the trust company, who was also superintendent of Marion's Sunday school and senior elder in the church to which she belonged, had known and respected Marion's father for a good many years and was also a kindly soul. So when Marion, fairly frightened out of her senses to think that she had dared to come into such a distinguished presence, was presently ushered into his inner sanctum, he greeted her with great cordiality and seated her in one of his big leather chairs.

"Good afternoon, Miss Marion," he said, beaming pleasantly upon her. He prided himself that he knew the entire Sunday school by name and never made a mistake, although there were some fifteen hundred on the roll. "I am glad to see you, although I have but a few minutes to spare before a most important meeting. Is there anything that I can do for you? Your father was a man whom I greatly honored and whose friendship I prized beyond most. He was a man of God if there ever was one."

Marion looked up with a sudden light in her eyes and forgot her fright.

"And he had a great admiration for you, Mr. Radnor," she said shyly. "He once said he would rather ask a favor of you than of any man he knew, because he said you treated a poor man as if he was a prince."

"Well, he was a prince if there ever was one," said the bank president heartily, "and I feel honored that he so honored me. Now, if there is any service I can render his daughter, I shall be doubly pleased."

"Well," said Marion with a sudden return of her embarrassment, "I want to get a position as a saleswoman in a department store. Could you give me a letter of introduction somewhere to someone you know? I think I could be a salesgirl. It seems to me the work would be easy to learn, and I would try with all my ability to do credit to whatever recommendation you feel you can give me."

"Why, surely," beamed Mr. Radnor heartily.

He delighted to do favors to members of his Sunday school, and it happened that this request was one that he was peculiarly able to grant just at that time. One of the chiefs in a great department store was under heavy obligation to him. He felt reasonably sure that anything he asked of the man at that time would be readily granted. Moreover, he was one who delighted to please others, especially when it cost him little trouble. He turned to his telephone and called up his man.

Marion's cheeks glowed with pleasure as she listened to the one-sided conversation and heard the glowing praise of her father's sterling character and the kindly words about herself. In wonder she listened and knew the gate of her desire had swung wide at the magic touch of this great man's word.

It was just one minute of three when the bank president hung up the receiver and turned to Marion, graciously smiling.

"It's all right, Miss Marion," he said in the same tone he used to announce the annual Sunday school picnic. "You can have a position as soon as you are ready to take it, I think. You'll need to answer a few questions, of course, but they are mere formalities. Mr. Chapman has promised to give you something worthwhile. You had better go right over and make out the application while it is fresh in his mind. He said he could see you in half an hour. You are to come to the second-floor office and inquire for Mr. Chapman. Here, I'll give you my card." He hastily wrote across the top of his card, INTRODUCING MISS MARION WARREN, and handed it to her.

"Don't think of thanking me. No trouble whatever. I'm only too glad that it was possible for me to do it.

It is fortunate that you caught me just at this time, as I am usually out of the office before this hour. Now I must go to my appointment. Sorry I can't visit with you a few minutes. I hope you'll have no trouble in securing just what you want at a good salary. He promised me he would do his best for you financially for a start and give you opportunity to rise. Come back if you have any trouble, but I don't think you will. Good afternoon. So glad you came."

It was over, the dreaded interview.

Marion stood on the steps of the great building and looked back at it with awe as an employee lazily closed and fastened the great gate of shining steel bars. The massive stone building seemed to tower kindly above her as if it had been a kind of church in which some holy ordinance had been observed, so truly she felt that God had been kind to her and helped her in her need.

Chapter 4

She hurried to the department store, full of tremors. As in a dream, she passed through the ordeal there. She came out a half hour later dazed with the swiftness of the system through which she had passed. She went to the waiting room and sat down for a minute or two to think it over and steady herself. She dared not go home to her sister-in-law with the strangeness of it all upon her. It seemed odd to her that people passing back and forth in the store did not look at her and see from her eyes that something unusual had happened to her. She was employed, regularly employed as a saleswoman, although it had been strongly impressed upon her that the size of the salary she was receiving was entirely due to the influence of the bank president and that, in the words of the brusque Mr. Chapman, it was "up to her" to get more pay as rapidly as she chose. It was at the ribbon counter that she was to begin, but perhaps someday she might attain to the book department. Mr. Chapman had intimated that there might be a vacancy there soon, and he would see. Her eyes shone in anticipation. To handle books! To know them as if they were people, acquaintances! To be among them all day long! What joy that would be!

She sat quietly thinking it over for at least ten minutes, looking around at the great store with its rising galleries and vaulted arches, listening to the heavenly music that came from the organ up in the heights somewhere among those tiers of white and gold pillars. It was her store. She was part of it. In a little while she was to be one of the wheels in the great mechanism that made this institution possible. She would be where she could watch the multitude of passing faces, hear the grand music, and now and then catch passing bits of uplifting conversation. It was wonderful, wonderful! How glad her father would have been! Of course he would have been sorry, grieved, that it must be just as a salesgirl she was to start out in life, and not as a teacher; but that could not be, and she knew he would have been glad of this opportunity for her.

Then, with a little quaking in her heart at the thought of Tom and Jennie and what they would say, she rose hurriedly and wound her way through the store, a little frail figure of a girl with shining eyes and a flower face, her plain, neat street suit and black felt hat attracting little attention beside the gaudy spring attire that flaunted itself on every hand.

She had to stand in the trolley car nearly all the way home; for it was after five o'clock, and cross, tired shoppers filled up every seat before the shy girl could reach them. The red had faded from her cheeks by the time she reached home, and Jennie noticed that she looked worn and tired, albeit the glow in the girl's eyes puzzled her.

"Where on earth have you been?" she questioned sharply. "I should think with all there is to do you might have hurried home."

"I have been to see someone," said Marion, as she had planned to say. "I came home as soon as I could."

"H'm!" said her sister-in-law significantly. "Well, I've taken down all the curtains and washed them this afternoon, and I'm tired; so you can get supper. You better hurry, for Tom has to go out this evening early."

Without answering, Marion laid aside her hat and coat and obediently went into the kitchen, tying on her apron as she went. In spite of her, she could not get rid of a feeling of guilt in the presence of her sister-in-law, but out in the kitchen by herself she felt like singing at the thought of the prospect before her. She would not have to take orders from Jennie anymore, nor bear her frowns and sharp words. She would be her own mistress. There might be orders in the store, of course there would, but she would have her hours and her times when she might do as she pleased. Her whole life would not be under unsympathetic surveillance.

But Jennie was not nearly as unconcerned as she tried to appear. She was genuinely worried. Had Marion somehow found that will? Did she suspect that it had been hidden? She longed to go to the old desk and see whether it was still where she had hidden it, but she did not dare lest Marion should see her and suspect something.

"Do you suppose she's been to see a lawyer about whether she's got to sign away her part of the house?" questioned Jennie in a whisper when Tom came home.

"Nonsense! Jennie," exclaimed her husband, "what's got into you? Marion won't make a fuss. She never did in her life. She's a meek little thing. She wouldn't dare. You'll find her as interested in the plans as you are in a few days."

"Well, I'm not so sure," said his wife with set lips. "I shall breathe easier when that deed is signed."

"Fiddlesticks!" said her husband. "You leave Marion to me, and for pity's sake don't talk to her about it. Half the trouble in this world is made by this continual haranguing. Women always have to yammer a lot about everything. It makes a man sick!"

Nevertheless, at the dinner table he eyed his sister

surreptitiously and seemed anxious to appease her. He talked a lot in a loud, breezy tone and tried to make them all laugh. He laughed a great deal himself and spoke of what nice times they were going to have on the farm. He passed Marion the cake twice instead of eating the last piece himself as he usually did.

"How about it, girls?" he asked jovially as he carefully picked up some crumbs on the tablecloth beside his plate. "Can we get packed up in three weeks?"

"Of course!" said Jennie sharply, not daring to look at Marion.

"How about it, Marion, do you think we can?" asked her brother as Marion arose to clear off the table.

"Why, I should think so," said Marion coolly as she gathered up a stack of dishes.

She felt as if she were shouting it and marveled at how willing she was now to have the house sold, if sold it must be, since she had a new life before her. Not that she was at all reconciled to leaving her home; but she had decided that it was the right thing to do to let Tom get his farm, and having decided, she had put it away from her thoughts. She knew the wrench was going to be very great when it came, but she did not feel quite so bitter about it now that she had a prospect of something besides the desolation of a farm life in Jennie's continual company.

But she did not want her brother to discover her

secret yet, so she hurried out of the room lest he suspect something in her acquiescence to his plans. She knew that the traditions of the family made it imperative that she should be taken care of. Tom was old-fashioned. He would not think it right to leave her alone in the city. He would feel he was not doing his duty by her. Tom was determined to do right by her, though his ideas of what were right for her were sometimes out of focus. She had not yet planned how to carry out the rest of the project, nor how to break the news to her brother that she was not going with him to Vermont. But if he found it out too soon, he would surely manage to upset all her plans and perhaps make it necessary for her to go after all.

But Tom was not of a suspicious nature and was too conceited to think that his sister would stand out long against him. So he only raised his eyebrows at his wife with a knowing "See, Jennie?" and began to whistle.

After that the packing went merrily forward, and no one could complain that Marion did not do her share, though all the time her heart was exceedingly sorrowful at leaving her old home.

❧

When Wednesday evening came, Marion hurried through the dishes and put on her coat and hat.

"Marion, you're never going to prayer meeting tonight

after the way you've worked today!" exclaimed Jennie disapprovingly. "I think you owe it to us to stay at home and rest if you won't consider your own feelings. There's more yet to do tomorrow. You ought to stay at home and go to bed."

Marion turned in dismay at this new obstacle to her plans. She had been troubled to seem to dissemble about the prayer meeting, but it was the only way to get a chance to go out and hunt a boarding place without being questioned, and a whole week was gone already. She looked at her sister-in-law in distress.

"I would rather go, Jennie," she said, and felt as if she were uttering a lie. "You know I am used to going out Wednesday night—"

"Well there's such a thing as carrying religion too far and making it ridiculous. You're going away from here soon now, anyway, and it doesn't matter one prayer meeting more or less. From now on I think you'll be plenty busy without prancing off to that church where the folks don't care a straw about you, anyway. Besides, if you have any strength left, I wish you'd stay home and help me let down Nannie's dress for traveling. She's grown so tall it won't do at all."

Marion stood uncertainly by the door. Was it possible she must stay at home this evening? Just then help arose from an unexpected source.

"Oh, let her go if she wants to, Jennie. She always

was a great one for church, and we're going off in the country where she can't get to church often. She might as well take her fill before we leave. As for letting down Nannie's dress, I'd wait till I got there, for she'll have trouble in going on a half-fare ticket if you make her look a day older. Run along, Marion; you've earned your evening. Do as you like with it."

Marion cast a grateful look at her brother and hurried out into the darkness, still feeling guilty with the knowledge that she was not going to church tonight, yet afraid to say anything lest she should be stopped.

Tom retired behind his paper while his wife informed him that he made a perfect little goose out of Marion. No wonder she was spoiled. If he was half as good to his wife, he'd have kept his sister at home to help her this evening. She was too tired to put the children to bed.

Whereupon he informed her dryly that Marion was nearly twenty-three years old and didn't have to do as she was told; in fact, didn't have to live with them at all, so he didn't exactly see the point. After which he folded up his paper and put the children to bed himself, which mollified his wife somewhat but also gave him a period in which to reflect on the usefulness of unmarried sisters.

~◠◡~

Marion's evening was a fruitless search. She could not find anywhere in the neighborhood a room that was not far beyond her pocketbook. And it began to seem as if boardinghouses, at least any that looked at all possible, were only for multimillionaires.

Marion felt that her disappointment was a just reward for staying away from prayer meeting, and she went home more downcast than she had been since her brother announced his intention of selling the house. How could she find a place to live without explaining the whole matter to her brother? Perhaps that would yet be the only way out of her difficulty. But now to her uncertainty was added the fear that there were no places where she could possibly afford to live that would not be intolerable for one reason or another. They were either too hot or too cold or too unsanitary or too utterly distasteful in some way, when they were not too expensive. Once in a while she would find one that she thought could be made to do, and then she would discover some terrible drawback and have to move on to another place. So she came home, a trifle later than she usually came from prayer meeting, and had to meet Jennie's sharp eyes and prying questions about why she was so late.

Two days later, however, Jennie announced her intention of taking the children and making a flying farewell visit to her sister, who lived in a small town thirty miles away. She would go early Friday morning and return Monday. She felt that the packing was well started and Marion could do a good deal while she was gone. Marion's attitude had been so pleasant and willing that her fears were somewhat set at rest, and she longed to have a little ease herself, for she had worked very hard. She knew, too, that Marion could pretty well be counted on to do the work of two people in her absence, so she went with a mind free to enjoy her vacation.

Marion had agreed to the suggestion readily enough. She knew she could work early and late and still have time free for what she wanted to do for herself, and Jennie's absence seemed really providential. Tom was away all day from breakfast until evening settling up his business affairs, not even coming home to lunch on Friday or Saturday, he said, so she was free to do as she pleased.

So Marion hurried through the breakfast dishes and locked the door on the duties Jennie had suggested, and made her way downtown to hunt a place to live.

She had several plans. There was a girl who used to be in the same Sunday school class who worked downtown, a secretary or something. She boarded somewhere.

She would go and ask her some questions.

But the girl was very busy taking dictation and could not be seen for a long time, and when she did appear she gave very little help. Yes, she boarded not far from her office, but it was rotten board, she said, and not a very pleasant bunch of boarders. She was thinking of making a change herself. Lots of girls took a room and got their meals at restaurants or did some cooking in their rooms, but she couldn't see that after working all day. She suggested several places where Marion might look for rooms, and Marion finally went away armed with addresses, much wiser and more anxious.

She longed inexpressibly for a room of her own, no matter how tiny it might be. The idea of a small gas stove appealed to her tremendously. Even without a gas stove she felt sure she could manage her breakfasts and perhaps an occasional evening meal. Or, if she took a good meal at a restaurant in the middle of the day, she might make her evening meal, usually very simple, milk and fruit and crackers or cereal, and that could be managed in her own room of course. She disliked the thought of constant daily contact with other boarders, especially since her talk with the other girl, who made it plain what kind of people she had to mingle with in a cheap boardinghouse. A restaurant was different. One did not have to be so intimate with a crowd as with individuals at the same table.

She went to one of the restaurants the girl had suggested and ordered a glass of milk and some crackers, and while she was eating them studied the menu. It seemed from the card to be quite easy to select a substantial meal for a very small sum if one was careful about counting the cost. If the lack of variety palled, she could always try another restaurant.

Before the morning was over, she had gone into many dreary little halls and climbed many steep, narrow flights of stairs in her search, till she began to feel that nowhere in the wide world was her little refuge to be found at any price that she could hope to pay; and her promised wages, that at first had seemed so large, began to dwindle. How very little her pay was going to be able to purchase in the way of comfort for her. Oh, if her father had foreseen this, how troubled he would have been! Perhaps she was doing wrong. Perhaps she ought to go with Tom.

But no, she had her own life to live, and her father would have been just as disappointed to have had her lose the other things of life, which were only to be had if she remained near the city with its music and art and libraries and evening schools. She must have a chance.

Now and then a feeling of a sob came in her throat. It ought not to be so hard for her. She ought to have her part of what her father had left. But she shrank inexpressibly from Tom's look when he told her, as he surely would, that she was spoiling all his prospects in life by her silly whims, and that of course, if she wanted her half of the money it would be impossible for him to get the land he wanted, but together they could have a nice home. No, let him have the home and be satisfied. She would take her chance without the money. Then he had nothing for which to blame her.

So she toiled on from apartment house to apartment house, in fruitless search.

About the middle of the afternoon, and just as she was beginning to think with sinking heart that she would have to take a little hall bedroom without heat or give up her plan entirely, she came at last upon a room that seemed to have possibilities.

It was on the third floor back in the saddest of all the sad little houses she visited, and its roof sloped at the sides.

It had no heat, but there were two lovely dormer windows looking toward the river, and the spring was coming on. She need not think of heat. Besides, the sad-faced woman who took lodgers said there was a pipe-hole in the chimney, and she had an old wood-stove that she wouldn't mind putting up in the winter if the young lady would bring up her own wood. Seeing as the young lady had her own furniture and wouldn't even require a carpet, she would let her have it very cheap.

Marion joyfully accepted the proposition. The land-lady had reluctantly agreed that she might move her things in as soon as was convenient, but the rent was not to begin until the first of the month, which was a little more than a week off.

All the way home, the girl was trying to think what would be best to do about moving her things. She knew her brother would make serious objection to her remaining in the city. He might even go so far as to refuse to let her take her things out of the house. Not that he had any right, of course, for the things were her own; but she knew he would use any method to pre-vent her staying if he took the whim to be obstinate about it. Marion felt she could afford to run no risks now. She must get her furniture moved at once and then keep her door locked. There was no other way.

As soon as dinner was out of the way, she shut herself into her room and went to work. Tom had gone out again as soon as he finished his dinner, so she was not hindered by anything, and he had not thought to ask her what she had been doing all day. Her eyes were bright with excitement and unshed tears. But she had no time to cry. Tenderly and hurriedly she took down the few pictures and little ornaments and packed them into the bureau drawers with as many of her other belongings as she could get in. She packed the china washbowl and pitcher carefully, wrapping them in an old quilt, and tied newspapers about the white bed and other furniture until the room resembled a ghostly edition of itself.

When all was done, she lay down upon the bare mattress, her head upon the tied-up pillows and her raincoat spread over her. She was not sure how she was going to sleep the rest of the nights they stayed in the house, but she was too tired to care. She meant to get her own things into her own little room before her brother and sister-in-law found out anything about it. After they were once safely out of the house, she could work with a free mind.

She carried out her purpose the next morning, securing a wagon to take her furniture and then hurrying in the trolley car to her new quarters to receive her things and see them safely housed. The landlady had had the room swept and the floor wiped up. The spring sunshine was flooding the windows, and all together Marion felt that it was not a bad prospect for a home.

As soon as the furniture was all carried in, she locked the door and sped back to her neglected work. The rest of the day she worked as if her life depended on getting things done, not even stopping to get any lunch for herself. She had paid the first month's rent and the mover out of her own small hoard, which had been saved from time to time during many years. She had but fifteen dollars left on which to live until she should receive her first week's pay, but she felt confident she could make it do, and she was happy in a way, happier than she had been since the death of her father.

She hurriedly improvised a temporary bed for herself from the old cot used during her father's illness, stored away in the loft. Then, taking care to lock her door, she went at the duties that her sister-in-law had suggested she should do.

It was not until Tuesday morning that Jennie discovered the locked door.

Chapter 5

It was the afternoon before the goods were to be taken away. Marion had been hoping against hope that she could keep her secret until a few loads had left the house. Then surely no one would notice her room was practically empty, or think anything of it. She had suggested to Jennie that it would be a good time for her to go to the stores for a few last things that she needed for the journey and that she herself would stay and direct the men what to take first. It seemed as if everything were going all right with her plans. But she had not calculated on the whims of her sister-in-law.

Marion was in the kitchen packing pot and pans, salt cellars, and kitchen cutlery, labeling each box carefully so that those who unpacked it would have no trouble in finding everything. Suddenly Jennie appeared in the doorway with her eyes blazing angrily and a sneer on her tired, dirty face.

"Marion, what on earth do you keep your door locked all the time for? You act as if you expected us to steal something!"

Marion turned and tried to smile in the face of Jennie's fury.

"Why, it looked so untidy up there. All my things are spread out, you know. I started to pack my clothes this morning."

If only she could keep Jennie in good humor so that Tom would not have to know yet!

"Well you certainly are a prude if there ever was one. Give me the key. I want to go in there and throw these pillows and a rug out of your window. It will save lugging them downstairs."

Marion turned, wondering what to do.

"Why, let me go up and throw them down," she said pleasantly. "Here, you sit down in this chair and finish wrapping these little things. You look tired to death."

But Jennie turned on her almost in a fury.

"Give me that key!" she said. "I believe you are afraid I'll pry into your things or maybe take something. But I'm not standing anything more from you, and I haven't time to argue. Where is the key?"

"Jennie!" said Marion in distress, "you know that isn't true. I just thought it would rest you to sit down awhile."

"Oh yes, *rest!*" sniffed Jennie. "I haven't time for rest. And I hate doing that little finicky work anyway. Finish what you've begun, and give me the key."

Marion, with set lips and cheeks turned suddenly scarlet, handed over the key and went on with her work. Perhaps the revelation might as well come this way.

"How strangely you look at me," said Jennie as she grabbed the key. "I actually believe you don't want me to go into your room."

Jennie hurried upstairs, and Marion could hear her dragging the heavy rug to the door, fitting in the key, and unlocking it. There was an instant's silence—ominous silence, and then angry footsteps hurried down the stairs and Jennie burst into the kitchen again.

"What on earth does all this mean?" screamed Jennie, her eyes fairly snapping. "I knew you were up to some tricks; you were so meek and quiet. And now I see why you locked your door. People don't keep locked doors in their own house unless they have something they're ashamed of to hide. What have you done with your furniture, Marion Warren?"

Marion turned around and faced her angry sister-in-law, her face white but calm, her voice as gentle as her state of nervous excitement would admit.

"Listen, Jennie, it was my own furniture. I had a right to do what I liked with it. I have done nothing I am ashamed of."

"No, I don't suppose you are ashamed. You don't know enough to know when you ought to be ashamed. Well, what have you done with it? Sold it? Because if you have, I'm sure I don't know where you're going to get any more to furnish your room. Are you intending to sleep on a cot all your life and keep your hairbrush and comb on the floor?"

"No, I haven't sold it, Jennie," said Marion, trying to steady the involuntary tremble that would creep into her voice. It always made her tremble to face Jennie in one of her fits of anger.

"Well, what have you done with it? For mercy's sake don't waste all the afternoon telling me. I'd be glad to know the worst at once."

"It isn't dreadful, Jennie," said Marion, looking at her wistfully. "I really think perhaps it will be a relief to you in the end. I've sent it away to a room I've rented."

"A room you've rented! Indeed! And what have you rented a room for, I'd like to know!"

"To live in," answered Marion simply.

"To live in!" screamed Jennie. "You don't say! And who is going to support you while you live in it, may I ask? Or is that a secret? Perhaps that's something you'd like to hide behind locked doors, too!"

There was a covert sneer in Jennie's words that brought the vivid color to Marion's cheeks, sweeping up over her brow and then receding again, leaving it white as death. Her eyes, too, had grown cold with hurt dignity.

"I have taken a position in Ward's store," she said almost haughtily, and turned back to her work again, trying to down the stinging tears that threatened.

The angry sister-in-law stood speechless for a moment, too taken aback for words. At last she spoke, biting words that stung as they fell about the troubled girl.

"And you call that right, do you? You think you're a Christian, don't you? You're always going to church and prayer meeting and pretending to be better than anybody else, and you're always so hypocritically sweet and patient. Oh yes, but you're sly! The idea of your going to work and sneaking your furniture out of the house as if you thought we might steal it, and going about it in an underhanded way, just to make your brother trouble. Here he's slaving and planning to make a nice, permanent home for you, where you will be cared for all your life and be safe and comfortable, and you act up like this! Why didn't you come out straight and tell him you didn't like him? Answer me that! Why didn't you tell him all about it? There must be some hidden reason why you want to stay. You're afraid to tell your brother. I understand."

Jennie was so angry now that she did not really know what she was saying.

"There's probably some man at the bottom of this. There's always a man!"

But suddenly Marion turned and took hold of her furiously, her face white, her eyes black with indignation. She took hold of Jennie and shook her.

"You shall not say a thing like that! You shall not! It is not true, and you know it is not true! I could not go to Vermont. My father wanted me to stay here and get an education! I couldn't go away! You have no right to say such things about me!"

Marion had caught Jennie unaware and for a moment had been able to punctuate her sentences by shaking her as if she had been a child too astonished to recover herself. But her slender hold had not a chance in the world against Jennie's stout arms, and in a moment more, Jennie had wrenched herself free and dealt a resounding slap on Marion's white cheek.

Stinging with pain and humiliation, Marion buried her face in her hands, and moaning, turned and fled up to her room, blindly stumbling over the heavy rug that Jennie had left in a heap in the doorway. Falling headlong, she lay for a moment, too crushed to do anything but lie there shaking with silent sobs.

Then suddenly she realized that she must not let herself be defeated this way. She had done wrong perhaps to shake her sister-in-law, even though she had insulted her, but she was in the right in demanding her freedom. She must go down and face Jennie again and explain.

Hastily dashing the tears away, she got up and went downstairs to the furious Jennie.

"Jennie, I am sorry I shook you," she said gently, "although you said something that made me very, very angry."

"Oh yes, you're sorry now," flashed Jennie, gloating over Marion's humiliation. "You're afraid of what your brother will say, laying hands on his wife. It doesn't look very well for a Christian to go around shaking people just because she doesn't like to hear them tell her the truth and call a spade a spade, but you'll have to learn that the world won't stand for your sly ways, and Tom won't either. Well, as far as I'm concerned, I'm glad it came out for once. Tom always thinks you are so sweet and meek and gentle. I wonder what he'll think now. The idea of attempting to shake me! Tell me what I shall say and what I shan't. You sly little minx—you. Get out of my sight! You make me sick, getting up a scene like this and planning to upset all your brother's plans."

"Jennie, that isn't true," said Marion boldly. "It can't possibly make any difference to you whether I go to Vermont or not, and I have not done anything wrong, either. I have only taken away the furniture that my father gave me when I was a little girl. I have not even asked for my share of the money from this house or from my father's life insurance or from his other property, although I'm sure I must have had a perfect right to do so. I thought it over and decided that I did not want to have Tom disappointed about the farm he meant to buy, and I could not see why it should make any difference to either of you if I stayed behind, so long as I gave up my share of the property."

"Property! Property!" babbled Jennie, too angry to reason, "as if property were everything. As if, of course, the property wouldn't be a man's to look after. As if your father didn't expect you would stay with your brother and behave yourself like a decent girl and not try to run around alone and set up your own apartment like these common flappers! As if you weren't leaving me with all the work of settling and the children to care for and everything, and me off alone there on the farm without any company or anyone to relieve me day in and day out!" She raged on, but Marion had control of herself now.

"Listen! Jennie, you didn't have to go on a farm if you didn't want to, and you had no right to demand that I go, anyway. Tom is perfectly able to hire help for you if you want it!"

"Yes, hire, hire, hire help! As if Tom was made of money! You're perfectly willing your brother should go to a great expense while you lie around and have a fine time!"

"Jennie! Stop! I'm not going to lie around and have a good time. I'm going to work hard and earn my living and get more education. And at least you will have the price of my board and keep extra, if you don't count that I had any right in my father's property. You don't seem to realize that you have taken away the home that I love from me. My father always said—"

But Jennie, with a frightened look at Marion, had fled to her room and locked the door behind her, and Marion could hear her sobbing aloud for a long time.

Marion, feeling that she had made a mess of everything and disgraced her Christian profession as well by losing her temper, went around finishing the rest of her work with sorrowful heart and troubled eyes in which were many unshed tears.

She tried to get together a nice little supper with the few utensils that were not packed, but when Tom came in the storm raged again, and nobody attempted to eat anything until it was all cold. Jennie came down to meet her husband in a perfect torrent of angry tears as soon as she heard his step in the house, and Marion had the added sorrow of seeing her brother turn horrified unbelieving eyes in her direction and reprove her bitterly.

"Marion! I never thought this of you. Is that really true? Did you lay hands on my wife and shake her?"

Marion opened her white lips to protest, but no

words came from her parched throat. She could only stare at her brother with wretched eyes. How could she speak up and say that Jennie had slapped her in the face? How could she tell that they had come to a common low-down fight, like two fish-wives, she a Christian, and her brother's wife! How could she justify herself? And because her heart was almost broken that Tom, her brother, should believe all that and not know that there was something to be said in her defense, she could not speak. Her throat refused her breath to clear herself.

So she had to stand there speechless and hear Jennie tell the whole miserable story over in her own version, blaming her and never telling what she herself had done.

And finally she had to see her brother soothing his wife and comforting her clumsily, and telling her she was all worn out and that she must go upstairs and lie down and he would bring her some supper, that she needed to rest; and then he helped her up the stairs, with cold reproachful looks at Marion, who had caused all this trouble.

After a long, long time, Tom came down and harshly called to her.

"Now, Marion, let me hear what you have to say. What is all this nonsense about you hiring a room? Of course you know I can't permit it."

Marion stood up straight and slim and white to the lips and tried to say the things she had planned to say to her brother, but her lips trembled so she almost broke down.

"Tom, I'm not a little girl; I'm of age. You have no right to say 'permit' to me. I have a right to stay here where Father planned that I should stay. And I am not doing wrong. I have deliberately planned to give up whatever share of property I should have had and to earn my own living—"

"So you think I'm so mercenary, do you, that all I will care about will be the property?" he interrupted, the hard, cold look in his eyes.

"Oh, Tom!" cried Marion. "Why won't you understand?"

"No, I can't understand," he said coldly. "This is merely a streak of stubbornness in you, and I suppose I shall have to let you go and try it before you will believe what a fool you are making of yourself. Everyone knows that father was visionary—!"

"Tom!" cried Marion. "Don't! Don't!"

"No, I won't," said Tom, "because it is of no earthly use. You have that streak in you, and I suppose you can't help it. It will have to be taken out of you, and I guess it won't take long working for your living before you find out. Very well, go your own gait and learn your lesson to your sorrow. You are of age, of course, and I can't prevent you forcibly. You've got the bug of education in your head, and you don't realize that you're too old now to make anything out of that. You've got all the education any reasonable woman, who is decent and stays in her own respectable home, needs. But you've got to find it out, so stay and learn your lesson. But remember that when you've learned it, your brother is ready to forgive you and take you back. There'll be a nice, comfortable home waiting for you with plenty of all that any woman needs to make her happy. You don't see it now, but the time will come when you'll be sorry and ashamed that you have treated your only brother this way. And you don't think for a minute, do you, that Father would want you to desert us and live by yourself in the city? Answer me that?"

"Tom, I think he would," said Marion sorrowfully. "The last thing he said was that I would have a home here in this house."

"Oh, you're going to harp on that again, are you? You are trying to punish me for selling this house. Well, you should have said so before it was sold. It is too late now. You had a perfect right not to sign your name to the deed if you didn't want to, but you never even mentioned—"

"Tom, I begged you that first night—"

"Oh yes, I know you went into hysterics at first. I expected that. But after you knew all the story, about what a wonderful place we were getting—"

"Well, Tom, I haven't blamed you about the house. I only—"

"Oh yes, you have blamed me. You said that Father said you were to have this house, and I had taken it away from you. You as much as said that. Come now, didn't you?"

"Tom, if you twist what I said that way, I can't talk any more about it. I—"

"Very well, young lady, don't talk! I won't talk either! No, I don't want to hear any more of your explanations. They are all insulting to me. I'm done! You go and do what you've planned, and when you find out what a mistake you've made, let me know, and we'll have some basis to go on. As things are, I've nothing further to say. Of course, if you change your mind before we leave, why you can go along yet, but I suppose that's too much to expect of a little silly head like you. You've made your bed, and you'll have to lie on it. No, don't say another word! I'm done!" And he stalked off upstairs without even looking at the nice supper she had prepared at such pains.

That last night in her dear old home was a most unhappy one for Marion. She did not sleep until almost daybreak, and then from sheer exhaustion. It was worse than even her wildest fears, but there was some relief that at last it was out and there was nothing more to dread.

The next morning she came down pale and sorrowful and prepared the last meal in the old home, and then slipped up the back stairs as the others came down the front ones and began to roll up the mattresses and fold sheets and pillow cases and stuff them into the drawers that had been left unlocked to receive them.

She was everywhere at once, it seemed, helping, bringing labels when they were needed, always knowing where the hammer and scissors and cord had been laid down, always knowing just which article of furniture Tom wanted the men to take next to pack in the car.

It was thus she happened to be in the den when the movers came in to take her father's desk out. It was covered in burlap, and Marion's eyes filled with wistful tears as the men lifted it up to carry it out of the room. Her father's desk, and she would likely see it no more. Why hadn't she asked Tom to let her have it? Still, there would scarcely be room for it in her tiny room. She must let it go. Perhaps, later when Tom became more reconciled to her new life, he might be willing she should send for it. She could pay the freight on it herself. But now she must let it go.

As the movers passed her, she noticed a brown envelope slipping down farther and farther from behind the drawers at the back of the desk. It was more than two-thirds protruding when they reached the door, and impulsively she stepped forward and twitched it out, stuffing it down inside her blouse without looking to see what it was. Probably nothing but an old empty envelope, but it had been her dear father's, and it was something she could keep and look at. Anyhow, whatever it was, it would only be lost on the way to the car if it were left sticking out that way. Then, because she was afraid Jennie might notice the stiff bulging and crackling of the envelope, she ran up to her room and slipped it into her little handbag, still without taking time to glance at it.

Tom made one more attempt to reason with Marion after the last load was gone and he had time to look around and see that everything was in order for the new tenants. Jennie and Marion had thoroughly cleaned the house, and there was nothing left to be done but to sweep where the men had brought in dust. So Tom followed Marion into the parlor, where she was brushing up nails and papers and making all clean and neat, and began to reproach her once more. Suddenly she turned on him desperately.

"Tom! Stop! You've always known Father meant me to study. He expected me to stay here in this home that he made for us, and it just breaks my heart to leave it. But since that could not be, I've made no fuss about selling the house because I saw it would break your heart not to have that farm, and you had to have the money to buy it. Now, please, please let me stay without being unkind to me. I cannot bear it. But anyway, I've got to stay. I've got to go to lectures and concerts and to night school, perhaps. I've got to have a chance. I would smother if I can't."

Tom, looking into his sister's pleading brown eyes, was startled by her likeness to their father, and he seemed to see something of the spirit of that father, who through all his gentleness had known how to be firm on occasion. So Tom knew it was of no use to say anything more. Marion could not be reasoned out of her "notions."

"It's no use to talk to her, Jen," he said, coming back to his wife. "She's set on getting more education, and you can't argue her out of it. Father put it into her head, and she's got to try it before she'll be satisfied. It won't take her long to get homesick for us all, and she'll be glad enough to come to us after a few weeks. The best way's to let her see how hard it is to live alone and earn her own living. That's the only way to cure her. She'll soon see her mistake and come running up to the farm."

"Yes, after all the hard work of settling is over," grumbled Jennie, dissatisfied. "You always were too soft-hearted about Marion. I might have known you'd give in. It's lucky the house is sold and the goods gone, or she might make you stay here yet."

The next two hours were filled with work and discomfort for Marion; but they were over at last, and the girl was glad to bid them all good-bye. She was tired of Jennie's alternate sharp words and icy silences; and the parting sarcasms were worst of all. It was only when the babies gave her sweet, sticky kisses and Tom gave a burly hug that a sense of coming loneliness swept over her. But she brushed away the gathering tears and waved a farewell.

Chapter 6

She was very tired, more so than she ever remembered to have been before, but there was a kind of elation upon her. She still felt the burden of the sorrow through which she had passed, the strain of the last few days, and the sudden desolation that had swept over her at parting with Tom, the only one on earth to whom she could rightfully say she belonged. Yet she realized that she was standing upon the threshold of a new life, and the whole world lay at her feet. It was not in any sense self-will that had brought her to this place. It was an honest desire, a fervid longing, to get for herself the things her father had striven to give her and failed. She felt that she owed it to him, and to the longings that were within her. They seemed a holy call. Perhaps she was wrong—if she was, she wanted to find it out—but she felt she was right.

If she had stayed in the city for her own pleasure, to participate in forbidden pleasure, to dress and gallivant and be generally selfish, she told herself this would not have been the case. But she had not. She had stayed to make herself the best that herself could be made—for the glory of God, she added under her breath. Just how her life could possibly be for the glory of God, she did not understand; only she had been taught early in her youth that it was, and she had grown up in the firm conviction. She earnestly desired to give God as much glory as possible.

So here she was her own mistress. She might apportion her hours, at least as many of them as she was not using for the store, in doing what she liked. It seemed wonderful. Some girls would have bought an ice cream cone at once and then gone straight to the movies, but Marion entered her freedom with bated breath and wonder in her eyes. Now that she was on her own responsibility, she felt she must walk carefully.

She stopped in the station restaurant and indulged in a cup of hot tea and a sandwich, looking about upon her new world with interest.

Over there in the corner were two girls about her own age laughing over the events of the day. Did they care for the great things for which she longed? Or were they trifling away? From some of their conversation that drifted her way she judged the latter. But anyway, whatever they were, she felt a sudden kinship with them and with all the universe of young, independent beings like herself. It was a little touch of the modern reaction that had reached her, perhaps, after all her years of patient, sweet subservience; or perhaps it was only her way of choking down the sob that came in her throat when she thought of the dark, empty house standing alone that had been her home for so many precious years, and of the only brother, harsh though he had been, who was speeding toward a new home far away.

She was such a conscientious child that she had to struggle with herself, now that the thing was done, not to reproach herself and feel after all that she had been wrong.

It was very dark climbing up her little, steep stairway. The landlady held a candle and apologized for a broken gas fixture that made the candle necessary. She said the last lodger had broken it off one night in a drunken rage because he ran into it.

Marion shuddered and escaped into her room, which looked weird and desolate with a single gas jet wavering over her paper-wrapped furniture. Her first glance about seemed to warn her that life was not to be all roses yet. She locked her door, remembering with horror a possible drunken neighbor in the room next door. Removing her hat and coat, she untied the mattress and pillows and placed them on the bed, which she had had the expressman set up when he brought it. She got out some blankets and without further ado dropped herself on the bed under the blankets and was soon asleep.

It was quite late in the morning before she awoke, for she had been thoroughly worn out and needed the sleep. There had been no rousing voice of her sister-in-law to waken her, no sense of duties calling, no clatter of the children.

It was wonderful just to lie still and gradually realize where she was and that no one had a right to call her or demand that she get up till she was ready. This feeling might not last, but it was good, for she had been mortally weary, soul and body.

When she finally did get up and went rummaging in her handbag for her watch to see what time it was, she came upon the envelope so hurriedly thrust there the day before and not thought of since. Tenderly she took it out and smoothed its rumpled surface, and was startled to see written on the outside in her father's neat, painstaking hand, "My Will."

For a moment, she sat looking at the words with an almost frightened feeling. There had been a will then, and Tom had not found it! What should she do with it now? Send it to him? Open it? Or would it be better not even to read it, just destroy it now, since all that had been done with the house was now irrevocable? It would only make Tom feel terrible if he had transgressed any of his father's directions, and it was too late to remedy that. Besides, it affected no one but herself probably, for Tom had all there was. Perhaps it might promote more ill feeling between them than there already was. Perhaps she ought to destroy it. Just destroy it without reading it. Perhaps that would be the Christian way.

She held it in her hand, looking at it, half inclined to feel that perhaps it was something she had no right to have.

But then, it wouldn't be right to destroy it either. There might be something in it that they didn't know about, something sweet and precious of which she, at least, would treasure the thought all her life, and surely she had a right to that since she had relinquished all the rest. It could do no possible harm for her to read it if she kept it to herself. Of course she must not let it influence her in any way nor let her mind dwell upon anything it might have given her. She had given up her inheritance of her own free will. There was no possible reason why the will should make the slightest difference now.

Slowly, almost reluctantly, she pressed back the unsealed flap of the envelope, took out the single sheet of paper that it contained, and read it through.

The familiar wording of the homemade will filled her throat with sobs and her eyes with tears, but she read it through to the end. Her father had left the house and all its furnishings and his savings fund account, amounting to several thousand dollars, entirely to herself. The life insurance money went to Tom. He called her "my dear daughter," and there was a tender sentence in the will appealing to Tom's chivalry to look out for his sister and see that she was enabled to carry out the plan that he had always had in mind for her education.

She dropped her face on the paper and covered it with kisses and tears. Her precious father! It was like a voice from the other world.

For a long time she sat there on the disheveled bed, her slender body shaking with sobs, as this tenderness brought back all the years of his constant care.

But gradually she grew calmer and, wiping her eyes, sat up and read the paper over again, taking in every detail till it was graven on her mind. She was glad she had read it. Glad her father had been so thoughtful for her. It would make no difference, of course. She had chosen her life. She was carrying out the spirit of her father's wishes, though she did not have his protecting care that he had done his best to make sure for her. But not for worlds would she let her brother know about the will. It could only bring him pain. He had bought his farm, and she knew him well enough to know that while he might not have approved of his father's "notions," as he called them, he was conscientious enough to have carried them out to the letter and said not a hesitant word about it. Jennie would have had her say, of course, and a good deal of it, but Tom would have been magnanimous and beautiful about it. He probably would have given up his own desire for a farm, too, and stayed in town to live with her that she might have her home as her father planned.

But perhaps it was just as well that things had turned out as they had. Tom had his wish, and she would be able to carry out hers somehow. God would help her. She felt confident that she could do it. So she would put away the will and keep it among her most treasured possessions, and sometimes when she was lonely and desolate, she would take it out and read it just to get the comforting feel of her father's voice to hearten her. But she would leave it where Tom never, never could find it to make him feel uncomfortable.

She bent her head to lay her lips on the signature once more before she slipped the paper back into its envelope, and a whiff of something pleasant and familiar came to her. What was it? Peppermint. How strange. Her father hated peppermint. The odor of it made him really ill. It was likely only the smell of the adhesive on the envelope flap or perhaps some peculiar kind of paper. Some paper had a strange odor. But it seemed odd that her father's will should smell of it; it seemed somehow a desecration. They never used to eat any candy flavored with peppermint when he was there because he disliked the smell of it so. It was just a little idiosyncrasy of his. Not that he objected to other people eating it, but she had always planned for his comfort not to have the odor of it around when he was in the house.

Her mother had been very fond of chocolate peppermints, and so was Jennie. Jennie had made some only a few days before her father died. It had hurt her terribly to think that Jennie would deliberately do what she must know would annoy the patient. Jennie had been eating a piece of candy when she came into their father's room that day after dinner, and Marion had motioned her away quickly. Jennie laughed. She thought it was nonsense. She said people ought not to be humored in such whims; it spoiled them. She had gone away in a huff. There had been smears of chocolate on her fingers and her dress. Marion remembered how untidy and disagreeable she had looked. Oh, she must stop thinking such things about Jennie! Mr. Stewart had preached about that—some verse from Second Peter about "exercising your mind in covetousness." He had said that people exercised their mind in evil thoughts of other people, and that was not the way to add to their faith, virtue, and to virtue, knowledge, and all those other things. She must add to her faith, self-control, and keep from thinking unpleasant thoughts about Jennie. She must pray to be kept from having anything in her heart but love for Jennie.

She folded the paper and slipped it into the envelope. Something seemed to catch one corner so that it did not go in smoothly; perhaps it was crumpled from being crushed into her bag. She put her finger inside to smooth it out gently and came in contact with something rough and hard. She looked, and a strange, cold feeling came in her throat. It was a tiny piece of chocolate and cream peppermint candy hardened onto the paper. How did it get into that envelope? Her father's envelope! Her father who hated it and never would have touched any. Jennie! The candy she had made and that she was eating when she left the sick room and went downstairs! Oh, it was unthinkable! But how could she help thinking about it?

There was another thing—how would that will get out of the little strongbox where Father always kept his papers? He was always so careful. It must have fallen down behind the drawer. Of course, he might have laid it in the drawer sometime and thought he had put it back in the box. Surely that must have been it. But if it had been locked in the box, how could Jennie—how could the peppermint? Oh, she must not think about it! She must not get to feeling that Jennie had done this despicable thing! She would hate her if she kept on this way. And hating, the Bible said, was equal to murder in God's eyes. No, she must not think this of Jennie. But how could she help it? What other explanation could there be? Why had Jennie done it?

A wave of anger swept over her, so that for the instant she was half ready to take the next train up to Vermont and face her sister-in-law with the will and the evidence of her guilt and demand her rights.

But of course she would not do that. If Jennie had been so untrue, Tom must not know it. Tom was honest whatever else he might be lacking in. And if he thought Jennie had done this thing, even with the best of intentions, he would be very severe with her. He might lose all his love for her. And she was the mother of his children. Tom must not know what Jennie had done, if she had done it.

Over and over again she turned the matter, now blaming, now excusing Jennie. Probably Jennie felt that she, Marion, would not suffer. She would have a good home, and all would be well without any financial complications. Mothers looked out for their children in these things, and Jennie was likely to have thought that the will was unfair, that perhaps Marion had influenced her father. Well, perhaps in a way it was not fair to Tom. But her father had always felt that Tom, being a man, could better look out for himself. Well, whatever it was, of course she was going to do nothing about it. Of course she was going to have to destroy that will. For now she must not keep it. Tom might find it someday if anything happened to her, and it would make trouble all around. Trouble for Tom and trouble for Jennie. No, she must live peaceably. And what was a little money?

And so, before her courage failed her, she laid her lips tenderly once more upon that will, and then resolutely carried it over to the little woodstove that her landlady had had set up in her room and struck a match from the box on the little shelf by the chimney. She held the will in the stove until it was burned to a crisp. Then she knelt down by her bed and prayed, "Dear Father, help me to keep from thinking about this. Help me not to blame Jennie unjustly and to be able to forgive her if she did it; and help me never to mention it or make any trouble about it."

Quite simply she arose and put it away forever from her mind as a question that had been settled once for all and must not be opened again. It was the kind of thing her father had taught her to do, to be what he called "square" and "Christian." That word *Christian* in his opinion covered everything that a meek and quiet spirit should have before God, living in this world but not of it. Of course there would be temptations to think hard thoughts of Jennie now and again, but she must resolutely put them from her each time they came and pray for strength. That was the only way to live at peace with all men in this world.

And so, when she was dressed, she tried to turn her thoughts to the new life before her and keep them from straying back to that will.

Two whole days she had before her, besides Sunday, before she must begin her work in the store. In that time she could get nicely settled and know just how to arrange her daily plans. She arose with a zest for life that the night before she had not dreamed she could feel.

Her breakfast was a ten-cent box of crackers from the little grocery around the corner and an apple that Nannie had pressed upon her at parting. Nannie more than the other children had cared for her aunt Marion.

Scrubbing was the order of the morning, but after everything was clean and shining, Marion decided to invest a little of her precious money in brightening up those dingy walls. If she only could find some cheap paper, she could put it on herself. Jennie and she had often done it. Sometimes one could get paper for very little if the pattern was out of fashion. And a very tiny can of paint would freshen up the dirty woodwork. The walls and paint were smoky, and she could not feel comfortable with them that way. With quick resolve, she hurried out to the stores and came back in an hour armed with rolls of paper, a tiny pot of gray paint, a bucket containing ten cents' worth of paste, and a great paste brush that the paperhanger had good-naturedly lent her.

That night saw the dingy walls covered with a pretty creamy paper in simple design. It made a wonderful difference in the room, and the wavering gaslight seemed to give forth twice as much light as before. When she had made up her bed and crept sleepily into it, she felt that she had accomplished a great deal. Tomorrow she would paint the woodwork and arrange the furniture. Then she would be ready to live.

The old landlady looked in toward noon, opening cautiously the door in its fresh coat of paint. Marion was putting down her rugs. On a chair by the window stood a hyacinth in bloom, one that the girl had been nursing all the spring. Its pale pink blossoms gave forth a rich fragrance, not altogether hidden by the clean smell of the paint. Over the footboard of the white bed hung two white muslin curtains ready to be put up when the paint was sufficiently dry. The white bureau was dressed up with small accessories, and the china pitcher and bowl were washed and in their places. Near the other window stood the willow rocker and the little writing desk close by, with its modest array spread out and a small rack of books atop. The old woman looked and looked again.

"My land!" she exclaimed in an awed voice. "I didn't suppose you could make it look like that! It's worth having you up here just to think there's a place like this in the house. I believe it'll kind of rest me to remember it."

Marion laughed happily and looked around upon her home. It was better than she dared hope, and she rejoiced in it. There might be trials ahead of her, but there would be this quiet, sweet spot away from everything.

"I just stopped up to say I'd be pleased to have you take Sunday dinner with me tomorrow if you care to. You ain't barely settled yet, and I don't suppose you'll mind not going out this first Sunday. It'll be quite a thing to have a pretty young lady like you at my table."

Marion thanked her and accepted the invitation, reflecting that she not only had a home but also had already gained a friend in her strange-looking landlady.

The new life was full of novelty, and Marion entered upon her duties in the store with a zest and energy that would have amazed her scornful family, who were hourly expecting her repentant return to their protection. The ribbons were a constant source of delight to her. She loved all beautiful things; and her shy, accommodating ways made her at once a favorite with her customers.

This would have brought her enemies among her coworkers had she been less humble or less willing to learn.

When she had her lunch hour, one of the girls in

the aisle, perhaps sent by the head of the department, Marion was not sure, smiled at her and asked if she would like to go with her to lunch that day.

She was a girl with closely cropped hair and a flimsy little black satin dress made very short and tight. Marion felt that it was not quite modest, but the girl had a pleasant smile and a hearty voice, and she was really frightened at the idea of making her way alone to the lunchroom in the store where most of the girls ate their noonday meal.

"You don't know the ropes, do ya?" asked the other girl. "I'll put ya wise. You don't wanna order rice pudding—it's the limit—but the coconut pie is a humdinger. You order coconut pie. You like coconut, dontcha?"

"Oh, I like almost anything," laughed Marion to cover her embarrassment. "But don't they have anything but desserts? I've got to be economical till I get started. I'm quite on my own, you see."

"Oh, we're all in that boat, sister. But gimme the pie every time. I havta eat just plain food enough at home. Pie and coffee's what I eat every day. I can't stand soups and slops, and I'm sick ta death of sandwiches of any kind. Meat ur cheese, ur some kinda vegetable, it's all the same to me. They stick in my throat. Gimme my pie an' coffee, an' I'm okay."

"But I should think you'd get sick living on things like that all the time. I haven't been used to it. I'm sure it wouldn't be good for me."

"Sick? Me sick? I should worry. Get off a day then. You're 'llowed a sick day now an' then, you know, an' b'lieve me, I get 'em every time. Nothin' coming to me I don't take. It don't pay not to. Ya havta look out for yerself. Nobody else's goin' to look out for ya. Here we are. Now, where you wanta sit? There's a place over there. Some of the crowd from my department there, too. I'll introduce ya. Say, whyn't ya bob yer hair? Make ya a lot more popular. I know they say it ain't being done anymore, but look around. I tell ya, look around. Do ya see another girl ain't got her hair bobbed? Besides, if the fashion really changes, it'll be easy enough to tie some on. Keep yer own an' tie it on with a net over it an' nobody'll ever know. Besides, when that time comes, you'll have plenty o' company. Everybody else gotta grow hair, too. Say, yer awful pale. Dontcha wantta borrow some of my lipstick? Ya won't get anywhere with some of the fellas if yer not upta date."

"Thank you," said Marion with a smile, inwardly aghast. "I don't think I'll bother. Tell me, why should I want to get anywhere with the fellows? I don't go out much, and I don't know any of them, you know."

The girl laughed loudly.

"Oh, that's a good one. You gotta good sense of humor, ain't you? Say, I b'lieve I'm gonna like you, but I do wish you'd bob yer hair. I'll take ya to my barber if ya will. They do a dandy cut; makes ya look just like a boy."

"Oh, but I don't think I care to look like a boy," smiled Marion. "I prefer to look like what I am."

"Aw, get out. You look just like a last-century school ma'am. You don't wantta, do ya?"

"Well, why not?" asked Marion brightly. "I've been trying for several years to be a school teacher."

"Good night! You? A school teacher? Wha-for?"

"Why, I think I'd like it. I love to teach anything."

"Good night! I don't. I hadta go down and teach a new girl how ta tie up packages before I left that department, and I thought I'd pass out. Why she was the dumbest thing you ever saw. She didn't even know how to curl the string around her finger to break it. Actually! Yes, that's right! I certainly was glad when I got her off my hands. Whadda ya wantta teach for? We have lots better times here. D'ya play any instrument? They have an orchestra here, an' ya get time off ta practice, an' there's a lot of dandy men there. There's one fella there, he's married, but he don't care; he carries on just like he was a young fella, an' he brings us chocolates, and we certainly have the time of our life. We write notes, too, an' good night! You oughtta see the note I got last night! He's some baby, the man that wrote it. He don't care what he says. I said, 'Ya think yer smart, dontcha?' but he knows I won't stand fer everything that baby does. Say, didn't you meanta order coffee?

743

Just milk? My word, you're a good little girl, ain't ya? But you'll get all over that here. Say, you got pretty eyes. When I first saw ya, I says to myself, 'I b'leeve I am gonta like that girl. I'll get her fer my buddy.' The girl I been goin' with was jealous of a man I know, an' I'm off her for life. Say, will you wait fer me when we go home? They'll let you off early 'cause it's your first day, an' you wait down by the girls' dressing room, right by the lockers, ya know. I'll be out as soon as I can, but you wait! Oh yes my name's Gladys Carr. What's yours? Marion? Say, that sounds real old-fashioned. It sorta fits yer eyes. But I think you oughtta put on some rouge. You're too pale."

She rattled on during the whole noon hour, with just a nod of assent now and then from Marion, and Marion went back to her counter rather shaken in her ideas, but wholly entertained and somewhat refreshed on the whole. After all, wasn't this girl going to be rather good for her in a way? One ought to know all sides of the world to understand what they were thinking about, and now she came to think of it, perhaps she was a bit old-fashioned. Certainly she didn't look much like the rest of the girls in the store, and perhaps that would work against her in the long run. She might lose her position. They might not want a strange-looking girl around.

On their way back to their department, they passed

one of the long mirrors with which the store abounded, and Marion studied her own slim little figure in its ill-shaped brown dress that she had worn for at least two years. It never had been an attractive brown, and Marion's artistic soul would not have chosen it, but it was made out of an old dress of her mother's, which she had felt she ought to use up. She had helped a neighboring dressmaker to make it just before her father was taken sick, and it had seemed a very nice dress at the time. It was too long, of course. Strange she hadn't noticed how much longer her dresses were than those the other girls were wearing. Of course, some of them wore outrageously short dresses, but one didn't have to go to the extreme in anything; and now that she saw herself through Gladys Carr's eyes, she realized that some changes could be made to great improvement and were perhaps due her employer. Not that she meant that Gladys Carr was fitted to be her mentor, but Gladys had spoken frankly from her point of view, and it had really opened her eyes to defects in herself that she ought to remedy.

She watched people all the afternoon, when she was not actually employed, and studied her own clothing, thinking how she might improve it. She had not realized how out of date she had allowed herself to get while she was shut up in the house. Perhaps that was the reason those girls in the church had looked at her so scornfully. Well, that was something that must be remedied. Everyone ought to be as good looking and fittingly clad as was possible under their circumstances, and there were things she certainly could do if she set about to remedy her defects, although she had no intention of painting her lips or wearing earrings or making her dresses as short as those her new friend wore. Her own fine sense taught her better.

Following the innate guidance of her own artistic soul, the next day, when she had a few minutes off, she found her way to where the imported dresses were on display and hastily reviewed them. She selected three or four from the motley array that appealed to her as being modest and lovely and fulfilling all the lines of beauty and form and color that should be in a dress and studied them carefully.

That evening she sat up late by the light of her little gas jet sewing a deeper hem into her gown and laying a couple of pleats that brought it more into fashion's subjection, and the result really did seem to justify her hard work.

It was lucky for her that she had fingers that could fashion almost anything she saw out of whatever material was put before her. Of course, she had little material with which to work and no money at all to buy any, but she managed to do wonders with her old dresses.

This occupation served two purposes. It gave a new interest to the first few days of loneliness, and it made her look much more like other girls. She resolved that as soon as she could conscientiously afford it, she would buy herself one or two of the cheap, pretty little dresses that were for sale in the basement. As an employee, she could get a discount, so it would not cost so very much, and, of course, she must not look dowdy.

She learned to dress her hair, too, in a more modern way, and it was wonderful how attractive it was.

"Oh, I like your hair, Marion Warren," cried out Gladys Carr the first morning she appeared with it waved away from her face, piled high in the back, and fastened with an old tortoise-shell hairpin of her mother's. "Oh, isn't that just precious, girls! Look at her! Say, isn't that the cat's?"

Marion colored a little at the expression of her friend's interest but was encouraged and made to feel less shy by the kindly approval of the other girls.

Gladys gave her another hint about lipstick and rouge that day, but she shook her head decidedly.

"No, Gladys, I don't like it," she said firmly. "I'll never do it. It doesn't seem nice to me. And excuse me, but really it doesn't even seem beautiful. It looks so unnatural. It really seems kind of ghastly, just as if a person had died and had been painted up to look like life. I can't bear those dead whites and vivid reds, nor the Indian colors, either. You never saw a living soul look like that. You can't imitate pink and white health; it has to grow. I'm going to take some exercises at night, perhaps take some walks and breathing exercises and see if I can't get some real pink in my cheeks, but if I don't, I'm not going to paint it on!"

"My soul!" said Gladys Carr, looking at her earnestly. "You're awful strange, but yer nice. I b'leeve I like ya just as ya are! There ain't many I'd say that to though, I can tell ya."

Then, spying another girl passing out the door, she lifted up her voice and yelled.

"Say, Totty Frayer, was it you took my pencil off my counter this morning when I had my back turned getting that spool of silk? I'd likta know where ya got the nerve! I never done nothing like that ta you. I'd be pleased to have ya return it. I need that pencil. Get me?"

It was not many days before Marion began to feel more at home in the store and had other friends besides Gladys Carr. And little by little, even the most flapperish flappers among her fellow workers began to be nice to her. For was she not unfailingly nice to them? She was always ready with a smile to stay after hours in the place of some girls who had a headache or wanted to go to a moving-picture show that evening and had to hurry home. She never complained when it was her turn to stay, and she would always cut short her precious lunch hour five minutes at the request of someone who wanted a bit more time and asked her to come back early. The ripples in her brown hair and tender lights in her brown eyes were pleasing to look upon and have about.

She was the kind of girl that men admired from a distance, yet not the kind they asked to go with them to the theater or presented with flowers and candy; nor did they dare joke with her. They respected her and let her alone. She made no advances and answered all their conversation shyly, and never thought of lingering about in their way. They thought she was above them, and she was. Nevertheless, she missed much pleasant companionship she might have had, and they missed her guiding presence, which might have been an inspiration to them if they had but understood.

So she passed in and out among them, handling her pretty ribbons, smiling cheerily always to customers and fellow workmen alike, eating her cheap meals gratefully, and hoarding her pennies most carefully.

She drank a good deal of milk; that was cheap, and it gave a pretty roundness to her cheeks and a clearness to her complexion that made her all the more attractive. It had been scarce at home since her father died; there were so many babies to drink milk that there had been very little left for Marion. Besides, Jennie told her she was too old to drink milk; that was children's food, and it was extravagant for a grown person to drink it. After that Marion drank no more milk. But now it was the cheapest thing on the menu. A little bottle of rich, creamy milk and a dainty bundle of shredded-wheat biscuit or crackers done up in waxed paper made a cheap and attractive breakfast or supper.

Then it was a real relief to feel that when her day's work was over her time was really her own. There were no little stockings to mend or dishes to wash or endless demands upon her precious evenings; and she might read to her heart's delight. Sometimes she felt selfish in her joy over this; yet her conscience told her it was her right to have a little time to herself for improvement, and the books she chose were good and helpful ones, not always just for amusement. Biography, history, and stories were well blended in her self-prescribed course. She joined a summer class in English literature and took real pleasure in going further in the study that had been interrupted when her school days suddenly came to an end.

The summer drew on, and the days grew hotter. The little third-story room with its pretty dormer windows was absolutely breathless. She kept the fact from her inner consciousness as long as possible, and then one stifling night when she slept but little, she acknowledged it to herself and accepted it along with the great loneliness that was gradually growing in her heart, and decided she was glad to be here anyway in spite of heat and solitude.

There were wonderful concerts in the department store, and sometimes the sound of them floated faintly as far as the ribbon counter. Then it seemed that angels might be lingering above and watching over her work.

But the summer was long and the heat intense. Sometimes even her enthusiasm lagged, and her step grew less elastic. Shredded wheat and cheap dinners palled, and everything in the restaurant smelled alike. Cooking over gas was hot work, and trying to read in the tiny oven that her little top-floor room had become was impossible. She took one or two evening trolley rides to cool off because the heat at home seemed unbearable, but the getting home alone late frightened her. She was timid about going out at night alone.

She might have had company among her acquaintances in the church, perhaps, but she was so far away now that she seldom went except on Sundays. And besides, the ones who would have appreciated her fine, sweet friendship did not know her and knew not what they missed; and the others would have voted her "slow."

It was September when the symphony concerts were brought to her notice by the conversation that she overheard between two customers who had the same seats from year to year and were enthusiastic music lovers. This fired Marion with a desire to get a season ticket and go herself. Why had she not thought of it before?

She inquired about the sale of tickets and arranged to be among the first in line at the office the morning the sale began.

A young man who stood just behind her in the line watched her eager face as she asked questions about the seats. Her simple acknowledgment to the apathetic boy behind the ticket window that this was the first time she had attended the concerts and that she did not know how to choose her seat interested him. He felt like shaking the youth into a sense of his duty and was relieved when the girl quietly selected for herself one of the very best seats of those open for sale, an end chair on the middle aisle, about halfway up in the top gallery. As she counted out the dimes and quarters and a worn bill or two, the watcher somehow felt they were won with the girl's lifeblood, and her eager, speaking face told how much the tickets meant to her as she folded them into her small, cheap purse and slipped away from the rail. The man who followed her promptly bought a seat for the season one row up and across the aisle from the one she had taken instead of the balcony seat he had intended to get. He was interested to see the look of this girl when she should hear her first symphony. Would it bear out the impression her face had already given him? It was an idle whim, but because it pleased him, he followed it, even though it meant the extra climb to the highest gallery.

It was the night of the second symphony concert when the wonderful thing happened.

Chapter 7

Marion had come early and was among the first to enter. She loved to watch the vast space blossom into light and life. It was a great world of its own, full of light and sound and beauty. It held her enchanted from the first moment. Tonight she had an old pair of opera glasses that her landlady had hunted out from among her relics of former days. She seemed pleased to let the girl have them, and Marion handled them carefully as if they had been gold set with precious jewels. As a matter of fact, they were covered with worn, faded purple velvet and looked exceedingly shabby and old-fashioned; but the wonders that they opened up to the girl were just as great as if they had been fine and new.

She climbed the great staircase and stole down the velvet-covered steps to her seat as if entering a sacred area. But she started and looked around when she came to her chair. The seat was turned down as if someone had been sitting there, while all the other seats were still turned up, awaiting their occupants. But the strangest thing of all was that on the seat lay a great long-stemmed rose, half open. It was one of those rare, dark crimsons whose shadows have hints of black velvet and whose lights glow like hidden fire. From out of its heart there stole a fragrance, subtle, heavenly, reminding one of gardens long ago, of rare old lace and lavender and fair, fine ladies of an ancient type.

Marion caught her breath in ecstasy and stooped as if the rose had been a little child, then looked around again to see to whom it might belong. But there was no one around except two elderly women away around the horseshoe circle at the end and a man on the other side, to whom obviously it could not belong. She had the whole middle section to herself just now, and the lights were not turned up yet to their full power.

Perhaps someone had mistaken his seat, and going away, had forgotten the flower and might be coming back for it in a moment. Surely no one would forget a bud so exquisite. She lifted it and breathed its fragrance, then looked furtively toward the elderly women. Finally, she made her way over to the corner where the two women sat and asked whether they had lost a flower; but they looked at her coldly and answered, "No," as if they thought her intruding. She went back to her seat, and, turning down the next chair, laid the rose carefully on it with many a tender look and touch and a wistful breath of its sweetness.

The hall was filling up now, and she found great pleasure in using her opera glasses, watching all the people who came in, noting their beautiful gowns and wraps, or trying to think out the stories of them all in their relation one to the other. But all the time there was the breath of the rose and the pleasant consciousness that it was beside her. She never doubted that its owner would return and perhaps through some mistake try to claim her seat as well as the rose. But until he or she came, she would enjoy the luxury of the presence of the flower.

She was absorbed in watching the musicians come to their seats with their instruments, when suddenly the owner of the next chair appeared beside her. She stood haughtily in the aisle, a large woman with a wide sweep of a cloak trimmed with imitation fur. Marion, suddenly aware of her presence, dropped her opera glasses into her lap and shrank into insignificance; but the large lady still waited.

"Please remove your flowers from my chair," she demanded icily; and Marion, feeling that the rose was a friend she must guard till it came to its own, quickly lifted the lovely flower and laid it on her own lap, while the ponderous person settled herself to her own satisfaction and ignored her.

No one came to claim the rose, and Marion felt that the concert had been a double pleasure because of having it. But she waited after others had gone out and looked about in a troubled way. What should she do with it? Surely the owner must have discovered its loss by this time. She went shyly, hesitantly, toward one of the guards in the hall and told him someone had left the flower on her chair. He looked at the stately flower and at the plain young woman who held it and smiled indulgently.

"I guess it's yours, lady," he said. "Nobody would come back after them kind of things. Whoever dropped it has plenty more where that came from."

"Oh, do you think so?" sighed Marion, and she sped away with her treasure out into the darkness.

Up in the little top-floor room, the rose glorified everything. She put it in a slim glass vase that had belonged to her father's mother; it was one that Jennie had always called old-fashioned. The dusky velvet warmth of the rose seemed to be at home. The girl hovered around it, taking little whiffs of its intoxicating sweetness; she had laid her cheek softly against its wonderful petals and was happy. She went to sleep making up stories of how it got into her chair, but never by any chance did she happen on the right explanation.

The next day she wore the rose to the store. It must

stay with her while it lasted. She could not let it waste its sweetness all alone. That day everyone came to smell her rose and ask her where she got it, and when she said, "I found it," they thought she was joking and rallied her upon her friend, the giver, wondering why she was not willing to confess and speculating on who it could be.

There are some people whose physical makeup is so constructed that a flower cannot live long near them but seems to be burned up, smothered, choked, just by lying on their chests. But that rose seemed to love to lie near Marion and to gain extended life from contact with hers. She kept the rose in her washbowl under a wet newspaper that night, and the next day it was almost as fresh as ever. Again she wore it, making all the girls marvel and declare it was another flower. The third day she still wore its crimson softness, no longer stiff and fresh, yet beautiful in its fading limpness. The fourth day she gathered its dropped petals wistfully and laid them in a drawer with her handkerchiefs. She would keep their fragrance after their beauty had departed.

The rose was still a pleasant memory on the night of the next symphony concert, and as she came down the velvet stairs to her seat, she was smiling at the thought of it and wondering again how it came there.

Then suddenly she paused beside her seat and drew a quick breath, passing her hand over her eyes. Did she see correctly? It was there again! The great, dark, burning rose. Every curl of the petals seemed the same. Was she dreaming, or was this a hallucination?

As before, there was no one near who seemed to have any connection whatsoever with the flower, and finally she managed to gather it up softly and sit down in a little limp heap with the flower lying against her chest where her lips could just touch it and its breath steal up into her face. If anyone were watching, he must have thought it a lovely picture. It was as if the first flower had been human and beloved and had come back to its own from the dust of the grave. This time the girl took the flower to herself, and without trying to fathom its secret, delighted in the thought that it was hers. It seemed to her now that it had a personality of its own and that it had come to her there of its own will.

When the music began, she rested her head against the high back of the seat and closed her eyes. It seemed the voice of the rose speaking to her inmost soul, telling of wonders she had never known, great secrets of the earth: the grave of the seed and the resurrection of the leaf and flower, the code of the wind's message, the words of a brook, the meaning of the birds' twitter, the beating of the heart of the woods, the whisper of the moss as it creeps, and the sound of flying clouds on a summer's day. All this and more the rose told her through the music, until her heart was stirred deeply and her face spoke eloquently of how her whole being throbbed in tune to the sound.

The girls in the store exclaimed with laughter and jokes over the second rose; but it seemed too sacred to talk about, and Marion said little, letting them think what they pleased. For herself she tried not to think how the rose came to be in her chair. Since she had looked into the handkerchief box and found the dead rose petals still lying sweet and withered—and two days later when she laid the second rose in its lovely death beside the first—she resolutely refused to think how it came to be hers. She did not want to think that perhaps they had been meant for another and someone was missing what had made her so happy.

The night of the fourth concert her heart beat excitedly. She had told herself a hundred times that of course there would be no rose this time, that whatever happening had given her the two roses could not of course in reason continue; yet she knew that she was expecting another rose, and her limbs trembled so that she could hardly climb the stairs to the gallery.

It was later than she had ever come before. She had felt that she must give some other one a chance to claim the flower if it were really there. There were people sitting all around the middle aisle. The large lady with a fur wrap lying across her lap was there, bulging over into Marion's seat. Marion tried not to look at her own chair until she was close beside it; and she walked down the steps slowly, taking long, deep breaths to calm her tripping heart. But every breath she imagined heavy with rose perfume, and before she had quite reached her place, she saw the chair was down, and a great green stem stuck out into the aisle three inches!

There it lay in all its dusky majesty. Her rose! As like the other two as roses could be. It nestled to her heart as if it knew where it belonged, and no one seemed to think it strange that she had taken it as her own.

Marion wore tonight her last winter's black felt hat with a new black grosgrain ribbon put on in tailored fashion by her own skillful fingers. She was learning rapidly how to look like other people—nice people, without spending much money for it. The severe little hat was most attractive on her.

More than one music lover turned to look again at the fresh, sweet face of the girl with the great dark rose against her cheek. Her lips moved softly on the petals as if caressing them, and her eyes glowed dark and beautiful.

That night there grew in her the consciousness that there was intention in this flower, and behind it someone. Who?

The thought made her tremble with fear and delight. Who in all the wide world could care enough for her to put a flower in her chair every night? She was half frightened over it. It seemed not quite proper, yet what was wrong about it? And how could she possibly help it? Throw the flower on the floor? Crush it? Leave it where she found it? Impossible. The flower appealed to every longing of her nature, and she could not more resist the gift of the rose than the rose itself could resist the rays of the sun and turn away from shadow.

Surely the most scrupulous could not find anything wrong in her accepting this anonymous gift of a single wonderful blossom, so long as no further attempt at acquaintance was made. It might be some girl like herself, who liked to do a kind act; or some dear old lady who had seen the loneliness in her face; or some— well, it didn't matter who. There never seemed to be anyone seated around her who was not nice and refined and respectable looking and utterly beyond any such thing as flirting with a shabby little person like herself. She would just take the flower as a part of her concert and be happy over it, letting it sing to her again, during the days that it lasted, the melodies that lifted her soul beyond earthly disappointments and trials.

She looked around again as she went slowly out with the others, this time holding her rose boldly close to her face and taking deep breaths of its sweetness. She wanted to make sure to herself that there was no one around her from whom she would not like to have taken the rose.

As she looked up, her eyes met those of a young man just ahead of her in the throng. He was good looking enough to be noticeable even in such a crowd. There was something about him that gave instant impression of refinement and culture. Though his eyes met hers, it was but for an instant, with a pleasant, unintimate glance, as one regards the casual stranger who for the time has been a partner in some pleasure.

Yet somehow in that glance she sensed the fact that he was of another world, a world where roses and music and friendships belonged by right, and where education and culture were a natural part of one's birthright like air and food and sunshine. It was a world where she could only steal in by sufferance for an hour, and that at the price of her little savings and much self-denial. Yet it was a world that she could have enjoyed to the utmost. She sighed softly and touched her rose gently once more with her lips as if to assure herself that so much of that world was really hers, at least for tonight.

That night she slept with the rose on a chair beside her, and she dreamed that a voice she had never heard before whispered softly to wonderful music, "Dear, I love you." She could not see who spoke, because the air was gloomed with dark rose leaves falling and shutting out the light; only amid that soft, velvety fall she could hear the echo, "Dear, I love you." It was very foolish, the whole thing, she told herself the next morning with glowing cheeks. She positively must stop thinking about who put the flowers in her chair and just enjoy them while they lasted. Very likely there wouldn't be any more, anyway. She must expect that, of course. If anyone was doing it for fun, it would not last much longer.

She went humming down the stairs toward her work that day, with the rose on her chest and a happy light in her eyes in spite of all her philosophy. Somehow those roses made her little top floor seem more like home and drove the loneliness from her heart.

The roses did not stop; they kept coming, one every symphony night. The good-looking stranger was usually in his place, but their eyes never met. She glanced back once or twice shyly, just to see who was near her, and always he seemed in his cultured aloofness to be a type of the world of refinement. But he never looked her way. He did not even know she was there, of course. His was another world.

She felt quite safe to glance at him occasionally, as one glances at an ideal. It could do him no harm, and it was good to know there were such men in the world. It made one feel safer and happier about living, just as it was good to know there was a great symphony orchestra to which she might listen occasionally.

One night it rained, but not until after the concert had begun. The sky had been clear at eight o'clock, with the stars shining and no hint of a coming storm. When the concert was out and the stream of people had reached the great marble entrance where the cream of society lingered in delicate attire awaiting their automobiles, the rain was pouring down in sheets and the heavens were rent with vivid flashes of lightning and crashing thunder.

Marion, in dismay, with no umbrella or overshoes, lingered until all but a few were gone. Then, stepping outside under the metal awning that covered the sidewalk to the curbing, she decided that she must go home. It was getting very late, and there seemed no sign of a letup.

She did not like to linger longer alone. There were only men left now, and they were glancing at her. She felt uncomfortable. In a moment more, the doors of the Academy of Music would close, and she would be left standing in the dark, wet street. She could not walk home and must sacrifice a few cents of that hoarded sum that was growing toward next winter's symphony concerts and perhaps a lecture or two in between.

The car came, and she made a dash through the wet and gained the platform. It was only a step; yet she was very wet, and her heart sank at the thought of her garments. She could not afford to replace them if they were spoiled.

The car was full, and she could barely get a seat, squeezed in between two cross, fat women. Marion thought with a sinking heart of the half block she must walk in this driving storm when she reached her own corner. She could not hope to protect herself. She must make up her mind to face it, for the rain was pelting down as hard as ever.

The car stopped at her corner, and she stood for just an instant, gasping on the step before she made the plunge into the downpour, expecting to be soaked to the skin at once; but to her surprise she felt only a few sharp spatters in her face now and then and the instant chill of water on her ankles as she hurried down the street.

Suddenly she realized that a shelter was over her. Someone, whom she could not see because of the rain in her eyes when she turned her head, and because of the slant of the blackness before her, was holding an umbrella over her as she flew along. She dared not turn to look and had no breath to speak and thank him. Indeed, so black was the night—for the electric streetlamps were gone out—that it seemed as if an umbrella had stepped impersonally off the car and was conducting her to her home in the teeth of the storm.

A moment more, and she was safe in the vestibule of her abiding place; and the dark form who had protected her, umbrella and all, was rushing on through the blackness. Oh, why hadn't she drawn him into the shelter until the rain stopped?

"Come back!" she called, but the wind tossed her words scornfully into her face. Then "Thank you!" she flung out into the darkness, and was it her imagination or only the wind that seemed to voice the word *Welcome*?

She put the thought away with others to keep and went slowly, smiling, up the stairs, her cheek against the wet rosebud. Someone had taken the trouble in all this storm to protect her. It mattered not who it was; it might be God. It *was* God, of course. The protector had passed on, but it warmed the girl's lonely heart to know that he had cared, that she was not all alone in the wide universe with no one who knew or thought of her.

Out of the night and blackness had come a helping hand holding an umbrella, and passed on unknown. Why not a rose the same way? She must get over the idea that someone was picking her out from the world and bestowing flowers upon her. It was utterly absurd and ridiculous, and would put wrong notions into her head and make her dissatisfied with life.

But the next morning, Marion was sick. A cold the day before, combined with the wetting and excitement, had been too much for her. She was not able to go to the store and had to pay the little colored maid downstairs to send a telephone message for her to the head of her department.

About ten o'clock that morning, a boy from the florist's rang the doorbell of the small, unpretentious house where Marion lodged. He carried a large pasteboard box under his arm and whistled to keep up a brave front. He was to earn half a dollar if he performed his errand thoroughly. He made a low bow to the tattered little maid of all work who held the door half open and giggled at him.

"Hey, kid," he began in the familiar tone of an old friend, "do me a favor? What's the name of the good-lookin' lady you got livin' here? She's had some flowers sent to her, and I can't for the life of me remember her name. It's got away from me somehow, and I can't get it back. Just mention over the names of the pretty girls you've got boarding here, and I might recognize it."

"It ain't Miss M'rion, is it?"

"Miss Marion, Miss Marion? That sounds as if it might be it. Is she small and wears a little black hat?"

"Sure!" answered the girl. "That's her. An' anyway, she's the only girl here now anymore. All the rest is just old women, 'ceptin' the 'lect'ic lightmen an' the vacuum-cleaner agent. It couldn't be no other girl, 'cause there ain't no other here now."

"What'd you say her last name was? Marion what? I just want to be sure, you know."

"Miss M'rion War'n," replied the girl, and held out her hands eagerly for the box.

"Just give Miss Warren that box, please, and I'll dance at your wedding. So long!" And he dashed away before the girl could get a chance to ask him any questions.

The box contained two dozen great crimson roses, the exact counterpart of those that had been laid in Marion's chair at the concerts.

Chapter 8

Marion sat up in bed and opened the box in amazement, almost fright. There was no card, nothing even on the box to identify the florist. Just the sweet, mute faces of the lovely flowers.

The astonished, gaping maid stood by in wonder but could give no explanation except the many-times-reiterated account of her conversation with the boy.

Marion laughed into the box and cried into it. She had been feeling so lonely, and her head and limbs ached so fearfully before this box came. Almost she had repented staying in the city. Almost she had decided that probably, after all, her place had been in Vermont, caring for the children and endlessly helping Jennie for the rest of her life. Education and culture were not for her, ever. It was too lonely and too hard work. Too few promotions and too many extra expenses. The loss of this day might cut down her money a little, too, although she was allowed a certain time for sick leave.

Now, however, things seemed different. The roses had come, and behind the roses must be someone— someone who cared a little. Her cheeks glowed scarlet at the thought. She gave the astonished maid a rose and sent three more down to her sad old landlady. Then after she had laughed over the roses and cried over them again, she put them into the washbowl beside her bed and went to sleep. Someone cared! *Someone cared!* No matter who, someone cared! It was like the refrain of a lullaby. She slept with a smile on her face; and while she dreamed, her father came and kissed her and said as he used to say long ago, *I'm glad for you, little girl,* real glad.

When she awoke, the roses were smiling at her, and she felt better. The next day, she was able to go back to the store. She wore a bundle of roses this time and had some to give away, which doubled her own pleasure in them.

It was two days later, while still a dusky red rose was brightening the blouse of Marion's somber little dress, that a young man walked slowly down the aisle in front of the ribbon counter and looked earnestly at the array of ribbons as if they possessed a kind of puzzled interest for him. He walked by twice; and the third time, when he turned and came back, two of the girls at the counter whispered about him. They thought he had been sent on an errand for ribbon and didn't know just how to go about it. They had seen his kind before. They presented themselves to his notice with a tempting, "Would you like to be waited upon?" but the young man replied gravely, "Not yet, thank you," and went on with his investigation. He seemed to be interested in the articles in the display case below the counter, and after watching him amusedly for a minute, the two salesgirls retired to a distance to comment on him.

It happened that during the winter Marion had developed quite a talent for making ribbon flowers and tying bows. During the last three weeks, she had been promoted regularly to the little counter where a line of people stood endlessly all day long with anxious, hurried looks and bolts of ribbon to be tied for "Mary's lingerie" or "a little girl's sash" or "my daughter's graduating dress" or "a young woman's headdress" or "rosettes for the baby's bonnet."

Marion liked it. Especially she liked the forming of the satin flowers. It was next to working among the flowers themselves to touch the bright petals and form them into shape around the tiny stamens. She was peculiarly successful with ribbon roses and almost every day had several orders for them for corsages or shoulder pins.

This afternoon she was sitting as usual before her

bit of counter, scissors at her side, spools of wire and bunches of centers close at hand, and a stack of rainbow ribbons in front of her.

The young man gradually progressed down the length of the ribbon counter till he came to where the bows were being tied; and there he stood a little to one side, watching with absorbed interest as the skillful fingers finished the lovely knots and rosettes and buds.

The counter was busy now, and there was a line of anxious mothers and hurried shoppers waiting to get ribbons made up. The young man watched and waited awhile, and finally, to the immense amusement of the girls at the main counter who had been watching him, he edged up to Marion and spoke to her.

"Are you too busy to select the right ribbon for me and make a rose the color of the one you are wearing? I can wait until you are free if you think you can do it."

Marion looked up. She had not noticed him before, and something in his eyes reminded her of the man at the symphony concerts; but she had never seen that man clearly, except one brief glance. Of course it could not be him. But she answered graciously.

"Certainly, I think I can find that color for you if you can wait till I finish these flowers. A customer is waiting for them."

He bowed and stepped back out of the way, watching

the passing throng and waiting until she came to him with the ribbon, matching it to the rose on her chest. His face lit up with a puzzled kind of relief.

"That looks exactly like it," he said.

"You want a single rose?" she asked, her sweet eyes looking directly at him in that pleasant way she had with all her customers, as if they were her friends. "Is it for the shoulder?"

"Why, yes," said he, a little puzzled. "I don't know how it should be. Make it like some of those in the case. Make it just as you would like to have it." He smiled helplessly, and she answered his appeal with another smile, distant and delicate as a passing bird's might be.

"I understand," she said brightly. "I'll make it pretty," and she went at the lovely task, deftly measuring and twisting the ribbon into what seemed like a living, breathing rose, and then another tiny bud by its side with a stem and a bit of green leaf. Then she held it out to him. Did that suit him? He said that it did, entirely; and his eyes showed plainly that he spoke the truth.

"How would you...put it on?" he asked hesitatingly, and the girls at the other end of the counter beat a hasty retreat behind the cash desk to laugh.

"O, what d' ye think o' that?" cried one.

"The dear innocent; is he goin' to wear it himself, or will he stick it on for her?" asked the other, mopping the tears of mirth from her eyes.

But Marion, oblivious, was holding the damask satin rose against her shoulder and showing how it should be worn.

"Say, it would be the cat's to be that man's wife, wouldn't it?" said one of the girls to Marion as her customer received his package and departed with a courteous bow. "Just see the trouble he took to get her something pretty."

Marion's eyes glowed, and all the afternoon she meditated on the careless question. "To be that man's wife," what must it be? How she would like to see the wife who was to wear those roses she had just made! What a dear, beautiful woman she must be! What a charmed life she must live, with someone like that to care for her, anticipate her needs, prepare surprises and pleasures for her! It was something like her own beautiful roses; only, of course there could be no one like that behind her roses, only some dear old lady perhaps who had seen her and maybe loved her a little for the sake of a lost daughter or friend or a fancied likeness to someone. Well, it was good that she had her dear roses, and she was glad the beloved wife had someone to care for her. She would like to see her sometime with the roses on her chest. She wondered what she would be like.

And then the day's work was finished, and Marion went home to her fading roses.

There was another church reception early that spring, and a few days before, Mrs. Shuttle happened to pass the ribbon counter and spied Marion.

"Well, I declare. Marion Warren! Is this where you have been hiding all these months? I've wondered why you don't come to prayer meeting anymore, and you weren't at the last two church suppers. I thought you promised to help on our committee. Do you know, we have just as hard a time getting someone to wash dishes as ever. Old Mrs. Brown won't come anymore, and none of the girls are willing to stick in the kitchen and wear old clothes and keep their hands in dishwater. Can't you come down and help us Friday night? We need you badly. There isn't a girl left on the committee has a brain in her head. They're all for beaux and making eyes at the men. I haven't any time for 'em. Do come back Marion just this once and help me. I'm all tired out."

Marion, with her usual willingness to oblige, finally promised to come. She still felt uncomfortable and humiliated when she remembered that last social she had attended, but what difference did it make? She had grown a little beyond such things, she hoped. She had made a new life of her own and ought to be big enough not to be troubled by being ignored by a girl she used to know just because she was not as well dressed as the rest of them. Well, they could find no fault with her now. Thanks to the store, she now knew what one ought to wear and exactly how to accomplish it on a very small income. She had learned that the most expensive models almost invariably chose lines of simplicity, both in cut and decoration, and therefore she had been enabled to select from among the cheaper garments those which followed this simplicity of good taste. Here in the store, also, she was able to purchase really fine material at very low cost because of the many opportunities to buy remnants, and also because of her employee's discount. Therefore Marion no longer felt embarrassed by her awkward garments.

But even though she knew she had a pretty and suitable dress to wear, she did not relish going back among a set of girls who had tried to snub her. It roused feelings that she felt were unchristian and unworthy of herself. Nevertheless, she had promised, and for this once she meant to go. It would be nice at least to meet the minister's wife again and have a little talk with her. Perhaps she would come down to see her sometime, too. That would be delightful. She might even get an afternoon off and ask her to take a cup of tea with her in her tiny third-story room. Of course, it was not palatial, but it was neat and cozy, and she was sure Mrs. Stewart would not mind having to climb two pairs of stairs just for once. She would not want to ask everybody to come up there, but it would be dear to have Mrs. Stewart. It would be like having a visit from a mother. Perhaps she would even dare to ask her about some of the problems that had been perplexing her.

So Marion agreed to go and to wash dishes.

When the evening came, Marion dressed with special care in a little satin dress of dark garnet that she had bought because it reminded her of the depths of shadow in her roses. It was wonderfully attractive and set off her dark eyes and hair and delicate features perfectly. The sleeves were georgette and showed the roundness of her arms prettily. She took care to arrange the wrists so that she might unfasten them and roll the sleeves above her elbows when she washed dishes. Also she had provided a pretty white rubber apron with little rubber frills around the edges that covered her satin gown amply and was attractive enough in itself so that she would not feel out of place among the well-dressed women.

As she got out of the trolley in front of the church and walked down the pavement to the side entrance, which was brightly lighted, a sudden feeling of the old panic came upon her. She seemed to feel herself about to become the scorn of all eyes, and in spite of all her resolves, a longing to flee took possession of her. She looked down at her pretty, new patent leather shoes with their modest steel buckles and her slim gray silk ankles and remembered that there was nothing noticeable about her garments. She was as well dressed as anyone. There was no reason why she should be singled out for scorn on that account. She looked up to the deep dark blue of the sky above her, set with sparkling stars, and breathed a little prayer. "Dear Father, I'm Your child. Help me that I shall behave in a way to bring glory to Your kingdom and not discredit. Help me not to be frightened or be a fool."

Then she stepped into the brightly lighted vestibule and looked around her.

Mrs. Shuttle was there, looking anxiously for some-one. She grabbed her at once eagerly.

"Oh, you've come. I was afraid you wouldn't. My! I'm so glad! My daughter has the flu and couldn't come at all, and I'm all beat out waiting on her all day. Say, you'll take charge of the aides when they come in and tell them where to put their wraps and what to do first, won't you? I've simply got to run home and give Mary her medicine. I forgot to put it where she could reach it, and she's got an awful high fever, and I don't like to leave her without it. And say, after things are pretty well served, would you mind staying just tonight and see that all the dishes are washed and put away right? You know we've got a new janitor, and he doesn't know a thing about where things belong."

Marion promised, though with sinking heart. She had been hoping to get away early and do a little studying before she went to bed. She had joined a literature class and a class in current events early in the winter, and they were to have examinations soon. She did want at least an hour before she slept in which to study. But it could not be helped of course. She couldn't say no to Mrs. Shuttle when her daughter was so sick. So Marion went into the big, bright room resolved to take off her coat and hat and then go at once to the kitchen and stay there. At least she would have plenty to do to fill the evening and need not bother about having to sit around alone with no one speaking to her. Likely she wouldn't even get a chance to see the minister's wife and give her invitation.

As she came out of the ladies' parlor, where she left her wraps, and started across the main Sunday school room to the kitchen, two men stood talking together over by the platform. One of them was the bank president, Mr. Radnor. The other was a stranger whom she did not even notice. She was thinking that she ought to go over and speak to Mr. Radnor and tell him how grateful she was for his influence, which had given her such a fine position. Could she do it now while there were only a few people in the room? Or must she wait until he was done speaking to the stranger?

While she hesitated, the eyes of the two were upon her.

"Who is that girl, Radnor?" the stranger was saying with almost a note of eagerness in his voice.

"Where? Over there by the door? Why, who is she? Let me see. Can that be—? Why, yes, I guess it is that little Warren girl, Marion Warren. Nice little thing. Good girl. She came to me for a recommendation to get a job last spring. I guess she's made good. She's been a member of this Sunday school ever since she was a little tot in the primary. We have a lot of that sort here, you know, good, plain, respectable people, never very well off, but make a good living and are good, sturdy stock. Makes a pretty good foundation for a church, you know. And you'd be surprised how that class of people give. Better in proportion sometimes than the really well-to-do."

"I'd like to meet her," said the younger man.

"Why, yes, certainly," said the kindly superintendent, a bit perturbed, "but, you know, Lyman, she really isn't in your class. Do you think it wise? It might put notions in her head, and she's a nice little thing. Her father was a good man, a sort of saint in his way, you know."

"She looks it," said the younger man earnestly. "And you're mistaken, Radnor—she is in my class. We've been attending the symphony concerts all winter, not exactly together, but her seat was just across the aisle from mine, and I've been noticing how she enjoyed the music. So, you see, we have a common interest. I'd really like to meet her if you don't mind. I'll try not to put any wrong notions in her head." And he laughed amusedly.

"Why, of course, if you wish it. She is a nice child, as I told you. I didn't know she cared especially for music. Somebody, probably, gave her the tickets. She couldn't afford to get them herself, I'm quite sure, and I can scarcely think she'd have the inclination of herself. But we can manage the introduction casually, of course. You can see what she is for yourself. I don't imagine she's had more than a common-school education. The father was a hard worker, and they lived on one of the smaller streets. But see, she is coming this way. It will be quite all right, I am sure."

Marion had decided to get her duty over quickly before the arrival of those obnoxious girls and was walking straight across the room to Mr. Radnor, stranger or no stranger. She wouldn't interrupt them but a second, and she might not get another chance after she went to the kitchen.

She did not have to interrupt them by saying excuse me, as she had planned to do, for she found the two men waiting for her as if they had expected her, and the bank president, with his most presidential air, greeted her with his smile.

"Why, good evening, Miss Marion, I've been

wondering how you are getting on. This is Mr. Lyman. You have met him before, haven't you? And how did you make out at the store? Did you get what you wanted?"

He scarcely gave Marion and the young man an opportunity to acknowledge the offhand introduction before he plied her with his questions. But he found to his relief that Marion was not especially interested in the young stranger. She acknowledged the introduction with a smile and a slight inclination of her head and turned her eyes at once back to Mr. Radnor's face, saying in a businesslike tone, "Yes, Mr. Radnor. I came over here to thank you. I have wanted to tell you before how well I am doing and how much I owe to your kind introduction, but I hesitated to take your time at the bank, and you are always so surrounded after Sunday school that I haven't been able to speak to you."

"You're quite welcome, I'm sure," he said genially, almost pompously, young Lyman thought. "I'm very glad it all came out right. Call on me again anytime I can help in any way. I'm always glad to help any of our school, you know. That's what the church is for. Ah, Lyman, Stewart has come at last. Shall we go over and talk that matter over with him? Good evening, Miss Warren. We'll see you again, I'm sure, before the evening is over. This is a pleasant occasion, isn't it? So nice to get all classes together on a common footing."

They moved away, and Marion had somehow the

same feeling she had known at the last church social—
a feeling of having been put in her place, this time
nicely and sweetly, with a smile and an offer of friendliness, but still put in her place.

She did not notice at the moment that the young
man had said as he moved away, with a pleasant friendly
smile, "Well, we shall see you again this evening, Miss
Warren."

It would have made little impression anyway. Of
course, he was just being polite, a nice, pleasant stranger.
Why was there something about his eyes that looked
familiar? Mr. Radnor had spoken as if perhaps they had
known each other before. He must be some member of
the church who had moved away and was back for the
evening. Of course, she had never seen him before, yet
his eyes had looked familiar. He probably resembled
someone she knew in the store.

Humanity seemed to be cut off in strips, and some
belonged to one strip and some to another. This young
man belonged to a pleasant type that had the faculty of
making one feel at ease. But what difference? She would
probably never see him again, anyway. She would go
at once to the kitchen and would not come out again
that night if she could help it. It was probably her own
fault somehow that people treated her so condescend-
ingly. But it didn't matter. She was getting too sensitive. She must not care whether people liked her or

not. Her lot in life was a lonely one, and she must get used to it.

So she made her way at once to the kitchen without further hindrance, and Mr. Radnor, having piloted his man to the minister and talked a few minutes, wandered off to talk to another businessman who had just arrived, congratulating himself on the tactful way in which he had managed that introduction. It certainly would have been unfortunate for Lyman to show any attention to that little mouse of a Warren girl. He was fully aware that his own niece, Isabel, was openly out for that young man's attentions, and he would not like to incur her enmity by having been the one to bring about even a casual friendship between Lyman and a little salesgirl from his Sunday school. If Isabel married Lyman, she would be well off in his hands and have made a most fitting match for herself, pleasing to the entrie family connection, as well as himself. Lyman was certainly a most unusual young man, wealthy as anyone need ever care to be and upright in every way. Interested in the church, too, which was most commendable in this modern age of indifference, especially among the young. He certainly was an unusual young man!

Marion reached the kitchen and found three or four women ahead of her, bustling around arranging salad on plates, cutting cakes, making coffee.

They greeted her with relief.

"Oh, here's Marion Warren! Now we'll be all right. She'll do it. Say, Marion, will you go out there and hunt up Mrs. McGovern and ask her which of these cakes she wants cut first? She told me, but I've forgotten. It's either the chocolate or the coconut, and I don't know which. She'll be mad as a hornet if I make a mistake. And while you're about it, won't you see if you can find Isabel Cresson anywhere? We haven't enough wait-resses, and I promised to ask her, but I've got this apron on and my sleeves rolled up, and I hate to go out now."

Marion, with heightened color, turned to do their bidding, wishing almost that she had not come if she had to carry a message to Isabel Cresson. However, that of course was beneath her. She must conquer such feelings. She hastened out, hoping that the Cresson girl had not yet arrived and she might be able to put the errand off on somebody else. She found Mrs. McGovern easily enough, discovered that the chocolate cake was to be cut first, and after a swift glance around, decided to her relief that Isabel Cresson had not yet arrived. She was just skirting the groups that were standing about talking when a lot of girls burst noisily into the room from the dressing room, and Isabel was foremost among them.

"Oh," said Marion. "Isabel, I've got a message for you." Isabel turned and stared at her coldly.

"Aw! It's Marion War'n, again, isn't it? I hardly knew ya!"

Marion's cheeks were pink with the slighting tone, but she went on briefly.

"Mrs. Forbes wants to know if you will help out as an aide. She says they haven't enough aides."

"What? Me? Naw indeedly! I nevah tie myself up like that, not this baby. I came to have a good time. Besides, I've got a new imported dress on. I'd be sure to ruin it. Just run back to Mrs. Forbes and ask her, what does she think I am? Ask her that for me!" And Isabel's laugh rang out in scorn, which somehow seemed to be turned against Marion, and all the other girls joined in the laugh and looked at Marion as if she were a doormat. At least that was the way it seemed to Marion.

The color came in a tide into her cheeks now. For a minute, she wanted to stand still there and turn on those girls and tell them just what she thought of them. Tell them how rude they were.

Well, what good would that do? And those ugly feelings that came into her heart—they were altogether unworthy of a child of the King. She was routed again. She must not let these girls have such power over her that they could trouble her soul even to having sinful thoughts, for somehow before she realized it, she was saying to herself how she hated Isabel Cresson.

Then instantly came the thought that she had

a refuge from all such things. One who was a very present help in time of trouble, and she could cry to Him even in this crowded, noisy social room. So she lifted her heart for help, and with her head raised in a sweet dignity, she began making her way between the people who were coming in very fast now and filling the room. Then suddenly the minister's wife slipped her arm around her and greeted her with a smile as if she were really glad to see her, and she felt a sudden rush of comfort. What a silly she was! Was she going to cry right there before all those people? Oh, Jennie and Tom had been right. She was not fit to go among people. She belonged out on a farm somewhere, where she wouldn't come in contact with the world at all! She must get over such foolishness and learn not to care what those rude girls did. Just because she used to know them at school and had expected them to be friendly. She must not let such things upset her so.

The minister's wife was talking to her, saying dear things about her father, telling her how badly she had felt when her own father had been taken away. Her sympathetic tone seemed healing in its touch. The tight lines around Marion's lips relaxed, and she began to look almost happy.

And suddenly the minister loomed in her way in a group of other men.

"Why, here is Miss Warren!" he said heartily. "Glad

to see you. You're getting to be quite a stranger here, do you know it? Though you're pretty faithful on Sundays, yet, aren't you? I always see you and try to get down to speak to you, but you slip away too quickly for me. By the way, Marion, you know this man, don't you? Jefferson, you know Miss Warren, surely."

Marion looked up to meet the eyes of the same young man to whom Mr. Radnor had so casually introduced her a few minutes before, and she could not help seeing that his eyes were full of interest. Where had she seen those eyes before? Surely she must have seen him somewhere.

She looked up with a natural little smile to acknowledge the introduction, wondering what to say, suddenly embarrassed by the unexpected sight of Isabel Cresson and her gang bearing down upon them between two groups of people.

Panic took hold upon her again. No, she would not meet those girls now—they would be sure to humiliate her before this pleasant stranger!

The minister was talking in answer to something Lyman had said.

"Yes, I suppose you must have been away at that time. I hadn't realized how long it had been. And you were but a boy when you left. Of course, you wouldn't know the older members of the church well. But your father did. And this young woman's father was one of the salt of the earth, one of our saints, you know. He has just recently been called home."

Marion's heart warmed and went on beating with something like its normal rhythm, and her eyes lost something of their panicky look. Somehow her glance was drawn involuntarily to the eyes of the stranger, and she saw that his face was full of sympathy. She gave him a trembling little smile of thanks. That was a beautiful thing for a young man to do, to seem to care about a stranger who was dead, a man whom he had never seen.

She would probably never see this young man again: he was likely a visitor in the town; but she would always remember his look that was a tribute to her father's name.

But there was no time to summon words to answer. Those girls were close at hand, and she could see by the look in Isabel's eyes that she was bearing down upon the young stranger as one hails an old friend.

She lifted her firm little chin and tried to smile and said hurriedly, "Please excuse me now. I've promised to help in the kitchen, and I think they must be waiting for me!" And she was gone, slipping between the people and gliding down the kitchen passageway out of sight.

Chapter 9

To the young man who watched her hasty retreat, she seemed a lovely thing. He noted the delicate profile of her face, the profile with which he had grown familiar in the Academy of Music, watching it to the accompaniment of the world's great music exquisitely rendered. Somehow she seemed to him to be naturally associated with all things fine and exquisite and lovely.

He noticed, too, with brightening eye, the color of her plain little gown, deep crimson, like the shadows in old-fashioned damask roses, and how it brought out the shell-pink tinting of her cheeks and the clear, straight penciling of lovely brow. To the young man, the shy lifting of her serious eyes had satisfied all his expectations. If what Radnor had said about her coming from a common family had been true, where and how had such a lovely, unspoiled spirit come up through the soil and rudeness of this present world? She was so very different from the girls he saw around him.

He turned about and faced Isabel Cresson, in blue and silver, with her long earrings and her ropes of pearl, her gold boy-bob, and her carmine lips and rouged cheeks. Isabel was vivacious and sparkling, cheerful and full of banter, bold and wise and able to take care of herself, like the present day and generation. But oh, what a contrast! The young man's eyes followed wistfully the girl in the garnet satin and wished she would come back and talk to him.

"Hello, Jeff!" greeted Isabel. "Never see you anymore unless I come to church. You must have got converted over in Europe; you only seem to be on exhibition at a church social. Why don't you come out to the country club and have a try at things? Got the darlingest floor now, the best dancing anywhere around, and the greatest orchestra! It's precious! You haven't heard it yet, have you? And you've been home almost a year! What did they do to you over there? Make an old man out of you? Have you forgotten our old friends? What's that? You're too busy? Oh, bologna! So's your old man! Come on out on the links Sunday morning, and let's play a few holes. Lately I've been shooting down the eighties! Not so bad, right? Come and try me, Jeffy! I'd like a chance to even up some of the old scores when you laid me out at tennis. Swing a racket anymore? We just got four more new courts. The turf is peachy. I can play a precious game at that, too. You ought to try me now! And I've just got the darlingest new racket. I'm dying to try it on somebody. What do you say? Is it a go Sunday morning? What? You got to go to church? Applesauce! Cut it out for once! Well then, make it six in the morning, and we'll have coffee at the club house and get back in plenty of time. Church isn't till eleven. Or I'll get up at five if you like that better. What? Why, Jeff Lyman! You're not such an old granny yet that you won't take refined exercise on Sunday? I'd like to know why. I thought you were progressive. Why, I thought you'd been abroad and got rid of all your narrow notions. They're just traditions, anyway, handed down from your family. You know you don't really think there can be anything wrong in going out into the lovely air, walking around after a ball a little while. Why nobody stops at anything like that anymore, at least not any of our old crowd. Why, the minister where friends of mine go even has church real early in the morning so his members can go and then have all the rest of the day for recreation. He says he thinks that's what the Bible means. The Sabbath was made for man. You don't really mean, Jeff, that you object yourself? Well, of course, in that case we might play Saturday. I have an engagement, but I'll break it for you. Will you do that much for me?"

"I'm afraid not, Isabel," said the young man amusedly. "I've something quite different in mind for that day, too, if it materializes. By the way, didn't I hear somebody say you were going to sing tonight? That will be interesting. You used to have a fine voice when you were a kid. I suppose you've been studying hard?"

Isabel made a wry face.

"Who? Me? Did you ever know me to work hard at anything? Oh, I've been taking lessons, of course. Had a few from that stunning tenor. He's an Italian, and he has the most gorgeous eyes. All the girls have a crush on him. But he's married unfortunately, and his wife won't give him a divorce. Isn't that tragic? If I was married to a man that wanted his freedom, I'm sure I wouldn't object. It seems common to hang on to a person when they want to be free. Don't you think so? I think Europeans are so much more sophisticated in those things. Say, I'm wild to hear all about your experience in Siberia. Wasn't it terrifying? But you were always so brave! Jeff, it's just great to have you home again, and you really must come to the dance next Sunday night. It's going to be simply darling. The decorations alone are costing—"

But Jefferson Lyman's eyes were off at the other side of the room, where a girl in a satin dress the color of old-fashioned damask roses was arranging a table with cups and saucers and sugar bowls and cream pitchers.

"Excuse me a minute, Isabel," said the young man suddenly. "I want to speak to someone." And he disappeared among the crowd.

A sudden blank look overspread Isabel's face as she watched him go.

"Oh, for cat's sake!" she exclaimed to Aline Baines, who acted the part of shadow to Isabel. "How do you suppose he got to know her? Probably that fool Stewart introduced them. He hasn't any more idea of the fitness of things! For a minister, he's the limit! I do wish we could go to another church! Now isn't that just enough to make you pass out? And the poor dear doesn't know the difference, of course! Men never do. Imagine! Marion Warren! Aline, we've simply got to rescue the poor man from her clutches. But imagine Marion Warren aspiring to Jeff Lyman! I ask you, did you ever hear the like? I didn't think she had the nerve. But I saw her rolling those big old eyes of hers at him as we came up. Isn't it vexatious? And he hadn't told me yet when he was ready to play golf with me. Come, darling, we've got to go to the rescue."

Isabel and her followers filed hastily through the crowd toward the table where Marion was arranging cups for the expeditious pouring of coffee when the time came to serve everyone at once. Lyman saw them coming, too, and he walked boldly up to Marion and spoke.

"Aren't you going to be free after a while? I'd like to talk with you. I know you've been enjoying the concerts this winter, and I'm longing for a kindred spirit to talk them over with me."

Marion looked up with a sudden light in her eyes. Could she believe her ears? Of course he didn't know what a very humble person she was or he wouldn't likely have spoken to her, selecting her from the whole roomful of girls; but it was so good to have someone speak to her like that, as if she were an equal, as if her opinion on anything so great as music was of any worth!

"Why—" She hesitated shyly with a smile that lit her face into new beauty and fired the soul of Isabel Cresson, coming on in the distance, into new fury. "Why—I—really—I don't know! But I'd love to," she finished impulsively. "I'll try. I've never had anyone to talk over the concerts with. It would be so nice."

"Jeff! You didn't say when you'd be ready to play golf!" broke in Isabel peremptorily. "I'm not going to let you get away without setting a definite date! Oh, is that you, Marion? I just met Mrs. Shuttle, and she wants you to go to the kitchen at once!"

The tone was most disdainful, as if Isabel were commanding a poor minion, but for some reason Marion was not frightened. The look in the eyes of the pleasant stranger who had just said he wanted to talk with her about the symphony concerts gave her strength, and she had a quick flash of revelation that God was answering her prayer and standing by her. She flashed a funny little smile at Isabel and answered.

"Oh, you're mistaken, Isabel. Mrs. Shuttle has gone home to take care of her sick daughter, and I'm taking her place for a while. Perhaps you will go into the kitchen yourself and tell the girls I'm ready for them to bring the coffee urn now if they have it filled."

The young man's eyes were dancing with fun, but he stood quietly by, watching this little tilt and thinking what a dead contrast these two girls were.

"Oh, really?" said Isabel scornfully. "No, I can't be bothered. What do you think I am? A servant?" and she turned her back on Marion and tried to press her challenge for a game on Lyman.

Marion went on coolly placing coffee cups and giving low-toned orders to the aides who came back and forth bearing dishes, but she was wondering if she had been unchristian in her reply to Isabel. More than anything else, she desired that her life should show forth the glory of God. She had a quiet feeling that God had stood by her, and she must not do the least little thing by word or deed, or even thought, that would not be according to His purpose for her life. Her life was meant to show forth His glory, not her own, and perhaps her tongue had gotten away with her. It would have done no harm for Isabel to think that she had scored a triumph.

Then she heard Lyman's good-natured answer to Isabel.

"Thanks, awfully, Isabel, but I'm afraid I'm not in the market for a game just now. The fact is my time is pretty well taken up." Lyman was leading Isabel away from the table now, and Marion smiled quietly to herself. Somehow she felt as if she had a champion, someone to take her part against the world. It was a new feeling, for since her father had been taken away, she had felt she would never have anyone to care much again. Of course, Tom cared in a way. But Tom was angry with her. In all the winter she had had only one or two brief, curt letters from him, and Jennie had written not at all, though she had written to them regularly once a week for a long time until she saw she got no reply. Even then she had tried to keep up a form of correspondence. It might be one-sided, but they should not have it to say that she had not kept in touch with them. And she had sent many pretty little presents, useful things and play things, to the children—out of her small salary, too. But still, she had a feeling that she was alone in the world, and if anything hard happened to her, there was not anybody who would care very much. Therefore it was wonderful to have someone be as kind and courteous as this stranger had been.

Presently Lyman disappeared from the group of

girls, and she thought perhaps he had gone home. She spied him later when she slipped into the classroom where all the younger boys had congregated to see if they had all been served, and found him with a group around him while he told them stories of his travels.

There was an extra plate of ice cream left on the tray she carried, and Lyman made room for her beside himself and begged her to sit down for just a few minutes and eat it with them. There really was not any good reason why she should refuse. The rush at the coffee table was over, and the aides were serving themselves. There was no immediate hurry about beginning on the dishes, and Mrs. Shuttle had returned and would take command for the time, so she sat down, glad that she was in an inconspicuous classroom, rather than out where everybody else was. She did not care to be in the public eye, not while Isabel was about.

It was thus she came to hear some of his wonderful stories and to listen while he described marvelous pictures he had seen in some of the world's most famous galleries. It was noteworthy that he described those pictures in such a way that even the youngest boy in the group did not grow restless or lose interest, but kept an admiring eye on his face and hung on his every word.

He was describing a picture he had seen in a great art gallery abroad when there came a general stir in the room outside, and the distant clatter of dishes reminded

Marion of her duty.

"They are bringing the dishes back!" she exclaimed contritely. "I must go at once. What will they think of me? I promised, you know; but oh, I thank you so much for this! It has been beautiful."

She gathered up the dishes on the tray, and he rose to let her pass but detained her just an instant.

"Have you someone you must go home with, or may I wait and go with you?" he asked in a low tone.

The soft flush of her cheeks mounted to her forehead, and her eyes were filled with half-frightened pleasure.

"Oh no! There is no one anymore"—her voice had a faint quiver as she spoke—"but indeed you must not wait for me. I shall be very late, and it isn't at all necessary. I am quite used to going alone now. But I thank you very much just the same." She hurried away to the kitchen with a smile, her heart beating high at the thought of what it would have meant to her to have a man like that escort her home. It helped to keep her smile sweet and her eyes unhurt through all the clatter of the kitchen and the reproachful voices that met her and demanded to know where she had been.

The young man lingered idly, watching her for a moment as she slipped away, pondering on the wistfulness of her eyes as she declined his offer. There was a look of resolution in his own eyes.

"I shall wait all right!" he murmured to the red and black figures of the church carpet at his feet.

Marion, in the kitchen tying on her little frilled rubber apron, was reflecting that the evening had been a rare treat after all its bad beginning, one that she would treasure among her happiest memories. This was the kind of talk for which her beauty-loving soul had longed. Now she would go the very next night to the public library and find some books about those galleries and read and read and read until she knew all that could be known about those pictures and could talk about them intelligently. She wished she might have written down some of the names of the galleries and the artists he had mentioned. If she ever had opportunity to meet him again, she would try to summon courage to ask him to write them down for her. He would think her an awful ignoramus, of course, but it would be wonderful to know.

At last the company in the chapel broke up and the big room was cleared as if by magic.

Lyman walked in a leisurely way around the room examining the inscriptions on the brass plates underneath some memorial pictures that hung on the walls. He could hear the gentle clink of china and silver in the kitchen. Only a group of Ladies Aiders were left in the big room holding a discussion in the middle of the room about their next bazaar.

The janitor was picking up the lost handkerchiefs and gloves that always accumulate after an affair like this, and the voices of the younger people were heard in the hall saying cheerful good nights.

A burst of hilarious laughter came through the swinging door as someone went out, and then a group of pretty girls in bright evening cloaks looked in, jostling one another in the doorway.

"Oh, here he is!" called one, and they all bore down upon him.

"Come on, Jeff!" called Isabel Cresson. "You didn't come in your car, did you? Uncle Rad says it isn't parked outside anywhere. He wants you to come with us. We'll drop you at your place."

"Thank you," said Lyman politely, "but you see, I'm waiting for a friend."

"Oh!" said Isabel, slightly baffled for a moment. "Well bring him along. There's plenty of room. Uncle Rad has the big car."

"Impossible," said Lyman, smiling. "My friend may not be ready to go for some time, and besides, I have my car. It is parked around the corner tonight. The street was full when I came. Thank you just the same."

Isabel gave up, somewhat crestfallen, with many a

lingering glance backward to discover if possible who was the favored friend.

But at last even the Ladies Aiders departed, and Lyman approached the kitchen cautiously.

Marion thought she was all alone in the building with only the janitor out arranging the chairs in orderly rows for Sunday school. When she heard Lyman's voice, she started.

"I've come to wipe dishes for you!" he said cheerfully. "Give me a towel. I know how. I used to do it when I was a little boy."

Marion's heart leaped, and then her pleasure was shown in her eyes. He had stayed. Everybody else was gone, and he had stayed to talk to her! Of course, he did not realize what an insignificant little girl she was, but that didn't matter for just once. She did so want to ask him some questions about those wonderful pictures and where she could find out more about them. And he was kind. He wouldn't mind if he did find out that she was only an ignorant girl who worked in a store. He seemed to like to help people.

She protested against his working, but he took the towel and went at it as if he really knew how, polishing glasses like an old hand in the kitchen. Marion tied a clean apron around his neck, one that Mrs. Shuttle had left lying on the table, and they worked away as blithely as if they had known each other all their lives.

Of course, it was like Isabel Cresson to make out she had left her gloves or her handkerchief or something and come back for them, just to find out if she could who that mysterious friend of Lyman's was, just to get another word with Lyman himself, perhaps.

She pushed open the silent swinging door and looked in just as Marion was tying the apron around Lyman's neck, and she heard their laughter ringing out in unison and saw that they were having a genuinely good time together. But they did not see her, and she let the door swing quickly back into place and searched no further for gloves that were not lost, but went back angrily to the waiting car. So that was what Marion Warren was up to, chasing Jeff! Well, that had to be looked into. That was not to be. Somebody had to warn Jeff. And somebody had to squelch that little upstart of a Marion. The idea! Marion Warren! What could he possibly see in her?

"He's wiping dishes for that egg of a Marion Warren," she announced as she got into the car. "I think you've got to get busy about that, Uncle Rad. I didn't know she was such a sly little cat! Of all the nerve! She was perfectly insulting to me tonight. Answered me back when I brought her a message and tried to make me out in a lie right before Jeff. Was it you who introduced her to him, Uncle Rad? I should think you'd better watch out what you do. Of course, he doesn't know anything about her. He doesn't know what common people they are, though I should think he might see if he has any discernment. She doesn't belong in our set at all."

"Well, you see, he asked to be introduced," said the uncle apologetically. "It's strange how men will be taken with a pretty face sometimes, and I told him about her. I informed him that she came from plain, respectable people, and I really warned him. I shouldn't like her to get any false notions about him. She's a nice little thing, and I had a great respect for her father."

"Oh, you needn't worry about her!" said Isabel caustically. "If you had seen her vamp him tonight, you'd know she could take care of herself. She's the slyest thing. She kept following him around. Everywhere he turned, there she was. Pretty? I don't see how you can say she is pretty! She looks as if she came out of the ark. She looks as if she was so innocent she belonged back in the Dark Ages. Look at her sallow cheeks and her white lips. She doesn't even know how to make herself look stylish. She just depends on old stuff, rolling those great brown eyes of hers and looking demure. Old stuff, all of it. I don't see what makes Jeff fall for it, but he's so fearfully afraid of hurting people's feelings, of course, he'll stand anything. I really think it's up to you Uncle

Rad to warn Jeff. He'll get her talked about, you see. And I'll make it my business to see that Marion cuts out that kind of thing from now on, or I'll make it too hot for her in this church. I won't stand for it, having Jeff made a goat of."

"There, there! Isabel! Don't get excited," said her pacifying uncle. "I'll manage it that Lyman will understand. You keep out of this. It'll all blow over. Lyman doesn't want to get mixed up with a plain little thing like that, of course, so don't you worry. He'll never likely see her again. It seems he was interested in her because he saw her at a symphony concert and saw how interested she was in music. That's his line, you know, music and uplift and all that. He would be interested in a girl who was trying to uplift herself, you see, purely from a philanthropic point of view; that's his line, Isabel; that's his line."

"Yes, and that's her line, too, Uncle Rad. She always was poking around trying to learn something more about everything. Nobody thought anything of her in school; she was a regular bookworm. She wasn't in the least popular. Of course, we had to be nice to her because she was in our classes, but she never was really taken in among the girls. Only now and then to speak to her about the lessons or something like that."

"Yes," spoke up Aline, who was riding home in the Radnor car and who was noted for always saying the wrong thing. "She used to do all our algebra problems for us, didn't she, Isabel? I remember once—"

But Isabel gave her a warning dig in the ribs and went loudly on.

"She used to be the most demure little thing. I never dreamed she'd develop into a man hunter. But I'm done with her from now on, and I'll take care everybody knows just what she is."

But Isabel Cresson had yet to discover that perhaps she had but just begun with the young woman in question.

Chapter 10

The dishes were finished in about half the time it usually took to do them, for the helper proved most efficient. Marion closed and locked the cupboards and handed the key to the janitor with a feeling of elation that was utterly new to her. She felt like a little girl who was going out to play.

They stepped out together into the starlight.

"My car is just around the corner," said Lyman. "Will you wait here till I bring it, or shall we walk?"

"Walk, of course," said Marion joyously. To think of going home in a car! There had been few automobile rides in Marion's life, and it seemed almost as great an event to her as a trip to Europe might have been to some people.

"Shall we go the long way or the short way? I'd like to show you a beautiful moonrise if you don't mind being a few minutes later getting home," he said.

"Oh, that will be lovely!" gasped Marion. "I have had very few rides lately; I certainly shall enjoy it."

"I hope you will allow me to take you again soon, then." He smiled, and they whirled away into what seemed to Marion like enchantment.

They went through the park and out a little way into the country, through a suburb with lofty estates on either hand, and rolling golf greens lying like dark velvet. They saw the moon rise, too, over the crest of a hill, and saw it rippling over a stream down in the valley; and Lyman told her how he had watched it rise in Switzerland once, describing the rosy glow on the snowcapped mountains until she almost held her breath with the delight of it.

And even then they were not very late coming home, for the little clock on Marion's bureau pointed only to half past twelve, and all that delight and wonder packed into one short hour since they had left the church. What a wonderful thing a high-powered car was. And Mr. Lyman wasn't a stranger in the city, after all. He had said they would ride soon again.

When she climbed the stairs to her little third-story room, her cheeks were glowing and her eyes were bright.

"Oh, I mustn't, mustn't, be so happy as this!" she told herself in the mirror as she caught a glimpse of her own happy face. "It isn't right! I am making too much of a small courtesy. He is only being kind and polite. He probably saw how unpleasant those girls were being, and he wanted to make me forget it. I must realize that this doesn't mean a thing but Christian courtesy. Oh, I won't presume upon it; it was beautiful, and even if I never do see him again, I shall always remember him with gratitude for the beautiful time he gave me tonight, and for the way he sort of championed me before Isabel.

"Is it wicked, I wonder, to be glad that that other girl didn't get him tonight, and that he stayed and helped me?" she asked herself slowly. "I don't begrudge her the nice times she has; but she has so many of them, and I had just this one. No, that isn't true, either. I just will not be ungrateful."

She went to a pretty little box on her bureau and peeped in at the shriveled rose leaves lying in rich heaps; and a soft fragrance stole out and sweetened the air. There were a great many beautiful things in her life, for which she was deeply thankful; and she would just take this beautiful evening and enjoy the memory of it, setting out all the disagreeable part and remembering only that which was pleasant.

But sleep did not come quickly to her eyes that night despite the fact that she was very tired. Every experience of the wonderful evening had been gone over again and again. She thrilled anew with the delight of having someone care to stay and help her and talk to her, and lived again the beautiful ride.

She told herself many times that she just simply must not let this bit of attention turn her head or make her discontented with her simple life. She would read and study the harder so that, if ever another opportunity came of talking with anyone like Mr. Lyman, she would be better able to do it. Then there was the last concert of the season to look forward to, and it promised to be the best of all. Altogether, the world was a happy place, and she was glad to be in it. Yet underneath it all ran the pleasant consciousness of Lyman's last words to her. He had hoped that they might meet soon again. Did he really mean it? It seemed as if he did. And would they ever meet? When and where would there ever be an opportunity?

But her harmless little triumph was but for the night. The next morning about eleven o'clock, Isabel Cresson sailed down upon her, clad in a stunning fur coat, with orchids for a boutonniere, and demanded in a loud, imperative voice to see her.

Marion rose from the seat behind her special counter where she was fashioning some exquisite pink satin petals for a shoulder rose for a well-dressed woman who stood waiting, and greeted Isabel with a courteous smile. She had a premonition that Isabel meant no good in coming thus to her, but while she was not over cordial, there was a sweet dignity about her that seemed to command respect.

Marion still held the lovely pink folds of ribbon in her fingers, and the needle was partly pulled through a stitch. There was that about her attitude that showed Isabel that she had no time to waste, so Isabel plunged in, regardless of listeners, not even troubling to hush her voice. She spoke haughtily, as to one beneath her, and more than that, as if she had the right to talk, the right of a near friend or relative.

"I just came in to wahn you, Marion, foah yoah own good," she began. "You can't get away with the stuff you pout ovah last evening. It won't go down."

There was a curious blending of loftiness and modern slang in her speech. But having got under way, she forgot her practiced accent. She raised her voice and became a little more explicit.

"You know you can't expect people like those over in that church not to gossip, and, of course, *everybody* noticed you. I was so *ashamed* for you, I didn't know what to do, to make yourself so conspicuous and fairly fling yourself at a young man like that. Of course, he's a gentleman and couldn't do a thing but be polite, or you'd have soon found out your mistake. And, of course, you know a young man in his position couldn't show attention to a girl like you without making talk. It simply isn't being done. And if he did, he wouldn't mean a thing by it, but I don't suppose you knew that. I thought I'd better come and tell you."

Marion had been simply frozen into dumbness by the thing that was happening to her, her smile congealed where it had been when Isabel first started her tirade. It didn't occur to her that she could do anything to stop it. It didn't even occur to her to try and answer. What was there to say to such cruelties? She just stood there and grew whiter, and her eyes grew larger and darker. A little slender, straight figure like a lance standing there before that avalanche of damaging words!

"You know just what kind of a girl they'll think you are! You understand, don't you? You've always posed as being so terribly good, but you don't put that over any longer. We're wise to you now, and my advice to you is—"

But Isabel got no further, for the aisle man suddenly appeared and stepped up to her politely.

"Is there anything the matter, madam, anything that we can set straight? Something about a purchase?" And Isabel looked up to see quite a crowd collecting nearby. For Gladys Carr, who had chanced to pass that way as Isabel's tirade began, went scowling after the aisle man and, happening to find him close at hand, pulled him back with her.

"It's one of these here fierce swells," she explained, "got a line of talk t'beat the band, and little Warren isn't saying a thing! Not a darned thing! You better go quick or there won't be any little Warren left." So the aisle man came at once. Marion with her quiet ways was somewhat of a relief in his busy days.

It was a delicate matter, interceding between a customer and an employee, but he was a brave man and came courageously to the front. Isabel turned upon him haughtily and replied in a tone that was intended to suppress him and send him off apologetically, "No, merely a personal mattah! You needn't intafeah!" And then she turned back to Marion with a malicious glance.

"Now, you're warned, Marion, and I wash my hands if you get into any furthah trouble. But remembah! We won't stand for anothah such performance!"

Then Isabel turned regardless of the staring onlookers and sailed away with her head in the air and her fur coat swaggering insolently behind her.

But Marion stood still where Isabel had left her, staring blankly, the needle held in her inert hand, the rose falling from the fingers of the other hand, almost as if she had been dead. She was white as death.

It was the voice of the customer who was waiting for her rose that recalled her to her senses and saved her from the whirling feeling that threatened to take her away entirely from the world of sense.

"My dear," she said, "my dear, don't mind her! Anyone can see what she is at a glance. Such a tirade! She ought to have been arrested."

Marion suddenly came back from the borderland and sat down, taking up her half-finished rose and trying to set a stitch with her trembling hands.

"Never mind, Miss Warren. I wouldn't pay any attention to that," said the aisle man kindly, looking over his glasses at Marion's white face. He was an elderly man and had a young daughter of his own growing up. "If she comes back, just you send for me."

Marion thanked him with her eyes, but she could not utter a word yet. Her throat seemed dry and cold. She felt numb all over.

"Who was that poor girl?" asked Gladys, making a trip past the counter as the aisle man turned away. "Some lady, I'll say! Say, M'rian, you shouldn't worry about her! She can't put anything over on any of us; we're wise to you, see? The poor fish must be blind not to know you ain't that kind of a baby! Great cats! I'd like to meet her on a dark night and teach her a few. It's my opinion she's jealous, an' that's the whole story!"

Marion lifted a grateful glance toward Gladys as she hurried away and then turned to her customer.

"I'm so ashamed," she said, with a catch in her breath as though she were going to cry. "There wasn't—any— occasion—whatever!"

"Of course not!" said the customer sympathetically. "That was an outrageous attack. That girl ought to have been arrested. You could have her arrested, you know. You needn't be ashamed at all. If you decide to have her arrested, I'll be glad to be a witness for you. You have my address; just let me know. I shouldn't let her get away with a thing like that."

Marion sat and worked silently through the long afternoon like one crushed. She felt so humiliated that it seemed to her she never could rise again and look anybody in the face.

And all the time Isabel's cruel arraignment was going over and over in her mind, and she was reviewing moment by moment the evening before and trying to see what it could have been in her conduct that had merited such an attack. Of course, she knew that she had done nothing wrong. Could it be true that people were talking about her? If so, why? Was it such an unheard of thing that a young man should be nice to a girl, even if she wasn't of his social degree? Just for one evening. And of course he couldn't be expected to know who she was. She looked nice and behaved herself; what more was necessary at a church affair where all were supposed to be family? But it seemed that was not enough. She should not have gone to the social. She should not have allowed anyone to speak to her. She ought not to have any good times at all, she told herself bitterly.

She tried to rise above the shock of it and be her

natural self. But continually the trouble returned no matter what line of reasoning she used. What had Isabel meant, for instance, by saying "in his position"? Was there something peculiar about Mr. Lyman? Was he perhaps married? Or divorced? There were a great many people divorced in these days of course. Perhaps that was what Isabel meant. Of course, that might have been what made people talk if they all knew it. But if he was divorced, who had he bought the ribbon roses for? She had always supposed they were for his wife. But perhaps they were for some girl. Perhaps he had a great many girlfriends. Well, why not? Most young men had. Would that then make it a sin for another girl to sit and talk with him a little while? He had only been kind and stayed to help her afterward. He had been sorry for the way that the other young people treated her. That was why he took her for that ride. Her cheeks burned red at the thought. What more might not Isabel have said if she had known about the ride? But of course she could not possibly have known that.

Well, she must learn a terrible lesson by this, not to have anything more to do with young men as long as she lived, not even if all the superintendents and ministers of the universe introduced her. Not even if they appeared to be angels come down to earth.

As for this Mr. Lyman, she would think no more about him. She would likely never see him again anyway, in spite of what he had said. That was only a polite way of saying good night. Perhaps she would go to another church for a while so that she would not have to see any of the people who had been talking about her so dreadfully. Or no, that would only be to make them think she was ashamed of herself. No, she would go, quietly, as she always had gone, attend service, and go home alone. Let them think what they pleased for a while. It could not really injure her. They would soon discover that it was not true, and it would be forgotten.

But as for this Mr. Lyman, she could see that he was far above her in every way, of course, cultured and traveled and wealthy, and it was far better for her to keep out of his sight. He was likely only studying her type. Writers did that, she had read. Perhaps he was a writer. Now that she had thought of it, it seemed quite to fit him. Well, she would keep entirely away from him from this time forth, and just as soon as she felt she could reasonably withdraw from the church without causing more gossip, she would do so. It would come hard to leave her Sunday school class and the minister and his wife, for they were the only two real friends she was sure of in the city.

So she gradually lifted her little head like a lily that had been stricken and was trying hard to revive, and tried to look as if nothing had happened.

The next time she saw Lyman was two days later, Sunday night after church. He had been sitting three seats behind her all the service, but she had not been aware of it.

For a moment, her heart beat wildly, and she wondered what to do. But she could not turn and flee in the church with people coming down the aisle. If she waited in her seat, that would only make her more conspicuous, and she could not go up and talk to the minister, for he was down at the front door shaking hands with people. Even Mrs. Stewart was nowhere to be seen. She had no excuse but to walk out and down the aisle as everybody else was doing.

He was waiting for her in his pew with the evident intention of walking by her side, and she did not know how to prevent it. She could not walk by with downcast eyes and pretend not to see him or know him. He had already seen the recognition in her face as their eyes met when she turned to go out of her pew. And after all, why should she not walk down the aisle by his side? Was there anything wrong in that?

At the door, they came upon Isabel and her uncle talking with a group of people, and Isabel darted her a meaningful look that pierced her like an arrow. She longed to slip out the open door and run down the street away in the dark. But of course she could not do that.

She was so overwrought that she could not think of a way to dismiss Lyman, and before she realized it, he was helping her down the steps and leading her toward his car, which was parked almost in front of the door.

"Oh, I mustn't," she said, shrinking away from him. "I thank you so much, but I mustn't trouble you any more."

"But I don't understand," he said, looking at her disappointedly. "Aren't you going home? Well, it's right on my way to drop you there, so please don't suggest trouble. It will be a pleasure."

She was too embarrassed to know what to do and only anxious to get out of sight of the people who were streaming out of the church now and looking in their direction. She could see Isabel coming toward the door, too, peering out. She got into the seat quickly and shrank back out of sight only anxious to end the scene, but not before Isabel had spotted her, she feared. She must find some way to let Mr. Lyman know that he could not attend her anymore. She would tell him her humble origin on the way home, and that would end it.

But while she was thinking about it, trying to frame a sentence that would not sound too much as if she were presuming upon his slight attentions, she found herself at her own door, and she merely found words to thank him for the ride and say good night. After all, perhaps this was best. She would just stay away from the church and from every other place where he would be likely to be, and he would soon forget her.

As for herself, would anything ever make her forget this taste of another life that she had enjoyed for a brief season? Well, perhaps the time might come when the horror of what she had passed through would blow away like a death-laden fog, and she might have for her own the memory of those interesting talks and the glimpses into travel and literature that he had given her.

Chapter 11

From time to time Monday morning, as she sat and wrought her flower work, Isabel's glance of hate recurred to her. It seemed a glance that needed thinking about. There had been recrimination in it. Marion had seemingly transgressed again, she supposed, by walking down the aisle with Lyman, although it was perfectly plain that there was nothing else for her to do unless she made a scene out of it and refused to speak to him. But what would Isabel do next? Was it conceivable that she would go to Lyman with some tale about herself? Well, she must endure that, too, perhaps. But what was all this happening to her for? She had always tried to do right. Even in this matter of staying in the city when the others went to the farm, her conscience was clear. It could not be punishment for her selfishness, could it?

Dr. Stewart had once preached about tests. He

had said that every Christian had to be tried by fire in some way, just as steel rails were tested before they were put in a railroad, to see if they were strong enough to bear the weight that was to be put upon them. Just as bridges were tested, and steam engines, and all sorts of machinery. God tested us by hard things. Well, if she were sure that was it, she might be able to endure it better. He had promised to be near and help. The words kept coming to her: "God is faithful, who will not suffer you to be tempted above that ye are able; but will with the temptation also make a way to escape, that ye may be able to bear it." And apparently the way of escape did not mean getting out of the testing entirely when it began to seem too hard, because it said, "that ye may be able to bear it." Well, if she was being tested, she wanted to come through it in a way that would give God the glory. She didn't want to be a miserable, weak failure of a Christian.

All that morning as she worked away, the words kept going over in her heart, "God is faithful, God is faithful," and they comforted her.

"What makes ya so silent this morning, M'rian?" asked Gladys, lingering by her counter. "Ya ain't worried about that tough egg of a high flyer yet, are ya? She ain't worth it, M'rian. I give you my word. She can't touch you."

But just then there came a call from the velvet

ribbon counter. "Miss Warren is wanted on the phone," and Marion was relieved that she did not have to reply. When she returned, the giddy Gladys would have forgotten all about it.

It was a strange voice on the telephone, a young man. He said he was president of the Christian Endeavor Society in her church, and he gave his name, Dick Struthers. That she knew was the name of the young man who was the present president. But the voice did not sound familiar. However, she had seldom heard Dick Struthers speak. He was a shy, quiet fellow, not inclined to words.

The voice said that there was to be a Christian Endeavor dinner held that evening at a nice, quiet little hotel, some sort of a celebration of something; he seemed vague as to what it was for. He said Mrs. Stewart, the minister's wife, had asked him to call her up and make a special request that Marion Warren attend. They needed a few of the older young people along to give dignity to the affair, and Mrs. Stewart had especially wanted Marion. She would have called herself, but she was just leaving with Doctor Stewart for New York to attend a wedding and hadn't time. No, it didn't cost anything. It was paid for out of the treasury. It was to be a real nice time. Marion would go, wouldn't she? One of the boys would call for her in a car at half past six. Could she be ready then? Where would she be? At home or at the store? Well, just what was her present address? He had forgotten. No, she didn't need to go home to dress up; it wasn't a dress affair. Come right from the store if she wanted to.

When Marion returned to her ribbons, she had a troubled look. She did not want to go to that dinner. She was not in the Christian Endeavor Society now, had not been for several years, not since her mother was taken sick. She did not know the members very well, but they were just boys and girls, of course, from fourteen up. Of course it wasn't like going among older strangers. She hated to say no when Mrs. Stewart had made it a special request, and now she was committed to it, when she would so much rather have spent the evening studying in her room. She had meant not to have anything more to do with affairs at the church, not for a long time anyway, till gossip had been forgotten and her reputation was established again—if such a thing were possible.

But this was only boys and girls.

Well, she had promised anyway, and it was too late to back out.

So she hurried home the minute she was free and donned a fresher dress and smoothed her hair.

She was scarcely ready when Mrs. Nash came up to say her car was at the door. The sad old landlady patted her cheek and told her she was looking real pretty and to have a good time, and Marion went down somehow cheered by her friendliness.

She got into the car before she noticed that there was no one in it whom she knew. There were two young men in the front seat, and she was put into the backseat with two girls in long cloaks, sitting back in the shadow. They merely nodded when they were introduced, and neither of them spoke a word the whole way except to answer in monosyllables indifferently when Marion suggested that it was a pleasant evening and that this dinner was something she had not heard about until that morning. She began to think they were a grumpy lot. The two boys continually smoked cigarettes, and she could get no responses from any of them. At last she gave up the effort, deciding that they were very young and embarrassed, and she lapsed into silence and her own thoughts.

They had gone a good many miles and had been traveling what she judged must be nearly three quarters of an hour when they finally drew up beside a wide, rambling building set among tall trees, with what looked in the darkness like beautiful grounds around them. There were red-shaded lamps in the windows, and a sound of music and laughter came through the wide-swung door.

The young men helped the girls out, and they all went inside. The look of the place bewildered Marion.

It did not seem like a hotel nor yet a home, but they went up a staircase, and there was a room with many comfortable-looking chairs and couches and a piano. There were red-shaded lamps here, too. A jazz orchestra was playing, and two young people, a man and a girl, were dancing in the middle of the room. Was this the kind of thing she had been sent to guard against? Did Mrs. Stewart want her to see that none of the wild young things whom she was supposed to be chaperoning did anything unseemly for young people belonging to a church organization? Her heart sank, because she felt that she would be most ineffectual in stopping anything that anybody wasn't to do if many of the society were like the two girls who had ridden with her.

Much troubled in mind, she followed the young people with whom she had come, threw off her wraps in the dressing room, and turned to find the two girls who accompanied her dressed in a most unsuitable manner. They were wearing indecently short dresses of chiffon, and when she saw the girls in the light, they were not young; they had an old, coarse look. She wondered where they came from. Some new members perhaps that the minister's wife was trying to get hold of.

They paid no attention to Marion but went to the mirror and began to apply cosmetics freely. Marion went and looked out of the window at a wide stretch of dim blue hills and starry sky and wished she had not come. This was the last, the very last social affair of that church that she would ever attend. She would tell Mrs. Stewart all about it, and then she would never go to any more things among the young people again. She felt very unhappy.

When the two young women were ready, she went with them across the wide room where now were several couples dancing in a way that Marion felt was not at all nice. She knew very little about dancing herself, but it seemed to her that this was some kind of super-dancing of which no one who was decent could approve.

She was glad to get across the room and out on a long, glassed-in porch set with small tables, some of which were occupied by people who were being served with food. Marion noted with startled surprise that there were wine bottles on some of the tables, and that one company of four that they passed was very loud and hilarious. One of the men looked up into her face as she went by and said insolently, "Here's my baby!" She was glad to escape into the private dining room at the end of the glass corridor. But just as she was entering behind the other two girls, someone came roughly out singing in a high key and jostled against her rudely, disarranging her dress as he brushed past her. She did not notice till afterward that the deep crimson ribbon rose that she had made for herself that day to brighten up her somber little dress had been torn from her shoulder. She was too much engaged otherwise to notice it was gone.

For the room was blue with cigarette smoke, and as she looked around in amazement, she saw that not only the men but the women also were smoking, and that she could not recognize a single face that she had ever seen before.

There were bottles on this table, too—a long table with about twenty people seated about it. They had begun to eat, or rather to drink, and were very noisy about it.

"Why, we've gotten into the wrong room," said Marion suddenly, clutching at the dress of the girl who stood next to her. "Let's get out quick! This is a terrible place!"

The girl turned and gave her a wise, evil leer, and suddenly a man's voice cried out in a thick, unsteady voice, "Why, there's Marry'n, little Marry'n. Precious Child! Come 'ere an' sit by me, Marry'n, pretty li'l Marry'n. Les' have a drink an' then we'll sing, 'She's my baby! Marry'n's my baby!'" His voice trailed off drunkenly as a door at the far end of the room opened and someone came in. Marion turned wild eyes of hope toward her. She was clad in an inadequate sheathing of cloth of gold, and her gold hair was bound about her forehead with a green jeweled serpent. She came steadily on toward Marion with a cold, hard look in her eyes, and suddenly Marion saw that it was Isabel.

"Get her good and drunk, boys!" cried out Isabel in a tone like a scimitar. "Nothing short of drunk will do. We've got to teach her a few lessons."

And suddenly Marion felt she was surrounded by these strange, hilarious men, each with a glass in his hand, and she stood at bay, her back against the wall, her lips moving soundlessly. The words they were speaking, without her conscious volition were: *God is faithful, who will not suffer you above that ye are able. God is faithful! Oh, God! Come! Help me!* And amid the wild screams of laughter at her last words, which had been audible, she sank white and still to the floor.

"Yes, God'll help her a lot! She'll find out!" said Isabel, cool and steady and sneering. "Dan, hand me that glass. Did you mix it the way you said first? Now, hold up her head. I'll make her drink it. Ted, you pry open her teeth. No, lift her head higher. That's right!"

Jefferson Lyman had found the two books that he had promised Marion he would lend her. That was one of the things he had said Sunday night, which she had not taken in because she was so distraught. If she had realized that he was coming to bring her some books, she would have been more worried than ever and have felt that she must plan something more decisive than merely to be out.

But he had thought to forestall missing her by going to her boardinghouse about the time he thought she would reach there from the store. He had even considered asking her to go out to dinner somewhere with him if she seemed in the mood and had nothing else to do.

He reached the house door in his own car, just in time to see another car driving away. He remembered it because he thought he recognized the driver and wondered what he was doing in that neighborhood. As he waited at the door for his ring to be answered, he looked up the street after the car, which was halted for the moment by a traffic light and idly wondered again whose it was.

Mrs. Nash appeared at the door almost instantly, for she had been watching at the parlor window to see Marion go away and had been astonished to see a second car drive up as the first left.

"No, she ain't here," she said in answer to his question. "She's just left this minute. You can catch her if you want to. They can't be far. Ain't been gone a minnit! She's gone to some kind of a Chrishun Dever spread out in the country. They come fur her. Ain't you one of their crowd? Was she expectin' you?"

But Lyman, with a sudden intuition, had excused himself and was back in his car before she had finished her sentence. "My land but he's tall!" said Mrs. Nash aloud to herself. "But he's better lookin' than the other one. I kinda wisht she'd waited fur this one."

Lyman sprang into his car and threw in the clutch. The lights had changed, and the car ahead leaped on with a jerk and was rounding the next corner. Lyman dashed after it.

During that long, hard ride in pursuit of the car ahead, Lyman wondered at himself. Why was he doing this? In the first place, he wasn't altogether certain he had followed the right car. In the gathering dusk with the crowded condition of traffic in the city, there had been two or three turnings when he was not sure he was following the right speck of ruby light. And now since they were out on the lonely highway, though he had sprinted forward several times to get a good look at the car, his quarry had also started up madly and torn along at a pace that worried him. The road they were taking as well as the speed they were making perplexed him. And it seemed altogether ridiculous to suppose that quiet little Marion Warren would be riding with people who drove like that. Of course, if it were some young boy who was driving—but somehow his conviction kept him going even against his better sense.

That they should have turned in at the roadhouse

where they finally arrived was altogether fitting with Lyman's instincts for that car; but by this time, he had decided that he was a fool, and that, of course, Marion Warren would not be in that car. She was probably at this minute sitting around some quiet, pleasant table partaking of a homely supper of cold ham and Saratoga potatoes and pickles and cake and canned peaches. It was absurd that he should make such a fool of himself and probably get into a mix-up and maybe see someone that he would rather not have recognize him in a place like this. He would go back. As soon as he had a good look at that car to make sure that his first guess about its owner was right, he would turn around and go back. He would not try to go in on so slender a chance as the mere hunch that he thought he had.

But when he had confirmed his suspicions about the car, some inner light drew him further. Now that he was here, he would be sure. He saw another car on the edge of the parking space that gave him another idea. Drunken men were not to be trusted. At least, if Marion Warren were in such a place and such company of her own free will, he wanted to know the truth before he went any further in his acquaintance. He was going in rather for what he hoped he would not find than for what he would.

So he went inside.

"Got any private dinners on tonight, Jack?" he asked

casually of the proprietor, who stood about respectably and eyed him.

"One or two." He eyed the newcomer up and down and clamped his lips shut.

"Atkins here?" he hazarded.

A knowing gleam responded and a slight lifting of the left eyebrow. "You belong to the crowd?" The proprietor was a bit doubtful.

"I'll just go up. Want to see him in a hurry."

"First room beyond the balcony," murmured the proprietor and turned on his heel. If it wasn't all right, he didn't want to know anything about it.

"Is this a practical joke or a case of kidnapping for the police?" asked a cool, incisive voice above the wild babel in the room beyond the glass corridor.

There was instant silence, and a stealthy melting away toward the door at the far end of the room. When Lyman raised his eyes to ask for a glass of water, there was no one else in the room but Marion lying white and still on the floor where she had fallen. Had he seen Isabel Cresson but an instant before in a golden garment that left bare the greater portion of her back—or was it only a figment of his imagination?

He reached for a glass of water from the table and dashed it into the unconscious girl's face. Then as he saw her eyelids quiver, he gathered her up in his arms and carried her rapidly down the corridor, across the deserted dance floor, and out the door to his car. The tables were strangely free from bottles as he passed them, though he might not have noticed them had there been ten thousand, and all the people who sat about eating were decorously sober. The other rooms were entirely empty, and he did not see the proprietor anywhere about, but he did not stay to hunt for him. He laid Marion gently in the backseat and drove like mad toward the city.

Halfway back she came to herself fully and sat up, more frightened than ever to find herself moving through the darkness at such a rapid rate. Had her tormentors taken her yet further from her home? Was there no help anywhere? Wouldn't it be better to risk opening the door softly and jumping out rather than to stay and take what might be ahead? Her nerves were so unstrung that she could not think.

But Lyman became aware of her almost instantly and, turning, reassured her.

"Lie still, Marion," he said gently. He called her Marion and did not know it. She held her breath in wonder. Was she ill, or dreaming? How could he possibly have come here?

"You are perfectly safe. Just close your eyes and try to rest. You are all right. Don't try to think about anything yet."

After a moment of wonder, she asked him in a faint voice, "How did you come to be there?"

"I didn't come to be there," he answered grimly. "I don't frequent such places. But I didn't like the way your driver was swerving all over the road, and I came to find out if you were there. Your landlady told me you were in the car."

She was silent a moment, and then she said in an awed voice, "Then He did help. He was faithful!"

Lyman considered this a moment before he asked, "Just who are you talking about?"

"God!" said Marion, a ring of triumph in her voice.

"Yes," said Lyman reverently, "He did. I didn't know what made me keep going on against my better judgment, but I guess that was it."

"And I can never thank you!" she exclaimed, remembering how she had planned never to see him again. What if he had not come?

"Don't try," he said lightly. "You've come through too much, and so have I."

"But I don't understand how you knew I was there. Did anyone tell you?"

"No, I just had a hunch, as they say. I went in to make sure you were not there, and when I got to a closed door with a regular fracas going on behind it, I almost turned back. It was this made me open the door, and there you were!"

To her amazement, he laid a little crushed satin rose in her lap.

"My rose!" she exclaimed in wonder. "I must have lost it off my dress when that man pushed past me!" She dropped back wearily on the cushion, looking white and spent.

"Don't talk!" he commanded. "You've had a shock. You need a rest!" He was gravely silent, almost tender as he helped her out of the car, but when he left her with the command to go straight to sleep and not think about the affair, she found Mrs. Nash waiting for her in the front hall.

"Well, you came back with the right fella, anyhow," she said with satisfaction. "I didn't like that first fella you went off with at all."

"No," said Marion decidedly, "I didn't either, and I shall never go with him again if I can help it."

"Well, I'm glad this other man found ya. He was powerful disappointed when he found you had gone. You'd oughtta waited fur him. He's real nice."

"I didn't know he was coming," said Marion softly, looking down at the two books he had left in her hand at parting. But when she went up to her room and sat down to face the situation, her eyes began to fill with horror and her cheeks to burn. It had suddenly occurred to her that perhaps he thought she had gone to that awful place of her own free will. As she recalled his constrained manner, his reserved, almost distant tone, his silence, her agitation grew. Oh, why had she not explained fully? How could she bear to have him think that of her?

She tried to sleep but could not. Perhaps she would never have another opportunity to explain. Sometime in the night she began to pray, "Dear Lord, I put this all in Your hands to straighten out as You see fit. I guess I've been an awful fool!" Then peace descended and she slept.

Chapter 12

With all the excitement that had been going on, Marion had almost lost sight of the thrill she usually felt in wondering whether there would be another rose in her chair at the next concert. She went early, however, that last night because she wanted to enjoy every minute from the time the doors were opened. There would be a long summer without these wonderful breaks in the monotony of work, and she must store it all up to help her through the heat and weariness.

Slowly she climbed the stairs, trying not to think it was the last time this year, glancing in as she passed the empty balcony and boxes where the favored great would come later to lend their countenance and clothing to the evening for a little while, and wondering as she had done many times before how it would seem to belong in that velvet grandeur always instead of up in the highest gallery.

Softly she trod the deep carpet of the hallway and went down the steps to her chair, and there, yes, there lay *two roses!* Two wonderful, great, crimson buds! There had never been two before.

She looked hurriedly around. There was no one on that floor yet and no one in the audience room that she could see from where she stood, except a man up in the top box next to the stage. He was almost hidden by the heavy crimson hangings of the box, and he seemed to be studying the fresco work of the ceiling through an opera glass. He seemed as far away from her as a man on Mars might be. She stooped and caught the rosebuds to her face and kissed them and whispered, "Oh, you dear things. You *dear* things! You lasted all the way through, didn't you?"

With a quick glance behind her to be sure no one had come in yet, and with the roses still caught to her heart, she made a tiny, graceful curtsey and a wave of her free hand toward the great empty room, whispering softly, "I thank you! I thank you!" It seemed as if her full heart must give some expression to her feelings; and, as she knew no one to thank, she threw her little grateful rejoicing out into the wide universe, trusting that it would somehow be brought home to its rightful owner.

Then she nestled down quietly in her seat with the

roses fastened in her dress. They seemed to soothe away all the pain of the past weeks with their soft, cool fragrance and make her happy again. At least she would forget all her perplexities for this one night and enjoy everything to the full. She had ceased to wonder where they came from. They were the more beautiful that they were a mystery. She shrank from the thought of finding out their donor, lest it should bring her disappointment of some kind.

She sat in a dream of joy as one by one the people stole in and the orchestra began to tune their instruments. It seemed to her as if this, too, were a part of the beauty of the evening, as if these magicians of harmonies were calling together one by one each note and melody, like sweet, reluctant spirits that together were presently to bring forth divine harmonies.

She took little notice of anyone around her that night. The roses and the music were enough. She wanted to take it all in and seal it up for memory's serving in the days of music famine that were almost upon her.

With the little black hat in her lap and the deep, burning roses nestling on her chest, where their glow was reflected upon the whiteness of her sweet face, she sat with closed eyes and shapely dark head covered with shining ripples, leaning back against the crimson of the high-backed chair. She listened as if she were out in a tide of melody, floating, floating with the melody where it would, her soul palpitating, quivering, feeling every suggestion the music conveyed, seeing every fair picture that it carried on its breath.

～

Down in a box below sat Isabel Cresson, attired in a costly gown, several diamonds easily visible. She was gazing through an exquisitely mounted pair of opera glasses. She was cross with all the people who sat around her, for she had searched every spot in the floor and lower balcony for a certain man and found him not; and then she had turned her attention reluctantly to the rest of the house and found him not, because a broad woman with a towering hat completely hid him from her view. But she found with her powerful lenses the vision of a sweet face leaning back and listening with closed eyes above two exquisite crimson rosebuds. Rosebuds that she knew could be found only at the best florists. It vexed her beyond endurance, and she heard not a note of that whole wonderful concert. Perhaps, however, she had not come to listen. For she had been most uneasy in her mind ever since the roadhouse episode. Just how much did Jefferson Lyman see in that inner room? Did he know she had been there? She would have given her best diamond to find out.

～

The last sweet note died away, and the musicians had

stolen out one by one before Marion put on her hat with a happy sigh and turned to go, taking a deep breath of her roses as she bent her head.

Then she raised her eyes, and there he stood, tall and smiling before her, just in front of the chair where the man had sat that she had noticed once or twice; and with a gasp of astonishment, she suddenly realized that it had been him all the time.

And she had wondered who it was he resembled!

He smiled down into her eyes with that deep understanding that made her heart quiver with a glad response and caused her to forget all her nice little resolutions and phrases.

He was just a part of the wonder of it all that night, and the air was still full of the music that he and she had both been in and lived through and understood. Its heartbreaks and its ecstasies were their common experience, and there could be no question of their right to talk it over and feel anew the thrill of the evening's pleasure.

"It was without a flaw tonight, was it not?" he said as he bent courteously to assist her up the steps, and somehow that low-spoken sentence seemed to bring all the symphony nights into one and make them theirs. She forgot she had not meant to let him take her home again.

They were talking of the music, comparing one

selection with another, calling attention to the exquisite emotion of one passage or the magnificent climax of another; and so, before Marion had realized it, they were on her shabby doorstep, and all the words she had planned were left unsaid.

"I want to explain about last Tuesday," she said earnestly. "I did not know those awful people nor where I was going. I got a telephone message that Mrs. Stewart wanted me to chaperone a Christian Endeavor party and they would call for me."

He looked at her with something in his eyes that thrilled her. "Of course," said he, "I understood as soon as I saw who they were. There ought to be some way to bring them to justice, but let's forget them for the present.

"Is it ever possible for you to get away from the store on Saturday afternoons?" It was the first time he had hinted that he knew she was in the store. He knew, then, that she had to work for her living!

"Why—I—yes, I suppose I could," she found herself saying. "Yes, I think I could. I haven't asked any time off; we are entitled to a few days during the year."

"Well, then suppose you try for next Saturday afternoon. I have tickets for a recital that I am sure you will enjoy. It promises to be far finer than anything we have had among the soloists this winter. It is Paderewski, the great pianist. Have you ever heard him?"

"Oh!" She caught her breath. "Oh no! I have never heard him, but I have read of him a great many times. He is very wonderful, more than all the others, isn't he? You have heard him?"

"Yes," he said smiling. "I have heard him, here and abroad; and I think he is the greatest. There are people who criticize him, but then there are those who would criticize that!" He waved his hand toward the brilliant bit of night that hung over the street, a wonderful, dark azure path between the rows of tall houses, luminous with a glorious silver moon and studded with myriads of stars.

She looked up and understood and then met his glance with delighted comprehension. She knew that he felt she would understand.

"Oh, thank you!" she said. "I hope I can get away. It would be the greatest pleasure I can think of to hear him."

He looked into the depths of her eyes for an instant and exulted in their starry shine. She seemed so utterly sweet and natural.

"Then shall we arrange for it, unless I hear from you that you cannot get away?" he asked. "And may I call for you here, or will some other place be more convenient?"

"I could not get away until the last minute," she said thoughtfully. "There would not be time to come home, I'm afraid; and, dear me! I'll not be very fine to go to a concert straight from the store without a chance to freshen up."

"You always look nice," he said admiringly. "Then suppose I meet you in the Chestnut Street waiting room at half past two. Will that be quite convenient, or is there some other place you would prefer?"

Before she realized it was all settled, he was gone, and she was on her way up to the little room at the top of the house.

But somehow in spite of her happiness over her coming pleasure, there seemed to be an undertone of self-accusation in her heart. She had not revealed her station in life to him thoroughly, and she ought to have done so. Even though he did know she was working in a store for the present, he might think it was on account of some sudden reverse of fortune, and that because Mr. Radnor had introduced her among other girls, she must necessarily have come of a fine old family and be a girl of education and refinement. The dull old wallpaper on the hall seemed to cry out *Shame!* to her as she passed by; the very cheap pine stair banisters mocked her with their bony spindles and reminded her that he thought her more than she was, and she had not undeceived him.

He has not been in this shabby house, they seemed to say. *He does not know how you live in poverty. If he could see us all as we are—we, your surroundings—he would never be inviting you to go to grand concerts. He will only turn your head and make you discontented, and then when he found out*—when he finds out—*WHEN HE FINDS OUT!* They fairly shouted it through the keyhole at her as she shut her door sharply and lighted her gas, trying to solace her troubled mind with a glimpse of the dainty refuge she had made.

She tried to forget these things in looking at her roses as she unpinned them before her glass and laid them tenderly on the white bedspread.

"You dears," she said, "if you could only last till next Saturday, but you won't. And you're the very last. There'll be no more chances for you anymore. Bless the dear old lady, whoever she is." She had settled it long ago that the donor of the roses was a dear old lady with white hair, like the one who sat in the balcony below and sometimes looked up in her direction, and who probably sent her servant up to leave the rose in her seat. She never troubled anymore to explain just how or why. It was like a sweet fairy tale that one took on faith. She told herself, "The dear old lady will never know where to find me anymore: at least, unless I get the same seat next year; and I'm afraid that is not possible, for they told me that former holder wanted it again next year. Perhaps, now, perhaps—that's an idea. What if somebody has been putting flowers in that former owner's seat and doesn't know she is gone away? Maybe they have been meant for her all the time. Well, she was off to Europe or somewhere, and I have enjoyed the roses for her. If I had not, they might have withered unnoticed. But isn't it great, great, *great* that I'm to hear the real Pader—how *did* he pronounce that name? I wonder? I must listen when he speaks it again and remember just how it was."

Thus communing with herself she managed to silence for a time the voices of her poverty that were crying out against her. But when she was alone upon her pillow in the dark, once more her conscience arose and reminded her that she did not know a thing about this stranger except that he was kind. Of course, Mr. Radnor had introduced him, and also the minister, who had seemed very fond of him, but they did not expect her to go trailing off everywhere with him, and mercy—he might be married! Married men nowadays did sometimes pay attention to girls. But she was not that kind of a girl. She resolved that she would tell him all about herself plainly the next time she saw him. Perhaps it would be after church tomorrow night; and, if it was, she would be brave and tell him quickly before he could make her fear to lose the joy of that wonderful concert.

She might, of course, wait for just this one more great pleasure; to go to a real concert with a man like that would be a thing to remember all one's life. But if one took a forbidden pleasure, what could there be in the memory but shame and bitterness?

There was no way but to tell him all about it at once. If he did not come to church Sunday evening, perhaps she ought to write him a note and decline to go to the concert. But then that would seem to be making so much of the whole matter, as if she were taking his small attentions too seriously. What should she do? Oh for her dear father to advise her! He had not been highly educated, nor much used to the ways of the world, but somehow he had always seemed to possess a keen sense to know what to do on every occasion; and his love for his one daughter had made him highly sensitive to help her on all occasions.

Between her joy over the prospective pleasure and her worrying over this matter, she had a week of most intense excitement. Sometimes she thought she would go for this once and have her good time, telling him afterward. Once more could do no harm. And yet in spite of all her questionings she went steadily forward with her preparations.

Her problem was by no means solved by the fact that Lyman did not appear in church Sunday evening and that early Monday morning a note was brought to her door from him, saying that he had found urgent business awaiting him the evening before, which had called him away from the city immediately, not to return until Friday evening; but he hoped that she would arrange matters satisfactorily for the concert on Saturday, for he was counting on the pleasure of her company.

When she opened the envelope, her heart gave a wild throb of pleasure. It was so wonderful to be receiving notes like other girls, so marvelous that he cared to be kind to her!

Yet it troubled her and frightened her to think she cared so much. If her dear father were with her, she felt certain he would warn her against losing her heart to this man. It was out of the question that he could be her intimate friend, so far apart they were in everything. If her father had lived, and she could have gone on with her studies, it might have been possible in time that she could have been fitted to be a worthy friend of such a one.

She sighed and pressed back the tears that smarted in her eyes. She would not give in to discontent. She would take this one pleasure yet, this concert. It was too late now to stop it. He had given her no address except his home, and he was to be away all the week. It was not quite polite to send a refusal at the last minute when perhaps he could get no one else to accompany him, though of course he could probably always get good company. There was no sense in blinding herself; she might just as well admit that she was weak enough to want this one more real pleasure before she stopped altogether her friendliness with the only worthy man who had ever sought her out and seemed to care for her company. She would go to the concert, and then on the way home she would briefly and quietly tell him all about herself. That would end it. It was better ended before her whole life was spoiled with useless longing for a companionship that could never be hers. She must stop it before it was too late, and save herself.

Yet the tears that wet her pillow that night ought to have made her doubt whether it was not already too late.

That noon she took time from her lunch hour to hover around the remnant counters and make a few modest purchases, and that evening she began to evolve a charming little afternoon dress for herself modeled after one in the French department—a blouse from a remnant of silk and a bit of chiffon she had bought. Marion was skillful with her needle, and she had wonderful imported creations to copy. The dress was an exquisite triumph of art when completed and fit her admirably besides being most attractive.

Browsing around in the millinery department, she discovered a table of last year's hats, and among them a very fine imported one whose brim was slightly damaged; and the price was merely nominal. The artist in the girl saw the possibilities in that hat. She bought it at once and that night remedied the defect by a deft bit of trimming. The result was most charming.

"If I only had some of those wonderful roses," she sighed. "I should really look quite grand for once." But of course there would be no more roses.

The new dress and the pretty hat went to the store the next morning, the dress in a small pasteboard box. Marion appeared in her place behind the counter in her plain dress as usual, and only her shining eyes like two stars and the soft flush on her cheek told that anything unusual was to happen that day.

About eleven o'clock there appeared at the ribbon counter a boy with a large box asking loudly for Miss Warren. Marion was making ribbon violets for a fussy old lady, patiently trying to please her, and did not notice the boy; but the other girls were not oblivious. They brought the box to her in great excitement.

"That's the boy from Horton's!" said one girl. "Say M'rion Warren, you must have a swell friend to send you flowers from that place. Seems to me you keep it mighty quiet."

But Marion only smiled at them and laid the box on the floor beside her. "Thank you," she said, and went on making her violets quite as if she had expected this box, though her fingers were trembling and her face had grown white with excitement. Could it be that

the box contained more roses? Could it be that someone really knew her and was sending them to her? Yes,
it must be, for this was the second time they had come
in a box and directly from a florist.

She had never been able to explain the other time,
the day after she had come home in the rain and caught
cold. But now she must face the question that she had
been putting aside. Who could be sending her flowers?

It was someone who knew her actions, who cared
when she was ill, and who knew she was going to a
concert. No one knew that but her old landlady, who
had happened up to the door while she was making her
new dress. She had showed her the hat and dress and
told her that a friend had invited her to go to a concert.
But that poor old lady would never have thought of
lovely roses, even if she had desired to do something
pleasant, and she certainly never could have afforded
them. What was Marion to think?

It had never occurred to her to connect the roses
with her new friend. They were part of her life before
he came into it, and of course he could not have sent
them. She would have been too humble to think such
a thing possible.

But the rest of the morning she worked in a tremor
of delicious excitement. She slipped the box, unopened,
under the lower shelf and went on with her ribbons,
much to the disappointment of the other girls, who

wanted a glimpse of what it contained. But she could not bear to open it before them all.

However, at half past one, when she was excused for the day, she hurried up to the privacy of the small dressing room set aside for employees; and finding the box contained far more roses than she could possibly wear at once, she hurried back with her arms full of lovely buds and bestowed one on each of her comrades.

"I don't care," said one of the loudest-voiced of them all, after they had thanked her and she had slipped away again. "I don't care! I think she's just a sweet little thing, if she is awful quiet and private about herself. She deserves to have nice friends. She's different somehow from most folks, and she seems to fit those roses. I'm glad she's got the afternoon off, even if I do have to look after some of her customers. She was awful good to me when I had the flu, and I hope she has a good time with her roses and her swell friends."

"Yes, she's all right," assented another girl, burying her nose deep in her rose. And the others all chorused, "Sure, she is!" as they separated to their various places, each breathing the perfume of her rose.

Marion ate no lunch. She was much too excited. The great hour was here at last, and after it would come the time of self-humiliation. But she was going to forget all about it until the concert was over. She was going to enjoy to the full the joy that had been set before her.

She hurried to the dressing room and donned the new dress and hat. The old dress was tucked away in the box to stay in her locker until Monday.

She thought with a qualm of conscience as she turned away from the glass that perhaps she ought not to have made herself look quite so much like a girl of his own class, and then the task before her would have been easier.

It seemed very strange to her to sit in a luxurious chair in the waiting room, dressed like a lady, and see the whirl of life go on around her, while off in the distance she could glimpse the ribbon counter, with the girls going busily about, now and then stopping to smell their roses. A happy smile came into Marion's eyes as she noticed this, and she bowed her face to her own glorious roses fastened on her chest. She was glad over the roses, that they had come that special day in time for the concert and that there had been enough to give the other girls some—the other girls, who were not going to have her good time. She wished she might thank the giver.

He came exactly on the minute appointed; and when she stood up quietly at his approach, he half paused and caught his breath at the lovely vision she made—the soft cream-colored dress, the attractive hat, the shining of her eyes, the glow of her cheeks above the velvet of the gorgeous roses. He had not known how beautiful she was before, he told himself, though he had always thought her lovely. Did the roses or the clothes or the joy in her face make all the difference, wondered he? How he should like to spend his life making her look like that!

Chapter 13

A sweet shyness came down upon Marion as they went on their way to the Academy of Music. Her companion seemed to see and understand, and he did most of the talking himself, making her forget the strangeness of it all.

But when they entered the Academy by the great front door, where only the select who frequented the boxes might enter, she was filled with awe.

They mounted only one low flight of broad, marble stairs and entered the enchanted areas of the first balcony, and he led her to one of the luxurious boxes in the semicircle, set apart by crimson curtains. When she sank into her velvet chair down close to the front rail and looked out over the great room and down upon the platform that she had seen only from afar, she realized that everything was different from this point of view.

For an instant, her soul quivered before the thought that her other world where she belonged, which was represented by the highest gallery, would perhaps be spoiled for her by this brief stay in luxury. Then she put it all aside joyously. Never mind if her own world seemed not so grand by contrast. She would always know hereafter how it felt to be one of those favored ones down here. She was having her taste of the delights of luxury, and she would enjoy concerts all the more after having this broader view of life.

Sitting thus with the crimson background, the crimson roses against the soft cream of her dress, Marion was beautiful. Isabel Cresson, on the other side of the house in a gloomy proscenium box, attended by her aunt, was unable to recognize her. There was nothing about her outfit that could be criticized. It had the stamp of a foreign maker just because the owner had learned the art of the great originators of her models.

Isabel was baffled by the sight and much disquieted within her. She studied the other girl again and again through the afternoon, but not once did she dream that she was the plain, despised Marion Warren, sitting in the seat of the mighty and looking as lovely as one of them. She tried once to signal Lyman to bring his friend around to meet her, but he did not seem to see her, and she had to solace herself with watching his devotion to his beautiful companion.

~~~

From the moment when the great pianist came to the platform until the last lingering note of the last encore was over and the last bow was received with jubilant applause, Marion was utterly unconscious of self. The strong, fine personality of the musician, which seemed to fill the great auditorium and dominate every being in it from the moment of his entrance, charmed her.

Marion's heart swelled with wonder at the miracle of the music. No player or players, no singer or instrument, had ever affected her quite as this great man did.

She listened with her soul in her eyes as the master fingers struck the keys and the instrument responded as if it were glad of the hand that touched it. The music seemed to drip from his fingertips like liquid jewels, flashing as they fell. The young, untaught girl drank it in most eagerly, forgetting everything besides; and the man who had brought her forgot to listen in watching her intense delight. The great master of the keys might be at his best, and at another time this man would have rejoiced in it, but today the music was but a lovely setting for his love, which shone like priceless pearls amid it all.

After the program was over, they called the pianist

back, seven, eight times; and each time he played again as if he could not bear to deny them the gift to which they had accorded so great applause. When at last he was gone, the reluctant audience came down to earth again and began to pick up their belongings. Marion turned to her companion with a radiant face and a sigh of ecstasy.

"Oh, it has been like being in heaven for a little while and hearing someone who had learned of God."

"Perhaps he has," said Lyman reverently. "It seems as if no other man could so nearly reach our ideals of the heavenly music."

"I shall remember it always," said the girl, her eyes shining like two stars.

Then suddenly, as they passed from the hall into the thronged street, she realized that it was over and her task time had come.

She must tell him. But all the simple speech she had fashioned took flight and left her trembling so that she tottered as she went down the wide stone steps to the pavement; Lyman put out his hand and steadied her courteously.

"You have no call to hurry home, have you?" he said. "Suppose we go somewhere and have dinner together. I always like to talk it out after hearing a concert like that, and I want to know your impressions."

"That would be beautiful," she said wistfully. "But

I oughtn't to. I must go right home, I think."

Because he had very much set his heart upon this little dinner together, and would be greatly disappointed not to have it, he urged her.

"Oh, why? Is someone expecting you? Have you promised?"

"Oh no!" she answered quickly. "No, there is no one, but—"

"But what? Can't you give me this little pleasure? I had quite counted on it, you see—but perhaps I should have told you beforehand. Of course, if it isn't convenient—"

"Oh no!" she said desperately. "It's not anything like that, and it's very kind of you to ask me and to say it would be a pleasure to you, but—"

"Well, it *would* be a pleasure, a great, big pleasure," he said pointedly; and she felt that there was something more than ordinary feeling behind the words. Then she plunged blindly in.

"It's just that I felt that I have been having too good a time lately, and I must stop it, or I shall be spoiled. You see, I'm not used to many good times, and I might get very much discontented with my life." She stumbled along, hardly knowing what she was saying, and he smiled indulgently down into her face and drew her arm gently within his own in a protecting way as they came to the street crossing, guiding her skillfully between the crowding, impatient cars that were huddled in the street.

"I'd like a chance to spoil you a little," he said, and his voice was very tender. The glance of his eyes even in the electric glow of the street made her heart stand still, as if she looked into a mighty joy upon which she must herself shut the door.

"Oh, but you don't understand!" she said desperately. "It's very kind and nice, and it's been so beautiful, but I ought to have told you before. I ought not to have let you think—" She paused, unable to find words, and another congested street crossing interrupted their conversation for a moment. She never noticed that he was guiding her steps toward the region of the better class of downtown tearooms and restaurants. She was not familiar with these places and would never have thought of it if she had noticed.

"Let me think what, please?" he asked gravely when they were safe on the other side of the street. His own heart was beating hard now. Was she going to tell him that she had a beau somewhere struggling to earn enough for her support and that she could not accept his attentions any longer? His hand trembled as he laid it upon her little gloved one that rested on his arm so lightly.

"I have let you think I'm just like those other girls you know."

"Oh, you're mistaken about that," he answered quickly. "I never thought you were like them. Thank God you are not. If you had been, I should not have cared to have your company. You knew that the first night at the church reception."

"Oh that is not it, either," she said desperately. It seemed so very hard to make him understand. And she felt a great sob swelling up through her throat. What should she do when it arrived?

"Look here," he said, and his voice was very peremptory, "tell me this." He paused at the corner and detained her a little out of the crowd of passers. "Just tell me this one thing. Do you belong to someone else? Is there any reason why it is not right for you to go with me tonight?"

"Oh no," she gasped, almost laughing, "there isn't anyone at all. I don't belong to anyone in the whole wide world anymore, and there's nobody who belongs to me except my brother Tom and his family; but they have each other, and they haven't time to think about me. I certainly am making a terrible mess of telling you, and you will think I am very stupid to make so much out of it all; only I've enjoyed it so much, and I knew I ought to explain it for your sake."

"There!" said Lyman, laughing joyously and drawing her onward again. "There, don't say another word about it till we've had something to eat. If there isn't anyone else, I'm sure what you have to say won't matter in the least. Anyway, it can wait until we're out of the crowd."

He guided her carefully through the maze of people hurrying away from business or pleasure to their homes and dinners. All the time, his strong, firm hand was held close over her little, trembling one, steadying and seeming to want to comfort and reassure her. And in a moment more, he led her into a great, brilliant room lined with palms and set with little tables where snowy linen, glittering glass and silver, and delicate china glowed under the warm light of rosy candle shades. Low-voiced men and women were seated here and there conversing while a sweet-stringed orchestra, concealed somewhere not too nearby, sent forth delicious sounds like some sweet, subtle perfume filling the air.

He seated her at one of the little tables in a far corner, where a screen of palm half hid them from the room and yet revealed its beauties to them. She felt as if she were suddenly plunged into a wonderful fairyland where she had no right to be yet could not get away. Delight and distress were struggling for the mastery in her face, and the pretty color came and went, making her more vividly beautiful than he had ever seen her yet. He looked at her with deep satisfaction and admiration as he hung up his coat and seated himself opposite her.

"I wonder what you like," he said, smiling. "May I

try and see if I can please you?"

"Oh, anything!" she said, embarrassed. What would he think of her way of ordering, always looking at the figures in the right-hand column of the menu first to pick out the cheapest foods and then choosing from those?

With the ease of one accustomed, Lyman took up the menu, and, running down the list, in a low voice rapidly mentioned what he wanted to the deferential waiter, who seemed to understand at once and vanished, leaving them alone.

"Now," said Lyman, "if you will feel better to tell me at once, I will listen. What is it that you thought I ought to know?" His kindly eyes were upon her, and the color flamed into her cheeks until they rivaled the roses on her chest.

"I think you ought to know that I am a very poor girl who has to earn my own living—and—" She paused for more words.

"I surmised as much," he said. "Did you think I was mercenary, that I had to choose my friends from among wealthy people only?"

"Oh no," she said in great distress. "You do not understand yet! I am not only poor, but I am uneducated. I have had very few opportunities. I have never been to college. All those other girls have."

He laughed.

"Why, I have been to college myself, and I'm not so sure that I'm much better off for it, either. The fact is, I fooled much of my time away in college and learned more outside afterward. I hadn't learned what college was for before I went, perhaps. As for those other girls, I doubt if Isabel Cresson is the wiser for her college course. I myself heard her tell a woman, a friend of mine, that all she went for was to get into the sororities. She could not possibly have enjoyed that music as you did this afternoon."

But Marion was struggling with her task. How could she overcome his great kindness and make plain to him what she meant?

"Thank you," she said gently, "but there is something she has that I have not, and that must always be a great lack in the eyes of everybody. She comes of a fine old family, and she has culture and refinement behind her. She is used to going among people. She knows how to move and speak and act. My father was a plain mechanic. He worked in the Houghton Locomotive Works. We were not so very poor while he lived, because he earned good wages. He meant to give me a good education. That was what he wanted above everything else, but he died before he was able to accomplish it. He was only a mechanic, but he was a good man and a dear father—"

"I know," said Lyman gently. "He had the accident

from which he died through doing a kindness for another man who was in trouble. I have stood beside his own machine at Houghton's and heard the foreman tell the whole story. He described the scene when your father was found hurt and they were about to take him home. He said there wasn't a dry eye in the room. He said that for days afterward the men kept coming to him and telling him of little things that Mr. Warren had done for them. Some told how he'd followed them into a saloon and persuaded them to come out, how he'd stayed with them and walked out of his way night after night to go home with them and get them safely by temptation till they were strong enough to go alone. Some told how he'd stayed after hours and done their work when their wives or children were sick and they needed to be away from the shop; and one man told how your father divided his pay with him for weeks when he was getting over an operation and could work only half-time.

"You are mistaken, Miss Warren; your father was a gentleman, and yours was a royal family if there ever was one. Do you know how Miss Cresson's father died? It was in a drunken row in some fine banquet hall; and before he died, he had killed another man. Perhaps she is not so much to blame for being what she is with such a father, but tell me, which is the fine old family, yours or hers? I should prefer yours."

Chapter 14

The tears had come now in spite of all Marion's struggles, though they were happy tears, and she tried to hurry them away with smiles.

"Oh," she said, "how beautiful of you, how beautiful to say that about my dear father! I knew he was all that and a great deal more, too, but I thought—I thought you would not count—"

"You thought that I was a snob," he said, smiling.

"Oh no!" she said aghast. "Oh no! I never thought that."

"Yes, yes, you did. There's no use in denying it. You thought because I had enjoyed advantages that had not been yours that I would count those advantages greater than all other noble things in earth, and that I would despise you when I knew that you had been without them. Isn't that so?"

"No, not that exactly," she said with a troubled look. "It was just that I thought you did not know, and that, when you found out, you would think I had not been honest with you to let you put yourself in that light before people. Isabel Cresson and all those girls know who I am. They probably thought it very strange of you to sit and talk with me when they were nearby, and when they knew that I was such an insignificant little thing. It was not that I did not think you noble enough to be kind to me, even if you did know about me; but I was not one you would be likely to pick out for a friend, I knew, and I felt that I must make you understand it at once. It has troubled me all week that I did not tell you last Saturday evening, but I did so want to go today— just this once more before—before. . ." She stopped in dismay and knew not what to say.

"Before what?" he asked, watching her with gentle indulgence in his eyes.

"Why, before it ended," she finished bravely with scarlet cheeks.

"Then you thought I would drop you as soon as I knew?"

"Why, I supposed. . .that would be the end," she answered lamely.

"Answer me truly, and look right in my eyes," he insisted teasingly. "Did you really think I would drop you as soon as I knew? Please look up while you answer.

You can't possibly deceive yourself into saying the wrong thing while you're looking at me, you know."

She raised her eyes in beautiful embarrassment to his and wavered under his steady gaze.

"I thought. . .you. . .*ought* to."

"You thought I *ought*?" he laughed merrily. "Ah! Now, then, the question just once more; and please, if you don't mind, look up again for a minute. Did you *really* think I would drop you?"

"I—" There was a long pause, and then her eyes dropped in deep embarrassment. "I do not. . .know," she finished.

"Ah! Then you will admit just a little doubt of my criminality?" Her troubled eyes gave him one beautiful look of reproach, and then her long lashes drooped on her crimson cheeks.

"Forgive me!" he said quickly. "I did not mean to tease you. I am sorry. I only wanted to be sure whether you thought me that kind of a fellow or not. Now let me assure you that I do not intend to drop you in the least. If there's any dropping, it will have to be done by you and not me. By the way, have you any idea where I first saw you?"

His ordinary tone reassured her, and she lifted her gaze once more shyly, the light coming into her eyes at the remembrance.

"Oh yes, I shall never forget that; it was at the

church—Mr. Radnor introduced you. I thought it so kind of him, because nobody else ever noticed me much. Mr. Radnor appreciated Father a little, I think."

"He did, yes. I'm sure he did from some things he said to me," said Lyman thoughtfully; then, frowning slightly at the memory of some other things Mr. Radnor had said, "but I don't think he appreciates his daughter as much as I do. He has never gotten well enough acquainted. Someday I hope he will."

Marion smiled.

"I don't suppose he'll ever see enough of me to know more than he does now about me. He is a very busy man, and I'm quite inconspicuous."

She spoke with a sweet humility, and the young man thought how very lovely she looked as she said it.

"Time changes all things," said Lyman, smiling. "You might find the order reversed, and Mr. Radnor may one day find you conspicuous enough on his horizon to warrant the time for appreciation. However, just at present I don't care much, do you? I prefer to appreciate you myself. And, by the way, you're all off about where I first saw you. I did not see you that night for the first time, by any means."

"Oh, you mean at the store when you bought the ribbon roses," she said. "Of course! How stupid of me! But I felt you did not recognize me then."

"Oh, but I did," he said, "but that wasn't the first

time either. I had seen you on several different occasions before that, besides once when I couldn't see you very well."

"Oh, what can you possibly mean?" she said looking at him with such an air of utter bewilderment, as if her world had suddenly turned upside down, that he laughed joyfully again; and the deferential waiter, appearing just then to serve the first course, was relieved to see that his delay had not been noticed.

Marion sat wondering and watching while the waiter served them, laying so carefully before her the delicate china, heavy silver, and crystal as if she were a queen. How did it come that all this beauty and honor were for her even for a night? She could not understand it; and looking up at the man across the table, she found her answer in his eyes, and her own drooped once more, while her heart beat rapid, joyous time in tune with the orchestra.

She dared not put into thoughts the thing she had seen in his eyes, yet it had entered her consciousness with a thrill that lifted the heavy weight she had been carrying all the week and made her feel it was right to be happy in this good time, at least for tonight.

"Isn't it strange that there should be roses on the table just like mine tonight?" she said, suddenly laying her hand lovingly on the flowers on her chest.

The waiter was fussing with the silver covers of the

soup tureen that he had just brought, but he gave her a quick, knowing glance.

"Well, yes, that is a coincidence," said Lyman with a twinkle in his eye toward the solemn black man, who never stirred a muscle of his ebony countenance, though Lyman could see by the roll of his eyes that he was enjoying the little secret immensely. Then the soup was served, and the waiter took himself to a suitable distance.

Now, Marion had eaten no lunch, and she had starved herself during the week as much as she dared for the sake of buying the new dress and hat, so that the delicious, rich soup and the courses that followed were fully appreciated by her. But still the delightful new dishes kept appearing, and still the pleasant conversation kept up its charm, until the girl dreaded the thought that the evening must soon be over—this great, wonderful, beautiful evening in which there had been given to her a glimpse of the world of beauty she had never thought to enter.

"But what did you mean?" she dared shyly when they had finished a most delectable salad and were waiting for dessert. She had hoped her companion would answer this without her having to ask again; but when the waiter left them, he had introduced another subject as if he delighted to leave it unanswered. "Where did you first see me?"

"At Harley's music store, when you bought your first symphony tickets," he answered, watching her changing face delightedly.

Her eyes kindled with the happy memory.

"Oh! Were you there?"

"I was standing just behind you in the line and heard you say you had never been before. I did a very bold thing, I'm afraid. I bought my ticket and selected a seat as near the one you had chosen as possible, so that I might have the added delight of hearing a symphony in the vicinity of one who had never heard one before. Will you think I was very much to blame if I confess that I wanted to watch your face as you listened?"

"Oh!" said Marion with wonder in her eyes; and then she suddenly became terribly confused and dropped her gaze from his. Why did this most unusual man say such strange things to her? Did he say them to other girls? Was it quite right to let him? Of course he meant nothing wrong by it; his face was too fine and pure to admit of a doubt about his having other than the noblest motives in all that he did, but did he quite understand how a girl felt when a man looked at her like that and said such things? Perhaps girls who were used to society and heard these nice things said to them every day would not think anything about it, but she felt embarrassed and did not know what to do. She lifted troubled eyes to his, and seeing her embarrassment, he said in an easy tone, "When are you going to tell me about your roses? I've been hoping for a long time that you would speak of them."

She was at her ease at once.

"Oh, would you care to know about them? Aren't they beautiful? Aren't they *dear*? Almost like human faces! And such a deep, wonderful velvet! I've wanted to tell you about them two or three times, but I haven't had the courage, because, you see, it's kind of a strange story, and you might not understand. For, you see, I don't know where they come from."

She touched the roses lightly, caressingly, with the tips of her fingers, and looked up to see what he would say.

"You don't know where they come from?"

She could not tell whether this was a question or an exclamation.

"No," she went on, "I don't know in the least. They come to me from time to time. I always think each time is the last, but today they came again."

"And you haven't the least suspicion who sends them?"

"No, not the least. At first I thought they were not sent to me at all, and it was all just a happening or mistake that I got them; but now the concerts are over, and these came to the store this morning, and there were lots of them. I was so glad. There were enough to wear all these and give one to each one of the girls in our department. I liked having them to give even better than wearing them, and I had wished so much the last one could have lived for me to wear today. Then, once before, some came to the house a day when I was not well enough to go to the store, and how could anyone know that? I don't understand it."

"Tell me about it. When did they begin to come?" His tone was low, and he was toying with his glass of water. He was not looking directly at her now. He seemed to be thinking hard.

"Why, I found the first one in my seat the night of the second symphony concert. I thought someone had dropped it and laid it in the chair next to mine, but no one came to claim it. I asked an usher about it, but he only laughed and said that the owner probably had plenty more. But when it happened again the next concert, I tried to find out who had left it there. I asked some women in the same gallery, but they acted as if I were impertinent to speak to them; so after that I kept the roses for myself, and they came every symphony night. I always found one there, all but the last night; and then there were two. I thought it was a kind of good-bye, and I kept them in water until every leaf fell. I couldn't bear to put them away in the box with the rest of the dead ones. I made them last as long as possible. And then these came today just when I wanted them."

"Who do you think sent them?" His tone was still

quiet and his gaze downward.

"I don't know at all," she said. "At first I tried to think of someone I could see who might have done it. Down in the balcony where we went today there was a beautiful old lady with a silvery dress and lovely white hair. I pleased myself by thinking maybe someone like that had sent them because she saw I was a girl alone, and perhaps she thought I looked like someone she had loved or something. Then it came to me that perhaps someone had my seat last year who had a friend who used to send roses and didn't know she was gone away, and so the roses kept coming; but that wouldn't explain those that came to the house and the store. And so I didn't know what to think, and I just thought God knew I needed them and so He sent them; and I thanked Him, for I hadn't anyone else to thank."

Her voice had grown low and sweet, and the eyes across the table looked at her with reverence, and when she looked up, his tenderness almost blinded her. It seemed so very much what she needed and yet couldn't expect to have, of course.

"I have something to tell you," he said very gently and with a voice full of feeling. "Suppose we take a walk. Do you like to walk? Do you feel like walking? Or would you prefer to stay here awhile?"

"I love to walk," said Marion with delight. "I haven't had a good walk for a long, long time. Father and I used to go when he had a Saturday afternoon off, or sometimes when he came home early in the evenings and wasn't too tired."

"Then let us walk," said Lyman with satisfaction, rising from his chair. "The moon is almost full, and the Avenue will not be crowded by this time. There will be opportunity to talk."

"It will be beautiful," said the girl wistfully, "but I have already taken a great deal of your day."

"I shall be only too pleased to give you the rest of it," he said smiling, "and as many more as you will take."

Then he turned to the waiter and said in a low tone, "Just put this on my account."

It was a common enough sentence, but it startled Marion.

"Put this on my account!" Then this man was accustomed to come to this wonderful place and partake of such meals! Nothing that he could have said would have so impressed the girl who listened with a sense of the difference between his station and hers. And a man like this had been giving her his time and attention!

Doubtless it was but a passing whim. Very likely he brought other girls to this beautiful place after other concerts. She was to him but a psychological study; and, when he had examined her little life awhile and analyzed and tabulated her species, she would soon be forgotten. But need she resent that? Might she not take this pleasant spot in life, knowing it was fleeting, and enjoy it while it lasted? Would it leave a pain greater than the pleasure when it was gone because of what she missed? Well, she must look well to herself that she did not let the joy enter into her soul too deeply. It was to be like her roses, fleeting but sweet.

With this thought passing through her mind, she walked the length of the palm-girded rooms and out into the lovely night.

It was lovely even in the city, for the moon was nearly full, and the air was balmy with the promise of spring yet held a tang of bracing air left over from the winter to give a zest to the walk.

Lyman led her quickly through the more crowded part of the streets and out to the Avenue, where pedestrians were not too many for comfort and where the fine pavement and the brilliant lighting made a beautiful place for a promenade.

He had drawn her hand firmly within his arm when they started and dropped his step into unison with her own, and she could not but feel the exhilaration of walking so.

"Now!" said he when they had come into the broad part of the Avenue, where they did not have to thread their way so carefully between people and it was quieter for talking. "Now would you like *me* to tell *you* about your roses?"

"Oh, do *you* know where they came from? Do you know who sent them?"

He felt her hand trembling on his arm, and her eyes looked anxiously into his. She knew the time of revelation had come, and she dreaded to hear about them, lest it would make them less her own. With a tenderness, he laid his own hand over hers and kept it there. Looking down into her eyes, he said in a low tone, "Don't you know now? Can't you guess who it was?"

She searched his face and hesitated then read his answer there.

"Oh, it was not. . . . It could not have been. . . . It—was—you!"

There was awe and delight and then real alarm in her voice, as her conviction became a certainty and she began to realize what it all meant.

He was troubled at her silence.

"Are you glad or sorry it was me?" he asked anxiously.

She did not answer for a moment; and then, looking down with troubled air, she said half tremblingly, "Oh, why—why—did—you—do—it?"

He felt the moment had come, and he was not half so sure of her as he had been a little while before.

"Because I loved you from the first minute I saw you, and I wanted to win you for my wife," he answered in a low, intense voice.

Chapter 15

For your wife!" she repeated in wonder, as if she had not heard correctly. "You would not choose *me* for your *wife*!"

"I surely do," he said tenderly. "I want it more than I ever wanted anything in my life before. I tell you, I have loved you ever since that first morning. I could not get the vision of your fresh, sweet face out of my mind. It stayed with me all day long, and I looked for you eagerly at the first concert."

"How wonderful!" answered Marion in a low, sweet voice as if she had just received a message from a heavenly visitant and angel wings were still visible to her eye.

"Didn't the roses tell you that someone loved you?"

"They tried to, but I wouldn't let them."

"Why wouldn't you let them?"

"Because I was afraid. I didn't see how it could ever come true. I was sure no one for whom I could care would ever care for me."

"And now that you know, do you think you could care for me?" He asked the question tenderly, looking down into her face as they walked slowly down the bright avenue, utterly oblivious of the other pedestrians.

She lifted her eyes to him wonderingly.

"How could I help it?" she asked. "I've cared from the first minute you spoke to me, and I have been so troubled about it I did not know what to do. I almost decided to go to Vermont and live with my brother and get away from the temptation. It seemed so terrible in me to dare to care for you—*you*! Oh, I don't see how I'm ever to believe it. And I don't think it can be right for me to accept this great thing. I'm sure you don't understand how ignorant and untrained I am."

"My darling!" said he. "Don't! I cannot bear to hear you say those things about yourself. I love you for yourself and not for your achievements. Those things are only outside matters. We will study together, you and I."

"Oh!" breathed the girl. "I could not think of anything more beautiful in life than that—"

"You darling!" he said again. "If you keep on looking at me like that, I shall be obliged to kiss you right here on the street, and that would be scandalous, I suppose."

"Oh!" gasped Marion, dropping her eyes in alarm, while the lovely waves of color rushed into her cheeks.

"There! Don't be frightened," he laughed. "I'll remember the conventionalities, only you really make it very hard work when you put on that adorable look. Tell me, did you like the roses?"

"Like them! I—*loved* them. But how did you do it? It is so wonderful! It is all wonderful."

"Oh, it was easily managed. I just went early and got in as soon as the doors were open. In fact, I bribed one of the doorkeepers to let me in early and then put the rose in your chair and went down to the proscenium box to watch you. You almost caught me once when you came so early. I was just going up the last step at the left-hand door when you entered the middle door. I waited to watch you through the crack that time. And do you remember when you asked the usher what to do with your first rose? I was standing boldly in the doorway, talking to the other usher all the time. I wanted to be sure that you took my rosebud home with you."

"Oh!" said Marion. It seemed to be her one available word.

"Do you remember a night when it rained, and you went home in the car? Did you know I walked home with you from the corner and held my umbrella over you? I doubt if you realized it, for you must have gotten just as wet as if you had been alone, it was blowing so hard."

"Oh, was it you?" Her eyes glowed at him again. "I called a 'thank you' into the darkness. Did you hear me? I always thought I heard an answer."

"I answered you," he said eagerly. "I said, 'You're welcome, dear.' To be sure, I whispered the 'dear' to myself, but didn't your heart hear it, dear?"

"I believe it did," she answered softly, "only I didn't know what made me so happy. I thought it was the rose."

They walked on fully absorbed in each other, the blocks counting into one, two, three miles.

"And did you know from the first that I worked in the store?" she asked once.

"No, I had to search that out. After that night in the rain when I found out where you lived, I was determined to make a way to be introduced. I made errands down that way day after day, changing the hour and walking up and down the street, or riding past, hoping to catch a glimpse of you. At last it occurred to me that, coming from that neighborhood and a plain house, you very likely had to earn your living. Your interest in the concerts made me think of music, naturally, but careful listening could never even imagine a sound of music coming from your abiding place. I felt sure you could not be a music teacher, or there would have been a piano heard sometimes. I thought perhaps you taught school—"

"That was what Father wanted for me," she interrupted sadly.

"So I went very early to the street, but not early enough to catch you yet. Then I thought of stenography and bookkeeping."

"All too high for me to attempt," she murmured humbly.

"At last, about a week after I began to watch, I went one morning before it was quite daylight and tramped up and down, always in sight of the house, until I was rewarded by seeing you come out. You haven't any idea how my heart pounded as I turned to follow you at a discreet distance. I never felt so shy in my life. I met a policeman a few blocks on the way, and he looked at me half suspiciously, I thought, as if I must appear guilty. But you walked calmly on and never seemed to notice that your steps were being followed."

"Oh, how frightened I should have been if I had known!" she exclaimed.

"Am I so formidable?"

Then they both laughed, and he began again.

"I saw you enter the door for employees, and then I had a long search through the departments until I found you. I began at last to despair and to suspect that you were hidden away in some mysterious workroom on a top floor or in some dull office; but I finally came upon you, all by chance, right in the midst of the beautiful colors of all those ribbons. That day I celebrated by having you make me some roses. Have you forgotten?"

"Forgotten! How could I? I've often wondered about them. I thought then they were for your wife. The girls all said so. They said your wife must be very happy to have you care so much for her."

"I hope she will be happy," he said reverently. "I shall make it my business to do all I can in that direction. Yes, I guess the roses were for my wife, though I wanted them for myself till she came to me. I will give them to you, my wife, on our wedding morning. How soon can that be?"

"Oh!" said Marion softly. "Oh!" and then, "Oh, I don't know." Her eyes drooped, and her whole countenance took on a troubled look.

"Couldn't we be married right away?" he asked. "Is there anything or anybody to hinder? I haven't told you a bit about myself yet, have I? Perhaps you won't feel like trusting me until you've known me longer, though."

"Oh, it isn't that!" said the girl quickly. "It never could be that. It's only that I...that there are so many things ...so much for me to do first before I could be fit... ready...ever to marry you...if I ever really could be."

"What things? Clothes, do you mean?"

"Yes, clothes, and other things, and I'd have a great deal to learn. I don't know that I could ever learn it all."

"And why should you? I thought we were going to

study together. What right would you have to go off and study things by yourself? And, as for the clothes, I always thought that was the silliest of all silly reasons to keep a man away from his wife for weeks and weeks after they have found out they love each other and decided to get married. I don't want a lot of fine clothes for a wife; I want you, now, just as you are. You're sweet enough and pretty enough and fine enough to please me always; and if you need a lot of new things, it shall be my pride and pleasure to buy them for you. You'll have plenty of time to select what you want and can go about it in a leisurely way. I can assure you I'm not going to be a bit patient about this. I want you right away. Couldn't you arrange to marry me some day next week? I've got to go up to Boston on a business trip, and I want to take you with me. I can't bear to go and leave you—"

"Oh no!" gasped Marion. "I couldn't possibly. Oh! Why, you've only just told me about it—"

"Dear," said he, tenderly pressing the hand he held. "I'm not going to frighten you with my haste—and we'll do things decently and in order as you wish it, of course—but you forget that I've been thinking of this all winter; and perhaps you don't know it, but I'm a very lonesome man. I need you tremendously. I've nobody to love me and nobody to love except the world at large. Mother died two years ago. She had been an invalid for ten years, and she and I had traveled together a great deal whenever she was able. I have missed her more than I can tell you since she went away. I live in a great big house with two old servants who have been with us since I was a boy. They do their best to make it comfortable, but they cannot make a home, and I want you there with your brightness and beauty. I want to be with you and have your companionship in my work and pleasure. Must I wait? Couldn't you make it next week? Are you afraid of me? Don't you love me enough to come to me right away?"

As he told of his mother, her other hand had stolen up and touched his gently, as if she wanted to console him for his loss, and he gathered it with the other in his clasp.

"I love you enough to come right away, of course," she said, and her voice was clear and steady now. "It isn't that; it's only that I feel so unready in mind and ways; and then, I've really no thing such as other people get married in. I shouldn't feel right not to get *some* things ready, and then, besides, there's the store. You know when we sign the contract we promise to give a month's notice if we are going to leave. It wouldn't be fair to them."

"Don't worry about the store," he said joyously. "Chapman's a good friend of mine. It would need only a word from me to get you off in a hurry. I'll see to that if you'll give me permission. I want you. I need you; why, I—*love* you, dear! Can't you see? You wouldn't let clothes and things stand in the way of that, would you?"

In the end, he had his way. When did a man not have his way who talked like that? Marion had the feeling that she had suddenly been invited to enter heaven all as she was, arrayed in earthly garments; nevertheless, a great joy and sweetness came down upon her. She could scarcely realize her own gladness, it was so great. She had not yet gotten used to knowing that he loved her and that he had been the giver of the roses that had gladdened her heart all winter, and here was the great question of marriage pushed in, for which she felt so unfit.

"I'm not at all the kind of wife you ought to have," she said faintly after her last protest had been silenced. "People will pity you and think you have demeaned yourself to marry a lowly person. Isabel will think—"

"Never mind what Isabel thinks. I'll warrant you one thing: she will be among the first to call upon my wife."

"And oh, what shall I do? How shall I act?" Marion almost stopped in her walk, aghast at the prospect.

"You'll act just your own sweet, natural self, dear," he said, "and she will go away and say how very charming you are and how she has known you and admired you all her life. Oh, don't I know her? She is a cunning one, and she will not leave you off her calling list. There are reasons why she will prefer to pose as your intimate friend. As for other people, I'm not afraid that my wife will not win her sweet way wherever she goes; and, if any dare to think in my presence any such things as you have mentioned, I shall be glad to teach them otherwise. Now, dear, you are not to think this thing about yourself another minute. You are yourself, and just what I want. You are the only woman in the whole world that I love and want for my wife. Besides that, you're tired, for we've walked miles, and now we're going home in a taxi, and you're going to rest tonight. And tomorrow afternoon you're going to let me come and take you out in my car, where we shall be alone and can talk together. Then perhaps in the evening we'll go to church together and horrify dear Isabel just once more before she finds she has to change her tactics."

An hour later in her room, Marion stood before her mirror and surveyed herself critically. The new dress was undeniably pretty and the new hat attractive. Roses and cheeks vied with each other in glowing crimson, and her eyes had not lost their starry look. But she was not admiring herself as she stood and looked earnestly. She was looking into the soul of this self that smiled back to her and searching it to see whether she could find the old self anywhere, and whether it was really Marion Warren, the little ribbon girl who had lived her lonely life for a whole year, struggling upward toward the great things she had longed for. And was this life suddenly to be all changed, and she to be put down in the midst of the larger life, where she was to be not an insignificant learner merely, but a most important part of a truly great man's life? Could it be true? Wasn't she dreaming?

Then the searching went deeper, and she looked into the eyes in the glass to see whether she could find any trace of the woman who was to be, out of the self that she was. Was it possible for her to fulfill the great ideal of the man who had chosen her out of all the world to be his wife? Then her great love answered for her, and she smiled back an assurance to the girl in the glass who questioned.

"I will do my best, and if he is satisfied, nothing else matters," she murmured softly to herself.

Then she turned to look about on her little room with new eyes. There it all was just as she had left it in the early morning, everything in order, only her scissors and some bits of silk scraps on the desk betraying her last bit of preparation for this wonderful afternoon. There was the small box of provisions standing by the partly open window from which she had expected to get her meager supper after the concert should be over.

To think now how superfluous any supper seemed after that wonderful dinner!

As she looked around her room, it seemed but half familiar, as if it had been weeks instead of hours since she left it. Could it be that it was but this morning that she had gone out from here expecting to return at night with the burden of a closed friendship on her heart? And now here she stood, the promised wife of the man she loved, and a whole story of revelation wrapped up in the crimson buds on her chest to be read and reread at her leisure, and all the tomorrows of more beautiful pages still to be written for her in the future!

There came slow steps up the stairs, and the tired voice of the landlady called out, "Here's a letter fer ye, Miss Warren. The postman brung it this mornin', an' I thought you might like it right off, so I come up. It was layin' on the hall table, but I guess you didn't take notice to it when you come along by."

"Oh, thank you, Mrs. Nash. That's very kind," she said. "No, I didn't notice any letter for me. I wasn't expecting one tonight."

Her radiant face and happy voice attracted the tired woman.

"You're lookin' most awful pretty tonight," she said, lingering. "Them roses is like some my grandmother used to raise on a little bush by her kitchen window. I ain't seen none exactly that color since I was a girl till you sent me down them that day. My, but that's a nice hat, and you look real good in it."

She surveyed the girl admiringly.

The old woman came into the room and dropped into the nearest chair, wrapping her hands in her checked apron as if she had something on her mind. "I been noticing them roses you get so often," she began again. "Some man'll be tryin' to carry you off purty soon. I've seen it comin'. No such pretty, sweet girl as you would stay long by herself lonesome like. It ain't accordin' to nature, an' I s'pose it's all right; but it's a terrible lottery, marriage is. I hope the man you been keepin' comp'ny with ain't got no bad habits. If he should turn out to drink, don't have him, Miss Warren, no matter how fair he speaks. It's no use trustin' 'em; the poor things can't help it once drink gets at 'em. I hope he makes a good livin' an' you won't have to work no more. I hope you'll turn out to get a good man, my dear. You certainly deserve it more 'n most."

Marion's cheeks flamed scarlet, but she answered smilingly, "You needn't worry about me, Mrs. Nash. He's all right, and I shall not have to work anymore."

"Well, my dear, I s'pose you'd think so anyway, whatever he was. But I hope your belief comes true, I do. You've been a good lodger, and I'll not get another as good in many a long day; I am sure of that."

When the old woman had toiled downstairs again, Marion opened her letter.

Chapter 16

The letter seemed remote from her, as if it were written to her in a former state of existence and had no relation to her present circumstances. She knew it was Tom's writing. Jennie had written occasionally since they went away, but usually it was to ask about fashions or request her sister-in-law to make some purchases for her, with always a sharp dig at the end of the letter because Marion chose to stay in the city. The girl felt almost too happy tonight to be interested in a letter from anywhere; but as she read, her face softened and tears gathered in her eyes.

Dear Marion (it read):
   I've made up my mind to write and tell you
that we think it is about time you quit the business
of staying in the city alone and came up to live

*with us. Father wouldn't like you to be off like that.
My conscience has troubled me ever since we went
away. I think I ought to have stayed in the city
another year for your sake and given you a little
more schooling if you wanted it so much. I thought
you'd soon see how foolish it was and come to us, but
you've got pluck. I always knew that, and I ought
to have seen you'd get what you wanted. I never
could understand why you wanted it, but seeing
you did, you ought to have had it. Now I've got a
proposition to make. You come home this summer
and help with the housework, especially during
harvest, and help Jennie sew things up and teach
the children a little; and then, if you don't like it up
here, we'll all go down to the village to live. There's
a real good teachers' school there, and you can study
winters if you want to and be home summers.*

*There's another thing, too. I've felt mean about
the money for the house. It was half yours, you
know, and you had a right to it. Father always said
he'd made a will, and I can't help thinking by what
he said at the last that he meant to leave the house
to you. Anyhow, half of it was yours, and I oughtn't
to have taken it. Of course it's all in the house now,
and I can't very well get it out for four or five years
yet; but I'll pay you interest on your part, and if you
don't want to live here, you shall have your share,*

*if I'm prospered, as soon as I can conveniently take
it out. I'm sending you a check for a hundred and
fifty dollars. Things went pretty well with us,
better than I expected for a first year; and I can
spare this just as well as not. Get yourself anything
you need, and live comfortably; but I hope you'll
decide to accept my proposition and come home
for the summer anyway. Then we'll try to fix things
to suit somehow. Jennie says she wishes you'd come,
too. I don't like to think of my little sister all alone
in a big city. It isn't the thing in these days when
so many things happen. Of course I don't want to
hinder you in what you want to do, but I think you
better decide to come home.*

Your affectionate brother,
Tom

It was the longest letter Tom had ever written, and it
warmed his sister's heart to have it come now in the
midst of her other joy, that she might feel that her own
were loving toward her also.

She was glad to the depths of her soul that she did
not have to accept his proposition and go to that home
to live. But he had asked her in a humble, loving way
and sent that generous check.

She would be able now to buy a number of necessities
and a few luxuries to replenish her meager wardrobe.

For it hurt her pride terribly to think of going to her husband like a shabby little beggar girl. And the savings from her tiny salary were so very small that she knew she could get very few, even simple wedding garments with it.

Also, there was another reason why she was glad of that letter. It made it seem reasonably sure that Tom never knew about the will, else he would not have written as he had. She rejoiced that she might once more have faith in her brother.

When she lay down to sleep, it was with a great joy in her heart. She felt again the thrill of Lyman's hand upon hers; his voice when he first said, "I love you"; his lips upon hers in good night.

He came the next afternoon, and the gloomy little parlor wore its most dustless front, with three crayon portraits of Landlady Nash's deceased husband, son, and daughter respectively, smiling down upon it all.

Mrs. Nash herself, with most unexpected fineness of soul, sent in, when they returned from their ride, a tray containing hot biscuits, pressed chicken, honey, two cups of tea, and a plate of sugar cookies. She had said to herself, *What if me own daughter had lived an' been alone in a strange boardin'house!—and this had been the result.*

The pretty new hat and the dress went to church that evening with two quiet roses nestling among its folds. Miss Cresson, seated across the aisle, spent the hour of service in thoughtful meditation, and the theme of her cogitation was, "Is *that* who she was?"

"How long have you gone to this church?" asked Marion of Lyman as they were on their way home. "I don't remember having seen you before that reception."

"My grandfather was one of the founders of that church," he said. "I've always gone there when I was at home. But I've been away a good many years altogether, counting school and college and war and travel afterward. I spotted you the first thing when I got back, however. You must have been a very small girl when I went away."

"It is all just a fairy dream," said the girl joyfully. "How could it ever have happened to me?"

"Because you are the princess," said Lyman smiling.

The fairy story continued to unfold the next morning. Just a little before her lunch hour she was sent for to come to the office, where she was told that her services had been most valuable to the firm, and that, while deep regret was felt at the thought of losing her, she was at liberty to leave them immediately if she felt it imperative. They would, however, take it as a great favor if she would remain for two or three days to instruct a substitute. Also she was handed a generous check, which she was told was the office's appreciation of her unique work in the store. Mr. Chapman said some very pleasant things, which brought the rosy flush to her cheeks; and the tone in which he spoke of Lyman made her heart throb with pride. The esteem with which he treated her was a marked contrast to his brief, abrupt manner of their first interview.

She knew that Lyman had been to see Mr. Chapman as he had promised to do the night before. It was beautiful to her that he had cast the mantle of his own personality about her.

With the pleasant, kindly wishes of the official head of the firm ringing in her ears, Marion went from the office to meet Lyman, as had been agreed upon.

They took lunch in a quiet little restaurant this time, where a sheltered table at the end of the room gave them opportunity for conversation.

After the order had been given, Lyman took from his pocket a tiny white leather box and handed it to the wondering girl.

She opened it shyly, not guessing what it contained.

Inside was a crimson velvet case with a white pearl spring. The crimson of the velvet was the same shade as the rose she wore. Had he matched it on purpose? Still wondering, she took out the case and touched the spring. There against its white velvet lining flashed a glorious diamond.

She caught her breath and looked at him, almost frightened by the magnificence of it.

"Put it on," he said. "It may not fit, and then I'll have

to have it changed. I stole your glove last night when you dropped it on the floor as we said good night. I had to get the measurement from that."

"Is it for me?" she asked with such an illumination of her whole face that he was almost awed by the effect of his gift.

"Surely! Who else could it be for? Put it on quick, before the waitress comes. Here, hide the box." And he reached out and took possession of the box and case in time to prevent the waitress from enjoying a bit of delightful gossip with her fellow workers.

The ring fit perfectly, and after the waitress had left them alone, once more the little hand with its unusual adornment stole out to the edge of the table and revealed itself; but when Marion lifted her eyes, they were glittering with unshed tears.

"What is it, dear?" he asked anxiously. "Have I hurt you in any way? Don't you like it?"

"Oh, it is wonderful, wonderful!" she said, "and I was thinking how pleased Father would be to have you care for me like that."

"Dear little girl!" said the man, reverently leaning toward her and speaking in a low voice. "That is only a small symbol of how much I love you. I hope to make my life tell you plainer than that."

She gave him a smile of radiant brightness.

The precious lunch hour was soon over, and she felt

that she must hasten back to the store. As they rose to go out, he said, "I want you to promise me one thing. Don't get a lot of clothes, please. Just fix up what you want for the wedding, and let's buy anything else you need in New York. It will be delightful to go shopping with you and help you pick out things, if you don't mind having me around."

He was rewarded with another brilliant smile of reassurance.

"It will be beautiful, inexpressibly so, to have you always around," she said with shining eyes.

She went back to her ribbons as quietly that afternoon as if nothing wonderful had happened, but there was a light in her eyes and a glow on her cheeks that were presently detected by her coworkers; and it was not many minutes before they had discovered the flashing of the beautiful diamond on her finger. It was whispered from one to another, till finally the boldest of them all laughingly challenged her to tell where it came from. She smiled shyly over the rosette she was making and acknowledged that she was engaged, and they kissed her and congratulated her and said they hoped she would not leave them soon.

Their kindness was very pleasant. They had not all seemed to be so very friendly before this, except when they wanted a favor, but it was pleasant to have them be nice to her, even though she did recognize that her roses and her diamond had paved the way for their affection.

Late that afternoon, when customers were growing less and the new girl she was teaching did not need her help for a few minutes, she stole away for a little while and refigured for the purchases she must make.

It was almost closing time when Lyman came down the aisle and stopped before her counter.

"I may walk home with you, may I not?" he asked in a low tone, his eyes answering her glad look in greeting. "Where shall I meet you?"

"Why, I can go with you now in just a minute. I've closed up my book and sent it in. Wait by the door at the end of the aisle while I run up to the coatroom for my things."

He watched her as she rapidly and skillfully rolled the ends of two or three bolts of ribbon smoothly and pinned them in place, putting them on the shelf and touching them gently as if she loved their rosy tints and silken texture, the ring flashing on her white hand caressingly.

She turned brightly to the other girls, who were huddled together at the upper end of the counter watching and whispering softly about her.

"Good night, girls; it's my turn to go early tonight."

"Good night!" they chorused eagerly as if they wished to show their goodwill before her friend.

They watched Marion and Lyman walk together down the aisle.

"She's in luck!" remarked one girl. "He's one of the swellest of the swells. He's no snob, either. He's the real thing. Did you notice that diamond, girls? Wasn't it a peach? He's some classy bridegroom, all right."

"Well, she deserves it!" unexpectedly snapped a sharp-faced, elderly saleswoman whose plain face and plainer speech were not relished by the girls, and who seldom had a pleasant word for anyone.

"She certainly does," agreed the rest. "If anybody can have good times and not be spoiled by them, she can. She's an angel if there ever was one, and she'll never be too proud to speak to her old friends, I'll bet."

"I don't believe she will," said another. "Gee! Wasn't that a diamond, though? I'd like to get on to a job like that myself, but they aren't just lying around loose."

"If they were, you'd never get one, Fan. It wouldn't go with all those glass rings and bracelets you've got on!"

The girl in question looked down on her cheap jewelry, contemplatively chewing her gum.

"Well, I s'pose I wouldn't fit," she said, "but I'm real glad she's got him, anyway. It makes you feel kind of good inside to have things like that happen once in a while. There goes the bugle. Good night, girls; I'm booked for a movie tonight. Billy asked me, and I s'pose Billy's good enough for me. Anyhow, I like him. Good night."

❧

The next two days went like a sweet dream. Marion had fully made up her mind what she needed for her wedding day and the journey, and with her two checks, she found it quite possible to get these things of the best. The gown she had set her heart upon in her dreams for several weeks was still in a glass case up in the French department. It was a simple affair of dark blue cloth with lines that only imported things from great artists seem able to achieve, and she knew it was to be marked down on account of the approach of spring. Her discount as an employee would bring it down still lower and put it quite within her means; and she knew its distinguished simplicity would give her the quiet, suitable appearance that Lyman's wife should have. A black hat from the French room went well with it.

An attractive little dinner gown of georgette; some fine, well-chosen lingerie; and a few other dainty accessories completed her modest outfit. She had promised not to get much, but what she got should be of the best and worthy of the position she was to occupy as the wife of a man of wealth and influence.

She had as yet no adequate idea of how wealthy or influential Lyman was. He dressed quietly, and he never spoke of his circumstances. Indeed, she thought little about it herself except to feel her own unworthiness.

One fact, however, served to open her eyes somewhat. On Tuesday evening, when she reached her lodging place, she found two large packages that had arrived during the day, addressed to herself. She opened them eagerly and found that one contained a set of beautiful, heavy silver spoons of the latest pattern, engraved with her own initials and bearing the personal card of Mr. Chapman. The other, when unwrapped, proved to be a massive bowl of solid silver, costly and magnificent, and bearing the congratulations of the firm.

She had heard stories of the fine wedding gifts that had been given to employees in the past, but nothing to equal these, and she had sense enough to see that for her own sake such costly gifts would never have been hers. These did more than anything else to fill her with awe and almost dread for her new position, and to make her feel the wide gulf, social and financial, that existed between herself and the man who had chosen her for his wife.

She placed the glittering array of silver on her little white bed and sat down on the floor before it. Then suddenly her head bowed beside it. How could she ever live up to those elegant wedding gifts? Oh, it was all a mistake, a dreadful mistake. She was just a plain little common girl, and she never could be a rich man's wife.

Then in the midst of her agitation, the maid of all work brought up Lyman's card with three great crimson roses, and she hurried down to him, all fearful as she was.

He heard her protest and, gathering her in his arms, laid his lips upon hers in token of his love for her and his strength that should be hers to overcome all such difficulties and differences.

"But won't you be sorry by and by when you know me better and see the difference?" she asked, fearful even yet.

"Will you?" he asked. "Dear, there's just as much difference between you and me as there is between me and you. Did you never think of that? If there's anything to feel, you'll feel it just as much as I."

"No," said Marion, shaking her head, "I'm sure you feel it *down* more than you feel it *up*."

"It looks to me as though you were trying to feel it 'up,' as you call it, more than I do what you are pleased to say is 'down,' though that, dear, remember, I deny. You are not down. In real things, I know you are far ahead of me. You have much to teach me, dear, of faith in God. What difference does the rest make? It was nice of the firm to send us that. I've known them all always, and they were friends of Father's. Chapman is a good friend also. He would of course send you something nice. There'll be a lot more things when people find it out. I'll be interested to see what Miss Cresson will send. If it were in the days of the ancients, it might perhaps be a serpent ring with eyes of rubies and a secret spring concealing a drop of poison, but I scarcely think in these days there'll be danger of that. She'll probably content herself with a silver pheasant or a pair of andirons. Come on, let's sit down and talk business."

Chapter 17

The next morning, Marion told the girls that it was her last day with them, and many were the outcries of dismay. They could not get over it and hovered around her between customers, until people looked curiously and wondered why that extremely pretty girl in the plain black dress wore so gorgeous a diamond and how she made her hair wave so beautifully. Before night the news of her marriage on the morrow had spread among all her acquaintances in the store, and they kept coming one by one to wish her well and leave with her some gift or remembrance, until the shelves around her were overflowing with packages little and big, and she had to send a lot of them up to the cloakroom to make room for the ribbons.

It seemed that Marion had more friends than she had known.

There was the pale little girl who carried up the ribbon bows to the millinery department on the eighth floor. She brought Marion a lovely, fine handkerchief with hand embroidery. Marion had taken ten minutes of her lunch hour once to run up in her place when the girl had a headache.

There was the sharp-faced maiden lady who made things unpleasant for the others at the ribbon counter. Her gifts were a collar and cuffs of real lace.

The girl who chewed gum and wore glass rings presented her with a handsome silk umbrella with a silver handle of the latest model. She knew a good thing when she saw it if she did prefer "Billy."

The floor walker in her vicinity brought a bronze clock; the head man of the department offered a silver-link handbag; and one little errand boy, whom Marion had kindly helped out of several scrapes brought on by his love of fun, brought her a gold thimble.

There were handkerchiefs and scarfs and pins and bracelets, jardinières and candlesticks and lamps, a book or two, and three pictures, not always well chosen, but all bringing to her a revelation of goodwill and kindly fellowship that made her heart leap with joy. These with whom she had been working during the past year were all her friends. How nice it would have been if she could have understood it all along!

It was being whispered about that she was to marry

someone of high degree in social circles, and all of them showed her that they were proud of her for having done so well. There did not seem to be one among them all who felt jealous or hard toward her for having the opportunity to pass into an easier life than theirs. Even the old janitor, who had every day cleared away the trash from the spent ribbon bolts, came with his offering, a little brown bulb in a pretty clear glass of pebbles and water. He told her it would bloom for them in the store, God bless her.

And Marion put her hand into his rough one and thanked him as she might have thanked her own dear father.

But the day was over at last, and weary and happy, Marion went back to her little top-floor room for the last night.

Lyman had promised to come for her at half past eight, and long before he arrived, she was ready with her modest outfit packed in her handsome new suitcase and looking as pretty as a bride would wish to look.

Mrs. Nash had sent up a nice breakfast, but Marion was too excited to eat much, though she tried to do so to please the old landlady. Most of the time she spent quietly kneeling beside her white bed, praying to be made fit for the place she was going to try to fill in the world and thanking her heavenly Father.

With the blessings of her landlady ringing loudly

in her ears, Marion stepped from that door to behold a handsome limousine waiting at the curbstone. The small children of the street were drawn up in frank amazement to stare. The dark, quiet elegance of the car, its silver mountings and inconspicuous monogram, proclaimed its patrician ownership. A chauffeur in livery stood awaiting orders.

The girl hesitated on the doorstep. Was she to ride in that great, beautiful car to her wedding? A sudden fearful shyness took possession of her. Lyman helped her into the tonneau and, with a word to the chauffeur, took his place beside her. The seat in front of them held a great sheaf of white roses, and beyond the roses loomed the immaculate back of the chauffeur.

She felt out of place amid all this elegance. The newness of her own attire made her feel still stranger. Would she ever be at home in the new world that she was about to enter? Perhaps she had been wrong to accept; perhaps he would be sorry. Oh, perhaps—

Then quietly a hand was laid upon hers.

"Darling," he said in a low tone, "don't be frightened! See the roses. They are white for my bride, but I had one great red one hidden underneath them all. Look!" He reached over with his free hand and lifted the upper rows of heavy white buds; and there, nestling in the hidden green, lay one great deep, dark crimson bud.

The sight of it reassured the girl. With a rush of

gladness, she turned to him.

"Oh, you are so good to me!" she cried. "Won't you ever be sorry it was only I? Won't you ever wish it was somebody wiser and better?"

"Never, darling!" he said, and the look in his eyes reassured her more than his words could have done.

Then in a moment it seemed they were at the church.

One white bud broke off as they were taking the flowers from the car, and Marion gave it to a little lame child who was leaning on her crutch to watch them. She smiled on the child, and the little girl answered with such a ravishing smile of thanks that Marion felt it was a kind of benediction.

There were beautiful lights in the empty church from the great stained-glass windows. The spring sunshine lit up the face of the Christ in the window behind the pulpit. There were ferns and palms and white and crimson roses, a few of them around the platform; and the minister stood gravely, smiling with his eyes. The organ was playing, too, softly, as they came in, yet with a note of triumph in the sweet, old wedding march.

Marion, coming shyly up the aisle, her hand resting on the arm of the man she loved, was filled with wonder and awe over it all. Who trimmed the church with roses for her? How did it happen that the organist was there for her quiet little wedding? Oh, it was all his love, his great, wonderful love around her. It was a miracle of love for her. Could she ever be worthy of it all?

As she turned from the minister's final words and blessing, she felt that the wedding ceremony was the most beautiful she had ever heard. Every word seemed written in her heart, and with her whole soul she echoed the vows she had made.

The minister's wife blessed her lovingly, and Marion felt as if she were not so friendless after all.

A moment more, and they were back in the car and speeding away. Marion did not question where until they stopped once more, and she looked up in surprise.

"We're going to have our wedding breakfast now, dear," said Lyman. "I was hoping you would not eat anything before you left the house. Did you? Come, confess!"

He led her laughing into a small, lovely room where a round table was set for two; and here, too, the table was smothered in red and white roses and asparagus ferns. From a quick glance as they entered, she recognized it as the most exclusive hotel in the city, and again her foolish fears came down upon her. She was fairly afraid of the silent servants who did everything with such machine-like perfection. She found her only safety in keeping her eyes on her husband's face and realizing that he was master of the situation and she belonged to him; therefore she need not fear. He would see that she did not do anything out of the way.

After they had been served and were about to go away, Marion looked at the roses lovingly and bent her face down to the table.

"You dear things! I'm sorry to leave you behind, though I've so many more," she said, smiling. Then she said, looking at Lyman, "How I wish the girls at the ribbon counter could have a glimpse of them! They would think this table so wonderful."

"A good idea!" said Lyman. "It isn't far from here. Symonds," he said, turning to the headwaiter, "can you leave this table just as it is, only putting on more places, and serve lunch for some ladies here? Serve the same menu we had. Marion, you call them up and give the invitation. I'll 'phone to Chapman to let them off together. He can put two or three people there for an hour while they are gone, I'm sure. Tell them to take the roses with them."

Marion's eyes shone with her delight. He stood for a moment watching her before he went into the office to another telephone. It was one of the greatest pleasures the girl had ever had thus to pass on her beautiful time to those who had no part in it.

"Is that you, Gladys?" she said. She had chosen her first friend in the store to give the invitations. She knew what pleasure it would give her to convey it to the rest.

"This is Marion Warren—" she paused, remembering that was no longer her name. "This *was* Marion

Warren," she corrected, laughing. "I want to invite you girls at the counter to take lunch at the B— today. I am sorry not to be able to be here and receive you, but we are going right away. Mr. Lyman has telephoned to Mr. Chapman about allowing you all to go together for once, and you are to take the roses on the table when you leave. Divide them among you."

"Gee! Is that straight goods, Mar—I mean, Mrs. Lyman? You're just fooling, aren't you? Well, there's some class to that invite. Come? 'Course we will, every last one of us. Say, you're a real lady; do you know it? You're the bee's knees! Gee, I wish I could think of some way to let you know how much we all like this. When you get back, we'll come and see you and tell you about it."

Marion turned to greet her husband with a laughing face but eyes in which the tears were very near. She knew just how much those girls would enjoy that. She had been one of them.

"Will he let them go?" she asked anxiously.

"Yes," said Lyman. "He hesitated at first, wanted them to go in stages, but I held out and told him he must for our wedding celebration; and he finally said he would. He said to tell you he would put Miss Phipps and Jennie and Maria in charge, and you would know that things would go all right."

They were like two children playing with new toys,

this happy bride and groom.

With a few directions to the headwaiter about the luncheon they were giving, they went on their way; and now, when they came out to the car, it had somehow been transformed. It no longer had a little glass room behind, with a stately chauffeur's seat in front. Its roof had been folded back, its glass doors disappeared entirely somewhere, and it was just an open car with two seats, the back one of which was covered with roses. Marion was put in the front seat, and Lyman got in beside her. The chauffeur stood smiling on the sidewalk.

"All right, Terence. You have the directions and the address. Very well, that's all. You put in the suitcases? Well, we'll meet you in New York sometime this afternoon if all goes well. Good-bye."

Then the fine machinery of the car responded to its master's touch and moved smoothly off down the street, leaving the respectful chauffeur bowing and smiling on the sidewalk.

"Why!" said Marion when she could get her breath from amazement, "is this car yours?"

"It is *ours*," he said with tender emphasis.

"Oh!" said Marion. "Oh! It is so wonderful! How can I ever get used to it?" After a moment's silence, in which her husband carefully guided his car through a tangle of moving vehicles and turned into a quieter street, she said, "Oh, I suppose heaven will be like this.

There will be so much, and all ours! And we won't know how to adjust ourselves to it all, not right at first."

"Dear child!" said Lyman, giving her a look of almost worship. "Does this seem that way to you? You make me feel humble. I never felt that I had so much. Perhaps you will teach me to be more thankful."

It was a wonderful trip for the two. Spring skies and cheerful little scurrying spring clouds overhead; in the distance soft purple hazels touched by tender green willows were coming into spring beauties, or starred with hepatica and bloodroot, and a smell of earth and moist-growing things all about. Birds were hurrying about to secure the best locations, and everything in nature seemed joyous and happy.

To the girl who had never been outside her own city farther than the suburbs or some nearby woodland park on a picnic, the whole experience was wonderful, of course; but the greatest thing of all was to keep realizing that the man beside her was her husband and that she was to be privileged to stay beside him as long as they both should live. It seemed too wonderful to be true.

There followed long, delightful days of sightseeing and shopping in New York, when Marion felt that at last she was realizing her heart's desire and beginning to see and know "things," as she had often expressed it to herself in her lonely meditations.

Then one bright morning the chauffeur, who had seemed always to know just when to appear and take the car, brought it to the hotel door, and they started up to the Vermont farm to visit Tom and Jennie and the children.

Marion had carefully considered the idea of inviting at least Tom to the wedding but decided against it. There would be so many endless explanations, perhaps wranglings and delays. Tom might object. Why worry him until it was all done and he could see for himself what a wonderful brother-in-law he had acquired?

Packed carefully in the ample storage of the car were gifts: a new dress for Jennie, ready-made in a style that Marion knew would please her; a hat that she would consider a dream; gloves; and a number of other dainty, feminine articles that Marion's experience with Jennie made her sure would be welcome; all sorts of pretty wearable and usable things for the children besides a wonderful doll that could talk, an Irish mail toy vehicle, and a bicycle. For Tom a fine watch; several pictures carefully selected to be interesting and uplifting to the whole family; some of the latest books on scientific farming; and a large, beautiful reading lamp. Marion was anxious that a little of her delight in higher things should reach these who were nearest to her in the world.

Lyman had seemed to enjoy the selection of these gifts as much as his wife did and was helpful with suggestions. He seemed to understand at once all about Tom and Jennie and to accept them as they were, and not expect any great things of them. Gradually Marion's fear of having them meet was wearing off. She began to understand that the true gentleman was always ready to see the true man, no matter how rough an exterior, and Tom was not so rough as he might have been. He had a little touch of his father in him with all his disappointing qualities.

The chauffeur had been sent back home, and they took this trip alone. Lyman seemed to realize that his wife wanted no strange eyes to witness the meeting between her husband and her brother, and with fine perception he made the way as easy for her as possible.

It was a great morning at the farm when they arrived.

Marion had written her brother of her coming marriage, but only in time for him to receive the letter a few hours before the ceremony. He could not have written her in time and was little likely to telegraph about a matter of that sort. She had said in the letter that she and Lyman were going to Boston and they might find it possible to stop over for a few hours and see them all, but nothing definite had been arranged.

So Tom and Jennie were in a state of sulkiness over the ingratitude of Marion. Jennie especially was out of humor about it. Marion was missed more and more. Jennie found it impossible to get hired help who could take her place. And now she had gone and gotten married! That was the end of it. But no, that might not be not be the end of it, either. Perhaps this new brother-in-law thought it would be a good thing to settle down upon them and take things easy. It might be that they would have Marion and her husband to look after now. Jennie suggested this snappishly that morning just after breakfast, but Tom only sighed and said, "Yes, I don't suppose she's got anyone worthy of her. She was always so trustful of people, and she never had any business caution about her. I ought to have stayed in the city and looked after her."

"Nonsense!" said Jennie sharply. "She isn't a baby, and you couldn't look after her. She would have her own way. It isn't your fault. And getting married isn't a business, either. But if I were you, I'd make her understand plainly that he can't stay here long loafing on us unless he helps in the planting. We can't afford to have him. He's most likely a lazy, good-for-nothing—"

It was just at that moment that the eldest child called from the front doorstep.

"Ma, oh, Ma, there a 'mobile stopping at our big gate!"

"It's just someone wanting to know the way to the village, I suppose," said Jennie discontentedly, hurrying, nevertheless, to the door to look out. "Tom, you go down and tell them. I'm sure I don't see why people can't read the signposts."

Then almost instantly her voice changed.

"Tom, they've opened the big gate and are coming in. You go out and see who it is, for pity's sake, while I take down my curlpapers. Goodness! Suppose they should want to come in and rest, and the spare room not finished yet. I washed the curtains yesterday, but they're lying on the bed. If it's tourists to stay, we'll put them in the parlor, and you'll have to come up and help me put the curtains up quick."

Jennie's tongue went no faster than her hands. The curlpapers were out of sight in a twinkling, and her hairstyle settled into its company appearance. Three aprons, a rubber doll, and a little sunbonnet were swept into a closet with one movement; and the hall table received a swift dusting with the apron she wore, while it was yet in a process of being snatched off to share the seclusion of the other three. Then a chorused shout from the children outside the door made her pause and listen.

"Aunt Marion! It's Aunt Marion!" they warbled gleefully, and Jennie's hasty preparations relaxed into grim dignity.

But how in the world did Marion come to arrive in such a fine automobile? This was her first thought. Very likely they had lost their way and some kind chauffeur had offered to give them a lift in their long walk. If it had been a farm wagon, now, that would have been quite likely; but chauffeurs and automobile owners, what few of them there were about that neighborhood, were not likely to be so kindly. However, that was probably the explanation.

It was to be hoped that neither Marion nor her good-for-nothing husband had met with an accident such as a sprained or broken ankle or leg, which made it necessary for even the iron heart of a limousine to relent and pause for them. A broken leg would be an excellent reason for living at the farm gratis for several weeks. Jennie had set her lips firmly. If anyone had broken a leg, he could go to the hospital in the village. There were excellent nurses and a good doctor there. She, Jennie, had no time or strength to wait on invalids.

With this thought she went out to greet her unwelcome guests.

Chapter 18

The car stood in front of the great flat stone by the side door, and a tall, handsome man with a long, fur-lined coat was helping a lady out. Jennie hurriedly glanced about but, not seeing any other travelers, concluded the children had made a mistake and brought her eyes back to the lady.

Marion wore a long fur coat also, for the air in that northern climate was still cold for a long drive. Jennie's discerning eyes made out that the coat was real mink and that the crimson roses she was wearing were not artificial, even before her eyes rested on the face beneath the attractive hat. The three children surrounded the newcomer, climbing upon her as if she were their long-lost property, regardless of mink and roses. Jennie started forward in horror to reprove them; but Marion, having stooped to kiss the baby, lifted laughing eyes to greet her sister-in-law, and Jennie suddenly recognized her.

"Why, Marion Warren! What on earth?" she exclaimed, starting back. Then Tom came to the front. Men take astonishing things with less surprise. He had grasped the fact of his sister's bettered condition like a flash as he stood watching the car drive into the yard. His practiced eye knew at once that it was a private car and that the man who sat beside his sister was no freeloader who could be put to work in the hay field if he lingered too long for convenience. By the time the car stopped at the door, he was ready with a hearty greeting for both his sister and her husband, and he already felt on intimate terms with his new brother-in-law, for Lyman's hearty grasp and pleasant smile had won his frank, open-hearted nature at once.

"Jennie, this is Marion's husband, Mr. Lyman. Lyman, this is my wife," he said loudly. "Jennie, why don't you open the door and let these travelers in? I know they are tired and cold. Nannie, let go of your Aunt Marion's hand. Don't you see you are crowding her off the step? Come, children; get out of the way. Run into the house and get some chairs ready for them to sit on."

Tom's loud tone of deference showed Jennie that the new brother-in-law had made an impression on her husband already. Not so easily convinced herself, she looked at Lyman sharply and was somewhat abashed to meet his pleasant gaze and to see the twinkle in his eye. Her face suddenly grew very red at the remembrance of what she had said about putting this new relative to work planting potatoes. She perceived at once that he would be as much out of place at that occupation as a silk gown on wash day.

But it was characteristic of Jennie that it vexed her to be taken by surprise. Although she had pictured a most undesirable brother-in-law, whose coming could but bring trouble and dissension to their home, she was annoyed that it had turned out otherwise than her prophecy, so that it was with an ill grace that she shook hands stiffly with Lyman and preceded him into the house, where she felt quite ill at ease. How was she to manage for this grand company with no one to help her? One could scarcely expect such a dressed-up minx of a Marion to help get dinner. It was just as she had expected, after all. Marion had arranged things so that she would have everything easy and be a lady living on her brother's wife. She looked belligerently at the bride, who was surrounded again by the three adoring children, being freed of fur coat and chic hat and roses as fast as six little hands could accomplish it. Tom beamed joyously over the whole and loudly told his new brother-in-law to make himself at home at once. There seemed no place in the whole setting for the ill-used Jennie.

It was Marion whose sharp eyes saw and understood, and freeing herself from the little detaining hands, arose.

"Come, Jennie," she cried, "get me an apron, and I'll help get dinner. It was mean of us to come down upon you this way without a warning, but we were not quite sure whether we could get here so early; and, besides, I did enjoy surprising you so much. What a lovely, big house this is! I'm in a great hurry to see the whole of it. Is this the way to the kitchen? Come on and get me an apron."

Jennie, somewhat mollified by the offer of help, followed her, protesting stiffly that she must not think of helping, but relieved, nevertheless, and more than curious about the bride's attire, her husband, and, most of all, the car in which they had come.

"Where did you get it?" she demanded as soon as they reached the kitchen, her eyes meanwhile traveling over the bride's clothing with comprehensive glance and resting scrutinizingly on the diamond that now guarded Marion's wedding ring.

Marion, smiling, held out her hand.

"My ring, do you mean?" she said pleasantly. "Isn't it beautiful? I never expected to have even the tiniest diamond, and to have this great beauty was wonderful. I was so surprised when he gave it to me."

"No, I didn't mean that," said Jennie bluntly. "I hadn't

noticed that yet, though it's big enough to see a mile off, goodness knows. Is it real?"

Marion felt indignant, but she managed to say, "Yes," very gently, though she withdrew her hand from inspection. It seemed to desecrate her new joy to have unsympathetic eyes and tongue at work upon it. Perhaps pretty soon Jennie would ask whether Lyman's love was genuine. She probably would if it occurred to her to do so. Marion shrank from the ordeal.

"It must have cost a lot of money if it's real. In my opinion, people better put their money away for a rainy day than to flaunt it in trinkets, but tastes differ. As for me, I never expect to have even a fake diamond. Though I don't know but it's a good thing he gave it to you. If you ever get in need, you could sell it."

"Jennie!" Marion could not keep the horror from her voice.

"Well, it's just as well to think of those things. You never know how a marriage is going to turn out. Are you sure he's all right? Where'd you meet him, anyway?"

Marion controlled her feelings, although her cheeks were very red, and answered gently, "Mr. Radnor introduced us at a church social."

"Well, it's plain to be seen why you married him," grudged Jennie. "You always did like pretty things and pretty people, and he certainly isn't bad looking. And you seem to have blossomed out in stylish clothes on the strength of it. I hope you had the money to pay for them."

"They are all paid for," said Marion quietly.

"Hm!" said Jennie. "They must have cost a lot. But what I was asking you about at first was the automobile. Where did you get it? Did you rent it in the village? I didn't know they had them to rent in the village."

Marion smiled.

"Oh no. It is our car," she said. "We came all the way from New York since yesterday morning in it. The ride was beautiful. I have enjoyed the trip so much—"

"Your car!" interrupted Jennie. "What on earth do you mean, Marion Warren? Are you telling me the truth?"

"I certainly am," said Marion, laughing now at the comical expression of her sister-in-law's face. "Come, Jennie; let's hurry and get dinner, for I've brought a few things for the children and I want to open them. Is Nannie as fond of dolls as ever?"

"Are you sure it's paid for, Marion?" asked Jennie anxiously. "They say hardly anybody that owns an automobile pays for it. They say they just mortgage their houses to get them or go in debt. You can't be sure about anybody."

"Well, you needn't worry, Jennie. This is all paid for, and my husband has money enough left to make us entirely comfortable. Come, Jennie, where is an apron?

Were you going to peel these potatoes? Let me do them."

"Marion Warren, have you married a real rich man? Tell me at once."

"I suppose I have," answered the bride meekly with a dimple in each cheek. "I never understood how it happened, but it's true."

"Well, then you can go right out of this kitchen. I'm not going to have a rich sister-in-law peeling potatoes for dinner in my kitchen. I know what is fitting if I am blunt in my speech."

"Nonsense, Jennie! I'm no different because my husband has a little money. I'm just the same girl I was a year ago."

"Indeed you're not!" said Jennie, taking the knife from her and going at the potatoes furiously. "Look at your shoes and your dress; it looks as if a tailor made it. And you're wearing roses in the morning. If you've really got the money to pay for it all, why, you've a right to be waited on, I suppose. Anyhow, you're not going to sit down in that dress and peel potatoes in my kitchen. And wasn't that a real mink coat you wore? Goodness! It's a wonder you weren't ashamed to bring your fine husband up here."

In vain did Marion protest. Jennie would have none of her assistance. She worked rapidly and soon had a good dinner in preparation. She brought forth her best preserves and pickles and the last of the fruitcake she had been saving for the church sewing society when it would meet with her the following week. Jennie was not so bad, after all, when she really was impressed, and she was impressed at last.

She went about with a martyr-like attitude, treating Marion with a deferential stiffness that was as unpleasant as her former attitude had been. When Marion insisted upon setting the table, Jennie sent Nannie to perform the task, saying with a heavy sigh, "I have done my own work and set my own table for a good many years and shall probably have to continue to do so all my life. One setting of a table more or less will make little difference. It's not with me as it is with you."

And this style of conversation continued until Marion was almost sorry she had come, and she retreated at last to the parlor, which had been made delightful with a great open fire in the old-fashioned fireplace. Then Nannie abandoned her table setting and nestled down close to her, and the other two children climbed into her lap and demanded a story just where she had left off the year before. Lyman, talking politics to the delight of Tom, who had missed his city friends when it came to election time, yet found time to watch his wife as she made a pretty picture of herself with the little ones around her.

The dinner would have been a trying affair with Jennie sitting up straight and stiff and dispensing her hospitalities without a smile, and Marion shy and embarrassed, wondering what her husband would think of it all, if it had not been for Lyman, who adapted himself to the situation with the most charming simplicity, talking intimately with Tom about the farm, admiring the view from the windows, discussing the possibilities of crops, then turning to the children with the story of a little dog they saw on the way, and even bringing a softened expression to Jennie's mouth when he admired her plum jam.

Marion watched him with growing pride and love, and Jennie watched her surreptitiously and marveled. What a lady she had become! Did a few costly garments make all the difference there was between them, or had it been there all the time? These were the thoughts that were troubling Jennie.

As soon as dinner was over, Marion coaxed them all into the parlor, and Lyman brought the things from the car into the room. Thinking the gifts were all for the children, the father and mother gathered eagerly around to watch them untied. Jennie had thawed in her manner somewhat but was not yet altogether cordial. She sat stiffly in one of the parlor chairs and watched Nannie's eager fingers untie the cord of a large box, and then suddenly the child threw back the lid of the box and screamed with delight over the beautiful doll. The mother's face relaxed then into real pleasure as she saw the costly doll and her little girl's delight. Tom entered into the excitement as if he had been a boy and helped the two little boys undo their packages, even shouting with them over what they brought to light, and beginning at once to set up the little electric railway that the new uncle had brought them.

In the midst of the tumult, Marion brought the hatbox and the suit box and the packages containing the other things she had for Jennie around to the couch and motioned her sister-in-law to come to her. Thinking these were more things for the children, and thoroughly mollified now, Jennie came and helped with untying the strings. When she saw the beautiful dress and understood that it was for herself, her face was a study of conflicting emotions; amazement, doubt, shame, and delight contended for mastery.

"Do you like it?" asked Marion. "If you would rather have something else, I think I could change it on my way back and send it to you."

Jennie laid eager hands on the soft, silken material and smoothed it lovingly.

"Well, I should think I did like it," said Jennie, at last melted out of her frigidity. "I never expected to have anything half so fine; and the color is just what I always wanted and never could seem to find except in expensive stuff. I'm sure I'm very much obliged to you, Marion."

"Oh, I'm so glad you like it!" said Marion, pleased, "and I do hope it fits you. I tried it on, but I used to be smaller than you, and I wasn't sure it would fit you. It was large for me."

"Oh, I'm sure it'll fit. It looks good and large. I'm just glad to have it made; the dressmaker out here isn't very good, and they never see anything as stylish as this. I'm real pleased."

But when Marion opened the hatbox and brought forth the hat, graceful and simple in its lines, yet beautiful and bearing that unmistakable stamp of the lady, Jennie succumbed entirely. It was the last straw that broke her barriers down. She looked and looked and could say nothing, and then looked again as Marion set it on her own head.

Then Marion put the hat on Jennie and sent her to the glass to see; and Jennie walked solemnly from the room, her kitchen apron still tied around her waist but her head borne regally, mindful of its crowning glory. Tom and Lyman stopped talking, and Tom shouted out his hearty approval till his wife's face grew rosy with pleasure. She stayed a long time in the guest room before the mirror; and Marion, fearful lest she did not like the hat, followed shyly and found Jennie looking at herself intently in the glass, and two great tears rolling down her flushed cheeks.

"Don't you like it, Jennie?" she asked anxiously.

"Like it!" said Jennie, turning full upon her. "I like it better than anything I ever had in my life before, and I don't deserve it. I've been awful mean to you sometimes, and I've almost hated you because you didn't come up here and help us get settled, and because you always held yourself away from things and seemed to think nothing was good enough for you; but I'm ashamed now, and I oughtn't to take these nice things. They don't belong to me, and I don't deserve to have you bring such nice presents to me or the children. I'm sorry, and I ask you to forgive me."

And suddenly Jennie, the grim and forbidding, burst into tears and fell upon her astonished sister-in-law's neck. But Marion's loving heart was equal to the occasion. With abounding forgiveness, she received Jennie's overtures and folded her arms lovingly around her, rejoicing that at last she had won her sister.

"But you don't know it all yet," sobbed out Jennie, lifting her head from Marion's shoulder. "You'll never forgive me, but I've got to tell. I can't sleep nights thinking of it. I stole your father's will and hid it so it wouldn't be found. I didn't destroy it, but I hid it so you'd never know the house was all yours. And now I can't find the will anymore; it's gone."

Marion's hand rested softly on Jennie's head. Marion's voice was very gentle as she said, "That's all right, Jennie. I forgave it long ago."

Jennie lifted her astonished head and stared.

"You forgave it? Then you knew it?"

"Yes, I knew it. The will fell out from behind the desk when the movers were carrying it out of the house."

"But you didn't know *I* did it."

"Yes, Jennie, you had dropped a bit of your peppermint candy into the envelope. I knew it must have been you. But it's all right now. I burned it up. Let's forget it. I've got something far better than the old house. You must come and see me in my new one."

"You knew I'd done it, and yet you forgave me!" marveled Jennie. "And you never *told*, either! You're an angel, Marion Warren, and I'm a devil. But I'll love you always, and I'll do anything in the world for you. We'll sell this farm and give you back your money. Tom hasn't been happy about it either, but he didn't know what I'd done."

"You will not sell this farm, Jennie dear, and Tom is *never* to know about that will. I don't want the money, and I *do* want you to have the farm. I've more money than I know how to spend, so please, please forget it. I have, and let us have a good time!"

They came into the other room in a few minutes with shining faces.

"We may as well open the rest of these things," said Lyman, producing the packages meant for Tom; and

Tom, enthusiastic and unsuspecting, took the small box handed him and presently found the fine watch and the books and the other things; and the two sat down and had a real brotherly chat over the good cheer that had been brought.

Lyman, as he watched the brother, caught little gleams of resemblance to his wife in the rougher, heartier features, little tricks of speech and mannerisms that were pleasant to recognize, and he saw at once that the brother was no blockhead. He might not care for music and art and philosophy, but he would make a sharp businessman and was a good talker. His arguments in politics were well put and the points sharp and original. He might be of far coarser mold than his fair and delicate sister, but there was nothing about him to be ashamed of, and the new brother-in-law was enjoying himself immensely.

Finally, Lyman and Tom went out to look over the farm while Marion and Jennie cleared off the table, and there was no more talk about rich and poor, for there was a final truce between and Jennie and Marion.

They rode away the next morning into a sunlit world, having left happy hearts and pleasant feelings behind them, and really sorry that it was not possible to have planned to accept the urgent invitations of both host and hostess to remain a few days longer. How they would have shouted with merriment if they could have known how Jennie feared they were coming to live on them, and of her plans to put her new brother-in-law to work on the farm to earn his board!

But as they waved a good-bye to the group on the side porch and turned into the broad highway with the prospect of a glorious spring day before them, and just their two selves in all the great, beautiful world, Lyman felt that now indeed his bride belonged to him entirely. Until he had seen her people he knew she felt ill at ease with him whenever she thought of the wide difference in their birth. But he had somehow managed to make it plain to her that all the world is kin and that he felt no such gulf as she had feared. He could see that her heart was light from the burden lifted, and now she felt that she might rest in his love and be happy.

Also there was a feeling of exhilaration upon them both, for they had won a victory over Jennie and made her their devoted admirer. It gave Marion a great sense of peace to know this. Jennie might not be any pleasanter for daily living than before, when the newness wore off, but she did not have to live with her; and it was good to know that Jennie bore no grudges.

Marion enjoyed thinking of the pleasant surprises she would send them all, and so make up to Jennie for any imagined wrongs of the past. So Marion sat beside her husband, happy and smiling, as they flew along the great, wide road and drew in the morning breath of spring sweetness and delighted in the glance of each other's eyes.

At New York they found the chauffeur and a lot of letters.

Lyman had taken care to have announcement cards sent to all their friends before they left home, and now the congratulations were pouring down upon them. Marion gasped as she opened one exquisitely perfumed epistle written in exceedingly tall handwriting on the latest style of paper with a gold-embossed monogram.

> *You dear little Marion* (it began familiarly)*:*
> *How you have surprised us all! Though I'll tell you a secret. I suspected long ago what was going on and have been perfectly delighted over the prospect; but I didn't tell a soul. Wasn't I good?*
> *I am charmed that you are to enter our circle and be one of us. It is a real pleasure to think of you as mistress of that lovely home. I shall be so pleased to be "near neighbors" and run in often. I have always admired you greatly and wanted to see more of you, and have often grieved over the separation*

that circumstances made necessary as we grew older. And now you are coming right into our set, and there will be nothing to hinder our being bosom friends. Your husband and I have always been very intimate, and so I have a double claim upon you, you see; and I do hope my note will be the first you receive to tell you how glad we all are to have you among us. I intend to give a large dinner for you just as soon as you are settled at home and ready for your social duties.

It is not necessary for me to tell you what a wonderful husband you have married, for you probably know that. Tell him for me that he is to be congratulated upon the bride he has chosen.

Yours always lovingly,
Isabel Cresson

The gift that came with the note was a paperweight of green jade in the form of an exquisitely carved little idol with a countenance like a foreign devil.

"Oh!" gasped Marion, helplessly letting the note slip from her fingers to the floor. "Oh!"

"What is the matter, dear?" asked Lyman, turning from a letter from a business friend.

"Oh!" said Marion. "I am ashamed to have misjudged her so. She is very kind, I'm sure; but—but—I don't think I shall ever really quite enjoy her; she's such an awful hypocrite. I shall always think of her in that gold dress!"

Lyman picked up the letter and read it with growing amusement.

"Don't worry, dear," he said, laughing. "This is just what I've expected, and you've yet to learn that this young woman can be several very different people. It suits her just now to pose as my intimate friend—and yours. But no one is thereby deceived. Everyone of our circle knows that she has always been my special aversion. There are reasons why she will never be likely to say any disagreeable things to you, and you need not fear her; but, as for making her your intimate friend, that will never be necessary. Be your own sweet self, gracious and simple to her; but never let her deceive you into thinking you are wrong in your own intuition about her. She has no right to claim even toleration from you. She is a cruel, selfish, rotten-hearted woman. She is simply showing you that she is robbed of her power to hurt you and prefers to make the best of it and be as intimate as you will allow."

Two days later they returned, and Marion entered the great, handsome house and looked about upon the beauty and luxury that were henceforth to be hers. Everywhere, in all the rooms, there were roses to welcome her—great crimson roses, glowing in masses, in crystal bowls and jardinières and costly vases. But on her dressing table in the little white boudoir he had prepared for her, standing in a clear glass vase so that its long green stem was clearly seen, there nodded and glowed a single crimson bud.

GRACE LIVINGSTON HILL (1865–1947) is known as the pioneer of Christian romance. Grace wrote more than a hundred faith-inspired books during her lifetime. When her first husband died, leaving her with two daughters to raise, writing became a way to make a living, but she always recognized storytelling as a way to share her faith in God. She has touched countless lives through the years and continues to touch lives today. Her books feature moving stories, delightful characters, and love in its purest form.

LOVE ENDURES

3-in-1 Collection of Classic Romance

Treasure an exclusive collection of three timeless stories from America's best-loved storyteller, Grace Livingston Hill.

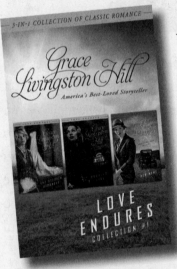

A stranger salvages a wedding gone awry for one desperate bride in *The Beloved Stranger*.

Believing he is a murderer, a young man hides his identity in *A New Name*.

A rebellious teenager's escape brings more than she bargained for in *The Prodigal Girl*.

With charming 1920s settings, these beloved romances capture the enduring power of faith—and love.